THE HARPER HALL OF PERN

DRAGONSONG

DRAGONSINGER

DRAGONDRUMS

Anne McCaffrey

Nelson Doubleday, Inc.   Garden City, New York

Contents

HIGH
REACHES

RUATHA

TILLEK

FORT

BOLL

PERN

Rivers

Lakes

Weyrs

Holds

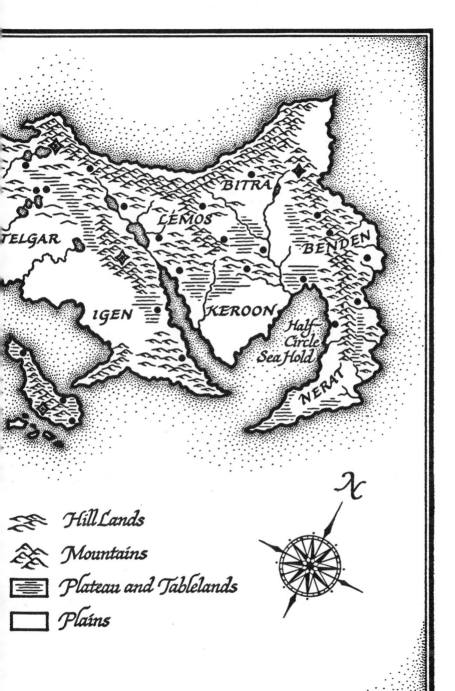

BITRA

LEMOS

TELGAR

BENDEN

IGEN

KEROON

Half-
Circle
Sea Hold

NERAT

Hill Lands

Mountains

Plateau and Tablelands

Plains

DRAGONSONG

TO BETH BLISH

who stands first in line

for a dragon—behind me!

AT Half-Circle Sea
  Hold, in Benden Hold

Yanus, Sea Holder,
Mavi, Sea Holder's Lady
Menolly, their youngest child and daughter
Sella, the next oldest daughter
Alemi, the third son of six

Petiron, the old Harper
Elgion, the new Harper

Soreel, wife of First Holder
Old Uncle, Menolly's great-grandfather

AT Benden Weyr

F'lar, Weyrleader—bronze Mnementh
Lessa, Weyrwoman—queen Ramoth
N'ton, a wingleader—bronze Lioth
T'gellan, a wingleader for Half-Circle Sea Hold—bronze Monarth
T'gran, dragonrider—brown Branth
T'sel, dragonrider—green Trenth, bronze fire lizard Rill
F'nor, wing-second—brown Canth, gold fire lizard Grall
Brekke, queenrider—queen Wirenth, killed, bronze fire lizard Berd

Manora, Headwoman of the Weyr's Lower Caverns
Felena, her second in charge
Oharan, Weyr Harper

Mirrim, fosterling of Brekke, (3 fire lizards)
     green   Reppa
             Lok
    brown   Tolly
Sanra, in charge of children in living cavern

Masterharper Robinton
Masterminer Nicat

Menolly's fire lizards: gold   Beauty
                   bronze   Rocky
                          Diver
                   brown   Lazybones
                          Mimic
                          Brownie
                     blue   Uncle
                   green   Auntie One
                          Auntie Two

Foreword

Rukbat, in the Sagittarian Sector, was a golden G-type star. It had five planets, two asteroid belts, and a stray planet it had attracted and held in recent millennia. When men first settled on Rukbat's third world and called it Pern, they had taken little notice of the stranger planet, swinging about its adopted primary in a wildly erratic elliptical orbit. For two generations, the colonists gave the bright red star little thought, until the path of the wanderer brought it close to its stepsister at perihelion.

Then, the spore life, which proliferated at an incredible rate on the Red Star's wild surface, spun off into space and bridged the gap to Pern. The spores fell as thin threads on the temperate, hospitable planet, and devoured anything organic in their way, seeking to establish burrows in Pern's warm earth from which to set out more voracious Threads.

The colonists suffered staggering losses in terms of people scored to death, and in crops and vegetation wiped out completely. Only fire killed Thread on land: only stone and metal stopped its progress. Fortunately it drowned in water, but the colonists could scarcely live on the seas.

The resourceful men cannibalized their transport ships and, abandoning the open southern continent where they had touched down, set about making the natural caves in the northern continent habitable. They evolved a two-phase plan to combat Thread. The first phase involved breeding a highly specialized variety of a life-form indigenous to their new world. The "dragons" (named for the mythical Terran beast they resembled) had two extremely useful characteristics: they could get from one place to another instantly by teleportation, and when they had chewed a phosphine-bearing rock, they could emit a flaming gas. Thus the flying dragons could char Thread to ash midair and escape its ravages themselves.

Men and women with high empathy ratings or some innate telepathic ability were trained to use and preserve these unusual animals, partnering them in a lifelong and intimate relationship.

The original cave-Fort, constructed in the eastern face of the great West Mountain range, soon became too small to hold either the colonists or the great "dragons." Another settlement was started slightly to the north, by a great lake, conveniently nestled near a cave-filled cliff. Ruatha Hold, too, became overcrowded in a few generations.

Since the Red Star rose in the East, it was decided to start a holding in the eastern mountains, provided suitable accommodations could be found. The ancient cave-pocked cones of extinct volcanoes in the Benden mountains proved so suitable to the dragonmen and women that they searched and found several more throughout Pern, and left Fort Hold and Ruatha Hold for the pastoral colonists, the holders.

However, such projects took the last of the fuel for the great stonecutters, originally thought to be used for the most diffident mining since Pern was light on metals, and any subsequent holds and weyrs were handhewn.

The dragons and their riders in their weyrs, and the people in the cave holdings, went about their separate tasks and each developed habits that became custom, which solidified into tradition as incontrovertible as law.

By the Third Pass of the Red Star, a complicated social, political and economic structure had developed to deal with the recurrent evil of Thread. There were now six Weyrs, pledged to protect all Pern, each Weyr having a geographical section of the northern continent literally under its wings. The rest of the population, the Holds, agreed to tithe to support the Weyrs, since these fighters, these dragonmen, did not have any arable land in their volcanic homes, nor did they have time for farming while protecting the planet from Passes of the Thread.

Holds developed wherever natural caves could be found: some, of course, were extensive or strategically placed near good water and grazing, others were smaller and less well placed. It took a strong man to keep frantic, terrified people in control in the Holds during Thread attacks: it took wise administration to conserve food supplies for times when nothing could be safely grown. Extraordinary measures controlled population, keeping its number healthy and useful until such time as the Thread should pass. And often children from one Hold were raised in another Hold, to spread the genetic pool and keep the Holds from dangerous inbreeding. Such a practice was called "fostering" and was used in both Hold and Crafthalls, where special skills such as metalworking, animal breedings, farming, fishing and mining (such as there was) were preserved. So that one Lord Holder could not deny the products of a Crafthall situated in his Hold to others, the Crafts were decreed independent of a Hold affiliation, each Craftmaster at a hall owing allegiance only to the Master of that particular craft who, as the need arose, took likely students in as fosterlings.

Except for the return of the Red Star approximately every two hundred years, life was pleasant on Pern.

There came a time when the Red Star, due to the conjunction of Rukbat's five natural satellites, did not pass close enough to Pern to drop the dreadful spores. And the Pernese forgot about the danger. The people prospered, spreading out across the rich land, carving more Holds out of solid rock and becoming so busy with their pursuits, that they did not realize that there were only a few dragons in the skies, and only one Weyr of dragonriders left on Pern. In a few generations, the descendants of the Holders began to wonder if the Red Star would ever return. The dragonriders fell into disfavor: why should all Pern support these people and their hungry beasts? The legends of past braveries, and the very reason for such courage, became dishonored.

But, in the natural course of events, the Red Star again spun close to Pern, winking with a baleful red eye on its intended victim. One man, F'lar, rider of the bronze dragon, Mnementh, believed that the ancient tales had truth in them. His half brother, F'nor, rider of brown Canth, listened to his arguments and came to believe. When the last golden egg of a dying queen dragon lay hardening on the Benden Weyr Hatching Ground, F'lar and F'nor seized the opportunity to gain control of the Weyr. Searching Ruatha Hold, they found a strong woman, Lessa, the only surviving member of the proud bloodline of Ruatha Hold. She Impressed young Ramoth, the new queen, and became Weyrwoman of Benden Weyr. And F'lar's bronze Mnementh became the new queen's mate.

The three young riders, F'lar, F'nor and Lessa forced the Lord Holders and the Craftsmen to recognize their imminent danger and prepare the almost defenseless planet against Thread. But it was distressingly obvious that the scant two hundred dragons of Benden Weyr could not defend the wide-spread and sprawling settlements. Six full Weyrs had been needed in the olden days when the settled land had been much less extensive. In learning to direct her queen *between* one place and another, Lessa discovered that dragons could teleport *between* times as well. Risking her life as well as Pern's only queen, Lessa and Ramoth went back in time, four hundred Turns, to the days before the mysterious disappearance of the other five Weyrs, just after the last Pass of the Red Star had been completed.

The five Weyrs, seeing only the decline of their prestige and bored with inactivity after a lifetime of exciting combat, agreed to help Lessa, and Pern, and came forward to her time.

Dragonsong begins seven Turns after the Five Weyrs came forward.

Chapter 1

Drummer, beat, and piper, blow
Harper, strike, and soldier, go
Free the flame and sear the grasses
Til the dawning Red Star passes.

Almost as if the elements, too, mourned the death of the gentle old Harper, a southeaster blew for three days, locking even the burial barge in the safety of the Dock Cavern.

The storm gave Sea Holder Yanus too much time to brood over his dilemma. It gave him time to speak to every man who could keep rhythm and pitch, and they all gave him the same answer. They couldn't properly honor the old Harper with his deathsong, but Menolly could.

To which answer Yanus would grunt and stamp off. It rankled in his mind that he couldn't give voice to his dissatisfaction with that answer, and his frustration. Menolly was only a girl: too tall and lanky to be a proper girl at that. It galled him to have to admit that, unfortunately, she was the only person in the entire Half-Circle Sea Hold who could play any instrument as well as the old Harper. Her voice was true, her fingers clever on string, stick or pipe, and she knew the Deathsong. For all Yanus could be certain, the aggravating child had been practicing that song ever since old Petiron started burning with his fatal fever.

"She will have to do the honor, Yanus," his wife, Mavi, told him the evening the storm began to slacken. "The important thing is that Petiron is properly sung to rest. One does not have to record who did the singing."

"The old man knew he was dying. Why didn't he instruct one of the men?"

"Because," replied Mavi with a touch of sharpness in her voice, "you would never spare him a man when there was fishing."

"There was young Tranilty . . ."

"Whom you sent fostering to Ista Sea Hold."

"Couldn't that young lad of Forolt's . . ."

"His voice is changing. Come, Yanus, it'll have to be Menolly."

Yanus grumbled bitterly against the inevitable as he climbed into the sleeping furs.

"That's what everyone else has told you, haven't they? So why make so much of a necessity?"

Yanus settled himself, resigned.

"The fishing will be good tomorrow," his wife said, yawning. She preferred him fishing to stomping around the Hold, sullen and critical with enforced inactivity. She knew he was the finest Sea Holder Half-Circle had ever had: the Hold was prospering, with plenty for bartering set by in the storage caves; they hadn't lost a ship or a man in several Turns either, which said much for his weather-wisdom. But Yanus, at home on a heaving deck in foul weather, was very much adrift when taxed with the unexpected on land.

Mavi was keenly aware that Yanus was displeased with his youngest child. Mavi found the girl exasperating, too. Menolly worked hard and was very clever with her fingers: too clever by half when it came to playing any instrument in the Harper Craft. Perhaps, Mavi thought, she had not been wise to permit the girl to linger in the old Harper's constant company once she had learned all the proper Teaching Songs. But it had been one less worry to let Menolly nurse the old Harper, and Petiron had wished it. No one begrudged a Harper's requests. Ah well, thought Mavi, dismissing the past, there'd be a new Harper soon, and Menolly could be put to tasks proper to a young girl.

The next morning, the storm had cleared off: the skies were cloudless, the sea, calm. The burial barge had been outfitted in the Dock Cavern, Petiron's body wrapped in harper-blue on the tilter board. The entire Fleet and most of the Seahold followed in the wake of the oar-driven barge, out into the faster moving current above Nerat Deep.

Menolly, on the barge prow, sang the elegy: her clear strong voice carrying back to the Half-Circle Fleet; the men chanting the descant as they rowed the barge.

On the final chord, Petiron went to his rest. Menolly bowed her head, and let drum and stick slide from her fingers into the sea. How could she ever use them again when they had beaten Petiron's last song? She'd held back her tears since the Harper had died because she knew she had to be able to sing his elegy and you couldn't sing with a throat closed from crying. Now the tears ran down her cheeks, mingled with sea spray: her sobs punctuated by the soft chant of the steersman, setting about.

Petiron had been her friend, her ally and mentor. She had sung from the heart as he'd taught her: from the heart and the gut. Had he heard her song where he had gone?

She raised her eyes to the palisades of the coast: to the white-sanded harbor between the two arms of Half-Circle Hold. The sky had wept itself out in the past three days: a fitting tribute. And the air was cold. She shivered in her thick wherhide jacket. She would have some protection from the wind if she stepped down into the cockpit with the oarsmen. But she couldn't move. Honor was always accompanied by responsibility, and it was fitting for her to remain where she was until the burial barge touched the stones of Dock Cavern.

Half-Circle Hold would be lonelier than ever for her now. Petiron had tried so hard to live long enough for his replacement to arrive. He'd told Menolly he wouldn't last the winter. He'd dispatched a messge to Masterharper Robinton to send a new Harper as soon as possible. He'd also told Menolly that he'd sent two of her songs to the Masterharper.

"Women can't be harpers," she'd said to Petiron, astonished and awed.

"One in ten hundred have perfect pitch," Petiron had said in one of his evasive replies. "One in ten thousand can build an acceptable melody with meaningful words. Were you only a lad, there'd be no problem at all."

"Well, we're stuck with me being a girl."

"You'd make a fine big strong lad, you would," Petiron had replied exasperatingly.

"And what's wrong with being a fine big strong girl?" Menolly had been half-teasing, half-annoyed.

"Nothing, surely. Nothing." And Petiron had patted her hands, smiling up at her.

She'd been helping him eat his dinner, his hands so crippled even the lightest wooden spoon left terrible ridges in the swollen fingers.

"And Masterharper Robinton's a fair man. No one on Pern can say he isn't. And he'll listen to me. He knows his duty, and I am, after all, a senior member of the Crafthall, being taught up in the Craft before him himself. And I'll require him to listen to you."

"Have you really sent him those songs you made me wax down on slates?"

"I have. Sure I have done that much for you, dear child."

He'd been so emphatic that Menolly had to believe that he'd done what he'd said. Poor old Petiron. In the last months, he'd not remembered the time of Turn much less what he'd done the day before.

He was timeless now, Menolly told herself, her wet cheeks stinging with cold, and she'd never forget him.

The shadow of the two arms of Half-Circle's cliffs fell across her face. The barge was entering the home harbor. She lifted her head. High above, she saw the diminutive outline of a dragon in the sky. How lovely! And how had Benden Weyr known? No, the dragonrider was only doing a routine sweep. With Thread falling at unexpected times, dragons were often flying above Half-Circle, isolated as it was by the bogs at the top of Nerat Bay. No matter, the dragon was awing above Half-Circle Hold at this appropriate moment and that was, to Menolly, the final tribute to Petiron the Harper.

The men lifted the heavy oars out of the water, and the barge glided slowly to its mooring at the far end of the Dock. Fort and Tillek might boast of being the oldest Sea-Holds, but only Half-Circle had a cavern big enough to dock the entire fishing fleet and keep it safe from Threadfall and weather.

Dock Cavern had moorings for thirty boats; storage space for all the nets, traps and lines; airing racks for sail; and a shallow ledge where hulls could be scraped free of seagrowths and repaired. At the very end of the immense Cavern was a shelf of rock where the Hold's builders worked when there was sufficient timber for a new hull. Beyond was the small inner cave where priceless wood was stored, dried on high racks or warped into frames.

The burial barge lightly touched its pier.

"Menolly?" The first oarsman held out a hand to her.

Startled by the unexpected courtesy to a girl her age, she was about to jump down when she saw in his eyes the respect due her at this moment. And his hand, closing on hers, gave silent approval for her singing of the Harper's elegy. The other men stood, too, waiting for her to disembark first. She straightened her shoulders, although her throat felt tight enough for more tears, and she stepped proudly down to the solid stone.

As she turned to walk back to the landside of the Cavern, she saw that the other boats were discharging their passengers quickly and quietly. Her father's boat, the biggest of the Half-Circle fleet, had already tacked back into the harbor. Yanus's voice carried across the water, above the incidental sounds of creaking boats and muted voices.

"Quickly now, men. We've a good breeze rising and the fish'll be biting after three days of storm."

The oarsmen hurried past her, to board their assigned fishing boats. It seemed unfair to Menolly that Petiron, after a long life's dedication to Half-Circle Hold, was dismissed so quickly from everyone's mind. And yet . . . life did go on. There were fish to be caught against winter's hungry months. Fair days during the cold months of the Turn were not to be squandered.

She quickened her pace. She'd far to go around the rim of the Dock

Cavern and she was cold. Menolly also wanted to get into the Hold before her mother noticed that she didn't have the drum. Waste wasn't tolerated by Mavi any more than idleness by Yanus.

While this was an occasion, it had been a sad one and the women and children and also the men too old to sea-fish observed a decorous pace out of the Cavern, making smaller groups as they headed towards their own Holds in the southern arc of Half-Circle's sheltering palisade.

Menolly saw Mavi organizing the children into work groups. With no Harper to lead them in the Teaching Songs and ballads, the children would be kept occupied in clearing the storm debris from the white-sanded beaches.

There might be sun in the sky, and the dragonrider still circling on his brown, but the wind was frigid and Menolly began to shiver violently. She wanted to feel the warmth of the fire on the great Hold's kitchen hearth and a cup of hot klah inside her.

She heard her sister Sella's voice carrying to her on the breeze.

"She's got nothing to do now, Mavi, why do *I* have to. . . ."

Menolly ducked behind a group of adults, avoiding her mother's searching glance. Trust Sella to remember that Menolly no longer had the excuse of nursing the ailing Harper. Ahead of her, one of the old aunts tripped, her querulous voice raised in a cry for help. Menolly sprinted to her side, supporting her and receiving loud protestations of gratitude.

"Only for Petiron would I have dragged these old bones out on the cold sea this morning. Bless the man, rest the man," the old woman went on, clinging with unexpected strength to Menolly. "You're a good child, Menolly, so you are. It is Menolly, isn't it?" The old one peered up at her. "Now you just give me a hand up to Old Uncle and I'll tell him the whole of it, since he hasn't legs to leave his bed."

So Sella had to supervise the children and Menolly got to the fire: at least long enough to stop shivering. Then old auntie would have it that the Uncle would be grateful for some klah, too, so when Mavi entered her kitchen, her eyes searching for her youngest daughter, she found Menolly dutifully occupied serving the oldster.

"Very well then, Menolly, while you're up there, see that you set the old man comfortably. Then you can start on the glows."

Menolly had her warming cup with the Old Uncle and left him comfortable, mournfully exchanging tales of other burials with the aunt. Checking the glows had been her task ever since she had grown taller than Sella. It had meant climbing up and down the different levels to the inner and outer layers of the huge Sea Hold, but Menolly had established the quickest way to finish the job so that she'd have some free time to herself before Mavi started looking for her. She had been accustomed to spending those earned minutes practicing with the Harper. So Menolly was not surprised to find herself, eventually, outside Petiron's door.

She was surprised, however, to hear voices in his room. She was about to charge angrily through the half-open door and demand an accounting when she heard her mother's voice clearly.

"The room won't need much fixing for the new Harper, so it won't."

Menolly stepped back into the shadow of the corridor. The new Harper?

"What I want to know, Mavi, is who is to keep the children up in their learning until he comes?" That voice was Soreel's, the wife of the First Holder and therefore spokeswoman for the other Hold women to Mavi as Sea Holder's lady. "She did well enough this morning. You have to give her that, Mavi."

"Yanus will send the message ship."

"Not today, nor tomorrow he won't. I don't fault Sea Holder, Mavi, but it stands to reason that the boats must fish and the sloop's crew can't be spared. That means four, five days before the messenger gets to Igen Hold. From Igen Hold, if a dragonrider obliges by carrying the message—but we all know what the Oldtimers at Igen Weyr are like so let's say, Harper drums to the Masterharper Hall at Fort is another two–three days. A man has to be selected by Masterharper Robinton and sent overland and by ship. And with Thread falling any time it pleases, no one travels fast or far in a day. It'll be spring before we see another Harper. Are the children to be left without teaching for months?"

Soreel had punctuated her comments with brushing sounds, and there were other clatters in the room, the swishing of bed rushes being gathered up. Now Menolly could hear the murmur of two other voices supporting Soreel's arguments.

"Petiron has taught well . . ."

"He taught *her* well, too," Soreel interrupted Mavi.

"Harpering is a man's occupation . . ."

"Fair enough if Sea Holder'll spare a man for it." Soreel's voice was almost belligerent because everyone knew the answer to that. "Truth be told, I think the girl knew the Sagas better than the old man this past Turn. You know his mind was ranging back in time, Mavi."

"Yanus will do what's proper." The finality in Mavi's tone firmly ended that discussion.

Menolly heard footsteps crossing the old Harper's room, and she ducked down the hall, around the nearest bend and down into the kitchen level.

It distressed Menolly to think of anyone, even another Harper, in Petiron's room. Obviously it distressed others that there was no Harper. Usually such a problem didn't arise. Every Hold could boast one or two musically able men and every Hold took pride in encouraging *these* talents. Harpers liked to have other instrumentalists to share the chore of entertaining their Holds during the long winter evenings. And it was also the better part of wisdom to have a substitute available for just such an emergency as Half-Circle was experiencing. But fishing was hard on the hands: the heavy work, the cold water, the salt and fish oils thickened joints and calloused fingers in the wrong places. Fishermen were often away many days on longer hauls. After a Turn or two at net, trap and sail line, young men lost their skill at playing anything but simple tunes. Harper Teaching Ballads required deft quick fingers and constant practice.

By putting to sea to fish so quickly after the old Harper's burial, Yanus thought to have time enough to find an alternative solution. There was no doubt that the girl could sing well, play well, and she'd not disgraced Hold or Harper that morning. It was going to take time to send for and receive a new Harper, and the youngsters must not lose all progress in the learning of the basic Teaching Ballads.

But Yanus had many strong reservations about putting such a heavy responsibility on the shoulders of a girl not fifteen Turns old. Not the least of these was Menolly's distressing tendency toward tune-making. Well enough and amusing now and again in the long winter evenings to hear her sing them, but old Petiron had been alive to keep her to rights. Yanus wasn't sure that he could trust her not to include her trivial little whistles in the lessons. How were the young to know that hers weren't proper songs for their learning? The trouble was, her melodies were the sort that stayed in the mind so a man found himself humming or whistling them without meaning to.

By the time the boats had profitably trawled the Deep and tacked for home, Yanus had found no compromise. It was no consolation to know that he wouldn't have any argument from the other holders. Had Menolly sung poorly that morning . . . but she hadn't. As Sea Holder for Half-Circle, he was obliged to bring up the young of the Hold in the traditions of Pern: knowing their duty and how to do it. He counted himself very lucky to be beholden to Benden Weyr, to have F'lar, bronze Mnementh's rider, as Weyrleader and Lessa as Ramoth's Weyrwoman. So Yanus felt deeply obliged to keep tradition at Half-Circle:

and the young would learn what they needed to know, even if a girl had the teaching.

That evening, after the day's catch had been salted down, he instructed Mavi to bring her daughter to the small room off the Great Hall where he conducted Hold business and where the Records were stored. Mavi had put the Harper's instruments on the mantel for safekeeping.

Appropriately Yanus handed Menolly Petiron's gitar. She took the instrument in a properly reverential manner, which reassured Yanus that she appreciated the responsibility.

"Tomorrow you'll be excused from your regular morning duties to take the youngsters for their teaching," he told her. "But I'll have no more of those finger-twiddlings of yours."

"I sang my songs when Petiron was alive and you never minded them . . ."

Yanus frowned down at his tall daughter.

"Petiron *was* alive. He's dead now, and you'll obey me in this . . ."

Over her father's shoulders, Menolly saw her mother's frowning face, saw her warning headshake and held back a quick reply.

"You bear in mind what I've said!" And Yanus fingered the wide belt he wore. "No tuning!"

"Yes, Yanus."

"Start tomorrow then. Unless, of course, there's Threadfall, and then everyone will bait longlines."

Yanus dismissed the two women and began to compose a message to the Masterharper to go when he could next spare the sloop's crew. They'd sail it to Igen Hold. About time Half-Circle had some news of the rest of Pern anyway. And he could ship some of the smoked fish. The journey needn't be a wasted trip.

Once in the hallway, Mavi gripped her daughter's arm hard. "Don't disobey him, girl."

"There's no harm in my tunes, mother. You know what Petiron said . . ."

"I'll remind you that the old man's dead. And that changes everything that went on during his life. Behave yourself while you stand in a man's place. No tuning! To bed now, and mind you turn the glowbaskets. No sense wasting light no eye needs."

Chapter 2

Honor those the dragons heed
In thought and favor, word and deed.
Worlds are lost or worlds are saved
From those dangers dragon-braved.

Dragonman, avoid excess:
Greed will bring the Weyr distress:
To the ancient Law adhere,
Prospers thus the Dragonweyr.

It was easy enough, at first, for Menolly to forget her tuning during the Teachings. She wanted to do Petiron proud so that when the new Harper came, he'd find no fault in the children's recitations. The children were attentive: the Teaching was always better then gutting and preserving fish, or net mending, and longline baiting. Then, too, winter storms, the severest in many Turns, kept the fishing fleet docked and the Teaching eased the boredom.

When the fleet was in, Yanus would stop by the Little Hall where Menolly held her class. He'd scowl at her from the back of the Hall. Fortunately, he'd only stay a little while because he made the children nervous. Once she actually saw his foot tapping the beat; he scowled when he realized what he was doing and then he left.

He had sent the message sloop to Igen Hold three days after the burial. The crew brought back news of no interest to Menolly but the adults went around looking black: something about the Oldtimers and Menolly wasn't to worry her head, so she didn't. The crew also brought back a message slate addressed to Petiron and signed with the imprint of Masterharper Robinton.

"Poor old Petiron," one of the aunties told Menolly, sighing and dabbing affectedly at her eyes. "He always looked forward to slates from Masterharper. Ah well, it'll keep til the new Harper comes. He'll know what to do with it."

It took Menolly a while to find out where the slate was: propped up conspicuously on the mantel in her father's Records room. Menolly was positive that the message had something to do with her, with the songs

that Petiron had said he'd sent to the Masterharper. The notion so
obsessed her that she got bold enough to ask her mother why Yanus
didn't open the message.

"Open a sealed message from the Masterharper to a man dead?"
Mavi stared at her daughter in shocked incredulity. "Your father would
do no such thing. Harpers' letters are for Harpers."

"I only remembered that Petiron had sent a slate to the Masterharper. I thought it might be about a replacement coming. I mean
. . ."

"I'll be glad when the new Harper does come, m'girl. You've been
getting above yourself with this Teaching."

The next few days were full of apprehension for Menolly: she conceived the idea that her mother would make Yanus replace her as
Teacher. That was, of course, impossible for the same reasons that had
forced Yanus to make her the teacher in the first place. But it was a fact
that Mavi found all the smelliest, most boring or tedious jobs for Menolly once her teaching duty was done. And Yanus took it into his head
to appear in the Little Hall more frequently.

Then the weather settled down into a clear spell and the entire Sea
Hold was kept at a run with fish. The children were excused from the
Teaching to gather seaweeds blown up by the high tides and all the
Hold women set to boiling the weed for the thick juice in the stalks:
juice that kept back many sicknesses and bone ailments. Or so the old
aunties said. But they'd find good out of any bad and the worst of any
blessing. And the worst of the seaweed was its smell, thought Menolly,
who had to stir the huge kettles.

Threadfalls came and added some excitement: the fear in being
Holdbound while the dragons swept the skies with their fiery breath,
charring Thread to impotence. (Menolly wanted to see that grand sight
one day, instead of just singing about it, or knowing it was taking place
outside the thick stone walls and heavy metal shutters of the Hold's
windows.) Afterward she joined the flame-thrower crews that checked
for any possible Thread that might have escaped dragon flame. Not that
there was much for Thread to eat on the windswept bare marshes and
bogs around Half-Circle Sea Hold. The barren rock palisades that made
Half-Circle bore no greenery at all, winter or summer, but it was wise to
check the marshes and beaches. Thread could burrow into the seagrass
stalks, or slide down the marshberry and seabeachplum bushes, burrow
into the roots, multiply and eat anything green and growing until the
coast was as bare as rock.

Flame-crewing was cold work, but it was a distinct pleasure for Menolly to be out of the Hold, in the rough air. Her team got as far as the

Dragon Stones to the south. Petiron had told her that those stones, standing offshore in the treacherous waters, had once been part of the palisade, probably hollowed with caves like all this stretch of cliff.

The crowning treat for Menolly was when the Weyrleader, F'lar, himself, on bronze Mnementh, circled in for a chat with Yanus. Of course, Menolly wasn't near enough to hear what the two men said, but she was close enough to smell the firestone reek of the giant bronze dragon. Close enough to see his beautiful eyes catching all colors in the pale wintry sunlight: to see his muscles knot and smooth under the soft hide. Menolly stood, as was properly respectful, with the other flame-thrower crews. But once, when the dragon turned his head in a lazy fashion to peer in her direction, his eyes whirled slowly with their changing colors and she was certain that Mnementh looked at *her*. She didn't dare breathe, he was so beautiful!

Then, suddenly, the magic moment was over. F'lar gave a graceful leap to the dragon's shoulder, caught the fighting straps and pulled himself into place on the neck ridges. Air whooshed around Menolly and the others as the great bronze opened his fragile-looking wings. The next moment, he seemed to be in the air, catching the updraft, beating steadily higher. Abruptly the dragon winked from view. Menolly was not the only one to sigh deeply. To see a dragonrider in the sky was always an occurrence: to be on the same ground with a dragon and his rider, to witness his graceful takeoff and exit *between* was a marvel.

All the songs about dragonriders and dragons seemed inadequate to Menolly. She stole up to the little cubicle in the women's dormitory that she shared with Sella. She wanted to be alone. She'd a little pipe among her things, a soft, whispery reedpipe, and she began to play it: a little whistle composed of her excitement and her response to the day's lovely event.

"So there you are!" Sella flounced into the room, her face reddened, her breath rough. She'd obviously run up the steep stairs. "Told Mavi you'd be here." Sella grabbed the little pipe from Menolly's fingers. "And tuning, too."

"Oh, Sella. It's an old tune!" Menolly said mendaciously and grabbed her pipe back.

Sella's jaw worked with anger. "Old, my foot! I know your ways, girl. And you're dodging work. You get back to the kitchen. You're needed now."

"I am not dodging work. I taught this morning during Threadfall and then I had to go with the crews."

"Your crew's been in this past half-day or more and you still in smelly, sandy clothes, mucking up the room I have to sleep in. You get below or I'll tell Yanus you've been tuning."

"Ha! You wouldn't know a tune if you had your nose rubbed in it."

But Menolly was shedding her work clothes as fast as she could. Sella was just likely to slip the word to Mavi (her sister was as wary of Yanus as Menolly) about Menolly piping in her room—a suspicious action on its own. Though Menolly hadn't sworn not to tune at all; only not to do it in front of people.

However, everyone was in a good mood that night: Yanus, because he'd spoken to F'lar the Weyrleader and because there'd be good fishing on the morrow if the weather held. Fish always rose to feed from drowned Thread, and half the Fall had been over Nerat Bay. The Deep would be thick with schools. With Yanus in a good mood, the rest of the sea holders could also rejoice because there'd been no Thread on the ground at all.

So it wasn't any wonder that they called on Menolly to play for them. She sang two of the longer Sagas about dragons; and then did the Name-Song for the current wingleaders of Benden Weyr so her Sea Hold would know their dragonmen. She wondered if there'd been a recent Hatching that Half-Circle mightn't have heard about, being so isolated. But she was certain that F'lar would have told Yanus if that were so. But would Yanus have told Menolly? She wasn't the Harper to be told such things as courtesy.

The sea holders wanted more singing, but her throat was tired. So she played them a song they could sing, bellowing out the words in voices roughened by wind and salt. She saw her father scowling at her, though he was singing along with the rest of them, and she wondered if he didn't want her—a mere girl—to play men's songs. It galled her because she'd played them often enough when Petiron was alive. She sighed at this injustice. And then wondered what F'lar would have said if he'd known that Half-Circle Sea Hold was dependent on a mere girl for their harpering. She'd heard everyone say that F'lar was a fair man, a farseeing man, and a fine dragonrider. There were even songs about him and his Weyrwoman, Lessa.

So she sang them, in honor of the Weyrleader's visit, and her father's expression lightened. She sang on until her throat was so tight that not a squeak would come out. She wished that someone else could play to give her a rest but, as she scanned the faces of the holders, there wasn't any of them who could beat a drum properly, much less finger a gitar or pipe.

That was why the next day it seemed only logical for her to start one of the children learning the drum rolls. Plenty of songs could be sung just to drumbeat. And one of Soreel's two children still in Teaching was sensitive enough to learn to pipe.

Someone, Sella perhaps, Menolly thought bitterly, informed Mavi of Menolly's activity.

"You were told no tuning . . ."

"Teaching someone drum beats is not tuning . . ."

"Teaching anyone to play is Harper business, not yours, m'girl. Just your good fortune Sea Holder is out in the Deep or you'd have the belt across your shoulders, so you would. No more nonsense."

"But it's not nonsense, Mavi. Last night another drummer or piper would have . . ."

Her mother raised her hand in warning, and Menolly bit shut her lips.

"No tuning, Menolly!"

And that was that.

"Now girl, see to the glows before the fleet gets back."

That job took Menolly inexorably to the Harper's room: swept clean of everything that had been personal to Petiron. She was also reminded of the sealed message on the Record room mantel. What if the Masterharper were expecting a message from Petiron about the songmaker? Menolly was so very sure that part of that unopened message was about her. Not that thinking about it did Menolly any good. Even knowing it for a fact would be no help, Menolly decided gloomily. But that didn't stop her from going past Yanus's Record room and peering in at the tempting package on the mantel.

She sighed, turning from the room. By now the Masterharper would have heard of Petiron's death and be sending a new Harper. Maybe the new man would be able to open the message, and maybe, if it was about her, maybe if it said that the songs she'd sent were good ones, Yanus and her mother wouldn't put such restrictions on her about tuning and whistling and everything.

As the winter spun itself out, Menolly found that her sense of loss when she thought of Petiron deepened. He had been the only person in the Sea Hold who had ever encouraged her in anything: and most especially in that one thing that she was now forbidden to do. Melodies don't stop growing in the mind, tapping at fingers, just because they're forbidden. And Menolly didn't stop composing them—which, she felt, was not precisely disobeying.

What seemed to worry Yanus and Mavi most, Menolly reasoned to herself, was the fact that the children, whom she was supposed to teach only the proper Ballads and Sagas, might think Menolly's tunes were Harper-crafted. (If her tunes were that good in her parents' ears, what was the harm of them?) Basically they didn't want her to play her songs aloud where they would be heard and perhaps repeated at awkward times.

Menolly could, therefore, see no harm in writing down new tunes. She played them softly in the empty Little Hall when the children had left, before she began her afternoon chores, carefully hiding her notations among the Harper records in the rack of the Hall. Safe enough, for no one but herself, til the new Harper came, would discover them there.

This mild deviation from the absolute obedience to her father's restriction about tuning did much to ease Menolly's growing frustration and loneliness. What Menolly didn't realize was that her mother had been watching her closely, having recognized the signs of rebellion in her. Mavi didn't want the Hold to be disgraced in any way, and she feared that Menolly, her head turned by Petiron's marked favor, was not mature enough to discipline herself. Sella had warned her mother that Menolly was getting out of hand. Mavi put some of that tale down to sisterly envy. But, when Sella had told Mavi that Menolly had actually started to teach another how to play an instrument, Mavi had been obliged to intervene. Let Yanus get one whisper of Menolly's disobedience and there'd be real trouble in the Hold for the girl.

Spring was coming and with spring, the quieter seas. Perhaps the new Harper would arrive soon.

And then spring did come, a first glorious day. The sweet scents of seabeachplum and marshberry filled the seaward breezes and came in through the opened shutters of the Little Hall. The children were singing loudly, as if shouting got them through the learning faster. True, they were singing one of the longer Sagas, word perfect, but with far more exuberance than was strictly needed. Perhaps it was that exuberance that infected Menolly and reminded her of a tune she'd tried to set down the day before.

She did not consciously disobey. She certainly was unaware that the fleet had returned from an early catch. She was equally unaware that the chords she was strumming were not—officially—of the Harper's craft. And it was doubly unfortunate that this lapse occurred just as the Sea Holder passed the open windows of the Hall.

He was in the Little Hall almost at once, summarily dismissing the youngsters to help unload the heavy catch. Then he silently, which made the anticipation of the punishment worse, removed his wide belt, signaled Menolly to raise her tunic over her head and to bend over the high harper's stool.

When he had finished, she had fallen to her knees on the hard stone flags, biting her lips to keep back the sobs. He'd never beaten her so hard before. The blood was roaring in her ears so fiercely that she didn't hear Yanus leave the Little Hall. It was a long while before she could ease the tunic over the painful weals on her back. Only when she'd got slowly to her feet did she realize that he'd taken the gitar, too. She knew then that his judgement was irrevocable and harsh.

And unjust! She'd only played the first few bars . . . hummed along . . . and that only because the last chords of the Teaching Ballad had modified into the new tune in her head. Surely that little snitch wouldn't have done any lasting harm! And the children knew all the Teaching Ballads they were supposed to know. She hadn't *meant* to disobey Yanus.

"Menolly?" Her mother came to the classhall door, the carrying thong of an empty skin in her hand. "You dismissed them early? Is that wise . . ." Her mother stopped abruptly and stared at her daughter. An expression of anger and disgust crossed her face. "So you've been the fool after all? With so much at stake, and you had to tune . . ."

"I didn't do it on purpose, Mavi. The song . . . just came into my mind. I'd played no more than a measure . . ."

There wasn't any point in trying to justify the incident to her mother. Not now. The desolation Menolly had felt when she realized her father had taken the gitar intensified in the face of her mother's cold displeasure.

"Take the sack. We need fresh greens," Mavi said in an expressionless voice. "And any of the yellow-veined grass that might be up. There should be some."

Resignedly, Menolly took the sack and, without thinking, looped the thong over her shoulder. She caught her breath as the unwieldy sack banged against her scored back.

Before Menolly could avoid it, her mother had flipped up the loose tunic. She gave an inarticulate exclamation. "You'll need numbweed on some of those."

Menolly pulled away. "What good's a beating then, if it's numbed away first chance?" And she dashed out of the Hall.

Much Mavi cared if she hurt, anyhow, except that a sound body works harder and longer and faster.

Her thoughts and her misery spurred her out of the Hold, every swinging stride she took jarring her sore back. She didn't slow down because she'd the whole long track in front of the Hold to go. The faster she went, the better, before some auntie wanted to know why the children were out of lessons so soon, or why Menolly was going green-picking instead of Teaching.

Fortunately she encountered no one. Everyone was either down at the Dock Cave, unloading, or making themselves scarce to the Sea Holder's eyes so they wouldn't have to. Menolly charged past the smaller holds, down aways on the marshroad, then up the righthand track, south of the Half-Circle. She'd put as much distance between herself and Sea Hold as she could: all perfectly legitimate, in search of greenery.

As she jogged along the sandy footpath, she kept her eyes open for fresh growth, trying to ignore the occasional rough going when she'd jar her whole body. Her back began to smart. She gritted her teeth and paced on.

Her brother, Alemi, had once said that she could run as well as any boy of the Hold and outdistance the half of them on a long race. If only she had been a boy . . . Then it wouldn't have mattered if Petiron had died and left them Harperless. Nor would Yanus have beaten a boy for being brave enough to sing his own songs.

The first of the low marsh valleys was pink and yellow with blooming seabeachplum and marshberry, slightly blackened here and there: more from the low-flying queens catching the odd Thread that escaped the main wings. Yes, and there was the patch that the flame-thrower had charred: the one Thread infestation that had gotten through. One day, Menolly told herself, she'd just throw open a window's steel shutters and *see* the dragons charring Thread in the sky. What a sight that must be for certain!

Fearful, too, she reckoned, having seen her mother treat men for Threadburn. Why, the mark looked as if someone had drawn a point-deep groove with a red-hot poker on the man's arm, leaving the edges black with singed skin. Torly would always bear that straight scar, puckered and red. Threadscore never healed neatly.

She had to stop running. She'd begun to sweat heavily and her back was stinging. She loosened her tunic belt, flapping the soft runner-beast hide to send cooling draughts up between her shoulder blades.

Past the first marsh valley, up over the rocky hump hill into the next valley. Cautious going here: this was one of the deep, boggy places. No sign of yellow-veined grasses. There had been a stand last summer two humpy hills over.

She heard them first, glancing up with a stab of terror at the unexpected sounds above. Dragons? She glanced wildly about for the telltale gray glitter of sky-borne Thread in the east. The greeny blue sky was clear of that dreaded fogging, but not of dragonwings. She heard dragons? It couldn't be! They didn't swarm like that. Dragons always flew in ordered wings, a pattern against the sky. These were darting, dodging, then swooping and climbing. She shaded her eyes. Blue flashes, green, the odd brown and then . . . Of course, sun glinted golden off the leading, dartlike body. A queen! A queen that tiny?

She expelled the breath she'd been holding in her amazement. A fire lizard queen? It had to be. Only fire lizards could be that small and look like dragons. Whers certainly didn't. And whers didn't mate midair. And that's what Menolly was seeing: the mating flight of a fire lizard queen, with her bronzes in close pursuit.

So fire lizards weren't boy talk! Awed, Menolly watched the swift, graceful flight. The queen had led her swarm so high that the smaller ones, the blues and greens and browns, had been forced down. They circled now at a lower altitude, struggling to keep the same direction as the high fliers. They dipped and dashed in mimicry of the queen and bronzes.

They had to be fire lizards! thought Menolly, her heart almost stopping at the beauty and thrill of the sight. Fire lizards! And they *were* like dragons. Only much, much smaller. She didn't know all the Teachings for nothing. A queen dragon was gold: she mated with the bronze who could outfly her. Which was exactly what was happening right now with the fire lizards.

Oh, they were beautiful to behold! The queen had turned sunward and Menolly, for all her eyes were very longsighted, could barely pick out that black mote and trailing cluster.

She walked on, following the main group of fire lizards. She'd bet anything that she'd end up on the coastline near the Dragon Stones. Last fall her brother Alemi had claimed he'd seen fire lizards there at dawn, feeding on fingertails in the shallows. His report had set off another rash of what Petiron had called "lizard-fever." Every lad in the Sea Hold had burned with plans to trap a fire lizard. They'd plagued Alemi to repeat his sighting.

It was just as well that the crags were unapproachable. Not even an experienced boatman would brave those treacherous currents. But, if anyone had been *sure* there were fire lizards there . . . Well no one would know from her.

Even if Petiron had been alive, Menolly decided, she would not have told him. He'd never seen a fire lizard, though he'd admitted to the children that the Records allowed that fire lizards did exist.

"They're seen," Petiron had told her later, "but they can't be captured." He gave a wheezing chuckle. "People've been trying to since the first shell was cracked."

"Why can't they be caught?"

"They don't want to. They're smart. They just disappear . . ."

"They go *between* like dragons?"

"There's no proof of that," said Petiron, a trifle cross, as if she'd been too presumptuous in suggesting a comparison between fire lizards and the great dragons of Pern.

"Where else can you disappear to?" Menolly had wanted to know. "What is *between?*"

"Some place that isn't." Petiron had shuddered. "You're neither here nor there," and he gestured first to one corner of the Hall and then towards the Sea Dock on the other side of the Harbor. "It's cold, and it's nothing. No sight, no sound, no sensations."

"You've ridden dragonback?" Menolly had been impressed.

"Once. Many Turns ago." He shuddered again in remembrance. "Now, since we're touching on the subject, sing me the Riddle Song."

"It's been solved. Why do we have to know it now?"

"Sing it for me so I'll know that you know it, girl," Petiron had said testily. Which was no reason at all.

But Petiron had been very kind to her, Menolly knew, and her throat tightened with remembered regret for his passing. (Had he gone *between?* The way dragons did when they lost their riders or grew too infirm to fly? No, one left nothing behind, going *between.* Petiron had left his body to be slipped into the deeps.) And Petiron had left more behind than his body. He'd left her every song he'd ever known, every lay, every ballad, saga, every fingering, chord and strum, every rhythm. There wasn't any way a stringed instrument could be played that she didn't know, nor any cadence on the drums at which she wasn't time-perfect. She could whistle double-trills as well as any wherry with her tongue or on the reeds. But there had been some things Petiron wouldn't—or perhaps couldn't—tell her about her world. Menolly wondered if this was because she was a girl and there were mysteries that only the male mind could understand.

"Well," as Mavi had once told Menolly and Sella, "there are feminine puzzles that no mere man could sort, so that score is even."

"And one more for the feminine side," said Menolly as she followed the fire lizards. A mere girl had seen what all the boys—and men—of the Sea Hold had only dreamed of seeing, fire lizards at play.

They'd ceased following the queen and her bronzes and now indulged in mock air battles, swooping now and then to the land itself. And seemingly under it. Until Menolly realized that they must be over the beaches. The sand was slipping under her feet. An unwary step could plunge her into the holes and dips. She could hear the sea. She changed her course, keeping to the thicker patches of coarse marsh grasses. The ground would be firmer there, and she'd be less visible to the fire lizards.

She came to a slight rise, before the bluff broke off into a steep dive onto the beaches. The Dragon Stones were beyond in the sea, slightly hidden by a heat haze. She could hear fire lizards chirping and chattering. She crouched in the grasses and then, dropping to her full length, crept to the bluff edge, hoping for another glimpse of the fire lizards.

They were quite visible—delightfully so. The tide was out, and they were exceedingly busy in the shallows, picking rockmites from the tumbled exposed boulders, or wallowing on the narrow edging of red and white sand, bathing themselves with great enthusiasm in the little pools, spreading their delicate wings to dry. There were several flurries as two fire lizards vied for the same choice morsel. In that alone, she decided, they must differ from dragons; she'd never heard of dragons fighting amongst themselves for anything. She'd heard that dragons feeding among herds of runner-beasts and wherries were something horrible to behold. Dragons didn't eat that frequently, which was as well or not all the resources of Pern could keep the dragons fed.

Did dragons like fish? Menolly giggled, wondering if there were any fish in the sea big enough to satisfy a dragon's appetite. Probably those legendary fish that always eluded the Sea Hold nets. Her Sea Hold sent their tithe of sea produce, salted, pickled or smoked, to Benden Weyr. Occasionally a dragonrider came asking for fresh fish for a special feasting, like a Hatching. And the women of the Weyr came every spring and fall to berry or cut withies and grasses. Menolly had once served Manora, the headwoman of Benden Lower Caverns, and a very pleasant gentle woman she'd been, too. Menolly hadn't been allowed to stay in the room long because Mavi shooed her daughters out, saying that she had things to discuss with Manora. But Menolly had seen enough to know she liked her.

The whole flock of lizards suddenly went aloft, startled by the return of the queen and the bronze who had flown her. The pair settled wearily in the warm shallow waters, wings spread as if both were too exhausted to fold them back. The bronze tenderly twined his neck about his queen's and they floated so, while blues excitedly offered the resting pair fingertails and rockmites.

Entranced, Menolly watched from her screen of seagrass. She was utterly engrossed by the small doings of eating, cleaning and resting. By and by, singly or in pairs, the lesser fire lizards winged up to the first of the sea-surrounded bluffs, lost quickly from Menolly's sight as they secreted themselves in tiny creviced weyrs.

With graceful dignity, the queen and her bronze rose from their bathing. How they managed to fly with their glistening wings so close together, Menolly didn't know. As one, they seemed to dart aloft, then glided in a slow spiral down to the Dragon Stones, disappearing on the seaside and out of Menolly's vision.

Only then did she become conscious of discomfort; of the hot sun on her welted back, sand in the waistband of her trousers, seeping into her shoes, dried as sweaty grit on her face and hands.

Cautiously, she wriggled back from the edge of the bluff. If the fire lizards knew they'd been overseen, they might not return to this cove. When she felt she'd crawled far enough, she got to a crouching position and ran for a way.

She felt as rarely privileged as if she'd been asked to Benden Weyr. She kicked up her heels in an excess of joy and then, spotting some thick march grass canes in the bog, snicked one off at the waterline. Her father may have taken her gitar away, but there were more materials than strings over a sounding box to make music.

She measured the proper length barrel and cut off the rest. She deftly made six holes top and two bottom, as Petiron had taught her, and in moments, she was playing her reed pipe. A saucy tune, bright and gay because she was happy inside. A tune about a little fire lizard queen, sitting on a rock in the lapping sea, preening herself for her adoring bronze.

She'd a bit of trouble with the obligatory runs and found herself changing keys, but when she'd rehearsed the tune several times, she decided she liked it. It sounded so different from the sort of melody Petiron had taught her, different from the traditional form. Furthermore, it sounded like a fire lizard song: sprightly, cunning, secretive.

She stopped her piping, puzzled. Did the dragons know about fire lizards?

Chapter 3

Holder, watch; Holder, learn
Something new in every Turn.
Oldest may be coldest, too.
Sense the right: find the true!

When Menolly finally got back to the Sea Hold, the sky was darkening. The Hall was bustling with the usual end of day activity. The oldsters were setting the dinner tables, tidying the great Hall and chattering away as if they hadn't met for Turns instead of only that morning.

With luck, thought Menolly, she could get her sack down to the water rooms . . .

"Where did you go for those greens, Menolly? Nerat?" Her mother appeared in front of her.

"Almost."

Immediately Menolly saw that her pert words were ill-timed. Mavi roughly grabbed the sack and peered inside critically.

"If you'd not made the trip worth the while . . . Sail's been sighted."

"Sail?"

Mavi closed the sack and shoved it back into Menolly's hands. "Yes, sail. You should have been back hours ago. Whatever possessed you to take off so far with Thread . . ."

"There weren't any greens nearer . . ."

"With Thread due to fall anytime? You're a fool twice over."

"I was safe enough. I saw a dragonrider doing his sweep . . ."

That pleased Mavi. "Thank heavens we're beholden to Benden. They're a proper Weyr." Mavi gave her daughter a shove towards the kitchen level. "Take those, and be sure the girls wash every speck of sand off. Who knows who's sailing in?"

Menolly slipped through the busy kitchen, countering orders flung at her by various other women who saw in her a capable assistant at their own tasks. Menolly merely brandished the sack and proceeded down to the water rooms. There some of the older but still able women were busily sandscouring the best metal plates and trays.

"I must have one basin for the greens, auntie," said Menolly, pushing up to the rank of stone sinks.

"Greens is easier on old skin than sand," said one of the women in a quavering, long-suffering voice and promptly deposited her pile of plates into the sink beside her and pulled her plug.

"More sand in greens than cleaning," another woman remarked in an acid tone.

"Yes, but take it *off* greens," said the obliging one. "Oh, what a lovely mess of yellow-veins, too. Where did you find them this time of year, daughter?"

"Halfway to Nerat." Menolly suppressed her grin at their startled shrieks of dismay. The furthest they'd stir from the Hold was the ledge in front on a sunny day.

"With Thread falling? You naughty girl!" "Did you hear about the sail?" "Who do you suppose?" "The new Harper, who else?" There was a wild chorus of cackling laughs and great wonderings about the appearance of the new Harper.

"They always send a young one here."

"Petiron was old!"

"He got *that* way. Same as we did!"

"How would you remember?"

"Why not? I've lived through more Harpers than you have, my girl."

"You have not! I came here from Red Sands in Ista . . ."

"You were born at Half-Circle, you old fool, and I birthed you!"

"Ha!"

Menolly listened to the four old women arguing back and forth until she heard her mother demanding to know if the greens had been washed. And where were the good plates and how was she to get anything done with all the gossip?

Menolly found a sieve large enough to hold the washed greens and brought them up for her mother's inspection.

"Well, that'll be enough for the head table," Mavi said, poking at the glistening mound with her fork. Then she stared at her daughter. "You *can't* appear like that. Here you, Bardie, take the greens and put the dressing on them. The one in the brown flask on the fourth shelf in the cool room. You, Menolly, have the goodness to get yourself sandfree and decently dressed. You're to attend Old Uncle. The moment he opens his mouth, shove something into it or we'll be hearing him all night long."

Menolly groaned. Old Uncle smelled almost as much as he chattered. "Sella's much better handling him, Mavi . . ."

"Sella's to attend head table. You do as you're told and be grateful!"

Mavi fixed her rebellious daughter with a stern eye, tacitly reminding her of her disgrace. Then Mavi was called away to check a sauce for the baking fish.

Menolly went off to the bathing rooms, trying to convince herself that she was lucky she hadn't been banished completely from the Hall this evening. Though tending Old Uncle came as close as could be to banishment. Honor obliged the Sea Holder to have all his household there to greet the new Harper.

Menolly shucked off the dirty tunic and breeches, and slipped into the warm bathing pool. She swung her shoulders this way and that for the water to wash the sand and sweat as painlessly as possible from her sore back. Her hair was all gritty with sea sand, too, so she washed that. She was quick because she'd have her hands full with Old Uncle. It'd be much better to have him all arranged in his hearth seat before everyone else assembled for dinner.

Draping her dirty clothes around her, Menolly took the calculated risk that few people would be in the High Hold at this hour and charged up the dimly lit steps from the bathing pools to the sleeping level. Every glow in the main corridor was uncovered, which meant that the Harper, if such it were, would have a guided tour of the Hold later. She dashed down to the narrow steps leading to the girls' dormitories, and got into her cubicle without a soul the wiser.

When she got to Old Uncle's room, later, she had to clean his face and hands and slip a clean tunic over his bony shoulders. All the while he was chattering about new blood in the Hold and hee-hee who was the new Harper going to marry? He'd a thing or two to tell the Harper, give him the chance, and why did she have to be so rough? His bones ached. Must be a change in the weather because his old legs never failed to give warning. Hadn't he warned them about the big storm a while back? Two boats had been lost with all crew. If they'd paid attention to his warning, it wouldn't have happened. His own son was the worst one for not listening to what his father said and why was she hurrying him so? He liked to take his time. No, couldn't he have the blue tunic? The one his daughter had made him, matching his eyes, she'd said. And why hadn't Turlon come to see him today as he'd asked and asked and asked, but who paid him any heed anymore?

The old man was so frail that he was no burden to a strong girl like Menolly. She carried him down the steps, he complaining all the way about people who'd been dead before she was born. Old Uncle's notion of time was distorted, that's what Petiron had told her. Brightest in Uncle's memory were his earlier days, when he'd been Sea Holder of Half-Circle, before a tangled trawler line had sliced off his legs below the knee. The great Hall was almost ready for guests when Menolly entered with him.

"They're tacking into Dock," someone was saying as Menolly arranged Old Uncle in his special seat by the fire. She wrapped him well in the softened wherhides and tied the strap that would keep him upright. When he got excited, Old Uncle had a tendency to forget he had no feet.

"Who's tacking into Dock? Who's coming? What's all the hubble-bubble about?"

Menolly told him, and he subsided, moments later wanting to know in a querulous tone of voice if anyone was going to feed him or was he supposed to sit here dinnerless?

Sella, in the gown she'd spent all winter making, swirled past Menolly, pressing a small packet into her hand.

"Feed him these if he gets difficult!" And she skimmed away before Menolly could say a word.

Opening the packet, Menolly saw balls of a sweet made from seaweed, flavored with purple grass seed. One could chew these for hours, keeping the mouth fresh and moist. Small wonder Sella'd been able to keep Old Uncle happy. Menolly giggled and then wondered why Sella was being so helpful. It must have pleased Sella no end to learn Menolly had been displaced as Harper. Or would she know? Mavi wouldn't have mentioned it. Ah, but the Harper was here now, anyhow.

Now that she had Old Uncle settled, Menolly's curiosity got the better of her and she slipped over to the windows. There was no sign of the sail in the harbor now, but she could see the cluster of men, glows held high, as they walked around the shore from the Dock to the Hold proper. Keen though her eyes were, Menolly could not pick out the new faces and that was that.

Old Uncle began one of his monologues in a high-pitched voice, so Menolly scooted back to his side before her mother could notice she'd left her post. There was so much bustle, putting food on the tables, pouring the welcoming cups of wine, all the Hold arranging itself to meet the guests, no one noticed what Menolly was or wasn't doing.

Just then, Old Uncle came to himself again, eyes bright and focused on her face. "What's the stir today, girl? Good haul? Someone getting spliced? What's the lay?"

"There's a new Harper coming, everyone thinks, Old Uncle."

"Not another one?" Old Uncle was disgusted. "Harpers ain't what they used to be when I was Sea Holder, not by a long crack. I mind myself of one Harper we had . . ."

His voice fell clearly in the suddenly quiet Hall.

"Menolly!" Her mother's voice was low, but the urgency was unmistakable.

Menolly fumbled in her skirt pocket, found two sweetballs and popped them into Old Uncle's mouth. Whatever he'd been about to say was stopped by the necessity of dealing with two large round objects. He mumbled contentedly to himself as he chewed and chewed and chewed.

All the food had been served and everyone seated before Menolly got so much as a glimpse of the new arrivals. There had been a new Harper. She heard his name before she ever saw his face. Elgion, Harper Elgion. She heard that he was young and good-looking and had brought two gitars, two wooden pipes and three drums, each carried separately in its own case of stiffened wherhide. She heard that he'd been very seasick across Keroon Bay and wasn't doing justice to the lavish dinner spread in his honor. With him had come a craftmaster from the Smithcrafthall to do the metal work required on the new ship and other repairs beyond the metalman in the Sea Hold. She heard that there was urgent need at Igen Hold for any salted or smoked fish the Sea Hold might have to spare on the return voyage.

From where Menolly sat with Old Uncle, she could see the backs of heads at the high table and occasionally a profile of one of the visitors. Very frustrating. So was Old Uncle and the other elderly relatives whose old bones rated them a spot near the fire. The aunts were, as usual, squabbling over who had received the choicer portions of fish, and then Old Uncle decided to call them to order, only his mouth was full at that moment and he choked. So the aunts turned on Menolly for trying to stuff him to an early death. Menolly could hear nothing over their babble. She tried to content herself with the prospect of hearing the Harper sing, as he surely would once the interminable meal was ended. But it was hot so close to the big fire and the heat made Old Uncle smell worse than ever, and she was very tired after the day's exertions.

She was roused from a half doze by a sudden hallwide thudding of heavy seaboots. She jerked fully awake to see the tall figure of the new Harper rising at the head table. He had his gitar ready and was taking an easy stance, one foot on the stone bench.

"You're sure this Hall isn't rocking?" he asked, strumming a few chords to test the instrument's pitch. He was assured that the Hall had been steady for many, many Turns, never known to rock at all. The Harper affected not to be reassured as he tuned the G-string slightly higher (to Menolly's relief). He made the gitar moan then, like a seasick soul.

As laughter rippled through the eager audience, Menolly strained to see how her father was taking this approach. The Sea Holder had little humor. A Harper's welcome was a serious occasion, and Elgion did not appear to realize this. Petiron had often told Menolly how carefully Harpers were chosen for the Hold they were assigned to. Hadn't anyone warned Elgion about her father's temperament?

Suddenly Old Uncle cut across the gentle strumming with a cackle of laughter. "Ha! A man with humor! That's what we need in this Hold—some laughter. Some music! Been missing it. Let's have some rollicking tunes, some funny songs. Give us a good rib-popping ditty, Harper. You know the ones I like."

Menolly was aghast. She fumbled in her skirt pocket for some of the sweetballs as she shushed Old Uncle. This was exactly the sort of incident that she was supposed to prevent.

Harper Elgion had turned at the imperious order, bowing with good respect to the old gentleman by the hearth.

"I would that I could, Old Uncle," he said most courteously, "but these are serious times," and his fingers plucked deep sombre notes, "very serious times and we must put lightness and laughter behind us. Square our backs to the problems that face us . . ." and with that he swung into a new exhortation to obey the Weyr and honor the dragonrider.

The sticky sweetballs had got warmed and stuck to the fabric of her pocket, but Menolly finally got some out and into Old Uncle's mouth. He chewed angrily, fully aware that his mouth was being plugged and resenting it. He chewed as fast as he could, swallowing to clear his mouth for more complaints. Menolly was only just aware that the new tune was forceful, the words stirring. Harper Elgion had a rich tenor voice, strong and sure. Then Old Uncle began to hiccup. Noisily, of course. And to complain, or try to, through the hiccups. Menolly hissed at him to hold his breath, but he was furious at not being allowed to talk, at getting hiccups, and he started to pound the arm of his chair. The thumps made an out-of-tempo counterpoint to the Harper's song and brought her furious glances from the head table.

One of the aunts gave her some water for the old man, which he overturned on Menolly. The next thing, Sella was beside her, gesturing that they were to take the old man back to his quarters instantly.

He was still hiccuping as they put him back to bed, and still beating the air with punctuated gestures and half-uttered complaints.

"You'll have to stay with him until he calms down, Menolly, or he'll fall out of bed. Whyever didn't you give him the sweetballs? They always shut him up," Sella said.

"I did. They're what started him hiccuping."

"You can't do anything right, can you?"

"Please, Sella. You stay with him. You manage him so well. I've had him all evening and not heard a word . . ."

"*You* were told to keep him quiet. *You* didn't. *You* stay." And Sella swept out of the room, leaving Menolly to cope.

That was the end of the first of Menolly's difficult days. It took hours for the old man to calm down and go to sleep. Then, as Menolly wearily got to her cubicle, her mother arrived to berate her soundly for the inattention that had given Uncle a chance to embarrass the entire Hold. Menolly was given no chance to explain.

The next day, Thread fell, sequestering them all within the Hold for hours. When the Fall was over, she had to go with the flame-thrower crews. The leading edge of Thread had tipped the marshes, which meant hours of plodding through sticky marsh mud and slimy sand.

She was tired enough when she returned from that task, but then they all had to help load the big nets and ready the boats for a night trawl. The tide was right then.

She was roused before sunrise the next morning to gut and salt the phenomenal catch. That took all the livelong day and sent her to bed so weary she just stripped off her dirty clothes, and dropped into her sleeping furs.

The next day was devoted to net-mending, normally a pleasant task because the Hold women would chat and sing. But her father was anxious for the nets to be repaired quickly so that he could take the evening tide again for another deep-sea cast. Everyone bent to his work without time for talk or singing while the Sea Holder prowled among them. He seemed to watch Menolly more often than anyone else, and she felt clumsy.

It was then that she began to wonder if perhaps the new Harper had found fault with the way the youngsters had been taught their Ballads and Sagas. Time and again Petiron had told her that there was only one way to teach them and, as she had learned properly from him, she must have passed on the knowledge correctly. Why then did her father seem to be so annoyed with her? Why did he glare at her so much? Was he still angry with her for letting Old Uncle babble?

She worried enough to ask her sister about it that evening when the ships had finally set sail and everyone else could relax a little.

"Angry about Old Uncle?" Sella shrugged. "What on earth are you talking about, girl? Who remembers that? You think entirely too much about yourself, Menolly, that's your biggest problem. Why should Yanus care one way or another about *you?*"

The scorn in Sella's voice reminded Menolly too acutely that she was only a girl, too big for a proper girl, and the youngest of a large family, therefore of least account. It was in no way a consolation to be insignificant, even if her father was, for that reason, less likely to notice her. Or remember her misdeeds. Except that he'd remembered about her singing her own songs to the youngsters. Or had Sella forgotten that? Or did Sella even know that?

Probably, thought Menolly as she tried to find a comfortable spot in the old bed rushes for her weary body. But then, what Sella said about Menolly thinking only of herself applied even more to Sella, who was always thinking about her appearance and her self. Sella was old enough to be married to some advantage to the Hold. Her father had only three fosterlings at the moment, but four of Menolly's six brothers were out at other Sea Holds, learning their trade. Now, with a Harper to speak for them all again, perhaps there'd be some rearrangements.

The next day the Hold women spent in washing clothes. With Threadfall past, and a good clear sunny day, they could count on fast drying. Menolly hoped for a chance to speak to her mother to find out if the Harper had faulted her teaching, but the opportunity never arose. Instead, Menolly came in for another scolding from Mavi for the state of her clothes, unmended; her bed furs, unaired; her hair, her sloppy appearance and her slothfulness in general. That evening Menolly was quite content to take a bowl of soup and disappear into a shadowy corner of the big kitchen rather than be noticed again. She kept wondering why she was being singled out for so much misunderstanding.

Her thoughts kept returning to the sin of having strummed a few bars of her own song. That, and being a girl and the only one who could teach or play in the absence of a real Harper.

Yes, she finally decided, that was the reason for her universal disfavor. No one wanted the Harper to know that the youngsters had been schooled by a girl. But, if she hadn't taught them right, then Petiron had taught her all wrong. That didn't hold water. And, if the old man had really written the Masterharper about her, wouldn't the new Harper have been curious, or sought her out? Maybe her songs hadn't been as good as old Petiron had thought. Probably Petiron had never sent them to the Masterharper. And that message hadn't said anything about her. At any rate, the packet was now gone from the mantel in the Records room. And, the way things were going, Menolly would never get close enough to Elgion to introduce herself.

Sure as the sun came up, Menolly could guess what she'd have to do the next day—gather new grasses and rushes to repack all the beds in the Hold. It was just the sort of thing her mother would think of for someone so out of favor.

She was wrong. The ships came back to port just after dawn, their holds packed with yellow-stripe and packtails. The entire Hold was turned out to gut, salt and start the smoke-cave.

Of all the fish in the sea, Menolly detested packtails the most. An ugly fish, with sharp spines all over, it oozed an oily slime that ate into the flesh of your hands and made the skin peel off. Packtails were more head and mouth than anything else but hack the front end off and the rounded, blunt tail could be sliced off the backbone. Grilled fresh it was succulent eating: smoked it could be softened later for baking or boiling and be as tasty as the day it was caught. But packtails were the messiest, hardest, toughest, smelliest fish to gut.

Halfway through the morning, Menolly's knife slipped across the fish she was slicing, gashing her left palm wide open. The pain and shock were so great that Menolly just stood, stupidly staring at her hand bones, until Sella realized that she wasn't keeping pace with the others.

"Menolly, just dreaming . . . Oh, for the love of . . . Mavi! Mavi!" Sella could be irritating, but she could keep her wits. As she did now, grabbing Menolly's wrist and stopping the spurt of blood from the severed artery.

As Mavi came and led her past the furiously working holders, Menolly was seized with a sense of guilt. Everyone glared at her as if she'd deliberately wounded herself to get out of working. The humiliation and silent accusations brought tears to her eyes, not the pain nor the sick feeling in her hand.

"I didn't do it on purpose," Menolly blurted out to her mother as they reached the Hold's infirmary.

Her mother stared at her. "Who said that you did?"

"No one! They just looked it!"

"My girl, you think entirely too much about yourself. I assure you that no one was thinking any such thing. Now hold your hand, so, for a moment."

The blood spurted up as Mavi released the pressure on the tendon in Menolly's wrist. For one instant Menolly thought she might faint, but she was determined not to think of herself again. She pretended that she didn't own the hand that Mavi was going to have to fix.

Mavi now deftly fastened a tourniquet and then laved the wound with a pungent herbal lotion. Menolly's hand began to numb, increasing her detachment from the injury. The bleeding ceased, but somehow Menolly couldn't bring herself to look into the wound. Instead she watched the intent expression on her mother's face as she quickly stitched the severed blood vessel and closed the long slice. Then she slathered quantities of salve on the cut and bound the hand in soft cloths.

"There! Let's hope I got all that packtail slime out of the wound."

Concern and doubt caused Mavi to frown, and Menolly became fearful. Suddenly she remembered other things: women losing fingers and . . .

"My hand will be all right, won't it?"

"We'll hope so."

Mavi never lied, and the small hard ball of sick fear began to unknot in Menolly's stomach.

"You should have some use of it. Enough for all practical purposes."

"What do you mean? Practical purposes? Won't I be able to play again?"

"Play?" Mavi gave her daughter a long, hard stare, as if she'd mentioned something forbidden. "Your playing days are over, Menolly. You're way past the teaching . . ."

"But the new Harper has new songs . . . the ballad he sang the first night . . . I never heard all of it. I don't know the chording. I want to learn . . ." She broke off, horribly frightened by the closed look on her mother's face, and the shine of pity in her eyes.

"Even if your fingers will work after that slice, you won't be playing again. Content yourself that Yanus was so indulgent while old Petiron was dying . . ."

"But Petiron . . ."

"That's enough *buts.* Here, drink this. I want you in your bed before it puts you to sleep. You've lost a lot of blood, and I can't have you fainting away on me."

Stunned by her mother's words, Menolly barely tasted the bitter wine and weed. She stumbled, even with her mother's help, up the stone steps to her cubicle. She was cold despite the furs, cold in spirit. But the wine and weed had been liberally mixed, and she couldn't fight the effect. Her last conscious thought was of misery, of being cheated of the one thing that had made her life bearable. She knew now what a dragonless rider must feel.

Chapter 4

Black, blacker, blackest
And cold beyond frozen things.
Where is between when there is naught
To Life but fragile dragons' wings?

Despite her mother's care in cleaning the wound, Menolly's hand was swollen by evening and she was feverish with pain. One of the old aunts sat with her, placing cool cloths on her head and face, and gently crooning what she thought would be a comforting song. The notion was misplaced since, even in her delirium, Menolly was aware that music had now been forbidden her. She became more irritated and restless. Finally Mavi dosed her liberally with fellis juice and wine, and she fell into a deep slumber.

This proved to be a blessing because the hand had so swollen that it was obvious some of the packtail slime had gotten in the bloodstream. Mavi called in one of the other Hold women deft in such matters. Luckily for Menolly, they decided to release the coarse stitches, to allow better drainage of the infection. They kept Menolly heavily dosed and hourly changed the hot poulticing of her hand and arm.

Packtail infection was pernicious, and Mavi was dreadfully afraid that they might have to remove Menolly's arm to prevent a further spread. She was constantly by her daughter's side, an attention that Menolly would have been surprised, and gratified, to receive, but she remained unconscious. Fortunately the angry red lines faded on the girl's swollen arm on the evening of the fourth day. The swelling receded, and the edges of the terrible gash assumed the healthier color of healing flesh.

Throughout her delirium, Menolly kept begging "them" to let her play just once more, just once again, pleading in such a pitiful tone that it all but broke Mavi's heart to realize that unkind fortune had made that impossible. The hand would always be crippled. Which was as well since some of the new Harper's questions were provoking Yanus. Elgion very much wanted to know who had drilled the youngsters in their Teaching Songs and Ballads. At first, thinking that Menolly had been

nowhere near as skilled as everyone had assumed, Yanus had told Elgion that a fosterling had undertaken the task and he'd returned to his
own Hold just prior to the Harper's arrival.

"Whoever did has the makings of a good Harper then," Elgion told
his new Holder. "Old Petiron was a better teacher than most."

The praise unexpectedly disturbed Yanus. He couldn't retract his
words, and he didn't want to admit to Elgion that the person was a girl.
So Yanus decided to let matters stand. No girl could be a Harper, any
way the road turned. Menolly was too old now to be in any of the
classes, and he'd see that she was busy with other things until she came
to think of her playing as some childish fancy. At least she hadn't
disgraced the Hold.

He was, of course, sorry that the girl had cut herself so badly, and not
entirely because she was a good worker. Still it kept her out of the
Harper's way until she forgot her silly tuning. Once or twice though,
while Menolly was ill, he missed her clear sweet voice in counter-song,
the way she and Petiron used to sing. Yet he dismissed the matter from
his mind. Women had more to do than sit about singing and playing.

There were exciting doings in the Holds and Weyrs, according to
Elgion's private report to him. Troubles, too, deep and worrisome
enough to take his mind from the minor matter of a wounded girl.

One of the questions that Harper Elgion often posed concerned the
Sea Hold's attitude towards their Weyr, Benden. Elgion was curious as
to how often they came in contact with the Oldtimers at Ista Weyr.
How did Yanus and his holders feel about dragonriders? About the
Weyrleader and Weyrwoman of Benden? If they resented dragonmen
going on Search for young boys and girls of the Holds and Crafthalls to
become dragonriders? Had Yanus or any of his Hold ever attended a
Hatching?

Yanus answered the questions with the fewest possible words, and at
first this seemed to satisfy the Harper.

"Half-Circle's always tithed to Benden Weyr, even before Thread fell.
We know our duty to our Weyr, and they do theirs by us. Not a single
burrow of Thread since the Fall started seven or more Turns ago."

"Oldtimers? Well, with Half-Circle beholden to Benden Weyr, we
don't much see any of the other Weyrs, not as the people in Keroon or
Nerat might when the Fall overlaps two Weyrs' boundaries. Very glad
we were that the Oldtimers would come *between* so many hundreds of
Turns to help our time out."

"Dragonmen are welcome any time at Half-Circle. Come spring and
fall, the women are here anyway, gathering seabeachplums and
marshberries, grasses and the like. Welcome to all they want."

"Never met Weyrwoman Lessa. I see her on her queen Ramoth in the sky after a Fall now and then. Weyrleader F'lar's a fine fellow."

"Search? Do they find any likely lad at Half-Circle, it will be to our honor, and he's our leave to go."

Although the problem had never worried the Sea Holder; no one from Half-Circle had answered a Search. Which was as well, Yanus thought privately. If a lad happened to be chosen, every other lad in the Hold would take to grumbling that he should have been picked. And on the seas of Pern, you had to keep your mind on your work, not on dreams. Bad enough to have those pesky fire lizards appearing now and then by the Dragon Stones. But as no one could get near enough to the stones to catch a fire lizard, no harm was done.

If the new Harper found his Holder an unimaginative man, hardworking and hidebound, he had been well prepared for it by his training. His problem was that he must provoke a change, subtle at first, in what he found; for Masterharper Robinton wanted each of his journeymen to get every Holder and Craftmaster to think beyond the needs of their own lands, Hall and people. Harpers were not simply tellers of tales and singers of songs; they were arbiters of justice, confidants of Holders and Craftmasters, and molders of the young. Now, more than ever, it was necessary to alter hidebound thinking, to get everyone, starting with the young and working on the old, to consider more of Pern than the land they kept Threadfree or the problems of their particular area. Many old ways needed shaking up, revising. If F'lar of Benden Weyr hadn't done some shaking up, if Lessa hadn't made her fantastic ride back four hundred Turns to bring up the missing five Weyrs of dragonriders, Pern would be writhing under Thread, with nothing green and growing left on the surface. The Weyrs had profited and so had Pern. Similarly the holds and crafts would profit if they only were willing to examine new ideas and ways.

Half-Circle could expand, Elgion thought. The present quarters were becoming cramped. The children had told him that there were more caves in the adjacent bluffs. And the Dock Cavern could accommodate more than the thirty-odd craft now anchored so safely there.

By and large, though, Elgion was rather relieved at his situation, since this was his first post as Harper. He had his own well-furnished apartments in the Hold, enough to eat, though the diet of fish might soon pall on a man accustomed to red meat, and the Seaholders were generally pleasant people, if a little dour.

Only one thing puzzled him: who had drilled the children so perfectly? Old Petiron had sent word to the Harper that there was a likely songmaker at Half-Circle, and he had included two scored melodies that had greatly impressed the Masterharper. Petiron had also said that there'd be some difficulty in the Sea Hold about the songmaker. A new Harper, for Petiron had known that he was dying when he wrote the Masterharper, would have to go carefully. This was a Hold that had kept much to itself and observed all the old ways.

So Elgion had kept his counsel on the matter of the songmaker, certain that the lad would make himself known. Music was hard to deny and, based on the two songs Elgion had been shown, this lad was undeniably musical. However, if the chap were a fosterling and away from the Hold, he'd have to await his return.

Elgion had soon managed to visit all the different smaller holds in the Half-Circle palisade and gotten to know most people by name. The young girls would flirt with him or gaze at him with sorrowful eyes and sighs when he played in the evenings at the Great Hall.

There was really no way in which Elgion would have realized that Menolly was the person he wanted. The children had been told by the Sea Holder that the Harper would not like to know that they'd been drilled by a girl, so they were not to bring disgrace on the Hold by telling him. After Menolly cut her hand so badly, it was rumored that she'd never use it again, so everyone was told that it would be heartless to ask her to sing in the evenings.

When Menolly was well of the infection and her hand healed but obviously stiff, no one was thoughtless enough to remind her of her music. She herself stayed away from the singing in the Great Hall. And since she could not use her hand well and so many occupations in the Hold required two, she was frequently sent away in the day to gather greens and fruits, usually alone.

If Mavi was perplexed by the quietness and passivity of her youngest child, she put it down to the long and painful recovery, not to loss of her music. Mavi knew that all manner of pain and trouble could be forgotten in time, and so she did her best to keep her daughter occupied. Mavi was a very busy woman, and Menolly kept out of her way.

Gathering greens and fruit suited Menolly perfectly. It kept her out in the open and away from the Hold, away from people. She would have her morning drink, bread and fish quietly in the great kitchen when everyone was dashing around to feed the men of the Hold, either going out to fish or coming back in from a night's sailing. Then Menolly would wrap up a fishroll and take one of the nets or skin slings. She'd tell the old aunt in charge of the pantry that she was going out for whatever it was, and since the old aunt had a memory like a seine net, she wouldn't remember that Menolly had done the same thing the day before or realize that she would do the same the day after.

When spring was fully warming the air and making the marshes brilliant with green and blossom color, spiderclaws began to walk in from the sea to lay their eggs in the shallower cove waters. As these plump shellfish were a delicacy in themselves, besides adding flavor to every dish when dried or smoked, the young people of the Hold— Menolly with them—were sent off with traps, spades and nets. Within four days the nearby coves were picked clear of spiderclaws and the young harvesters had to go farther along the coast to find more. With Thread due to fall anytime, it was unwise to stray too far from the Hold, so they were told to be very careful.

There was another danger that concerned the Sea Holder considerably: tides had been running unusually high and full this Turn. Much higher water in the harbor and they'd not get the two big sloops in or out of the Cavern unless they unstepped the masts. Due notice was taken of the high-tide lines, and there was much shaking of heads when it was observed that the line was two full hands higher than ever before recorded.

The lower caverns of the Hold were checked against possible seepage. Bags of sand were filled and placed along the lower portions of the seawalls around the harbor.

A good storm and the causeways would be awash. Yanus was concerned enough to have a long chat with Old Uncle to see if he remembered anything from his earlier and clearer days of Sea Holding. Old Uncle was delighted to talk and ranted on about the influence of the stars, but when Yanus, Elgion and two of the other older shipmasters had sifted through what he'd said, it was not to any great increase in knowledge. Everyone knew that the two moons affected the tides, not the three bright stars in the sky.

They did, however, send a message about these curious tides to Igen Hold to be forwarded with all possible speed to the main Seacraft Hold at Fort. Yanus didn't want to have his biggest boats caught out in the open, so he kept careful check on the tides, determined to leave them within the Dock Cavern if the tide rose another hand higher.

When the youngsters went out to gather spiderclaws, they were told to keep their eyes open and report back anything unusual, especially new high-water marks on the coves. Only Thread deterred the more adventurous lads from using this as an excuse for ranging far down the coast. Menolly, who preferred to explore the more distant places alone, mentioned Thread to them as often as possible.

Then, after the next Threadfall, when everyone was sent out for spiderclaws, Menolly made certain that she got a headstart on the boys, making good use of her long legs.

It was fine to run like this, Menolly thought, putting yet another rise between her and her nearest pursuers. She altered her stride for uneven ground. It wouldn't do to break an ankle now. Running was something even a girl with a crippled hand could do well.

Menolly closed her mind to that thought. She'd learned the trick of not thinking about anything: she counted. Right now she counted her strides. She ran on, her eyes sweeping ahead of her to save her feet. The boys would never catch her now, but she was running for the sheer joy of the physical effort, chanting a number to each stride. She ran until she got a stitch in her side and her thighs felt the strain.

She slowed, turning her face into the cool breeze blowing offshore, inhaling deeply of its freshness and sea odors. She was somewhat surprised to see how far she had come down the coast. The Dragon Stones were visible in the clear air, and it was only then that she recalled the little queen. Unfortunately, she also remembered the tune she'd made up that day: that last day, Menolly now realized, of her trusting childhood.

She walked on, following the line of the bluffs, peering down to see if she could spot new high-water marks on the stone escarpments. Tide was halfway in now, Menolly decided. And yes, she could see the lines of sea debris from the last tide, in some places right up against the cliff face. And this had been a cove with a deep beach.

A movement above, a sudden blotting of the sun, made her gaze upwards. A sweep rider. Knowing perfectly well that he couldn't see her, she waved vigorously anyhow, watching the graceful glide as the pair dwindled into the distance.

Sella had told her one evening when they were preparing for bed that Elgion had flown on dragons several times. Sella had given a quiver of delighted terror, vowing that she wouldn't have the courage to ride a dragon.

Privately Menolly thought that Sella wouldn't likely have the opportunity. Most of Sella's comments, and probably thoughts, were centered on the new Harper. Sella was not the only one, Menolly knew. If Menolly could think how silly all the Hold girls were being about Harper Elgion, it didn't hurt so much to think about harpers in general.

Again she heard the fire lizards before she saw them. Their excited chirpings and squeals indicated something was upsetting them. She dropped to a crouch and crept to the edge of the bluff, overlooking the little beach. Only there wasn't much beach left, and the fire lizards were hovering over a spot on the small margin of sand, almost directly below her.

She inched up to the edge, peering down. She could see the queen darting at the incoming waves as if she could stop them with her violently beating wings. Then she'd streak back, out of Menolly's line of sight, while the rest of the creatures kept milling and swooping, rather like frightened herdbeasts running about aimlessly when wild wherries circled their herd. The queen was shrieking at the top of her shrill little voice, obviously trying to get them to do something. Unable to imagine what the emergency could be, Menolly leaned just a little further over the edge. The whole lip of the cliff gave way.

Clutching wildly at sea grasses, Menolly tried to prevent her fall. But the sea grass slipped cuttingly through her hand and she slid over the edge and down. She hit the beach with a force that sent a shock through her body. But the wet sand absorbed a good deal of the impact. She lay where she'd fallen for a few minutes, trying to get her breath into her lungs and out again. Then she scrambled to her feet and crawled away from an incoming wave.

She looked up the side of the bluff, rather daunted by the fact that she'd fallen a dragon length or more. And how was she going to climb back up? But, as she examined the cliff face, she could see that it was not so unscalable as she'd first thought. Almost straight up, yes, but pocked by ledges and holds, some fairly large. If she could find enough foot and hand holds, she'd be able to make it. She dusted the sand from her hands and started to walk towards one end of the little cove, to begin a systematic search for the easiest way up.

She'd gone only a few paces when something dove at her, screeching in fury. Her hands went up to protect her face as the little queen came diving down at her. Now Menolly recalled the curious behavior of the fire lizards. The little queen acted as if she were protecting something from Menolly as well as the encroaching sea, and she looked about her. She was within handspans of stepping into a fire lizard clutch.

"Oh, I'm sorry. I'm sorry. I wasn't looking! Don't be mad at me," Menolly cried as the little fire lizard came at her again. "Please! Stop! I won't hurt them!"

To prove her sincerity, Menolly backtracked to the far end of the beach. There she had to duck under a small overhang. When she looked around, there wasn't a sign of the little queen. Menolly's relief was short-lived, for how was she to find a way up the cliff if the little fire-lizard kept attacking her every time she approached the eggs. Menolly hunched down, trying to get comfortable in her cramped refuge.

Maybe if she kept away from the eggs? Menolly peered up the cliff directly above her. There were some likely looking holds. She eased herself out the far side, keeping one eye on the clutch, basking in the hot sun, and reached for the first ledge.

Immediately the fire lizard came at her.

"Oh, leave me alone! Ow! Go away. I'm trying to."

The fire lizard's talons had raked her cheek.

"Please! I won't hurt your eggs!"

The little queen's next pass just missed Menolly, who ducked back under the ledge.

Blood oozed from the long scratch, and Menolly dabbed at it with the edge of her tunic.

"Haven't you got any sense?" Menolly demanded of her now invisible attacker. "What would I want with your silly eggs? Keep 'em. I just want to get home. Can't you understand? I just want to go home."

Maybe if I sit very still, she'll forget about me, Menolly thought and pulled her knees up under the chin, but her toes and elbows protruded from under the overhang.

Suddenly a bronze fire lizard materialized above the clutch, squeaking worriedly. Menolly saw the queen swooping to join him, so the queen must have been on the top of the ledge, waiting, just waiting for Menolly to break cover.

And to think I made up a pretty tune about you, Menolly thought as she watched the two lizards hovering over the eggs. The last tune I ever made up. You're ungrateful, that's what you are!

Despite her discomfort, Menolly had to laugh. What an impossible situation! Held under a cramped ledge by a creature no bigger than her forearm.

At the sound of her laughter, the two fire lizards disappeared.

Frightened, were they? Of laughter?

"A smile wins more than a frown," Mavi was fond of saying.

Maybe if I keep laughing, they'll know I'm friendly? Or get scared away long enough for me to climb up? Saved by a laugh?

Menolly began to chuckle in earnest, for she had also seen that the tide was coming in rather quickly. She eased out of her shelter, flung the carry-sack over her shoulder, and started to climb. But it proved impossible to chuckle and climb. She needed breath for both.

Abruptly both the little queen and the bronze were back to harry her, flying at her head and face. The fragile looking wings were dangerous when used as a weapon.

No longer laughing, Menolly ducked back under her ledge, wondering what to do next.

If laughter had startled them, what about a song? Maybe if she gave that pair a chorus of her tune, they'd let her go. It was the first time she'd sung since she'd seen the lizards, so her voice sounded rough and uncertain. Well, the lizards would *know* what she meant, she hoped, so she sang the saucy little song. To no one.

"Well, so much for that notion," Menolly muttered under her breath. "Which makes the lack of interest in your singing absolutely unanimous."

No audience? Not a fire lizard's whisker in sight?

As fast as she could, Menolly slipped from her shelter and came face to face, for a split second, with two fire lizard faces. She ducked down, and they evidently disappeared because when she cautiously peered again, the ledge where they'd been perched was empty.

She had the distinct impression that their expressions had registered curiosity and interest.

"Look, if wherever you are, you can hear me . . . will you stay there and let me go? Once I'm on the top of the cliff, I'll serenade you til the sun goes down. Just let me get up there!"

She started to sing, a dutiful dragon song as she once again emerged from her refuge. She was about five steps upward when the queen fire lizard emerged, with help. With squeaks and squeals she was driven back down. She could even hear claws scraping on the rock above her. She must have quite an audience by now. When she didn't need one!

Cautiously she looked up, met the fascinated whirling of ten pairs of eyes.

"Look, a bargain! One long song and then let me up the cliff? Is that agreed?"

Fire lizard eyes whirled.

Menolly took it that the bargain was made and sang. Her voice started a flutter of surprised and excited chirpings, and she wondered if by any possible freak they actually understood that she was singing about grateful holds honoring dragonriders. By the last verse she eased out into the open, awed by the sight of a queen fire lizard and nine bronzes entranced by her performance.

"Can I go now?" she asked and put one hand on the ledge.

The queen dived for her hand, and Menolly snatched it back.

"I thought we'd struck a bargain."

The queen chirped piteously, and Menolly realized that there had been no menace in the queen's action. She simply wasn't allowed to climb.

"You don't want me to go?" Menolly asked.

The queen's eyes seemed to glow more brightly.

"But I have to go. If I stay, the water will come up and drown me." And Menolly accompanied her words with explanatory gestures.

Suddenly the queen let out a shrill cry, seemed to hold herself midair for a moment and then, her bronzes in close pursuit, she glided down the sandy beach to her clutch. She hovered over the eggs, making the most urgent and excited sounds.

If the tide was coming in fast enough to endanger Menolly, it was also frighteningly close to swamping the nest. The little bronzes began to take up the queen's plaint and several, greatly daring, flew about Menolly's head and then circled back to the clutch.

"I can come there now? You won't attack me?" Menolly took a few steps forward.

The tone of the cries changed, and Menolly quickened her step. As she reached the nest, the little queen secured one egg from the clutch. With a great laboring of her wings, she bore it upward. That the effort was great was obvious. The bronzes hovered anxiously, squeaking their concern but, being much smaller, they were unable to assist the queen.

Now Menolly saw that the base of the cliff at this point was littered with broken shells and the pitiful bodies of tiny fire-lizards, their wings half-extended and glistening with egg fluid. The little queen now had raised the egg to a ledge, which Menolly had not previously noticed, about a half-dragon length up the cliff-face. Menolly could see the little queen deposit the egg on the ledge and roll it with her forelegs towards what must be a hole in the cliff. It was a long moment before the queen reappeared again. Then she dove towards the sea, hovering over the foamy crest of a wave that rolled in precariously close to the endangered clutch. With a blurred movement, the queen was hovering in front of Menolly and scolding like an old aunt.

Although Menolly couldn't help grinning at the thought, she was filled with a sense of pity and admiration for the courage of the little queen, single-handedly trying to rescue her clutch. If the dead fire lizards were that fully formed, the clutch was near to hatching. No wonder the queen could barely move the eggs.

"You want me to help you move the eggs, right? Well, we'll see what I can do!"

Ready to jump back if she had mistaken the little queen's imperious command, Menolly very carefully picked up an egg. It was warm to the touch and hard. Dragon eggs, she knew, were soft when first laid but hardened slowly on the hot sands of the Hatching Grounds in the Weyrs. These definitely must be close to hatching.

Closing the fingers of her damaged hand carefully around the egg, Menolly searched for and found foot and hand holds, and reached the queen's ledge. She carefully deposited the egg. The little queen appeared, one front talon resting proprietarily on the egg, and then she leaned forward, towards Menolly's face, so close that the fantastic motion of the many-faceted eyes were clearly visible. The queen gave a sort of sweet chirp and then, in a very businesslike manner, began to scold Menolly as she rolled her egg to safety.

Menolly managed three eggs in her hand the next time. But it was obvious that between the onrushing tide and the startling number of eggs in the clutch, there'd be quite a race.

"If the hole were bigger," she told the little queen as she deposited three eggs, "some of the bronzes could help you roll."

The queen paid her no attention, busy pushing the three eggs, one at a time, to safety.

Menolly peered into the opening, but the fire lizard's body obscured any view. If the hole was bigger and the ledge consequently broader, Menolly could bring the rest of the eggs up in her carry-sack.

Hoping that she wouldn't pull down the cliffside and bury the queen, clutch and all, Menolly prodded cautiously at the mouth of the opening. Loose sand came showering down.

The queen took to scolding frantically as Menolly brushed the rubble from the ledge. Then she felt around the opening. There seemed to be solid stone just beyond. Menolly yanked away at the looser rock, until she had a nice tunnel exposed with a slightly wider opening.

Ignoring the little queen's furious complaints, Menolly climbed down, unslinging her sack when she reached the ground. When the little queen saw Menolly putting the eggs in the sack, she began to have hysterics, beating at Menolly's head and hands.

"Now, look here," Menolly said sternly, "I am not stealing your eggs. I am trying to get them all to safety in jig time. I can do it with the sack but not by the handful."

Menolly waited a moment, glaring at the little queen who hovered at eye level.

"Did you understand me?" Menolly pointed to the waves, more vigorously dashing up the small beach. "The tide is coming in. Dragons couldn't stop it now." Menolly put another egg carefully in the sack. As it was she'd have to make two, maybe three trips or risk breaking eggs. "I take this," and she gestured up to the ledge, "up there. Do you understand, you silly beast?"

Evidently, the little creature did because, crooning anxiously, she took her position on the ledge, her wings half-extended and twitching as she watched Menolly's progress up to her.

Menolly could climb faster with two hands. And she could, carefully, roll the eggs from the mouth of the sack well down the tunnelway.

"You'd better get the bronzes to help you now, or we'll have the ledge stacked too high."

It took Menolly three trips in all, and as she made the last climb, the water was a foot's width from the clutch. The little queen had organized her bronzes to help, and Menolly could hear her scolding tones echoing in what must be a fair-sized cave beyond the tunnel. Not surprising since these bluffs were supposed to be riddled with caverns and passages.

Menolly gave a last look at the beach, water at least ankle deep on both ends of the little cove. She glanced upward, past the ledge. She was a good halfway up the cliff now, and she thought she could see enough hand and foot holds ahead.

"Good-bye!" She was answered by a trill of chirps, and she chuckled as she imagined the scene: the queen marshalling her bronzes to position her eggs just right.

Menolly did not make the cliff top without a few anxious moments. She was exhausted when she finally flopped on the sea grasses at the summit, and her left hand ached from unaccustomed gripping and effort. She lay there for some time, until her heart stopped thudding in her ribs and her breath came more easily. An inshore breeze dried her face, cooling her; but that reminded her of the emptiness of her stomach. Her exertions had reduced the rolls in her pouch to crumby fragments, which she gobbled as fast as she could find them.

All at once the enormity of her adventure struck her, and she was torn between laughter and awe. To prove to herself that she'd actually done what she remembered, she crept cautiously to the bluff edge. The beach was completely underwater. The sandy wallow where the fire lizard eggs had baked was being tideswept smooth. The rubble that had gone over the edge with her had been absorbed or washed away. When the tide retreated, all evidence of her energies to save herself and the clutch would be obliterated. She could see the protuberance of rock down which the queen had rolled her eggs but not a sign of a fire lizard. The waves crashed with firm intent against the Dragon Stones when she gazed out to sea, but no bright motes of color flitted against the somber crags.

Menolly felt her cheek. The fire lizard's scratch was crusted with dried blood and sand.

"So it did happen!"

However did the little queen know I could help her? No one had ever suggested that fire lizards were stupid. Certainly they'd been smart enough for endless Turns to evade every trap and snare laid to catch them. The creatures were so clever, indeed, that there was a good deal of doubt about their existence, except as figures of overactive imaginations. However, enough trustworthy men had actually seen the creatures, at a distance, like her brother Alemi when he'd spotted some about the Dragon Stones, that most people did accept their existence as fact.

Menolly could have sworn that the little queen had understood her. How else could Menolly have helped her? That proved how smart the little beast was. Smart enough certainly to avoid the boys who tried to capture them . . . Menolly was appalled. Capture a fire lizard? Pen it up? Not, Menolly supposed with relief, that the creature would stay caught long. It only had to pop *between.*

Now why hadn't the little queen just gone *between* with her eggs, instead of arduously transporting them one by one? Oh, yes, *between* was the coldest place known. And cold would do the eggs harm. At least it did dragon eggs harm. Would the clutch be all right now in the cold cavern? Hmmm. Menolly peered below. Well, if the queen had as much sense as she'd already shown, she'd get all her followers to come lie on the eggs and keep them warm until they did hatch.

Menolly turned her pouch inside out, hoping for some crumbs. She was still hungry. She'd find enough early fruits and some of the succulent reeds to eat, but she was curiously loath to leave the bluff. Though, it was unlikely that the queen, now her need was past, would reappear.

Menolly rose finally and found herself stiff from the unaccustomed exercise. Her hand ached in a dull way, and the long scar was red and slightly swollen. But, as Menolly flexed her fingers, it seemed that the hand opened more easily. Yes, it did. She could almost extend the fingers completely. It hurt, but it was a stretchy-hurt. Could she open her hand enough to play again? She folded her fingers as if to chord. That hurt, but again, it was a stretchy-hurt. Maybe if she worked her hand a lot more . . . She had been favoring it until today when she hadn't given it a thought. She'd used it to climb and carry and everything.

"Well, you did me a favor, too, little queen," Menolly called, speaking into the breeze and waving her hands high. "See? My hand is better."

There was no answering chirp or sound, but the soft whistle of the seaborn breeze and the lapping of the waves against the bluff. Yet Menolly liked to think that her words had been heard. She turned inland, feeling considerably relieved and rather pleased with the morning's work.

She'd have to scoot now and gather what she could of greens and early berries. No point in trying for spiderclaws with the tide so high.

Chapter 5

Oh, Tongue, give sound to joy and sing
Of hope and promise on dragonwing.

No one, as usual, noticed Menolly when she got back to the Hold. Dutifully she saw the harbormaster and told him about the tides.

"Don't you go so far, girl," he told her kindly. "Thread's due any day now, you know. How's the hand?"

She mumbled something, which he didn't hear anyway, as a shipmaster shouted for his attention.

The evening meal was hurried since all the masters were going off to the Dock Cavern to check tide, masts and ships. In the bustle Menolly could keep to herself.

And she did—seeking the cubicle and the safety of her bed as soon as possible. There she hugged to herself the incredible experience of the morning. She was certain that the queen had understood her. Just like the dragons, fire lizards knew what was in the mind and heart of a person. That's why they disappeared so easily when boys tried to trap them. They'd liked her singing, too.

Menolly gave herself a squeeze, ignoring the spasm of pain in her now stiff hand. Then she tensed, remembering that the bronzes had been waiting to see what the queen would do. She was the clever one, the audacious one. What was it Petiron was always quoting? "Necessity breeds solution."

Did fire lizards really understand people, even when they kept away from them, then, Menolly puzzled again. Of course, dragons understood what their riders were thinking, but dragons Impressed at Hatching to their riders. The link was never broken, and the dragon would only hear that one person, or so Petiron had said. So *how* had the little queen understood her?

"Necessity?"

Poor queen! She must have been frantic when she realized that the tide was going to cover her eggs! Probably she'd been depositing her clutches in that cove for who knows how long? How long did fire lizards live? Dragons lasted the life of their rider. Sometimes that wasn't so long, now that Thread was dropping. Quite a few riders had been so badly scored they'd died and so had their dragons. Would the little fire lizards have a longer life, being smaller and not in so much danger? Questions darted through Menolly's mind, like fire lizards' flashing, she thought, as she cuddled into the warmth of her sleeping fur. She'd try to go back tomorrow, maybe, with food. She rather thought fire lizards would like spiderclaws, too, and maybe then she'd get the queen's trust. Or maybe it would be better if she didn't go back tomorrow? She should stay away for a few days. Then, too, with Thread falling so often, it was dangerous to go so far from the safety of the Hold.

What would happen when the fire lizard eggs hatched? What a sight that would be! Ha! All the lads in the Sea Hold talking about catching fire lizards and she, Menolly, had not only seen but talked to them and handled their eggs! And if she were lucky, she might even see them hatching, too. Why, that would be as marvelous as going to a dragon Hatching at one of the Weyrs! And no one, not even Yanus, had been to a Hatching!

Considering her exciting thoughts, it was a wonder that Menolly was able to sleep.

The next morning her hand ached and throbbed, and she was stiff from the fall and the climbing. Her half-formed notion of going back to the Dragon Stones' cove was thwarted by the weather, of all things. A storm had blown in from the sea that night, lashing the harbor with pounding waves. Even the Dock Cavern waters were turbulent, and a wind whipped with such whimsical force that walking from Hold to Cavern was dangerous.

The men gathered in the Great Hall in the morning, mending gear and yarning. Mavi organized her women for an exhaustive cleaning of some of the inner Hold rooms. Menolly and Sella were sent down to the glow storage so often that Sella vowed she didn't need light to show her the way anymore.

Menolly worked willingly enough, checking glows in every single room in the Hold. It was better to work than to think. That evening she couldn't escape the Great Hall. Since everyone had been in all day, everyone needed entertainment and was going. The Harper would surely play. Menolly shuddered. Well, there was no help for it. She had to hear music sometime. She couldn't avoid it forever. And at least she could sing along with the others. But she soon found she couldn't even have that pleasure. Mavi gestured to her when the Harper began to tune his gitar. And when the Harper beckoned for everyone to join in the choruses, Mavi pinched Menolly so hard that she gasped.

"Don't roar. You may sing softly as befits a girl your age," Mavi said. "Or don't sing at all."

Across the Hall, Sella was singing, not at all accurately and loud enough to be heard in Benden Hold; but when Menolly opened her mouth to protest, she got another pinch.

So she didn't sing at all but sat there by her mother's side, numb and hurt, not even able to enjoy the music and very conscious that her mother was being monstrously unfair.

Wasn't it bad enough she couldn't play anymore—yet—but not to be allowed to sing? Why, everyone had encouraged her to sing when old Petiron had been alive. And been glad to hear her. Asked her to sing, time and again.

Then Menolly saw her father watching her, his face stern, one hand tapping not so much to the time of the music but to some inner agitation. It was her father who didn't want her to sing! It wasn't fair! It just wasn't fair! Obviously they knew and were glad she hadn't come before. They didn't want her here.

She wrenched herself free from her mother's grip and, ignoring Mavi's hiss to come back and behave herself, she crept from the Hall. Those who saw her leave thought sadly that it was such a pity she'd hurt her hand and didn't even want to sing anymore.

Wanted or not, creeping out like that would send Mavi looking for her when there was a pause in the evening's singing. So Menolly took her sleeping furs and a glow and went to one of the unused inner rooms where no one would find her. She brought her clothes, too. If the storm cleared, she'd be away in the morning to the fire lizards. *They* liked her singing. They liked *her!*

Before anyone else was up, she had risen. She gulped down a cold klah and ate some bread, stuffed more in her pouch and was almost away. Her heart beat fast while she struggled with the big metal doors of the Hold entrance. She'd never opened them before and hadn't appreciated how very solid they were. She couldn't, of course, bar them again, but there was scarcely any need.

Sea mist was curling up from the quiet harbor waters, the entrances to the Dock Cavern visible as darker masses in the gray. But the sun was beginning to burn through the fog, and Menolly's weather-sense told her that it would soon be clear.

As she strode down the broad holdway, mist swirled up and away from her steps. It pleased Menolly to see something give way before her, even something as nebulous as fog. Visibility was limited, but she knew her path by the shape of the stones along the road and was soon climbing through the caressing mists to the bluff.

She struck somewhat inland, towards the first of the marshes. One cup of klah and a hunk of bread was not enough food, and she remembered some upstripped marshberry bushes. She was over the first humpy hill and suddenly the mist had left the land, the brightness of the spring sun almost an ache to the eyes.

She found her patch of marshberry and picked one handful for her face, then one for the pouch.

Now that she could see where she was going, she jogged down the coast and finally dropped into a cove. The tide was just right to catch spiderclaws. These should be a pleasant offering to the fire lizard queen she thought as she filled her bag. Or could fire lizards hunt in fog?

When Menolly had carried her loaded sack through several long valleys and over humpy hills, she was beginning to wish she'd waited a while to do her netting. She was hot and tired. Now that the excitement of her unorthodox behavior had waned, she was also depressed. Of course, it was quite likely that no one had noticed she'd left. No one would realize it was she who had left the Hold doors unbarred, a terrible offense against the Hold safety rules. Menolly wasn't sure why— because who'd want to enter the Sea Hold unless he had business there? Come all that dangerous way across the marshes? For what? There were quite a few precautions scrupulously observed in the Sea Hold that didn't make much sense to Menolly: like the Hold doors being barred every night, and unshielded glows never being left in an unused room, although it was all right in corridors. Glows wouldn't burn anything, and think of all the barked shins that would be saved by leaving a few room glows unshielded.

No, no one was likely to notice that she was gone until there was some unpleasant or tedious job for a one-handed girl to do. So they wouldn't assume that *she'd* opened the Hold door. And since Menolly was apt to disappear during the day, no one would think anything about her until evening. Then someone might just wonder where Menolly was.

That was when she realized that she didn't plan to return to the Hold. And the sheer audacity of that thought was enough to make her halt in her tracks. Not return to the Hold? Not go back to the endless round of tedious tasks? Of gutting, smoking, salting, pickling fish? Mending nets, sails, clothes? Cleaning dishes, clothes, rooms? Gathering greens, berries, grasses, spiderclaws? Not return to tend old uncles and aunts, fires, pots, looms, glowbaskets? To be able to sing or shout or roar or play if she so chose? To sleep . . . ah, now where would she sleep? And where would she go when there was Thread in the skies?

Menolly trudged on more slowly up the sand dunes; her mind churning with these revolutionary ideas. Why, everyone had to return to the Hold at night! The Hold, any hold or cot or weyr. Seven Turns had Thread been dropping from the skies, and no one travelled far from shelter. She remembered vaguely from her childhood that there used to be caravans of traders coming through the marshlands in the spring and the summer and early fall. There'd been gay times, with lots of singing and feasting. The Hold doors had not been barred then. She sighed, those had been happier times . . . the good old days that Old Uncle and the aunties were always droning on about. But once Thread started falling, everything had changed . . . for the worse . . . at least that was the overall impression she had from the adults in the Hold.

Some stillness in the air, some vague unease caused Menolly to glance about her apprehensively. There was certainly no one else about at this early hour. She scanned the skies. The mist banking the coast was rapidly dispersing. She could see it retreating across the water to the north and west. Towards the east the sky was brilliant with sunrise, except for what were probably some traces of early morning fog in the northeast. Yet something disturbed Menolly. She felt she should know what it was.

She was nearly to the Dragon Stones now, in the last marsh before the contour of the land swept gently up towards the seaside bluff. It was as she traversed the marsh that she identified the odd quality: it was the stillness. Not of wind, for that was steady seaward, blowing away the fog, but a stillness of marsh life. All the little insects and flies and small wrigglers, the occasional flights of wild wherries who nested in the heavier bushes were silent. Their myriad activities and small noises began as soon as the sun was up and didn't cease until just before dawn, because the nocturnal insects were as noisy as the daytime ones.

It was this quiet, as if every living thing was holding its breath, that was disturbing Menolly. Unconsciously she began to walk faster and she had a strong urge to glance over her right shoulder, towards the northeast—where a smudge of gray clouded the horizon . . .

A smudge of gray? Or silver?

Menolly began to tremble with rising fear, with the dawning knowledge that she was too far from the safety of the Hold to reach it before Thread reached her. The heavy metal doors, which she had so negligently left ajar, would soon be closed and barred against her, and Thread. And, even if she were missed, no one would come for her.

She began to run, and some instinct directed her towards the cliff edge before she consciously remembered the queen's ledge. It wasn't big enough, really. Or she could go into the sea? Thread drowned in the sea. So would she, for she couldn't keep under the water for the time it would take Thread to pass. How long would it take the leading edge of a Fall to pass over? She'd no idea.

She was at the edge now, looking down at the beach. She could see her ledge off to the right. There was the lip of the cliff that had broken off under her weight. That was the quick way down, to be sure, but she couldn't risk it again, and didn't want to.

She glanced over her shoulder. The grayness was spreading across the horizon. Now she could see flashes against that gray. Flashes? Dragons! She was seeing dragons fighting Thread, their fiery breath charring the dreaded stuff midair. They were so far away that the winking lights were more like lost stars than dragons fighting for the life of Pern.

Maybe the leading edge wouldn't reach this far? Maybe she was safe. "Maybes seldom are" as her mother would say.

In the stillness of the air, a new sound made itself heard: a soft rhythmic thrumming, something like the tuneless humming of small children. Only different. The noise seemed to come from the ground.

She dropped, pressing one ear to a patch of bare stone. The sound was coming from within.

Of course! The bluff was hollow . . . that's why the queen lizard . . .

On hands and knees, Menolly scooted to the cliff edge, looking for that halfway ledge of the queen's.

Menolly had enlarged the entry once. There was every chance she could make it big enough to squirm through. The little queen would certainly be hospitable to someone who had saved her clutch!

And Menolly didn't come empty-handed as a guest! She swung the heavy sack of spiderclaws around to her back. Grabbing handfuls of the grasses on the lip of the cliff, she began to let herself slowly down. Her feet fumbled for support; she found one toehold and dug half that foot in, the other foot prodding for another place.

She slithered badly once, but a rock protrusion caught her in the crotch before she'd slipped far. She laid her face against the cliff, gulping to get back her breath and courage. She could feel the thrumming through the stone, and oddly, that gave her heart. There was something intensely exciting and stimulating about that sound.

Sheer luck guided her foot to the queen's ledge. She'd risked only a few glances beneath her—the aspect was almost enough to make her lose her balance completely. She was trembling so much with her exertions that she had to rest then. Definitely the humming came from the queen's cavern.

She could get her head into the original opening. No more. She began to tear at the sides with her bare hands until she thought of her belt knife. The blade loosened a whole section all at once, showering her with sand and bits of rock. She had to clean her eyes and mouth of grit before she could continue. Then she realized that she'd gotten to sheer rock.

She could get herself into the shelter only up to her shoulders. No matter how she turned and twisted, there was an outcropping that she could not pass. Once again she wished she were as small as a girl ought to be. Sella would have had no trouble crawling through that hole. Resolutely, Menolly began to chip at the rock with her knife, the blows jarring her hand to the shoulder, and making no impression at all on the rock.

She wondered frantically how long it had taken her to get down the cliff. How long did she have before Thread would be raining down on her unprotected body?

Body? She might not get past the bobble in the wall with her shoulders . . . but . . . She reversed her position, and feet, legs, hips, all right up to the shoulders passed into the safety of solid rock. Her head was covered, but only just, by the cliff overhang.

Did Thread *see* where it was going when it fell? Would it notice her, crowded into this hole as it flashed by? Then she saw the thong of the carry-sack where she'd looped it over the ledge to keep it handy but out of her way. If Thread got into the spiderclaws.

She pulled herself far enough out of the hole to cast an eye above. No silver yet! No sound but the steadily increasing thrumming. That wouldn't have anything to do with Thread, would it?

The carry-sack thong had bitten into the ledge and she had a job freeing it, having to yank rather hard. The next thing she knew the sack came free, the force of her pull threw her backwards, cracking her head on the roof of her tunnel, and then the surface beneath her buttocks started to slide, out and down. Menolly clawed her way into the tunnel, as the ledge slowly detached itself from the face of the cliff and tumbled down onto the beach.

Menolly scrambled back quickly, afraid more of the entrance would go, and suddenly she was in a cave, wide, high, deep, clutching the carry-sack and staring at the greatly widened mouth.

The thrumming was behind her and, startled at what she could only consider to be an additional threat, she whirled.

Fire lizards were perched around the walls, clinging to rock spur and ledge. Every eye glinted at the mound of eggs in the sandy center of the cave. The thrumming came from the throats of all the little fire lizards, and they were far too intent on what was happening to the eggs to give any heed to her abrupt appearance.

Just as Menolly realized that she was witnessing a Hatching, the first egg began to rock and cracks appeared in its shell.

It rocked itself off the mound of the clutch and, in hitting the ground, split. From the two parts emerged a tiny creature, not much bigger than Menolly's hand, glistening brown and creeling with hunger, swaying its head back and forth and tottering forward a few awkward steps. The transparent brown wings unfolded, flapping weakly to dry, and the creature's balance improved. The creel turned to a hiss of displeasure, and the little brown peered about defensively.

The other fire lizards crooned, encouraging it to some action. With a tiny shriek of anger, the little brown launched itself towards the cave opening, passing so close to Menolly she could have touched it.

The brown fire lizard lurched off the eroded lip of the cave, pumping its wings frantically to achieve flight. Menolly gasped as the creature dropped, and then sighed with relief as it came into sight briefly, airborn, and flew off, across the sea.

More creeling brought her attention back to the clutch. Other fire lizards had begun to hatch in that brief period, each one shaking its wings and then, encouraged by the weyrmates, flopping and weaving towards the cave mouth, defiantly independent and hungry.

Several greens and blues, a little bronze and two more browns hatched and passed Menolly. And then, as she watched a little blue launch itself, Menolly screamed. No sooner had the blue emerged from the safety of the cliff than she saw the thin, writhing silver of Thread descending. In a moment, the blue was covered with the deadly filaments. It uttered one hideous shriek and disappeared. Dead? Or *between?* Certainly badly scored.

Two more little fire lizards passed Menolly, and she reacted now.

"No! No! You can't! You'll be killed." She flung herself across their path.

The angry fire lizards pecked at her unprotected face and while she covered herself, made their escape. She cried aloud when she heard their screams.

"Don't let them go!" She pleaded with the watching fire lizards. "You're older. You know about Thread. Tell them to stop!" She half-crawled, half-ran to the rock where the golden queen was perched.

"Tell them not to go! There's Thread out there! They're being killed!"

The queen looked at her, the many-faceted eyes whirling violently. The queen chuckled and chirped at her, and then crooned as yet another fledgling spread its wings and began to totter towards sure death.

"Please, little queen! Do something! Stop them!"

The thrill of being the witness to a Hatching of fire lizards gave way to horror. Dragons had to be protected because they protected Pern. In Menolly's fear and confusion, the little fire lizards were linked to their giant counterparts.

She turned to the other lizards now, begging them to do something. At least until the Threadfall was over. Desperately she plunged back to the cave mouth and tried to turn the little fire lizards back with her hands, blocking their progress with her body. She was overwhelmed with pangs of hunger, belly-knotting, gut-twisting hunger. It took her only a moment to realize that the driving force in these fire lizards was that sort of hunger: that was what was sending them senselessly forth. They had to eat. She remembered that dragons had to eat, too, when they first Hatched, fed by the boys they Impressed.

Menolly wildly grabbed for her carry-sack. With one hand she snatched a fire lizard back from the entrance, and with the other, a spiderclaw from the sack. The little bronze screeched once and then bit the spiderclaw behind the eye, neatly killing it. Wings beating, the bronze lifted itself free of Menolly's grasp and with more strength than Menolly would have thought the newborn creature could possess flew its prey to a corner and began tearing it apart.

Menolly reached out randomly now and, with some surprise, found herself holding the one queen in the clutch. She snagged two spider-claws from the sack in her other hand, and deposited them and the queen in another corner. Finally realizing she couldn't handfeed the whole clutch, she upended the sack, spilling the shellfish out.

Newly hatched fire lizards swarmed over and after the spiderclaws. Menolly caught two more lizards before they could reach the cave mouth and put them squarely in the center of their first meal. She was busy trying to make sure that each new fire lizard had a shellfish when she felt something pricking her shoulder. Surprised, she looked up to find the little bronze clinging to her tunic. His round eyes were whirling and he was still hungry. She gave him an unclaimed spiderclaw and put him back in his corner. She tossed the little queen another and snared several other spiderclaws for her "specials."

Not many more of the newly-hatched got out, not with a source of food so nearby. She'd had a fair haul in the sack, but it didn't take long for the hungry fire lizards to devour every last morsel. The poor things were still sounding starved as they creeled about, tipping over claws and body shells, trying to find any scraps overlooked. But they stayed in the cave and now the older fire lizards joined them, nuzzling or stroking, making affectionate noises.

Utterly exhausted, Menolly leaned back against the wall, watching their antics. At least they'd not all died. She glanced apprehensively at the entrance and saw no more writhing lengths of Thread falling past. She peered further. There wasn't even a trace of the menacing gray fog on the horizon. Threadfall must be over.

And not a moment too soon. Now she was experiencing hunger thoughts from all the fire lizards. Rather overpoweringly, in fact. Because she realized how hungry she herself was.

The little queen, the old queen, began to hover in the cave, squeaking an imperious command to her followers. Then she darted out and the old clutch began to follow her. The fledglings, moving awkwardly, made their virgin flight, and within moments, the cave was empty of all but Menolly, her torn sack, and a pile of empty spiderclaw and fire lizard shells.

With their exit, some of Menolly's hunger eased and she remembered the bread she'd tucked in her pocket. Feeling a bit guilty at this belated discovery, she gratefully ate every crumb.

Then she made herself a hollow in the sand, pulled the torn carrysack over her shoulders, and went to sleep.

Chapter 6

Lord of the Hold, your charge is sure
In thick walls, metal doors, and no verdure.

Threadfall was well past, the flame-thrower crews safely back in Half-Circle Hold before anyone missed Menolly. Sella did because she didn't want to have to tend Old Uncle. He had had another seizure, and someone had to stay by his bedside.

"That's about all she's good for now anyway," Sella told Mavi and then hastily demurred at her mother's stern look. "Well, all she does is drag about, cradling that hand of hers as if it were precious. She gets off all the *real* work . . ." Sella let out a heavy sigh.

"We've enough trouble this morning what with someone leaving the Hold doors unfastened and Thread falling . . ." Mavi shuddered at the thought of that brace of horrors; the mere notion of Thread cascading down, able to wriggle within the Hold, turned her stomach. "Go find Menolly and see that she knows what to do in case the old man has another fit."

It took Sella the better part of an hour to realize that Menolly was neither in the Hold nor among those baiting longlines. She hadn't been among the flame-thrower crews. In fact, no one could remember having seen or spoken to her all day.

"She couldn't have been out hunting greens like she usually does," said an old auntie thoughtfully, pursing her lips. "Threadfall was on directly we'd our morning klah. Didn't see her in the kitchen then, either. And she's usually so good about helping, one-handed and all that she is, poor dear."

At first Sella was just annoyed. So like Menolly to be absent when needed. Mavi was a good deal too lenient with the child. Well, if she'd not been in the Hold in the morning, she'd been caught out in the Thread. And that served her right.

Then Sella wasn't so sure. She began to feel the first vestige of fright. If Menolly had been out during Threadfall, surely there'd be . . . something . . . left that Thread couldn't eat.

Gulping back nausea at that thought, she sought out her brother, Alemi, who was in charge of the flame-throwers.

"Alemi, you didn't see anything . . . unusual . . . when you were ground checking?"

"What do you mean by 'unusual'?"

"You know, traces . . ."

"Of what? I've no time now for riddles, Sella."

"I mean, if someone were caught out during Threadfall, how would you know?"

"Whatever are you tacking around?"

"Menolly's nowhere in the Hold, or the Dock, or anywhere. She wasn't on any of the teams . . ."

Alemi frowned. "No, she wasn't, but I thought Mavi needed her in the Hold for something."

". . . There! And none of the aunties remember seeing her this morning. *And* the Hold doors were unbarred!"

"You think Menolly left the Hold early?" Alemi realized that a strong, tall girl like Menolly could very easily have managed the door bars.

"You know how she's been since she hurt her hand: creeping away every chance she gets."

Alemi did know, for he was fond of his gawky sister, and he particularly missed her singing. He didn't share Yanus's reservations about Menolly's ability. And he didn't honestly agree with Yanus's decision to keep knowledge of it from the Harper, especially now that there was a Harper in the Hold to keep her in line.

"Well?" Sella's prompting irritated him out of his thoughts.

"I saw nothing unusual."

"Would there *be* something? If Thread did get her?"

Alemi gave Sella a long hard look. She sounded as if she'd be glad if Menolly did get Threaded.

"There'd be nothing left if she'd been caught by Thread. But no Thread got through the Benden wings."

With that he turned on his heel and left his sister, mouth agape. His reassurance was curiously no consolation to Sella. However, since Menolly was so obviously missing, Sella could take some pleasure in informing Mavi of this fact, adding her theory that Menolly had committed the enormous crime of leaving the Hold doors unbarred.

"Menolly?" Mavi was handing out sea salt and spiceroot to the head cook when Sella imparted her news. "Menolly?"

"Yes, Menolly. She's gone. Not been seen, and she's the one left the Hold doors unbarred. With Thread falling!"

"Thread wasn't falling when Yanus discovered the doors open." Mavi corrected Sella mechanically. She shuddered at the thought of anyone, even a recalcitrant daughter, caught out in the silvery rain of Thread.

"Alemi said no Thread got through the dragons, but how can he be sure?"

Mavi said nothing as she locked up the condiment press and spun the rollers. "I'll inform Yanus. And I'll have a word with Alemi, too. You'd better take care of Old Uncle."

"Me?"

"Not that that's real work, but it is suited to your temperament and ability."

Yanus was silent for a long moment when he heard of Menolly's disappearance. He didn't like untoward things happening, such as the Hold doors being left unbarred. He'd worried about that all during the Fall and the fishing after the Fall. It wasn't good for a Sea Holder to have his mind diverted from the task at hand. He felt some relief that the mystery had been solved, and a keen annoyance and anxiety about the girl. Foolish thing for her to have done—leave the Hold that early. She'd been sulking ever since that beating. Mavi hadn't kept her busy enough to make her forget the nonsense of tuning.

"I've heard that there're plenty of caves in the cliffs along the coast," Elgion said. "The girl probably took shelter in one."

"She probably did," said Mavi briskly, grateful to the Harper for such a sensible suggestion. "Menolly knows the coast very well. She must know every crevice by now."

"She'll be back then," Yanus said. "Give her time to get over the fright of being out during Threadfall. She'll be back." Yanus found relief in his theory and turned to less distressing business.

"It *is* spring," said Mavi, more to herself than to the others. Only the Harper caught the anxious note in her voice.

Two days later Menolly had not returned, and the entire Sea Hold was alerted to her disappearance. No one remembered seeing her on the day of Threadfall. No one had seen her since. Children sent out for berries or spiderclaws had encountered no trace of her, nor had she been in any of the caves they knew.

"Not much point in sending out a search," said one of the shipmasters, mindful that there was more surety of catching fish than finding any trace of a foolish girl. Particularly one with a crippled hand. "Either she's safe and doesn't choose to come back, or . . ."

"She could be hurt . . . Threadscored, a broken leg or arm . . ." said Alemi, "unable to make her way back."

"Shouldn't've been out anyway without letting someone know where she'd gone." The shipmaster's eyes moved towards Mavi, who did not catch this implied negligence on her part.

"She was used to going out for greens first thing in the morning," Alemi said. If no one else would defend Menolly, he would speak up.

"Did she carry a belt knife? Or a metal buckle?" asked Elgion. "Thread doesn't touch metal."

"Aye. We'd find that much of her," said Yanus.

"If Thread got her," said the shipmaster darkly. He rather favored the notion that she'd fallen into a crevice or over the edge of the bluff, in terror at finding herself out during Threadfall. "Her body'd wash up around the Dragon Stones. Current throws up a lot of sea trash down that way."

Mavi caught her breath in a sound very like a sob.

"I don't know the girl," Elgion said quickly, seeing Mavi's distress. "But if she did, as you say, stay out a good deal of the time, she'd know the land too well to go over the edge of a cliff."

"Threadfall's enough to rattle anyone's wits . . ." said the shipmaster.

"Menolly is not stupid," said Alemi with such feeling that everyone looked at him in surprise. "And she knew her Teaching well enough to know what to do if she were caught out."

"Right enough, Alemi," said Yanus sharply and rose to his feet. "If she were able and of a mind to return, she'd have done so. Everyone who is abroad is to keep a sharp eye for any trace of her. That includes sea as well as land. As Sea Holder, I cannot in conscience do more than that, under the circumstances. And the tide is making. To the boats now."

While Elgion did not actually expect the Sea Holder to institute an intensive search for a lost girl, he was surprised at the decision. Mavi, even, accepted it, almost as if she were glad of an excuse, as if the girl were an embarrassment. The shipmaster was obviously pleased by his Sea Holder's impartiality. Only Alemi betrayed resentment. The Harper motioned to the young man to hang back as the others filed out.

"I've some time. Where would you suggest I look?"

Hope flashed in Alemi's eyes, then as suddenly wariness clouded them.

"I'd say it's better if Menolly remains where she is . . ."

"Dead or hurt?"

"Aye." Alemi sighed deeply. "And I wish her luck and long life."

"Then you think she's alive and chooses to be without Hold?"

Alemi regarded the Harper quietly. "I think she's alive and better off wherever she is than she would be in Half-Circle." Then the young Sea

Man strode after the others, leaving the Harper with some interesting reflections.

He was not unhappy at Half-Circle Hold. But the Masterharper had been correct in thinking that Elgion would have to make quite a few adjustments to life in this Sea Hold. It would be a challenge, Robinton had told Elgion, to try to broaden the narrow outlook and straitened thinking of the isolated group. At the moment Elgion wondered if the Masterharper had not vastly overrated his abilities when he was unable to get the Sea Holder, or his family, to even try to rescue a blood relation.

Then, shifting through the tones of voices, rather than the words spoken, Elgion came to realize that this Menolly posed some sort of problem to her Hold beyond the crippled hand. For the life of him, Elgion couldn't remember seeing the girl, though he thought he could recognize every member of the Hold. He'd spent considerable time now with every family unit, with the children in the Little Hall, with the active fishermen, with the honorably retired old people.

He tried to recall when he'd seen a girl with an injured hand and had only the fleetingest recollection of a tall, gawky figure hurrying out of the Hall one evening when he'd been playing. He hadn't seen the girl's face, but he'd recall her slumping figure if he saw it again.

It was regrettable that Half-Circle Hold was so isolated that there was no way to send a drum-message. He could signal the next dragonrider he saw, as an alternative, and get word to Benden Weyr. The sweep riders could keep their eyes open for the girl, and alert any Holds beyond the marshes and down the coast. How she could have gotten that far with Thread falling, Elgion didn't know, but he'd feel better taking some measures to find her.

He had also made no headway in discovering the identity of the song-maker. And Masterharper had charged him to have that lad in the Harpercrafthall for training as soon as possible. Gifted songmakers were a rare commodity. Something to be sought and cherished.

By this time Elgion understood why the old Harper had been so cautious about identifying the lad. Yanus thought only of the sea, of fishing, of how to use every man, woman and child of his Sea Hold to the Hold's best advantage. He had them all well-trained. Yanus would certainly have looked askance at any able-bodied lad who spent too much time tuning. There was, in fact, no one to help Elgion with the evening task of entertainment. One likely lad had a fair sense of rhythm, and Elgion had already started him on the drum, but the majority of his students were thick-fingered. Oh, they knew their Teachings, spot-on, but they were passive musically. No wonder Petiron had been so effusive about the one really talented child among so many deadheads. Too bad the old man had died before he received Robinton's message. That way the boy would have known that he was more than acceptable as a candidate to the Harpercrafthall.

Elgion watched the fishing fleet out of the harbor and then rounded up several lads, got meatrolls from an auntie in the Hold kitchen, and set off on, ostensibly, a food gathering mission.

As Harper he was acquainted with them; but mindful that he was the Harper, the boys regarded him with respect and kept him at a distance. The moment he told them that they should keep their eyes open for Menolly, for her belt knife, if they knew it, or belt buckle, the distance widened inexplicably. They all seemed to know, though Elgion doubted that the adults had told them, that Menolly had been missing from the Hold for some days. They all seemed equally reluctant to look for her, or to suggest to him possible areas in which to search. It was as if, Elgion told himself with frustrated anger, they were *afraid* the Harper would find her. So he tried to regain their confidence by telling them that Yanus had suggested that everyone who went outside the Hold should keep their eyes open for the lost girl.

He came back with his charges to the Hold, with sacksful of berries, greens and some spiderclaws. The only information the boys had volunteered about Menolly during the entire morning was that she could catch more spiderclaws than anyone.

As it turned out, Elgion didn't have to signal for a dragonrider. The next day a bronze wingleader came circling down to the beach at Half-Circle, greeting Yanus affably and asking if he might have a few words with the Harper.

"You'll be Elgion," said the young man, raising his hand in greeting. "I'm N'ton, rider of Lioth. I heard you were settling in."

"What can I do for you, N'ton?" and Elgion tactfully walked the bronze rider out of Yanus's earshot.

"You've heard of fire lizards?"

Elgion stared at N'ton in surprise for a moment before he laughed. "That old myth!"

"Not really a myth, friend," said N'ton. Despite the laughing mischief in his eyes, he was speaking in earnest.

"Not a myth?"

"Not at all. Would you know if the lads here have spotted any along the coast? They tend to leave their clutches in beach sands. It's the eggs we want."

"Really? Actually it isn't the lads who've seen them, but the Sea Holder's son, not the fanciful sort, although I didn't really credit . . .

he saw some around some rock crags known as the Dragon Stones. Down the coast some ways." Elgion pointed the direction.

"I'll go have a look myself. But this is what has happened. F'nor, brown Canth's rider, has been injured." N'ton paused. "He's been convalescing at Southern Hold. He found, and Impressed," and again N'ton paused significantly to emphasize his last word, "a fire lizard queen . . ."

"Impressed? I thought only dragons . . ."

"Fire lizards are much like dragons, only smaller."

"But this would mean . . ." And Elgion was lost in the wonder of that meaning.

"Yes, precisely, Harper," said N'ton with a wide grin. "And now everyone wants a fire lizard. I can't imagine Yanus Sea Holder wasting the time and energy of his men looking for fire lizard clutches. But if fire lizards have been seen, any cove with warm sand might just hide a clutch."

"The high tides this spring have been flooding most of the coves."

"Too bad. See if you can't organize the Hold youngsters to search. I don't think you'd have much resistance . . ."

"None at all." And Elgion realized that N'ton, dragonrider though he now was, must have been susceptible to the same boyhood designs on fire lizards that Elgion had once planned. "When we find a clutch, what do we do?"

"*If* you find one," N'ton said, "fly the signal banner and the sweep rider will report. If the tide is threatening, put the clutch in either warm sand or warmed hides."

"If they should hatch, you did mention they can be Impressed . . ."

"I hope you're that lucky, Harper. Feed the fledglings. Stuff their faces with as much as they can eat, talking all the time. That's how you Impress. But then, you've been to a Hatching, haven't you? So, you know how to go about it. Same principle involved."

"Fire lizards." Elgion was enchanted with the prospect.

"Don't Impress them all, Harper. I'd like one of the little beasties myself."

"Greedy?"

"No, they're engaging little pets. Nothing as intelligent as my Lioth there," and N'ton grinned indulgently at his bronze who was scrubbing one cheek in the sand. As he turned back to Elgion, N'ton noticed the line of awed children, lining the seawall, all eyes on Lioth's action. "You'll have no lack of help, I suspect."

"Speaking of help, Wingleader, a young girl of the Sea Hold is missing. She went out the morning of the last Fall and hasn't been seen since."

N'ton whistled softly and nodded sympathetically. "I'll tell the sweep riders. She probably took shelter, if she'd any sense. Those palisades are riddled with caves. How far have you searched?"

"That's it. No one has bothered to."

N'ton scowled and glanced towards the Sea Holder. "How old a girl?"

"Come to think of it, I don't know. His youngest daughter, I believe."

N'ton snorted. "There are other things in life than fish."

"So I used to believe."

"Don't be so sour so young, Elgion. I'll see you come to the next Hatching at Benden."

"I'd appreciate that."

"I suspect so." With a farewell wave, N'ton strode back to his bronze dragon, leaving Elgion with an easier conscience and the prospect of some relief from the monotony of the Sea Hold.

Chapter 7

Who wills,
Can.
Who tries,
Does.
Who loves,
Lives.

It took Menolly four days to find the right sort of rocks to spark a fire.
She'd had plenty of time before that to dry seaweeds and gather dead
marshberry bushes for fuel, and to build a little hearth in the side of the
big cavern where a natural chimney took the smoke up. She'd gathered
a generous pile of sweet marsh grasses for bedding and picked out the
seam of the carry-sack to make herself a rug. It wasn't quite long
enough unless she curled up under it, but the fire lizards insisted on
sleeping about and around her and their bodies made up the lack. In
fact, she was quite comfortable at night.

With fire, she was very comfortable. She found a stand of young
klahbark trees, and though the resultant brew was harsh, it woke her up
very well. She went to the clay deposits that Half-Circle Hold used and
got sufficient clay to make herself several cups, plates and rude containers for storage, which she hardened in the ashes of her fire. And she
filled in the holes of a dishlike porous rock in which she could boil
water. With all the fish she needed in the sea in front of her, she ate as
well as, if not better than, she would have in the Hold. Although, she
did miss bread.

She even made herself a sort of path down the cliff face. She carved
out footrests and staked in some handholds, to make both ascent and
descent safer.

And she had company. Nine fire lizards were constantly in attendance.

The morning after her hectic adventure, Menolly had been absolutely
stunned to wake with the unaccustomed weight of warm bodies about
her. Scared, too, until the little creatures roused, with strong thoughts
of renewed hunger and love and affection for her. Driven by their need,
she had climbed down the treacherous rock face to the sea and gathered

fingertails, trapped in the shallow tidal pools. She wasn't quite able to dig rockmites, but when she showed her charges where they could get them out with their long, agile tongues, the creatures found their instinct adequate for the job. Having fed her friends, Menolly was too tired to go in search of sparking rocks and had eaten a flat fish raw. Then she and the fire lizards had crept back into the cavern and slept again.

As the days went by their appetite drove Menolly to lengths she wouldn't have attempted for her own comfort. The result was that she was kept entirely too busy to feel either sorry for or apprehensive about herself. Her friends had to be fed, comforted and amused. She also had to supply her own needs—as far as she was able—and she was able to do a lot more than she'd suspected she could. In fact, she began to wonder about a lot of things the Hold took for granted.

She had automatically assumed, as she supposed everyone did, that to be caught without shelter during Threadfall was tantamount to dying. No one had ever correlated the fact that the dragonriders cleared most of the Thread from the skies before it fell—that was the whole point of having dragons—with the idea that as a result there was very little Thread to fall on the unsheltered. Hold thinking had hardened into an inflexible rule—to have no shelter during Threadfall was to experience death.

In spite of her increasing independence, however, had Menolly been alone, she might have regretted her foolishness and crept back to the Sea Hold. But the company and wonder of the fire lizards gave her all the diversion she needed. And they loved her music.

It was no great trick at all to make one reed pipe, and a lot more fun to put five together so she could play a counter-tune. The fire lizards adored the sounds and would sit listening, their dainty heads rocking in time with the music she played. When she sang, they'd croon, at first off-key; but gradually, she thought, their "ear" improved, and she had a soft chorus. Menolly sang, in amused duty, all the Teaching Ballads, particularly the ones about dragons. The fire lizards might understand less than a child three Turns old, but they responded with small cries and flapping wings to any of the dragon songs, as if they appreciated the fact that she was singing about their kin.

There was no doubt in Menolly's mind that these lovely creatures were related to the huge dragons. How, she didn't know and didn't really care. But if you treated them the way weyrmen treated their dragons, the fire lizards responded. She, in turn, began to understand their moods and needs, and insofar as she was able, supplied them.

They grew quickly, those first days. So quickly that she was hard pressed to keep their mouths full. Menolly didn't see too much of the other hatchlings, the ones she hadn't fed or had fed only casually. She saw them now and again, smaller creatures, as the entire weyr fed on the rockmites at low tide. The little queen and her bronze mate would often hover, watching Menolly and her small group. The queen sometimes scolded Menolly or perhaps berated the fire lizard Menolly was holding. Menolly wasn't sure which. And occasionally the queen would even fly at one of the fledglings, beating it soundly with her wings. For what reason, Menolly could never figure out, but the little ones meekly submitted to her discipline.

Occasionally Menolly offered food to one of the others, but they'd never take it if she remained near. Nor would any of the older fire lizards, including the queen. Menolly concluded that that was as well, otherwise she'd have to spend every single waking moment feeding lazy fire lizards. The nine she'd Impressed were quite enough to keep sated.

When she saw the first skin lesion on the little queen, Menolly wondered where she would find oil. They'd all need it. Cracks in the skin would be deadly for the young fire lizards if they had to go *between*. And with natural enemies around, like wherries and eager boys from nearby Holds, *between* was a needed refuge.

The closest source of oil swam in the sea. But she'd no boat to catch the deep-sea oily fishes, so she searched the coast for dead fish and found a packtail washed up during the night. She slit the carcass, carefully, always working the knife blade away from her, and squeezed the oil from the skin into a cup. Not the most pleasant of jobs; and by the time she'd finished, she had a bare cupful of unpleasantly fishy yellow oil. Yet it did work. The queen might not smell very pleasant, but the oil did coat the crack. For good measure, she smeared all her friends.

The stench in the cavern that night was almost more than she could endure, and she fell asleep trying to think of alternatives. By morning the possibilities had narrowed down to one: sweetening the fish oil with certain marsh grasses. She couldn't get the pure sweet oil they used in the Hold because that was traded from Nerat; it was pressed from the flesh of a hot-climate fruit that grew abundantly in the rain forests there. The oily seed pod that grew from a sea bush would not be available until fall; and while she could get some oil from black marshberries, it would take immense quantities, which she'd prefer to eat.

With her fire lizards as winged escort, she made her way south and inland, towards country little penetrated by the Sea Holders as being too far, these days, from shelter.

Menolly set out as soon as the sun was up and varied her pace between a striding walk and an easy jog. She decided to go on as far as she could until the sun was mid-heaven; she couldn't risk being too far from her cave when night fell.

The fire lizards were excited, darting about until she scolded them for wasting their energy. They took enough feeding without all that flying and all they could count on in this flat marsh area were berries and a few early sour plums. They took turns clinging to her shoulders and hair, then, until the little brown pulled at her once too often, and she shooed them all off.

She was soon past any familiar terrain and began to proceed more slowly. It wouldn't do to be bogged down. Midday found her deep in the marshes, gathering berries for herself, her friends and her basket. She'd managed to harvest some of the aromatic grasses she wanted, but not enough for her purpose. She had decided to sweep in a wide circle back towards her cliff cave when she heard distant cries.

The little queen heard them, too, landing on Menolly's shoulder and adding her agitated comments.

Menolly told her to be quiet so she could hear, and to her surprise, the little queen instantly obeyed. The others subsided, and all seemed to wait expectantly. Without diversion Menolly recognized the distinctive and frantic noise of a distressed wherry.

Following the sound, Menolly crossed the slight rise into the next bog valley and saw the creature, wings flapping, head jerking but its legs and body firmly captured by treacherous sinking sands.

Oblivious to the excitement of the fire lizards who recognized the wherry as an enemy, Menolly ran forward, drawing her knife. The bird had been eating berries from the bushes edging the boggy sands and stupidly stepped into the mire. Menolly approached the sands cautiously, making certain that she was stepping on firm land. She got close enough—the frightened bird not even aware of her proximity—and plunged her knife into its back, at the base of the neck.

One more frightened squawk and the thing was dead, limp wings settling on the surface and rapidly submerging.

Menolly unbuckled her belt to make a loop of the buckle end. Grabbing the tough branches of a berry bush, she leaned out just far enough to snap the loop around the head of the bird. She tightened the loop and slowly began to pull.

Not only was there wherry meat here to feed herself and the fire lizards, but the layer of fat under its tough hide would provide her with the best possible grease for her friends' fragile skins.

Again, to Menolly's surprise, the fire lizard queen appeared to understand the situation. She sank her tiny talons into a wherry wing and pulled the tip out of the mud. She squeaked shrilly at the others, and before Menolly realized it, all of them had seized some tenable part of the wherry and were exerting their efforts to pull it from the bogsand.

It took a lot of pulling and shrill fire lizard orders, but they managed to get the wherry out of the sands and onto firm ground.

The rest of her day was spent in sawing through the tough outer hide to disembowel and dress the carcass. The fire lizards made an enthusiastic meal of the entrails and the blood that flowed from the wherry's neck. The sight somewhat nauseated Menolly, but she set her jaw and tried to ignore the voracity with which her otherwise gentle companions attacked the unexpected delicacy.

She hoped the taste of hot raw meat wouldn't change their temperaments, but she reckoned that dragons didn't become savage from their diet of live meat so it was fair to assume that the fire lizards wouldn't. At least, they were well fed for the day.

The wherry had been a good-sized bird, doubtless feeding somewhere in the lower reaches of Nerat for its fatty layer was juicy. It couldn't be a northern bird. Menolly skinned it, stopping twice to hone her knife sharp. She carved the meat from the bones, stuffing it into the hide to carry home. When she had finished, she had a hefty burden, and the bones were by no means stripped clean. Too bad she couldn't tell the old queen where they were.

She was rigging a forehead sling of her belt and the leg skin when suddenly the air was alive with fire lizards. With creels of shrill delight, the old queen and her bronzes settled on the bones. Menolly backed hastily away before the fire lizards decided to attack her for the meat she carried.

She had plenty of time on her long and tiring march back to the sea cave to wonder about their appearance. She could easily believe that the little queen could understand what she was thinking, and the others she had been taking care of. But had the young queen told the others? Or had Menolly some tenuous contact with the old queen, too?

Her special group showed no inclination to remain with the others, but kept her company, sometimes disappearing or making lazy figures in the sky. Sometimes the little queen sat on her shoulder for a few dragon lengths, chirruping sweetly.

It was fully dark long before Menolly reached her refuge. Only the moonlight and familiarity with the access route helped her down the cliff face. Her hearth fire was sullen embers, which she wearily coaxed into a cheery blaze. She was too tired to do more than wrap a piece of wherry meat in a few leaves of seaweed and stick it in the heated sands by the fire to cook for the morning. Then she wrapped herself up in her carry-sack and fell asleep.

She rendered the fat over the next several days, wishing time and again for one decent cooking pot. She heaped aromatic herbs into the hot fat and poured the mixture into clay pots for cooling. The wherry meat had a slightly fishy taste, which suggested that the stupid bird had been of a seaside flock rather than an inland or mountain group. But the cooled grease smelled of the herbs. Not, Menolly supposed, that the fire lizards minded how they smelled so long as their itching skin was soothed.

They loved to be oiled, lying on their backs, their wings spread for balance, curling around her hand as she spread oil on their softer belly hide. They hummed with delight at the attention, and when she had finished each one, the creature would stroke her cheek with its small triangular head, the glistening eyes sparkling with brilliant colors.

She was beginning to find individual traits among her nine charges. The little queen was exactly as she should be: into everything, bossing everyone else, as imperious and demanding as a Sea Holder. She'd listen, however, very quietly to Menolly. And she'd listen to the old queen, too. But she paid no heed to any of the others, although they were expected to obey anything she said. She'd peck them fast enough if they disobeyed her.

They were two bronzes, three browns, a blue and two greens. Menolly felt a little sorry for the blue. He seemed to be left out or picked upon by the others. The two greens were always scolding him. She named him Uncle, and the greens became Auntie One and Auntie Two. Two was slightly smaller than One. Because one of the bronzes preferred to hunt for rockmites while the other was deft at diving into pools for fingertails, they became Rocky and Diver. The browns were so much alike that for a long time they remained nameless, but gradually she found that the largest of the trio usually fell asleep, given any opportunity to do so, so she called him Lazybones. The second was Mimic because he always did what he saw the other doing; and the third was Brownie for lack of any other distinguishing feature.

The little queen was Beauty because she was and because she took such elaborate pains with her grooming and required much more attention and oiling than the others. She was forever digging at her talons with her teeth, spreading them to clean between the toes, or licking any specks of dust from her tail, burnishing her neck ridges in the sand or grass.

At first Menolly talked to her creatures to hear the sound of her own voice. Later she spoke with them because they seemed to understand what she was saying. They certainly gave every indication of intelligent listening, humming, or crooning an encouraging response when she paused. And they never seemed to get enough of her singing to them, or playing her pipes. She couldn't exactly say that they harmonized with her, but they did hum softly in tune as she played.

Chapter 8

Wheel and turn
Or bleed and burn.
Fly between,
Blue and green.
Soar, dive down,
Bronze and brown.
Dragonmen must fly
When Threads are in the sky.

As it turned out, Alemi sailed Elgion to the Dragon Stones to search there for the elusive fire lizards. One windy day, not long after the visit of N'ton, the young Sea Man broke a leg bone when the rough seas tossed him against the pilot house of his ship. They were coming into harbor and the high tide made for heavier waters there than he'd expected. Yanus grumbled a good deal about Alemi being too experienced a seaman to get injured, but his grumbling subsided when Mavi pointed out that here was a chance to see if Alemi's first mate would be capable of assuming command of the ship being finished in the building Cavern.

Alemi tried to take the injury in good part, but after four days in bed, with the swelling eased, he was heartily bored and restless. He plagued Mavi so constantly that she handed him the crutch she had not meant to give him for a full sevenday more, and suggested that if he broke his neck, too, he would have only himself to blame.

Alemi had more sense than that and navigated the inner stairways, narrow and dark, slowly and carefully; he kept to the wider outer stairs and the Sea Hold's main rooms and the holdway whenever possible.

While he had some mobility, he didn't have much activity if the fishing fleet was out, so he was soon attracted by the sound of the children learning a new ballad from the Harper. He caught Elgion's eye and received a courteous wave to enter the Little Hall. If the children were startled to hear a baritone suddenly take up the learning, they had too much respect for the Harper to do more than hazard a quick peek and the class progressed.

To Alemi's pleasure he found himself as quick to memorize the new words and tune as the youngsters, and he thoroughly enjoyed the session; he was almost sorry when Elgion excused them.

"How's the leg, Alemi?" the Harper asked when the room had emptied.

"I'll have a weather-wise ache now for sure."

"Is that why you did it?" Elgion said with a broad grin. "I'd heard you wanted to be sure Tilsit got a chance at command."

Alemi let out a snort of laughter. "Nonsense. I haven't had a rest since the last five-day gale. That's a fine ballad you're teaching."

"That's a fine voice you were singing it with, too. Why don't you sound out more often? I was beginning to think the sea wind snatches the voice of everyone at about twelve Turns."

"You should have heard my sis . . ." and Alemi stopped, flushed, and clamped his lips tight.

"Which reminds me: I took the liberty of asking N'ton, Lioth's rider, to spread the word at Benden Weyr that she's missing. She may still be alive, you know."

Alemi nodded slowly.

"You Sea Holders are full of surprises," said Elgion, thinking to switch to a less painful topic. He went to the racks of wax tablets and removed the two he sought. "These must have been done by that fosterling who took over when Petiron died. The other slates are all in the older script notations, which the old Harper used. But these . . . A lad who can do this sort of work is needed in the Harper's craft. You don't know where the boy is now, do you?"

Alemi was torn between duty to the Hold and love of his sister. But she wasn't in the Hold anymore, and commonsense told Alemi that she must be dead if, in this length of time, with dragonriders looking for her, she hadn't been found. Menolly was only a girl, so what good did it do that her songs found favor with the Harper? Alemi was also reluctant to put the lie to his father. So, despite the fact that Elgion was impressed by the songs, since the songmaker was beyond them, Alemi answered truthfully that he didn't know where "he" was.

Elgion wrapped the waxed slates carefully, and with a noticeable sigh of regret. "I'll send them on to the Harper Crafthall anyway. Robinton will want to use them."

"Use them? They're that good?" Alemi was startled and regretted the lies still more.

"They're cracking good. Maybe if the lad hears them, he'll come forward on his own." Elgion gave Alemi a rueful smile. "Since it's obvious there's some reason you can't name him." He chuckled at the Sea Man's reaction. "Come now, man, the lad was sent away in some sort of disgrace, wasn't he? That happens, as any harper worth his salt knows—and understands. Hold honor and all that. I won't tease you anymore. He'll surface to the sound of his own music."

They talked of other things then, until the fishing fleet returned—two men of the same age but different background: one with an inquisitive interest in the world beyond his Sea Hold, and the other quite willing to satisfy it. Elgion was, in fact, delighted to find none of Yanus's denseness and inflexibility in Alemi, and the Harper began to feel that after all he might be able to follow Master Robinton's ambitious plan of broadening understanding beyond the limits of this Sea Hold.

Alemi was back the following day after the children had been dismissed, with more questions. He stopped midsentence finally, apologizing profusely for taking so much of Elgion's time.

"I tell you what, Alemi, I'll teach you what you'd like to know if you'll teach me how to sail."

"Teach you to sail?"

Elgion grinned. "Yes, teach me to sail. The smallest child in my class knows more about that than I do, and my professional standing is in jeopardy. After all, a Harper is supposed to know everything.

"I may be wrong but I can't imagine that you need both legs to sail one of those little skiffs the children use."

Alemi's face lit up, and he pounded the Harper on the back with enthusiasm.

"Of course I can. By the First Shell, man, I'd be glad to do it. Glad."

And nothing would satisfy Alemi but to take the Harper down to the Dock Cavern immediately and give him the fundamentals of seamanship. In his own subject, Alemi was as good an instructor as the Harper; and Elgion was able to tack across the Harbor by himself by the end of the first lesson. Of course, as Alemi remarked, the wind was from the right quarter and the sea calm, ideal sailing conditions.

"Which rarely prevail?" asked Elgion; and he was rewarded by Alemi's tolerant chuckle. "Well, practice makes perfect, and I'd better learn the practical."

"And the theory."

So their friendship was cemented by mutual exchanges of knowledge and long visits together. Although their conversation touched many subjects, Elgion hesitated to bring up the subject of fire lizards, or the fact that the Weyr had asked him to search for traces of the elusive little creatures. He had, however, searched as much of the accessible coastline as he could on foot. There were some beaches that should be checked now from the seaside. With Alemi teaching him how to handle the skiff, he hoped he'd soon be able to do it himself. Elgion knew with certainty that Yanus would be completely scornful of any search for fire lizards, and the Harper didn't want to implicate Alemi in any plan that would bring Yanus's anger down on his head. Alemi was in bad enough straits over breaking his leg.

One clear bright morning, Elgion decided to put his solution to the test. He dismissed the children early, then sought out Alemi and suggested that today was not only a fine day but the sea was rough enough to test his ability. Alemi laughed, cast a wise eye at the clouds, and said that it would be mild as a bathing pool by afternoon but that the practice now would be useful to Elgion's progress.

Elgion wheedled a large package of fish rolls and spicecakes from a kitchen auntie, and the two men set off. Alemi was agile enough now with his crutch and splint-bound leg on land, but he was glad of any excuse to be on the sea.

Once beyond the protecting arms of the Half-Circle cliffs, the sea was choppy with crosscurrent and wind; Elgion's skill would be well tested. Alemi, disregarding an occasional wetting as the skiff plunged in and out of the wave troughs, played silent passenger while the Harper fought tiller and sheet to keep them on the course Alemi had set down the coast. The Sea Man became aware of the windshift some moments before Elgion, but it was the mark of his abilities as a teacher that Elgion was quick enough to notice the change.

"Wind's slacking off."

Alemi nodded, adjusting his cap slightly for the wind's new direction. They sailed on, the wind slackening to a gentle pressure against the sail, the skiff's speed aided more by the deep current than the wind.

"I'm hungry," Alemi announced as he and Elgion saw the stumpy violet crags of the Dragon Stones to leeward.

Elgion released the sheet line, and Alemi pulled the sail down, furling it with absent skill against the boom. At his direction, Elgion lashed the tiller so that the current carried them idly downcoast.

"Don't know why," Alemi said through a mouthful of fishroll, "food always tastes better on the sea."

Elgion contented himself to a nod since his mouth was full. He also had a good appetite; not, he qualified to himself, that he had been working overhard, just hanging on to the tiller and adjusting the sail sheet now and then.

"Come to think, don't often have time to eat on the sea," Alemi added. He gestured to include their leisurely bobbing, the skiff itself and the informal meal. "Haven't been this lazy on a sail since I was old enough to haul a net." He stretched and then adjusted his splinted leg slightly, grimacing against the awkwardness and discomfort. Suddenly he leaned away from the bulwark, to reach into the small locker fitted against the curve of the hull. "Thought so." Grinning, he held up fishline, hook and dry worm.

"Can't you leave off?"

"What? And have Yanus give out about unproductive hands?" Alemi deftly threaded line to hook and baited it. "Here. You might as well try hook line and bait. Or does the Masterharper object to cross-crafting?"

"The more crafts the better, says Master Robinton."

Alemi nodded, his eyes on the current. "Aye, sending lads away to other Sea Holds for fostering doesn't quite answer, does it?" Deftly he threw the line from him, watched the cast carry it well away from the drifting skiff and sink.

Elgion gave a fair imitation of that cast and settled himself, as Alemi had, to wait for results.

"What would we be catching out here?"

Alemi drew his mouth up in a grimace of indifference. "Probably nothing. Tide's full, current's strong, midday. Fish feed at dawn, unless there's Thread."

"Is that why you use the dry worm? Because it resembles Thread?" Elgion couldn't suppress the shudder that went down his spine at the thought of loose Thread.

"You're right."

The silence that often grips fishermen settled comfortably in the boat.

"Yellow-stripe, if anything," Alemi finally said in answer to the question that Elgion had almost forgotten he'd asked. "Yellow-stripe or a very hungry packtail. They'll eat anything."

"Packtail? That's good eating."

"Line'll break. Packtail's too heavy for this."

"Oh."

The current was inexorably drawing them closer to the Dragon Stones. But, although he wanted to get Alemi talking about them, Elgion couldn't find the proper opening. At about the point where Elgion felt he'd better speak or they'd be pulled by the current into the Stones, Alemi casually glanced around. They were only several dragon lengths from the most seaward of the great crags. The water now lapped peacefully against the base, exposing occasionally the jagged points of submerged rock, eddying around others. Alemi unfurled the sail and hauled on the sheet line.

"We need more sea room near those. Dangerous with sunken rock. When the tide's making, current can pull you right in. If you sail this way by yourself, and you'll soon be able to, make sure you keep your distance."

"The lads say you saw fire lizards there once." Elgion found the words out of his mouth before he could censor them.

Alemi shot him a long amused look. "Let's say I can't think what else it could've been. They weren't wherries: too fast, too small, and wherries can't maneuver that way. But fire lizards?" He laughed and shrugged his shoulders, indicating his own skepticism.

"What if I told you that there are such things? That F'nor, Canth's rider, Impressed one in Southern and so did five or six other riders? That the Weyrs are looking for more fire lizard clutches, and I've been asked to search the beaches?"

Alemi stared at the Harper. Then the skiff rocked in the subtle cross currents. "Mind now, pull the tiller hard aport. No, to your left, man!"

They had the looming Dragon Stone comfortably abaft before further conversation.

"You can Impress fire lizards?" If Alemi's voice was incredulous, an eager light sparkled in his eyes, and Elgion knew he'd made an ally; he told as much as he, himself, knew.

"Well, that would explain why you rarely see grown ones, and why they evade capture so cleverly. They *hear* you coming." Alemi laughed, shaking his head. "When I think of the times . . ."

"Me, too." Elgion grinned broadly, remembering his boyhood attempts to rig a successful trap.

"We're to look on beaches?"

"That's what N'ton suggested. Sandy beaches, sheltered places, preferably hard for small active boys to find. There're plenty of places where a fire lizard queen could hide a clutch around here."

"Not with the tides so high this season."

"There must be some beaches deep enough." Elgion felt impatient with Alemi's arguments.

The Sea Man motioned Elgion out of the tiller seat, and deftly tacked about.

"I saw fire lizards about the Dragon Stones. And those crags'd be right good weyrs. Not that I think we'd have a chance of seeing them today. They feed at dawn: that's when I saw them. Only," and Alemi chuckled, "I thought my eyes were deceiving me since it was the end of a long watch and a man's eyes can play tricks with him at dawn."

Alemi sailed the little skiff far closer to the Dragon Stones than Elgion would have dared. In fact the Harper found himself gripping the weatherboard very hard and edging his body away from the towering crags as the skiff breezed lightly by. There was no doubt that the crags were riddled with holes, likely weyrs for fire lizards.

"I wouldn't try this tack except when the tide is full, Elgion," said

Alemi as they sailed between the innermost crag and the tide-washed land. "There's a right mess of bottom-reaming rocks here even at half-tide."

It was quiet, too, with the waves softly caressing the narrow verge of sand between sea and cliff. Quiet enough for the unmistakable sound of piping to carry across the water to Elgion.

"Did you hear that?" Elgion grabbed Alemi's arm.

"Hear what?"

"The music!"

"What music?" Alemi wondered briefly if the sun were strong enough to give the Harper a stroke. But he sharpened his ears for any unusual sound, following the line of Elgion's stare to the cliffs. His heart leaped for a moment, but he said, "Music? Nonsense! Those cliffs are riddled with caves and holes. All you hear is the wind . . ."

"There isn't any wind now . . ."

Alemi had to admit that because he'd let the boom out and was even beginning to wonder if they had enough wind to come about on a tack that would clear the northern side of the stones.

"And look," said Elgion, "there's a hole in the cliff face. Big enough for a person to get into, I'd wager. Alemi, can't we go inshore?"

"Not unless we walk home, or wait for high tide again."

"Alemi! That's music! Not wind over blow holes! That's someone playing pipes."

An unhappy furtive thought crossed Alemi's face so plainly that Elgion jumped to a conclusion. All at once, all the pieces fell into place.

"Your sister, the one who's missing. *She* wrote those songs. She taught the children, not that conveniently dismissed fosterling!"

"Menolly's not playing any pipes, Elgion. She sliced her left hand, gutting packtail, and she can't open or close her fingers."

Elgion sank back to the deck, stunned but still hearing the clear tone of pipes. Pipes? You'd need two whole hands to play multiple pipes. The music ceased and the wind, rising as they tacked past the Dragon Stones, covered his memory of that illusive melody. It could have been the land breeze, sweeping down over the cliffs, sounding into holes.

"Menolly did teach the children, didn't she?"

Slowly Alemi nodded. "Yanus believed the Sea Hold disgraced to have a girl taking the place of a Harper."

"Disgraced?" Once again Elgion was appalled at the obtuseness of the Sea Holder. "When she taught so well? When she can turn a tune like the ones I've seen?"

"She can play no more, Elgion. It would be cruel to ask now. She wouldn't even sing in the evenings. She'd leave as soon as you started to play."

So he'd been right, thought Elgion, the tall girl had been Menolly.

"If she's alive, she's happier away from the Hold! If she's dead . . ." Alemi didn't continue.

In silence they sailed on, the Dragon Stones falling away, back into violet indefiniteness as each man avoided the other's gaze.

Now Elgion could understand many things about Menolly's disappearance and the general reluctance at the Hold to discuss her or find her. There was no doubt in his mind that her disappearance was deliberate. Anyone sensitive enough to compose such melodies must have found life in the Sea Hold intolerable: doubly so with Yanus as Sea Holder and father. And then to be considered a disgrace! Elgion cursed Petiron for not making the matter plain. If only he had told Robinton that the promising musician were a girl, she might have been at the Harperhall before that knife had a chance to slip.

"There'd be no clutches on the Dragon Stones' cove," Alemi said, breaking into Elgion's rueful thoughts. "Water's right up to the bluff at high tide. There is one place . . . I'll take you there after the next Threadfall is past. A good long day's sail down the coast. You *can* Impress a fire lizard, you say?"

"I'll set the signal for N'ton to talk to you after Fall." Elgion was happy enough to use any subject to break the restraint that had fallen between them. "Evidently you or I can Impress, though lowly Harpers and young Sea Men may be far down on the list for available eggs."

"By the dawn star, when I think of the hours I spent as a small fellow . . ."

"Who hasn't?" Elgion grinned back, eager too for the chance.

This time their silence was companionable, and when they exchanged glances, it was for remembered boyish fancies of capturing the elusive and much desired fire lizard.

As they tacked into the Dock Cavern late that afternoon, Alemi had a final word for Elgion.

"You understand why you're not to know it was Menolly who did the teaching?"

"The Sea Hold is not disgraced." Elgion felt Alemi's hand tighten on his arm so he nodded. "But I would never betray that confidence."

If his solemn response reassured the Sea Man, it reinforced Elgion's determination to find out who had made that pipe music. Was it possible to play multiple pipes with one hand? He was convinced that he'd heard music, not wind over blowholes. Somehow, whether on the pretext of searching for fire lizards or not, he must get close enough to examine that cave in the Dragon Stones' cove.

The next day was rainy, a thin soft drizzle that did not deter the fishermen but that made both Elgion and Alemi unwilling to take a long and possibly fruitless journey in an open boat.

That same evening Yanus asked Elgion to excuse the children from lessons the following morning as they'd be needed to gather seaweed for the smoke-cave. Elgion granted considered permission, masterfully suppressing a desire to thank the Sea Holder for a free day, and determined to rise early and be off to seek the answer to the music mystery. He was up as soon as the sun, first in the Great Hall, so that he had to unbar the metal doors, little realizing as he did so that he would be following an unnerving precedent. With fish rolls and dried fruit in his pouch, his own pipe slung across his back, a stout rope about his middle (for he rather thought he might need it climbing down that cliff face), Elgion was away.

Chapter 9

*Oh, Tongue, give sound to joy and sing
Of hope and promise on dragonwing.*

The hunger of the fire lizards roused Menolly from sleep. There was nothing in the cave to eat because the previous day had been wet enough to keep them all inside. She saw that the tide was well out, and the day was clear.

"If we scramble, we can get down coast and pick us up a nice lot of spiderclaws. They'll be gone soon," she told her friends. "Or we can look for rockmites. So come along, Beauty." The little queen hummed from her warm nest in the rushes, and the others began to stir. Menolly reached down and tickled Lazy's neck where he lay by her feet. He slapped at her, rousing enough to let out a huge yawn. His eyelids peeled back and his eyes sparkled faintly red.

"Now, don't you all start in on me. I got you up so we could be off. You won't be hungry long if we all stir smartly."

As she descended agilely to the beach, her friends swooping gracefully from the cave, some of the other fire lizards were feeding in the shallows. Menolly called out a greeting to them. She wondered, as she often did, if the other fire lizards, with the notable exception of the queen, were at all aware of her. She felt it rude not to acknowledge their presence whether they responded or not. Maybe one day they would have grown so used to her, that they'd answer.

She slipped on the wet rocks at the far end of the cove, wincing as a sharp edge made itself painfully felt through the thinning soles of her boots. *That* was a matter she'd have to attend to soon, new boot soles. With such rough surfaces, she couldn't go barefoot. And she certainly couldn't climb barefooted, not if she had toes like a watchwher. She'd have to get another wherry, tan its leg hide to a proper toughness. But how could she sew the new leather to her old bootsole? She looked down at her feet, placing them carefully, as much to save the leather as her feet.

She took her band to the furthest cove they'd yet explored, far enough down the coast for the Dragon Stones to be knobs on the horizon. But the long walk was worth the effort for spiderclaws scurried wildly up and down the wide, gently curving beach. The bluff had dwindled to a height just above her head in some places, and at the far end of the cresent sands, a stream fed into the sea.

Beauty and the others were soon playing havoc with the spiderclaws, diving down on their intended prey, then darting up to the cliffs to eat. When her net was full, Menolly searched for enough sea wreckage to start a fire. That was how she found the clutch, covered as it was and almost level with the beach surface. But she saw the faint outline of a mound, supiciously circular. She brushed away enough sand to expose the mottled shell of a hardening fire lizard egg. She glanced around carefully, wondering if the queen was anywhere about; but she saw only her own nine. She put a gentle finger on the exposed egg: it was softish. Quickly she patted the sand back into place and hurried from the clutch. The high-tide mark on this beach was a long way from threatening the eggs. It pleased her to realize that this beach was a long way from any Hold so these fire lizard eggs were safe.

She gathered sufficient wood, made a rude hearth, started her fire, killed the spiderclaws deftly and laid them on a conveniently flat stone and went exploring while they baked.

The stream flowed broad into the sea; sand banks had formed and reformed to judge by the myriad channels. Menolly followed the stream inland, looking for the sweet cresses that often grew where the water freshened. Submarine bodies moved upstream, too, and she wondered if she could catch one of the big specklers. Alemi often boasted that he could tickle them into his grasp as they fought the current. Thinking of the spiderclaws roasting on her fire, Menolly decided to leave that exercise until another day. She did want some greens; succulent cresses with their odd tangy aftertaste would make a good addition to spiderclaws.

She found the greens well above the tidewater, where the stream was fed by tiny trickles from the flat marshy lands through which it looped. She was greedily stuffing a handful of greens into her mouth before she really took in her surroundings. In the distance, low on the horizon, were lightning flashes against a gray sky.

Thread! Fear rooted her to the ground; she nearly choked on the half-chewed mouthful of greens. She tried to talk herself out of terror by counting the flashes of dragon fire that made a pattern across the sky: a wide, long pattern. If the dragonriders were already at work, the Thread wouldn't get as far as here. She was a long way from it.

But how far away was safe? She'd just made it to the cave before that other Fall. She was too far away, run as fast as ever she could, to reach the cave's safety now. She'd the sea behind her. Water! She'd the stream beside her. Thread drowned in water. But how deep did it fall before it drowned?

She told herself firmly that now was not the time to panic. She forced herself to swallow the last of the cress juices. Then she had no control over her legs; they took off with her and she was running, towards the sea and towards the rock safety of her cave.

Beauty appeared above her head, swooping and chittering as she caught Menolly's fear. Rocky and Diver arrived with Mimic popping in a half-breath later. They experienced her alarm, circling around her head as she ran, calling out with the piercingly sweet tenor bugle of challenge. Then they all disappeared. Which made running easier for Menolly. She could concentrate on where she was putting her feet.

She made diagonally for the beaches, wondering briefly if it wouldn't be smarter to go along the shore line. She'd be that much nearer the dubious safety of the water. She hurdled a ditch; managed to keep her balance as her left foot twisted on landing; staggered a few paces before she found her stride again. No, there'd be more rocks on the shore, cutting down her speed and increasing the danger of a badly twisted ankle.

Two queens gleamed golden in the air above her, and Rocky and Diver were back, with Lazybones, Mimic and Brownie. The two queens chittered angrily, and the males, to Menolly's surprise, flew ahead of her now, and high enough not to be a nuisance. She ran on.

She came to a height, and the incline robbed her of breath so that she staggered to the summit and had to drop to a walk, clutching her right side against the nagging stitch, but somehow moving forward. Ahead of her the Dragon Stones were more than knobs but too distant to reassure. One look over her shoulder at the sky bursts of dragon fire told her that the Thread was gaining on her.

She broke into a run again, the two queens gliding right over her head, and she felt oddly protected. She had her second wind now, and her stride, and felt as if she could run forever. If she could only run fast enough to stay beyond the reach of Thread . . . She kept her eyes on the Dragon Stones, refusing to look over her shoulder: that unnerving sight caught the breath she needed for running.

She ran as close to the bluff edge as she dared. She'd slithered down one cliff without desperate damage to herself: she'd risk it again to get into the water if she had to.

She ran, one eye on the Dragon Stones, one for the ground ahead of her feet.

She heard the whoosh, heard the fire lizards' startled chirrups, saw the shadow and fell to the ground covering her head instinctively with her hands, her body taut for the first feel of flesh-scoring Thread. She smelt fire-stone, and felt the air heavy against her body.

"Get on your feet, you silly fool! And hurry. Leading edge is nearly on us!"

Incredulous, Menolly looked up, right into the whirling eyes of a brown dragon. He cocked his head and hummed urgently.

"Get up!" said his rider.

Menolly wasted no time after a frantic look at the fire blossoms and the sight of a line of dragons swooping and disappearing. She scrambled to her feet, dove for the brown rider's extended hand and one of the fighting strap ends, and got herself firmly astride the brown's neck behind his rider.

"Hang on to me tightly. And don't be afraid. I'm to take you *between* to Benden. It'll be cold and dark, but I'll be with you."

The relief of being rescued when she was fearing injury or death was too overwhelming for speech. The brown dragon half-ran to the bluff edge, dropped down briefly to get wing room, and then surged up. Menolly felt herself pressed against the soft warm flesh and burrowed into the hide-clad back of her rescuer, struggling for a lungful of air to ease her tight chest. She had one brief glimpse of her little fire lizards trying vainly to follow when the dragon winked into *between.*

Sweat froze on her forehead and cheeks, down her back, on her calves, her wet and ragged boots and her sore feet. There was no air to breathe and she felt she would suffocate. She tightened her hands convulsively on the dragonrider, but she couldn't feel him or the dragon she knew she was riding.

Now, she thought with that part of her mind that wasn't frozen in panic, she fully understood that Teaching Song. In terror, she fully understood it.

Abruptly, sight, sound, feeling, and breath returned. They were spiralling down at a dizzying height above Benden Weyr. As big as Half-Circle was, this place of dragons and dragonmen was bigger by half again as much. Why, the immense harbor of Half-Circle would have fitted with dragon lengths to spare in the Bowl of the Weyr.

As the dragon circled, she saw the giant Star Stones, and the Eye Rock, which told when the Red Star would make its fateful Passes. She saw the watch dragon beside the Stones, heard him trumpet a greeting to the brown she rode. Between her legs she felt the rumble of response in the brown's throat. As they glided down, she saw several dragons on the Bowl floor, with people gathered about them; saw the steps leading to the queen's weyr, and the yawning maw of the Hatching Ground. Benden was vaster than she'd imagined.

The brown landed near the other dragons, and Menolly now realized that the dragons had been Threadscored and were being treated. The brown dragon half-folded his wings, craning his neck around to the two on his back.

"You can relax your death hold, lad," said the brown rider with tolerant amusement as he unfastened the fighting straps from his belt.

Menolly jerked her hands free with a muttered apology. "I can't thank you enough for finding me. I thought Thread would get me."

"Whoever let you out of your Hold so near to Threadfall?"

"I was catching spiderclaws. Went out early."

He accepted that hurried explanation, but now Menolly wondered how she could make it plausible. She couldn't remember the name of the nearest Hold on the Nerat side of Half-Circle.

"Down you go, lad, I've got to rejoin my wing to mop up."

That was the second time he'd called her "lad."

"You've a fine pace on you. Ever think of going for a hold runner?"

The brown rider swung her forward so she could slide down the brown's shoulder. The moment her feet touched the ground, she thought she'd faint with the pain. She grabbed frantically at the brown's foreleg. He nuzzled her sympathetically, humming to his rider.

"Branth says you're hurt?" The man slid down quickly beside her.

"My feet!" She'd run the boots to uppers without knowing it, and her lacerated feet were bloody from toe to heel.

"I'll tell the world. Here we go!"

He grabbed her by the wrist, gave a practiced yank and laid her over his shoulder. As he made for the entrance to the lower Caverns, he called out for someone to bring a pot of numbweed.

She was uprighted into a chair, the blood singing in her ears. Someone was propping her damaged feet onto a stool while women converged on her from several sides.

"Hey, Manora, Felena," yelled the brown rider urgently.

"Just look at his feet! He's run them raw!"

"T'gran, wherever . . ."

"Saw him trying to outrun Thread down Nerat way. Bloody near did!"

"Bloody's quite accurate. Manora, could you spare a moment, please?"

"Should we wash the feet first or . . ."

"No, a cup of weed first," was T'gran's suggestion. "You'll have to cut the boots off . . ."

Someone was holding a cup against her lips, bidding her drink it all down. On a stomach empty of anything but a few blades of cress, the fellis juice acted so quickly that the circle of faces about her became a confused blur.

"Good heavens, the holders have gone mad, going out in Threadfall." Menolly thought the speaker sounded like Manora. "This is the second one we've rescued today."

After that, voices became indistinguishable mumbles. Menolly was unable to focus her eyes. She seemed to be floating a few handspans off the ground. Which suited her because she didn't want to use her feet anyway.

Seated at a table on the other side of the kitchen cavern, Elgion at first thought the boy had fainted with relief at being rescued. He could appreciate the feeling certainly, having been sighted by a dragonrider as he was pelting back towards Half-Circle, fully winded and despairing of life. Now, with his stomach full of good weyr stew, his wits and breath restored, he was forced to face his folly in going outside the Hold so close to a Fall. And, more daunting to contemplate, the reception on his return to Half-Circle. Talk about disgracing the Sea Hold! And his explanation that he was searching for fire lizard eggs would not go down well with Yanus. Even Alemi, what would he think? Elgion sighed and watched as several weyr-women carried the boy off towards the living caverns. He half-rose, wondering if he should have volunteered to help. Then he saw his first fire lizard and forgot everything else.

It was a little golden queen, swooping into the cavern, calling piteously. She seemed to hover motionless in midair, then winked out of sight. A moment later, she was diving into the kitchen cavern again, less agitated but looking for something or someone.

A girl emerged from the living cavern, saw the fire lizard and held up her arm. The little queen delicately landed, stroking the girl's face with her tiny head while the girl evidently reassured her. The two walked out into the Bowl.

"You've never seen one, Harper?" asked an amused voice, and Elgion came out of his trance to attend the weyrwoman who'd been serving him food.

"No, I hadn't."

She laughed at the wistfulness in his voice. "That's Grall, F'nor's little queen," Felena told him. Then abruptly she asked Elgion if he'd like more stew.

He politely declined because he'd already had two platefuls: food being the weyr's way of reassuring those they rescued.

"I really should be finding out if I can get back to Half-Circle Sea Hold. They'll have discovered my absence and . . ."

"Don't worry on that account, Harper, for word was passed back through the fighting wings. They'll let Half-Circle know you're safely here."

Elgion expressed proper gratitude, but he couldn't help fretting over Yanus's displeasure. He would simply have to make it clear that he'd been following Weyr orders, and Yanus was nothing if not obedient to his Weyr. Nonetheless, Elgion did not relish his return to the Sea Hold. He also couldn't politely insist on going when he chose because the dragons were tired as they returned to their Weyr, Thread successfully obliterated on this Fall.

Some of the young Harper's worst apprehensions were relieved by T'gellan, the bronze wingleader in charge of that Fall.

"I myself told them you were safe, and a good thing, too. They were all ready to mount a search. Which, for old Yanus, is a remarkable concession."

Elgion grimaced. "I suppose it wouldn't look well to lose two Harpers in a short time."

"Nonsense. Already Yanus prizes you above fish! Or so Alemi said."

"Was he angry?"

"Who? Yanus?"

"No, Alemi."

"Why? I'd say he was better pleased than Yanus to hear you were safe and scoreless at Benden. More important, *did* you see any signs of fire lizard clutches?"

"No."

T'gellan sighed, stripping off his wide riding belt and opening the heavy wherhide jacket. "How we need the silly creatures."

"Are they that useful?"

T'gellan gave him a long look. "Possibly not. Lessa thinks them a real nuisance; but they look, and act, like dragons. And they give those narrow-minded, hide-bound, insensitive Lord Holders just that necessary glimpse of what it is to ride a dragon. *That* is going to make life . . . and progress . . . easier for us in the Weyrs."

Elgion rather hoped that this had been made plain to Yanus; and he was going to tactfully suggest that he was ready to go back to the Sea Hold when the bronze rider was called away to check a dragon's wing injury.

Elgion found the additional delay instructive. He decided he would put his observations to good use in getting back into Yanus's favor—for he had an opportunity to see Weyr life as unsung in Saga and Ballad. An injured dragon cried as piteously as a child until his wounds were salved with numbweed. A dragon also cried distressingly if his rider was injured. Elgion watched the touching sight of a green dragon, crooning anxiously at her rider as he leaned against her forearm, while the weyrwomen dressed his Threadscored arm. Elgion saw the weyrlings bathing and oiling their young beasts, the Weyr's several fire lizards assisting. He saw the youngsters of the Weyr refilling firestone sacks for the next Fall, and couldn't fail to notice that they made less work of the onerous chore than Sea Hold lads would have done. He even ventured to peer into the Hatching Ground where golden Ramoth lay curled protectively around her eggs. He ducked out of sight, hoping she hadn't seen him.

Time passed so quickly that Elgion was surprised to hear the kitchen women calling everyone in to eat. He hovered at the entrance, wondering what to do when T'gellan grabbed him by the arm and propelled him to an empty table.

"G'sel, come over here with that bronze nuisance of yours. I want the Half-Circle Harper to see him. G'sel has one of the original clutch F'nor discovered in Southern," T'gellan said in an undertone as they watched the stocky young man weaving his way through the tables towards them, balancing a bronze fire lizard on his forearm.

"This is Rill, Harper," G'sel said, extending his arm to Elgion. "Rill, be courteous; he's a Harper."

With great dignity the fire lizard extended his wings, executing what Elgion construed to be a bow, while the jeweled eyes regarded him intently. Not knowing how one saluted a fire lizard, Elgion tentatively extended his hand.

"Scratch his eye ridges," G'sel suggested. "They all love that."

To Elgion's delight and amazement, the fire lizard accepted the caress, and as Elgion's stroking eased an itch, Rill's eyelids began to close in sensuous pleasure.

"He's another convert," said T'gellan, laughing and pulling out his chair. The noise roused the fire lizard from somnolence and he hissed softly at T'gellan. "They're bold creatures, too, you'll notice, Harper, with no respect for degree."

This was evidently an old jibe, for G'sel, seating himself, paid it no heed, but coaxed Rill to step onto a padded shoulder rest so he could eat the dinner now being served.

"How much do they understand?" Elgion asked, taking the chair opposite G'sel so he could see Rill better.

"To hear Mirrim talk about her three, everything."

T'gellan snorted with good-natured derision.

"I can ask Rill to carry a message to any place he's already been. No, to a *person* he knows at another Hold or Weyr I've taken him to. He follows me no matter where I go. Even during Threadfall." At T'gellan's snort, G'sel added, "I told you to watch today, T'gellan. Rill was with us."

"Yes, so tell Elgion how long it takes Rill to come back from delivering a message."

"All right, all right," said G'sel with a laugh as he stroked Rill affectionately. "And when you've one of your own, T'gellan . . ."

"Possibly, possibly," the bronze rider said easily. "Unless Elgion here finds us another clutch, we'll just have to stay jealous of you."

T'gellan changed the subject then to ask about Half-Circle Hold, general questions that did not embarrass or compromise Elgion. T'gellan evidently knew Yanus's reputation.

"If you feel too isolated there, Harper, don't fail to fly the signal and we'll pop you up for an evening here."

"Hatching's soon," G'sel suggested, grinning and giving Elgion a wink.

"He'll be here for that certainly," T'gellan agreed.

Then Rill creeled for a bite to eat while the bronze rider chided G'sel for turning the lizard into an importunate beggar. Elgion noticed T'gellan, himself, finding a titbit for the little bronze, however, and he, too, offered Rill some meat, which the creature daintily accepted from the knife.

By the end of the meal Elgion was ready to brave Yanus's worst displeasure and wrath to find a fire lizard clutch and Impress a fire lizard of his own. That prospect made his inevitable return easier.

"I'd better do you the honors, Elgion," T'gellan said, rising at last from the table. "And I'd also better get you back early. No sense aggravating Yanus more than necessary."

Elgion wasn't certain how to take that remark or the wink that accompanied it, particularly as it was now full dark and for all he knew, the Hold doors were already barred for the night. Too late now to wish he'd gone back as soon as the dragonriders had returned from the Fall. But then he wouldn't have met Rill.

They were aloft, Elgion reveling in the experience, craning his head to see as much as possible in the clear night air. He had only a glimpse of the Higher Benden Range hills before T'gellan asked Monarth to take them *between*.

Suddenly, it was no longer full dark: the sun was a handspan above the glowing sea as they burst into the air above Half-Circle Harbor.

"Told you I'd get you back early," T'gellan said, turning to grin at the Harper's startled exclamation. "We're not supposed to time it, but all in a good cause."

Monarth circled down lazily so that everyone in the Sea Hold was gathered on the holdway when they landed. Yanus strode a few paces ahead of the others while Elgion searched the faces for Alemi's.

T'gellan leaped from the bronze's shoulder and made a show of assisting Elgion as the entire Hold cheered loudly for their Harper's safe return.

"I'm neither crippled or old," Elgion muttered under his breath, aware of Yanus's approach. "Don't overdo it."

T'gellan laid his arm across Elgion's shoulders in a comradely fashion, beaming at the oncoming Sea Holder. "Not at all," he said out of the corner of his mouth. "The Weyr approves!"

"Sea Holder, I am profoundly embarrassed at the inconvenience . . ."

"No, Harper Elgion," T'gellan interrupted him, "any apologies are the Weyr's. You were adamant in wishing to return to Half-Circle immediately. But Lessa needed to have his report, Yanus, so we had to wait."

Whatever Yanus had been about to say to his erring Harper was neatly blocked by T'gellan's obvious approval. The Sea Holder rocked a bit on his feet, blinking as he reorganized his thoughts.

"Any fire lizard sign you discover must be made known to the Weyr as soon as possible," T'gellan continued blithely.

"Then that tale is true?" Yanus asked in a grumble of disbelief. "Those . . . those creatures do exist?"

"They do indeed, sir," Elgion replied warmly. "I have seen, touched and fed a bronze fire lizard; his name is Rill. He's about as big as my forearm . . ."

"You did? He is?" Alemi had pushed through the crowd, breathless from excitement and the exercise of hobbling as fast as he could down the holdway. "Then you did find something in the cave?"

"The cave?" Elgion had forgotten all about his original destination that morning.

"What cave?" demanded T'gellan.

"The cave . . ." and Elgion gulped and then boldly embroidered on the lie T'gellan had begun, "I told Lessa about. Surely you were in the room then."

"What cave?" demanded Yanus, stepping close to the younger men, his voice half-angry because he was being excluded from the conversation.

"The cave that Alemi and I spotted on the shore near the Dragon Stones," Elgion said, trying to give the proper cues. "Alemi," Elgion had to address T'gellan now, "is the Sea Man who saw the fire lizards last spring near the Dragon Stones. Two—three days back, we sailed down the coast and saw the cave. That's where I think it's likely we'll find fire lizard eggs."

"Well, then, since you're now safely in your Hold, Harper Elgion, I will leave you." T'gellan couldn't wait to get back to Monarth. And the cave.

"You'll let us know if you find anything, won't you?" Elgion called after him and received only a wild arm gesture before the bronze rider swung himself up to Monarth's back.

"We offered him no hospitality for his trouble in returning you," Yanus said, worried and somewhat aggrieved by the bronze rider's precipitous departure.

"He'd just eaten," Elgion replied, as the bronze dragon beat his way upward above the sunset-lit waters of the harbor.

"So early."

"Ah, he'd been fighting Thread. And he's wingleader, so he must be back at the Weyr."

That did impress Yanus.

Rider and dragon winked out, drawing a startled exclamation of delight from everyone. Alemi caught Elgion's eye, and the Harper had to suppress his grin: he'd share the full jest with Alemi later. Only would the joke be on himself if after all the half-truths T'gellan found fire lizard eggs . . . or a piper . . . in the cave?

"Harper Elgion," said Yanus firmly, waving the rest of the holders away from them as he pointed to the Hold door. "Harper Elgion, I'd be grateful for a few words of explanation."

"Indeed, sir, and I've much to report to you of happenings in the Weyr." Elgion respectfully followed the Sea Holder. He knew now how to deal with Yanus with no further recourse to evasions or lies.

Chapter 10

Then my feet took off and my legs went, too,
So my body was obliged to follow
Me with my hands and my mouth full of cress
And my throat too dry to swallow.

When Menolly roused, she was in a quiet dark place and something crooned comfortingly in her ear. She knew it was Beauty, but she wondered how she could be so warm all over. She moved, and her feet felt big, stuffed and very sore.

She must have made some sound because she heard a soft movement and then the glow in the corner of the room was half-unshielded.

"Are you comfortable? Are your feet painful?"

The warmth beside Menolly's ear disappeared. Clever Beauty, Menolly thought with approval after an instant's fear of discovery.

Someone was bending over Menolly now, securing the sleeping furs about her shoulders; someone whose hands were gentle, soothing, who smelled of clean herbs and faintly of numbweed.

"They only hurt a little," Menolly replied untruthfully because her feet had taken to throbbing so hard she was afraid the woman could hear them.

Her soft murmur and her gentle hands denied Menolly's stoicism.

"You must surely be hungry. You've slept all day."

"I have?"

"We gave you fellis juice. You'd run your feet to ribbons . . ." There was a slight hesitation in the woman's voice. "They'll be fine in a sevenday. No serious cuts." The quiet voice held a ripple of amusement. "T'gran is convinced you're the fastest . . . runner in Pern."

"I'm not a runner. I'm just a girl."

"Not 'just' a girl. I'll get you something to eat. And then it's best if you sleep again."

Alone, Menolly tried not to think of her throbbing feet and a body which felt stone-heavy, immobile. She worried for fear Beauty or some of the others would come and be discovered by the weyrwoman, and what would happen to Lazy with no one to make him hunt for himself and . . .

"I'm Manora," the woman said as she returned with a bowl of steaming stew and a mug. "You realize that you're at Benden Weyr? Good. You may stay here, you know, as long as you wish."

"I can?" A relief as intense as the pain in her feet flooded Menolly.

"Yes, you can," and the firmness of that reply made that right inalienable.

"Menolly is my name . . ." She hesitated because Manora was nodding. "How did you know?"

Manora motioned for her to continue eating. "I've seen you at Half-Circle, you know, and the Harper asked the wingleader to keep search for you . . . after you disappeared. We won't discuss that now, Menolly, but I do assure you that you can stay at Benden."

"Please don't *tell* them . . ."

"As you wish. Finish your stew and take all the drink. You must sleep to heal."

She left as noiselessly as she'd come, but Menolly was reassured. Manora was headwoman at Benden Weyr, and what she said was so.

The stew was delicious, thick with meat chunks and satisfying with herb flavors. She'd almost finished it when she heard a faint rustle and Beauty returned, piteously broadcasting hunger. With a sigh, Menolly pushed the bowl under the little queen's nose. Beauty licked it dry, then hummed softly and rubbed her face against Menolly's cheek.

"Where are the others?" Menolly asked, worriedly.

The little queen gave another hum and began to curl herself up in a ball by Menolly's shoulder. She wouldn't have been so relaxed if the others were in trouble, Menolly thought, as she sipped the fellis juice.

"Beauty," Menolly whispered, nudging the queen, "if anyone comes, you go. You mustn't be seen here. Do you understand?"

The queen rustled her wings irritably.

"Beauty, you mustn't be seen." Menolly spoke as sternly as she could, and the queen opened one eye, which whirled slowly. "Oh dear, won't you understand?" The queen gave a soft reassuring croon and then closed both lids.

The fellis juice was already melting Menolly's limbs into weightlessness. The dreadful throb of her feet eased. As her eyes relentlessly closed, Menolly had one last thought: how had Beauty known where she was?

When Menolly woke, it was to hear faint sounds of children laughing, an infectious laughter that made her grin and wonder what caused such happiness. Beauty was gone but the space where she'd lain by Menolly's head was warm to the touch. The curtain across the cubicle parted and a figure was silhouetted against the light beyond.

"What's the matter with you all of a sudden, Reppa?" the girl said softly to someone Menolly couldn't see. "Oh, all right. I'm well rid of you for now." She turned and saw Menolly looking at her. "How do you feel today?" As she adjusted the glow for full light, Menolly saw a girl about her own age, dark hair tied primly back from a face that was sad, tired and oddly mature. Then she smiled, and the impression of maturity dissolved. "Did you really run across Nerat?"

"I really didn't, although my feet feel as if *they* had."

"Imagine it! And you holdbred and out during a Fall!" There was a grudging respect in her voice.

"I was running for shelter," Menolly felt obliged to say.

"Speaking of running, Manora couldn't come to see you herself right now so you're in my charge. She's told me exactly what to do," and the girl grimaced with such feeling that Menolly had a swift vision of Manora delivering her precise and careful instructions, "and I've had a lot of experience . . ." An expression of pain and anxiety crossed her face.

"Are you Manora's fosterling?" asked Menolly politely.

The expression deepened for a moment, and then the girl erased all expression from her face, drawing her shoulders up with pride. "No, I'm Brekke's. My name is Mirrim. I used to be in the Southern Weyr."

She made the statement as if that should make all plain to Menolly.

"You mean, in the Southern Continent?"

"Yes," and Mirrim sounded irritated.

"I didn't know anyone lived there." The words were no sooner out of her mouth than Menolly remembered some snippet of information overheard in conversations between Petiron and her father.

"Where have you *been* all your life?" demanded Mirrim, exasperated.

"In Half-Circle Sea Hold," Menolly replied meekly because she didn't wish to offend the girl.

Mirrim stared at her.

"Haven't you ever heard of it?" It was Menolly's turn to be condescending. "We have the biggest dock cavern on Pern."

Mirrim caught her eye, and then both girls began to laugh, the moment in which their friendship began.

"Look, let me help you to the necessary, you must be bursting . . ." and Mirrim briskly threw back the sleeping fur. "You just lean on me."

Menolly had to because her feet were incredibly sore, even with Mirrim supporting most of her weight. Fortunately the necessary was no more than a few steps beyond the sleeping cubicle. By the time Menolly crawled back into her bed, she was shaking all over.

"Stay on your stomach, Menolly; it'll be easier to change your bandages," Mirrim said. "I haven't had to do many feet, it's true; but if you don't have to see what's going on, that makes it easier. Everyone at Southern said my hands are gentle, and I'll drown your feet in numbweed. Or would you want some more fellis juice? Manora said you could."

Menolly shook her head.

"Brekke . . ." and here Mirrim's voice faltered briefly, "Brekke taught me how to change sticky bandages because I . . . Oh, dearie me, your feet look just like raw meat. Ooops, that's not the right thing to say, but they do. They *will* be all right, Manora said," and there was such confidence in that statement that Menolly preferred to believe it, too. "Now Threadscore . . . that's nasty. You've just lost all the skin on your feet, that's all, but I expect you feel that's quite enough. Sorry. Caught you there. Anyway, you'll not even have scars once the new skin grows, and it's really amazing how quickly skin does grow. Or so I've observed. Now Threadscore, that's nasty for healing. Never quite fades. Lucky for you T'gran's Branth spotted you running. Dragons are very longsighted, you know. There, now, this should help . . ."

Menolly gasped involuntarily as Mirrim slathered cool numbweed on her right foot. She'd been biting her lips against the pain while Mirrim, with very gentle hands indeed, had removed the blood-caked bandages but the relief from pain was almost a shock. If she'd only lost the skin from her feet, why did they hurt so much more than her hand had?

"Now, we've only the left foot to go. The numbweed does help, doesn't it? Did you ever have to boil it?" Mirrim asked with a groan and, as usual, didn't wait for an answer. "For three days I just grit my teeth and close my nose and firmly remind myself that it would be so *much* worse if we *didn't* have numbweed. I suppose that's the bad with the good Manora's always saying we have to have. But you'll be relieved to know that there's no sign of infection . . ."

"Infection?" Menolly jerked herself up on her elbows, craning her head about.

"Will you keep still?" Mirrim glared so authoritatively that Menolly forced herself to relax. All she could see of her feet were salve-smeared heels. "And you're very, very lucky there isn't any infection. After all, you'd been running shoeless over sand, dirt and goodness knows what. It took us forever to wash the grit off." Mirrim made a sympathetic sound. "Just as well we'd dosed you good."

"You're sure there's no infection this time?"

"This time? You haven't done this before, have you?" Mirrim's voice was shocked.

"No, not my feet. My hand," and Menolly turned on her side, holding out her scarred hand. She was considerably gratified by the concerned pity in Mirrim's face as she examined the wound.

"However did you do that?"

"I was gutting packtail, and the knife slipped."

"You were lucky to miss the tendons."

"Miss?"

"Well, you are using those fingers. A bit drawn that scar, though." Mirrim clucked her tongue with professional dismay. "Don't think much of your Hold's nursing if that's any sample."

"Packtail slime is difficult, as bad as Threadscore in its own way," Menolly muttered, perversely defending her Hold.

"Be that as it may," and Mirrim gave the foot bandage a final twitch, *"we'll* see you don't have any such trouble with your feet. Now, I'll bring you something to eat. You must be starved . . ."

Now that the worst of the dressing was over and the numbweed had deadened the pain in her feet, Menolly was definitely aware of the emptiness in her stomach.

"So I'll be right back, Menolly, and if you need anything after that, just shout for Sanra. She's below on the Floor, minding the little ones, and she knows she's to listen for you."

As Menolly worked her way through the generous meal Mirrim brought, she reflected on some harsh truths. Definitely Mavi had given her the distinct impression that she'd never be able to use her hand again. Yet Mavi was too skilled a healer not to have known that the knife had missed the finger tendons. She had deliberately let the hand heal with drawn flesh. It was painfully clear to Menolly that Mavi, as well as Yanus, had not wanted her to be able to play again.

Grimly Menolly vowed that she'd never, never return to Half-Circle. Her reflections made her doubt Manora's assurance that she could stay at Benden Weyr. No matter, she could run away again. Run she could, and live holdless. And that's what she'd do. Why, she'd run across all Pern . . . And why not? Menolly became pleased with the notion. Indeed, there was nothing to stop her running right to the Masterharperhall in Fort Hold. Maybe Petiron *had* sent her songs to Masterharper Robinton. Maybe they were more than just twiddles. Maybe . . . but there was no maybe about returning to Half-Circle Hold! That she would not do.

The issue did not arise over the next few days while her feet itched—

Mirrim said that was a good sign of healing—and she found herself beginning to fret with impatience at her disability.

She also worried about her fire lizards now she wasn't able to forage for them. But the first evening when Beauty reappeared, her little eyes darting about the chamber to be sure Menolly was alone, there was nothing of hunger in her manner. She daintily accepted the morsels that Menolly had carefully saved from her supper. Rocky and Diver appeared just as she was drifting off to sleep. However, they promptly curled themselves up to sleep against the small of her back, which they wouldn't have done if they'd been hungry.

They were gone the next morning, but Beauty lingered, stroking her head against Menolly's cheek until she heard footsteps in the corridor. Menolly shooed her away, telling her to stay with the others.

"I know it's boring to stay abed," Mirrim agreed the third morning with a weary sigh that told Menolly Mirrim would gladly have swapped places, "but it's kept you out of Lessa's way. Since the . . . well," and Mirrim censored what she'd been about to say. "With Ramoth broody over those eggs, we're all treading hot sands until they Hatch, so it's better you're here."

"There must be something I can do, now that I'm better. I'm good with my hands . . ." and then Menolly, too, halted uncertainly.

"You could help Sanra with the little ones if you would. Can you tell any stories?"

"Yes, I . . ." and Menolly all but blurted out what she'd done at the Sea Hold, ". . . can at least keep them amused."

Weyrbred children were not like Hold children, Menolly discovered: they were more active physically, possessed of insatiable curiosity for every detail she cared to tell them about fishing and sailing. It was only when she taught them to fashion tiny boats of sticks and wide root leaves and sent them off to sail the skiffs in the Weyr lake that she had any rest the first morning.

In the afternoon, she amused the younger ones by recounting how T'gran had rescued her. Thread was not as automatically horrifying to Weyr children as it would be to Holders, and they were far more interested in her running and rescue than in what she was running from. Unconsciously she fell into a rhyming pattern and caught herself up sharply just before she'd conceived a tune. The children didn't seem to notice fortunately, and then it was time to peel tubers for the evening meal.

It was difficult to subdue that little tune as she worked. Really it had exactly the cadence of her running stride . . .

"Oh!"

"Did you cut yourself?" asked Sanra from the other side of the table.

"No," replied Menolly, and she grinned with great good humor. She had just realized something very important. She wasn't in the Sea Hold any longer. And no one here knew about her harpering. Likewise no one would know if it were her own songs she hummed when she felt like humming. So she began to hum her running song, and was doubly pleased with herself because the tune matched her paring strokes, too.

"It's a relief to hear someone happy," remarked Sanra, smiling encouragingly at Menolly.

Menolly realized then that she'd been vaguely aware all day of the fact that the atmosphere in the living cavern reminded her of those times when the fishing fleet was overdue in a storm and everyone was "waiting." Mirrim was very worried about Brekke but she wouldn't say why, and Menolly was reluctant to broach the girl's sad reserve.

"I'm happy because my feet are healing," she told Sanra and then hurried on, "but I wish someone would tell me what's wrong with Brekke. I know Mirrim's worried sick about her . . ."

Sanra stared at Menolly for a moment. "You mean, you haven't heard about . . ." she lowered her voice and glanced about to make sure they weren't overheard, ". . . about the queens?"

"No. No one tells girls anything in the Sea Hold."

Sanra looked surprised but accepted the explanation. "Well, Brekke used to be at Southern, you did know that? Good. And when F'lar banished all the rebellious Old-timers to Southern, the Southerners had to go somewhere. T'bor became Weyrleader at Fort Hold, Kylara . . ." and Sanra's usually gentle voice became hard, "Kylara was Weyrwoman for Prideth, with Brekke and Wirenth . . ." Sanra was having enough trouble telling the tale so Menolly was very glad she hadn't asked Mirrim. "Wirenth rose to mate, but Kylara . . ." and the name was spoken with intense hatred, "Kylara hadn't taken Prideth far enough away. She was close to mating, too, and when Wirenth flew the bronzes, she rose, and . . ."

There were tears in Sanra's eyes, and she shook her head, unable to continue.

"Both queens . . . died?"

Sanra nodded.

"Brekke's alive, though . . . Isn't she?"

"Kylara lost her mind, and we're desperately afraid that Brekke will lose hers . . ." Sanra mopped the tears from her face, sniffing back her sorrow.

"Poor Mirrim. And she's been so good to me!"

Sanra sniffed again, this time from pique.

"Mirrim likes to think she's got the cares of the Weyr on her shoulders."

"Well, I've a lot more respect for her the way she keeps on going when she's worried sick than if she crept off someplace and just felt sorry for herself."

Sanra stared at Menolly. "No need to bristle at me, girl, and if you keep on stabbing your knife that way, you will cut yourself."

"Will Brekke be all right?" asked Menolly after a few minutes' strict attention to her peeling.

"We hope so," but Sanra didn't sound confident. "No, we do. You see, Ramoth's clutch is about to hatch, and Lessa is certain that Brekke could Impress the queen. You see, she can speak to any of the dragons, the way Lessa can, and Grall and Berd are always with her . . . Here comes Mirrim."

Menolly had to admit that Mirrim, who only numbered the same Turns as she did, did assume an officious manner. She could understand that an older woman like Sanra might not take kindly to it. Yet Menolly had no fault to find with Mirrim's ministrations. And she let the girl bustle her off to her cubicle to change the bandages.

"You've been on them all day, and I want to be sure no dirt's in the scabs," she said, briskly.

Menolly obediently lay on her stomach in the bed and then tentatively suggested that perhaps tomorrow she could change her own bandages and save Mirrim some work.

"Don't be silly. Feet are very awkward, but *you're* not. You should just hear C'tarel complain. He got Threadscored during the last Fall. You'd think he was the only one ever in the world scored. And besides, Manora *said* I was to take care of you. You're easy, you don't moan, groan, complain, *and* swear like C'tarel. Now, these *are* healing nicely. In spite of the way it might feel to you. Manora says that feet hurt worse than any part of your body, but hands. That's why it seems much worse to you, I expect."

Menolly had no argument and breathed a sigh of relief that the painful session was now over.

"*You* taught the weyrlings how to make those little boats, didn't you?"

Menolly flipped over, startled, and wondering if she'd done wrong, but Mirrim was grinning.

"You should have *seen* the dragons snorting them about the lake." Mirrim giggled. "Having the grandest time. I haven't laughed so much in weeks. There you are!" And Mirrim bustled away on some other errand.

The following day Mirrim hovering beside her, Menolly walked slowly and not too painfully through the living cavern and into the main kitchen cavern for the first time.

"Ramoth's eggs are just about to Hatch," Mirrim told her as she placed Menolly at one of the worktables along the back side of the huge cave. "There's nothing wrong with your hands, and we'll need all the help we can get for the feast . . ."

"And maybe your Brekke will be better?"

"Oh, she's got to be, Menolly, she's got to be." Mirrim scrubbed her hands together anxiously. "If she isn't, I don't know what will become of her and F'nor. He cares so much. Manora's as worried about him as she is about Brekke . . ."

"It'll all come right, Mirrim. I'm sure it will," Menolly said, putting all the confidence she could muster into her voice.

"Oh, do you really think so?" Mirrim dropped her pose of bustling efficiency and was briefly a young, bewildered girl in need of reassurance.

"I most certainly do!" And Menolly was angry with Sanra's unkind statements of the day before. "Why, when I thought I'd be scored to death, T'gran appeared. And when I thought they'd all be Threaded . . ." Menolly hastily shut her mouth, frantically trying to think of something to fill that gap. She'd almost told Mirrim about saving the fire lizards.

"They must belong to somebody," a man said in a loud, frustrated tone of voice.

Two dragonriders entered the kitchen cavern, slapping dusty gloves against sandy boots and loosening their riding belts.

"They could be attracted by the ones we have, T'gellan."

"Considering how badly we need the creatures . . ."

"In the egg . . ."

"It's a raking nuisance to have a whole flaming fair that no one will claim!"

The next thing Menolly knew, Beauty appeared over her head, gave a terrified squawk and landed on Menolly's thinly clad shoulder. Beauty wrapped her tail, choking tight, about Menolly's neck and buried her face into her hair. Rocky and Diver seized the cloth of her shirt in their claws, struggling to burrow into her arms. The air was full of frightened fire lizards, diving at her; and Mirrim, who made no attempt to defend herself, stared with utter amazement at Menolly.

"Mirrim? Do they belong to you after all?" cried T'gellan as he strode towards their table.

"No, they're not mine." Mirrim pointed to Menolly. "They're hers."

Menolly was speechless, but she managed to contain Rocky and Diver. The others took refuge on ledges above her, broadcasting fear and uncertainty. She was just as confused as the fire lizards, because why were they in the Weyr? And the Weyr seemed to know about fire lizards, and . . .

"We'll soon know whose they are," said a woman's angry voice, carrying clearly in the pause. A small, slim woman in riding gear came striding purposefully into the main section of the kitchen cavern. "I asked Ramoth to speak to them . . ."

She was followed by another rider.

"Over here, Lessa," T'gellan said, beckoning, but his gaze did not leave Menolly's.

At the sound of that name, she struggled out of the chair, with the fire lizards squawking and trying to retain their balance and hold on her. All Menolly could think of was to keep out of Lessa's way, but she got tangled up in the chairs about the table and painfully stubbed her toes. Mirrim grabbed her arm, trying to make her sit down, and there seemed to be more fire lizards than Menolly could claim circling over her head and chittering wildly.

"Will someone quiet this lot?" demanded the small, dark woman, confronting Menolly, her fists on her riding belts, her eyes snapping with anger. "Ramoth! if you would . . ."

Abruptly, complete silence reigned in the huge kitchen cavern. Menolly felt Beauty trembling more violently than ever against her neck, and the talons of the two bronzes dug into her arms and sides.

"That's better," said Lessa, her eyes brilliant. "And who are you? Are these all yours?"

"My name is Menolly, please and," Menolly glanced up nervously at all the fire lizards perched silently with whirling eyes on ledges and hanging from the ceiling, "not all of these are mine."

"Menolly?" Some of Lessa's anger abated in her perplexity. "Menolly?" She was trying to place the name.

"Manora told you about her, Lessa," said Mirrim, which Menolly thought greatly daring and very much appreciated. "T'gran rescued her from Threadfall. She'd run her feet raw."

"Ah, yes. So, Menolly, how many fire lizards do look to you?"

Menolly was trying to figure out whether Lessa was annoyed or pleased, and if she had too many fire lizards would she be sent back to Half-Circle. She felt Mirrim prod her in the ribs.

"These," Menolly indicated the three clinging to her and felt Mirrim dig her again, "and only six of those up there."

"Only six of those up there?"

Menolly saw Lessa's fingers drumming on her wide riding belt; she heard one of the dragonriders muffling a sound; and glancing up saw that he had his hand over his mouth. But his eyes were dancing with laughter. Then she dared look at Lessa's face and saw the slight smile on the Weyrwoman's face.

"That makes nine, I think," Lessa said. "Just how did you contrive to impress nine fire lizards, Menolly?"

"I didn't contrive. I was in the cave when they hatched, and they were hungry, you see. I'd a sackful of spiderclaws so I fed them . . ."

"Cave? Where?" Lessa's words were crisp but not unkind.

"On the coast. Above Nerat, by the Dragon Stones."

T'gellan uttered an exclamation. "You were living in that cave? I found jars and pots . . . no sign of fire lizard shells."

"I didn't think fire lizards clutched in caves," Lessa remarked.

"It was only because the tide was high and the clutch would have been washed away. I helped the queen put them into the cave."

Lessa regarded Menolly steadily for a long moment. "You helped the fire lizard?"

"Yes, you see I'd fallen over the cliff, and they—the queen and her bronzes, from the old clutch, not these here," and Menolly jerked her chin at Beauty, Rocky and Diver, "they wouldn't let me get off the beach until I helped them."

T'gellan was staring at her, but the other two riders were grinning broadly. Then Menolly saw that Mirrim, too, was smiling with delight. More unbelievable to Menolly in her confusion, was the fact that a little brown fire lizard was perched on Mirrim's shoulder, intently staring at Beauty who wouldn't take her head out of Menolly's hair.

"I'd like to hear the whole story, in sequence, one day," Lessa said. "Right now, will you please keep your lot under control and with you? They're upsetting Ramoth and all the others. Nine, eh?" And Lessa sighed, turning away. "When I think where I could use nine eggs to good purpose . . ."

"Please . . . do you need more fire lizard eggs?"

Lessa whirled so fast that Menolly took an involuntarily backward step.

"Of course we need fire lizard eggs! Where have you been that you don't know?" She turned on T'gellan. "You're wingleader. Didn't you inform all the sea holds?"

"Yes, I did, Lessa," and T'gellan looked straight at Menolly now, "just about the time Menolly first disappeared from her hold. Right, Menolly? The sweep riders have been on the lookout for her ever since, but she was holed up snug as you please in that cave, with nine fire lizards."

Menolly hung her head in despair.

"Please, Weyrwoman, don't sent me back to Half-Circle Hold!"

"A girl who can impress nine fire lizards," said Lessa in a sharp rippling tone that made Menolly look up, "does not belong in a Sea Hold. T'gellan, find out from Menolly where that clutch is and secure it for us immediately. Let us fervently hope it hasn't hatched." To Menolly's intense relief, Lessa actually smiled at her, obviously in a much improved temper. "Remember to keep those pesky creatures away from Ramoth. Mirrim can help you train them. Hers are quite useful now."

She swept away, leaving the entire cavern breathless. Activity suddenly picked up on all sides of the kitchen. Menolly felt Mirrim pressing her into a chair; she sank weakly down. She found a cup of klah in her hands and heard T'gellan urging her to take a few sips.

"One's first encounter with Lessa is apt to be unnerving."

"She's . . . she's so small," Menolly said dazedly.

"Size is irrelevant."

Menolly turned anxiously to Mirrim. "Did she really mean it? I can stay, Mirrim?"

"If you can impress nine fire lizards, you belong here. But why didn't you tell me about them? Didn't you see mine? I've only the three . . ."

T'gellan clicked his tongue at Mirrim, who stuck hers out at him.

"I told mine to stay in the cave . . ."

"And here we've been wracking our brains," Mirrim went on, "accusing riders of hoarding eggs . . ."

"I didn't *know* you people needed fire lizards . . ."

"Mirrim, stop teasing her; she's unnerved. Menolly, drink your klah and relax," T'gellan told her.

Menolly obediently sipped her klah, but she felt obliged to explain about the boys in her Sea Hold who could think of nothing but snaring fire lizards; and she felt so strongly that that was wrong that she hadn't even mentioned seeing them mating.

"Under the circumstances, you did just as you should, Menolly," said T'gellan. "But let's get to that clutch and rescue it. Where did you see it? How close do you think it is to Hatching?"

"The eggs were still pretty soft when I found them the day T'gran rescued me. And it's about a half-morning's walk from the Dragon Stones."

"A few minutes' glide by dragonback; but south? north? Where?"

"Well, south, where a stream feeds into the sea."

T'gellan raised his eyes in exasperation. "That describes too many places. You'd better come with me."

"T'gellan," Mirrim sounded shocked. "Menolly's feet are in shreds . . ."

"So is Lessa's temper. We'll wrap her feet in hides, but we must get those eggs. And you're not headwoman yet, my girl," T'gellan said, waggling a finger at Mirrim.

It didn't take long to outfit Menolly. Mirrim, as if to make up for her officiousness, brought her own wherhide riding jacket and headgear and a pair of vastly oversized boots. They were eased over Menolly's sore and bandaged feet and fastened tightly around her legs with leather strips.

Rocky and Diver were reassured by tidbits of meat, but Beauty refused to unwrap her tail from Menolly's neck. She chattered angrily at T'gellan when he half-carried Menolly to Monarth, waiting patiently just outside the kitchen cavern.

T'gellan threw Menolly up the dragon's shoulder. She hauled herself up to his neck ridges by the fighting straps, giving her feet one or two painful knocks.

T'gellan started to settle himself in front of Menolly, but Beauty came alive, hissing menacingly and lashing out at the dragonrider with one foreleg, talons unsheathed.

"She's never been so bad mannered," Menolly said apologetically.

"Monarth, will you speak to her?" asked T'gellan good-naturedly.

The next instant, Beauty stopped mid-hiss, chirped experimentally, her eyes whirling less frantically, and her tail relaxed from its choke hold on Menolly's throat.

"That's a sight better. She does have a baleful stare!"

"Oh dear!"

"I'm teasing you, Menolly. Now, look, I shall have Monarth tell your fair of fire lizards exactly what we're going to do so they don't go mad when we take off."

"Oh, would you?"

"I would, and I . . ." T'gellan paused, "I have. We're away!"

This time Menolly could enjoy the sensations of flying. She couldn't imagine why Petiron had found the experience so horrible. She didn't even fear the lack of all sensation as they went *between*. She did feel the bitter, bitter cold in the soles of her half-healed feet, but the pain lasted such a fleeting second. Abruptly, they were low over the Dragon Stones, coming in from the sea. The sheer thrill of the flight took Menolly's breath away.

"There is a chance that the first queen might lay another clutch in that cave," T'gellan said over his shoulder. "But it should be cleared of your things."

So they landed on the beach with Monarth peering rather disapprovingly at the little cove while the water lapped gently on his feet.

Her group arrived, carolling in wild delight at coming home. A single fire lizard appeared above and to one side of them.

"Look, T'gellan, that's the old queen!"

But she'd gone when T'gellan looked up.

"I'm sort of sorry she saw us here. I was hoping . . . Where was the clutch when you rescued it?"

"We're standing on the place."

Monarth moved to one side.

"Does he hear what I'm telling you?" Menolly whispered anxiously in T'gellan's ear.

"Yes, so be careful how you speak of him. He's very sensitive."

"I haven't said anything, have I, that would hurt his feelings?"

"Menolly!" T'gellan looked back at her, grinning, "I was teasing you."

"Oh!"

"Hmmm. Yes. Well, so you managed to climb that cliff face?"

"It wasn't so hard. If you'll look, you'll see there're plenty of hand and foot holds, even before I made a regular path."

"A regular path? Hmmm. Yes. Monarth, can you get us a bit closer, please?"

Monarth obligingly angled against the cliff face and raised himself to his haunches; Menolly was amazed to see that they could step off his shoulders right into the cave.

Her nine came arrowing into the opening, trumpeting and squealing, their bugles abruptly amplified by the vaulting height of the inner cavern. Just as she and T'gellan reached it, the light was suddenly blocked. Turning, she saw Monarth's head in the opening, his great eyes whirling idly.

"Monarth, get your great, bloody, big head out of the light, will you?" asked T'gellan.

Monarth blinked, gave a little wistful rumble, but removed his great head.

"Why didn't anyone find you on Search, young lady?" T'gellan asked, and she saw that he'd been watching her intently.

"No one's ever been Searched at Half-Circle Sea Hold."

"That shouldn't surprise me. Now, where did the old queen have her clutch?"

"Right where you're standing."

T'gellan jumped sideways, giving her a second admonitory look, which she couldn't interpret. He knelt, running his fingers through the sand, making pleased noises in his throat.

"You tossed out the old shells?"

"Yes. Was that wrong?"

"I don't think so."

"Would she come back here again?"

"She might. If the cove waters remain high the next time she mates. D'you happen to remember when you saw her mating flight?"

"Yes, I do. Because we had Threadfall just after. The one when the leading edge hit the marshes halfway to Nerat."

"Good girl!" T'gellan tipped his head back, pressing his lips together, and Menolly thought he was doing some rapid mental calculations. Alemi had a similar habit when he was charting a course. "Yes. And when did these hatch?"

"I lost track of my sevendays, but they hatched five Falls ago."

"That's great. She may mate before high summer, if fire lizards follow the same sort of cycle the dragons do during a Pass." He glanced around him at the bits and pieces with which she had made the cave livable. "D'you want any of these things?"

"Not many," Menolly said and dove for her sleeping rug. Her pipes were still there, so he hadn't seen them in his first visit to the cave. She bundled the rug round the pipes again. "My oil . . ." she said, grabbing up the pot. I'll need that."

"Not really," said T'gellan with a grin, "but bring it along. Manora's always interested in such things."

She took her dried herbs, too, and made a neat package, which she could tie on her back. Ruthlessly then she began to chuck her homemade crockery out of the cave entrance.

"Oh!" Aghast, she rushed to the mouth, looking about for Monarth.

"You missed him! He's got more sense than to stay around when there's a cleaning." With that T'gellan launched her boiling pot into the air.

"That's everything, I think," she said.

"Let's go!"

At the entrance, Menolly turned for one last look at the cave and smiled to herself. She'd never thought to leave it, certainly not to step to the shoulders of a dragon. But then, she'd never thought she'd live in a cave like this at all, much less ride a dragon. Nothing now marked that anyone had ever sheltered in this cave. Even the dry sand was falling back into the depressions their feet had made. T'gellan held out his hand to help her to Monarth's back, and then they were away to find the fire lizard's clutch.

Chapter 11

The little queen, all golden
Flew hissing at the sea.
To keep it back,
To turn it back
She flew forth bravely.

Menolly and T'gellan brought the thirty-one eggs of the clutch safely to Benden Weyr without so much as cracking a shell in the double, furred sack that had been provided for the journey *between*. Their return caused a flurry of excitement, the weyrfolk crowding around to examine the eggs. Duly informed, Lessa arrived, imperiously ordering a basket of warm sand from the Hatching Ground; directing it to be placed by the small sauce hearth and scrupulously turned at intervals to distribute the heat evenly. She judged that the eggs were a good sevenday from hatching hardness.

"As well," she said in her dry fashion. "One hatching at a time is enough. Better still, we can present the worthies with their eggs at the Impression." She seemed inordinately pleased with that solution and smiled on Menolly. "Manora says that your feet aren't healed yet, so you're in charge of the clutch. And, Felena, get this child out of those ridiculous boots and into some decent clothes. Surely we have something in stores that'll make her look less disreputable."

Lessa departed, leaving Menolly the object of intense scrutiny. Felena, a tall, willowy woman with very beautiful, curved black eyebrows and green eyes, gave her a long appraisal, sent one helper off for clothing from a special press, another to get the tanner to take Menolly's measure for footwear, a child for her shears because Menolly's hair must be trimmed. Who had hacked it off? They must have used a knife. And such pretty hair, too. Was Menolly hungry? T'gellan had snatched her out of the cavern without a nay—yea or maybe. Bring that chair here and push that small table over! Don't stand there gawking, get the girl something to eat.

"How many Turns do you have?" Felena asked on the end of that long series of orders.

"I've fifteen, please," answered Menolly, dazed and trying very hard not to cry. Her throat ached and her chest was tight and she couldn't believe what was happening to her: people fussing over how she looked and what she wore. Above all, Lessa had smiled at her because she was so pleased about the clutch. And it seemed as if she didn't have to worry about being sent back to Half-Circle. Not if the weyrfolk were ordering her shoes and giving her clothes. . . .

"Fifteen? Well, you wouldn't need much more fostering, would you?" Felena sounded disappointed. "We'll see what Manora has in mind for you. I'd like you as mine."

Menolly burst into tears. That provoked more confusion because her fire lizards began swooping dangerously close to people's faces. Beauty pecked at Felena, who was only trying to offer comfort.

"Let us have some order here," said a fresh, authoritative voice. Everyone, except the fire lizards, obediently subsided, and room was made for Manora. "And you be quiet, too," she said to squealing Beauty. "Go on," and she waved at the others, "go sit quietly somewhere. Now, why is Menolly crying?"

"She just burst into tears, Manora," said Felena, as perplexed as everyone else.

"I'm happy, I'm happy, I'm happy," Menolly managed to blurt out, each repetition punctuated by a heaving sob.

"Of course you are," said Manora understandingly, and made gestures to one of the women. "It's been a very exciting and tiring day. Now you just drink this." The woman had returned with a mug. "Now, everyone will go about their duties and let you catch your breath. There, that's better."

Menolly obediently sipped the drink. It wasn't fellis juice, but there was a slightly bitter taste. Manora urged her to drink deeply, and gradually Menolly felt her chest loosen, her throat stop aching and she began to relax.

She looked up to see that Manora was the only one at the little table, sitting with her hands folded serenely in her lap, her aura of calm patience very soothing.

"Feel more like yourself? Now, you just sit quietly and eat. We don't take in many new people, so there's bound to be a fuss about you. Soon enough to do everything else. How many fire lizard eggs did you find in that clutch?"

Menolly found it easy to talk to Manora, and soon she was showing the headwoman the oil and explaining how she'd made it.

"I think you did wonderfully well all on your own, Menolly, not but what I'd expect it of someone Mavi has trained."

Menolly's ease disappeared at the sound of her mother's name. Involuntarily she clenched her left hand, feeling the scar tissue pull painfully from the intensity of her grip.

"You wouldn't like me to send a message to Half-Circle?" asked Manora. "To say that you're safely here?"

"I don't want you to, please! I'm no use to them there." She held up her scarred hand. "And . . ." she halted, she'd been about to add "a disgrace." "I seem to be useful here," she said quickly, pointing to the basket of fire lizard eggs.

"So you are, Menolly, so you are." Manora rose. "Now eat your meat, and we'll talk again later."

When she had finished her food, Menolly felt much better. She was content to sit in her hearth corner, watching the industry of others. And in a little while, Felena came over with her shears and trimmed Menolly's hair. Then someone watched the fire lizard eggs while Menolly changed into the first brand new garments she'd ever had, being the youngest in a large family. The tanner came and not only measured her feet for proper boots but by evening he'd also made up some soft hide slippers that fit loosely over her bandaged feet.

She was so changed in appearance that Mirrim, passing her table just before the evening meal, almost failed to recognize her. Menolly had been worrying that Mirrim was deliberately avoiding her because Menolly had Impressed nine fire lizards, but there was no restraint in Mirrim's manner. Flopping into a chair across the table, she heartily approved the hair trim, the clothing and the slippers.

"I heard all about the clutch, but I've been so busy, up, down, in, out, running errands for Manora that I simply haven't had a moment."

Menolly suppressed a grin. Mirrim sounded exactly like Felena.

Then Mirrim cocked her head at Menolly. "You know, you look so much nicer in proper clothes that I didn't recognize you. Now, if we can only get you to smile once in a while . . ."

Just then a little brown lizard glided in to land on Mirrim's shoulder, snuggling affectionately up to her neck, and peering at Menolly from under her chin.

"Is he yours?"

"Yes, this is Tolly, and I have two greens, Reppa and Lok. And I'll make it very plain that three is quite enough for me. How ever did you manage to feed nine? They're so ravenous all the time!"

The last of Menolly's awkwardness with her friend disappeared as she recounted how she had coped with her fair of fire lizards.

The evening meal was then ready, and Mirrim, ignoring Menolly's protests that she was able to fetch her own, served them both. T'gellan joined their table and managed to coax Beauty, much to Menolly's amazement, to accept some food from his knife.

"Don't be surprised," Mirrim told Menolly with just a touch of condescension. "These greedy guts will eat what's offered from anyone. But that doesn't mean that they'll *look* to whoever feeds them. Besides, with nine . . ." She rolled her eyes so expressively that T'gellan chuckled.

"She's jealous, so she is, Menolly."

"I am not. Three's quite enough, though . . . I would've liked a queen. Let's see if Beauty will come to me. Grall does."

Mirrim concentrated on coaxing Beauty to accept a piece of meat while T'gellan teased her, rather unfairly Menolly thought; but Mirrim returned his jibes with a few tart remarks of her own in a way that Menolly would never have dared address an older man, much less a dragonrider.

She was very tired, but it was pleasant to sit in the big kitchen cavern, listening to T'gellan, watching Mirrim coax Beauty, though it was Lazybones who finally ate from her hand. There were other small groups, chatting late over their evening meal, the women pairing with dragonriders. Menolly noticed wineskins being passed. She was surprised, at first, because the Sea Hold served wine only on very special occasions. T'gellan sent one of the weyrboys to get him cups and a skin and insisted that Menolly, as well as Mirrim, have a cup.

"Good Benden wine is not to be refused," he told her, filling her cup. "There, now, isn't that the best you've ever tasted?"

Menolly forebore to mention that, barring wine laced with fellis juice, it was the first. Living was certainly conducted on different rules in the Weyr.

When the Weyr's Harper began to play softly, more for his own pleasure than to entertain anyone in the cavern, Menolly did not restrain her fingers from tapping the rhythm. It was a song she liked, though she felt his chords were dull, which was why she began to hum her harmony when it did not discord with his. She wasn't even aware of what she was doing until Mirrim looked up with a smile on her face.

"That was just lovely, Menolly. Oharan? Come over here; Menolly has a new harmony for that one."

"No, no, I couldn't."

"Why not?" demanded T'gellan, and poured a bit more wine in her glass. "A little music would give us all heart. There're faces around here as long as a wet Turn."

Timidly at first, because of the older injunction against singing in front of people, Menolly joined her voice to Harper Oharan's baritone.

"Yes, I like it, Menolly. You've got a sure sense of pitch," said Oharan so approvingly that she started to worry again.

If Yanus knew she was singing at the Weyr . . . But Yanus wasn't here and he would never know.

"Say, can you harmonize to this one?" And Oharan broke into one of the older ballads, one in which she had always sung a counter-tune against Petiron's melody.

Suddenly there were other voices humming along, softly but surely. Mirrim looked around, stared suspiciously at T'gellan, and then pointed at Beauty.

"She's humming in tune. Menolly, however did you teach her to do that? And the others . . . some of them are singing, too!" Mirrim was wide-eyed with amazement.

Oharan kept on playing, nodding at Mirrim to be quiet so they could all hear the fire lizards while T'gellan craned his head and cocked his ears, first at Beauty, then at Rocky and Diver and Brownie who were near him.

"I don't believe it," said T'gellan.

"Don't scare them! Just let them do it," said Oharan in a low voice as he modulated his chords into another verse.

They finished the song with the fire lizards humming obediently along with Menolly. Mirrim demanded then to know how on earth Menolly had gotten her lizards to sing with her.

"I used to play and sing for them in the cave, you know, to keep us company. Just little twiddles."

"Just little twiddles! I've had my three much longer, and I never even knew they liked music."

"Just shows that you don't know all there is to know, doesn't it, young Mirrim?" teased T'gellan.

"Now that isn't fair," Menolly interceded and then hiccuped. To her embarrassment she hiccuped again.

"How much wine have you been giving her, T'gellan?" demanded Mirrim, frowning at the bronze rider.

"Certainly not enough to put her in her cups."

Menolly hiccuped again.

"Get her some water!"

"Hold your breath," Oharan suggested.

T'gellan brought water and, with quick sips, Menolly managed to stop her hiccuping. She kept insisting that she didn't feel the wine, but she was very tired. If someone would watch the eggs . . . it was so late . . . With solicitous help, T'gellan and Oharan supported her to her sleeping chamber, Mirrim fussing at them that they were two great big numbwits who hadn't a lick of sense between them.

Menolly was very glad to lie down and let Mirrim remove the slippers and the new clothes and cover her. She was asleep before the fire lizards had disposed themselves about her for the night.

Chapter 12

Dragonman, dragonman,
Between thee and thine,
Share me that glimpse of love
Greater than mine.

Mirrim roused Menolly early the next morning, impatiently shushing the fire lizards who hissed at her rough shaking of their mistress.

"Menolly, wake up. We need every hand in the kitchen. The eggs will Hatch today and half Pern's invited. Turn over. Manora's coming to look at your feet."

"Ouch! You're too rough!"

"Tell Beauty . . . ouch . . . I'm *not* hurting you. Beauty! Behave or I'll tell Ramoth!"

To Menolly's surprise, Beauty stopped diving at Mirrim and retreated with a squeak to the far corner of the room.

"You were hurting me," said Menolly, too sleepy to be tactful.

"Well, I said I was sorry. Hmmm. Your feet really do look a lot better."

"We won't use such heavy bandages today," said Manora, entering at that moment. "The slippers give enough protection."

Menolly craned her head about as she felt Manora's strong gentle fingers turn first one foot and then the other.

"Yes, lighter bandages today, Mirrim, and salve. Tonight, no bandages at all. Wounds must have fresh air, too, you know. But you've done a good job. The fire lizard eggs are fine this morning, Menolly."

With that she left, and Mirrim quickly set about dressing the feet. When she'd finished and Menolly rose to put on her clothes, her fingers lingering in the soft folds of the overshirt, Mirrim sank onto the bed with an exaggerated sigh.

"What's the matter with you?" Menolly asked.

"I'm getting all the rest I can while I can," Mirrim replied. "You don't know what a Hatching is like, with all those holders and crafters stumbling about the Weyr, poking here and there where they're NOT supposed to be and getting scared of and scaring the dragons and the weyrlings and the hatchlings. And the way they eat!" Mirrim rolled her eyes expressively. "You'd think they'd never seen food and . . ." Mirrim flopped over on the bed and started to sob wildly.

"Mirrim, what's the matter? Oh, it's Brekke! Isn't she all right? I mean, won't she re-Impress? Sanra said that's what Lessa hoped . . ."

Menolly bent to comfort her friend, herself upset by those heart-rending sobs. Mirrim's words were garbled by her weeping, although Menolly gathered that Mirrim didn't want her foster-mother to re-Impress and the reason was obscure. Brekke didn't want to live, and they had to find some way to make her. Losing her dragon was like losing half herself, and it hadn't been Brekke's fault. She was so gentle and sensible, and she loved F'nor, and for some reason that was unwise, too.

Menolly just let Mirrim cry, knowing how much relief she had felt the day before when she'd wept, and hoping deep in her heart that there might be joyful tears, too, for Mirrim later that day. There had to be. She forgave Mirrim all her little poses and attitudes, aware that that was how Mirrim had masked her intense anxiety and grief.

There was a rattling of the cubicle's curtain, a squabble of fire lizard protest, and then Mirrim's Tolly crawled under the curtain, his eyes whirling with indignation and worry. He saw Menolly stroking Mirrim's hair and, raising his wings, made as if to launch himself at her when Beauty warbled sharply from the corner. Tolly sort of shook his wings, but when he leaped to the bed, he landed gently on the edge and remained there, his eyes first on Mirrim, then on Menolly. A moment later the two greens entered. They settled themselves on the stool, watchful but not obtrusive.

Beauty, in her corner, kept an eye on them all.

"Mirrim? Mirrim?" It was Sanra's voice from the living cavern. "Mirrim, haven't you finished Menolly's feet yet? We need both of you! Now!"

As Menolly rose obediently, Mirrim caught her hand and squeezed it. Then she rose, shook her skirts out and marched from the cubicle, Menolly following more slowly behind her.

Mirrim had by no means exaggerated the amount of work to be done. It was just past sunrise, but obviously the main cooks had already been up for hours, judging by the breads—sweet, spiced and sour—cooling on long tables. Two weyrmen were trussing a huge herdbeast for the main spit and at the smaller hearths, wild wherries were being cleaned and stuffed for roasting later.

For added protection in the busy kitchen, someone had placed the small table over her fire lizard egg basket. They were doing fine, the sand nice and warm all around. Felena caught sight of her, told her to

feed herself quickly from the sauce hearth and did she know anything
flavorful to do with dried fish? Or would she prefer to help pare roots?

Menolly instantly elected to cook fish, so Felena asked what ingredients she'd need. Menolly was a little dismayed to learn the quantity
she'd have to prepare. She had had no idea that so many people came to
a Hatching: the number coming was more than *lived* at Half-Circle Sea
Hold.

The knack in making the fish stew tasty was in the long baking so
Menolly applied herself to prepare the huge pots quickly, to give them
enough time to simmer into succulence. She did so with such dispatch
that there were still plenty of roots left to pare.

Excitement filled the air of the kitchen cavern. The mound of root
vegetables in front of Menolly melted away as she listened to the chatter
of the other girls and women. There was great speculation as to which
of the boys, and the girls for the queen egg, would Impress the dragons
to be hatched that day.

"No one has ever re-Impressed a dragon," said one woman wistfully.
"D'you think Brekke will?"

"No one's ever been given the chance before."

"Is it a chance we should take?" asked someone else.

"*We* weren't asked," said Sanra, glaring at the last speaker. "It's
Lessa's idea, but it wasn't F'nor's or Manora's . . ."

"Something has to help her," said the first woman. "It tears my heart
to see her lying there, just lying, like the undead. I mind me of the way
D'namal went. He sort of . . . well . . . faded completely away."

"If you'll finish that root quickly, we can put this kettle on," said
Sanra, briskly rising.

"Will all of this be eaten?" asked Menolly of the woman beside her.

"Yes, indeed, and there'll be some looking for more," she said with a
complacent smile. "Impression Days are good days. I've a fosterling
and a blood son on the Hatching Ground today!" she added with understandable pride. "Sanra!" she turned her head to shout over her shoulder, "just one more largish kettle will take what's left."

Then white roots had to be sliced finely, covered with herbs and
placed in clay pots to bake. The succulent odors of Menolly's fish con-
coction aroused compliments from Felena, who was in charge of the
various hearths and ovens. Then Menolly, who was told to keep off her
poor feet, helped decorate the spiced cakes. She giggled with the rest
when Sanra distributed pieces of one cake about, saying they had to be
certain the bake had turned out well, didn't they?

Menolly did not forget to turn the fire lizard eggs, or to feed her
friends. Beauty stayed within sight of Menolly, but the others had been

seen bathing in the lake and sunning themselves, scrupulously avoiding Ramoth, whose bugles punctuated the morning.

"She's always like that on Impression Day," T'gellan told Menolly as he grabbed a quick bite to eat at her table. "Say, will you get your fire lizards to hum along with you again this evening? I've been called a liar because I said you'd taught them to sing."

"They might turn difficult and shy in front of a lot of people, you know."

"Well, we'll wait till things get quiet, and then we'll give it a try, huh. Now, I'm to see you get to the Hatching. Midafternoon, I'd say, so be ready."

As it happened, she wasn't. She felt the thrumming before she heard it. She and everyone else in the cavern stopped working as one-by-one they became aware of the intensely exciting noise. Menolly gasped, because she recognized it as the same sort of sound the fire lizards had made when their eggs had hatched.

There was suddenly no time for her to return to her cubicle and change. T'gellan appeared at the cavern entrance, gesturing urgently to her. She made as much speed as her feet would permit because she could see Monarth waiting outside the entrance. T'gellan had already taken her hand when she exclaimed over the cooking stains and wet marks on her overshirt.

"I told you to be ready. I'll put you in a corner, pet, not that anyone will notice stains today," T'gellan reassured her.

A trifle resentful, Menolly noticed that he was dressed in new dark trousers, a handsomely overstitched tunic, a belt worked with metal and jewels, but she didn't resist.

"I have to get you in place first, because I'm to collect some visitors," T'gellan said, climbing nimbly into place in front of her on Monarth's neck ridges. "F'lar's filling the Hatching Ground with anyone who'll ride a dragon *between.*"

Monarth was awing, slanting up from the Bowl floor to an immense opening, high up on the Weyr wall, which Menolly had not noticed before. Other dragons were angling towards it, too. Menolly gasped as they entered the mouth, with a dragon before them and one abaft, so close that she had momentary fears of collision. The dark core of the tunnel was lit at the far end, and abruptly they were in the gigantic Hatching Ground.

The whole north quadrant of the Weyr must be hollow, thought Menolly, awed. Then she saw the gleaming clutch of dragon eggs and gasped. Slightly to one side was a larger egg, and hovering over it was the zealous golden form of Ramoth, her eyes incredibly brilliant with the coming of Impression.

Monarth dropped with distressing abruptness, then backwinged to land neatly on a ledge.

"Here you are, Menolly. Best seat in the Ground. I'll be back for you afterwards."

Menolly was only too glad to sit still after that incredible ride. She was in the third tier, by the outer wall, so she had a perfect view of the Hatching Ground and the entrance through which people were beginning to file. They were all so elegantly dressed that she brushed vainly at the stains and crossed her arm over her chest. At least the clothes were new.

Other dragons were arriving from the upper entrance, depositing their passengers, often three and four at a time. She watched the now steady stream of visitors coming in from the ground entrance. It was amusing to watch the elegant, and sometimes overdressed, ladies having to pick up their heavy skirts and run in awkward little steps across the hot sands. The tiers filled rapidly, and the excited thrumming of the dragons increased in pitch so that Menolly found it difficult to sit quietly.

A sudden cry announced the rocking of some of the eggs. Late arrivals began to hurry across the sands, and the seats beyond Menolly were filled with a group of minecraftsmen, to judge from their red-brown tunic devices. She crossed her arms again and then uncrossed them because she had to lean forward to see around the minecraftsmen's stocky bodies.

More eggs were rocking, all of them except the smallish gray egg that had somehow got shoved back against the inside wall.

Another rush of wings, and this time bronze dragons entered, depositing the girls who were candidates for the queen egg. Menolly tried to figure out which one was Brekke, but they all looked very aware and healthy. Hadn't the weyrwomen remarked that morning how Brekke just lay like someone dead? The girls formed a loose but incomplete semicircle about the queen egg while Ramoth hissed softly behind it.

Young boys marched in now from the Bowl, their expressions purposeful, their shoulders straight in the white tunics as they approached the main clutch.

Menolly did not see Brekke's entrance because she was trying to figure out which of the violently rocking eggs would hatch first. Then one of the miners exclaimed and pointed towards the entrance, to the slender figure, stumbling, halting, then moving onward, apparently insensitive to the hot sands underfoot.

"That would be the one. That would be Brekke," he told his comrades. "Dragonrider said she'd be put to the egg."

Yes, thought Menolly, she walks as if she's asleep. Then Menolly saw Manora and a man she didn't recognize standing by the entrance, as if they had done all they could in bringing Brekke to the Hatching Ground.

Suddenly Brekke straightened her shoulders with a shake of her head. She walked slowly but steadily across the sands to join the five girls who waited by the golden egg. One girl turned and gestured for her to take the space that would complete the semicircle.

The humming ceased so abruptly that a little ripple of reaction ran through those assembled. In the expectant silence, the faint crack of a shell was clear, and the pop and shatter of others.

First one dragonet, then another, awkward, ugly, glistening creatures, flopped and rolled from their casings, squawking and creeling, their wedge-shaped heads too big for the thin, sinuous short necks.

Menolly noticed how very still the boys were standing, as stunned as she'd been in that very little cave with those tiny fire lizards crawling from their shells, voracious with hunger.

Now the difference became apparent; the fire lizards had expected no help at their hatching, their instinct was to get food into their churningly empty stomachs as fast as possible. But the dragons looked expectantly about them. One staggered beyond the first boy who sidestepped its awkward progress. It fell, nose first at the feet of a tall, black-haired boy. The boy knelt, helped the dragonet balance on his shaky feet, looked into the rainbow eyes.

Emotion like a fist squeezed Menolly's heart. Yes, she'd her fire lizards, but to Impress a dragon . . . Startled, she wondered where Beauty, Rocky, Diver and the others were. She missed them acutely, wanted Beauty's affectionate nuzzling, even the choke-tight twist of the little queen's tail about her neck.

The crack of the golden egg was a summons for all attention to be centered on it. The egg split right down the center, and its inmate, protesting her abrupt birth, fell to the sand on her back. Three of the girls moved to assist it. They got the little queen to her four legs and then stepped back. Menolly held her breath as they all turned towards Brekke. She was unaware of anything. Whatever strength had sustained her to walk across the sands had now left her. Her shoulders sagged pathetically, her head listed to one side as if too heavy to hold upright. The queen dragonet turned her head towards Brekke, the glistening eyes enormous in the outsize skull. Brekke shook her head as if aware of the scrutiny. The dragonet lurched forward one step.

Menolly saw a bronze blur out of the corner of her right eye and for an unnerving moment thought it must be Diver. But it couldn't be, because the little bronze just hung above the dragonet's head, screaming defiantly. He was so close to her head that she reared back with a startled shriek and bit at the air, instinctively spreading her wings forward as protection for her vulnerable eyes.

Dragons bugled warnings from their perches at the top of the Hatching Ground, and Ramoth spread her wings, rising to her haunches as if to strike at the invader. One of the girls interposed her body between the queen and her small attacker.

"Berd! Don't!" Brekke, too, moved, her arm extended towards the irate bronze.

The dragonet queen creeled and hid her face in the girl's skirt. The two women faced each other for a moment, tense, worried. Then the other stretched her hand out to Brekke, and Menolly could see her smile. The gesture lasted only a moment because the young queen butted imperiously, and the girl knelt, her arms reassuringly encircling the dragonet's shoulders.

At the same instant, Brekke turned, no longer a somnolent figure, immersed in grief. She walked back to the entrance of the Cavern, the little bronze fire lizard whirring around her head, making noises that went from scolding to entreaty, just like Beauty when Menolly was doing something that had upset her.

Menolly didn't realize that she was weeping until tears dropped onto her arms. She glanced hastily to see if the miners had noticed, but they were concentrating on the main clutch. From their comments it seemed that a boy had been found on Search in one of their craftholds, and they were impatiently waiting for him to Impress. For a fleeting moment, Menolly was angry with them; hadn't they seen Brekke's deliverance? Didn't they realize how marvelous that was? Oh, think how happy Mirrim would be now!

Menolly sank wearily back against the stones, depleted by the emotionally-laden miracle. And the look on Brekke's face as she passed under the arched entrance! Manora was there, her face radiant, her arms outstretched in a joyful gesture. The man, who was surely F'nor, swept Brekke up in his arms, his tired face mirroring his relief and gladness.

A cheer from the miners beside her indicated that their lad had Impressed although Menolly couldn't be certain which of the boys he was. There were so many now paired off with wobbly-legged hatchlings, all creeling with hunger, lurching and falling towards the entrance. The miners were urging their favorite on; and when a curly-haired, skinny lad passed by, with a grin for their cheering, she saw that he had done rather well, Impressing a brown. When the exultant miners turned to her to share their triumph, she managed to respond properly, but she was relieved when they scrambled down the tiers to follow the pair out of the Hatching Ground.

She sat there, glowing over the resurgence of Brekke, the determination and fierceness of bronze Berd, his courage in braving Ramoth's ire at such a moment. Now, why, Menolly wondered, didn't Berd want Brekke to Impress the new queen? At all events, the experiment had successfully roused Brekke from her lethargy.

The dragons were returning, landing in the Hatching Ground so that their riders could help the weyrlings, or to escort guests outside. The tiers were emptying. Soon there was only a man in holder colors on the first tier with two boys. The man looked as tired as she felt. Then one of the boys rose, pointing to the little egg on the sand that wasn't even rocking.

Idly Menolly thought that it might not hatch, remembering the uncracked egg left in the fire lizard's sand nest the morning after her fire lizards had hatched. She'd shaken it and something hard had rattled within. Sometimes hold babies were born dead, so she'd supposed that it could happen to other creatures, too.

The boy was running along the tier now. To Menolly's astonishment, he jumped to the Hatching Ground and began kicking at the little egg. His cries and his actions attracted the notice of the Weyrleader and the small knot of candidates who had not Impressed. The Holder half-rose, one hand extended in a cautionary gesture. The other boy was shouting at his friend.

"Jaxom, what are you doing?" shouted the Weyrleader.

The egg fractured then, and the boy began tearing at the shell, ripping out sections and kicking until Menolly could see the small body pushing at the thick inner membrane.

Jaxom cut at the membrane with his belt knife, and a small white body, not much larger than the boy's torso, fell from the sac. The boy reached out to help the creature to his feet.

Menolly saw the little white dragon lift his head, his eyes, brilliant with greens and yellows, fastened on the boy's face.

"He says his name is Ruth!" the boy cried in amazed delight.

With a strangled exclamation, the older man sank back to the stone seat, his face a mask of grief. The Weyrleader and the others who had rushed to prevent what had just occurred halted. To Menolly it was all too obvious that Jaxom's Impression of the little white dragon was unprecedented and unwelcome. And she couldn't imagine why: the boy and the dragon looked so radiant, who could deny them their joyous union?

Chapter 13

Harper, your song has a sorrowful sound,
Though the tune was written as gay.
Your voice is sad and your hands are slow
And your eye meeting mine turns away.

When it became obvious to Menolly that T'gellan had forgotten his promise to return, she slowly climbed down from the tiers and made her way out of the deserted Hatching Ground, over the hot sand.

Beauty met her at the entrance, demanding caresses and reassurance. She was swiftly followed by the others, all chittering nervously and with many anxious dartings to the entrance to see if Ramoth was about.

Although Menolly had not had far to walk on the sands, the heat had quickly penetrated the soles of her slippers. Her discomfort was acute by the time she stepped onto the cooler earth of the Bowl. She edged to one side of the entrance and sank down, her fire lizards grouping themselves about her while she waited for the pain to subside.

As everyone was on the kitchen cavern side of the Bowl, no one noticed her, for which she was grateful since she felt useless and foolish. It would be a long walk across the Bowl to the kitchens. Well, she'd just take it in small sections.

She heard the faint cries of the herdbeasts at the farthest end of the Bowl valley and saw Ramoth hovering for a kill. The weyrwomen had said that Ramoth hadn't eaten for the past ten days, which was partly the cause of her irascible temper.

By the lakeside, hatchlings were being fed and bathed, and their riders shown how to oil the fragile skin. Their white tunics stood out among the gleaming green, blue, brown and bronze hides. The little queen was slightly removed from the others, with two of the bronze dragons in attendance. She couldn't see where the white dragon was.

On the weyr ledges dotting the Bowl's face, some dragons were curled in what remained of the afternoon sun. Above and to the left of her, Menolly saw great bronze Mnementh on the ledge of the queen's weyr. He was seated on his haunches, watching his mate choose her meal. Menolly saw him move slightly, glancing over his left shoulder.

Then Menolly caught a glimpse of a man's head as he descended the stairs from the queen's weyr.

Felena's voice, raised above the conversational babble, brought Menolly's gaze back to the kitchen cavern where tables were being erected for the evening's feasting. The dragonriders were doing it, for the bright colors of their best tunics were conspicuous, moving about while the soberer colors of Holder and Craft seemed to stay in stationary clumps at a polite distance from the workers.

The man had reached the Bowl floor now from the queen's weyr, and Menolly idly watched him start across. Auntie One and Two came sweeping down to her, chittering about something that had excited them and ducking their heads at her for reassurance. They needed to be oiled, and she felt guilty for not taking better care of them.

"Do you have *two* greens?" asked an amused voice, and the tall man was standing in front of her, his eyes friendly and interested.

"Yes, they're mine," she said and held up Two for him to inspect, responding to the kindness and good humor in his long face. "They like their eye ridges scratched, gently, like this," she added, showing him.

He dropped to one knee in the sand and obligingly caressed Two, who crooned and closed her eyelids in appreciation. Auntie One whistled at Menolly for attention, digging a jealous claw into her hand.

"Stop that, you naughty creature."

Beauty roused, and Rocky and Diver reacted as well, all three scolding Auntie One so fiercely that she took flight.

"Don't tell me the queen *and* the two browns are yours as well?" the man asked, startled.

"I'm afraid so."

"Then you must be Menolly," he said, rising to his feet and making such an elaborate bow that she blushed. "Lessa has just told me that I may have two eggs of that clutch *you* discovered. I'm rather partial to browns, you know, though I wouldn't actually object to a bronze. Of course the greens, like this lady here," and he smiled such a winning smile to the watching Two that she crooned responsively, "are such delicate darlings. That doesn't mean that I would object to a blue, however."

"Don't you want the queen?"

"Ah, now that would be greedy of me, wouldn't it?" He rubbed his face thoughtfully and gave her a wry half-smile. "All things considered, though, I'd be heartily embarrassed if Sebell—my Journeyman is to have possession of the other egg—secured a queen instead. But . . ." and he threw his long fingered hand upwards to signify his submission to chance. "Are you waiting here for some purpose? Or is the confusion on the other side of the Bowl too much for all your friends?"

"I should be there. The clutch must be turned; the eggs are in warm sand by the hearth; but T'gellan brought me into the Hatching Cavern and told me to wait . . ."

"And seems to have forgot you. Not surprising, considering today's surprises." The man hastily cleared his throat and extended his hand to her.

She accepted his aid because she couldn't have risen without it. He had taken three strides when he realized that she wasn't keeping up with him. Politely he turned. Menolly tried to walk normally, a feat she managed for about three strides when her heel came down so painfully on a patch of pebbles that she involuntarily cried out. Beauty whirled, scolding fiercely, and Rocky and Diver added their antics, which were of no help to anyone.

"Here's my arm, girl. Were you too long on the hot sands? Ah now, wait. You're a long child, but there's no meat on your bones."

Before Menolly could protest, he'd swung her up into his arms and was carrying her across the Bowl.

"Tell that queen of yours I'm helping you," he asked when Beauty disordered his silvering hair, diving at him. "After sober reflection, be sure you give me green eggs."

Beauty was too excited to harken to Menolly, so she had to wave her arms about his head and face to protect him. It was not astonishing then that their approach to the kitchen caverns attracted attention; but people made way so politely, bowing to them with such deference, that Menolly began to wonder who the man was. His tunic was a gray cloth with just a band of blue, so he must be a harper of some sort; probably weyrbound to Fort Weyr to judge by the yellow arm device.

"Menolly, did you hurt your feet?" Felena appeared before them, curious at the flurry of excitement. "Didn't T'gellan remember you? He's got no memory, drat the man. How good of you to rescue her, sir!"

"Think nothing of it, Felena. I discovered she was custodian of the fire lizard eggs. However, if you happened to have a cup of wine . . . This is thirsty work."

"I can stand, really I can, sir," Menolly protested, for something in Felena's manner told her that this man was too-important to be toting sore-footed girls. "Felena, I couldn't stop him."

"I'm only being my usual ingratiating self," the man told her, "and do stop struggling. You're too heavy!"

Felena was laughing at his exaggeration as she led the way to Menolly's table above the egg basket.

"You're a terrible fellow, Master Robinton, indeed you are. But you'll have your wine while Menolly picks out the best of the clutch. Have you spotted the queen egg, Menolly?"

"After the way Menolly's queen has been attacking me, I'd be safer with any other color, Felena. Now do get that wine for me, there's a good woman. I'm utterly parched."

As he gently settled her into her chair, Menolly heard Felena's teasing remark, ". . . terrible fellow, Master Robinton . . . terrible fellow, Master Robinton . . ." She stared at him, disbelieving.

"Now, what's the matter, Menolly? Did my exercise bring out spots on my face?" He mopped at his cheeks and brow and examined his hand. "Ah, thank you, Felena. You've saved my life. My tongue was quite stuck to the roof of my mouth. And here's to you, young queen, and thank you for your courtesy." He raised his cup to Beauty, who was perched on Menolly's shoulder, her tail firmly entwined as she glared at him. "Well?" he asked kindly of Menolly.

"You're the Masterharper?"

"Yes, I'm Robinton." He sounded quite casual about it. "And I think you need some wine, too."

"No, I couldn't." Menolly held up her hands in refusal. "I get hiccups. And go to sleep." She hadn't meant to say that either, but she had to explain why she was discourteous enough to refuse his cup. She was also acutely aware now of her stained overshirt, her sandy clothes and slippers, her complete disarray. This wasn't how she imagined her first meeting with the Masterharper of Pern, and she hung her head in embarrassment.

"I always advise eating *before* drinking," remarked Master Robinton in the nicest possible way. "I shouldn't wonder but that's half the problem right now," he added and then raised his voice. "This child is faint with hunger, Felena."

Menolly shook her head, denying his suggestion and trying to forestall Felena, but she was already ordering one of the lads to bring klah, a basket of breads, and a dish of sliced meats. When she was served, just as if she were one of the Weyrwomen, she kept her head bent over her cup, blowing to cool the contents.

"Do you think there's enough here for a starving man?" asked Masterharper Robinton, his voice so plaintive and faint with his pretended hunger that Menolly was startled into glancing up at him. His expression was at once so wistful, appealing and kind that, despite her deep chagrin, she smiled in response to his foolishness. "I'll need strength for this evening's work, and a base for my drinking," he added in a very quiet, worried voice.

She had the feeling that he had let her share his responsibilities, but she wondered at the sadness and anxiety. Surely everyone in the Weyr was happy today?

"A few slices of meat on a slab of that good bread," and Robinton made his voice quaver like a peevish old uncle's. "And . . ." his voice returned to his normal baritone range, "a cup of good Benden wine to wash it down . . ."

To her consternation, he rose then, bread and meat in one hand, the wine mug in the other. He bowed to her with great dignity and, with a smile, was off.

"But, Masterharper, your fire lizard eggs . . ."

"Later, Menolly. I'll come back later for them."

His tall figure, his head visible above the bustling activity, retreated across the cavern, away from her. She watched until he was out of sight amid the visitors, bewildered, and all too keenly aware that there was no way in which she would be able to ask Masterharper Robinton about her songs. Twiddles they were, as Yanus and Mavi had always said: too insignificant to be presented for serious consideration to such a man as Masterharper Robinton.

Beauty crooned softly and headstroked Menolly's cheek. Rocky hopped down from his wall perch to her shoulder. He nuzzled her ear, humming in a consoling tone.

Mirrim found her that way, and she roused from her apathy to rejoice with her friend.

"Oh, I'm so very happy for you, Mirrim. You see it did come right!" If Mirrim, with all her worries, had been able to keep a good face, surely Menolly, with much to be grateful for, could manage to follow her example.

"Did you see it? You *were* in the Hatching Ground? I was so terrified that I didn't dare watch," Mirrim said, no trace of terror now in her radiant face. "I made Brekke eat, the first food she's taken in just days. And she smiled at me, Menolly. She smiled at me, and she knew me. She's going to be perfectly all right. And F'nor ate every speck of the roast wherry I brought him." She giggled, all mischievous girl, not Mirrim-Felena, or Mirrim-Manora. "I snitched the best slices of the spiced wherry breast, too. And you know, he ate every bit of it! He'll probably eat himself sick at the Feast as well. Then I told him to take poor Canth down to feed because that dragon's just about transparent with hunger." Her voice dropped in awe. "Canth tried to protect Wirenth from Prideth, you know. Can you imagine that? A brown protecting a queen! It's because F'nor loves Brekke so. And now it's all right. It's well and truly all right. So tell me."

"Tell you? What?"

Irritation flashed across Mirrim's face. "Tell me exactly what happened when Brekke got on the Hatching Ground. I told you I didn't dare look myself."

So Menolly told her. And told her again until she ran out of answers to all the detailed questions Mirrim found to ask her.

"Now you tell me why everyone's so upset about this Jaxom Impressing the little white dragon. He saved his life, you know. The dragon would have died if Jaxom hadn't broken the shell and cut the sac."

"Jaxom Impressed a dragon? I didn't know!" Mirrim's eyes widened with consternation. "Oh! Now why would that kid do such a dreadful thing?"

"Why is it dreadful?"

"Because he's got to be Lord Holder of Ruatha Hold, that's why."

Menolly was a bit annoyed with Mirrim's impatience and said so.

"Well, he can't be Lord Holder *and* dragonrider. Didn't you learn anything in that Sea Hold of yours? And, by the way, I saw the Half-Circle Harper, I think his name is Elgion. Shall I tell him you're here?"

"No!"

"Well, no need to bite my head off." And with that Mirrim flounced off in a huff.

"Menolly, will you forgive me? I completely forgot to come back for you," T'gellan said, striding up to the table before Menolly had a chance to catch her breath. "Look, the Masterminer is supposed to have two eggs. He can't stay for the whole Feast, so we've got to fix something for him to carry the eggs home in. And the rest of the eggs as well. No, don't get up. Here, you, come be feet for Menolly," he ordered, beckoning to one of the weyrboys.

So Menolly spent most of that evening in the kitchen cavern sewing furry bags to carry eggs safely *between*. But she could hear all the jollity outside; and with no small effort, she made herself enjoy the singing. Five harpers, two drummers and three pipers made music for the Impression Feast. She thought she recognized Elgion's strong tenor in one song, but it was unlikely he'd look for her at the back of the kitchen cavern.

His voice made her briefly homesick for seawinds and the taste of salty air; briefly, too, she longed for the solitude of her cave. Only briefly; this Weyr was the place for her. Her feet would heal soon; she'd no longer be Old-Auntie-Sit-by-the-Fire. So how would she make her place in the Weyr? Felena had enough cooks, and how often would the Weyr, used to meat when it wished, want to eat fish? Even if she knew more ways of preparing it than anyone else? When she came down to it, the only thing in which she excelled was gutting fish. No, she would not think about harpering anymore. Well, there had to be something she could do.

"Are you Menolly?" asked a man tentatively.

She looked up to see one of the minercraftsmen who'd shared her tier at the Impression.

"I'm Nicat, Masterminer of Crom Hold. Weyrwoman Lessa said that I was to have two fire lizard eggs."

Beyond his stiff manner, Menolly could see he was restraining an eager impatience to hold fire lizard eggs of his own.

"Indeed I have sir, right here," she said, smiling warmly at him and indicating the table-protected basket.

"Well, my word," and his manner thawed visibly, "you're taking no chances, are you."

He helped her move the table and watched anxiously as she brushed back the top layer of sand and exposed the first of the eggs.

"Could I have a queen egg?" he asked.

"Master Nicat, Lessa explained to you that there's no way of telling which is which among the fire lizard eggs," said T'gellan, joining them to Menolly's intense relief. "Of course, Menolly might have a way of telling . . ."

"She might?" Masterminer Nicat regarded her with surprise.

"She's Impressed nine, you know."

"Nine?" Master Nicat frowned at her now, and she could practically read his mind: Nine for a child, and only two for the Masterminer?

"Pick Master Nicat two of the best, Menolly! We don't want him to be disappointed." Although T'gellan's face was sober, Menolly caught the expression in his eyes.

She managed to conduct herself with proper dignity and made a play of picking out just the right eggs for Masterminer Nicat, all the while being certain in her own mind that the queen egg was going to Masterharper Robinton only.

"Here you are, sir," she said, handing Masterminer Nicat the furry pouch with its precious contents. "You'd best carry them in your riding jacket, against your skin, on the way home."

"Then what do I do?" Master Nicat asked with humility as he held the sack in both hands against his chest.

Menolly looked at T'gellan, but both men were looking at her. She gulped.

"Well, I'd do exactly what we're doing here. Keep them near the hearth in a strong basket with either hot sand or furs. The Weyrwoman said they'd be hatching in about a sevenday. Feed them as soon as they break their shells, as much as they can eat, and talk to them all the time. It's important to . . ." She faltered; how could she tell this hard-faced man that you had to be affectionate and kind . . .

"You must reassure them constantly. They're nervous when they're first hatched. You saw the dragons today. Touch them and stroke them . . ." The Masterminer was nodding as he catalogued her instructions. "They must be bathed daily, and their skins must be oiled. You can always tell when a crack is developing from scaly patches on the hide. And they keep scratching themselves . . ."

Master Nicat turned questioningly to T'gellan.

"Oh, Menolly knows what to do. Why, she has her fire lizards singing tunes along with her and all . . ."

T'gellan's airy assurance did not sit too well with the Masterminer.

"Yes, but how do you get them to come to you?" he asked pointedly.

"You make them *want* to come back to you," Menolly said so firmly that she rated one of the Miner's daunting frowns.

"Kindness and affection, Master Nicat, are the essential ingredients," T'gellan said with equal force. "Now I see that T'gran is waiting to escort you, and your fire lizards, back to Crom." And he led the Masterminer off.

When T'gellan returned to Menolly, his eyes were dancing.

"I'll wager you my new tunic that one won't keep a fire lizard. Cold clod, that's what he is. Numbwit!"

"You shouldn't have said that about my fire lizards singing with me."

"Why not?" T'gellan was surprised at her criticism. "Mirrim hasn't done that much with her three, and she's had them longer. I told . . . Ah, yes, Craftmaster, F'lar did indeed say that you're to have a fire lizard egg."

And so the evening went, with lucky eager holders and craftsmen arriving to collect the precious fire lizard eggs. By the time only Masterharper Robinton's eggs remained in the warm sands of the basket, Menolly had become resigned to hearing T'gellan's wheeze that she had taught her fair of fire lizards to sing. Fortunately no one asked her to put it to the test, since her weary friends were curled up on their wall perches. They hadn't roused from sleep for all the singing and laughter at the merry tables in the Bowl.

Harper Elgion was thoroughly enjoying the Impression Feast. He hadn't realized how dour Half-Circle Hold was until this evening. Yanus was a good man, a fine Sea Holder to judge by the respect his holders accorded him, but he certainly knew how to take the joy out of living.

When Elgion had sat in the Hatching Ground, watching the young boys Impress, he'd determined that he'd find a fire lizard clutch of his own. That would alleviate the gloom at Half-Circle. And he'd see that Alemi got an egg, too. He'd heard from his neighbors in the tiers that the clutch being distributed this evening to the fortunate had been found down the coast from Half-Circle Sea Hold by T'gellan. Elgion had promised himself a chat with the bronze dragonrider; but T'gellan had had two passengers aboard Monarth when he'd collected Elgion at Half-Circle so there'd been no opportunity to talk. Elgion hadn't seen the man since the Hatching. But he'd bide his time.

Meanwhile, Oharan, the Weyr Harper, had Elgion playing gitar with him to amuse the visitors.

Elgion had just finished another tune with Oharan and some of the other visiting harpers when he caught sight of T'gellan, assisting a craftsman to mount a green dragon. It was then that Elgion noticed that the visitors were thinning out and this rare evening was drawing to a close. He'd speak with T'gellan, and then seek out the Masterharper, too.

"Over here, man," he said, beckoning to the bronze rider.

"Oh, Elgion, a cup of wine, please. I'm parched with talking. Not that it'll do those cold clods much good. They've no feeling for fire lizards at all."

"I heard you found the clutch. It wasn't in that cave by the Dragon Stones, was it?"

"By the Dragon Stones? No. Way down the coast in fact."

"Then there wasn't anything there?" Elgion was so bitterly disappointed that T'gellan gave him a long look.

"Depends on what you were expecting. Why? What did you think would be in that cave if it didn't hold fire lizard eggs?"

Elgion wondered briefly if he would be betraying Alemi's confidence. But it had become a matter of his professional honor to know if the sounds he'd heard from that cave had been made by pipes.

"The day Alemi and I saw the cave from the boat, I could have sworn I heard pipes. Alemi insisted it was wind over blowholes in the cliff, but there wasn't that much wind that day."

"No," T'gellan said, seeing a chance to tease the Harper, "you heard pipes. I saw 'em when I searched the place."

"You found pipes? Where was the player?"

"Sit down. Why're you so excited?"

"Where's that player?"

"Oh, here at Benden Weyr."

Elgion sat down again, so deflated and disappointed that T'gellan forbore to tease him further.

"Remember the day we rescued you from Thread? T'gran brought someone in as well."

"The lad?"

"That was no lad. That was a girl. Menolly. She'd been living in the cave . . . Now, what's the matter?"

"Menolly? Here? Safe? Where's the Masterharper? I've got to find Master Robinton. Come, T'gellan, help me find him!"

Elgion's excitement was contagious and though he was mystified, T'gellan joined the search. Taller than the young Harper, T'gellan spotted Master Robinton in deep conversation with Manora at a quiet table in the Bowl.

"Sir, sir, I've found her," Elgion cried, dashing up to them.

"Have you now? The love of your life?" asked Master Robinton amiably.

"No, sir. I've found Petiron's apprentice."

"Her? The old man's apprentice was a girl?"

Elgion was gratified by the Masterharper's surprise and grabbed at his hand, quite prepared to drag the man after him to search.

"She ran away from the Sea Hold, because they wouldn't let her make music, I think. She's Alemi's sister . . ."

"What's this about Menolly?" asked Manora, obstructing Elgion's flight with the Harper.

"Menolly?" Robinton raised his hand to silence Elgion. "That lovely child with the nine fire lizards?"

"What do you want of Menolly, Master Robinton?" Manora's voice was so stern that the Harper was brought up sharp.

He took a deep breath. "My much respected Manora, old Petiron sent me two songs written by his 'apprentice'; two of the loveliest melodies I've heard in all my Turns of harpering. He asked were they any good . . ." Robinton raised his eyes heavenward for patience, "I sent word back immediately, but the old man had died. Elgion found my message unopened when he got to the Sea Hold, and then he couldn't find the apprentice. The Sea Holder gave him some folderol about a fosterling who'd returned to his own hold. What's distressing you, Manora?"

"Menolly. I knew something had broken that girl's heart, but not what. She may not be able to play, Master Robinton. Mirrim says there's a dreadful scar on her left hand."

"She can, too, play," said T'gellan and Elgion together.

"I heard the sound of multiple pipes coming from that cave," Elgion said hurriedly.

"I saw her hide those pipes when we cleared out her cave," T'gellan added. "And furthermore, she's taught her fire lizards to sing, too."

"She has!" Bright sparks lit the Masterharper's eyes, and he turned purposefully towards the kitchen cavern.

"Not so fast, Masterharper," said Manora. "Go softly with that child."

"Yes, I saw that, too, when we were chatting this evening, and now I understand what was inhibiting her. So how to proceed cautiously?" The Masterharper frowned and gazed at T'gellan so long that the bronze rider wondered what he'd done wrong. "How do you know she's taught her fire lizards to sing?"

"Why, they were singing along with her and Oharan last night."

"Hmmm, now that's very interesting. Here's what we shall do."

Menolly was tired now, and most of the visitors had left. Still the Masterharper did not appear to collect his fire lizard eggs. She wouldn't leave until she'd seen him again. He'd been so kind; she hugged to herself the memory of their meeting. It was hard for her to believe that the Masterharper of Pern had carried her, Menolly of . . . Menolly of the Nine Fire Lizards. She propped her elbows up on the table and rested her head on her hands, feeling the rough scar against her left cheek and not even minding that at the moment.

She didn't hear the music at first, it was soft, as if Oharan was playing to himself at a nearby table.

"Would you sing along with me, Menolly?" asked Oharan softly, and she looked up to see him taking a place at the table.

Well, no harm in singing. It would help keep her awake until the Masterharper arrived. So she joined in. Beauty and Rocky roused at the sound of her voice, but Rocky went back to sleep after a peevish complaint. Beauty, however, dropped down to Menolly's shoulder, her sweet soprano trill blending with Menolly's voice.

"Do sing another verse, Menolly," said Manora, emerging from the shadows of the darkened cavern.

She took the chair opposite Menolly, looking weary, but sort of peaceful and pleased. Oharan struck the bridging chords and started the second verse.

"My dear, you have such a restful voice," Manora said when the last chord died away. "Sing me another one and then I'm away."

Menolly could scarcely refuse, and she glanced at Oharan to see what she should sing.

"Sing this one along with me," the Weyr Harper said, his eyes intent on Menolly's as his fingers struck an opening chord. Menolly knew the song, which had such an infectious rhythm that she began to sing before she realized why it was so familiar. She was also tired and not expecting to be trapped, not by Oharan and certainly not by Manora. That's why she didn't realize at first what Oharan was playing. It was one of the two songs she'd jotted down for Petiron: the ones he'd said he'd sent to the Masterharper.

She faltered.

"Oh, don't stop singing, Menolly," Manora said, "it's such a lovely tune."

"Maybe she should *play* her own song," said someone standing just behind Menolly in the shadow; and the Masterharper walked forward, holding out his own gitar to her.

"No! NO!" Menolly, half-rose, snatching her hands behind her back. Beauty gave a startled squawk and twined her tail about Menolly's neck.

"Won't you please play it . . . for me?" asked the Harper, his eyes entreating her.

Two more people emerged from the darkness: T'gellan, grinning fit to crack his face wide open, and Elgion! How did he know? From the gleam of his eyes and his smile, he was pleased and proud. Menolly was frightened and hid her face in confusion. How neatly she had been tricked!

"Don't be afraid now, child," said Manora quickly, catching Menolly's arm and gently pressing her back into her chair. "There's nothing for you to fear now: for yourself or your rare gift of music."

"But I can't play . . ." She held up her hand. Robinton took it in both of his, gently fingering the scar, examining it.

"You can play, Menolly," he said quietly, his kind eyes on hers, as he continued to stroke her hand, much as she would have caressed her frightened Beauty. "Elgion heard you when you were playing the pipes in the cave."

"But I'm a girl . . ." she said. "Yanus told me . . ."

"As to that," replied the Masterharper somewhat impatiently, though he smiled as he spoke, "if Petiron had had sense enough to tell me that that was the problem, you might have been spared a great deal of anguish: and I certainly would have been spared a great deal of trouble searching all Pern for you. Don't you *want* to be a harper?" Robinton ended on such a wistful, distressed note that Menolly had to reassure him.

"Oh yes, yes. I want music more than anything else in the world

. . ." On her shoulder, Beauty trilled sweetly and Menolly caught her breath sharply in distress.

"Now what's the matter?" asked Robinton.

"I've got fire lizards. Lessa said I belong in the Weyr."

"Lessa will not tolerate *nine singing* fire lizards in her Weyr," said the Harper in a voice that brooked no contradiction. "And they *do* belong in my Harperhall. You've a trick or two to teach me, my girl." He grinned down at her with such mischief dancing in his eyes that she smiled timorously back at him. "Now," and he waggled a finger at her, in mock seriousness, "before you can think of any more obstacles, arguments or distractions, will you kindly bundle up my fire lizard eggs, get whatever you have, and let us be off to the Harperhall? This has been a day of many tiring impressions."

His hand pressed hers reassuringly, and his kind eyes urged her acquiescence. All Menolly's doubts and fears dissolved in an instant.

Beauty bugled, releasing the stranglehold of her tail about Menolly's neck. Beauty called again, rousing the rest of the fair, her voice echoing Menolly's joy. She rose slowly to her feet, her hand clinging to the Harper's for support and confidence.

"Oh, gladly will I come, Master Robinton," she said, her eyes blurred by happy tears.

And nine fire lizards bugled a harmonious chorus of accord!

DRAGONSINGER

To ANDRE NORTON

this book is respectfully, admiringly,

lovingly dedicated

At the Harper Craft Hall

Robinton—Masterharper; bronze fire lizard, Zair

Masters Jerint—Instrument maker
       Domick—Composition
       Morshal—Musical Theory
       Shonagar—Voice
       Arnor—Archivist
       Oldive—Healer

Journeymen Sebell; gold fire lizard, Kimi
       Brudegan
       Talmor
       Dermently

Apprentices Piemur
       Ranly
       Timiny
       Brolly
       Bonz

Menolly; 9 fire lizards
       gold,   Beauty
       bronze, Rocky
              Diver
       brown, Lazybones
              Mimic
              Brownie
       blue,   Uncle
       green,   Auntie One

Auntie Two

Students Amania
   Audiva
   Pona
   Briala

Silvina—headwoman
Abuna—kitchen worker
Camo—half-witted kitchen drudge
Dunca—cotholder of girl's cottage

At Fort Hold

Lord Holder Groghe; gold fire lizard, Merga
Benis—son of Groghe
Viderian—fosterling
Ligand—journeyman tanner
Palim—baker
T'ledon—dragonrider

At Half-Circle Sea Hold

Yanus—Sea Holder
Mavi—Sea Holder's Lady
Alemi—son of Yanus
Petiron—old Harper
Elgion—new Harper

At Benden Weyr

F'lar—Weyrleader
Lessa—Weyrwoman
T'gellan—bronze dragonrider

F'nor—brown dragonrider; gold fire lizard Grall
Brekke—queenrider; bronze fire lizard Berd
Manora—Headwoman
Felena—second in charge
Mirrim—fosterling of Brekke; 3 fire lizards

Chapter 1

The little queen all golden
Flew hissing at the sea.
To stop each wave
Her clutch to save
She ventured bravely.

> *As she attacked the sea in rage*
> *A holderman came nigh*
> *Along the sand*
> *Fishnet in hand*
> *And saw the queen midsky.*

> > *He stared at her in wonder*
> > *For often he'd been told*
> > *That such as she*
> > *Could never be*
> > *Who hovered there, bright gold.*

> > > *He saw her plight and quickly*
> > > *He looked up the cliff he faced*
> > > *And saw a cave*
> > > *Above the wave*
> > > *In which her eggs he placed.*

The little queen all golden
Upon his shoulder stood
Her eyes all blue
Glowed of her true
Undying gratitude.

When Menolly, daughter of Yanus Sea Holder, arrived at the Harper Craft Hall, she came in style, aboard a bronze dragon. She was seated on Monarth's neck between his rider, T'gellan, and the Masterharper of Pern, Robinton. For one who had been told that girls could not become harpers, who had run away and actually lived holdless because she could not continue life without music, this was something of a triumphal success.

Yet it was also frightening. To be sure, music would not be denied her at the Harper Hall. True, she had written some songs that the Masterharper had heard and liked. But they were just tunings, not anything important. And what could a girl, even one who had taught her Hold's youngsters their Teaching Songs and Ballads, do at a Harper Hall from which all teaching songs originated? Especially a girl who had inadvertently Impressed nine fire lizards when everyone else on Pern would give a left arm to own just one? What *had* Master Robinton in mind for her to do here in the Harper Hall?

She couldn't think, she was so tired. She'd had a busy, exciting day at Benden Weyr on the opposite side of the continent where night now was well advanced. Here in Fort Hold, the sky was just darkening.

"Just a few minutes more," said Robinton in her ear. She heard him laugh because just then bronze Monarth trumpeted a greeting to the Fort Hold watch dragon. "Hang on, Menolly. I know you must be exhausted. I'll put you in Silvina's care the moment we land. See, there," and she followed the line of his pointing finger and saw the lighted quadrangle of buildings at the foot of the Fort Hold cliff. "That's the Harper Hall."

She shivered then, with fatigue, the cold of their passage *between* and apprehension. Monarth was circling now, and figures were pouring out of the Harper Hall into the courtyard, waving wildly to cheer the Masterharper's return. Somehow, Menolly hadn't expected that there'd be so many people in the Harper Craft Hall.

They kept well back, though their shouts of welcome didn't abate, while the big bronze dragon settled in the courtyard, giving him plenty of wingroom.

"I've got two fire lizard eggs!" shouted Master Robinton. Hugging the earthen pots tightly against his body, he slid from bronze Monarth's shoulder with the ease of considerable practice in dismounting dragons. "Two fire lizard eggs!" he repeated joyfully, holding the precious egg pots above his head and striding quickly to show off his prizes.

"My fire lizards!" Anxiously Menolly glanced up and about her. "Did they follow us, T'gellan? They're not lost *between.*"

"No chance of that, Menolly," T'gellan replied, pointing to the slated roof behind them. "I asked Monarth to tell them to perch there for the time being."

With infinite relief, Menolly saw the unmistakable outlines of her fire lizards on the rooftop against the darkening sky.

"If only they don't misbehave as they did at Benden . . ."

"They won't," T'gellan assured her easily. "You'll see to that. You've done more with your fair of fire lizards than F'nor has with his one little queen. And F'nor's a trained dragonrider." He swung his right leg over

Monarth's neckridge and dropped to the ground raising his arms to her. "Bring your leg over. I'll steady you so you won't jar those sore feet of yours," and his hands braced her as she slid down Monarth's shoulder. "That's the girl, and here you are, safe and sound in the Harper Hall." He gestured broadly as if only he could have accomplished this mission.

Menolly looked across the courtyard, where the Masterharper's tall figure and presence dominated those surrounding him. Was Silvina one of them? Wearily Menolly hoped that the Harper would find her quickly. The girl could put no reliance on T'gellan's glib assumption that her fire lizards would behave. They'd only just got used to being at Benden Weyr, among people who had some experience with winged antics.

"Don't worry so, Menolly. Just remember," said T'gellan, gripping her shoulder in awkward reassurance, "every harper on Pern has been trying to find Petiron's lost apprentice . . ."

"Because they thought that apprentice was a boy . . ."

"That made no difference to Master Robintón when he asked you to come here. Times are changing, Menolly, and it'll make no difference to the others. You'll see. In a sevenday you'll have forgotten you've ever lived anywhere else." The bronze dragonrider chuckled. "Great shells, girl, you've lived holdless, outrun Thread, and Impressed nine fire lizards. What's to fear from harpers?"

"Where is Silvina?" The Masterharper's voice rose above the others. There was a momentary lull and someone was sent to the Hall to find the woman. "And no more answers now. You've the bones of the news, I'll flesh it out for you later. Now, don't drop these egg pots, Sebell. Right now, I've more good news! I've found Petiron's lost apprentice!"

Amid exclamations of surprise, Robinton broke free of the crowd and beckoned T'gellan to bring Menolly forward. For a brief second, Menolly fought the urge to turn and run, impossible as it was with her feet barely healed from trying to outrun Thread and with T'gellan's arm about her. His fingers squeezed on her shoulder as if he sensed her nervousness.

"There's nothing for you to fear from harpers," he repeated in her ear as he escorted her across the court.

Robinton met them halfway, beaming with pleasure as he took her right hand. He flung up his other arm to command silence.

"This is Menolly, daughter of Yanus Sea Holder, late of Half-Circle Sea Hold, and Petiron's lost apprentice!"

Whatever response the harpers made was covered by an explosion of fire lizard cries from the rooftop. Fearful that the fair might wing down on the harpers, Menolly turned, saw that their wings were indeed spread and sternly commanded them to stay where they were. Then she had no excuse for not confronting the sea of faces: some smiling, some with mouths ajar in surprise at her fire lizards, but too many, many people.

"Yes, and those fire lizards are Menolly's," Robinton went on, his voice easily projecting above the murmurs. "Just as that lovely song about the fire lizard queen is Menolly's. Only it wasn't a *man* who saved the clutch from the sea, it was Menolly. And when no one would let her play or sing in Half-Circle Sea Hold after Petiron died, she ran away to the fire lizard queen's cave and Impressed nine of the eggs before she realized what she was doing. Furthermore," and he raised his volume above the ragged cheers of approval, "furthermore, she found another clutch, which provided *me* with two eggs!"

The second cheer was more wholehearted, reverberating in the courtyard and answered by shrill whistles from the fire lizards. Under cover of good-natured laughter at that response, T'gellan muttered, "I told you so" in her ear.

"And where is Silvina?" asked the Harper again, a note of impatience audible.

"Here I am and you ought to be ashamed of yourself, Robinton," said a woman, pushing through the ring of harpers. Menolly had an impression of very white skin and large expressive eyes set in a broad-cheeked face framed by dark hair. Then strong but gentle hands took her from Robinton's grasp. "Subjecting the child to such an ordeal. No, no, you lot calm down. All this noise. And those poor creatures up there too scared out of their wits to come down. Haven't you any sense, Robinton? Away! The lot of you. Into the Hall. Carry on all night there if you've the energy but I'm putting this child to bed. T'gellan, if you'd help me . . ."

As she upbraided everyone impartially, the woman was also making her way, with Menolly and T'gellan, through the crowd which parted respectfully but humorously before her.

"It's too late to put her with the other girls at Dunca's," said Silvina to T'gellan. "We'll just bed her in one of the guest rooms for the night."

Unable to see clearly in the shadows of the Hall, Menolly barked her toes on the stone steps, cried out involuntarily at the pain and grabbed at the supporting hands.

"What happened, child?" asked Silvina, her voice kind and anxious.

"My toes . . . my feet!" Menolly choked back tears that the unexpected pain had brought to her eyes. Silvina mustn't think her a coward.

"Here! I'll carry her," said T'gellan and swung Menolly up into his arms before she could protest. "Just lead the way, Silvina."

"That dratted Robinton," Silvina said, *"he* can go on all day and night without sleep but forgets that others—"

"No, it's not his fault. He's done so much for me . . ." Menolly began.

"Ha! He's deeply in *your* debt, Menolly," said the dragonrider with a cryptic laugh. "You'll have to have your healer see to her feet, Silvina," T'gellan continued as he carried Menolly up the broad flight of stairs that led from the main entrance of the Hall. "That's how we found her. She was trying to outrun the leading edge of Threadfall."

"She was?" Silvina stared over her shoulder at Menolly, her green eyes wide with respectful astonishment.

"She nearly did, too. Ran her feet raw. One of my wingmen saw her and brought her back to Benden Weyr."

"In this room, T'gellan. The bed's on the left-hand side. I'll just open the glow baskets . . ."

"I see it," and T'gellan deposited her gently in the bed. "I'll get the shutters, Silvina, and let those fire lizards of hers in here before they do get into trouble."

Menolly had let herself sink into the thick mattress of sweet rushes. Now she loosened the thong holding the small bundle of belongings to her back but she hadn't the energy to reach for the sleeping fur folded at the foot of the bedstead. As soon as T'gellan had the second shutter open, she called her friends in.

"I've heard so much about the fire lizards," Silvina was saying, "and had only the glimpse of Lord Groghe's little queen that. . . . Gracious goodness!"

At Silvina's startled remark, Menolly struggled out of the thick mattress to see the fire lizards dipping and wheeling about the woman.

"How many did you say you have, Menolly?"

"There are only nine," replied T'gellan, laughing at Silvina's confusion. She was twisting about, trying to get a good look at one or another of the gyrating creatures.

Menolly told them to settle down quickly and behave. Rocky and Diver landed on the table near the wall while the more daring Beauty took up her accustomed perch on Menolly's shoulder. The others came to rest on the window ledges, their jewelled eyes whirling with the orange of uncertainty and suspicion.

"Why, they're the loveliest creatures I've ever seen," said Silvina, peering intently at the two bronzes on the table. Rocky chirped back, recognizing that remarks were being made about him. He flipped his wings neatly to his back and cocked his head at Silvina. "And a good evening to you, young bronze fire lizard."

"That bold fellow is Rocky," said T'gellan, "if I remember correctly, and the other bronze is Diver. Right, Menolly?" She nodded, relieved in her weariness that T'gellan was ready to speak for her. "The greens are Aunties One and Two," and the pair began to chatter so like old women that Silvina laughed. "The little blue is Uncle but I haven't got the three browns sorted out . . ." and now he turned inquiringly to Menolly.

"They're Lazybones, Mimic and Brownie," Menolly said pointing at each in turn, "and this . . . is Beauty, Silvina," Menolly spoke the woman's name shyly because she didn't know her title or rank in the Harper Hall.

"And a Beauty she is, too. Just like a miniature queen dragon. And just as proud, I see." Then Silvina gave Menolly a hopeful look. "By any chance, will one of Robinton's eggs hatch a queen?"

"I hope so, I really do," said Menolly fervently. "But it's not easy with fire lizard eggs to tell which is the queen."

"I'm sure he'll be just as thrilled no matter what the color. And speaking of queens, T'gellan," and Silvina turned to the dragonrider, "do please tell me, did Brekke re-Impress the new queen dragon at your Hatching today? We've been so worried about her here, since her queen was killed."

"No, Brekke didn't re-Impress," and T'gellan smiled quickly to reassure Silvina. "Her fire lizard wouldn't let her."

"No?"

"Yes. You should have seen it, Silvina. That little bronze midget flew at the queen dragon, scolding like a wherry hen. Wouldn't let Brekke near the new queen. But she snapped out of that depression, and she'll be all right now, F'nor says. And it was little Berd who pulled the trick."

"Well, that really is interesting." Silvina regarded the two bronzes with thoughtful respect. "So they've a full set of wits . . ."

"They seem to," T'gellan went on. "F'nor uses his little queen, Grall, to send messages to the other Dragon Weyrs. Of course," and T'gellan chuckled disparagingly, "she doesn't always return as promptly as she goes . . . Menolly's trained hers better. You'll see." The dragonrider had been edging towards the door and now gave a huge yawn. "Sorry . . ."

"I'm the one who should apologize," replied Silvina, "indulging my curiosity when you two are all but asleep. Get along with you now, T'gellan, and my thanks for your help with Menolly."

"Good luck, now, Menolly. I know you'll sleep well," said T'gellan with a jaunty wink of farewell. He was out of the door, his boot heels clicking on the stone floor before she could thank him.

"Now, let's just have a quick look at these feet you ran ragged . . ." Silvina gently tugged off Menolly's slippers. "Hmmm. They're all but healed. Manora's clever with her nursing, but we'll have Master Oldive look at you tomorrow. Now, what's this?"

"My things, I don't have much . . ."

"Here, you two watch that and keep out of mischief," Silvina said, putting the bundle on the table between Rocky and Diver. "Now, slip off your skirt, Menolly, and settle down. A good long sleep, that's what you need. Your eyes are burned holes in your head."

"I'm all right, really."

"To be sure you are, now you're here. Living in a cave, did T'gellan say? With every harper on Pern looking for you in holds and crafthalls." Silvina deftly tugged at skirt tapes. "Just like old Petiron to forget to mention you being a girl."

"I don't think he forgot," Menolly said slowly, thinking of her father and mother and their opposition to her playing. "He told me girls can't be harpers."

Silvina gave her a long hard look. "Maybe under another Masterharper. Or in the old days, but surely old Petiron knew his own son well enough to—"

"Petiron was Master Robinton's father?"

"Did he never tell you that?" Silvina paused as she was spreading the sleeping fur over Menolly. "The old stubborn fool! Determined not to advance himself because his son was elected Masterharper . . . and then picking a place halfway to nowhere. . . . I beg your pardon, Menolly . . ."

"Half-Circle Sea Hold *is* halfway to nowhere."

"Not if Petiron found *you* there," said Silvina, recovering her brisk tone, "and sponsored you to this Craft. Now that's enough talking," she added, closing the glow basket. "I'll leave the shutters open . . . but you sleep yourself out, you hear me?"

Menolly mumbled a reply, her eyelids closing despite her effort to remain politely awake while Silvina was in the room. She let out a soft sigh as the door banged softly shut. Beauty immediately curled up by Menolly's ear, and the girl felt other small hard bodies making themselves comfortable against her. She composed herself for sleep, aware now of the dull throbbing of her feet and the aching of her banged toes.

She was warm, she was comfortable; she was so tired. The bag that enclosed the thick rushes was stout enough to keep stray edges from digging into her flesh, but she couldn't sleep. She also couldn't move because, while her mind turned over all the day's incredible events, her body wasn't hers to command but in some nether region of unresponsiveness.

She was conscious of the spicy odor of Beauty, of the dry sweet scent of the rushes, the earthy smell of wet fields borne in by the night wind, accented occasionally by the touch of acrid blackstone smoke. Spring was not advanced enough to dispense with evening fires.

Strange not to have the smell of sea in her nostrils, Menolly thought, for sea and fish odors had dominated all but the last sevenday of her fifteen Turns. How pleasant to realize that she had done with the sea, and fish, forever. She'd never have to gut another packtail in her life, or risk another infected cut. She couldn't use her injured hand as much as she wanted to yet, but she would. Nothing was impossible, not if she could get to the Harper Hall in spite of all the odds against it. And she'd play gitar again and harp. Manora had assured her she'd use the fingers properly in time. And her feet were healing. It amused Menolly, now, to think that she'd had the temerity to try to outrun the leading edge of Threadfall. Running had done more than save her skin from Threadscoring: it had brought her to Benden Weyr, to the attention of the Masterharper of Pern and to the start of a completely new life.

And her dear old friend, Petiron, had been Master Robinton's father? She'd known the old Harper had been a good musician, but it had never occurred to her before to wonder why he had been sent to Half-Circle Sea Hold where only she had profited from his ability as a teacher. If only her father, Yanus, had let her play gitar when the new Harper first arrived . . . but they'd been so afraid that she'd disgrace the Sea Hold. Well, she hadn't, and she wouldn't! One day her father, and yes, her mother, too, would realize that Menolly was no disgrace to the Hold of her birth.

Menolly drifted on thoughts of triumph until sound invaded her reflections. Male voices, laughing and rumbling in conversation, carried on the clear night air. The voices of harpers; tenor, bass and baritone, in amused, argumentative, cajoling tones, and one querulous, sort of quavery, older, whiny voice. She didn't like that one. Another, a velvet-soft, light baritone, rose above the cranky tenor, soothing. Then the Masterharper's deeper baritone dominated and silenced the others. Though she couldn't understand what he was saying, his voice lulled her to sleep.

Chapter 2

Harper, tell me of the road
That leads beyond this Hold,
That wends its way beyond the hill . . .
Does it go further on until
It ends in sunset's gold?

Menolly roused briefly, reacting to an inner call that had nothing to do with the sun's rising on this side of Pern. She saw dark night and stars through the window, felt the sleeping fire lizards tucked about her, and gratefully went back to sleep again. She was so tired.

Once the sun had cleared the roof of the outer side of the rectangle of buildings that comprised the main Harper Craft Hall, it shone directly at her windows, set in the eastern side of the Hall. Gradually the light penetrated the room, and the unusual combination of light and warmth on her face woke Menolly.

She lay, her body not yet responsive, wondering where she was. Remembering, she was uncertain what to do next. Had she missed some general waking call? No, Silvina had said that she was to sleep herself out. As she pushed back the sleeping furs, she heard the sound of voices chanting. The rhythm was familiar. She smiled, identifying one of the long Sagas. Apprentices were being taught the complicated timing by rote, just as she had taught the youngsters in Half-Circle Sea Hold when Petiron was sick, and later after he died. The similarity reassured her.

As she slid from the bed, she clenched her teeth in anticipation of touching the cool hard stones of the floor, but to her surprise, her feet only felt stiff, not painful, this morning. She glanced out the window at the sun. It was well into morning by the cast of shadow: she'd really slept. Then she laughed at herself, for, to be sure she had: she was halfway round Pern from Benden Weyr and Half-Circle Hold, and she had had at least six hours more rest than usual. Fortunately the fire lizards had been as tired as she or they'd have wakened her with their hunger.

She stretched and shook out her hair, then hobbled carefully to the jar and basin. After washing with soapsand, she dressed and brushed her hair, feeling able to face new experiences.

Beauty gave an impatient chirp. She was awake. And very hungry. Rocky and Diver echoed the complaint.

Menolly would have to find them food and right soon. Having nine fire lizards would prejudice enough people against her, without having unmanageably hungry ones who would irritate even the most tolerant of people.

Resolutely, Menolly opened the door to a silent hallway. The aromatic odors of *klah,* baking breads and meats filled the air. Menolly decided she need only follow the smells to their source to satisfy her friends.

On either side of the wide corridor were doors; those on the outside of the Hall were open to let sun and air flood the inside. She descended from the uppermost level into the large entranceway. Directly in front of the staircase were dragon-high metal doors with the most curious closings she'd ever seen: on the back of the doors were wheels, which evidently turned the heavy bars into floor and ceiling. At Half-Circle Sea Hold there had been the heavy horizontal bars, but this arrangement would be easier to lock and looked much more secure.

To the left was a double-doored entrance into a Great Hall, probably the room where the Harper had been talking last night. To the right, she looked into the dining hall, almost as large as the Great Hall, with three long tables parallel to the windows. Also to her right, by the stairwell, was an open doorway, leading to shallow steps and the kitchen, judging by the appetizing odors and familiar sounds.

The fire lizards creeled in hunger, but Menolly couldn't have the whole fair invading the kitchen and upsetting the drudges. She ordered them to perch on the cornices in the shadows above the door. She'd bring them food, she promised them, but they had to behave. Beauty scolded until the others settled meekly into place, only their glowing, jewel-faceted eyes giving evidence of their positions.

Then Beauty assumed her favorite perch on Menolly's shoulder, her head half-buried in Menolly's thick hair, and her tail wrapped securely about Menolly's throat like a golden necklace.

As Menolly reached the kitchen, the scene with the drudges and cooks scurrying about preparing the midday meal fleetingly revived memories of happier days at Half-Circle. But here, it was Silvina who noticed her and smiled, as Menolly's mother would not have done.

"You're awake? Are you rested?" Silvina gestured imperatively at a slack-featured, clumsy-looking man by the hearth. "Klah, Camo, pour a mug of klah, for Menolly. You must be famished, child. How are your feet?"

"Fine, thank you. And I don't want to bother anyone . . ."

"Bother? What bother? Camo, pour the klah into the mug."

"It's not for myself I'm here . . ."

"Well, you need to eat, and you must be famished."

"Please, it's my fire lizards. Have you any scraps . . ."

Silvina's hands flew to her mouth. She glanced about her head as if expecting a swarm of fire lizards.

"No, I've told them to wait," Menolly said quickly. "They won't come in here."

"Now, you are a thoughtful child," Silvina said in so firm a tone that Menolly wondered why and then realized that she was the object of a good deal of furtive curiosity. "Camo, here. Give me that!" Silvina took the cup from the man, who was walking with exaggerated care not to slop an overfull container. "And get the big blue bowl from the cold room. The big blue bowl, Camo, from the cold room. Bring it to me." Silvina deftly handed the cup to Menolly without spilling a drop. "The cold room, Camo, and the blue bowl." She turned the man by the shoulders and gave him a gentle shove in the proper direction. "Abuna, you're nearest the hearth. Do dish up some of the cereal. Plenty of sweetening on it, too, the child's nothing but skin and bones." Silvina smiled at Menolly. "No use feeding the fowl and starving the servant, as it were. I saved meat for your friends when we trussed up the roast," and Silvina nodded towards the biggest hearth where great joints of meat were turning on heavy spits, "since meat's what the Harper said fire lizards need. Now, where would the best place . . ." Silvina glanced about her undecidedly, but Menolly had noticed a low door that led up a short flight of steps to the corner of the courtyard.

"Would I disturb anyone out there?"

"Not at all, you are a considerate child. That's right, Camo. And thank you." Silvina patted the half-wit's arm kindly, while he beamed with the pleasure of a job properly done and rewarded. Silvina tipped the edge of the bowl towards Menolly. "Is this enough? There's more . . ."

"Oh, that's a gracious plenty, Silvina."

"Camo, this is Menolly. Follow Menolly with the bowl. She can't carry it *and* her own breakfast. This is Menolly, Camo, follow Menolly. Go right out, dear. Camo's good at carrying things . . . at least what doesn't spill."

Silvina turned from her then, speaking sharply to two women chopping roots, bidding them to slice, not stare. Very much aware of scrutiny, Menolly moved awkwardly to the steps, cup in one hand, bowl of warm cereal in the other, and Camo shuffling behind her. Beauty, who had remained discreetly covered by Menolly's hair, now craned her neck about, smelling the raw meat in the bowl Camo carried.

"Pretty, pretty," the man mumbled as he noticed the fire lizard. "Pretty small dragon?" He tapped Menolly on the shoulder. "Pretty small dragon?" He was so anxious for her answer that he almost tripped on the shallow steps.

"Yes, she is like a small dragon, and she is pretty," Menolly agreed, smiling. "Her name is Beauty."

"Her name is Beauty." Camo was entranced. "Her name is Beauty. She pretty small dragon." He beamed as he loudly declared this information.

Menolly shushed him, not wanting either to alarm or distract Silvina's helpers. She put down her mug and bowl and reached for the meat.

"Pretty small dragon Beauty," Camo said, ignoring her as she pulled the bowl so firmly clutched in his huge, thick-fingered hands.

"You go to Silvina, Camo. You go to Silvina."

Camo stood where he was, bobbing his head up and down, his mouth set in a wet, wide grimace of childish delight, too entranced by Beauty to be distracted.

Beauty now creeled imperiously, and Menolly grabbed a handful of meat to quiet her. But her cries had alerted the others. They came, some of them from the open windows of the dining hall above Menolly's head, others, judging by the shrieks of dismay, through the kitchen and out the door by the steps.

"Pretty, pretty. All pretty!" Camo exclaimed, turning his head from side to side, trying to see all the flitting fire lizards at once.

He didn't move a muscle as Auntie One and Two perched on his forearms, snatching gobbets of meat directly from the bowl. Uncle secured his talons to the fabric of Camo's tunic, his right wingtip jabbing the man in the neck and chin as the littlest fire lizard fought for his fair share of the meat. Brownie, Mimic, and Lazybones ranged from Camo's shoulders to Menolly's as she tried to distribute the meat evenly.

Alternating between embarrassment at her friends' bad manners and gratitude for Camo's stolid assistance, Menolly was acutely aware that all activity had ceased in the kitchen to watch the spectacle. Momentarily, she expected to hear an irate Silvina order Camo back to his ordinary duties, but all she heard was the buzz of whispered gossiping.

"How many does she have?" she heard one clear whisper out of the general mumble.

"Nine," Silvina answered, imperturbable. "When the two the Harper was given have hatched, the Harper Hall will have eleven." Silvina sounded smugly superior. The buzz increased in volume. "That bread's risen enough now, Abuna. You and Kayla shape it."

The fire lizards had cleared the bowl of meat, and Camo stared into its hollow, his face contorted by an expression of dismay.

"All gone? Pretties hungry?"

"No, Camo. They've had more than enough. They're not hungry anymore." In fact, their bellies were distended, they'd gorged so. "You go to Silvina. Silvina wants you, Camo," and Menolly followed Silvina's example: she took him by the shoulders, turned him down the steps, and gave him a gentle shove.

Menolly sipped the good hot klah, beginning to think that Silvina's marked attentions and kindness were deliberate. Or was that foolish? Silvina was just a kind, thoughtful person: look how she treated dull-witted Camo. She was patience itself with his inadequacy. Nonetheless, Silvina was obviously the headwoman at the Harper Craft Hall and, like serene Manora at Benden Weyr, undoubtedly wielded a good deal of authority. If Silvina was friendly, others would follow her lead.

Menolly began to relax in the warm sun. Her dreams last night had been troubled, though she couldn't remember details now in the bright morning, only a sense of uneasiness and helplessness. Silvina had done much to dissipate the lingering misgivings. *Nothing to fear from harpers,* T'gellan had repeatedly told her.

Across the courtyard, young voices broke into a lusty rendition of the Saga previously chanted. The fire lizards rose at the eruption of sound, settling again as Menolly laughingly reassured them.

Then a pure sweet trill from Beauty soared in delicate descant above the apprentices' male voices. Rocky and Diver joined her, wings half-spread as they expanded their lungs for breath. Mimic and Brownie dropped from the window ledge to add their voices. Lazy would not put himself to any such effort, and the two Aunties and blue Uncle were at best indifferent singers, but they listened, heads cocked, jeweled eyes whirling. The five singers rose to their haunches now, their throats thickening, their cheeks swelling as their jaws relaxed to emit the sweet pure notes. Their eyes were half-lidded as they concentrated, as good singers will, to produce the fluting descant.

They were happy then, Menolly thought with relief, and picked up the melody of the Saga, not that the fire lizards needed her voice with the apprentices supplying the tune and harmony.

They were on the last two measures of the chorus when Menolly suddenly realized that it was only herself and the fire lizards singing, that the male voices had ceased. Startled, she looked up and saw that almost every window about the courtyard was filled with faces. The exceptions were the windows of the hall from which the voices had come.

"Who has been singing?" demanded an irate tenor, and a man's head appeared at one of the empty windows.

"Why, that's a grand way to wake up, Brudegan," said the clear baritone of the Masterharper from some point above Menolly and to her left. Craning her head up, she saw him leaning out of his window on the upper story.

"Good morning to you, Masterharper," said Brudegan courteously, but his tone indicated that he was disgruntled by the intervention.

Menolly tried to sit small, heartily wishing herself *between:* she was certainly frozen motionless.

"I didn't know your fire lizards could sing," Silvina said, appearing on Menolly's right and absently retrieving mug and bowl from the steps. "A nice compliment to your chorus, eh, Brudegan," she added, raising her voice to carry across the courtyard. "You'd be wanting your klah now, Robinton?"

"It would be welcome, Silvina." He stretched, leaned further out to peer down at Menolly. "Enter a fair of fire lizards singing! A lovely way to be awakened, Menolly; and a good morning to you, too." Before Menolly could respond, a look of dismay crossed his face. *"My* fire lizard. My egg!" and he disappeared from sight.

Silvina chuckled and she regarded Menolly. "He'll be of no use to anyone until it's hatched and he's got one of his own."

At that point, Brudegan's singers renewed their song. Beauty chirruped questioningly at Menolly.

"No, no, Beauty. No more singing, not now."

"They need the practice," and Silvina gestured at the hall. "Now I've the Harper's meal to see to and you to settle . . ." She paused, glancing about at the fire lizards. "But what to do with them?"

"They usually sleep when they're as full as they are right now."

"All to the good . . . but where? Mercy!"

Menolly tried not to laugh at Silvina's astonishment, because all but Beauty, who took her usual perch on Menolly's shoulder, had disappeared. Menolly pointed to the roof opposite and the small bodies landing there, apparently out of thin air.

"They do go *between,* don't they?" Silvina said more than asked. "Harper says they're much like dragons?" That was a question.

"I don't know that much about dragons, but fire lizards can go *between.* They followed me last night from Benden Weyr."

"And they're obedient. I could wish the apprentices were half so willing." Then Silvina motioned Menolly to follow her back into the kitchen. "Camo, turn the spit. Camo, now turn the spit. I suppose the rest of you have been watching the yard instead of the food," she said, scowling indiscriminately about the kitchen. The cooks and drudges alike pretended industry, clanging, banging, splashing or bending with assiduous care over quieter tasks of paring and scraping. "Better yet, Menolly, *you* take the Harper his klah, and check that egg of his. He'll be roaring for you soon enough, so we might as well anticipate. Then I shall want Master Oldive to see your feet, not that Manora hasn't all but healed them anyway. And . . ." Silvina caught Menolly's left hand and scowled at the red mark. "Wherever did you get such a fierce wound? And who bungled the healing of it? There now, can you grip with that hand?" Silvina had been assembling on a small tray the various items of the Harper's breakfast, the last of which was a heavy pot of klah. Now she gave the tray to Menolly. "There now. His room is the second door on the right from yours, Menolly. Turn the spit, Camo, don't just hold on to it. Menolly's fire lizards are fed and sleeping. You'll have another gawk at them later. Turn the spit now!"

As briskly as Menolly could move on her stiff feet, she made her way out of the kitchen and up the broad steps to the second level. Beauty hummed softly in her ear, a gently disobedient descant to the Saga that Brudegan's pupils were singing lustily.

Master Robinton hadn't sounded annoyed about the fire lizards' singing, Menolly thought. She'd apologize to Journeyman Brudegan when she got the chance. She simply hadn't realized she'd cause a distraction. She'd been so pleased that her friends were relaxed enough to want to sing.

Second door on her right. Menolly tapped. Then rapped, then knocked, hard enough to make her knuckles sting.

"Come. Come. And, Silvina . . . oh, Menolly, you're just the person I wanted to see," the Harper said, throwing open the door. "And good morning to you, proud Beauty," he added, grinning at the little queen who chirped an acknowledgement as he took the tray from Menolly. "Silvina's forever anticipating me. . . . Would you please check my egg? It's in the other room, by the hearth. It feels harder to me . . ." He sounded anxious as he pointed to the farther door.

Menolly obediently entered the room, and he walked with her, setting the tray down as he passed the sandtable by the window and pouring himself a mug of klah before he joined her by the hearth in the next room where a small fire burned gently. The earthen pot had been set at the edge of the hearth apron.

Menolly opened it, carefully brushing aside the warm sand that covered the precious fire lizard egg. It was harder, but not much more so than when she had given it to the Masterharper at Benden Weyr the previous evening.

"It's fine, Master Robinton, just fine. And the pot is warm enough, too," she said, running her hands down the sides. She replaced the sand and the top and rose. "When we brought the clutch back to Benden Weyr two days ago, Weyrwoman Lessa said it would take a sevenday for them to hatch, so we've five days more."

The Harper sighed with exaggerated relief. "You slept well, Menolly? You're rested? Awake long?"

"Long enough."

The Harper burst out laughing as she realized how much chagrin she'd put into her tone.

"Long enough to set a few people by the ears, huh? My dear child, did you not notice the difference in the chorus the second time? Your fire lizards have challenged them. Brudegan was only gruff with surprise. Tell me, can your fire lizards improvise descants to any tune?"

"I don't really know, Master Robinton."

"Still not sure, are you, young Menolly?" He didn't mean the fire lizards' abilities. There was such kindness in his voice and eyes that Menolly felt unexpected tears behind her eyes.

"I don't want to be a nuisance . . ."

"Allow me to differ both to statement and content, Menolly . . ." Then he sighed. "You're overyoung to appreciate the value of nuisance, although the improvement in that chorus is a point in my argument. However, it's much too early in the morning for me to expound philosophy." He guided her back into the other room, quite the most cluttered place she had ever seen and in direct contrast to the neatness of his bedchamber. While musical instruments were carefully stored on hook and shelf in cases, piles of record skins, drawings, slates—wax and stone —littered every surface and were heaped in corners and against the walls of the room. On one wall was a finely drawn map of the Pern continent, with smaller detailed drawings of all the major Holds and Crafthalls pinned here and there on the borders. The long sandtable by the window was covered with musical notations, some of them carefully shielded by glass to prevent erasure. The Harper had set the tray on the center island, which separated the sandtable into two halves. Now he pulled a square of wood to protect the sand and positioned the tray so he could eat comfortably. He smeared a thick slice of bread with soft cheese and picked up his spoon to eat his cereal, motioning with the spoon for Menolly to seat herself on a stool.

"We're in a period of change and readjustment, Menolly," he said, managing to speak and eat simultaneously without choking on food or garbling his words. "And you are likely to be a vital part of that change. Yesterday I exerted an unfair pressure on you to join the Harper Hall. . . . Oh yes, I did, but you belong here!" His forefinger stabbed downward at the floor and then waggled out at the courtyard. "First," and he paused to swallow klah, washing down bread and cereal, "we must discover just how well Petiron taught you the fundamentals of our craft and what you need to further your gifts. And . . ." he pointed now to her left hand, ". . . what can be done to correct that scar damage. I'd still like to hear you *play* the songs you wrote." His eyes fell to her hands in her lap so that she was aware of her absentminded kneading of her left palm. "Master Oldive will set that right if anyone can."

"Silvina said I was to see him today."

"We'll have you playing again, more than just those pipes. We need you, when you can craft songs like those Petiron sent me and the ones Elgion found stuck away at the back of the harper's shelves in Half-Circle. Yes, and that's a matter I'd better explain . . ." he went on, smoothing the hair at the back of his neck and, to Menolly's amazement, appearing to be embarrassed.

"Explain?"

"Yes, well, you hadn't obviously finished *writing* that song about the fire lizard queen . . ."

"No, I hadn't actually . . ." Menolly felt that she was not hearing his words properly. For one thing, why did the Masterharper have to explain anything to *her*? And she'd only jotted down the little tune about the fire lizard queen, yet last night. . . . Now she remembered that he'd mentioned the song, as if all the harpers knew about it. "You mean, Harper Elgion sent it to you?"

"How else would I have got it? We couldn't find you!" Robinton sounded annoyed. "When I think of you, living in a cave, with a damaged hand, and you hadn't been *allowed* to finish that charming song. . . . So I did."

He got up, rummaged among the piles of waxed slates under the window, extracted one and handed it to her. She looked at the notations obediently but, although they were familiar, she couldn't make her mind read the melody.

"I had to have something about fire lizards, since I believe they're going to be far more important than anyone has yet realized. And this tune . . ." his finger tapped the hard wax surface approvingly, ". . . was so exactly what I needed, that I just brushed up the harmonics, and compressed the lyric story. Probably what you'd've done yourself if you'd had the chance to work on it again. I couldn't really improve on the melodic line without destroying the integral charm of. . . . What's the matter, Menolly?"

Menolly realized that she'd been staring at him, unable to believe that he was praising a silly tune she'd only scrawled down. Guiltily, she examined the slate again.

"I never did get a chance to *play* it. . . . I wasn't supposed to play my own tunes in the Sea Hold. I promised my father I wouldn't . . . so you see—"

"Menolly!"

Startled, she looked up at his stern tone.

"I want you to promise me—and you're now my apprentice—I want you to promise me to write down any tune that comes into your mind: I want you to play it as often as necessary to get it right . . . do you understand me? That's why I brought you here." He tapped the slate again. "That was a good song even before I tampered with it. I need good songs badly.

"What I said about change affects the Harper Hall more than any other craft, Menolly, because we are the ones who effect change. Just as we teach with our songs, so we also help people accept new ideas and necessary changes. And for that we need a special kind of harpering.

"Now, I still have to consider Craft principles and standards. Especially in your unusual situation, the conventional procedure must be observed. Once we've dispensed with the formalities, we can proceed with your training as fast as you want to go. But this is where you belong, Menolly, you and your singing fire lizards. Bless me but that was lovely to hear this morning. Ah, Silvina, good morning and to you, as well, Master Oldive . . ."

Menolly knew it was impolite to stare at anyone and looked away as soon as she realized that she was staring, but Master Oldive required a long look. He was shorter than herself but only because his head was awry on his neck. His great lean face tilted up from its permanent slant, and she had the impression of enormous dark eyes under very shaggy brows taking in every detail of herself.

"I'm sorry, Master Robinton, have we interrupted you?" Silvina paused on the threshold indecisively.

"Yes, and no. I don't think I've convinced Menolly but that will take time. Meanwhile, we'll get on with the basics. We'll speak again, Menolly," said the Harper. "Go along with Master Oldive now. Let him do his best, or his worst, for you. She must play again, Oldive." The Harper's smile as he gestured to Menolly to follow the man implied complete faith in his ability. "And Silvina, Menolly says the egg's safe enough for four or five days, but you'll please arrange to have someone—"

"Why not Sebell? He's got his egg to check, too, doesn't he? And with Menolly here in the Hall . . ." Silvina was saying as Master Oldive, ushering Menolly out of the room before him, closed the door.

"I'm to see to your feet as well, Silvina tells me," was the man's comment as he indicated Menolly should lead the way to her room. The Master's voice was unexpectedly deep. And while he might be shorter than herself in the torso, he'd as long a leg and arm and matched her stride down the corridor. As he pushed wider her door, she realized that his stature was due to a terrible malformation of his spine.

"By my life!" Oldive exclaimed, stopping abruptly as Menolly preceded him into the room. "I thought for a moment you were as blighted as myself. It is a fire lizard on your shoulder, isn't it?" He chuckled. "Now, there's one on me, so it is. Is the creature friendly?" He peered up at Beauty, who chirruped pleasantly back, since Oldive was patently addressing her. "As long as I'm friendly to your Menolly, I take it? You'll have to write another verse to your fire lizard song, proving the rewards of kindness," he added, gesturing her to sit on the window side of the bed as he pulled up the stool.

"Oh, that's not my song . . ." she said, removing her slippers.

Master Oldive frowned. "Not your song? But Master Robinton assigns it to you—constantly."

"He rewrote it . . . he told me so."

"That's not unusual," and Master Oldive dismissed her protest. "Proper mess you made of your feet," he said, his voice taking on a distant, thoughtful quality as he looked at first one, then the other foot. "Running, I believe . . ."

Menolly felt reproved. "I was caught out during Threadfall, you see, far from my cave and had to run . . . oooh!"

"Sorry, did I hurt? The flesh is very tender. And will remain that way awhile longer."

He began to smooth on a pungent-smelling substance, and she couldn't keep her foot still. He grabbed her ankle firmly to complete the medication, countering her embarrassed apology by remarking that her twitching proved that she'd done the nerves no harm with the pounding she'd given her feet.

"You're to keep off them as much as possible. I'll tell Silvina so. And use this salve morning and night. Aids healing and keeps the skin from itching." He replaced Menolly's slippers. "Now, this hand of yours."

She hesitated, knowing that his opinion of the bungled wound was likely to echo Manora's and Silvina's. Perversely she was afflicted by an obscure loyalty to her mother.

Oldive regarded her steadily, as if divining some measure of her reluctance, and extended his own hand. Compelled by the very neutrality of his gaze, she gave him her injured hand. To her surprise, there was no change of expression on his face, no condemnation or pity, merely interest in the problem the thick-scarred palm posed for a man of his skill. He prodded the scar tissue, murmuring thoughtfully in his throat.

"Make a fist."

She could just about do that but, when he asked her to extend her fingers, the scar pulled as she tried to stretch the palm.

"Not as bad as I was led to believe. An infection, I suppose . . ."

"Packtail slime . . ."

"Hmm, yes. Insidious stuff." He gave her hand another twist. "But the scar is not long healed, and the tissue can still be stretched. A few more months and we might not have been able to do anything to flex the hand. Now, you will do exercises, tightening your fingers about a small hard ball, which I will provide you, and extending the hand." He demonstrated, forcing her fingers upwards and apart so that she cried out involuntarily. "If you can discipline yourself to the point of actual discomfort, you are doing the exercise properly. We must stretch the tightened skin, the webbing between your fingers, and the stiffened tendons. I shall also provide a salve, which you are to rub well into the scar tissue to make it softer and more pliable. Conscientious effort on your part will determine the rate of progress. I suspect that you will be sufficiently motivated."

Before Menolly could stammer her thanks, the astonishing man was out of the room and closing the door behind him. Beauty made a sound —half quizzical chirp, half approving burble. She'd come loose from Menolly's neck during the examination, watching the proceedings from a depression in the sleeping furs. Now she walked over to Menolly and stroked her head against Menolly's arm.

From the apprentice's hall across the courtyard, the singing was renewed, with vigor and volume. Beauty cocked her head, humming with delight and then, when Menolly shushed her, looked wistfully up at the girl.

"I don't think we should sing again just now, but they do sound grand, don't they?"

She sat there, caressing Beauty, delighting in the music. Very close harmony, she realized approvingly, the sort only trained voices and well-rehearsed singers can achieve.

"Well," said Silvina, entering the room briskly, "you have stirred them up. It's good to hear that old rooter sung with some spirit."

Menolly had no time to register astonishment at Silvina's comment, for the headwoman poked at Menolly's bundle of things on the table, and twitched the sleeping rug into neat folds.

"We might just as well get you settled in Dunca's cottage now," Silvina continued. "Fortunately, there's an outside room unoccupied . . ." The headwoman wrinkled her nose in a slightly disparaging grimace. "Those holder girls are impossible about being outside, but it oughtn't to worry you." She smiled at Menolly. "Oldive says you're to keep off your feet, but some walking's got to be done. Still, you won't be in a chore section . . . another good reason to keep you at Dunca's, I suppose . . ." Silvina frowned and then looked back at Menolly's small bundle. "This is all you brought with you?"

"And nine fire lizards."

Silvina laughed. "An embarrassment of riches." She glanced out the window, peering across the courtyard to the far roof where the fire lizards were still sunning themselves. "They *do* stay where they're told, don't they?"

"Generally. But I'm not sure how good they are with too many people about or unusual noise."

"Or fascinating diversions . . ." Silvina smiled again at Menolly as she nodded towards the windows and the music issuing from the apprentices' hall.

"They always sang along with me . . . I didn't realize we shouldn't—"

"How should you? Not to worry, Menolly. You'll fit in here just fine. Now, let's wrap up your bundle and show you the way to Dunca's. Then Robinton wants you to borrow a gitar. Master Jerint is sure to have a spare usable one in the workshop. You'll have to make your own, you know. Unless you made one for Petiron at the Sea Hold?"

"I had none of my own." Menolly was relieved that she could keep her voice steady.

"But Petiron took his with him. Surely you . . ."

"I had the use of it, yes." Menolly managed to keep her tone even as she rigidly suppressed the memory of how she had lost the use, of the beating her father had given her for forbidden tuning, playing her own songs. "I made myself pipes . . ." she added, diverting Silvina from further questions. Rummaging in her bundle, she brought out the multiple pipes she had made in her cave by the sea.

"Reeds? And done with a belt knife by the look of them," said Silvina, walking to the window for more light as she turned the pipes in a critical examination. "Well done for just a belt knife." She returned the pipes to Menolly with an approving expression. "Petiron was a good teacher."

"Did you know him well?" Menolly felt a wave of grief at her loss of the only person in her home hold who had been interested in her.

"Indeed I did." Silvina gave Menolly a frown. "Did he not talk of the Harper Hall at all to you?"

"No. Why should he?"

"Why shouldn't he? He taught you, didn't he? He encouraged you to write. . . . Sent Robinton those songs . . ." Silvina stared at Menolly in real surprise for a long moment, then she shrugged with a little laugh. "Well, Petiron always had his own reasons for everything he did, and no one the wiser. But he was a good man!"

Menolly nodded, unable for a moment to speak, berating herself for ever once doubting, during those lonely miserable days at Half-Circle after Petiron's death, that he'd done what he said he'd do. Though the Old Harper's mind had taken to wandering. . . .

"Before I forget it," Silvina said, "how often do your fire lizards need to be fed?"

"They're hungriest in the morning, though they eat any time, but maybe that was because I had to hunt and catch food for them, and it took hours. The wild ones seemed to have no trouble . . ."

"Feed 'em once and they're always looking to you, is that it?" Silvina smiled, to soften any implied criticism. "The cooks throw all scraps into a big earthen jar in the cold room . . . most of it goes to the watchwhers, but I'll give orders that you're to have whatever you require."

"I don't mean to be a bother . . ."

Silvina gave her such a look that Menolly broke off her attempt to apologize.

"Be sure that when you *do* bother me, I'll inform you." Silvina grinned. "Just ask any of the apprentices if I won't."

Silvina had been leading Menolly down the steps and out of the cliffhold of the Harper Hall as she talked. Now they passed under an arch that gave onto a broad road of paving stones, never a blade of grass or spot of moss to be seen anywhere.

For the first time Menolly had a chance to appreciate the size of Fort Hold. Knowing that it was the oldest and largest Hold was quite different from seeing it, being outside the towering cliff.

Thousands of people must live in the cliffholds and cottages that hugged the rock palisade. Awed, Menolly's steps slowed as she stared at the wide ramp leading to the courtyard and main entrance of Fort

Hold, higher in the cliff face than the Harper Craft Hall, and with rows of windows extending upwards in sheer stone, almost to the fire heights themselves. In Half-Circle Sea Hold, everyone had been in the cliff, but at Fort Hold, stone buildings had been built out in wings from the cliff, forming a quadrangle similar to the Harper Craft Hall. Smaller cottages had been added onto the original wings, on either side of the ramp. There were dwellings bordering the sides of the broad paved road that led in several well-traveled directions; south to the fields and pastures, east down the valley towards the low foothills and west around to the pass in the cliff that would lead to the higher mountains of the Central Fort Range.

Silvina guided Menolly now towards a cottage, a good-sized one with five windows, all of them shuttered tight, on the upper floor. The cottage nestled against the slope of the ramp. As they got close enough, Menolly realized that the little cot was also quite old. And the cottage door was metal, too! Incredible! Silvina opened it, calling out for Dunca. Menolly had just time to notice that the metal door closed as the one at the Harper Hall did, with a small wheel throwing the thick rods into grooves in ceiling and floor.

"Menolly, come and meet Dunca who holds the cottage for the girls who study at the Harper Hall."

Menolly dutifully greeted the short, dumpy little woman with bright black eyes and cheeks like a puff-belly's sides. Dunca gave Menolly a raking look, at odds with her jolly appearance, as if measuring up Menolly to the gossip she'd already heard. Then Dunca saw Beauty peeking around Menolly's ear. She gave a shriek, jumping back.

"What's that?"

Menolly reached up to calm Beauty, who was hissing and raising her wings, getting one entangled in Menolly's hair.

"But, Dunca, surely you knew—" Silvina's voice chided the woman, "—that Menolly had Impressed fire lizards."

Menolly's sharp ear caught the edge to Silvina's voice, and so did the little queen, for Beauty thrummed softly and warningly in her throat as her eyes whirled at Dunca. Menolly silently called her to order.

"I'd *heard,* but I don't always credit things I'm *told,*" said Dunca, standing as far away from Menolly and Beauty as the hall permitted.

"Very wise of you," replied Silvina. The set of the headwoman's lips and the wary amusement in her glance told Menolly that Silvina was not overly fond of the little cotholder. "Now you've a windowed room vacant, have you not? I think it's best if we settled her there."

"I don't want another hysterical girl who'll panic during Threadfall and scare us all with imagining that Thread is actually *in* the cottage!"

Silvina's eyes danced with suppressed laughter as she glanced Menolly's way. "No, Menolly won't panic. She is, by the way, the youngest daughter of Sea Holder Yanus of Half-Circle Sea Hold, beholden to Benden Weyr. The sea breeds stern souls, you know."

Dunca's bright little eyes were almost lost in the folds of her eye flesh as she peered up at Menolly.

"So you knew Petiron, did you?"

"Yes, I did, Dunca."

The cotholder gave a disgusted snort and turned so quickly her full skirt followed in hasty swirls as she made for the stone steps carved into the wall at the back of the hallway. She kept twitching her skirt, grunting at the steepness of the risers as she heaved her small fat person upwards.

Two narrow corridors, lit at either end by dimming glows, went left and right from the stairwell. Dunca turned right, led them to the far end and threw open the last door on the outside.

"Lazy sluts," she said truculently, fumbling at the catch of the glowbasket. "They've cleared the glows."

"Where are they kept?" asked Menolly, wishing to ingratiate herself with the cotkeeper. Fleetingly she wondered if she'd always be trotting up and down narrow steps after glows.

"Where's your drudge, Dunca? It's her task to bring glows, not Menolly's," said Silvina as she walked past Dunca and flipped open first one, then a second set of shutters, flooding the room with sunlight.

"Silvina! What are you doing?"

"Threadfall's not for two more days, Dunca. Be sensible. The room's fusty."

Dunca's answer was a shriek as the other fire lizards swooped in through the opened window, diving about the room, chittering excitedly. There was nothing for them to cling to, since the walls were bare of hangings and the bed a frame, empty of rushes, the sleeping fur rolled up on the small press. The two green Aunties and blue Uncle fought for landing space on the stool and then zoomed out the window again as Dunca's screams startled them. The little cotholder cowered in the corner, skirts about her head, shrieking.

Menolly ordered the browns to stop diving, told Auntie One and Two and Uncle to stay on the window ledge, got Rocky and Diver to settle on the bedstead while Silvina calmed Dunca and led her from the corner. By the time the cotholder had been cajoled into watching Silvina handle Lazybones, who'd let anyone caress him so long as it involved no effort on his part, Menolly realized that Dunca would never be comfortable in their presence and that the woman disliked Menolly intensely for witnessing her fearfulness. For a long, sad moment, Menolly wished that she could have stayed at the Weyr where everyone could accept fire lizards equably.

She sighed softly to herself as she stroked Beauty, absently listening to Silvina's reassurances to Dunca that the fire lizards wouldn't harm anyone, not her, not her charges; that Dunca'd be the envy of every other cotholder in Fort to have nine fire lizards . . .

"Nine?" Dunca's protest came out in a terrified squeak, and she reached for her skirts to throw over her head. "Nine of those beastly things flitting and diving about *my* home—"

"They don't like to stay inside, except at night," said Menolly, hoping to reassure Dunca. "They're rarely all with me at one time."

From the horrified and malicious look Dunca gave her, Menolly realized that she herself would be rarely with Dunca if the cotholder had anything to say in the matter.

"We can stop here no longer now, Menolly. You've to pick a gitar from the workshop," said Silvina. "If you need more rushes, Dunca, you've only to send your woman to the Hall," she added as she motioned Menolly to precede her from the room. "Menolly will be more closely involved with the Hall than the other girls . . ."

"She's to be back here at shutter time, same as the others, or stay at the Hall," said Dunca as Silvina and Menolly went down the steps.

"She's strict with the girls," Silvina remarked as they emerged into the bright midday sun and started across the broad paved square, "but that's to the good with all those lads vying for their attention. And take no heed to her grumbles over Petiron. She'd hoped to wed him after Merelan died. *I'd* say Petiron resigned as Fort Hold Harper as much to get free of Dunca as to clear the way for Robinton. He was so very proud that his son was elected Masterharper."

"Half-Circle Sea Hold is a long way from Fort Hold."

Silvina chuckled. "And one of the few places isolated enough to prevent Dunca from following him, child. As if Petiron would ever have taken another woman after Merelan. She was the loveliest person, a voice of unusual beauty and range. Ah, I miss her still."

More people were about: field workers coming in for their midday meal; a party of men on leggy runners, slowing to an amble through the crowd. An apprentice, intent on his errand, ran right into Menolly. He was mouthing an apology when Beauty, peering through Menolly's hair, hissed at him. He yelped, ducked with an apprentice's well-developed instinct, and went pelting back the way he'd come.

Silvina laughed. "I'd like to hear his tale when he gets back to his hall."

"Silvina, I'm—"

"Not a word, Menolly! I will not have you apologizing for your fire lizards. Nor will Master Robinton. There will always be fools in the world like Dunca, fearful of anything new or strange." They had entered the archway of the Harper Hall. "Through that door, across the stairhall, and you'll find the workshop. Master Jerint is in charge. He'll find you an instrument so you can play for Master Domick. He'll meet you there." With an encouraging pat and a smile, Silvina left her.

Chapter 3

Speak softly to my lizard fair
Nor raise your hand to me.
For they are quick to take offense
And quicker to champion me.

Menolly wished that Silvina had stayed long enough to introduce her to Master Jerint, but she guiltily realized how much of the headwoman's valuable time she had already had. So, squaring her shoulders against her ridiculous surge of nervousness, Menolly entered the square stairhall and saw the door that must lead to the workshop of Master Jerint.

She could hear the sounds of workshop industry: hammering, the scrape of saw on wood, toots and thumps; but the instant she opened the door, she and Beauty got the full impact of various noises of tuning, sanding, sawing, pounding, the twanging of tough wherhide being stretched over drum frames and snapping back. Beauty let out a penetrating shriek of complaint and took off, straight for the bracing beams of the high ceilinged workshop. Her raucous call and her flight suspended all activity in the room. The sudden silence, and then the whisperings of the younger workers, all staring at Menolly, attracted the attention of the older man who was bent almost double, glueing a crucial piece of inlay on the gitar in his lap. He looked up and around at the staring apprentices.

"What? Well?"

Beauty gave another cry, launching herself from the rafter beam back to Menolly's shoulder now that the distressing sounds had ceased.

"Who made that appalling noise? It was animal, not instrumental."

Menolly didn't see anyone pointing at her, but suddenly Master Jerint was made aware of her presence by the door.

"Yes? What are you doing here? And what's that thing on your shoulder? You oughtn't to be carting pets about, whatever it is. It isn't allowed. Well, lad, speak up!"

Titters in various parts of the workroom indicated to the man that he was in some error.

"Please, sir, if you're Master Jerint, I'm Menolly . . ."

"If you're Menolly, then you're no lad."

"No, sir."

"And I've been expecting you. At least, I think so." He peered down at the inlay he'd been glueing as if accusing the inanimate object of his absentmindedness. "What is that thing on your shoulder? Did it make that noise?"

"Yes, because she was startled, sir."

"Yes, the noise in here would startle anyone with hearing and wit." Jerint sounded approving and now craned his head forward, withdrawing the instant Beauty gave one of her little chirps and frowning in surprise that she reacted to his curiosity. "So she is one of those mythical fire lizards?" He acted skeptical.

"I named her Beauty, Master Jerint," Menolly said, determined to win other friends for her fire lizards that day. She firmly unwound Beauty's tail from her neck and coaxed her to her forearm. "She likes to have her headknob stroked. . . ."

"Does she?" Jerint caressed the glowing golden creature. Beauty closed the inner lid of her brilliant eyes and submitted completely to the Master's touch. "She does."

"She's really very friendly, it's just all that noise and so many people."

"Well, I find her quite friendly," Jerint replied, one long calloused and glue-covered finger stroking the little queen with growing confidence as Beauty began to hum with pleasure. "Very friendly indeed. Are dragons' skins as soft as hers?"

"Yes, sir."

"Charming creature. Quite charming. Much more practical than dragons."

"She sings, too," said a stocky man sauntering from the back of the hall, wiping his hands on a towel as he came.

As if this newcomer released a hidden spring, a murmurous wave of half giggle, half excited whisperings rippled through the apprentices. The man nodded at Menolly.

"Sings?" asked Jerint, pausing in mid-caress so that Beauty butted her nose at his hand. He continued to stroke the now coyly curved neck. "She sings, Domick?"

"Surely you heard this morning's glorious descant, Jerint?"

This stocky man was Master Domick for whom she must play? True, he wore an old tunic with a faded journeyman's markings, but no journeyman would have addressed a master by his bare name nor would he be so self-assured.

"This morning's descant?" Jerint blinked with surprise, and some of the bolder apprentices chortled at his confusion. "Yes, I remember thinking the pitch was a bit unusual for pipes, and besides that Saga is traditionally sung without accompaniment, but then Brudegan is always improvising . . ." He gave an irritable wave of his hand.

Beauty reared up on Menolly's arm, startled into fanning her wings for balance and digging her hind talons painfully through Menolly's thin sleeve.

"Didn't mean you, you pretty thing," Jerint said by way of apology and caressed Beauty's headknob until she'd subsided to her former position. "But all that sound from this little creature?"

"How many were actually singing, Menolly?" asked Master Domick.

"Only five," she replied reservedly, thinking of Dunca's reaction to the figure nine.

"Only five of them?"

The droll tone made her glance apprehensively at the stocky Master, wondering if he were taunting her, since the half-smile on his face gave her no real hint.

"Five!" Master Jerint rocked back on his heels with amazement. "*You* . . . have five fire lizards?"

"Actually, sir, to be truthful . . ."

"It is wiser to be truthful, Menolly," agreed Master Domick, and he was teasing her, not too kindly either.

"I Impressed nine fire lizards," said Menolly in a rush, "because, you see, Thread was falling outside the cave, and the only way I could keep the hatchlings from leaving and getting killed by Thread was to feed them and that . . ."

"Impressed them, of course," Domick finished for her, when she faltered because Master Jerint was wide-eyed with astonishment and incredulity. "You will really have to add another verse to your song, Menolly, or possibly two."

"The Masterharper has edited that song as he feels necessary, Master Domick," she said with what she hoped was quiet dignity.

A slow smile spread across the man's face.

"It is wiser to be truthful, Menolly. Didn't you train all your fire lizards to sing?"

"I didn't actually train them, sir. I played my pipes, and they'd sing along . . ."

"Speaking of pipes, Jerint, this girl has to have an instrument until she can make one herself. Or didn't Petiron have enough wood to teach you, girl?"

"He *explained* how . . ." Menolly replied. Did Master Domick think Sea Holder Yanus would have wasted precious timber for a *girl* to make a harper's instrument?

"We'll see in due time how well you absorbed that explanation. In the meantime, Menolly needs a gitar to play for me and to practice on . . ." He drawled the last two words, his stern glance sweeping around the room at all the watchers.

Everyone was suddenly exceedingly occupied in their interrupted tasks, and the resultant energetic blows, twangs and whistles made Beauty spread her wings and screech in protest.

"I can hardly fault her," said Domick as Menolly soothed the fire lizard.

"What an extraordinary range of sounds she can make," remarked Master Jerint.

"A gitar for Menolly? So we can judge the range of sounds *she* can make?" Domick reminded the man in a bored tone.

"Yes, yes, there's any number of instruments to choose from," said Jerint, walking with jerky steps towards the courtyard side of the L-shaped room.

And indeed there were, Menolly realized as they approached the corner clutter of drums, pipes, harps of several sizes and designs, and gitars. The instruments depended from hooks set in the stone and cords attached to the ceiling beams, or sat dustily on shelves, the layers of dust increasing as the instruments went beyond easy range.

"A gitar, you said?" Jerint squinted at the assortment and reached for a gitar, its wood bright with new varnish.

"Not that one." The words were out before Menolly realized how brash she must sound.

"Not this one?" Jerint, arm still upraised, looked at her. "Why not?" He sounded huffy, but his eyes narrowed slightly as he regarded her; there was nothing of the slightly absent-minded craftsman about Master Jerint now.

"It's too green to have any tone."

"How would you know by looking?"

So, thought Menolly, this is a sort of test for me.

"I wouldn't choose any instrument on looks, Master Jerint, I'd choose by the sound, but I can see from here that the wood of that gitar is badly joined on the case. The neck is not straight for all it's been veneered prettily."

The answer evidently pleased him, for he stepped aside and gestured to her to make her own selection. She picked the strings of one gitar resting against the shelves and absently shook her head, looking further. She saw a case, its wherhide worn but well-oiled. Glancing back at the two men for permission, she opened it and lifted out the gitar; her hands caressed the thin smooth wood, her fingers curling appreciatively about the neck. She placed it before her, running her fingers down the strings, across the opening. Almost reverently she struck a chord, smiling at the mellow sound. Beauty warbled in harmony to the chord she struck and then chirruped happily. Menolly carefully replaced the gitar.

"Why do you put it back? Wouldn't you choose it?" asked Jerint sharply.

"Gladly, sir, but that gitar must belong to a master. It's too good to practice on."

Domick let out a burst of laughter and clapped Jerint on the shoulder.

"No one could have told her that one's yours, Jerint. Go on, girl, find one just bad enough to practice on but good enough for you to use."

She tried several others, more conscious than ever that she had to choose well. One sounded sweet to her, but the tuning knobs were so worn that the strings would not keep their pitch through a song. She was beginning to wonder if there was a playable instrument in the lot when she spotted one depending from a hook, almost lost in the shadows of the wall. One string was broken, but when she chorded around the missing note, the tone was silky and sweet. She ran her hands around the sound box and was pleased with the feel of the thin wood. The careful hand of its creator had put an intricate pattern of lighter shades of wood around the opening. The tuning knobs were of newer wood than the rest of the gitar but, except for the missing string, it was the best of all but Master Jerint's.

"I'd like to use this one, if I may?" She held it towards Jerint.

The Master nodded slowly, approvingly, ignoring Domick, who gave him a clout on the shoulder. "I'll get you a new E string . . ." And Jerint turned to a set of drawers at one end of the shelves, rummaged a moment and brought out a carefully coiled length of gut.

As the string was already looped, she slipped it over the hook, lined it over the bridge and up the neck into the hole of the tuning knob. She was very conscious of intent scrutiny and tried to keep her hands from trembling. She tuned the new string first to the next one, then to the others and struck a true chord; the mellowness of the sound reassured her that she had chosen well.

"Now that you have demonstrated that you can choose well, string and tune, let's see if you can *play* the gitar of your choice," said Domick, and taking her by the elbow, steered her from the workroom.

She had only time to nod her thanks to Master Jerint as the door slammed behind her. Still gripping her arm and unperturbed by

Beauty's hissing, Domick propelled her up the stairs and into a rectangular room built over the entrance archway. It must serve a dual purpose as an office and an additional schoolroom, to judge by the sandtable, the record bins, the wall writing board and the shelves of stored instruments. There were stools pulled back against the walls, but there were also three leathered couches, the first that Menolly had ever seen, with time-darkened armrests and backs, some patched where the original hide had been replaced. Two wide windows, with folding metal shutters, overlooked the broad road to the Hold on one side, the courtyard on the other.

"Play for me," Domick said, gesturing for her to take a stool as he collapsed into the couch facing the hearth.

His tone was expressionless, his manner so non-committal that Menolly felt he didn't expect her to be able to play at all. What little confidence she had gained when she had apparently chosen unexpectedly well ebbed from her. Unnecessarily she struck a tuning chord, fiddled with the knob on the new string, trying to decide what to play to prove her competence. For she was determined to surprise this Master Domick who teased and taunted and didn't like her having nine fire lizards.

"Don't sing," Domick added. "And I want no distraction from her." He pointed to Beauty still on Menolly's shoulder. "Just that." He jabbed his finger at the gitar and then folded his hands across his lap, waiting.

His tone stung Menolly's pride awake. With no further thought, she struck the opening chords of the "Ballad of Moreta's Ride" and had the satisfaction of seeing his eyebrows lift in surprise. The chording was tricky enough when voices carried the melody, but to pluck the tune as well as the accompaniment increased the difficulty. She did strike several sour chords because her left hand could not quite make the extensions or respond to the rapid shifts of harmony required, but she kept the rhythm keen and the fingers of her right hand flicked out the melody loud and true through the strumming.

She half-expected him to stop her after the first verse and chorus, but, as he made no sign, she continued, varying the harmony and substituting an alternative fingering where her left hand had faltered. She had launched into the third repetition when he leaned forward and caught her right wrist.

"Enough gitar," he said, his expression inscrutable. Then he snapped his fingers at her left hand, which she extended in slow obedience. It ached. He turned it palm up, tracing the thick scar so lightly that the tickling sensation made her spine twitch in reaction though she forced herself to keep still. He grunted, noticing where her exertions had split the edge of the wound. "Oldive seen that hand yet?"

"Yes, sir."

"And recommended some of his sticky smelly salves, no doubt. If they work, you'll be able to stretch for the fingerings you missed in the first verse."

"I hope so."

"So do I. You're not supposed to take liberties with the Teaching Ballads and Sagas—"

"So Petiron taught me," she replied with an equally expressionless voice, "but the minor seventh in the second measure is an alternative chording in the Record at Half-Circle Sea Hold."

"An old variation."

Menolly said nothing, but she knew from his very sourness that she had played very well indeed, despite her hand, and that Domick didn't want to be complimentary.

"Now, what other instruments did Petiron teach you to play?"

"Drum, of course."

"Yes, of course. There's a small tambour behind you."

She demonstrated the basic drum rolls, and at his request did a more complex drum dance beat, popular with and peculiar to seaholders. Though his expression remained bland, she saw his fingers twitch in time with the beat and was inwardly pleased by that reaction. Next, she played a simple lullaby on the lap harp, well suited to the light sweet tone of the instrument. He told her he would assume that she could play the great harp but the octave reaches would place too great a strain on her left hand. He handed her an alto pipe, took a tenor one and had her play harmony to his melody line. That was fun, and she could have continued indefinitely because it was so stimulating to play duet.

"Did you have brass at the Sea Hold?"

"Only the straight horn, but Petiron explained the theory of valves, and he said that I could develop a good lip with more practice."

"I'm glad to hear he didn't neglect brass." Domick rose. "Well, I can place your instrumental standard. Thank you, Menolly. You may be dismissed for the midday meal."

With some regret, Menolly reached for the gitar. "Should I return this to Master Jerint now?"

"Of course not." His expression was still cool, almost rude. "You got it to practice on, remember. And, despite all you know, you will need to practice."

"Master Domick, whose was this?" She asked the question in a rush, because she had a sudden notion it might be his, which could account for some of his curious antagonism.

"That one? That was Robinton's journeyman's gitar." Then, with a broad grin at her astonishment, Master Domick quit the room.

Menolly remained, still caught by surprise and dismay at her temerity, holding the now doubly precious gitar against her. Would Master Robinton be annoyed, as Master Domick seemed to be, that she had chosen his gitar? Commonsense reasserted itself. Master Robinton had much finer instruments now, of course, or why else would his journeyman's effort be hidden among Jerint's spares? Then the humor of her choice struck her: of all the gitars there, she had picked the discarded instrument of the Masterharper. Small wonder he was Harper here if this fine gitar had been made when he was still young. She strummed lightly, head bent to catch the sweet mellow quality, smiling as she listened to the soft notes die away. Beauty chirped approvingly from her perch on the shelf. Chirpy echoes about the room apprised her that the other fire lizards had sneaked in.

They all roused and took wing, squeaking, as a loud bell, seemingly right overhead, began to toll. The sharp notes punctuated a pandemonium that erupted from the rooms below and into the courtyard. Apprentices and journeymen, released from their morning classes, spilled into the courtyard, all making the best possible speed to the dining hall, jostling, pushing and shouting in such an excess of spirits that Menolly gasped in surprise. Why some of them must be over twenty Turns old. No seaholder would act that way! Boys of fifteen Turns, her age, were already serving on boats at the Sea Hold. Of course, an exhausting day at sail lines and nets left little energy to expend on running or laughing. Perhaps that was why her parents couldn't appreciate her music—it wouldn't appear to be hard work to them. Menolly shook her hands, letting them flap from her wrists. They ached and trembled from the constricted movements and tension of an hour of intensive playing. No, her parents would never understand that playing musical instruments could be as hard work as sailing or fishing.

And she was just as hungry as if she'd been trawling. She hesitated, gitar in hand. She wouldn't have time to take it back to her room in the cottage. No one in the yard seemed to be carrying instruments. So she put the gitar carefully in a vacant spot on a high shelf, told Beauty and the others to remain where they were. She could just imagine what would happen if she brought her fire lizards to that dining hall. As bad as the noise was now . . .

Suddenly the courtyard was empty of hurrying folk. She took the stairs as fast as her feet could go and crossed the courtyard with a fair approximation of her normal swinging stride, hoping to enter the dining room unobtrusively. She reached the wide doorway and halted. The hall seemed overly full of bodies, standing in rigid attention at the long tables. Those facing the windows stood taut with expectation while those facing the inner wall seemed to be staring hard at the corner on her right. She was about to look when a hissing to her left attracted her. There was Camo, gesturing and grimacing at her to take one of the three vacant seats at the window table. As quickly as possible, she slid in place.

"Hey," said the small boy next to her, without moving his head in her direction, "you shouldn't be here. You should be over there. With them!" He jerked his finger at the long table nearest the hearth.

Craning her head to peer past the screening bodies, Menolly saw the sedate row of girls, backs to the hearth. There was an empty seat at one end.

"No!" The boy grabbed at her hand. "Not now!"

Obeying some signal Menolly couldn't see, everyone was seated at that precise moment.

"Pretty Beauty? Where's pretty Beauty?" asked a worried voice at her elbow. "Beauty not hungry?" It was Camo, in each hand a heavy platter piled with roast meat slices.

"Take it quick," said the boy beside her, giving her a dig in the ribs. Menolly did so.

"Well, get yours and pass it," the boy went on.

"Don't just sit there like a dummy," added the black-haired lad opposite her, frowning fiercely and shifting his buttocks on the hard wood of the bench.

"Hey, grab; don't gab," ordered another lad, further up the table with considerable irritation at the delay.

Menolly mumbled something, and rather than waste time fumbling for her belt knife, she tweaked the topmost slice from the platter to her plate. The boy across from her deftly snagged four slices on his knife point and transferred them, dripping juices, to his plate. The boy beside her struggled with the heavy platter, taking four slices, too, as he passed it on.

"Should you take so much?" she asked, her surprise at such greed overcoming reticence.

"You don't starve in the Harper Hall." He said, grinning broadly. He sliced the first piece into halves, folded one half over neatly with his blade and then shoved it into his mouth, catching the juices with his finger, which he managed to lick despite the mouthful he was busy chewing.

His assurance was borne out by the deep bowl of tubers and roots, and the basket of sliced breads, which Camo deposited beside her. From these Menolly helped herself more liberally, passing the dishes along as quickly as she could.

"You're Menolly, aren't you?" asked the boy beside her, his mouth still full.

She nodded.

"Was it really your fire lizards singing this morning?"

"Yes."

Whatever lingering embarrassment for that incident Menolly retained was dispersed in the giggle from her table companion and the sly grins of those near enough to overhear the conversation.

"You should've seen Bruddie's face!"

"Bruddie?"

"Journeyman Brudegan to us apprentices, of course. He's choir leader this season. First he thought it was me pulling a stunt, 'cause I sing high treble. So he stood right beside me. I didn't know what was up, a'course. Then he went on to Feldon and Bonz, and that's when I could hear what was happening." The boy had so engaging a grin that Menolly found herself smiling back. "Shells, but Bruddie jumped about. He couldn't trace the sound. Then one of the basses pointed out the window!" The boy chortled, suppressing the sound when it rose above the general level of table noise. "How'd you train 'em to do that, huh? I didn't know you could get fire lizards to sing. Dragon'll hum, but only when it's Hatching time. Can *anyone* teach a fire lizard to sing? And do you really have eleven all your own?"

"I've only got nine—"

"Only nine, she says," and the boy rolled his eyes, encouraging his tablemates to second his envious response. "I'm Piemur," he added as an afterthought of courtesy.

"She shouldn't be here," complained the lad immediately opposite Menolly. He spoke directly to Piemur, as if by ignoring Menolly he could be rude. He was bigger and older looking than Piemur. "She belongs over there with them." And he jerked his head backwards, toward the girls at the hearth table.

"Well, she's here now, and fine where she is, Ranly," said Piemur with unexpected aggressiveness. "She couldn't very well change once we were seated, could she? And besides, I heard that she's to be an apprentice, same as us. *Not* one of them."

"Aren't they apprentices?" asked Menolly, inclining her head in the girls' general direction.

"Them?" Piemur's astonished query was as scornful as the look on

Ranly's face. "No!" The drawl in his negative put the girls in an inferior category. "They're in the special class with the journeymen, but they're not apprentices. No road!"

"They're a right nuisance," said Ranly with rich contempt.

"Yeah, they are," said Piemur with a reflective sigh, "but if they weren't here, I'd have to sing treble in the plays, and that'd be dire! Hey, Bonz, pass the meat back." Suddenly he let out a startled yip. "Feldon! I asked first. You've no right . . ." A boy had taken the last slice as he handed down the platter.

The other boys shushed Piemur vigorously, darting apprehensive glances towards the right corner.

"But it's not fair. *I* asked," Piemur said, lowering his voice slightly but not his insistence. "And Menolly only had one slice. She should get more than *that!*"

Menolly wasn't certain if Piemur was more outraged on her behalf or his own, but someone nudged her right arm. It was Camo.

"Camo feed pretty Beauty?"

"Not now, Camo. They're not hungry now," Menolly assured him because his thick features registered such anxiety.

"They're not hungry, but she is, Camo," Piemur said, shoving the meat platter at Camo. "More meat, Camo. More meat, please, Camo?"

"More meat please," Camo repeated, jerking his head to his chest; and before Menolly could say anything, he had shuffled off to the corner of the dining hall where sliding shelves brought food directly up from the kitchen.

The boys were sniggering with the success of Piemur's stratagem, but they wiped their faces clear of amusement when Camo shuffled back with a well-laden platter.

"Thank you very much, Camo," Menolly said, taking another thick slice. She couldn't fault the boys for their greed. The meat was tasty and tender, quite different from the tough or salted stuff she was used to at Half-Circle Sea Hold.

Another slab was dumped onto her plate.

"You don't eat enough," Piemur said, scowling at her. "Too bad she'll have to sit with the others," he told his tablemates as he passed the platter. "Camo likes her. And her fire lizards."

"Did he really feed them with you?" asked Ranly. He sounded doubtful and envious.

"They don't frighten him," Menolly said, amazed at how fast news of everything spread in this place.

"They wouldn't frighten me," Piemur and Ranly assured her on the same breath.

"Say, you were at Impression at Benden Weyr, weren't you?" asked Piemur, nudging Ranly to be silent. "Did you *see* Lord Jaxom Impress the white dragon? How big is he really? Is he going to live?"

"I was at the Impression . . ."

"Well, don't go off in a trance," said Ranly. "Tell us! All we get is secondhand information. That is, if the masters and journeymen *think* we apprentices ought to know." He sounded sour and disgusted.

"Oh, shell it, Ranly," Piemur suggested. "So what happened, Menolly?"

"I was in the tiers, and Lord Jaxom was sitting below me with an older man and another boy . . ."

"That'd be Lord Warder Lytol, who's raised him, and the boy was probably Felessan. He's the son of the Weyrleader and Lessa."

"I know that, Piemur. Go on, Menolly."

"Well, all the other dragon eggs had hatched, and there was just the little one left. Jaxom suddenly got up and ran along the edge of the tier, shouting for help. Then he jumped onto the Hatching Ground and started kicking the egg and slashing at the thick membrane inside. The next thing, the little white dragon had fallen out and . . ."

"Impression!" Piemur finished for her, bringing his hands together. "Just like I told you, Ranly, you simply have to be in the right place at the right time. Luck, that's all it is. Luck!" Piemur seemed to be pressing an old argument with his friend. "Some people got a lot of luck; some don't." He turned back to Menolly. "I heard you were daughter of the Sea Holder at Half-Circle."

"I'm in the Harper Hall now, aren't I?"

Piemur stretched out his hands as if that should end the discussion.

Menolly turned back to her dinner. Just as she finished mopping the last of the juices on her plate with bread, the shimmering sound of a gong brought instant silence to the hall. A single bench scraped across the stone floor as a journeyman rose from the top oval table at the far end of the hall.

"Afternoon assignments are: by the sections; apprentice hall, 10; yard, 9; Hold, 8; and no sweeping behind the doors this time or you'll do an extra half-day. Section 7, barns; 6, 5 and 4, fields; 3 is assigned to the Hold and 2 and 1 to the cothalls. Those who reported sick this morning are to attend Master Oldive. Players are not to be late this evening, and the call is for the twentieth hour."

The man sat down to the accompaniment of exaggerated sighs of relief, groans of complaint and mumbles.

Piemur was not pleased. "The yard again!" Then he turned to Menolly. "Anyone mention a section number to you?"

"No," Menolly replied, although Silvina had mentioned the term. "Not yet," she added as she caught Ranly's black stare.

"You have all the luck."

The gong broke through the rumble of reaction, and the bench under Menolly began to move out from under her. Everyone was rising, so Menolly had to rise, too. But she stood in place as the others swarmed by, milling to pass through the main entrance, laughing, shoving, complaining. Two boys started gathering plates and mugs, and Menolly, at a loss, reached for a plate to have it snatched out of her hand by an indignant lad.

"Hey, you're not in my section," he said in an accusing tone, tinged with surprise, and went about his task.

Menolly jumped at a light touch on her shoulder, stared and then apologized to the man who had come up beside her.

"You are Menolly?" he asked, a hint of displeasure in his tone. He had such a high-bridged nose that he seemed to have difficulty focusing beyond it. His face was lined with dissatisfaction, and a sallow complexion set off by greying locks tinged with yellow did nothing to alter the general impression he gave of supercilious discontent.

"Yes, sir, I'm Menolly."

"I am Master Morshal, Craftmaster in Musical Theory and Composition. Come, girl, one can't hear oneself think in this uproar," and he took her by the arm and began to lead her from the Hall, the throng of boys parting before him, as if they felt his presence and wished to avoid any encounter. "The Masterharper wants my opinion on your knowledge of musical theory."

Menolly was given to understand by the tone of his voice that the Masterharper relied on Master Morshal's opinion in this and other far more important matters. And she also gathered the distinct impression that Morshal didn't expect her to know very much.

Menolly was sorry she had eaten so heartily because the food was beginning to weigh uneasily in her stomach. Morshal was obviously already predisposed against her.

"Pssst! Menolly!" A hoarse whisper attracted her attention to one side. Piemur ducked out from behind a taller boy, jerked his thumb upwards in an easily interpreted gesture of encouragement. He rolled his eyes at the oblivious Morshal, grinned impudently and then popped out of sight in his group.

But the gesture heartened her. Funny-looking kid, Piemur was, with his tangle of tight black curls, missing half a front tooth and by far the smallest of the apprentice lot. How kind of him to reassure her.

When Menolly realized that Master Morshal must be taking her to the archroom, she sent a mental command to the fire lizards to stay quiet or go find a sunny roof until she called them again. There wasn't so much as a rustle or a chirp when she and Morshal entered. With a resigned attitude, he seated himself on the only backed chair at the sandtable. As he didn't indicate that she could seat herself, she remained standing.

"Now, recite for me the notes in a C major chord," he said.

She did so. He regarded her steadily for a moment, and blinked.

"What notes would comprise a major fifth in C?"

When she had answered that, he began to fire questions at her, irritable if she paused, however briefly, to reply, but Petiron had drilled her too often the same way. Morshal's bored expression was disconcerting but, as his queries became more and more complex, she suddenly realized that he was taking examples from various traditional Sagas and Ballads. Once he mentioned the signature and which chord, it was simple enough for her to visualize the record hide and recite from memory.

Suddenly he grunted and then murmured in his throat. Abruptly he asked her if she'd been taught the drum. When she admitted some knowledge, he asked tedious questions about basic beats in each time factor. How would she vary the beat? Now, as to finger positions on a tenor pipe, what closures did one make for a chord in F? He took her through scales again. She could have demonstrated more quickly, but he gave her no chance to suggest it.

"Stand still, girl," he said testily as she shifted her throbbing feet. "Shoulders back, feet together, girl, head up." He heard a soft twitter, but as he'd been glaring at Menolly, it was obvious she hadn't opened her lips. He glanced about, to seek the source, as Menolly silently reassured Beauty and urged silence. "Don't slouch. What was my question?"

She told him, and he continued the barrage. The more she answered, the more he asked. Her feet were aching so that she had to ask permission to sit, if only briefly. But, to her amazement, before she could, Morshal abruptly stabbed a finger at the stool next to him. She hesitated, not quite believing the gesture.

"Sit! sit! sit!" he said in an excess of irritation at her delay. "Now, let's see if you know anything about writing down what you've been repeating so glibly."

So she'd been answering correctly, and he was annoyed because she knew so much. Her flagging spirits lifted, and as Master Morshal dictated musical notations, her fingers drove the pointer quickly over the sands. In her mind, a different, kinder voice dictated; and the exercise became a game, rather than an examination by a prejudiced judge.

"Well, move back so I can see what you've written." Morshal's testy voice recalled her to the present.

He peered at her inscriptions, pursed his lips, humphed and sat back. He gestured peremptorily for her to smooth the sand surface and rapidly gave her another set of chords. They included some difficult modulations and time values, but after the first two, she recognized the "Riddle Song" and was very glad Petiron had made her learn the haunting tune.

"That's enough of that," Master Morshal said, drawing his overtunic about him with quick, angry motions. "Now, have you an instrument?"

"Yes, sir."

"Then get it and that third score from the top shelf. Over there. Be quick about it."

Menolly hissed to herself as she stepped on her throbbing feet. Sitting had not relieved the swelling, and her feet felt thick at the ankles and stiff.

"Hurry up, girl. Don't waste my time."

Beauty gave a soft hiss, too, from her perch on the top shelf, unlidding her eyes, and from the rustling sounds in the same general area, Menolly knew the other fire lizards had roused. With her back to Master Morshal, she gestured to Beauty to close her eyes and be quiet. She cringed at the thought of Master Morshal's probable reaction to fire lizards.

"I said to hurry, girl."

She shuffled to the place where she had laid the gitar and hurried back with instrument and music. The Master took the hides, his lips twitching with annoyance as he turned the thick leaves. This was new copying, Menolly saw, for the hide was almost white and the notes clear and easily read. The hide edges were neatly trimmed, too, the lines going from margin to margin, to be sure, but no notes lost in decayed edges.

"There! Play me that!" The music was slid across the sandtable with —Menolly thought, somewhat shocked—complete disregard for the value of the work.

By some freak of chance, Master Morshal had chosen the "Ballad of Moreta's Ride." She'd never manage the verse chords as written, and he'd fault her if she couldn't.

"Sir, my . . ." she began, holding out her left hand.

"I want no excuses. Either you can play it as written or I assume that you are unable to perform a traditional work to a creditable standard."

Menolly ran her fingers across the strings to see if the tuning had held.

"Come, come. If you can read written scores, you can play them."

That was assuming a lot, Menolly thought to herself. But she struck the opening chords and, mindful that he was undoubtedly waiting for her to falter, she played the so well-known Ballad according to the score before her, rather than by rote. There were variations in the chords: two of which were easily managed, but she flubbed the fourth and fifth because her scarred hand would not stretch.

"I see, I see," he said, waving her to stop, but he looked oddly pleased. "You cannot play accurately at tempo. Very well, that is all. You are dismissed."

"I beg your pardon, Master Morshal . . ." Menolly began, again extending her hand as explanation.

"You what?" He glared at her, his eyes wide with incredulity that she seemed to be defying him. "Out! I just dismissed you! What is the world coming to when *girls* presume to be harpers and pretend to compose music! Out! Great shells and stars!" His voice changed from scold to panic. "What's that? What are they? Who let them in here?"

Already making her way down the steps, Menolly lost her anger with him at the fright in his voice. His anger had roused her friends, and since she was apparently in danger, they had rushed to protect her, by squeaking and diving at him. She laughed as she heard the slamming of a heavy door, and as instantly regretted the scene. Master Morshal would be against her, and that would not make her life easy in the Harper Hall. "Nothing to fear from harpers?" Was that what T'gellan had said last night? Maybe not *fear,* but certainly she was going to have to be cautious with them. Perhaps she ought not to have been so knowledgeable about music; that had irritated him. But wasn't that knowledge what he was testing? Once again, she wondered if there really was a place for her here? *Presume to be a harper?* No, she hadn't, and it was up to Master Robinton, wasn't it? Were Master Morshal and Master Domick part of the conventional procedures Master Robinton had mentioned? Even if she needn't have much to do with them, she sensed their antagonism and dislike.

She sighed and turned on the landing for the second flight and stopped. Piemur was in the hall, motionless, his eyes enormous as he followed the excited flitting of the fire lizards. Lazy and Uncle had subsided to the banister.

"I'm not seeing things?" he asked her, watching Lazy and Uncle with apprehensive gaze. From the hand held rigid at his side, the forefinger indicated the two fire lizards.

"No, you're not. The brown one is Lazy, and the blue is Uncle."

His eyes followed the flight of the others a moment longer, trying to count. Then they popped out further as Beauty landed daintily on Menolly's shoulder, in her usual position.

"This is Beauty, the queen."

"Yes, she is, isn't she?" Piemur kept staring as Menolly descended to the floor level.

Beauty stretched her neck, her eyes whirling gently as she returned his look. Suddenly she blinked her eyes, and so so did Piemur, which made Menolly giggle.

"No wonder Camo was cracking his shell over her." Then Piemur shook himself, all over, like a fire lizard shedding seawater. "I was sent to bring you to Master Shonagar."

"Who's he?" asked Menolly, weary enough from the session with Master Morshal.

"Old Marshface give you a hard time? Don't worry about it. You'll like Master Shonagar; he's my Master, he's the Voice Master. He's the best." Piemur's face lit up with real enthusiasm. "And *he* said that if you can sing half as well as your fire lizards do, you're an assss . . . atest . . . ?"

"Asset?" It amused Menolly to be so considered by anyone.

"That's the word. And he said that it didn't really matter if you croaked like a watchwher, so long as you could get the fire lizards to sing. Do you think she likes me?" he added, for he hadn't stopped staring at Beauty. Nor had he moved.

"Why not?"

"She keeps staring at me so, and her eyes are whirling." He gestured absently with one hand.

"You're staring at her."

Piemur blinked again and looked at Menolly, smiling shyly and giggling a bit self-consciously. "Yeah, I was, wasn't I? Sorry about that, Beauty. I know it's rude, but I've always wanted to see a fire lizard! Hey, Menolly, c'mon," and now Piemur moved off at a half-run, gesturing urgently for Menolly to follow him across the courtyard. "Master Shonagar's waiting, and I know you're new here, but you don't ever keep a master waiting. And say, can you keep them from following us, 'cause they might sing, and Master Shonagar did say it was you he wanted to hear sing today, not them again."

"They'll be quiet if I ask them to."

"Ranly, he sat across the table from you, he's from Crom and he's so smart, he says they only mimic."

"Oh no, they don't."

"Glad to hear that, because I told him they're just as smart as dragons, and he wouldn't believe me." Piemur had been leading her towards the big hall where the chorus had been practicing that morning. "Hurry up, Menolly. Masters hate to be kept waiting, and I've been gone awhiles tracking you down."

"I can't walk fast," Menolly said, gritting her teeth at the pain of each step.

"You sure are walking funny. What's the matter with your feet?"

Menolly wondered that he hadn't heard that tidbit of news. "I got caught away from the cave just at Threadfall. I had to run for safety."

Piemur's eyes threatened to bulge out of their sockets. "You ran?" His voice squeaked. "Ahead of Thread?"

"I ran my shoes off my feet and the skin as well."

Menolly had no chance to speak further because Piemur had brought her to the hall door. Before she could adjust her eyes to the darkness within the huge room, she was told not to gawk but come forward at a proper pace, he detested dawdling.

"With respect, sir, Menolly's feet were injured outrunning Thread," said Piemur, just as if he'd always been in possession of this truth. "She's not the dawdling kind."

Now Menolly could see the barrel-shaped figure seated at the massive sandtable opposite the entrance.

"Proceed at your own pace then, for surely a girl who outruns Thread has learned not to dawdle." The voice flowed out of the darkness, rich, round, with the r's rolled and the vowel sounds pure and ringing.

The other fire lizards swooped in through the open door, and the Master's eyes widened slightly. He regarded Menolly in mock surprise.

"Piemur!" The single word stopped the boy in his tracks, and the volume, which startled Menolly, caused Piemur to flick her a grin. "Did you not convey my message accurately? The creatures were *not* to come."

"They follow her everywhere, Master Shonagar, only she says they'll be quiet if she tells them to."

Master Shonagar turned his heavy head to regard Menolly with hooded eyes.

"So tell them!"

Menolly detached Beauty from her shoulder and ordered them all to perch themselves quietly. And not to make a single sound until she said they could.

"Well," remarked Master Shonagar, turning his head slightly to observe the obedience of the fire lizards. "That is a welcome sight, surrounded as I generally am by mass disobedience." He glared narrow-eyed at Piemur, who had had the temerity to giggle, and, at Master Shonagar's stare, tried to assume a sober expression. "I've had enough of your bold face, Piemur, and your dilatory manner. Take them away!"

"Yes, sir," said Piemur cheerfully, and twisting about on his heels, he marched himself smartly to the door, pausing to give Menolly an encouraging wave as he skipped down the steps.

"Rascal," said the Master in a mock growl as he flicked his fingers at Menolly to take the stool opposite him. "I'm given to believe that Petiron ended his days as Harper at your Hold, Menolly."

She nodded, tacitly reassured by his unexpected willingness to address her by name.

"And he taught you to play instruments and to understand musical theory?"

Menolly nodded again.

"In which Masters Domick and Morshal have examined you today." Some dryness in his tone alerted her, and she regarded him more warily as he tilted his heavy head sideways on his massive shoulders. "And did Petiron," and now the bass voice rolled with a hint of coming displeasure, so that Menolly wondered if her original assessment of this man was wrong and he was just as prejudiced as cynical Domick and soured Morshal. "Did he have the audacity to teach you how to use your voice?"

"No, sir. At least, I don't think he did. We . . . we just sang together."

"Ha!" And the huge hand of Master Shonagar came down so forcefully on the sandtable that the drier portions jumped in their frames. "You just sang together. As you sang together with those fire lizards of yours?"

Her friends chirped inquiringly.

"Silence!" he cried, with another sand-displacing thump on the table.

Somewhat to Menolly's surprise, because Master Shonagar had startled her again, the fire lizards flipped their wings to their backs and settled down.

"Well?"

"Did I just sing with them? Yes, I did."

"As you used to sing with Petiron?"

"Well, I used to sing descant to Petiron's melody, and the fire lizards usually do the descant now."

"That was not precisely what I meant. Now, I wish you just to sing for me."

"What, sir?" she asked, reaching for the gitar slung across her back.

"No, not with that," and he waved at her impatiently. "Sing, not concertize. The voice only is important now, not how you mask vocal inadequacies with pleasant strumming and clever harmony. I want to hear the voice. . . . It is the voice we communicate with, the voice which utters the words we seek to impress on men's minds, the voice which evokes emotional response; tears, laughter, sense. Your voice is the most important, most complex, most amazing instrument of all. And if you cannot use that voice properly, effectively, you might just as well go back to whatever insignificant hold you came from."

Menolly had been so fascinated by the richness and variety of the Master's tones that she didn't really pay heed to the content.

"Well?" he demanded.

She blinked at him, drawing in her breath, belatedly aware that he was waiting for her to sing.

"No, not like that! Dolt! You breathe from here," and his fingers spread across his barrel-width midsection, pressing in so that the sound from his mouth reflected that pressure. "Through the nose, so . . ." and he inhaled, his massive chest barely rising as it was filled, "down the windpipe," and he spoke on a single musical note, "to the belly," and the voice dropped an octave. "You breathe from your belly . . . if you breathe properly."

She took the breath as suggested and then expelled it because she didn't know what to sing with all that breath.

"For the sake of the Hold that protects us," and he raised his eyes and hands aloft as if he could grasp patience from thin air, "the girl simply sits there. Sing, Menolly, sing!"

Menolly was quite willing to, but he had so much to say before she could start or think of what to sing.

She took another quick breath, felt uncomfortable seated, and without asking, stood and launched into the same song that the apprentices had been singing that morning. She had a brief notion of showing him that he wasn't the only one who could fill the hall with resounding tones, but some fragment of advice from Petiron came to mind, and she concentrated on singing intensely, rather than loudly.

He just looked at her.

She held the last note, letting it die away as if the singer were moving off, and then she sank down onto the stool. She was trembling, and now that she'd stopped singing, her feet began to throb in a dull beat.

Master Shonagar only sat there, great folds of chin billowing down his chest. Without lifting his head, he tilted his body backwards and stared at her from under his fleshy and black-haired brows.

"And you say that Petiron never taught you to use your voice?"

"Not the way you did," and Menolly pressed her hands demonstratively against her flat belly. "He told me always to sing with my gut and heart. I can sing louder," she added, wondering if that's why Shonagar was frowning.

He waggled his fingers. "Any idiot can bellow. Camo can bellow. But he *can't* sing."

"Petiron used to say, 'If you sing loud, they only hear noise, not sound or song.' "

"Ha! He told you that? My words! My words exactly. So he did listen to me, after all." The last was delivered in an undertone to himself. "Petiron was wise enough to know his limitations."

Silently Menolly bridled at the aspersion. From the window ledge, Beauty hissed, and Rocky and Diver echoed her sentiment. Master Shonagar raised his head and regarded them in mild perplexity.

"So?" and he fixed his deep eyes on her. "What the mistress feels the pretty creatures echo? And you loved Petiron and will hear no ill-word against him?" He leaned forward slightly, waggling a forefinger at her. "Know this, Menolly who runs, we all have limitations, and wise is he who recognizes them. I meant," and he settled back into his chair, "no disrespect for the departed Petiron. For me that was praise." He tilted his head again. "For you, the best thing possible; for Petiron had sense enough not to meddle but to wait until I could attend to your vocal education. Temper and refine what is natural—and produce . . ." now Master Shonagar's left eyebrow was jerking up and down, the one arching while the other remained unmoved, so that Menolly was fascinated by his control, ". . . produce a well-placed, proper singing voice." The Master exhaled hugely.

Then Menolly took in the sense of what he'd been saying, no longer distracted by his facial contortions.

"You mean, I *can* sing?"

"Any idiot on Pern can sing," the Master said disparagingly. "No more talk. I'm weary." He began brushing her away from him. "Take those other sweet-throated freaks along with you, too. I've had enough of their baleful looks and assorted noises."

"I'll see that they stay . . ."

"Stay away? No." Shonagar's eyebrows rose sharply. "Bring them. They learn from example, one assumes. So you will set them a good example." A distant look clouded his face, and then a slow smile tugged up the corners of his mouth. "Go, Menolly. Go now. All this has wearied me beyond belief."

With that, he leaned his elbow on the sandtable so heavily that the opposite end left the floor. He cushioned his head against his fist and, while Menolly watched bemused, began to snore. Although she didn't think any human could fall asleep so quickly, she obeyed the implicit dismissal and, beckoning to her fire lizards, quietly departed.

Chapter 4

Harper, your song has a sorrowful sound
Though the tune was written as gay.
Your voice is sad and your hands are slow,
And your eye meeting mine turns away.

Menolly would have liked to find someplace to curl up and sleep herself, but Beauty began to creel softly. Silvina had said something about saving scraps, so Menolly crossed the courtyard to the kitchen door. She couldn't see either Silvina or Camo with all the coming and going. Then she saw the half-wit staggering in from the storage rooms, his arms clasping a great round yellow cheese. He saw her, grinned and deposited the cheese on the only clear space at one of the worktables.

"Camo feed pretty ones? Camo feed?"

"Camo, get on with that cheese, there's a good fellow," said the woman Menolly remembered as Abuna.

"Camo must feed." And the man had grabbed up a bowl, unceremoniously dumping its contents onto the table, and marched back to the storeroom.

"Camo! Come back and take care of this cheese!"

Menolly was sorry she'd come to the kitchen, but Abuna saw her.

"So you're the problem with him. Oh, all right. He'll be no use till he's helped you feed those creatures! But keep them out of my kitchen!"

"Yes, Abuna. I'm sorry to bother you—"

"And so you should be in the middle of getting ready the supper but . . ."

"Camo feed pretty ones? Camo feed pretty ones?" He was back trailing gobbets of meat from an overfull bowl.

"Not in my kitchen, Camo. Outside with you. Outside now. And send him back in when they've et, will you, girl? One thing he can do is get the cheese ready!"

Menolly assured Abuna, and smiling at Camo, drew him out of the kitchen and up the steps. Beauty and the others immediately converged on them. The two Aunties and Uncle again perched on convenient portions of Camo. The man's face was ecstatic, and he stood rigid, as if the slightest motion on his part would discourage his unusual guests, as the other fire lizards swooped to snatch food or clung to him long enough to eat directly from the bowl. Beauty, Rocky and Diver fed by preference from Menolly's hands, but the bowl was soon empty.

"Camo get more? Camo get more?"

Menolly caught him, forcing him to look at her. "No, Camo. They've had enough. No more, Camo. Now you must work on the cheese."

"Pretty ones leave?" Camo's face became a mask of tragedy as he watched one after the other of the fire lizards circle lazily up to the gable points of the hall. "Pretty ones leave?"

"They're going to sleep in the sun now, Camo. They're not hungry anymore. You go back to the cheese now." She gave him a gentle shove towards the kitchen. He went, bowl in both hands, staring back over his shoulder at the fire lizards so intently that this time he did bang right into the doorframe, corrected his direction without ever taking his eyes from the fire lizards, and disappeared into the kitchen.

"Could I help feed them? Maybe? Once?" asked a wistful voice at her elbow. Startled, she whirled to see Piemur, fringe of hair damp about his face and a line of rearranged dirt on each side of his neck up to his ears.

Other lads and some of the journeymen were beginning to drift across the courtyard to the Hall. "Rascal," Master Shonagar had called Piemur, and Menolly agreed, for a gleam lurked in Piemur's eyes for all his plaintive voice.

"Got a bet on with Ranly?"

"Bet on?" Piemur gave her a searching look. Then he chuckled. "A small guy like me, Menolly, has got to stay a jump ahead of the big ones, like Ranly, or they put on me in the dorm at night."

"So what did you put up with Ranly?"

"That you'd let me feed the fire lizards because they like me already. They do, don't they?"

"You really are a rascal, aren't you?"

Piemur's grin became a calculated grimace, and he shrugged admission of the charge.

"I've already got Camo falling over himself to feed . . ."

". . . 'Pretty Beauty,' " and Piemur mimicked the older man's thick voice perfectly, " 'Feed pretty Beauty . . .' Oh, don't worry Menolly, Camo and me are friends. He won't object to me helping, too."

As if that had settled the matter, Piemur grabbed Menolly's hand to pull her up the steps. "Hey, you don't want to be late for the table again," he said, leading her towards the dining hall.

"Menolly!"

The two halted at the sound of the Harper's voice and turned to see him descending the stairs from the upper level.

"How's the day gone for you, Menolly? You've seen Domick, Morshal and Shonagar, have you? I must make you known to Sebell, too, very soon. Before the eggs hatch!" The Masterharper grinned, much as Piemur had just done, in anticipation of the event. "And this scamp has attached himself to you, has he? Well, maybe you can keep him out of trouble for a while. Ah, Brudegan, a word with you before supper."

"Quick . . ." Piemur had her by the arm and was hurrying her into the dining hall so that betwixt the Harper and Piemur, it looked to Menolly as if neither wished her to meet Journeyman Brudegan, whose practice her fire lizards had interrupted. "Sebell's a real clever fellow," Piemur added in such a casual fashion that Menolly berated herself for imagining things. "He's to get the other egg." Piemur whistled in his teeth. "You think you got troubles? Sebell's only just walked the tables—"

"Walked the tables?" Menolly was startled.

"That's what we say when you've been promoted a grade. It happens at supper. If you're an apprentice, a journeyman stands by your seat and then walks you to your new place." He was pointing from the long tables to the oval ones at the far end of the dining hall. "And a master escorts a journeyman from them to the round table. But it'll be a long time before any of that happens to me," he said, sighing. "If it ever does."

"Why? Don't all apprentices become journeymen?"

"No," replied the boy with a grimace. "Some get sent home as useless. Some get dull jobs around here, helping journeymen or masters, or sent to a smaller crafthall elsewhere."

Maybe that was what the Masterharper had in mind for her, helping a journeyman or a master in some hold or crafthall. That made good sense, at least, but Menolly sighed. A sigh echoed by Piemur.

"How long have you been here?" Menolly asked. He looked a poorly grown nine or ten Turns, the age at which boys were customarily apprenticed, but he sounded as if he'd been in the Hall a long time.

"Two Turns I've been apprenticed," he answered with a grin. "I got taken in early on account of my voice." He said that without the least bit of conceit. "Now, look, you go on over there where the girls sit. And don't worry. You rank 'em."

Without explaining that, he darted in between the first and second tables. Menolly tried not to hobble as she moved to the benches he had indicated, keeping her shoulders back, her head up, and walking slowly so as to disguise her pain-footed gait. She was aware of, and tried to ignore, the overt and covert glances of the boys already in position at the tables. She'd better let Piemur help her feed the fire lizards: keeping on his good side might be as important as staying in the Harper's good graces.

The seats evidently reserved for the girls were marked by flaps of cushion on the hard wood. She took the end position, away from the fiercest heat of the hearth fire and stood politely waiting.

The girls entered the dining hall together. Together in more than one sense, for all regarded her steadily as they crossed to the table. Their unity was also maintained in their blank expressions. Menolly swallowed against the dryness in her throat, glanced around her, anywhere but at the fast approaching girls. She caught Piemur's eyes, saw him grin impishly, and she had to smile back.

"You're Menolly?" asked a quiet voice. The girls were ranged beyond their spokesman, again in a line that betokened unity.

"She couldn't be anyone else, could she?" asked the dark girl just behind her.

"My name is Pona, my grandfather is Lord Holder of Boll." She held out her right hand, palm up, and Menolly, who had never had an opportunity to make the gesture of formal greeting, covered it with hers.

"I am Menolly," and, remembering Piemur's comment about rank, she added, "my father is Yanus, Sea Holder of Half-Circle Sea Hold."

There was a startled murmur of surprise from the others.

"She ranks us," said someone, rebellious and astonished.

"There's rank in the Harper Hall?" asked Menolly, disturbed and wondering what other elements of courtesy she might unwittingly have neglected. Hadn't Petiron always told her that the Harper Craft, in particular, laid stress on skill and musical achievement rather than natal rank? But Piemur had said, "You rank 'em."

"Half-Circle is not the oldest seahold. Tillek is," said the dark-complexioned girl, rather crossly.

"Menolly is daughter, not niece," said the girl who had mentioned outranking. She now extended her hand, less grudgingly, Menolly thought. "My father is Weaver Craftmaster Timareen of Telgar Hold. My name is Audiva."

The dark-complexioned girl was about to name herself, her hand extended, when a sudden shuffling of feet alerted them all, and they took their places at the bench as everyone in the hall stood straight and looked forward. Menolly was then facing a tall boy whose slightly protuberant eyes were bulging with interest in the little scene he had just witnessed. Looking over his left shoulder and through a gap, she saw

Piemur, rolling his eyes as far to his right as possible. Menolly tried peering in the same direction and decided it must be the Harper's table that Piemur watched. Then everyone was jumping over the benches to get seated, and she hastened to do the same.

Heavy pitchers of a thick, meaty, hot soup were passed, and trays of the yellow cheese, which Camo must eventually have taken care of, as well as baskets of crusty bread. Evidently meals were reversed here in the Harper Craft Hall, with the heaviest meal in the middle of the day. Menolly ate hungrily and quickly until she realized that the girls were all taking half-spoonsful and breaking their bread and cheese into dainty bite-sized portions. Pona and Audiva watched her surreptitiously, and one of the other girls tittered. So, thought Menolly grimly, her table manners differed from theirs? Well, to change would mean admitting that hers were faulty. She did slow down, but she continued to eat heartily, making no bones about asking for more while the girls were still but halfway through their first serving.

"I understand that you were privileged to attend the latest Hatching at Benden Weyr," Pona said to Menolly with all the air of one conferring a favor by such conversation.

"Yes, I was there." *Privileged?* Yes, she supposed it would be considered a privilege.

"I don't suppose you can remember who made Impression?" Pona was vitally interested.

"Some of them, yes. Talina of Ruatha Hold is the new queen's weyrwoman . . ."

"You're certain?"

Menolly glanced beyond her to Audiva and saw merriment in her eyes.

"Yes, I'm certain."

"Too bad those three candidates from your grandfather's Hold didn't Impress, Pona. There'll be other times," said Audiva.

"Who else do you remember?"

"A lad from Master Nicat's Craft Hall Impressed a brown . . ." For some reason that seemed to please Pona. "Master Nicat also received two of the fire lizards' eggs."

Pona turned her head to stare haughtily at Menolly. "How ever did it come about that *you* . . ." and Menolly was made intensely aware of her unworthiness ". . . have nine fire lizards?"

"She was in the right place at the right time, Pona," said Audiva. "Luck doesn't recognize rank and privilege. And it's thanks to Menolly that there were fire lizard eggs for Master Robinton and Master Nicat."

"How do you know that?" Pona sounded surprised but her tone lost its affectedness.

"Oh, I had a word or two with Talmor while you were busy trying to make up to Jessuan and Benis."

"I never . . ." Pona was evidently as quick to take offense as give it, but she lowered her tone at Audiva's warning hiss.

"Don't worry, Pona. Just so long as Dunca doesn't *catch* you flipping your skirts at a son of the Hold, I'll hold my peace."

Whether Audiva was subtly deflecting Pona from pestering Menolly with snide questions or not, Menolly didn't know, but the girl from Boll ignored her for the rest of the meal. As Menolly had been taught that it was impolite to talk through or around someone, she couldn't converse with the apparently friendly Audiva, and the boy beside her was talking to his mates, his back to her.

"My uncle of Tillek says that fire lizards are going to be nothing more than pets, and I thought pets weren't allowed in the cottages . . ." said the dark girl, her mouth setting primly, as she cast a sideways look towards Menolly.

"The Master Harper doesn't rate fire lizards as pets, Briala," said Audiva in her droll way, and she winked at Menolly over Pona's head. "Of course, you've only got one at Tillek Hold."

"Well, my uncle says the Weyrmen are spending too much time on those creatures when they ought to get down to basic problems and go after Thread on the Red Star. That's the only way to stop this dreadful menace."

"What are the dragonriders supposed to do?" asked Audiva scornfully. "Even you should know that dragons can't go *between* blind."

"They ought to just flame the Red Star clean of Thread, that's what."

"Could they really?" asked the girl beyond Briala, her eyes round with amazement and a sort of hopeful horror.

"Oh, don't be ridiculous, Amania," said Audiva in disgust. "No one's ever been to the Red Star."

"They could *try* to get there," replied Pona. "That's what my grandfather says."

"Who's to say the first dragonmen didn't try?" asked Audiva.

"Then why isn't there a Record of the attempt?" demanded Pona with haughty condescension.

"They'd certainly have written a song about it if they had," said Briala, pleased to see Audiva confounded.

"Well, the Red Star is not our problem," said Audiva.

"Learning songs is." Briala's voice had a wailing edge to it. "And *when* are we going to have a chance to learn that music Talmor set us today? We've got rehearsal tonight, and it'll go on and on because those boys are always—"

"The boys? Just like you to blame it on the boys, Briala," said Audiva. "You had plenty of time this afternoon to practice your lessons, same as the rest of us."

"I had to wash my hair, and Dunca had to let out the seams of my red gown. . . ."

"If you'd stop. . . . Oh, not redfruit again?" Pona sounded aggrieved, but Menolly eyed the basket of delicacies with surprised delight.

Pona might affect indifference, but she was quick to snatch the curiously shaped fruit from the basket when it was passed to her. Menolly took hers and ate it quickly, getting as much of the sweet, tangy juice as possible. She wished she had the courage to lick her fingers the way the boys were doing. But the girls were so stuffy and mannered, she knew they'd stare if she did.

Suddenly the demands of the day, the excitements and tensions, sapped the last of Menolly's energy. She found it almost unbearable to have to sit at the table amid so many unknown people, unable to guess what more might be asked of her before she could seek the quiet and solitude of her bed. She worried about her fire lizards, and then tried not to, for fear they would seek her out. She was conscious of her throbbing feet; her hand ached, and the scar begged to be scratched. She shifted on the bench, wondering why they were held here at table. Restlessly she craned her neck to peer around at the Harper's table. She couldn't see Master Robinton but the others were laughing, obviously enjoying an aftermeal conversation. Was that why everyone was being held so long? Until the masters had stopped talking?

She longed for the peace of her cave near the Dragon Stones. Even for the little cubicle in her father's Sea Hold. She'd usually been able to slip away to it without accounting to anyone for her disappearance. At least once the day's work was done. And somehow, she'd never thought of the Harper Craft Hall being so . . . so populated, with so much to be done and doing, and all the masters and Silvina and. . . .

She was caught unawares and had to struggle to her feet as the others rose more gracefully to theirs. She was so relieved to be able to go that at first she didn't realize no one was leaving the benches but masters and journeymen. Pona's hiss caught her attention before she'd moved more than a few strides. Embarrassed, she stood with all the girls glaring at her as if she had committed a far more heinous crime than moving out of turn. She edged back towards her vacated place. Then, as soon as the apprentices and the girls began to saunter out of the dining hall, she sat down again. She did not want to be among people, especially all these strange people who had odd notions and different manners, and seemingly, no sympathy for the newcomer. The Weyr had been as big and well-populated, but she had felt at home there, with friendly glances and uncritical, smiling faces.

"Your feet hurting again?" It was Piemur asking, his brows contorted in a worried scowl.

Menolly bit her lip.

"I guess I'm just suddenly very tired," she said.

He wrinkled his nose drolly and then twitched it to one side. "I'm not surprised, your first day here and all, and having the masters giving you a poke and prod. Look, you can lean on my shoulder across to Dunca's. I can still get back in time for rehearsal . . ."

"Rehearsal? Do I have to be somewhere else now?" Menolly fought an almost overwhelming desire to weep.

"Shouldn't think so, your first day here. Unless Master Shonagar said something? No? Well, they can hardly have sorted out what your standard is, even if you couldn't play note one. And you know, you look ruddy awful. Awful tired, I mean. C'mon, I'll help you."

"But you have a rehearsal . . ."

"Don't you worry your head about me, Menolly." He grinned mischievously. "Sometimes it's an astest . . . asset . . . to be small," and he made a weaving motion with his hand, then squared his shoulders and stood, radiating innocent attention. He was so comic that Menolly giggled.

She rose, excessively grateful to him. He rattled on about the rehearsal for the usual spring affair at Fort Hold. The rehearsal was usually fun because Brudegan was in charge this season. *He* was good at explaining exactly what he wanted you to do, so if you listened sharp, you didn't make mistakes.

The swift spring evening was settling over the complex of Hold and Hall so there were very few passers-by. Piemur's physical presence and his chatter, blithely ignoring her silence, were more supportive than his bony shoulder, but she couldn't have made the walk without it. Menolly was grateful that she'd only the short flight of steps to go. The fire lizards chirped sympathetically at her from the window ledge outside her fast-shuttered room.

"You're okay now, with them," said Piemur, grinning up at the fire lizards. "I'll dash off. You'll be fine in the morning, Menolly, with a good night's rest under your ear. That's what my foster-mother always told us."

"I'm sure I will, Piemur, and thank you so much . . ."

Her words trailed off because he was dashing and out of earshot. She opened the door, calling tentatively for Dunca, but there was no answer, nor any sign of the plump cotkeeper. Grateful for that unexpected mercy, Menolly began to climb the steep steps, one at a time, pulling herself along by the railing and taking as much pressure off her feet as she could. Halfway up, Beauty appeared, chirruping encouragement. Rocky and Diver joined her on the top step and added their comforting noises.

With a sense of utmost relief, Menolly closed the door behind her. She hobbled to the bed and sank down, fumbling with the ties of the sleeping furs, not really aware of the scratching on the closed shutters until Beauty let out an authoritative squawk. Fortunately, Menolly only had to stretch out her arm to open the shutters. Aunties One and Two fell in, catching themselves by wing just off the floor, scolding her soundly as they flew about the room. Lazy, Brownie and Uncle entered with more dignity and Mimic waddled to the window edge, yawning.

Menolly remembered to rub the salve on her feet, though they were so tender, tears jumped to her eyes. Briefly she wished that Mirrim was there, with her brisk chatter and gentle touch. Feet were indeed very awkward to tend yourself. She rubbed the other stuff into her hand scar, restraining the urge to scratch the itching tissue. She slipped out of her clothes and under the sleeping furs, only vaguely aware that the fire lizards were making themselves comfortable about her. *Nothing to fear from harpers,* huh? T'gellan's comment mocked her. As she fell deeply asleep, she wondered if envy was akin to fear?

Chapter 5

My nightly craft is winged in white;
A dragon of night-dark sea.
Swiftborn, dreambound and rudderless;
Her captain and crew are me.
I sail a hundred sleeping tides
Where no seaman's ever been
And only my white-winged craft and I
Know the marvels we have seen.

The next day did not start propitiously for Menolly. Her sleep was broken by shrieks: Dunca's, the girls, and the fire lizards. Dazed, Menolly at first tried to calm the fire lizards swooping about the room, but Dunca, standing in the doorway, would not be quiet; and her terror, whether assumed or real, only stimulated the fire lizards into such aerial acrobatics that Menolly ordered them all out the window.

This only changed the tone of Dunca's screams because the woman was now pointing at Menolly's nudity until she could snatch up the discarded shirt and cover herself.

"And where were you all night?" Dunca demanded in a sobbingly angry voice. "How did you get in? When did you get in?"

"I was here all night. I got in by the front door. You weren't in the cottage." Then, seeing the look of complete disbelief on Dunca's plump face, Menolly added, "I came here directly after supper. Piemur helped me across the court."

"He was at rehearsal. Which was just after supper," said one of the girls crowding in at the door.

"Yes, but he got there out of breath," Audiva said, frowning, "I remember Brudegan rounding him on it."

"You must always inform me when you come in," said Dunca, by no means pacified.

Menolly hesitated and then nodded her head in acquiescence; it was useless to argue with someone like Dunca, who had obviously made up her mind not to like Menolly and to pick every fault possible.

"When you are washed and decently attired," and the tone of Dunca's voice suggested that she doubted Menolly was capable of either, "you will join us. Come, girls. There is no reason for you to delay your own meal."

As the girls filed obediently past the open doorway, most of the faces reflected Dunca's disapproval. Except Audiva who winked solemnly and then grinned before she schooled her features into a blank expression.

By the time Menolly had attended to her feet, had a quick wash, dressed and found the small room where the other girls were eating, they were almost finished. As one, they stared critically at her before Dunca brusquely motioned her to take the empty seat. And as one, they all watched her so that she felt doubly awkward about the simple acts of chewing and swallowing. The food tasted dry and the klah was cold. She managed to finish what had been set before her and mumbled thanks. She sat there, looking down at her place, only then noticing the fruit stains on her tunic. So, they had reason to stare. And she had nothing to change into while this top was washed, except her old things from her cave days.

Though she had eaten, she was still conscious of hunger pangs. The fire lizards were waiting to be fed! She doubted that Dunca would supply her need, but her responsibility to her friends gave her the courage to ask.

"May I be excused, please? The fire lizards must be fed. I have to go to Silvina . . ."

"Why would you bother Silvina with such a detail?" demanded Dunca, her eyes popping slightly with indignation. "Don't you realize that she is the headwoman of the entire Harper Craft Hall? The demands on her time are enormous! And if you don't keep those creatures of yours under proper control. . . ."

"You startled them this morning."

"I'm not having that sort of carry-on every morning, frightening my girls with them flying at such dangerous speeds."

Menolly refrained from pointing out that it had been Dunca's screaming that had alarmed the fire lizards.

"If you can't control them. . . . Where are they now?" She looked wildly about her, her eyes bulging with alarm.

"Waiting to be fed."

"Don't get pert with me, girl. You may be the daughter of a Sea Holder, but while you are in the Harper Craft Hall and in my charge, you are to behave yourself. We'll have no ranking here."

Half-torn between laughter and disgust, Menolly rose. "If I may go, please, before the fire lizards come in search of me . . ."

That sufficed. Dunca couldn't get her out of the cot fast enough.

Someone sniggered, but when Menolly glanced up she wasn't sure if it had been Audiva or not. It was a small encouragement that someone had recognized Dunca's hypocrisy.

As she stepped out into the crisp morning air, Menolly realized how stuffy the cot had been and glanced over her shoulder. Sure enough, all the shutters, except her own, were closed tight. As she crossed the wide court, she received morning grins and greetings from the farmholders making their way to the fields, from apprentices dashing to their masters. She looked about her for her fire lizards and saw one wheeling down behind the outer wing of the Craft Hall. As she walked under the arch, she saw the others clinging to the kitchen and dining hall ledges. Camo was in the doorway, a great bowl in the crook of his left arm, a hunk of something dangling from his right hand as he tried to entice the fire lizards to him.

She was halfway across the courtyard before she realized that it was much easier to walk on her feet today. However, that was one of the few good things that happened. Camo was chastized by Abuna for trying to coax the fire lizards to eat when he should have been delivering the cereal to the dining hall (for fire lizards would not eat from his hands until Menolly arrived). Then the fire lizards were frightened away when the apprentices and journeymen came tearing out of the dining hall, filling the courtyard with yells and shrieks and wild antics as they made their way to their morning classes. Menolly looked vainly for Piemur, and then, as abruptly, the courtyard was clear. Except for some older journeymen. One of them paused by her, officiously demanding to know why she was hanging about the yard. When she said that she hadn't been told where to go, he informed her that she obviously should be with the other girls and to get herself there immediately. As he gestured in the general direction of the archroom, Menolly assumed that was where the girls met.

She reached the archway room to find the girls already practicing scales on their gitars with a journeyman, who told her she was late, to get her instrument and see if she could catch up with the others. She mumbled an apology, found her precious gitar, and took a stool near the others. But the chords were basic and even with her injured hand she had no trouble with the drill. Not so the others. Pona seemed unable to bridge strings with forefinger: the joint kept snapping up; and although the journeyman, Talmor, patiently showed her an alternative chording, she couldn't get to it fast enough to keep the rhythm of the exercise. Talmor had great patience, Menolly thought, and idly ran silent fingers down the neck of her gitar, doing his alternative placement. Yes, it was a bit awkward if you were after speed, but not as impossible as Pona was making it out to be.

"Since you are so good at it, Menolly, suppose you demonstrate the exercise. In the time . . ." and Talmor directed the beat.

She caught it with her eyes, keeping her head still, for Petiron abhorred a musician who had to use unnecessary body motion to keep a rhythm going. She went through the chords on the scale as directed and then saw Audiva regarding her with fierce intent. Pona and the others glowered.

"Now use the regular fingering," Talmor said, coming over to stand by Menolly, his eyes intent on her hands.

Menolly executed the run. He gave a sharp nod of his head, eyed her inscrutably, and then returned to Pona, asking her to try it again, though he outlined a slower time. Pona mastered the run the third time, smiling with relief at her success.

Talmor gave them another set of scales and then brought out a large copy of a piece of occasional music. Menolly was delighted because the score was completely new to her. Petiron had been, as he phrased it, a teaching Harper, not an entertainer, and though she had learned the one or two occasional pieces of music he had in his possession, he had never acquired more. The Sea Holder, Menolly knew, had preferred to sing, not listen; and most occasional music was instrumental. In the bigger Holds, Petiron had told her, the Lord Holders liked music during the dinner hour and at night when they entertained guests in conversation rather than song.

This was not a difficult piece, Menolly realized, scanning it and silently fingering the one or two transitional chords that might be troublesome.

"All right, Audiva, let's see what you can make of it today," Talmor said, smiling at the girl with encouragement.

Audiva gulped, exhibiting a nervousness that puzzled Menolly. As Audiva began to pick out the chords, nodding her head and tapping one foot at a much slower rhythm than the musical notation required, Menolly's perplexity grew. Well, she thought, charitably, maybe Audiva was a new student. If she was, she was far more competent than Briala, who apparently had trouble just reading the music.

Talmor dismissed Briala to the table to copy the score for later practice. Pona was no improvement on the other two. The sly-faced, fairhaired girl played with great banging against the gitar belly, at time, but with many inaccuracies. When it was finally her own turn, Menolly's stomach was roiled by frustrated listening.

"Menolly," said Talmor at the end of a sigh that expressed his own frustration and boredom.

It was such a relief to play the music as it should be that Menolly found herself increasing the time and emphasizing the chords with a variation of her own in the strum.

Talmor just looked at her. Then he blinked and exhaled heavily, pursing his lips together.

"Well, yes. You've seen it before?"

"Oh, no. We had very little occasional music in Half-Circle. This is lovely."

"You played that cold?"

Only then did Menolly realize what she'd done: made the other girls look inadequate. She was aware of their cold, chill silence, their hostile stares. But not to play one's best seemed a dishonesty that she had never practiced and could not. Belatedly she recognized that she could have hedged: with her scarred hand she could have faltered, missed some of the chordings. Yet it had been such a relief, after their limping renditions, to play the music as it was meant to be played.

"I was the last to go," she said in a lame effort to retrieve matters, "I'd more time to study it, and see. . . ." She'd started to say, "see where they went wrong."

"Yes, well, so you did," Talmor said, so hastily that Menolly wondered if he'd also realized what a break she'd made. Then he added in a rush of impatience and irritation. "Who told you to join this class? I'd rather thought . . ." A snigger interrupted his query, and he turned to glare at the girls. "Well?" he asked Menolly.

"A journeyman . . ."

"Who?"

"I don't know. I was in the courtyard, and he asked me why wasn't I in class. Then he told me to come here."

Talmor rubbed the side of his jaw. "Too late now, I suppose, but I'll inquire." He turned to the other girls. "Let's play it in . . ." The girls were staring pointedly at the doorway, and he looked about. "Yes, Sebell?"

Menolly turned, too, to see the man to whom the other coveted fire lizard egg had gone. Sebell was a slender man, a hand or so taller than herself: a brown man, tanned skin, light brown hair and eyes, dressed in brown with a faded Harper apprentice badge half-hidden in the shoulder fold of his tunic.

"I've been looking for Menolly," he said, gazing steadily at her.

"I thought someone ought to be. She was misdirected here." Talmor sounded irritated, and he gestured sharply for Menolly to go to Sebell.

Menolly slipped from the stool, but she was uncertain what to do about the gitar and glanced questioningly at Sebell.

"You won't need it now," he said so she quickly put it away on the shelf.

She felt the girls staring at her, knew that Talmor was watching and would not continue the lesson until she had gone, so it was with intense relief that she heard the door close behind her and the quiet brown man.

"Where was I supposed to be?" she asked, but he motioned her down the steps.

"You got no message?" His eyes searched her face carefully although his expression gave no hint of his thoughts.

"No."

"You did breakfast at Dunca's?"

"Yes . . ." Menolly couldn't suppress her distaste for that painful meal. Then she caught her breath and stared at Sebell, comprehension awakening. "Oh, she wouldn't have. . . ."

Sebell was nodding, his brown eyes registering an understanding of the matter. "And you wouldn't have known yet to come to me for instructions . . ."

"You . . ." Hadn't Piemur said something about Sebell walking the tables, to become a journeyman? ". . . sir?" she added.

A slow smile spread across the man's round face.

"I suppose I do rate a 'sir' from a mere apprentice, but the Harper is not as strict about such observances as other masters. The tradition here is that the oldest journeyman under the same master is responsible for the newest apprentice. So you are my responsibility. At least while I'm in the Hall and I'm enjoying a respite from my journeyings. I didn't have the chance to meet you yesterday, and this morning . . . you didn't arrive as planned at Master Domick's . . ."

"Oh, no." Menolly swallowed the hard knot of dismay. "Not Master Domick!" Even Piemur was careful not to annoy him. "Was Master Domick very . . . upset?"

"In a manner of speaking, yes. But don't worry, Menolly, I shall use the incident to your advantage. It doesn't do to antagonize Domick unnecessarily."

"Not when he doesn't like me anyhow." Menolly closed her eyes against a vision of Master Domick's cynical face contorted with anger.

"How do you construe that?"

Menolly shrugged. "I had to play for him yesterday, I know he doesn't like me."

"Master Domick doesn't like anyone," replied Sebell with a wry laugh, "including himself. So you're no exception. But, as far as studying with him is concerned . . ."

"I'm to study with him?"

"Don't panic. As a teacher, he's top rank. I know. In some ways I think Master Domick is superior, instrumentally, to the Harper. He doesn't have Master Robinton's flare and vitality, nor his keen perception in matters outside the Craft." Although Sebell was speaking in his customary impersonal way, Menolly sensed his complete loyalty and devotion to the Masterharper. "You," and there was a slight emphasis on the pronoun, "will learn a great deal from Domick. Just don't let his manner fuss you. He's agreed to teach you, and that's quite a concession."

"But I didn't come this morning . . ." The magnitude of that truancy appalled Menolly.

Sebell gave her a quick reassuring grin. "I said that I can turn that to your advantage. Domick doesn't like people to ignore his instructions. It is not *your* worry. Now, come on. Enough of the morning has been lost."

He had directed her up the steps into the Hall, and to her surprise opened the door into the Great Hall. It was twice the size of the dining hall, three times the size of the Great Hall at Half-Circle. Across the far end was fitted a raised and curtained platform that jutted into the floor space. Tables and benches were piled haphazardly against the inner walls and under windows. Immediately to her right were a collection of more comfortable chairs arranged in an informal grouping about a small round table. To this area Sebell motioned her and seated himself opposite her.

"I've some questions to put to you, and I can't explain why I need to have this information. It is Harper business, and if you're told that, you'll be wise to ask no further. I need your help . . ."

"*My* help?"

"Strange as that might seem, yes," and his brown eyes laughed at her. "I need to know how to sail a boat, how to gut a fish, how to act like a seaman . . ."

He was ticking off the points on his fingers, and she stared at his hands.

"With those, no one would ever believe you had sailed . . ."

He examined his hands impersonally. "Why?"

"Seaman's hands get gnarled quickly from popping the joints, rough from salt water and fish oil, much browner than yours from weathering . . ."

"Would anyone but a seaman know that?"

"Well, *I* know it."

"Fair enough. Can you teach me to act, from a distance," and his grin teased her, "like a seaman? Is it hard to learn to sail a boat? Or bait a hook? Or gut a fish?"

Her left palm itched, and so did her curiosity. Harper business? Why would a journeyman harper need to know such things?

"Sailing, baiting, gutting . . . those are a question of practicing . . ."

"Could *you* teach me?"

"With a boat and a place to sail, yes . . . with hook and bait, and a few fish." Then she laughed.

"What's funny?"

"Just that . . . I thought when I came here, that I'd never need to gut a fish again."

Sebell regarded her sardonically for a long moment, a smile playing at the corners of his mouth. "Yes, I can appreciate that, Menolly. I was landbred and thought I'd done with walking about. Just don't be surprised at anything you're asked to do here. The Harper requires us to play many tunes for our Craft . . . not always on gitar or pipe. Now," and he went on more briskly, "I'll arrange for the boat, the water and the fish. But when?" At this requisite, he whistled softly through the slight gap between his two front teeth. "Time will be the problem, for you have lessons, and there are the two eggs . . ." He looked her squarely in the eye then, and grinned. "Speaking of which, have you any idea what color mine might be?"

She smiled back. "I don't think you can really be as sure with fire lizard eggs as you can with the dragons', but I kept the two largest ones for Master Robinton. One ought to be a queen, and the other should turn out to be a bronze at least."

"A bronze fire lizard?"

The rapt expression on Sebell's face alarmed her. What if both eggs produced browns? Or greens? As if he sensed her apprehension, Sebell smiled.

"I don't really care so long as I have one. The Harper says they can be trained to carry messages. And sing!" He was a great teaser, this Sebell, thought Menolly, for all his quiet manner and solemn expressions, but she felt completely at ease with him. "The Harper says they can get as attached to their friends as dragons do to their riders."

She nodded. "Would you like to meet mine?"

"I would, but not now," he replied, shaking his head ruefully. "I must pick your brains about the seaman's craft. So, tell me how goes a day at a Sea Hold?"

Amused to find herself explaining such a thing in the Harper Hall, Menolly gave the brown journeyman a drily factual account of the routine that was all she'd known for so many Turns. He was an attentive listener, occasionally repeating cogent points, or asking her to elaborate others. She was giving him a list of the various types of fish that inhabited the oceans of Pern when the tocsin rang again and her explanation was drowned by shouts as apprentices erupted into the courtyard on their way to the dining hall.

"We'll wait until the stampede has settled, Menolly," Sebell said, raising his voice above the commotion outside, "just give me that rundown on deep water fishes again."

When Sebell escorted her to her place, the girls treated her with a stony silence, emphasized by pursed lips, averted eyes and then sniggers to each other. Buoyed by Sebell's reassurances, Menolly ignored them. She concentrated on eating the roast wherry and the crusty brown tubers, bigger than she'd ever seen and so fluffy inside their crust that she ate more of them than bread.

Since the girls were so pointedly snubbing her, Menolly looked about the room. She couldn't spot Piemur, and she wanted him to come help her feed the fire lizards in the evening. She'd better strengthen what friendships she could within the Harper Hall.

The gong again called their attention to announcements; and to her surprise, Menolly heard her own name called to report to Master Oldive. Immediately the girls fell to whispering among themselves, as if such a summons was untoward, though she couldn't imagine why, unless they were doing it to frighten her. She continued to ignore them. And then the gong released the diners.

The girls remained where they were, pointedly not looking in her direction, and she was forced to struggle from the bench.

"And where in the name of the first shell were you this morning?" asked Master Domick, his face set with anger, his eyes slitted, his voice low but projected so that the girls all cowered away from him.

"I was told to go to—"

"So Talmor informed me," and he brushed aside her explanation, "but *I* had left word with Dunca for you to report to me."

"Dunca told me nothing, Master Domick," Menolly flicked a glance beyond him to the girls and saw in their smug expression the knowledge that they, too, had known there'd been a message for her, which Dunca had deliberately neglected to pass on.

"She said she did," said Master Domick.

Menolly stared back at him, bereft of any response and heartily wishing for Sebell to produce his assistance.

"I realize," Domick went on sarcastically, "that you've been living holdless and without authority for some time, but while you are an apprentice here, you will obey the masters."

In the face of his wrath, Menolly bowed her head. The next moment, Beauty came diving into the room, with two bronze and two brown shapes right behind her.

"Beauty! Rocky! Diver! Stop it!"

Menolly jumped in front of Domick, arms outstretched, protecting him from the onslaught of winged retaliation.

"What do you mean, disobeying me? Attacking Master Domick? He's a Harper! Behave yourselves."

Menolly had to shout because the girls, seeing the fire lizards swooping down, screamed and tried variously to get under the table or off the benches, overturning them; anywhere away from the fire lizards.

Domick had sense enough to stand still, incredulous as he was at the attack. Despite the girls' shrieks, Menolly had the lungs to be heard when she wished to.

Twittering, Beauty circled once and then came to Menolly's shoulder, glaring balefully at Domick from behind her mistress. The others lined up on the mantel, wings still spread, hissing, their jewelled eyes whirling, looking ready and quite willing to pounce again. As Menolly stroked Beauty to calmness, she struggled with an apology to Domick.

"Back to work, you! The rest of you, along to your sections," Domick said, raising his own voice to energize the stragglers in the dining hall who had observed the strange attack, and the boys who were clearing the tables. "I'd forgot about your loyal defenders," he told Menolly in a tight but controlled voice.

"Master Domick, will you ever forgive . . ."

"Master Domick," said another voice near the floor, and Audiva crawled from under the table. Domick extended a hand to help the girl to her feet. She glanced towards the entrance, then gave Menolly a brief nod. "Master Domick, Dunca told Menolly nothing about your message, but *we* all knew about it. Fair's fair." With one more glance at Menolly, she hurried across the dining hall to catch up with the other girls in the courtyard.

"How did you contrive to alienate Dunca?" asked Domick, his expression sullen but less fierce.

Menolly gulped and glanced at the fire lizards.

"Oh, them! Yes! I can quite see her point." There was no flexibility in Master Domick's attitude. "They do not, however, intimidate me."

"Master Domick—"

"That's enough, girl. Since you haven't the native intelligence to be tactful, I shall have to—"

"Master Domick—" Sebell came hurrying up.

"I know, I know," and the Master cut off the journeyman's explanation. "You do seem to acquire some champions at any rate. Let's hope the end result is worth the effort. I'll see you tomorrow morning, promptly after breakfast, in my study, which is on the second level to the right, fourth door on the outside. You will take your pipes this afternoon to Master Jerint for the first hour. I'm told you made the pipes yourself in that cave of yours? Good! Then the second hour you're to see Master Shonagar. Now, get yourself off to Master Oldive. His office is at the top of the steps on the inside, to your right. No, Sebell, you do not need to hover about her so protectingly. I'm not so lost to common sense as to punish her for being the victim of envy." He gestured imperatively at the journeyman to accompany him and then strode out of the hall. Sebell gave her a quick nod and followed.

"Pssst!" Attracted by the sound, Menolly looked down and saw Piemur crouched under the table.

"Is it safe to come out?"

"Aren't you supposed to be in a chore section?"

"Yeah, but never mind. I've got a few seconds leeway. Hey, those fribbles have it in for you, don't they? Or maybe Dunca *made* them not tell you?"

"How much did you overhear?"

"All of it." Piemur grinned, getting to his feet. "I don't miss much around here."

"Piemur!"

"Menolly, can I help you feed the fire lizards tonight?" he asked, eyeing Beauty warily.

"I was going to ask you."

"Great!" He beamed with pleasure. "And don't worry about *them,*" he added, jerking his head towards the door, meaning the girls. "You're much nicer'n them."

"You just want to make friends with my fire lizards . . ."

"Too right!" His grin was impudence itself, but Menolly felt that he'd have been her friend without Beauty and the others. "Gotta scamper, or I'll be put on. See you!"

She made her way to Master Oldive's office. He had the hard-gum ball for her and showed her how to exercise her hand around it.

"Not," he said, giving her the grimace of his smile, "that your hand will lack exercise of other sorts around here. How much does it ache?"

She mumbled something, so he gave her a stern look and laid a small pot in her hand.

"There is only one excuse on this planet for the existence of that odorous plant known as numbweed, which is to ease pain. Use it when needed. The salve is mild enough to give you relief without loss of sensitivity."

Beauty, who'd observed everything from her perch on Menolly's shoulder, gave an admonitory chirp, as if agreeing with Master Oldive. The man chuckled, eyeing the little queen.

"Things are lively with you lot about, aren't they?" he said, addressing the fire lizard directly. She chittered in response, turning her head this way and that as if looking him over. "How much larger will she grow?" he asked Menolly. "I understand yours are not long out of the shell."

Menolly coaxed Beauty from her shoulder to her forearm so that Master Oldive could examine her closely.

"What's this? What's this?" he asked, glancing from Beauty to Menolly. "Patchy skin?"

Menolly was horrified. She'd been so engrossed in her own problems that she hadn't been taking proper care of her fire lizards. And here was Beauty, her back skin flaking. Probably the others were in trouble, too.

"Oil. They need to be oiled. . . ."

"Don't panic, child. The matter is easily taken care of," and with one long arm, he reached to the shelving above his head, and without seeming to look, brought down a large pot. "I make this for the ladies of the Hold, so if your creatures don't mind smelling like females fair . . ."

Shaking her head, Menolly grinned with relief, remembering the stinking fish oil she'd used first for the fire lizards at the Dragon Stones cave. Master Oldive scooped up a fingertip of the ointment and gestured towards Beauty's back. At Menolly's encouraging nod, he gently smoothed the stuff on the patchy skin. Beauty arched her back appreciatively, crooning with relief, and then she stroked her head against his hand in gratitude.

"Most responsive little creature, isn't she?" Master Oldive said, pleased.

"Very," but Menolly was thinking of Beauty's deplorable attack on Master Domick.

"Now, I'll have a look at your feet. Hmmm. You've been on them too much; there's quite a bit of swelling," he said sternly. "I want you off your feet as much as possible. Did I not make that clear?"

Beauty squeaked angrily.

"Is she agreeing with me or defending you?" asked the Master.

"Possibly both, sir, because I had to stand a lot yesterday. . . ."

"I suppose you did," he said, more kindly, "but do try to keep off your feet as much as possible. Most of the Masters will be understanding." He dismissed her then, giving her the extra jars and reminding her to return the next day after dinner.

Menolly was glad the Master had an inside office, or he'd have seen her trudging across the courtyard after her pipes; but there was no other way, if she was to report with them to Master Jerint. And she didn't wish to offend another Master today.

The chore sections were at work in the courtyard, sweeping, cleaning, raking and doing the general heavy drudgery to keep the Harper Hall in order. She was aware of furtive glances in her direction but affected not to notice them.

The door to the cot was half-closed when she reached it, but Menolly clearly heard the voices raised inside.

"She's an *apprentice,*" Pona was shouting in strident and argumentative tones. "He *said* she was an *apprentice.* She doesn't belong with *us.* We're not apprentices! We've rank to uphold. She doesn't belong in here with us! Let her go where she does belong . . . with the apprentices!" There was a vicious, hateful edge to Pona's voice.

Menolly drew back from the doorway, trembling. She lay flat against the wall, wishing she were anywhere but here. Beauty chirped questioningly in her ear and then stroked her head against Menolly's cheek, the perfumed salve a sweetness in Menolly's nostrils.

One thing was certain: Menolly did not want to go into the cottage for her pipes. But what would happen if she went to Master Jerint without them? She *couldn't* go into the cot. Not now. Her fair swirled about, deprived of their customary landing spot by the closed shutters of Menolly's disputed room, and she wished with all her heart that she could consolidate her nine fire lizards into one dragon and be borne aloft, and *between,* back to her quiet cave by the Dragon Stones. She did belong there because she'd made it *her* place. Hers alone! And really, what place was there for her in the Harper Hall, much less the cot? She might be called an apprentice, but she wasn't part of their group either. Ranly had made that plain at the dining table.

And Master Morshal didn't want her to "presume" to be a harper. Master Domick would as soon she disappeared, for all he'd been willing to teach her. She *had* played well for him, scarred hand and all. She was certain of that. And she was clearly a far better musician than the girls. No false modesty prompted that evaluation.

If her only use at the Harper Hall was to instruct people on being bogus seamen or turning fire lizard eggs, someone else could as easily perform those services. She'd managed to alienate more people than she'd made friends, and the few friends she'd acquired were far more interested in her fire lizards than they were in her. Briefly she wondered what welcome she would have received if she hadn't brought the fire lizards or the two eggs with her. Then there would have been no fire lizard song for the Masterharper to rewrite. And he'd apologized to her for that. The Masterharper of Pern had apologized to her, Menolly of Half-Circle Sea Hold, for improving on her song. Her songs were what he needed, he said. Menolly took in a deep breath and expelled it slowly.

She did have music in the Harper Hall, and that was important! There might not be girl harpers, but no one had ever said there couldn't be girl song-crafters and that mightn't be a bad future.

Not to think of that now, Menolly, she chided herself. Think what you're going to do when you appear before Master Jerint with no pipes. He might seem absentminded, but she doubted very much if he really was. The pipes were in her room, on the little press, and nothing, not even obedience to, and love of, the Masterharper would force her into the cot while those girls were raging on about her.

Beauty took off from her shoulder, calling to the other fire lizards, and when they were all midair above her, they disappeared. Menolly pushed herself away from the cot's wall and started back to the Harper Hall. She'd think of something to say to Master Jerint about the pipes.

The fire lizards exploded into the air above her, squealing so shrilly that she looked up in alarm. They were grouped in a tight cluster, hovered just a split second while her eye took in their unusual formation, and then they parted. Something dropped. Automatically she held out her hands, and the multiple pipes smacked into her palms.

"Oh, you darlings. I didn't know you could do that!" She clutched the pipes to her, ignoring the sting of her hands. Only the stiffness in her feet prevented her from dancing with the joy of relief and the discovery of this unexpected ability of her friends. How clever, clever they were, going to her room and bringing her the pipes. No one could ever again say in her presence that they were just pets and nuisances, good for nothing but trouble!

"The worst storm throws up some wood on the beach," her mother used to say; mostly to soothe her father caught holdbound during a storm.

Why, if she hadn't needed the pipes so badly, and if the girls hadn't been so nasty, she'd never have discovered how very clever her fire lizards could be!

It was with a considerably lightened heart that she entered Master

Jerint's workshop. The place was unexpectedly empty. Master Jerint, bent over a vise attached to his wide and cluttered worktable, was the only occupant of the big room. As she could see that he was meticulously glueing veneer to a harp shaft, she waited and waited. And waited until, bored, she sighed.

"Yes? Oh, the girl! And where have you been this long time? Oh, waiting, I see. You brought your pipes with you?" He held out his hand, and she surrendered them.

She was a bit startled by the sudden intensity of his examination. He weighed the pipes in his hand, peered closely at the way she had joined the sections of reed with braided seaplant; he poked a tool into the blow and finger holes. Muttering under his breath, he brought the pipes over to the rank of windows and examined them minutely in the bright afternoon sun. Glancing at her for permission, he arranged his long fingers appropriately and blew on the pipes, his eyebrows arching at the pure clear tone.

"Sea reeds? Not fresh water?"

"Fresh water, but I cured them in the sea."

"How'd you get this dark shine?"

"Mixed fish oil with sea grass and rubbed it in, warm. . . ."

"Makes an interesting hint of purple in the wood. Could you duplicate the compound again?"

"I think so."

"Any particular type of sea grass? Or fish oil?"

"Packtail," and despite herself, Menolly winced at having to mention the fish by name. Her hand twitched. "And shallow-water sea grass, the sort that clings to sandy bottoms rather than rock."

"Very good." He handed her back the pipes, gesturing for her to follow him to another table where drum rings and skins of varying sizes had been laid out, as well as a reel of the oiled cord necessary to secure drum hides to frame. "Can you assemble a drum?"

"I can try."

He sniffed, not critically—reflectively, Menolly thought—and then motioned for her to begin. He turned back to his patient woodworking on the harp.

Knowing that this was likely another test, Menolly examined each of the nine drum frames carefully for hidden flaws, for the dryness and hardness of the wood. Only one did she feel worth the trouble, and the drum would be a thin, sharp-sounding instrument. She preferred a drum with deep full notes, one that would cut through male voices in a chorus and keep them on the beat. Then she reminded herself that here she would scarcely have to worry about keeping singers in time. She set to work, putting the metal clips on the frame edge to hold the skin. Most of the hides were well cured and stretched, so that it was a matter of finding one the proper size and thinness for her drum frame. She softened the chosen hide in the tub of water, working the skin in her hands until it was flexible enough to draw across the frame. Carefully she made slits and skewered the hide to the clips, symmetrically, so that one side wasn't pulled tighter than another lest it make an uneven tone along the outside of the drum and a sour one in the center. When she was sure she had the hide evenly placed, she lashed it around the frame, two fingers from the edge of the surface. When the hide dried, she'd have a taut drum.

"Well, you do know some of the tricks of the trade, don't you?"

She nearly jumped out of her own hide at the sound of Master Jerint's voice right by her elbow. He gave her a little wintry smile. She wondered how long he'd been standing there watching her. He took the drum, examining it minutely, humphing to himself, his face making a variety of contortions that gave her no real idea of his opinion of her handiwork.

He put the drum carefully on a high shelf. "We'll just let that dry, but you'd better get yourself off to your next class. The juniors are about to arrive, I hear," he added in a dry, unamused tone.

Menolly became immediately conscious of exterior noise; laughter, yells and the dull thudding of many booted feet. Dutifully she made her way to the chorus room where Master Shonagar, seemingly not having moved since she'd left him the day before, greeted her.

"Assemble your friends, please, and have them dispose themselves to listen," he told her, blinking a bit as the fire lizards swept into the high ceilinged hall. Beauty took up her favorite position on Menolly's shoulder. "You!" And one long fat forefinger pointed directly to the little queen. "You will find another perch today." The forefinger moved inexorably towards a bench. "There!"

Beauty gave a quizzical cheep but obediently retired when Menolly silently reinforced the order. Master Shonagar's eyebrows ascended into his hair line as he watched the little fire lizard settle herself, primly flipping her wings to her back, her eyes whirling gently. He grunted, his belly bouncing.

"Now, Menolly, shoulders back, chin up but in, hands together across your diaphragm, breathe in, from the belly to the lungs . . . No, I do not want to see your chest heaving like a smith's bellows . . ."

By the end of the session, Menolly was exhausted: the small of her back and all her midriff muscles ached, her belly was sore, and she felt that dragging nets for offshore fishing would have been child's play. Yet she'd done no more than stand in one spot and attempt, in Master Shonagar's pithy phrase, to control her breathing properly. She'd been allowed to sing only single notes, and then scales of five notes, each scale done on the breath, lightly but in true tone and on pitch. She'd have gutted a whole net of packtail with less effort, so she was intensely grateful when Master Shonagar finally waved her to a seat.

"Now, young Piemur, come forward."

Menolly looked around in surprise, wondering how long Piemur had been sitting quietly by the door.

"The other morning, Menolly, our ears were assailed by pure sound, in descant to a chorus. Piemur here seems of the opinion that the fire lizards will sing for or with anyone. Do you concur?"

"They certainly sang the other morning, but I was singing, too. I do not know, sir."

"Let us conduct a little experiment then. Let us see if they will sing when invited to do so."

Menolly winced a little at his phrasing, but Piemur's wry smile told her that this was Master Shonagar's odd version of humor.

"Supposing I just sing the melody of the chorus we were doing the other morning," said Piemur, "because if you sing *with* me, they're still singing with you and not along with me?"

"Less chatter, young Piemur, more music," said Master Shonagar, sounding extremely bass and impatient.

Piemur took a breath, properly, Menolly noticed, and opened his mouth. To her surprise and delight, a true and delicately sweet sound emerged. Her astonishment registered in the twinkle in Piemur's eyes, but his voice reflected none of his inner amusement to her reaction. Belatedly she encouraged her fire lizards to sing. Beauty flitted to her shoulder, wrapping her tail lightly around Menolly's neck as she peered towards Piemur, cocking her head this way and that as if analyzing the sound and Menolly's command. Rocky and Diver were less restrained. They flew from their perch on the sandtable and, rearing to their haunches, began to sing along with Piemur. Beauty gave a funny scolding sound before she sat up, one forepaw resting lightly on Menolly's ear. Then she took up the descant, her fragile voice rising sure and true above Piemur's. His eyes rolled in appreciation and, when Mimic and Brownie joined in, Piemur backed up so that he could see all of the singing fire lizards.

Anxiously, Menolly glanced at Master Shonagar, but he sat, his fingers shading his eyes, engrossed in the sounds, giving absolutely no indication of his reception. Menolly made herself listen critically, as the Master was undoubtedly doing, but she found little to criticize. She hadn't taught the fire lizards how to sing: she had only given them melody to enjoy. They had enjoyed it, and were expressing that enjoyment by participation. Their voices were not limited to the few octaves of the human voice. Their piercingly sweet tones resonated through their listeners. She could feel the sound in her ear bones, and, from the way Piemur was pressing behind his ears, he felt it as well.

"There, young fellow," said Master Shonagar as the echo of the song died away, "that'll put you in your place, won't it?"

The boy grinned impudently.

"So they will warble with someone besides yourself," the Master said to Menolly.

Out of the corner of her eye, Menolly saw Piemur reach out to stroke Rocky who was nearest him. The bronze immediately rubbed his head along Piemur's hand, whether in approval of the singing or in friendship was irrelevant, judging by the charmed expression on the boy's face.

"They're used to singing because they like it, sir. It's difficult to keep them quiet when there's music about."

"Is that so? I shall consider the potentialities of this phenomenon," and with a brusque wave, Master Shonagar dismissed them all. He settled his head against his propped arm and almost immediately began to snore.

"Is he really asleep? Or shamming?" Menolly asked Piemur when they were out in the courtyard.

"Far's anyone's been able to tell, he's asleep. The only thing that'll wake him is a flat tone or meals. He never goes out of the chorus hall. He sleeps in a little room at the back. Don't think he could climb steps anyway. He's too fat. Hey, you know, Menolly, even in scales, you got a pretty voice. Sort of furry."

"Thanks!"

"Don't mention it. I like furry voices," Piemur went on, undismayed by her sarcasm. "I don't like high, thin, screechy ones like Briala or Pona . . ." and he jerked his thumb toward the cot. "Say, hadn't we better feed the fire lizards? It's nearly suppertime, and they look kinda faded to me."

Menolly agreed, as Beauty, riding on her shoulder, began to creel piteously.

"I sure hope that Shonagar wants to use the fire lizards with the chorus," Piemur said, kicking at a pebble. Then he laughed, pointing to the kitchen. "Look, Camo's ready and waiting."

He was there, one thick arm wrapped about an enormous bowl,

heaped high with scraps. He had a handful raised to attract the fire lizards who spiraled in on him.

Uncle and the two green Aunties had decidedly adopted Camo as their feeding perch. They took so much of his attention that he didn't notice that Rocky, Lazy and Mimic draped themselves about Piemur to be fed. It certainly made it easier to apportion the scraps fairly, with three people feeding. So, when she caught Piemur glancing about the courtyard to see if anyone was noticing his new task, Menolly suggested that he'd be needed on a permanent basis if that didn't get him into any trouble with the masters.

"I'm apprenticed to Master Shonagar. *He* won't mind! And I sure as shells don't." Whereupon Piemur began to stroke the bronze and the two browns with an almost proprietary affection.

As soon as the fire lizards had finished gobbling, Menolly sent Camo back into the kitchen. There had been no loud complaints from Abuna, but Menolly had been conscious of being watched from the kitchen windows. Camo went willingly enough, once she assured him that he'd be feeding the fire lizards again in the morning. Sated, the nine lazily spiraled upwards to the outer roof of the Hall, to bask in the late afternoon sun. And not a moment too soon. They were only just settling themselves when the courtyard became full of boys and men filing into the Hall for their supper.

"Too bad you gotta sit with them," Piemur said, jerking his head at the girls seated at their table.

"Can't you sit opposite me?" asked Menolly, hopeful. It would be nice to have someone to talk to during the meal.

"Naw. I'm not allowed anymore."

"Not allowed?"

Alternating between sour disgust and pleased recollection, Piemur gave a shrug. "Pona complained to Dunca, and she got on to Silvina . . ."

"What did you do?"

"Oh, nothing much," Piemur's shrug was eloquent enough for Menolly to guess that he'd probably been downright wicked. "Pona's a sorry wherry-hen, you know, rank-happy and pleased to pull it. So I can't sit near the girls anymore."

She might regret the prohibition, but it enhanced her estimation of Piemur. As she reluctantly made her way toward the girls, it occurred to her that all she had to do to avoid sitting with them was to be late to meals. Then she'd have to sit where she could. That remedy pleased her so much that she walked more resolutely to her place and endured the hostility of the girls with fortitude. She matched their coldness with stony indifference and ate heartily of the soup, cheese and bread and the sweet pasty that finished the simple supper. She listened politely to the evening announcements of rehearsal times and the fact that Threadfall was expected midday tomorrow. All were to hold themselves close to the Hall, to perform their allotted tasks before, during and after Fall. Menolly heard, with private amusement, the nervous whispering of the girls at the advent of Threadfall and permitted herself to smile in disdain at their terror. They couldn't *really* be that afraid of a menace they'd known all their lives?

She made no move to leave the table when they did, but she was sure that she caught Audiva's wink as the girl followed the others out. When she judged them well away, she rose. Maybe she'd be able to get back into the cot again without confronting Dunca.

"Ah, Menolly, a moment if you please." The cheery voice of the Masterharper sang out as she reached the entrance. Robinton was standing by the stairs, talking to Sebell, and he gestured for Menolly to join them. "Come and check our eggs for us. I know Lessa said it would be a few more days but . . ." and the Harper shrugged his anxiety. "This way . . ." As she accompanied the two men to the upper level, he went on. "Sebell says that you're a mine of information." He grinned down at her. "Didn't ever think you'd have to talk fish in a Harper Hall, did you?"

"No, sir, I didn't. But then, I don't think I really knew what does go on in a Harper Hall."

"Well said, Menolly, well said," and the Harper laughed as well as Sebell. "The other crafts can jibe that we want to know too much about what is not strictly our business, but I've always felt knowledge of matters minor or major makes for better understandings. The mind that will not admit it has something more to learn tomorrow is in danger of stagnating."

"Yes, sir." Menolly caught Sebell's eye, anxiously hoping that the Harper had not heard the minor—or was it major—matter about her missing her scheduled lesson with Domick. An almost imperceptible shake of the brown man's head reassured her.

"Give me your opinion of our eggs, Menolly, for I must be out and about a great deal, but I don't wish to risk the hatching without me in attendance. Right, Sebell?"

"Nor do I wish two fire lizards instead of the one I'm entitled to have."

The two men exchanged knowing glances as Menolly obediently checked the eggs in their sand-filled, warm pots. She turned each one slightly so that the colder side faced the heat of the glowing embers on the hearth. Robinton added a few more blackstones and then eyed her expectantly.

"Well, sir, the eggs are hardening, but they are not hard enough to hatch today or tomorrow."

"So, will you check again tomorrow morning for me, Menolly? I must be away, although Sebell will always know where I can be reached."

Menolly assured the Masterharper that she would keep a watchful eye on the eggs and inform Sebell if there were any alarming changes. The Harper walked her back through his study to the door.

"Now, Menolly, you've played for Domick, been thoroughly catechized by Morshal and sung for Shonagar. Jerint says your pipes are quite allowable, and the drum is well-constructed and should dry out sound. The fire lizards will sing sweetly with others than yourself, so you've accomplished a very great deal in your first days here. Hasn't she, Sebell?"

Sebell agreed, smiling at her in a quiet, kind way. She wondered if either man knew how Dunca and the girls felt about her presence in the Harper Hall.

"And I can leave the matter of the eggs in your good hands. That's grand. That's very good, indeed," the Masterharper said, combing his fingers through his silvered hair.

For a fleeting moment, his usually mobile face was still, and in that unguarded moment, Menolly saw signs of strain and worry. Then he smiled so cheerfully that she wondered if she'd only imagined his weariness. Well, she could certainly spare him anxiety about the fire lizards. She'd check them several times during the day, even if it made her late to Master Shonagar.

As she returned to the cot, pleased that there was some small way in which she could serve the Masterharper, she recalled what he'd said about fish in a Harper Hall. For the first time, Menolly realized that she'd never really thought about life in a Harper Hall—except as a place where music was played and created. Petiron had spoken hazily about apprentices and his time as a journeyman, but nothing in detail. She had imagined the Harper Hall as some magical place, where people sang all conversations, or earnestly copied Records. The reality was almost commonplace, up to and especially including Dunca and the spiteful Pona. Why she had considered all Harpers, and harper people, above such pettiness, endowed with more humanity than Morshal or Domick had shown her, she did not know. She smiled at her naivety. And yet, harpers like Sebell and Robinton, even cynical Domick, were above the ordinary. And Silvina and Piemur were basically good, and certainly had been kind to her. She was in far better circumstances than she'd ever enjoyed in Half-Circle, so she could put up with a little unpleasantness, surely.

It was as well she had reached this conclusion because, no sooner was she inside the door, than Dunca pounced on her with a list of grievances. Menolly received a tirade about her fire lizards, how dangerous and unreliable the creatures were, how they must behave themselves or Dunca would not tolerate them, that Menolly had better realize how little rank mattered in Dunca's cot and that, as the newcomer, she must behave with more deference to those who had been studying far longer at the Harper Craft Hall. Menolly's attitude was presumptuous, uncooperative, unfriendly and discourteous, and Dunca was not having a tunnel-snake in her cot where the girls were as friendly and as considerate of one another as any fosterer could wish.

After the first few sentences, Menolly realized that she could put forth no defence of herself or her friends acceptable to Dunca. All she could do was say "yes" and "no" at appropriate intervals, when Dunca was forced to stop for breath. And every time Menolly thought the woman must surely have exhausted the subject, she would surge onto another imagined slight until Menolly seriously considered calling Beauty to her. The appearance of the fire lizard would certainly curtail the flow of abuse, but would irrevocably destroy any possibility of getting into Dunca's fair record.

"Now, have I made myself plain?" Dunca asked unexpectedly.

"You have," and since Menolly's calm acceptance momentarily robbed Dunca of speech, the girl flew up the steps, ignoring the stiffness of her feet and grinning at the explosive and furious reprimands Dunca made at her retreat.

Chapter 6

The tears I feel today
I'll wait to shed tomorrow.
Though I'll not sleep this night
Nor find surcease from sorrow.
My eyes must keep their sight:
I dare not be tear-blinded.
I must be free to talk
Not choked with grief, clear-minded.
My mouth cannot betray
The anguish that I know.
Yes, I'll keep my tears till later:
But my grief will never go.
          Menolly's "Song for Petiron"

Beauty woke her at sunrise. The other fire lizards were awake, too, though one thing was sure, no one else in the cot was awake yet.

Last night, when Menolly had reached the relative safety of her room, she had closed and barred the door, and then opened the shutters to admit her friends. She had recovered her composure by oiling their patchy skin with Master Oldive's salve. This was the first opportunity she'd had since they'd left the cave by the Dragon Stones to tend and fondle each one. They, too, were communicative. She got many impressions from them, mostly that they'd been bathing daily in the lakes above Fort Hold, which weren't much fun because there weren't any waves to sport in. Menolly caught pictures from their minds of great dragons and of a Weyr, differing in shape from Benden. Beauty's pictures were the sharpest. Menolly had enjoyed her quiet evening with them; it had made up for Dunca's irrational attitudes.

Now, as she became aware of the early morning stillness, she knew she'd have time to do a few tasks for herself. She could get a bath and wash the fruit stains out of her tunic. It ought to dry quickly on the window ledge in the morning sun. There should be time before Threadfall, for she remembered that would occur today.

Quietly she unbarred the door, listening in the corridor, and heard only the faintest echo of a snore. Probably Dunca. Adjuring her fire lizards to silence, she walked noiselessly down the steps to the bathing room at the back of the first level. She'd always heard of the thermal pools in the big Holds and Weyrs, but this was her first experience with them. The fire lizards came clustering in behind her, and she hushed their excited twitterings at the sight of the waist-high trough of steaming water. Menolly dipped her fingers in the pleasant warm water, checked to see if there were sandsoap and then, throwing her clothes on the floor, slipped into the bath.

The water was delightfully warm and soft to her skin, a change from the harsh sea or the mineral-heavy water in Half-Circle Sea Hold. Menolly submerged completely and came up, shaking her hair. She'd wash all over. One of the others pushed Auntie Two into the bath, and she let out a high-pitched squeal of protest and fright, then paddled happily about in the warm water. The next thing Menolly knew, all the fire lizards were splashing about, their talons unexpectedly catching her bare skin or tangling in her hair. She hushed them often and sternly, because she wasn't sure how far noise carried from the bathing room: all she'd need, after last night, was for Dunca to come charging in, roused from her night's rest by her least-wanted guests.

Menolly sandsoaped all of the fire lizards thoroughly, rinsed them well, got herself, her hair and finally her clothes well washed, then got back to her room without anyone the wiser for her early morning activity. She was oiling a rough patch on Mimic's back when she heard the first stirrings outside: the cheery greetings of the herdsmen going to attend their beasts who would be holdbound today with Threadfall due. She wondered how Fall would affect the business of the Harper Hall: probably the apprentices and journeymen were required to assist the holders in flame-thrower details. Thank goodness no one had asked her what she'd done after Fall in Half-Circle. She heard the slamming of a door below and decided that Dunca was up. Menolly slipped into her only other clothes, the patched tunic and trousers of her cave days. They were at least clean and neat.

They were not, however, it was pointed out to Menolly at the breakfast table, suitable attire for a young lady living in Dunca's cot. When Menolly explained that she had only the one other change, which was now drying, Dunca let out a shriek of outrage and demanded to know where the clothes were drying. Menolly was emphatically told that she had committed yet another unwitting sin by hanging her washing—like the commonest field worker—on the window ledge. She was ordered to bring down the offending garments, still damp, and shown by the fuming Dunca where such laundry was to be hung, in the inner recesses of the cot. Where, Menolly was sure, they would take days to dry and smell musty besides with no air to freshen them.

Very much aware of her disgrace and destitute condition, Menolly finished her breakfast as quickly as possible. But when she rose from the table, Dunca demanded to know where she thought she was going.

"I must feed my fire lizards, Dunca, and I was told to report to Master Domick this morning . . ."

"No message was received by me to such effect." Dunca drew herself up in officious disbelief.

"Master Domick told me yesterday."

"He made no mention of such instructions to me." Dunca's manner implied that Menolly was making up the order.

"Probably because yesterday's message went astray."

And, while Dunca stammered and stuttered, Menolly slipped out of the room and out of the cot, trotting across the road, the fire lizards gracefully swirling above her head until they were sure she was headed towards the Harper Hall. Then they disappeared.

They were perched on the window ledges when she reached the kitchen corner, their eyes whirling redly in anticipation of breakfast. There seemed to be more than the usual amount of confusion in the kitchen, but Camo, once he caught sight of her, immediately put down the side of herdbeast he'd been lugging and left the carcass, its legs obscenely dropping across the passage, while he disappeared back into the storeroom. He emerged with yet a bigger bowl, scraps spilling down its sides as he jogged to meet her. Suddenly he gave a startled cry; and Menolly, peering in the window, saw that Abuna, wooden spoon up-raised, was chasing after him. He slithered by, but her dress got caught on the extruding legs of the carcass.

Menolly ducked into the space between the windows, fervently hoping that Camo's preoccupation with the feeding of fire lizards was not going to cause a major breach with Abuna. There might be nothing to fear from harpers, but the women in the Harper Hall were certainly possible enemies.

"Menolly, am I too late . . ." Piemur came charging across the courtyard from the apprentice dormitory, his boots half-fastened, his tunic laces untied and his face and hair showing signs of half-hearted washing.

Before he could assemble his clothing properly, Rocky, Lazy and Mimic attached themselves to him: Camo came out of the kitchen to be assaulted by his three; and the three humans were exhorted by shrill hungry creelings to be fed.

Camo's great bowl was finally emptied, and as if on cue, Abuna's voice rose to command Camo back to his duties. Menolly hurriedly thanked the man and pushed him urgently down the kitchen steps, assuring him that he'd saved quite enough food for the pretties, that the pretties could not stuff in another mouthful.

When the breakfast gong sounded, Menolly stayed in the kitchen corner until the courtyard was cleared of the hungry harpers. She had to see Master Domick, for which interview she would need her gitar. She went to the archroom to collect it and lingered there, since everyone was still eating. She tuned the gitar, delighting afresh in its rich sweet tone. She attempted some of the bridges from the music she'd played in the abortive lesson with the girls, stretching and stretching against the pull of the scar until her hand muscles went into a spasm of cramping. All of a sudden, she remembered her other chore; to check the fire lizard eggs. But, if the Masterharper were still asleep. . . . No way of telling from here. She ran lightly down the steps, pleased that her feet were less stiff and tender this morning. She paused in the main hall, listening, and heard the distinctive sound of the Masterharper's voice at the round table. So she hurried up the steps and down the corridor to his room.

The fire lizard pots were warm on the side away from the fire, so they'd obviously just been turned. She uncovered each egg and checked the shells for hardness, for any sign of cracking or striation. They were fine. She gently covered them with sand and replaced the lids.

As she emerged from the Masterharper's rooms, she heard Master Domick's voice on the steps. With him were Sebell, carrying a small harp, and Talmor, gitar slung across his back.

"There she is," Sebell said. "You checked the eggs, Menolly?"

"I did, sir. They're fine."

"Come this way, then, step lively now . . . if you can. . . ." Domick said, frowning as he belatedly recalled her disability.

"My feet are nearly as good as new now, sir," she told him.

"Well, you're not to run any races with Thread today, hear?"

Menolly wasn't certain, as she followed the three men into the study, if Domick were teasing her or not. He sounded so sour, it was difficult to tell, but Sebell caught her eye and winked.

Domick's study, well-lit by huge baskets of glows, was dominated by the biggest sandtable Menolly had ever seen, with all its spaces glass-covered, though she politely averted her eyes from the inscriptions. Domick might not like people peering at his music. The shelves were jammed with loose record hides, and thin, white-bleached sheets of some substance evenly cut along the edges. She tried to get a closer look at them, but Master Domick called her to attention by telling her to take the middle stool.

Sebell and Talmor were already settling themselves before the music rack and tuning their instruments. So she took her place and cast a quick glance at the music before them. With a thrill of surprise, she saw that it was for four instruments, and no easy read.

"You're to play second gitar, Menolly," Domick said, with the smile of one who is conferring a favor. He picked up a metal pipe with finger stops, one of the flutes that Petiron had told her were used by more accomplished pipers. She politely suppressed her curiosity, but she couldn't control her delighted surprise when Domick ran a test scale. It sounded like a fire lizard's voice.

"You'll need to look through the music," he said, observing her interest.

"I will?"

Master Domick cleared his throat. "It *is* customary with music you've never seen before." He tapped the music with his pipe. "That," and his tone was very acid, "is no children's exercise. Despite your display for Talmor yesterday, you will not find this easy to read."

Rebuked, she skimmed the music, trying an alternative chording in one measure to see which would be easier on her hand at that tempo. The complexity of the chording was so fascinating that she forgot she was keeping three harpers waiting. "I beg your pardon." She turned the music back to the beginning and looked at Domick for him to give them the beat.

"You're ready?"

"I think so, sir."

"Just like that?"

"Sir?"

"Very well, young woman, at the beat," and Domick sternly tapped out the time with a strong stamp.

It had been fun, always, for Menolly to play with Petiron, particularly when he let her improvise around his melody. It had been a pleasure yesterday to see new music in Talmor's lesson, but now, the stimulation of playing with three keen and competent musicians gave her such impulsion that she seemed to be an irrelevant medium for fingers that had to play what her eager eyes saw. She was lost completely in the thrall of the music, so that when the rushing finale ended, she suffered a shock as keen as pain.

"Oh, that was marvelous. Could we play it again?"

Talmor burst out laughing, Domick stared at her, and Sebell covered his eyes with his hands as he bowed his head over his harp.

"I didn't believe you, Talmor," Domick said, shaking his head. "And I'd played with her myself. True, only basic things. I didn't think she was up to any demanding standard."

Menolly inhaled sharply, worried that she had somehow erred, as she had with the girls the previous day.

"And I know," Domick went on in that tight, dry tone, "that you can't ever have seen that piece of music before . . ."

Menolly stared at the Master. "It was fascinating. The interweaving of melody from flute to harp and gitar. I'm sorry about this section," and she flipped back the sheets. "I should have used your chords but my hand . . ."

Domick stared at her until her voice trailed off. "Did Sebell warn you what would happen this morning?"

"No, sir, only to say that I mustn't fail to come today."

"Enough, Domick. The child's worried sick that she's done something wrong. Well, you haven't, Menolly," Talmor said, patting her hand encouragingly. "You see," he went on, glaring in a good-natured fashion at Domick, "he just finished writing it. You've played the fingers off Sebell and me. Domick's panting for breath. And you've managed to plow through one of Domick's torturous inventions with . . . well, I did hear one faulty chording besides the one you just pointed out, but, as you say, your hand . . ."

Now Sebell lifted his head, and Menolly stared at him because his eyes were overflowing with tears. But at the same time, he was laughing! Convulsed with mirth he wagged an impotent finger at Domick, unable to speak.

Domick batted irritably at Sebell's hand and glared at both journeymen. "That's enough. All right, so the joke's on me, but you'll have to admit that there was good precedent for my skepticism. Anyone can play solo . . ." He turned on the bewildered Menolly. "Did you play a great deal with Petiron? Or any of the other musicians at Half-Circle?"

"There *was* only Petiron who could play properly. Fishing leaves a man's hands too stiff for any fine music." She flicked a glance at Sebell. "There were a few drummers and stickmen. . . ."

Her reply set Sebell laughing again. He hadn't seemed the sort, Menolly thought, being so calm and quiet. To be sure he was laughing without roaring but. . . .

"Suppose you tell me exactly what you did do at Half-Circle Sea Hold, Menolly. Musically, that is. Master Robinton's been too busy to confer with me at any length."

Domick's words implied that he had the right to know whatever it was she might tell Master Robinton, and she saw Sebell nodding his head in permission. So she thought for a moment. Would it be proper, now, to tell the harpers that she had taught the children after Petiron had died and before the new Harper had come? Yes, because Harper Elgion must have told Master Robinton, and *he* hadn't chided her for stepping into a man's duties. Further, Master Domick had taunted her with telling the truth once before. Rather than antagonize him for any reason, she had best be candid now. So she spoke of her situation at Half-Circle Sea Hold: how Petiron had singled her out when she was old enough to learn her Teaching Ballads and Sagas. He had taught her to play gitar and harp, "to help with the teaching," she assured her listeners, "and with the evening singing." Domick nodded. And how Petiron had shown her all the music he had, "but he'd only three pieces of occasional music because he said there wasn't need for more. Yanus, the Sea Holder, wanted music to sing to, not listen to."

"Naturally," Domick replied, nodding again.

And Petiron had taught her how to cut and hole reeds to make pipes, to stretch skin on drum frames, large and small, the principles involved in making a gitar or small harp, but there was no hardwood in the Sea Hold for another harp, and no real need for Menolly to have either harp or gitar. Two Turns ago, however, she'd had to take over the playing of the Teaching because Petiron's hands had become crippled with the knuckle disease. And then, of course, and now Menolly felt the lump of grief rising in her throat, she'd done all the teaching when Petiron had died because Yanus realized that the young must be kept up in their Teaching Ballads and Songs since he knew his duty to the Weyr, and she was the only person in the Hold who could be spared from the fishing.

"Of course," Domick had said. "And when you cut your hand?"

"Oh, the new Harper, Elgion, had arrived so I . . . wasn't required to play anymore. And besides," she held her hand up explanatorily, "it was thought I'd never be able to play again."

She wasn't conscious of the silence at first, her head bent, her eyes on her hand, rubbing the scar with her right thumb, because the intensive playing had caused it to ache again.

"When Petiron was here at the Hold, there was no finer musician, no better instructor," Master Domick said quietly. "I had the good fortune to be his apprentice. You've no need ever to be ashamed of your playing. . . ."

"Or of your joy in music," Sebell added, no laughter in his eyes now as he leaned towards her.

Joy in music! His words were like a release. How could he have known so acutely!

"Now that you're at the Harper Hall, Menolly, what would you like best to do?" Master Domick asked her, his tone so casual, so neutral that Menolly couldn't think what answer he expected of her.

Joy in music. How could she express that? In writing the kind of songs Master Robinton needed? How would she know what he needed? And hadn't Talmor said that Domick had composed the magnificent quartet they had just played? Why did Master Robinton need another composer if he already had Domick in the Hall?

"You mean, play or sing, or teach?"

Master Domick widened his eyes and regarded her with a half-smile. "If that's what you wish?"

"I'm here to learn, aren't I?" She avoided his taunt.

Domick acknowledged that that was true enough.

"So I'll learn the things I haven't had the chance to learn before because Petiron told me there were a lot of things he couldn't teach me. Like how to use my voice properly. That's going to take a lot of hard work with Master Shonagar. He only lets me breathe and sing five-note scales . . ." Talmor grinned so broadly at her, his eyes dancing as if he knew so exactly her feelings that she took encouragement from him. "I'd really love . . ." Then she hesitated because of what Domick might say and she dreaded his clever-edged tongue.

"What do you really want, Menolly?" asked Sebell kindly.

"You're frightening her, Domick," Talmor said at the same time.

"Nonsense, are you frightened of me, Menolly?" He sounded surprised. "It's having to train idiots that sours me, Menolly," said Master Domick, but his voice was suddenly gentler. "Now tell *me* what facet of music appeals to you most?"

He caught her gaze and would not release her eyes, but his phrasing had given her the answer.

"What appeals to me most? Why, playing like this, in a group." She got the words out in a rush, gesturing at the rack in front of her. "It's so beautiful. It's such a challenge, to hear the interweaving harmonies and the melody line changing from instrument to instrument. I felt as if I was . . . was flying on a dragon!"

Domick looked startled and blinked, a slow pleased smile lighting his otherwise dour face.

"She means it, Domick," Talmor said in the pause that followed.

"Oh, I do. It's the most exciting thing I've ever played. Only . . ."

"Only what?" urged Talmor when she faltered.

"I didn't play it right. I should have studied the music longer before I started playing because I was so busy watching the notes and time changes that I didn't, I couldn't, follow the dynamic markings. . . . I *am* sorry."

Domick brought his hand against his forehead in an exasperated smack. Sebell dissolved again into his quiet laughter. But Talmor just howled, slapping his knee and pointing at Domick.

"In that case, Menolly, we will play it again," Domick said, raising his voice to drown the amusement of the others. "And this time . . ." he frowned at Menolly, an expression which no longer distressed her because she knew that she had touched him, "watching those dynamic signs, which I put in for very good reason. Now, on the beat . . ."

They did not play the music through. Domick stopped them, time and again, insisting on a retard here, a variation of the designated time here, a better balance of the instruments in another section. In some respects, this was as satisfying as playing for Menolly, since Domick's comments gave her insights to the music as well as its composer. Sebell had been right about her studying with Domick. She had a lot to learn from a man who could write music like this, pure music.

Then Talmor began to argue interpretation with Domick, an argument cut short by the eerie sound that began softly and increased in volume and intensity so that it was almost unbearable in the closed room. Abruptly her fire lizards appeared.

"How did they get in here like that?" Talmor demanded, hunching his shoulders to protect his head as the study got overcrowded with nervous fire lizards.

"They're like dragons, you know," Sebell said, equally wary of claw and wing.

"Tell those creatures to settle down, Menolly," commanded Domick. "The noise bothers them."

"That's only the Threadfall alarm," said Domick, but the men were putting down their instruments.

Menolly called her fire lizards to order, and they settled on the shelves, their eyes wheeling with alarm.

"Wait here, Menolly," Domick said as he and the others made for the door. "We'll be back. That is, I will . . ."

"And I," "I, too," said the others, and then they all stamped out of the room.

Menolly sat uneasily, aware that the Hall was preparing for Threadfall, as she had prepared for the menace all her conscious years. She heard racing feet in the corridors, for the door was half ajar. Then the clanging of shutters, the squeal of metal, many shouts and a gradual compression of air in the room. The sudden throb as the great ventilating fans of the Hall were set into motion for the duration of Threadfall. Once again, she found herself wishing to be back in the safety of her seaside cave. She had always hated being closed in at Half-Circle Sea

Hold during Threadfall. There never seemed to be enough air to breathe during those fear-filled times. The cave, safe but with a reassuringly clear view of the sea, had been a perfect compromise between security and convention.

Beauty chirped inquiringly and then sprang from the shelf to Menolly's shoulder. She wasn't nervous at being closed in, but she was very much aware of Thread's imminence, her slim body taut, her eyes whirling.

The clatter and clangs, the shouts and stampings ceased. Menolly heard the low murmur of men's voices on the steps as Domick and the two journeymen returned.

"Granted that your left hand won't do octave stretches yet," Domick said, addressing Menolly but more as if he were continuing a conversation begun with the two journeymen, "how much harp instruction did Petiron give you?"

"He had one small floor harp, sir, but we'd such a desperate time getting new wire, so I sort of learned to . . ."

"Improvise?" asked Sebell, extending his harp to her.

She thanked him and politely proffered the gitar in its place, which he, with equal grave courtesy, accepted.

Domick had been riffling through music on the shelves and brought over another score, worn and faded in spots but legible enough, he said, for the purpose.

Menolly rubbed her fingertips experimentally. She'd lost most of the harp-string calluses, and her fingers would be sore but perhaps. . . . She looked up at Domick and receiving permission, plucked an arpeggio. Sebell's harp was a joy to use, the tone singing through the frame, held between her knees, like liquid sound. She had to shift her fingers awkwardly to make the octave run. Despite the fact that her scar made her wince more than once, she became so quickly involved in the music that the discomfort could be ignored. She was a bit startled when she reached the finale to realize that the others had been playing along with her.

"In the slow section," she asked, "is the major seventh chord accented throughout? The notation doesn't say."

"Whether it is or not must wait for another day," Domick said, firmly taking the harp from her and handing it back to Sebell. "You'll live to play harp another time, Menolly. No more now." He turned her left hand over so she was forced to notice that the scar had split and was bleeding slightly from the tear.

"But . . ."

"But . . ." Domick interrupted her more gently than he usually spoke, "it's time to eat. Everyone has to eat sometime, Menolly."

They were all grinning at her and, emboldened by the rapport she'd had with them during their practice, she smiled back. Now she smelled the aroma of roasted meat and spices and was mildly astonished to feel her stomach churning with hunger. To be sure, she hadn't eaten much at the cot, with everyone glaring at her so.

Some of her elation with the morning's satisfying work was dampened by the realization that she'd have to sit with the girls. But that was a small blemish on the pleasure of the hours gone past. To her surprise, however, there were no girls at the hearth table, and the great metal doors of the Hall were locked tight, the windows shuttered, the dining hall lit by the great central and corner baskets of glows; in some obscure way, the hall looked more friendly than she'd seen it before.

Everyone else was seated, though her quick glance did not show Master Robinton to be in his customary place at the round table. Master Morshal was and frowned at her until Master Domick gave her a shove towards her place as he drew out his own chair. Sebell and Talmor seemed in no way abashed as they went late to the oval journeymen's tables. But Menolly felt more conspicuous than ever as she walked awkwardly towards the hearth table. And it wasn't her imagination: every eye in the room was on her.

"Hey, Menolly," said a familiar voice in a harsh but carrying whisper, "hurry up so we can get fed." She saw Piemur slapping the empty place beside him. "See?" he said to his neighbor, "I told you she wouldn't be hiding in the Hold with the others." Then he added, under the cover of the noise of everyone taking their seats, "You aren't afraid of Thread, are you?"

"Why should I be?" Menolly was being truthful, but it obviously stood her in good credit with the boys near enough to hear her reply. "And I thought you said you weren't supposed to sit at the girls' table?"

"They're not here, are they? And you said you wanted someone to talk to. So here I am."

"Menolly?" asked the boy with the protuberant eyes who usually sat opposite her, "do fire lizards breathe fire like dragons and go after Thread?"

Menolly glanced at Piemur to see if he were back of the question. He shrugged innocence.

"Mine never have, but they're young."

"I told you so, Brolly," replied Piemur. "Dragonets in the Weyrs don't fight Thread, and fire lizards are just small dragons. Right, Menolly?"

"They do seem to be," she said, temporizing slightly, but neither debater noticed.

"Then where are they now?" Brolly wanted to know, slightly sneering.

"In Master Domick's study."

The meat reached them and further discussion was suspended. Today Menolly blithely speared four slices of juicy meat to her plate. She reached for bread, beating Brolly's grab for some. And she dished Piemur some of the redroots, which he wasn't going to take. He was much too small not to eat properly.

Whether it was Piemur's company or the absence of the girls, or both, Menolly didn't know, but suddenly she was included in the table conversations. The boys opposite her had question after question about her fire lizards: how she had accidentally discovered the queen's clutch in the sand; how she'd saved the hatchlings from destruction by Thread; how she had found enough food to support their voracious appetites; how she'd dragged a wherry from the mire to provide oil for her fire lizards' patchy skins. She sensed that the boys gradually became reconciled to her possession of so many fire lizards because it was obviously no gather day to take care of them. They had the most bizarre theories about fire lizards and a few unsubtle queries about when would her queen fly to mate and how soon would there be a clutch and how many in it.

"The masters and journeymen would get first crack anyhow," Piemur said, disgruntled.

"It ought to be free choice, the way the dragons choose their riders," said Brolly.

"Fire lizards aren't quite the same as dragons, Brolly," said Piemur, glancing at Menolly for support. "Look at Lord Groghe. What dragon would've picked him if it had had another choice?"

The boys shushed him, glancing nervously about to see if any one had overheard his indiscreet remark.

"The Weyrs have control of the fire lizards any road," said Brolly. "You can just bet the Weyrs're going to hand 'em out where they'll keep the Lord Holders and Craft Masters happy."

Menolly sighed for the truth of that surmise.

"Yes, but you can't *make* a fire lizard stay with you if you're mean to him," said Piemur flatly. "I heard that Lord Meron's disappears for days."

"Where do they go?" asked Brolly.

As Menolly didn't know, she was just as glad that the eerie sound, which Domick had said was the Thread alarm, sounded, effectively ending the conversation.

"That means Thread is directly over us," said Piemur, hunching his shoulders and pointing toward the ceiling.

"Look at that!" And Brolly's startled exclamation made everyone turn about.

On the mantel behind her were ranged all nine fire lizards, their eyes sparkling with rainbow reflections of intense agitation, their wings spread, talons unsheathed. They were hissing, retracting and extending their tongues as if licking imaginary Thread from the air.

Menolly half rose, glancing towards the round table. She saw Domick nodding permission to her as he, too, got to his feet. He was gesturing to someone at the journeymen's tables.

"The alarm chorus would be appropriate, Brudegan," he called as he crossed to the hearth, a wary eye on the fire lizards.

Menolly motioned to Beauty, but the little queen ignored her, rising to her haunches and starting to keen a piercing series of notes, up and down an almost inaudibly high octave. The others joined her.

"For the sake of our ears, Menolly, can you get your creatures to sing *with* the chorus now? Brudegan, where's your beat?"

Feet began to stamp, one, two, three, four, and suddenly the fire lizards' keen was covered by the mass chorus. Beauty fanned her wings in surprise, and Mimic backwinged himself off the mantel, only missing a drop to the floor by claws biting into the wood.

> *"Drummer, beat, and piper, blow,*
> *Harper, strike, and soldier, go . . ."*

sang the massed voices. Menolly joined in, singing directly to the fire lizards. She was aware of Brudegan, then Sebell and Talmor coming to stand beside her, but facing the boys. Brudegan directed, cueing in the parts, the descant on the refrain. Above the male voices, pure and piercingly thrilling, rang the fire lizards' tone, weaving their own harmonies about the melody.

The last triumphant note echoed through the corridors of the Harper Hall. And from the doorway to the outer hall, there came a sigh of pleasure. Menolly saw the kitchen drudges, an utterly entranced Camo among them, standing there, every face wreathed with smiles.

"I'd say that a rendition of 'Moreta's Ride' might be in order, if you think your friends would oblige us," Brudegan said, with a slight bow to Menolly and a gesture to take his place.

Beauty, as if she understood what had been said, gave a complacent chirp, blinking the first lids across her eyes so that those nearest laughed. That startled her, and she fanned her wings as if scolding them for impudence. That prompted more laughter, but Beauty was now watching Menolly.

"Give the beat, Menolly," said Brudegan, and because his manner indicated that he expected her obedience, she raised her hands and sketched the time.

The chorus responded at the upstroke, and she experienced a curious sense of power as she realized that these voices were hers to direct. Beauty led the fire lizards in another dizzy climb of sound, but they sang the melody, octaves above the baritones who introduced the first stanza of the Ballad, to the muted humming of the other parts. The baritones, Menolly felt, were not really watching her: she signaled for more intensity because, after all, the Ballad told of a tragedy. The singers gave more depth to their part. Menolly had often led the evening sings at the Half-Circle Sea Hold, so conducting was not new to her. It was the quality of the singers, their responsiveness to her signals, that made as much difference as chalk from cheese.

Once the baritones had finished telling of the dread sickness in the land, which had struck with incredible speed across the breadth of Pern, the full chorus quietly introduced the refrain, of Moreta secluded with her queen, Orlith, who is about to clutch in Fort Weyr, while the healers from all holds and Weyrs try to isolate the form of the disease and find a cure. The tenors take up the narration, with increasing intensity, the basses and baritones emphasizing the plight of the land, herdbeasts left untended, wherries breaking into crops as holders, crafters, dragonfolk alike are consumed by the dread fever.

A bass sings the solo of Capiam, Masterhealer of Pern, who isolates the illness and suggests its cure. Those dragonriders who are still able to stay on their beasts, fly to the rain forests of Nabol and Ista, to find and deliver to Capiam the all-important seeds that contain the cure, some riders dying with the effort as they complete their task.

A dialogue between baritone, Capiam, and the soprano; Moreta was sung, Menolly was only vaguely cognizant, by Piemur. Excitement builds as Moreta, once Orlith has clutched, is the only healthy dragonrider at the Fort and one of the few immune to the disease. It is up to her to deliver the medicine. Moreta, pushing herself and her queen to the limits of their endurance, flies *between* from hold to hold, crafthall to cot, from Weyr to Weyr. The final verse, a dirge with keening descant, this time so appropriately rendered by the fire lizards that Menolly waved the humans silent, ended in the sorrowful farewell of a world to its heroines as Orlith, the dying Moreta on her back, seeks the oblivion of *between.*

Such a deep silence followed the soft final chord that Menolly shook off the spell of the song with difficulty.

"I wonder if we could ever repeat that again," Brudegan said slowly, thoughtfully, after a further moment of almost unendurable silence. A sigh of release from the thrall of the music spread through the hall.

"It's the fire lizards," said the very soft voice of the usually impudent Piemur.

"You're right, Piemur," Brudegan replied, considering the suggestion, and there was a murmur of assent from the others.

Menolly had taken a seat, her knees shaking and her insides gripped by a rhythmic shuddering. She took a sip of the klah remaining in her cup; cold or not, it helped.

"Menolly, do you think they'd sing like that again?" Brudegan asked, dropping to the bench beside her.

Menolly blinked at him, as much because she hadn't had time to recover from the extraordinary experience of directing a trained group as because he, a journeyman, was asking the advice of the newest arrival in the Harper Craft Hall.

"They sang fine with me yesterday, sir," said Piemur. Then he giggled. "Menolly told Master Shonagar that it's hard to keep 'em quiet when you *don't* want 'em singing. Right, Menolly?" Piemur chortled again, all his impudence revived. "That's what happened the other morning, sir, when you didn't know who was singing."

To Menolly's relief, Brudegan laughed heartily, evidently reconciled. Menolly managed a shy and apologetic smile for that untoward incident, but the chorus leader was watching the fire lizards now. They were preening their wingtips or glancing about the room at all the people, oblivious to the sensation they had just caused.

"Pretties sing pretty," said Camo, appearing beside Menolly and Brudegan, a pitcher of steaming klah in one hand. He poured some into each empty cup, and then Menolly noticed that the drink was being served throughout the hall.

"You liked their singing, eh, Camo?" asked Brudegan, taking a judicious sip from his mug. "Sing higher than Piemur here, and he's got the best voice we've had in many a Turn. As if he didn't know it." Brudegan reached across the table to ruffle Piemur's hair.

"Pretties sing again?" asked Camo plaintively.

"They can sing any time they like for all of me," Brudegan replied, nodding to Menolly. "But right now, I want to get some practice done. We've that big chorale work to polish properly before Lord Groghe's entertainment." With a sigh, he pushed himself to his feet and tapped an empty klah pot for silence. "Don't stop them if they feel like singing, Menolly," he added, inclining his head towards the fire lizards. "Now then, you lot. We'll begin with the tenor solo, Fesnal, if you please . . ." And Brudegan pointed to one of the journeymen who rose to his feet.

Listening to the rehearsal was not quite the same involving experience as directing. Then, Menolly had felt herself to be an extension of the choral group. Now she found it objectively interesting to observe Brudegan's direction, and to think what she would do with the same passages. About the time she decided that he was an exceedingly clever director, she realized that she'd been setting herself in comparison with a man in every way superior in experience and training.

Menolly almost laughed aloud. Yet, she reflected, this was what life should be in a Harper Hall: music, morning, noon, afternoon and evening. She couldn't have enough of it, and yet, she could now see the logic of afternoons spent on other chores. Her fingertips ached from the harp strings, and her scar felt hot and pulsed. She massaged her hand, but that was too painful. She'd left the jar of numbweed in the cot, which meant she'd have to wait until after Threadfall to get easement. She wondered if the girls knew what went on in the Harper Hall during Threadfall. Hadn't Piemur said they were up at the Hold during Fall? She shrugged; she was far happier to be here.

Once more the eerie alarm cut through other sounds. Brudegan abruptly ended the practice, thanking his chorus members for their attention and hard work. Then he stood back politely as a tall older journeyman walked quietly to the fireplace, raising his hands unnecessarily for attention.

"Everyone remembers his duties now?" There was a murmur of assent. "Good. As soon as the doors are open, join your sections. With luck and Fort Weyr's usual efficiency, we'll be back in the Hall by suppertime . . ."

"I've meatrolls for the outside crews," announced Silvina, standing up at the round table. "Camo, take the tray and stand by the door!"

A second weird hooting, and then the clang and ring of metal and a ponderous creaking. Menolly half wished that she were in a position to see the Hall doors working as light began to flood the outer hallway. A cheer went up, and the boys surged towards the entrance, some going across the tide to take meatrolls from Camo's patiently held tray.

Then the dining hall shutters clanked back, the afternoon sunlight an assault on eyes accustomed to the softer illumination from glow baskets.

"Here they come! Here they come!" rose the shout, and the flow towards the door became a scramble, despite the attempts of masters and journeymen to keep an orderly pace.

"We can see as well from the windows, Menolly. Come *on!*" Piemur tugged at her sleeve.

The fire lizards reacted to the excitement, streaking through the open windows. Menolly saw the spiral of dragons descending in wings to the ground beyond the Hall courtyard. Truly they made a magnificent sight. The sky seemed to be as clogged with dragons as just recently it must have been with Thread. The boys let out a cheer, and Menolly saw the dragonriders lifting their arms in response to the hurray! She might have lost her fear of Thread, of being caught out holdless, but she would never lose that lift of heart at the sight of the great dragons who protected all Pern from the ravages of Thread.

"Menolly!"

She whirled at the sound of her name and saw Silvina standing there, a slight frown creasing her wide forehead. For the first time since morning, Menolly wondered what she had done wrong now.

"Menolly, has nothing been forwarded to you from Benden Weyr in the way of clothes? I know that Master Robinton dragged you out of there with scant time to assemble yourself . . ."

Menolly could say nothing, realizing that Dunca had complained about her tattered trousers to Silvina. The headwoman was giving her clothes a keen scrutiny.

"Well, for once," and Silvina's admission was grudging, "Dunca is right. Your clothes are worn to the woof. Can't have that. You'll give the Harper Craft a bad name, wandering about in rags, however attached to them you may be."

"Silvina, I . . ."

"Great shells, child, I'm not angry with *you!*" And Silvina took Menolly's chin firmly in her hand and made her look eye to eye. "I'm furious with myself for not *thinking!* Not to mention giving that Dunca a chance to snipe at you! Only don't go repeating *that,* please, for Dunca's useful to me in her own way. Not that you talk much anyhow. Haven't heard you put two sentences together yet. There now! What have I said to distress you? You just come along with me." And Silvina took Menolly firmly by the elbow and marched her towards the complex of storage rooms at the back of the Harper Hall on the kitchen level.

"There's been so much excitement these days, I haven't any more wit about me than Camo. But then, every apprentice is supposed to come with two decent sets of clothing, new or nearly new, so it never occurred to me. And you having come from Benden Weyr, I thought . . . though you weren't there long enough, now, were you?"

"Felena gave me the skirt and tunic, and they took my measure for boots . . ."

"And Master Robinton threw you a-dragonback before you could say a word. Well now, let's just see," and Silvina unlocked a door, flipped open a glow basket to illuminate a storeroom stacked from floor to ceiling with bolts of cloth, clothing, boots, hides made or uncut, sleeping furs and rolls of tapestries and rugs. She gave Menolly another appraising look, turning her from side to side. "We've more that's suitable for boys and men from the Weaver and Tanner Halls . . ."

"I'd really prefer trousers."

Silvina chuckled kindly. "You're lanky enough to wear them well, I must say, and since you're to be using instruments, trous will be handier than skirts. But you ought to have some finery, child. It does lift the spirit and there're gathers . . ." She was sorting through folded skirts of black and brown, which she replaced disdainfully. "Now this . . ." and she pulled out a bolt of a rich, dark red fabric.

"That's too fine for me . . ."

"You'd have me dress you in drudges' colors? Even they have something good!" Silvina was scornful. "You may not be proud in yourself, Menolly. In point of fact, your modesty has done you great service, but you will kindly consider the change in your circumstances. You're not the youngest child in a family of an isolated Sea Hold. You're an apprentice harper, and *we*"—Silvina tapped her chest smartly with her fingers—"have appearances to maintain. You will dress yourself as well as, and if I've my way, better than, those fumble-fingered females, or those musical midgets who will never be more than senior apprentices or very junior journeymen. Now, a rich red will become you. Ah, yes, this will suit you well," she said holding the red up against Menolly's shoulder. "Until I can have that made up, trous will have to do," and she held up a pair of dark blue hide pants to Menolly's waist. "You're all leg. And here." She shoved a pair of close-woven blue-green trousers at Menolly. "This should match the leather pants, and it does," she said tossing to Menolly a dark blue jerkin. "Put that lot on the chest there and try on this wherhide jacket. Yes, that's not too bad a fit, is it? Here's a hat and gloves. And tunics. Now these," and from another chest Silvina extracted breast bands and underpants, snorting as she passed them to Menolly. "Dunca was quite incensed that you'd no underthings at all." Silvina's amusement ended as she saw Menolly's face. "Whyever are you looking so stricken? Because you wore your underthings out? Or because Dunca's pried into your affairs? You can't honestly be worried what that fat old fool thinks or says or does? Yes, you can and you are and you would!"

Silvina pushed Menolly backwards until she sat abruptly on the chest behind her while Silvina, hands on her hips, regarded her with a curiously intense expression.

"I think," said Silvina slowly, in a very gentle voice, "that you have lived too much alone. And not just in that cave. And I think you must have been terribly bereft when old Petiron died. He seems to have been the only one in your Hold who understood what's in you. Though why he left it so long to tell Master Robinton I simply don't understand. Well, in a way I do, but that's neither here nor there. One thing certain, you're not staying on in that cot. Not another night . . ."

"Oh, but Silvina—"

"Don't 'oh but Silvina' me," the woman said sharply, but her expression was mocking, not stern. "Don't think I've missed Pona's little tricks, or Dunca's. No, the cot is the wrong place for you. I thought so when you first arrived, but there were other reasons for plunking you there at first. So we'll take the long view, as should be done, and shift you here. Oldive doesn't want you on your feet so much, and sure as Fall'll come again, the fire lizards are as unhappy at Dunca's as she is to have them. The old fool! No, Menolly," and now Silvina was angry with Menolly, "it is not your fault! Besides which, as a full harper apprentice, you really haven't anything to do with the paying students. Further, you ought to be near those fire lizard eggs until they hatch. So, you're staying here in the Hall! And that's the end of the matter." Silvina got to her feet. "Let's just gather these clothes, and we'll settle you right now. Back in the room you had the first night. It's handy to the Harper's and all—"

"That's much too grand a place for me!"

Silvina gave her a droll look. "I could, of course, move all the furniture out, take down the hangings, and give you an apprentice's cot and a fold stool . . ."

"I'd feel better about it . . ."

Silvina stared at her so that Menolly broke off, flustered.

"Why, you numbwit. You think I meant that?"

"Didn't you? Because the things in that room are far too valuable for an apprentice." Silvina was still staring at her. "Having nine fire lizards is causing enough trouble. The room would be just grand, and if I've only the furnishings of any other apprentice, why, that's proper, isn't it?"

Silvina gave her one more long, appraising look, shaking her head and laughing to herself.

"You're right, you know. Then none of the others could quibble about the change. But an apprentice's cot is narrow, and you've the fire lizards to consider."

"Two apprentice cots? If you have them to spare—?"

"Done! We'll tie the legs together and heap the rushes high."

Which is what they did. Without the rich hangings and heavy furniture, the chamber was echoingly empty. Menolly insisted that she didn't mind; but Silvina said it wasn't up to her because who was headwoman in this Hall? Hangings that Silvina had removed for shabbiness were recovered from storage, and Menolly was told that she could mend them when she had free time. Several small rugs were spread on the floor. A long table from the apprentices' study (with a leg mended after being damaged in a brawl), a bench and a small press for storage gave the room some homeyness. Silvina said that the place looked heartlessly plain but certainly no one could fault it for not displaying an apprentice's lowly state.

"Now then, that's settled. Yes, Piemur, you were looking for me?"

"No, Silvina. It's Menolly I'm after. For Master Shonagar. She's dead late for her lesson."

"Nonsense, there're no regular lessons on a Threadfall day. He should know that as well as anyone," Silvina said, taking Menolly by the arm as she started to leave the room.

"That's what I told him, Silvina," said Piemur, grinning from ear to ear, "but he asked me when had Menolly been assigned to a section. And, of course, I know she hasn't, so he said that she'd have nothing better to do with her time so she'd better learn something constructive. So . . ." And Piemur shrugged his helplessness in the face of such logic.

"Well, girl, you'd better go then. We're all settled here anyway. And you, Piemur, you pop over to Dunca's. Ask Audiva, politely, too, you imp, to bundle up Menolly's things . . . including the skirt and tunic Menolly washed today. What else did you have there, Menolly?"

Silvina smiled as if she knew perfectly well that Menolly was grateful not to have to return to the cot.

"Master Jerint has my pipes so there's only the medicines."

"Off with you, Piemur, and mind you make sure it's Audiva."

"I'd've asked for her anyhow, Silvina!"

"Bold as brass you are," Silvina called after him as he scampered down the steps. "A good lad at heart. You've heard him sing? He's younger than I like to have them in the Hall, but he does hold his own, rascal that he is, and where else should he be with a glorious treble voice like that? Planting tubers or herding the beasties? No, for such originals as Piemur and yourself, you're better here. Off with you now, before Master Shonagar starts bellowing. We don't really need a claxon with him in the Hall, so we don't."

Silvina had walked Menolly down the steps and now gave her a gentle shove towards the open Hall doors as she turned towards the kitchen. Menolly watched her for a moment, suffused by an inarticulate gratitude and affection for Silvina's understanding. The woman wasn't at all like Petiron, and yet Menolly knew that she could go to Silvina, as she had to Petiron, when she was perplexed or in difficulties. Silvina was like . . . like a storm anchor. Menolly, trotting obediently across the yard to Master Shonagar, smiled at such a seamanly metaphor for a landbound woman.

Master Shonagar did roar and bellow and carry on, but, buoyed by Silvina's courtesies, Menolly took the berating in silence until he made her promise faithfully that whatever else happened to her during the morning hours, the afternoon was his. Otherwise he'd never make a singer of her. So she was to report to him, please and thank you, through Fall, fog or fire, for how else was she to be a credit to his skill or the Craft Hall that had been pleased to exhibit its secrets for her edification and education?

Chapter 7

Don't leave me alone!
A cry in the night,
Of anguish heart-striking,
Of soul-killing fright.

The restlessness of the fire lizards about her woke Menolly from a deep sleep. She wished irritably that they didn't insist on sleeping with her; it had been an exciting and trying day, and she'd had a hard enough time getting to sleep. Her hand ached so from the day's playing that she'd had to slather the scar with numbweed to dull the pain. Beauty's tail twitched violently against Menolly's ear. She nudged the little queen, hoping to stir her out of whatever dream disturbed her. But Beauty was awake, not dreaming: her eyes, yellow and whirling with anxiety. All the fire lizards were awake and unusually alert in the dark of the night.

Seeing that Menolly's eyes were open, Beauty crooned, a half-fearful, half-worried sound. Rocky and Diver minced up Menolly's legs and crouched on her stomach, extending their heads towards her. Their eyes, too, were whirling with the speed and shade of fear. The rest, cuddling close against her, crooned for comfort.

Propping herself up on one elbow, Menolly peered toward the open windows. She could just distinguish the Fort Hold fire heights, black against dark sky. It took her some time to locate the dark bulk of the watch dragon. He was motionless, so whatever distressed the fire lizards did not apparently concern him.

"Whatever is your problem, Beauty?"

The little queen's croon increased its intensity. First Rocky, then Diver, added their notes. Aunties One and Two crept up and nuzzled to get under Menolly's left arm. Lazy, Mimic and Uncle burrowed into the fur at her right side, their twined tails latching fiercely onto her wrist while Brownie piteously paced across her feet. They were afraid.

"What's gotten into you?" Menolly couldn't for the life of her imagine anything within the Harper Craft Hall that would menace them. Covet them, yes: injure them, no.

"Shush a minute and let me listen." Beauty and Rocky gave little spurting sounds of fear, but they obeyed her. She listened as hard as she could, but the only sounds on the night air were the comfortable murmur of men's voices and an occasional laugh from the Hall beneath her. It wasn't as late as it had first seemed to her then, if the masters and older journeymen were still chatting.

Gently disengaging tails, Menolly slipped from her sleeping furs to the window. Several rectangles of light shone on the stones of the courtyard, two from the Great Hall and one above it, from Robinton's quarters, beyond hers.

Beauty gave a worried cheep and flew to Menolly's shoulder, wrapping her tail tightly around the girl's neck and burrowing into her hair, the slender little body trembling. The others set up an anxious clamor from the furs, so Menolly hurriedly returned to them. They were panic-stricken. The Masterharper might not approve of Silvina's moving her into this room if her fire lizards disturbed his studies at night. She tried to quiet them with a soft song, but now Beauty's voice rose querulously above her lullaby. Menolly gathered all of the fire lizards against her. Their tails twined about her arms so firmly that she couldn't use her hands to stroke them.

Now she felt a confused sense of imminent danger; clearly all the fire lizards were responding to a mutually experienced threat. Menolly fought against the panic their fear stirred in her.

"You're being ridiculous. What can harm us in the Harper Hall?"

Beauty on one side, Rocky on the other, stroked her face urgently with their heads, cheeping in mounting distress. Through their touch and minds, she got the distinct impression that they were reacting to a fear beyond them, beyond the walls, at a distance.

"Then how could it hurt you?"

Suddenly their terror erupted in her with such intensity that she cried out.

"Don't!" Her injunction was spontaneous. She tried to throw up her arms to protect herself from this unknown danger, but her hands were lizard-bound. Their fear was completely and utterly hers. And, incoherently, she repeated the cry, "Don't! DON'T!"

In her mind, out of nowhere, Menolly received an indelible impression of turbulence: savage, ruthless, destructive; a pressure inexorable and deadly; churning masses of slick, sickly grey surfaces that heaved and dipped. Heat as massive as a tidal wave. Fear! Terror! An inarticulate longing!

A scream, heard in her mind, a scream like a knife upon raw nerves!

''DON'T LEAVE ME ALONE!''

Menolly didn't think she had cried out. She was, as far as she could think sanely, certain that she hadn't heard the cry, but she knew that the words had been spoken at the extreme of someone's anguish.

Simultaneously the door to her room burst open, and the watch dragon on the Hold fire heights let out a shriek so like the one in her mind that she wondered if the dragon had called before. But dragons don't speak.

"Menolly! What's wrong?" Master Robinton was striding across the floor to her. The fire lizards took wing, darting out one window and back in the next, maniacal with fear.

"The dragon!" Menolly pointed, diverting Robinton's eyes to the window, to prove that she wasn't alone in alarm. They both saw the watch dragon launching himself, riderless, into the sky, bugling his distress. Robinton and Menolly heard, on the night air, the faint echo of answering bugles, a moment of silence and then the eerie screech of an hysterical watchwher from the Fort Hold court.

"Is every winged thing in the Hold out of its mind?" asked Robinton. "What made you scream, Menolly? 'Don't' what?"

"I don't know," Menolly cried, tears streaming down her face. She experienced a profound grief now and hugged herself against the chill of an awe-filled panic she couldn't explain and yet had experienced so profoundly. "I just don't know."

Robinton ducked as Beauty, leading the others, swooped past him and out the window. The queen was screaming at the others to follow. Menolly saw them outlined briefly by the light of the Masterharper's window and then the entire fair disappeared. Before Menolly, frightened for fear the fire lizards had gone completely from her, could tell Master Robinton, Domick came charging into the room.

"Robinton, what's going on—"

"Quiet, Domick!" The Masterharper's stern voice interrupted. "Whatever has frightened Menolly has also alarmed the watch dragon, and even the dead could hear that watchwher's howling. Furthermore, the dragon went *between,* without his rider!"

"What?" Domick was startled, no longer angry.

"Menolly," said Robinton, his hands warm and firm on her shoulders, his voice kindly calm, "take a deep breath. Now, take another . . ."

"I can't. I can't. Something terrible is happening," and Menolly was appalled at the sobs that tore at her, the cold terror that made her tremble so violently in the grip of this unknown disaster. "It's something terrible . . ."

Others were crowding into her room now, roused by her involuntary cries. Someone said loudly that there wasn't anything stirring in the court or on any of the roads. Another remarked that it was ridiculous to be startled out of a sound sleep by an hysterical child, trying to attract attention.

"Hold your silly tongue, Morshal," said Silvina, pushing through the crowd to Menolly's bed. "Better still, get off to your beds. All of you. You're no help here."

"Yes, if you'd please leave," said Robinton in a voice as close to anger as anyone had ever heard in him.

"It isn't the eggs hatching, is it?" Sebell asked anxiously.

Menolly shook her head, struggling to control herself and to stop the spasmodic shudders of fear that were depriving her of voice and wit enough to explain what was so inexplicable.

Silvina was soothing her. "Her hands are ice cold, Robinton," she said, and Menolly clung to the woman, as Robinton slipped to the other side of the double cot to support her shuddering body. "And these aren't hysterical tremors . . ."

Abruptly the spasms eased, then ceased completely. Menolly went limp against Silvina, gasping for breath, forcing herself to breathe as deeply as Robinton again urged her to do.

"Whatever was wrong has stopped," she said, spent.

Silvina and the Harper eased her against the bed rushes, Silvina drawing the fur up to her neck.

"Did the fire lizards take a fit?" the headwoman asked, glancing about the now-bright room. "They're not here . . ."

"I saw them go *between.* I don't know where. They were so afraid. It was incredible. There was nothing I could do."

"Take your time and tell us," said the Masterharper.

"I don't know all of it. I woke because they were so restless. They usually sleep quietly. And they got more and more frightened. And there wasn't anything . . . nothing. . . . I could *see* that . . ."

"Yes, yes, but something caused them to react." Robinton had captured her hand and was stroking it reassuringly. "Tell us the sequence."

"They were frightened out of their wits. And it got to me, too. Then," and Menolly swallowed quickly against that flash of vivid impression, "then, in my mind, I was aware of something so dangerous, so terrible, something heaving, and grey and deadly. . . . Masses of it . . . all grey and . . . and . . . terrible! Hot, too. Yes, the heat was part of the terror. Then a longing. I don't know which was the worst . . ." She clutched at the comforting hands and could not keep back the sobs of fright that rose from her guts. "I wasn't asleep either. It wasn't just a bad dream!"

"Don't talk anymore, Menolly. We can hope the terror has passed completely."

"No, I have to tell you. That's part of it. I'm supposed to tell. Then . . . I heard, only I didn't hear . . . except that it was as clear as if someone had shouted it right in this room . . . right inside my head . . . I heard something scream, 'Don't leave me alone!' "

The muscles in her body relaxed all at once now that she had spoken of the weight of terror.

" 'Don't leave me alone' ?" The Harper repeated the words half to himself, puzzling over the significance of the phrase.

"It's all gone now. Being afraid, I mean . . . and . . ."

The fire lizards swooped back into the room, aiming for the bed, but some of them dipped and darted for the window ledges, away from Master Robinton and Silvina, twittering, but only with surprise, not fear. Beauty and the two bronzes landed on the foot of the double cot, chirping at Menolly with little calls that sounded so normally inquisitive that Menolly let out an exasperated exclamation.

"Don't scold them, Menolly," said the Masterharper. "See if you can determine where they've just been."

Menolly beckoned to Beauty, who obediently crawled up to her arm and permitted Menolly to stroke her head and body.

"She's certainly not bothered by anything now."

"Yes, but where did she go?"

Menolly raised Beauty to her face, looking into the idly whirling eyes, laying the back of her hand against Beauty's cheek. "Where'd you go, pet? Where have you just been?"

Beauty stroked Menolly's hand, gave a smug chirrup, cocking her dainty head to one side. But an impression reached Menolly's mind, of a Weyr Bowl, and many dragons and excited people.

"I think they've been back to Benden Weyr. It must be Benden! They don't know Fort Weyr well enough to be that vivid. And whatever happened involved many dragons and lots of excited people."

"Ask Beauty what frightened her?"

Menolly stroked the little queen's head for a moment longer, to reassure her, because the question was sure to upset the little fire lizard. It did. Beauty launched herself from Menolly's arm so violently that her talons scratched deep enough to draw blood.

"A dragon falling in the sky!" Menolly gasped out the picture. "Dragons don't fall in the sky."

"She scratched you, child . . ."

"Oh, that's nothing, Master Robinton, but I don't think we'll get anything more out of her."

Beauty was clinging to the fireplace, chittering irritably, her eyes wheeling angrily orange.

"If something has happened at Benden Weyr, Master Robinton," remarked Silvina in a dry tone of voice, "they won't be overlong in sending for you." Silvina had to raise her voice to counteract the excited cries of the other fire lizards, who were reacting to Beauty's scolding. "We'd best not upset the creatures any further now. And I'm getting you a dose, young lady, or you'll never sleep tonight from the look of your eyes."

"I didn't mean to disturb everyone . . ."

Silvina gave her an exasperated snort, dismissing the need for an apology, although Menolly couldn't help but see, as Silvina opened the door, that harpers were lingering in the corridor. Menolly heard Silvina berating them and telling them to get off to their beds, what did they think they knew about fire lizards?

"The strangest aspect to this incident, Menolly," said the Masterharper, his forehead creased with thought lines, "is that the dragon reacted, too. I've *never* seen a dragon—short of a mating flight—go off without his rider. I shouldn't wonder," and Robinton smiled wryly, "if we don't have T'ledon over here demanding an explanation from you for the disappearance of his dragon."

The notion of a dragonrider compelled to ask her for advice was so absurd that Menolly managed a weak smile.

"How's that hand? You've been playing a lot, I hear," and the Harper turned her left hand over in his. "That scar's too red. You have been doing too much. Make haste a little more slowly. Is it painful?"

"Not much. Master Oldive gave me some salve."

"And your feet?"

"So long as I don't have to stand too much or walk too far . . ."

"Too bad your fire lizards can't combine to give you one little dragonpower."

"Sir?"

"Yes?"

"I think I ought to tell you . . . my fire lizards can lift things. They brought me my pipes the other day . . . to spare me the walk . . ." she added hastily. "They took it from my room at the cot, all in a cluster, and then dropped it into my hands!"

"Now that is very interesting. I didn't realize they had so much initiative. You know, Brekke, Mirrim and F'nor have got theirs to carry messages on a collar about their necks . . ." The Masterharper smiled with amusement, ". . . though they aren't always good about arriving promptly."

"I think you have to make certain *they* know how urgent the matter is."

"Like having your pipes for Master Jerint?"

"I didn't wish to be late, and I can't walk fast."

"We'll let that stand as the reason then, Menolly," said Robinton gently, and when Menolly glanced up at him startled, she saw the kind understanding in his eyes and flushed. He stroked her hand again. "What I don't *know*, I sometimes guess, knowing the way people interact, Menolly. Don't keep so much bottled inside, girl. And do tell me anything unusual that your fire lizards do. That's far more important than *why* they did it. We don't know much about these tiny cousins of the dragons, and I have a suspicion they'll be very important creatures to us."

"Is the little white dragon all right?"

"Reading my mind, too, Menolly? Little Ruth is all right," but the Harper's heavy, slightly hesitant tone gave the lie to his reassurance. "Don't fret yourself about Jaxom and Ruth. Just about everyone else on Pern does." He placed her hand back on the furs with a final pat.

Silvina returned, offering Menolly the mug she'd brought, and stood over her while she downed the dose, gagging a little at the bitterness.

"Yes, I know. I made it strong on purpose. You need to sleep. And Master Robinton, there's a messenger from the Hold for you below. Urgent, he said, and he's out of breath!"

"Sleep yourself out, Menolly," the Harper said as he rapidly left the room.

"Trouble?" Menolly asked Silvina, hoping to be told something.

"Not for you, or because of you, m'girl." Silvina chuckled, pushing the sleeping fur under Menolly's chin. "I understand that Groghe, Lord of Fort Hold, experienced the same unnerving nightmare, as he calls it, that you did and has sent for Master Robinton to explain it to him. Now rest and don't fuss yourself."

"How could I? You must have doubled that dose of fellis juice," said Menolly, relaxed and tactless in the grip of the drug. She couldn't keep her eyes open and effortlessly drifted to sleep to the sound of another chuckle from Silvina. One last thought let her slip easily into unconsciousness: Lord Groghe's fire lizard had reacted, so *she* wasn't hysterical.

She awoke slightly at one point, not quite conscious of her surroundings but aware of a rumbling voice, a treble response, and hungry creelings.

When she woke completely later, there was an empty bowl on the floor, and her friends were curled up about her in slumbering balls, wing-limp. The gnawing in her stomach suggested that she had slept well into the day, and the hunger was all her own. If the fire lizards had been that starved, they'd've been awake. Doubtless Camo and Piemur had done her the favor of feeding her friends. She grinned; Piemur and Camo must have been delighted at the chance.

The shutters were open and, with no sounds of music or voices, she guessed it must be afternoon and the Hall's population dispersed to their various chores. The watch dragon was back on the fire heights.

She sat upright in bed as the memory of the previous night's terror shattered her pleasant somnolence. At the same moment there was a tap on her door, and before she could answer, Silvina entered, carrying a small tray.

"My timing's very good," she said, pleased and smiling. "Do you feel rested?"

Menolly nodded in reply and thanked Silvina for the hot klah she was handed. "But, if I can be bold, you don't look as if you slept at all." Silvina's eyes were dark-circled and red-shot.

"Well, you're right and you're not bold, but I'm on my way to my bed, I can assure you, as soon as I've straightened up for Robinton. Now . . ." and Silvina nudged Menolly's hip so the girl made room for her to sit on the bed, "you ought to hear what disturbed your friends last night. No one else will think to tell you with the Harper away. Also, I've just checked the eggs, and I think you should take a look at them. . . . Not, however, until you've finished your klah," and Silvina put a restraining hand on Menolly's shoulder. "I want your wits in place and not fellis-fuddled."

"What happened?"

"The bare bones of the matter are that F'nor, brown Canth's rider, took it into his head to go to the Red Star last night . . ."

Menolly's gasp woke the fire lizards.

"Mind your thoughts, girl. I don't want them turning hysterical again, thank you." Silvina waited until the creatures had settled back into their naps.

"That's what seems to have set the fire lizards off, at any rate. And not just yours. Robinton said that anyone who has a fire lizard had the same trouble you did, only with your having nine, it was intensified. What happened was that Canth and F'nor went *between* to the Red Star. . . . Yes, small wonder you were terrified. What you told us about greyness and all that hideous heat and churning, that's what's on the Red Star. No one could land there!" She paused, gave a smug grunt. "That'll shut up the Lord Holders for wanting to *go* there!"

"Canth and F'nor?" Menolly felt fear stab coldly up her throat, and she remembered the scream.

"They're alive, but only just. And when you said, 'Don't leave me alone'? What you heard . . . and it had to be through your fire lizards . . . was Brekke calling out to F'nor and Canth." Silvina broke her narrative for effect. "Somehow they got back. Well, partway back from the Red Star. It must have been the most incredible sight . . ." Silvina's tired eyes narrowed, reconstructing that vision. "The reason the hold dragon took off was to help land Canth. It was like a path, Robinton tells us, of dragons in the air, catching Canth and F'nor, and braking their fall. They were both senseless, of course. Robinton says there isn't a scrap of hide left on Canth; as if some mighty hand had sanded his skin away. F'nor is not much better, for all he wore wherhide."

"Silvina, how could my fire lizards know what was happening at Benden Weyr?"

"Ramoth called the dragons . . . the Benden queen can do that, you know. Your fire lizards have been at Benden Weyr. Perhaps they heard her, too," Silvina dismissed that part of the mystery impatiently.

"But, Silvina, my fire lizards were afraid long before Ramoth called the Fort dragon, even before I heard Brekke call."

"Why, that's right. Ah well, we'll find the answer to that mystery in due time. We always do at the Harper Hall. If dragons can talk to dragons across distance, why can't fire lizards?"

"Dragons think sense," Menolly said, gently scratching her waking queen's little head, "and these beauties don't. At least not often."

"Babies don't make sense, and your fire lizards aren't all that long out of the shell. But think on it, Menolly. Camo doesn't make much sense, but he does have feelings."

"Was it he who fed my fire lizards this morning so I could sleep?"

"He and Piemur. Camo fussed and fussed before breakfast until I had to send him up here, with Piemur, to shut his moans." Silvina's chuckle was half amusement, half remembered irritation. "Nag, nag, nag about 'pretties hungry,' 'feed pretties.' Piemur said you didn't wake. Did you?"

"No." But the matter of fire lizard intelligence was more urgent in Menolly's estimation. "I suppose being at Benden Weyr might explain their reaction."

"Not entirely," Silvina replied briskly. "Lord Groghe's little friend responded, too. It wasn't hatched at Benden and has never been there.

There may well be more to these creatures than being silly pets after all. And making idiots of men who fancy themselves as good as dragonriders."

"I've finished my klah. Shall we see the eggs now?"

"Yes, by all means. If his egg should hatch without the Harper, we'd never hear the end of it."

"Is Sebell about?"

"Hovering!" Silvina's grimace was so maliciously expressive that Menolly laughed. "How're your feet today?"

"Only stiff."

"Just remember that that salve doesn't do you any good in the jar."

"Yes, Silvina."

"Don't you 'yes, Silvina' me meekly, m'girl," and there was unexpected warmth and affection in the woman's tone. Menolly smiled shyly back as the headwoman left the room.

She dressed quickly in one of the new tunics and the blue wherhide trousers, plumped up the rushes in their bag and smoothed the sleeping fur over all.

Silvina had just finished tidying up the Harper's room when Menolly entered, Beauty winging in gracefully behind her. She landed on Menolly's shoulder and, as Menolly checked both eggs, peered with equally curious interest. She chirped a question at Menolly.

"Well?" drawled Silvina, "now that you experts have conferred. . . ."

Menolly giggled. "I don't think Beauty knows any more than I do. She's never seen eggs hatch, but they are a good deal harder. They've been kept so nicely warm. I don't know for sure, but I suspect they'll hatch any time now."

Silvina drew in her breath sharply, startling Beauty. "That Harper! The problem will be keeping track of him." She gave the rush bag a final poke and twitched the sleeping fur straight. "If Lord Groghe," and Silvina jerked her head towards the Fort Hold palisade, "isn't sending for him, F'lar is. Or Lord Lytol for that white dragonet."

"If he wants to Impress his fire lizard, he'll have to make a choice, won't he?"

Silvina gaped at Menolly for a long moment and then burst out laughing.

"Might be the best thing that's happened since the queens were killed," Silvina said, mopping laugh tears from her eyes. "The man's had no more than a few hours sleep a day. . . ." Silvina gestured towards the study room, flicking her fingers at the scattered piles of records, the scrawls on the sandtable's surface, the half-empty wine sack with its pouring neck collapsed ludicrously to one side. "He won't miss the Impression of his fire lizard! But isn't there some sign to tell if the hatching is imminent? The dragonmen can tell. And what the Harper's doing is really urgent."

"When Beauty and the others hatched, the old queen and her flight hummed, sort of deep in the throat . . ." Menolly said cautiously, after a moment's thought.

Silvina nodded encouragingly.

"This isn't Beauty's clutch, so I don't know if she'll react, though the dragons at Benden Weyr hummed for Ramoth's clutch. So it seems logical that the fire lizards would react the same way."

Silvina agreed. "There'd be a slight interval in which we could track the Harper down? Supposing we can't get him to stay put here for the next day or two?"

Menolly hesitated, reluctant to agree to a conclusion achieved by guesswork.

"And they eat anything when they hatch?" asked Silvina who appeared content with the supposition.

"Just about." Menolly remembered the sack of spiderclaws, not the easiest of edibles, that had gone down the throats of her newly hatched friends. "Red meat is best."

"That will please Camo," Silvina said cryptically. "Now I think you'd best stay here. Well, what's wrong with that? Robinton would give up more than the privacy of his quarters to have a fire lizard. He's even threatened to forego his wine . . ." Silvina had a snort for that unlikely sacrifice. "Well, what is wrong with you?"

"Silvina . . . it's afternoon, isn't it?"

"Yes, indeed."

"I'm pledged to go . . . I must go . . . to Master Shonagar. He was very insistent . . ."

"Oh, he was, was he? And will he explain to Master Robinton that your voice is more important than the Harper's fire lizard? Oh, don't get yourself in a pucker. Sebell can sit in for you. And you tell your fire lizards to stand by . . ." Silvina walked to the open window and peered down into the courtyard. "Piemur! Piemur, ask Sebell to step up to the Harper's room, will you? Menolly? Yes, she's awake and here. No, she can't attend Master Shonagar until Sebell arrives. Yes? Well, go through the choir hall *to* the journeymen's quarters and give Master Shonagar *my* message. Menolly answers to Master Robinton first, me second and *then* any of the other masters who require her attention."

Menolly fretted about Master Shonagar's certain wrath while Silvina made her wait until Piemur had found and returned, at a run, with Sebell.

"They're hatching?" Sebell slithered to a stop in the doorway, breathing hard, his face flushed and anxious.

"Not quite yet," Menolly said, ready to speed to Master Shonagar but unwilling to brush impolitely past the journeyman blocking the entrance.

"How will I know?"

"Menolly says the fire lizards hum," replied Silvina. "Shonagar insists on her presence now."

"He would! Where's the Harper?"

"At Ruatha Hold by now, I think," Silvina said. "He went off to Benden Weyr when the dragonrider came for him. He said he'd stop off to see Mastersmith Fandarel at Telgar . . ."

Sebell's eyes went from Silvina to Menolly in surprise, as if Silvina were being indiscreet.

"More than any other, saving yourself, Menolly will need to know how many tunes a harper, much less *the* Harper, plays," she said. "I'll send more klah and . . ." now she chuckled, "have Camo lay about with that hatchet of his on the meat."

Menolly told the fire lizards to stay by Sebell, and then she scurried down the steps and across the courtyard to the chorus hall.

Despite Silvina's reassurance, Menolly was apprehensive as she made her tardy arrival before Master Shonagar. But he said nothing. That made her dereliction harder. He kept looking at her until she nervously began to shift her weight from foot to foot.

"I do not know what it is about you, young Menolly, that you can disrupt an entire Craft Hall, for you are not presumptuous. In fact, you are immodestly modest. You do not brag nor flaunt your rank nor put yourself forward. You listen, which I assure you is a pleasure and relief, and you learn from what you are told, which is veritably unheard of. I begin to entertain hope that I have finally discovered, in a mere slip of a girl, the dedication required of a true musician, an artist! Yes, I might even coax a real voice out of your throat." His fist came down with an almighty wallop on the sandtable, the opposite end flapping onto its supports. She jumped. "But even I cannot do much if you are not *here!*"

"Silvina said . . ."

"Silvina is a wonderful woman. Without her the Hall would be in chaos and our comfort ignored," Master Shonagar said, still in a loud tone. "She is also a good musician . . . ah, you didn't know that? You should make the occasion to listen to her singing, my dear girl. . . . *But,*" again the voice boomed, Master Shonagar's belly bouncing, although the rest of him seemed stationary, "I thought I had made it plain that *you are to be here without fail* every single day!"

"Yes, sir!"

"Come fog, fire or Fall! Have I made myself plain enough?"

"Yes, sir!"

"*Then . . .*" and his voice dropped to normal proportions, "let us begin with breathing . . ."

Menolly fought the desire to giggle. She mastered it by breathing deeply and then settled quickly to the discipline of the lesson.

When Master Shonagar had dismissed her with a further injunction to be on time not the next day, which was a rest day and he needed his rest, but the day following, the work parties were back from their chores. To her surprise, she was greeted by many of the boys as she raced past them to get back to the fire lizard eggs. She answered, smiling, unsure of names and faces but inwardly warmed by their recognition. As she took the steps to the higher level two at a time, she wondered if the boys all knew about the previous night's disturbance. Probably. News spread faster in this Craft Hall than Thread could burrow.

The sounds of soft gitar strumming reached her ears as she got to the upper hall. She slowed down, out of breath anyhow, and arrived at the Harper's quarters still breathing heavily, much as Sebell had done. He glanced up, grinned understandingly, and held up a hand to reassure her. Then his hand gestured to the sandtable. All her fire lizards were there, crouched, watching him.

"I've had an audience. What I can't tell is if my music has pleased them."

"It has," Menolly told him, smiling. She extended her arm for Beauty, who immediately glided to her. "See, their eyes tell you . . . the green is dominant, which is sleeping pleasure. Red means hunger, blue and green are sort of general shades, white means danger, and yellow is fright. The speed of the eye whirling tells you how intensely they feel about something."

"What about him then?" And Sebell pointed to Lazy whose eyes were first-lidded.

"He's called Lazybones for good reason."

"I wasn't playing a lullaby."

"Except when he's hungry, he's that way. Here," and Menolly scooped Lazy up from the sandtable and deposited him on Sebell's arm. Startled, the man froze. "Stroke his eye ridges and the back joints of the wings. There! See? He's crooning with delight."

Sebell had obeyed her instructions, and now Lazy collapsed about the journeyman's forearm, locked his claws loosely about the wrist and stretched his head across the back of Sebell's hand. Sebell caressed him, a shy and delighted smile on his face.

"I hadn't thought they'd be so soft to the touch."

"You have to watch for patchy skin and oil it well. I did a thorough job on these the other evening, but you can see where I'll have to do them again. Just stay there . . ." And Menolly quickly went down the hall to her room for the salve, Beauty complaining at the jouncing on her shoulder.

As they spread salve on the fire lizards, Sebell grew more confident of his handling of the creatures. He wore a half-smile, as if surprised to find himself at such a task.

"Do all fire lizards sing?" he asked, oiling Brownie.

"I don't really know. I suppose mine learned simply because I used to sing to them in the cave." Menolly smiled to herself, remembering the fire lizards perched attentively on the ledges about the cave, their little heads turning from side to side to catch the sounds of music.

"Any audience being better than none?" asked Sebell. "Did anyone think to tell you that Lord Groghe's little queen has recently started to sing along with the Hold Harper?"

"Oh no!"

"If Groghe could carry a tune," Sebell went on, enjoying her dismay, "it'd be understandable. Don't worry about it, Menolly. I heard also that Groghe's delighted." Then Sebell's expression altered subtly.

"I'll bet Lord Groghe wasn't so happy about last night, was he?" she hesitated, then blurted out. "Do you think Canth and F'nor will live?"

"They have much to live for, Menolly. Brekke needs them to stay alive. She's lost her queen already. She'll make them live. We'll know more when the Harper returns."

Camo entered the room, carrying a heavily laden tray. His thick-featured face changed from ludicrous anxiety to beams of joy as he saw first the fire lizards and then Menolly.

"Pretty ones hungry? Camo has food?" And Menolly saw two huge pans of meat in pieces among the other dishes on the tray.

"Thank you for feeding the pretties this morning, Camo."

"Camo very quiet. Very quiet." The man bobbed at Menolly in such a fashion that the pitcher of klah splashed.

Sebell deftly relieved him of the tray and set it on the sandtable center board.

"You're a good man, Camo," the journeyman said, "but go to the kitchen now. You must help Abuna. She needs you."

"Pretty ones hungry?" The disappointment was writ large on Camo's face.

"No, not now, Camo," Menolly said gently, smiling up at him. "See, they're asleep."

Camo turned himself in a circle towards the sandtable and then the window ledges where several of the fire lizards were sprawled on the sun-warmed stone, glistening with their recent oiling.

"We'll feed them again tonight, Camo."

"Tonight? Good. Don't forget? Promise? Promise? Camo feed pretties?"

"I promise, Camo," Menolly said with extra fervor. The wistful, piteous way in which the poor man asked her to promise suggested that too many promises made to Camo were conveniently forgotten.

"Now," Sebell said as the man shuffled from the room, "Silvina said you'd no time for more than klah when you woke. If I remember Shonagar's lessons, you'll be starved."

To Menolly's delight, there was redfruit on the tray as well as meatrolls, klah, cheese, bread and a sweet conserve. Sebell ate lightly, more to keep her company than because he was hungry, though he said he'd been studying. To prove that, he rattled off the names and descriptions of the fish she had given him the other morning.

"Did I remember them all correctly?" he asked, peering at her as she started at him in amazement.

"Yes, you did!"

"Think I can pose as a seaman now?"

"If you only have to name fish!"

"If only . . ." he paused dramatically, making a grimace for that restriction. "I had a chat with a bronze dragonrider I know at Fort Weyr. He's agreed to take us, on the quiet, to any body of water that you feel is adequate to teach me how to sail."

"Teach you how to sail?" Menolly was appalled. "In one easy lesson, like those fish names?"

"No, but I don't think I'll actually have to sail. I should know the fundamentals and leave . . ." he grinned at her, ". . . the doing to the experts in the craft."

She breathed a sigh of relief for she liked Sebell, and she'd been distressed to think that he might be foolhardy enough to attempt sailing on the ocean by himself. Yanus had often said that no one ever really learned all there was to know about the sea, the winds and the tides. Just when one got confident, a squall could make up and smash a ship to splinters.

"I do feel, that to be convincing, I'd better know how to gut fish as well. That seems a more integral part of the craft than actual sailing. So that will take priority in your instruction. N'ton said he could acquire some fresh fish for me with no problems."

Again Menolly suppressed her curiosity as to why a journeyman harper needed to be conversant with the seacraft.

"Tomorrow's a rest day," Sebell continued. "There may even be a gather if the weather holds, which to my landsman's eye, seems likely. So, if the fire lizards break shell, and if we can disappear circumspectly, perhaps some day after that . . ."

"I can't miss my lessons with Master Shonagar . . ."

"Has he got you dithering so soon?"

"He is so emphatic . . ."

"Yes, he usually is. But he really knows how to build a voice, if that's any consolation to you. I could always play an instrument . . ." and Sebell grinned in reminiscence, ". . . but I never thought I'd make a singer. I was terrified I'd be sent away from the Hall . . ."

"*You* were?"

"Oh, indeed I was. I'd wanted to be a harper since I learned my first Ballads. I'm landsman bred, so harpering is very respectable. My foster father gave me all the assistance I needed, and our Hold Harper was a good technician, not very creative," and Sebell waggled a hand, "but capable of teaching the fundamentals thoroughly. I thought myself a right proper musician . . . until I got here." Sebell uttered a self-deprecating noise at his boyish pretentions. "Then I learned just how much more there is to harpering than playing an instrument."

Menolly grinned with complete understanding. "Just like there's more to being a seaman than knowing how to gut a fish and trim sail?"

"Yes. Exactly. Which reminds me, Domick did excuse you from this morning's session, but he hasn't excused you from the work. . . . So, we might as well put waiting time to use. Incidentally, my compliments on your manner with Domick yesterday. You struck exactly the right note with him."

"I never play flat."

Sebell gave her a wide-eyed stare. "I didn't mean, playing." He stared at her a moment more. "You mean, you really like that sort of music? You weren't dissembling?"

"That music was brilliant. I've never heard anything like it." Menolly was a bit disconcerted by Sebell's attitude.

"Oh, I guess it would seem so to you. I only hope you have the same opinion several Turns from now after you've had to endure more of Domick's eternal search for pure musical forms." He gave a mock shudder. "Here . . ." and he spread out sheets of new music. "Let's see how you like this. Domick wants you to play first gitar, but you're to learn the second as well."

The occasional music for two gitars was extremely complex, switching from one time value to another, with chording difficult enough for uninjured hands. She and Sebell had to work out alternative fingering for the passages that her left hand could not manage. The repetitive theme had to dominate, but it swung from one gitar part to the other. They had gone through two of the three sections before Sebell called a break, laughing at his surrender as he stretched and kneaded tired fingers and shoulders.

"We won't get this music note-perfect in one sitting, Menolly," he protested when she wanted to finish the third movement.

"I'm sorry. I didn't realize . . ."

"Will you stop apologizing for the wrong things?"

"I'm sor—Well, I didn't mean to . . ." She had to rephrase what she wanted to say as Sebell laughed at her attempt to obey his injunction. "This sort of music is a challenge. It really is. For instance here . . ." and she turned to a quick time passage that had been extremely difficult to finger.

"Enough, Menolly. I'm bone tired, and why you aren't . . ."

"But you're a journeyman harper . . ."

"I know but this journeyman harper cannot spend all his time playing . . ."

"What do you do? Besides cross-craft."

"Whatever the Harper needs me to do. Primarily I journey . . . looking among the youngsters in hold and craft to see if there're any likely ones for the Craft Hall. I bring new music to distant harpers . . . your music most recently—"

"My music?"

"First to flush you out because we didn't know you were a girl. Second, because they were exactly the songs we need."

"That's what Master Robinton said."

"Don't sound so surprised . . . and meek. Admittedly it's nice to have one modest apprentice in this company of rampant extroverts . . . what's the matter?"

"Why isn't music like Master Domick's—"

"*Your* music can be played easily and well by any half-stringed harper or fumble-fingered idiot. Not that I'm maligning your songs. It's just that they're an entirely different kettle of fish—to use a seamanly metaphor—to Domick's. Don't you judge your songs against his standard! More people have already *listened* to your melodies and liked them, than will ever hear Domick's, much less like them."

Menolly swallowed. The very notion that her music was more accept-able than Domick's was incredible, and yet she could appreciate the distinction that Sebell was making. Domick was a musician's composer. "Of course, we need music like Master Domick's, too. It serves a different purpose, for the Hall, and the Craft. He knows more about the art of composing—which you have to learn—"

"Oh, I know I do." Then, because the problem had been weighting heavily on her conscience, she spilled the words out in a rush. "What do I do, Sebell, about the fire lizard song? Master Robinton rewrote it, and it's much, much better. But he's told everyone that *I* wrote it."

"So? That's the way the Harper wishes it to be, Menolly. He has his reasons." Sebell reached out to grip her knee and give her a little shake. "And he didn't change the song much. Just sort of . . ." Sebell ges-tured with both hands, compressing the space between them, ". . . tightened it up. He kept the melody as you'd written it, and that's what everyone is humming. What you have to do now is learn how to polish your music without losing its freshness. That's why it's so important for you to study with Domick. He has the discipline: you have the original-ity."

Menolly could not reply to that assessment. There was a lump in her throat as she remembered the beatings she'd taken for doing exactly what she was now encouraged to do.

"Don't hunch up like that," Sebell said, almost sharply. "What's the matter? You've gone white as a sheet. Shells!" This last word came out as an expletive and caused Menolly to look in surprise at the journey-man. "Just when I didn't want to be interrupted . . ."

She followed the line of his gaze and saw the bronze dragon circling down to land beyond the courtyard.

"That's N'ton. I've got to speak to him, Menolly, about our teaching trip. I'll be right back." He was out of the room at a trot, and she could hear him taking the steps in a clatter.

She looked at the music they'd been playing, and Sebell's words echoed through her mind. "He has the discipline; you have the original-ity." "Everyone's been humming it." People liking her twiddles? That still didn't seem possible, although Sebell had no more reason to lie to her than the Masterharper when he'd said that her music was valuable to him. To the Harper Craft. Incredible! She struck a chord on the gitar, a triumphant, incredible chord, and then modulated it, thinking how undisciplined that musical reaction had been.

They were still twiddles, her songs, unlike the beautiful, intricate musical designs that Domick composed. But if she studied hard with him, maybe she could improve her twiddles into what she could honestly call music.

Firmly she turned her thoughts towards the gitar duet and ran through the tricky passages, slowly at first and then finally at time. One of the chords modulated into tones that were so close to the agonized cry of the previous night that she repeated the phrase.

"Don't leave me alone" and then found another chord that fit, "The cry in the night/Of anguish heart-striking/Of soul-killing fright." That's what Sebell had said: that Brekke would not want to live if Canth and F'nor died. "Live for my living/Or else I must die/Don't leave me alone./A world heard that cry."

By the time Menolly had arranged the chords in the plaint to her satisfaction, Beauty, Rocky and Diver were softly crooning along with her. So she worked on the verse.

"Well, you approve?" she asked her fair. "Perhaps I ought to jot it down on something . . ."

"No need," said a quiet voice behind her, and she whirled on the stool to see Sebell seated at the sandtable, scribing quickly. "I think I've got most of it." He looked up, saw the startled expression on her face and gave her a brief smile. "Close your mouth and come check my notation."

"But . . . but . . ."

"What did I tell you, Menolly, about apologizing for the wrong things?"

"I was just tuning . . ."

"Oh, the song needs polishing, but that refrain is poignant enough to set a Hold to tears." He beckoned again to her, a crisp gesture that brought her to his side. "You might want to change the sequence, give the peril first, the solution next . . . though I don't know. With that melody . . . do you always use minors?" He slid a glass across the sand so the scribing couldn't be erased. "We'll see what the Harper thinks. Now what's wrong?"

"Leave it? You can't be serious."

"I can be and usually am, young Menolly," he said, rising from the stool to reach for his gitar. "Now, let's see if I put it down correctly."

Menolly sat, immersed in acute embarrassment to hear Sebell playing a tune of her making. But she had to listen. When her fire lizards began to croon softly along with Sebell's deft playing, she was about ready to concede—privately—that it wasn't a bad tune after all.

"That's very well done, Sebell. Didn't know you had it in you," said the Masterharper, applauding vigorously from the doorway. "I'd rather dreaded transferring that incident to music . . ."

"This song, Master Robinton, is Menolly's." Sebell had risen at the Harper's entrance, and now he bowed deferentially to Menolly. "Come, girl, it's why the harpers searched a continent for you."

"Menolly, my dear child, no blushes for that song." Robinton seized her hands and clasped them warmly. "Think of the chore you just saved me. I came in halfway through the verse, Sebell, if you would please . . ." and the Harper gestured to Sebell to begin again. With one long arm, Robinton snaked a stool out from under the flat-bottomed sand-table, and still holding Menolly by the hand, he composed himself to listen as Sebell's clever fingers plucked the haunting phrases from the augmenting chords. "Now, Menolly, think only of the music as Sebell plays, not that it is *your* music. Learn to think objectively, not subjectively. Listen as a harper."

He held her hand so tightly in his that she could not pull away without giving offense. The clasp of his fingers was more than reassuring: it was therapeutic. Her embarrassment ebbed as the music and Sebell's warm baritone voice flowed into the room. When the fire lizards hummed loud, Robinton squeezed her hand and smiled down at her.

"Yes, a little work on the phrases. One or two words could be altered, I think, to heighten the effect, but the whole can stand. Can you scribe. . . . Ah, Sebell, well done. Well done," said the Masterharper as Sebell tapped the protecting glass. "I'll want it transferred to some of those neat paper sheets Bendarek supplies us with, so Menolly can go over it at her leisure. Not too much leisure," and the Masterharper held up a warning hand, "because that fire lizard echo swept round Pern, and we must explain it. A good song, Menolly, a very good song. Don't doubt yourself so fiercely. Your instinct for melodic line is very good, very good indeed. Perhaps I should send more of my apprentices to a sea hold for a time if this is the sort of talent the waves provoke. And see, your fair is still humming the line . . ."

Menolly drew out of her confusion long enough to realize that the fire lizards' hum had nothing to do with her song: their attention was not on the humans but . . .

"The eggs! They're hatching!"

"Hatching!" "Hatching!" Both master and journeyman crowded each other to get through the door to the hearth and the fire-warming pots. "Menolly! Come here!"

"I'm getting the meat!"

"They're hatching!" the Harper shouted. "They're hatching. Grab that pot, Sebell, it's wobbling!"

As Menolly dashed into the room, the two men were kneeling at the hearth, watching anxiously as the earthen pots rocked slightly.

"They can't hatch IN the pots," she said with a certain amount of asperity in her voice. She took the pot from the protecting encirclement of Sebell's curved fingers and carefully upended it on the hearth, her fingers cushioning the egg until the sand spilled away from it. She turned to Robinton, but he had already followed her example. Both eggs lay in the light of the fire, rocking slightly, the striations of hatching marking the shells.

The fire lizards lined up on the mantel and the hearth, humming deep in their throats. The pulsing sound seemed to punctuate the now violent movements of the eggs as the hatchlings fluttered against the shells for exit.

"Master Robinton?" called Silvina from the outer room. "Master Robinton?"

"Silvina! They're hatching!" The Harper's jubilant bellow startled Menolly and set the fire lizards to squawking and flapping their wings in surprise.

Other harpers, curious about the noise, began to crowd in behind Silvina, who stood at the door to the Harper's sleeping quarters. If there were too many people in the room, Menolly thought . . .

"No! Stay out! Keep them out!" she cried before she realized she'd said anything.

"Yes. Stay back now," Silvina was saying. "You can't all see. You've got the meat, Menolly? Ah, so you have. Is it enough?"

"It should be."

"What do we do now?" asked the Harper, his voice rough with suppressed excitement as he crouched above the egg.

"When the fire lizard emerges, feed it," Menolly said, somewhat surprised, for the Harper must have been a guest at numerous dragon hatchings. "Just stuff its mouth with food."

"When *will* they hatch?" asked Sebell, washing his fingers in his palms with excited frustration.

The fire lizards' hum was getting more intense: their eyes whirling with participation in the event. Suddenly a second little golden queen erupted into the room, her eyes spinning. She let out a squeal which Beauty answered, lifting her wings higher, but in greeting, not challenge.

"Silvina!" Menolly pointed to the queen.

"Master Robinton, look!" said the headwoman and, as they all watched, the newly arrived queen took her place on the mantel beside Beauty, her throat vibrating as fast as the others.

"That's Merga, Lord Groghe's queen," said the Harper, and then he glanced over his shoulder at the door. "I hope it isn't an awkward time for him. This sort of summons could be inconvenient . . ."

Above the fire lizards' vibrant sounds, they all heard the Harper's name bellowed.

"Someone go and escort Lord Groghe," ordered the Harper, his eyes never leaving the hearth and the two eggs.

"Robinton!" It would seem that his order was unnecessary for the bellower was rapidly approaching. "Robin. . . . What? They are? D'you know what? That Merga of mine's in another taking. Forced me to come *here!* Here now, what's all this? Where *is* Robinton?"

Menolly tore her eyes from the two eggs, though she was certain she saw a widening crack in the one on the left, to see the entrance of the Fort Lord Holder. As his voice indicated, he was a big man, almost as tall as the Harper but much broader in the torso, with thick thighs and bulging calves. He walked lightly for all his mass although he was breathing heavily from having come to the Hall at a fair pace.

"There you are! What's this all about?"

"The eggs are about to hatch, Lord Groghe."

"Eggs?" The brows of the Holder's florid face were contracted into a puzzled scowl. "Oh, your eggs. They're hatching? And Merga's reacting?"

"I trust not at any inconvenience to you, Lord Groghe."

"Well, not so's I wouldn't come when she insisted. How'd the creature know?"

"Ask Menolly."

"Menolly?" And suddenly Menolly found herself the object of his intense, frowning scrutiny. "You're Menolly?" The brows went up in surprise. "Little bit of a thing, aren't you? Not at all what I expected. Don't blush. I don't bite. My fire lizard might. Wouldn't worry you, though, would it? These are all yours? Why, my queen's beside yours, friendly as can be. They're not dangerous at all."

"Menolly!" The Harper's exclamation brought her attention back to the hearth.

His egg had given a convulsive rock, all but spinning itself off the hearthstone. Gasping, he'd put out both hands to prevent its falling. The shell cracked wide open, and a little bronze fire lizard rolled into his hands, creeling with hunger, its body glistening.

"Feed it! Feed it!" Menolly cried.

Robinton, unable to take his eyes off the fire lizard, fumbled for the piled meat and shoved food into the fire lizard's open mouth. The little bronze, shaking its wings out for balance, snatched ferociously at the meat, gobbling so fast that Menolly held her breath for fear the creature would choke in its greed.

"Not too much. Make it wait! Talk to it. Soothe it," Menolly urged. Just then the other egg split.

"It's a queen!" shouted Sebell, rocking back on his heels in the excess of his surprise. Only Lord Groghe's quick hand on his back kept him from falling over.

"Feed her!" the Lord Holder barked.

"But I'm not to have the queen!" For one split second, Sebell started to turn and offer the queen to the Harper.

"Too late!" Menolly shouted, diving forward to intercept the gesture. She jammed meat on Sebell's seeking hand and then pushed it back to the frantically creeling queen. "You're supposed to have a fire lizard. It doesn't matter which!"

The Harper was oblivious to the interchange. He was intent on his bronze, stroking it, feeding it, crooning to it. The little queen had gobbled Sebell's initial offering, her tail wrapping so firmly about his wrist that he could not have disentangled himself had he managed to sustain his moment of sacrifice.

Menolly turned to assist the Harper, but Lord Groghe was kneeling beside him, encouraging him. When the two hatchlings were bulging with food, Menolly removed the meat bowls.

"They'll burst with another mouthful," she told the reproachful harpers. "Now, hold them against you. Stroke them. They should fall asleep. There now." As the men complied with her urgings, the new fire lizards, sated for the present, wearily closed their eyes, their little heads dropping to the protecting forearms. She'd forgotten what a scant handful a newly hatched fire lizard was. Her friends had grown so much since hatching. Lord Groghe's Merga was as tall in the shoulder as Beauty, but not so deeply chested. The two were now exchanging compliments, stroking heads and touching curved wings.

"It's incredible," the Harper said, his words no more than an articulated whisper, his eyes brilliant with joy. "It is absolutely the most incredible experience I have ever had."

"Know what you mean," Lord Groghe replied in an embarrassed mumble, ducking his head, but Menolly could see that the burly Holder's face was flushed. "Can't forget it myself."

Carefully Master Robinton rose from his knees, his eyes on the sleeping fire lizard, his free hand poised in case an incautious movement unsettled the little bronze.

"It explains so very much that I could never have understood about dragonriders. Yes, it opens a whole new area of understanding." He sat down on the edge of his bed. "Now I can sense, dimly, what Lytol, what Brekke must have suffered. And I know why young Jaxom must have Ruth." He smiled at Lord Groghe's grunt at that statement. "Yes, I have stood so long peering through a small opening into another Hold of understanding. Now I can see without obstruction." His chin had dropped to his chest as he spoke in soft reflective tones, more to himself than those close enough to catch the whispered words. He shook himself slightly and looked up, his smile again radiant. "What a gift you have made me, Menolly. What a magnificent gift!"

Beauty came to perch on Menolly's shoulder, her humming now diminished to a soft murmur of sound. Lord Groghe's queen, Merga, flew to his shoulder, wrapping her tail about his thick neck, just as Beauty did.

"I don't know how it happened, Master Robinton," Sebell said, rising from the hearth with exaggerated care. His manner was both defensive and apologetic. "The pots were in the wrong order. I don't understand. You should have had the queen."

"My dear Sebell, I couldn't care in the slightest. This bronze fellow is everything I could ever want. And frankly, I believe that it might be more advantageous for you to have the queen, going out and about the land as you'll have to do. Yes, I think chance has worked more for than against us. And I am quite content, oh, indeed I am, with my bronze man here. What a lovely, lovely creature!" He had eased himself back against the bolster, the fire lizard snuggled in the crook of his arm, his other hand protectingly cradling the open side. "Such a lovely big fellow!" His head fell back, his eyes heavy, all but asleep himself.

"Now that's a real miracle," said Silvina in a very soft voice. "Asleep without wine or fellis juice? Out! Out!" She shook her hands at those crowding the door, but her gesture to Lord Groghe to precede her from the room was a touch more courteous. The Lord Holder nodded agreement and made a great show of tiptoeing quietly across the room. His exit cleared the doorway of onlookers.

Silvina picked up the half-filled bowls by the fire and put one near the Harper's hand. Menolly beckoned to the rest of her fair and they flitted out the window.

"Got them well-trained, haven't you?" Lord Groghe said once Silvina had closed the door to the Harper's chamber. "Want to have a long chat with you about 'em. Robinton says they'll fetch and carry for *you.* D'you believe, as he does, that what one fire lizard knows, th'others do, too?"

Too disconcerted to reply, Menolly glanced frantically at Silvina and saw her nod encouragingly. "It would seem logical, Lord Groghe. Ah

. . . it would certainly account for . . . for what happened the other night. In fact, there's no other way to account for that, is there? Unless you can speak to dragons."

"Unless you can speak to dragons?" Lord Groghe laughed ponderously, poking Menolly's shoulder with his finger in good humor. "Speak to dragons? Hahaha."

Menolly felt herself grinning because his laughter was a bit contagious, and she didn't know what else to do. She hadn't meant to be funny. Then Silvina shushed them imperiously, pointing urgently at the Harper's closed door.

"Sorry, Silvina," Lord Groghe said, contritely. "Most amazing thing! Woke up out of a sound sleep, scared out of my wits. Never happened to me before, I can tell you." He nodded his head emphatically, and Merga chirped. "Wasn't your fault, pet," he said, stroking her tiny head with a thick forefinger. "Only doing the same as the others. That's what I want you to teach me, girl." The forefinger now pointed at Menolly. "You will, won't you? Robinton says you have yours trained a treat."

"It would be my privilege, sir."

"Well spoken." Lord Groghe turned his heavy torso in Silvina's direction, favoring the headwoman with a fierce stare. "Well-spoken child. Not what I expected. Can't trust other people's opinions. Never did. Never will. I'll arrange something with Robinton later. Not too much later. But later. Good day to you all." With that the Lord Holder of Fort strode from the room, nodding and smiling to the harpers still gathered in the corridor.

Menolly saw Sebell and Silvina exchanging worried glances, and she moved across the room to stand before them.

"What did Lord Groghe mean, Silvina? I'm not what he expected?"

"I was afraid you'd catch that," Silvina said, her eyes narrow with a contained anger. She patted Menolly's shoulder absently. "There's been loose talk, which has done them no good and you no harm. I've a few knees to set knocking, so I have."

Menolly was thoroughly and unexpectedly consumed with anger. Beauty chittered, her eyes beginning to whirl redly.

"Those cot girls stay up at the Hold during Threadfall, don't they?"

Silvina gave Menolly a long, quelling look. "I said I'll handle the matter, Menolly. You," and Silvina pointed at her, "will occupy yourself with *harper* business." She was clearly as furious as Menolly, and flicked imaginary dust from her skirt with unnecessary force. "You're to stay here, both of you, and be sure nothing disturbs the Harper. Nothing, you understand!" She pinned apprentice and journeyman with a stern glare. "He's asleep, and he's to stay asleep as long as that little creature lets him. That way he might get caught up on himself for a change before he's worn to death." She picked up the tray. "I'll send your suppers up with Camo. And their suppers as well."

She closed the door firmly behind her. Menolly looked at the closed door for a long moment, still feeling the anger in her guts. She'd not really done the girls any kind of harm, so why would they try to prejudice the Lord Holder against her. Or perhaps it was all Dunca's connivance? Menolly knew that the little cotholder hated her for the humiliation caused by the fire lizards. Now that Menolly was at the Hall, why should Dunca persist? She glanced back to Sebell, who was regarding her even as he cradled his sleeping little queen.

"Leave it, Menolly," he said in a quiet but emphatic tone. He gestured her to the sandtable. "Harper business is better business for you now. Master Robinton said you were to copy the song onto sheets." Moving carefully so as not to disturb his little queen, he got supplies from the shelves and put them on the center board. "So, copy!"

"I don't understand what they thought they'd accomplish, prejudicing Lord Groghe against me. What would he do?"

Sebell said nothing as he hooked a stool under him, and sat down. He pointed at the music.

"It's only right for me to know. The insult is mine to settle."

"Sit down, Menolly. And copy. That's far more important to the Harper and the Hall than any petty machinations of envious girls."

"They *could* do me a mischief, couldn't they? If they'd got Lord Groghe to believe what they said. I never hurt those girls."

"True enough but that is not harper business. The song is. Copy it! And one more word from you on any other subject and I'll—"

"If you're not quiet, you'll wake your fire lizard," Menolly said, but she sat down at the table and started copying. She could recognize obstinacy when she saw it, and it would do her no good to set Sebell against her. "What are you going to name her?" she asked.

"Name her?" Sebell was startled, and Menolly was dismayed to realize how much of his joy in his queen had been diminished by her silly concern over gossip. "Why, I can have the privilege of naming her, can't I? She's mine. I think . . ." and his eyes glowed with affection for the hatchling, "I think I'll call her Kimi."

"That's a lovely name," replied Menolly and then bent to her copying with a good heart.

Chapter 8

Gather! Gather! It's a gather day!
No work for us, and Thread's away.
Stalls are building, square's swept clear,
Gather all from far and near.
Bring your marks and bring your wares,
Bring your family for there's
Food and drink and fun and song.
The Hold flag flies: so gather along!

"What's wrong with the Hold?" Menolly asked Piemur the next morning as she, the boy and Camo were feeding the fire lizards. Piemur kept craning his neck past the roofs of the Harper Hall to see the fire heights of Fort Hold.

"Nothing's wrong. I want to see if the gather flag's up."

"Gather flag?" Menolly recalled that Sebell had mentioned a gather.

"Sure! It's spring, and sunny. It's a restday, Thread's not due, so there ought to be a gather!" Piemur regarded her a long moment, then his face screwed up into an incredulous expression. "You mean, you don't have gathers?"

"Half-Circle *is* isolated," Menolly replied defensively. "And with Thread falling . . ."

"Yeah, I forgot that. No wonder you're such a smashing musician," he said, shaking his head as if this were no real compensation. "Nothing to do but practice! Still," he added somewhat skeptical, "you must have had gathers *before* Thread started?"

"Of course we did. Traders came through the marshes three and four times a Turn." Piemur was unimpressed. Menolly realized that she herself had only the vaguest memories of such events. Threadfall had started when she was barely eight Turns old.

"We have gathers as often as it's sunny on a restday," Piemur said, chattering away, "and there isn't any Thread due. Of course, our being a Hold with several small crafthalls, as well as the main Harper Craft Hall, does make for great gathers. You don't happen," and he cocked his head slyly, "to have any marks on you?"

"Marks?"

Piemur was thoroughly disgusted with her obtuseness. "Marks! Marks! What you get in exchange for what you're selling at a gather?" He reached into his pocket and pulled out four small white pieces of highly polished wood, on which the numerals *32* had been incised on one side and on the other, the mark of the Smithcraft. "Only thirty-seconds, but with four I got an eighth, and Smithcraft at that."

Menolly had never actually seen marks before. All trading transactions had been carried out by her father, the Sea Holder. She was astonished that so young a boy as Piemur had possession of marks and said so.

"Oh, I sang, you know, even before I got apprenticed. I'd always get a mark of some amount or other. My foster mother kept them for me until I came here." Piemur wrinkled his nose in disgust. "But you don't get paid for singing at gathers if you're a harper, and you have to do your turn anyway. I haven't *anything* to give the marksmen here. I keep *trying,* but Master Jerint won't put his seal on my pipes, so I have to figure out other ways of turning the odd. . . . Hey, look, Menolly," and he grabbed her arm, "there goes the flag! There'll be a gather!" He went flying across the court as fast as he could to the apprentice dormitory.

On the top of the Fort Hold fire heights, Menolly now saw the bright yellow pennant, and flapping below it on the mast, the red and black barred streamer that apparently signaled a gather. She heard Piemur's cries echoing in the apprentice dormitory and the sounds of sleepers stirring in complaint.

As if Piemur's sighting of the pennant had been a signal, the drudges, herded by Abuna and Silvina, entered the kitchen. The flag and pennant on the Hold mast were duly noted and the meal preparations were conducted in a cheerful humor.

Menolly dispersed her fair to their sunning and bathing and, finding Silvina in the kitchen with Abuna, offered to take breakfast to the Harper and his bronze, whom he'd named Zair.

"I told you, Abuna, that with Menolly to help, two more fire lizards would be no problem," Silvina said, pushing the kitchen woman onto some other task as she smiled warmly at Menolly. "Not that the Harper will be here much with his, nor Sebell either," she called to Abuna who went off grumbling to herself. "Long as she's lived in the Harper Hall, you'd think she'd be used to change-about."

Menolly wanted to ask Silvina about the girls and their gossiping, but Silvina was avoiding her eye. Just then they both heard Menolly's name being called in a frantic voice. Sebell came crashing down the kitchen steps, holding up his trousers with one bare arm, wincing at the clutch of his fire lizard queen on the other. Kimi was creeling wildly with hunger.

"Menolly! There you are! I've been searching everywhere. What's the matter with her? Ouch!" Sebell was wide-eyed with anxiety.

"She's only hungry."

"*Only* hungry?"

"Here, come with me," and Menolly took Sebell by the arm, picked up the tray she had prepared for the Masterharper and pulled the journeyman out of the kitchen, to spare him Abuna's black scowl, and into the relative peace of the dining hall. "Now, feed her!"

"I can't. My pants!" Sebell nodded to his trousers, which, beltless, threatened to slip off his hips.

Stifling a giggle, Menolly unbuckled her own worn belt and secured Sebell's pants for him. He grabbed a handful of meat and held it out for Kimi. The ungrateful wretch hissed and lunged at the meat, digging her claws into his forearm.

Well, Menolly couldn't give him her tunic, too. She spotted a scrap of towelling by the service hatch. Deftly she disengaged the queen's legs from Sebell's forearm and wrapped the cloth about his scratched and bleeding arm, then managed to redeposit Kimi before the queen was aware of being shifted.

"Oh, thank you, thank you, thank you!" sighed Sebell, sinking to the nearest bench. "And you had nine of these creatures to feed every day?" He gave her a look of renewed respect. "I don't know how you did it! I really don't!"

Menolly pointed to his klah as she took up a handful of meat. Kimi didn't care whose hand held the meat, so Sebell gratefully gulped some klah.

"Menolly!" Another voice roared from the top of the stairs.

"Sir?" Menolly dashed to the foot of the steps.

"He's making the most outlandish noises," the Harper yelled. "Is he hurt or just hungry? His eyes are flaming red."

"Here you are," said Silvina, appearing from the kitchen with a second tray of food for human and fire lizard. "I thought we'd be hearing from him once Sebell appeared."

Menolly could not keep from laughing with Silvina. She took the steps two at a time without spilling so much as a drop of the klah or tumbling a glob of meat from the piled bowl.

The Harper had taken time to dress, and he'd thought to wrap his arm against the needle-sharp claws of his little bronze, but he looked not a whit less harried or distressed than Sebell.

"You're sure it's only hunger?" asked Master Robinton. But his fire lizard's creeling abated with the first mouthful of meat.

Robinton gestured Menolly towards his quarters, but the fire lizard, believing the food was being withdrawn, let out an indignant shriek and swatted at Menolly's hand.

"Here, here, eat, you greedy thing," said the Harper with great affection in his voice. "Just don't wake everyone. It's restday."

"Too late," remarked Domick, in an acid tone of voice, his sleeping rug pulled around him as he stood in the doorway of his room. "Between you howling like an injured dragon, Sebell sounding like a flight of 'em, and these pesky beasts with tones that could bend metal, no one's going to enjoy a restday."

"The gather flag is flying," the Harper said in a conciliatory way. He continued to feed Zair as he and Menolly proceeded to his room.

"A gather? That's all I need." Domick slammed his door.

"I trust there won't be a repetition of this," said Master Morshal as the Harper and Menolly came abreast of his room. He wore a loose robe, but he obviously had been drawn from his bed by the creelings and shouts. His sour gaze was directed fully on Menolly, as if she were the sole cause of the commotion.

"Probably," the Harper replied cheerfully, "until I figure out this precious creature's habits. He only hatched yesterday, Morshal. Do give him a few days' grace."

Morshal spluttered something, glared balefully and accusingly at Menolly, and then shut his door, pointedly without slamming it. Menolly all too clearly heard other doors closing along the corridor, and she was very grateful to be in the Harper's company.

"Don't let old Morshal upset you, Menolly," said Master Robinton in a quiet voice.

Menolly looked up quickly, grateful for his reassurance. He smiled again as he nodded for her to enter his room and gestured for her to set the tray down on the center of the sandtable.

"Fortunately," he went on, slouching in a chair, all the while supplying meat bits for Zair, "you don't have to sit classes with Morshal."

"I don't?"

Robinton chuckled at the note of relief in her voice and then laughed again as Zair missed a morsel, creeled anxiously until the Harper had retrieved it from the floor and deposited it neatly in the open mouth.

"No, you don't. Morshal teaches only at the apprentice level." The Master Harper sighed. "He really is adept at drilling basic theory into rebellious apprentice minds. But Petiron already taught you more than Morshal knows. Relieved, Menolly?"

"Oh, yes. Master Morshal doesn't seem to like me."

"Master Morshal has always considered it a waste of time and effort to teach any girls. What good would it do them?"

Menolly blinked, surprised to hear her father's opinion echoed in the Harper Hall. Then she realized that Master Robinton had been speaking in deft mimicry of Master Morshal's testy manner. Warm fingers caught her chin, and she was made to look up at the Harper. The lines of fatigue and worry were plainly visible, despite his good night's rest.

"Morshal's dislike of the feminine sex is a standing joke in this Hall, Menolly. Give him the courtesy due his rank and age, and ignore his biased thinking. As I said, you don't have to sit classes with him. Not that Domick will be any easier to study with. He's a hard taskmaster, but Domick will take over your tuition where Petiron left off in musical form and composition until I can. Unfortunately," and the Harper's smile of regret was sincere, "I am badly pressed for time with all that's happening, much though I would prefer to undertake the task myself. Still, Domick's understanding of the truly classical form is superior, and he's keen to monopolize any instrumentalist capable of playing his intricate music. Don't miss your lessons with Master Shonagar, for you must be able to sing your songs effectively, but," and he lifted a warning finger, "don't fall for Brudegan's importunings about fire lizard choruses. That can be scheduled for a later time when we've settled you properly in your craft.

"I'd like you to concentrate on your instruments . . . as far and as fast as that hand of yours permits. How is it healing, by the way?" And he reached for her left hand. "Hmmm, you've done too much by the look of those splits. Does it hurt? I won't have you crippling yourself in your zeal, Menolly, understand that!"

Menolly, sensing his kind concern, swallowed against the lump in her throat and managed a tentative smile.

"It is never easy, sweet child, to have a real gift: something else is withheld to compensate."

Menolly was startled at the sadness, that melancholy in his eyes and face, and he went on, almost to himself, "If you won't surrender the mark, you'll never be more than half-alive. Speaking of marks . . ." and his expression altered completely. He leaned forward, across the sandtable, rummaging in the compartments of the central bridge built above the actual sand level. "Ah, here," and he pressed something in her hand. "There's a gather today, and you deserve some relaxation. I suspect diversions were few and infrequent in your Sea Hold. Find something pretty to wear at the stalls . . . a belt perhaps . . . and buy some of the bubbly pies. Piemur will lead you to them, the scamp.

"But tomorrow," and Master Robinton waggled a finger at her, "back to work for you. Sebell says you make a good copyist. Did you have a chance to polish the Brekke song yesterday evening? I think you'll agree the melodic line falters in the fourth phrase . . ." and he hummed it. "Then I want you to rewrite the ballad observing all the traditional musical forms. Think of it as an exercise in musical theory. Mind you, I'm of the opinion that the strength of your work will lie in a looser, less formalized style. There are, however, purists in the Craft who must be mollified while you're an apprentice."

Zair, his belly so swollen that the individual lumps of meat could be discerned against his skin, gave a sudden burp and collapsed into sleep in the crook of the Harper's arm.

"I say, Menolly, how long will he do nothing but eat and sleep?" The Harper sounded disappointed.

"The first sevenday, and maybe a few days longer," Menolly answered, still trying to assimilate his astonishing instructions and philosophy. "He'll develop a personality in a very short time."

"That's a relief." The Harper heaved an exaggerated sigh. "I'd been worrying that perhaps his brains had got addled, going *between* so much in the egg. Not that I'd care for him any the less," and he smiled tenderly down at the sprawled form. "How did you ever manage to fill *nine* rapacious bellies?" Now his smile was all for her. "And what a relief to have you here to help us. In this I am your apprentice." His eyes held hers a moment longer, still twinkling with amusement although his face settled into a serious expression. "In all other matters, you are to consider yourself *my* apprentice, you know.

"Now, you may take the tray back to the kitchen, and you are dismissed to the gather. Unless, of course," he added with that winning smile, "something untoward happens to this fellow."

She brought the tray and empty dishes to the kitchen, where Abuna, with more than her usual courtesy, suggested that Menolly had better get some breakfast before it was all gone. They'd be clearing the tables soon, and if the lazybones hadn't eaten, too bad. Not but what they couldn't stuff themselves at the gather's stalls.

That reminded Menolly of the mark that the Harper had put in her hand. At first she thought it was the dim light of the passage, but when she got into the entrance hall, she could plainly see that the two was underscored: it wasn't a half-mark, which would have been scored above. She clenched the precious piece in her fist, amazed. The Master Harper had given her a whole two-mark piece to spend on herself. Two whole marks! Why, she could buy anything!

No, he'd said that she was to buy something pretty to wear. A belt.

The Harper's keen eye had noted the absence of hers. And it was a worn belt, anyhow. But a new one, instead of one handed down . . . a belt she could choose for herself! How very kind of Master Robinton. And he'd said she was to buy bubbly pies. She looked about the scattering of boys at the apprentice tables for Piemur's curly head of hair. He was, as usual, deep in conversation with several boys, and probably planning mischief to judge by the closeness of all the heads. There were no masters at the circular table and just a few journeymen at the oval ones, clustered about Sebell, admiring Kimi, asleep on his arm.

"She couldn't give 'em away if she wanted to," Piemur was saying in a strident tone as Menolly approached his group. Someone must have jabbed him in the ribs because he glanced over his shoulder and, while he looked in no way abashed, it was obvious from the expression of the others that Menolly had been the "she" he'd meant. "Can you?" he asked bluntly.

"Can I what?"

"Give anyone else one of your fire lizards?"

"No."

"I told you!" Piemur pointed an accusing finger at Ranly. "So Sebell couldn't have given Robinton the queen. Could he, Menolly?"

"But the Masterharper should have had the queen," said Ranly, rebellious and unconvinced.

"Sebell did offer the queen to Master Robinton when she hatched," Menolly said quickly, "but it was too late. Impression had occurred, and that can't be altered."

"Well, just how did Sebell get his hands on the queen egg?" Now Ranly's eyes hotly accused her of complicity.

"Completely by accident," she said, mastering her irritation at such an outrageous suggestion. "First, there really isn't any positive way of knowing which is the queen egg in a fire lizard clutch. Second, it isn't anyone's business but Master Robinton's and Sebell's." She'd just lay this divisive rumor into an early grave and repay a little of her great debt to both men. "Third, I picked the two biggest eggs in the clutch for Master Robinton," and the boys nodded with approval, "but they could both have been bronzes." Then she laughed. "It all happened so fast when the eggs started to hatch, no one bothered to see which pot was whose. Master Robinton and Sebell just grabbed because both pots were rocking fit to fall. The little bronze hatched first, right into Master Robinton's hands, and that was that, right then. He caught it just before it could fall from the hearthstone." The boys snatched in breath for that near catastrophe. "And then there was Sebell with a queen in his hands. Then, he *tried* to give her to the Harper, but Zair had Impressed and so had little Kimi. There's no way to change that. And I don't want to hear another word from any of you as to who got what and who shouldn't have. There's enough gossip flying about this Hall." She wished she could forget her worries about what those girls had told the Lord Holder.

"I kept trying to tell them," said Piemur, throwing his hands out, his eyes bright with injured innocence because Menolly was now glaring at him. Then he clutched dramatically at his throat because his voice had squeaked on the last word. "I've gone hoarse talking . . ."

"Can't have the golden throat hoarse, can we?" said Ranly sarcastically.

Piemur was testing klah pots on the table to see if there was any that was still warm. Finding one he poured two mugs, offering one to Menolly. He gurgled as he downed half a mug, rubbed his hand across his mouth and then told her that she'd better eat quickly because they'd be clearing any minute.

"Now, let's get *back* to the mark problem. This will be only the second gather of the Turn, so I figure that they'll be sending an older journeyman from the Smithcraft Hall, to keep an eye on the younger fellows and supervise the bargaining. And that journeyman is just likely to be my father's friend, Pergamol; and if it's Pergamol, then I can guarantee that you'll get top marks for your work. And . . ." he held up a silencing hand as Ranly opened his mouth to comment, "if it isn't Pergamol, it'll be someone who knows him."

"And if it's just a young journeyman who's on to you, Piemur?" Ranly asked in a caustic tone.

"Then I blubber!" Piemur dismissed this problem with all the disdain of the practiced dissembler. "I'm just a li'l feller, and I never have much and I . . ." Great tears welled up in his eyes, and his face was a mask of trusting and anxious innocence.

"If I may disturb this tactical meeting," said a different voice, and all the boys looked guiltily around to see Sebell, fire lizard cradled in his arm, "for a few words with Menolly . . ."

She rose and followed the journeyman to the window. He pressed her rolled-up belt in her hand, as he thanked her for saving his dignity that morning.

"Now, can I keep Kimi with me all the time?" he asked, lightly stroking the fire lizard's folded wings. Even in her sleep she responded to his touch with a sigh.

"The more she's with you the stronger the bond will grow. If not on you, near you."

"Is she too young to be taught to sit on my shoulder like your Beauty does? I've got to have both hands for a while today."

"When she wakes, put her on your shoulder." Menolly grinned. "And get used to having your neck throttled."

"How often does she eat?"

"She'll let you know." Menolly laughed at Sebell's consternation. "At least you don't have to go catch it. Keep a few meatrolls in your belt pouch, although I'm sure Camo will always be ready to chop-chop for you anytime." Sebell chuckled, too. "One thing you'll need to do daily is oil her skin."

"Does it have to stink like the stuff you use?" Sebell was dismayed.

Menolly suppressed a giggle. "Master Oldive had that oil on hand. He said he makes it for the ladies of the Hold to use on their faces . . ."

"Oh, no."

"But I'm sure he'd make you something more suitable for your . . ." She paused, not certain just how much she could tease Sebell.

"My male dignity and rank?" Sebell grinned at her. "I'll just have a word with him now," and he strolled off with a lilt in his step.

Menolly was very pleased that she'd suppressed the boys' misapprehension over the fire lizards' hatching. Sebell was so nice. And, it wasn't as if Master Robinton had been upset at Impressing the bronze. He genuinely hadn't cared a whit once Zair had Impressed and was his very own. And if Master Robinton was content, the rest of the Hall shouldn't quarrel!

Then she worried about the girls' gossip: if the apprentices could take a simple switch like the Hatching and derive deep insult from it, what had the girls done with her reputation at the Hold?

"Look, Menolly," Piemur said, popping up beside her, "I gotta couple of things to do now, but after dinner, you want me to take you round the gather? Seeing as how you haven't been to one . . . here, that is."

She readily agreed, curious to see just how his plans would affect his bargaining. He darted out of the Hall then, the other boys hard on his heels.

A few journeymen still lounged at the oval table, drinking klah, but most of the apprentices had dispersed. At the round table, Master Morshal now glowered darkly at her as he ate in solitary dignity. Menolly left the dining hall for the sanctuary of her room.

Her fire lizards were curled up on the deep window ledge, their wings glinting brilliantly in the sun but their jeweled eyes closed behind their several lids. Beauty stirred, raised her head, parted the outer lid, squeaked softly and, when Menolly stroked her reassuringly, sighed and resumed her interrupted nap.

From the vantage point of the second level, Menolly could see the square beyond the Harper Hall and the broad roadway. There was already considerable activity: burdenbeasts moving up the river road, their slow long stride one of indolence, rather than labor under heavy weight. Stalls were being assembled, forming a loose square about an open space. Tables and benches were already in place, facing the dance square. For dancing there would surely be, with a hundred or more harpers to do the playing. There'd be more dancing than she'd ever seen. And probably different dances from the ones popular in her Sea Hold. Oh, this would be a grand gather. Her first here, and her first since Thread started falling.

Menolly caught sight of the girls emerging from the cot, brightly clad, with filmy scarves to protect their hair from the light wind. Oh, what she'd like to do to their hair! Pona's hair, with its long neat plaits to be pulled out by the roots. . . . Menolly stopped her thoughts, a little appalled at the intensity of her dislike. After all, the girls had failed of their aim—to prejudice Lord Groghe against her. Why was she bothering her head about them? She'd better things to occupy herself with. She was an apprentice harper, not a sometime student. She was Masterharper Robinton's apprentice. Of course, since he was Master of the Harper Hall, everyone within was *his* apprentice.

But she was an apprentice. And she intended to remain one. More than ever now that the girls had made an effort to jeopardize her tenure. She was going to stay, to spite them, and her parents. She was going to make her place here because this was where she belonged, as Master Robinton had said. Here was where she could perfect her music. Here she could make her own place for herself, not slip into a spot left by someone else, anyone else. Just as she'd made the cave her own, she would make her own place here in the Harper Hall. And no one, particularly a sneaky little twitterhead whose only claim to importance was being someone's granddaughter, was going to dislodge her! Or a conniving coward like cotholder Dunca!

Menolly wondered if Silvina had done anything about settling the rumors. Really, it just wasn't important, Menolly told herself sternly. Particularly when Lord Groghe seemed to approve of her and had actually suggested that she help him train his queen, Merga.

Menolly laughed to herself. Just wait till those sissies heard about that! She, apprentice trainer of fire lizards, the only successful one on Pern. The teacher just one step ahead of the student. She giggled now, covering her mouth with her hands because she knew she was acting the wherry. But she'd been silly not to see before that she had several tunes to play in this Harper Hall: the tunes she made, her fire lizards—yes, and how to gut fish and trim sail whenever some harper needed to know. And why did Sebell need to know? She sighed gustily.

Too bad about those girls, though. She wished Audiva didn't have to stay with them; she was above the general sort at the cot, and it would have been nice to have a girl friend. Not that she didn't have a good friend in Piemur. When Piemur grew up and lost his brilliant voice, would he have to leave the Craft Hall? No, because they must surely be training him to play one of those "other" tunes. She didn't quite see him stepping into Master Shonagar's slippers . . .

She rose from the window ledge, reminded of the task that Master Robinton had set her as his apprentice. She tuned her gitar and began to rehearse the Brekke song, softly lest the Harper was busy in his rooms. Did he honestly think that song, a twiddle to while the time away until Sebell returned, was good enough to be perfected?

Of their own volition, her fingers were plucking out the melody. She found herself caught up once more in the poignancy of Brekke's anguished command! *Don't leave me alone!* She played the song through, agreeing with the Harper that the fourth phrase needed polishing . . . ah, yes, if she dropped to the fifth, it would intensify the phrase and compliment the chord.

The tocsin rang for mealtime finally, and shouts and laughter broke her concentration. She was almost angry with the disruption. But with a renewed awareness of her surroundings, she realized how her hand ached. Her back and neck muscles were stiff from crouching over the gitar. She'd no idea she'd been practicing that long, but the song was set in her mind and her fingers now. She would have it finished in next to no time once she had more ink and those paper sheets.

She changed into the clothes she wanted to wear to the gather: not as rich as the girls would be wearing, but new. The close-woven trousers and the contrasting colored tunic with the sleeveless hide jumper displaying the apprentice badge meant more to her than fine cloth and filmy scarves. As she pulled on her slippers, she noticed that the constant scuffing on the stone floors was wearing soles and toes out. At least here, she needn't fear to approach Silvina, and perhaps her feet were healed enough for proper boots, which would last longer.

Chapter 9

The fickle wind's my foe,
With tide his keen ally.
They're jealous of my sea's love
And rouse her with their lie.

Oh sweet sea, oh dear sea,
Heed not their stormy wile
But bear me safely to my hold
And from their watery trial.

Eastern Sea Hold Song

There was an excitement in the air of the dining hall, the boys chattering more loudly than ever, a conversational buzz that dropped off only slightly when they were seated and the heavy platters of steaming meat slices were brought around. She sat with Ranly, Piemur and Timiny, who all urged her to eat hearty for they'd be lucky to get stale bread for supper.

"Silvina counts on our stuffing ourselves on our own marks at the gather," Piemur told Menolly as he crammed meat into his mouth. He groaned as she heaped tubers on his plate. "I hate 'em."

"You're lucky to have 'em. They were treats where I come from."

"Then you have mine." He was generosity itself, but she made him eat his own.

No one spent time over the meal, and the diners were dismissed as soon as Brudegan had called out the list of names.

"Well, I'm not on a turn today," said Piemur with the air of a last minute reprieve.

"Turn?"

"Yeah, being Harper Hall and all, this Hold expects continuous music, but no one does more than one set, either singing or dance music. No great problem. You know, Menolly, you'd better tell your fire lizards to stay away," Piemur said as they all made their way across the courtyard to the archway. The other boys nodded in agreement. "No telling what ragtag is going to appear at a gather." He sounded darkly foreboding.

"Who'd hurt a fire lizard?" Menolly asked, surprised.

"Not hurt 'em. Just want 'em."

Menolly looked up and saw her friends sunning on the window ledges. As if her notice was sufficient, Beauty and Rocky came streaking down to her, chirping inquiringly.

"Couldn't I just take Beauty? No one sees her when she hides in my hair."

Piemur shook his head slowly from side to side. The other boys mimicked him with earnest expressions of concern.

"*We,*" and he meant Harpers, "know about you and having nine. There're some dimwits coming today who wouldn't understand. And you're wearing an apprentice badge: apprentices don't own nothing or count for anything. They're the lowest of the low and have to obey any journeyman, or master, or even a senior apprentice in any other craft. Shells, you know how Beauty acts when someone tries to rank you? You can't have Beauty taking a swipe at an honorable journeyman or craftmaster, now can you? Or someone from the Hold?" He jerked his thumb towards the cliffside as he dropped his voice to keep the mere possibility of such discourtesy from exalted ears.

"That would get Master Robinton in trouble?" Considering the gossip work already done at the Hold, Menolly would as soon remain anonymous to them.

"It could!" Ranly and Timiny nodded in solemn accord.

"How do *you* manage to stay out of trouble, Piemur?" Menolly asked.

" 'Cause I watch my step at a gather. One thing to cut up in the Hall when it's all Harpers, but . . ."

"Hey, Piemur." They all turned and saw Brolly and another apprentice whom Menolly did not know running towards them. Brolly had a brightly painted tambourine and the other a handsomely polished tenor pipe.

"Thought we might have missed you, Piemur," the boy gasped. "Here's my pipe, and Master Jerint stamped it and Brolly's tambourine. Will you take 'em to the marksman now?"

"Sure. And it's my father's friend, Pergamol, like I told you it would be."

Piemur took charge of the instruments, and with a quirk of a smile at Menolly, led the way towards the loosely arranged stalls on the perimeter of the gather's square.

For the first time Menolly realized how many people lived in this

Hold area. She would have liked to watch a bit on the sidelines, to get used to such a throng of people, but grabbing her hand, Piemur led her right into their midst.

She nearly piled into Piemur when he came to a sudden complete stop in the space between two booths. He glanced warningly over his shoulder, and Menolly noticed that he had the instruments behind his back as he composed his face into an expression of wistful ingenuousness. A tanner journeyman was bargaining with the well-dressed marksman in the stall, his Smithcraft badge gleaming with a gold thread in the design.

"See, it is Pergamol," Piemur said out of the side of his mouth. "Now you lot go on, across there to the knife stand until I'm finished. Men don't like a lot of hangers about when they're agreeing the mark. No, Menolly, you can stay!" Piemur snatched her back by the jerkin as she obediently started to follow the others.

Although Menolly could see Pergamol's lips moving, she heard nothing of his speech and only an occasional murmur from the bargaining journeyman. The Smithcraft marksman continually stroked the finely tanned wherhide as he dickered, almost as if he hoped to find some flaw in the hide so he could argue a further reduction. The hide was a lovely blue, like a summer sky when the air is clear and the sun setting.

"Probably dyed to order," Piemur whispered to her. "Selling it direct neither has to pay turnover fee. With us, once Jerint has stamped the instrument, the marksman doesn't *have* to say it was apprentice-made. So we get a better price not selling at the Harper booth, where they have to say who made it."

Now Menolly could appreciate Piemur's strategy.

The bargain was handsealed, and marks slipped across the counter. The blue hide was carefully folded and put away in a travel bag. Piemur waited until the journeyman had chatted, as courtesy required, and then he skipped to the front of the stall before anyone else could intervene.

"Back so soon, young rascal. Well, let's have a look at what you've brought. Hmm . . . stamped as you said . . ." Pergamol examined more than the stamp on the tambourine, Menolly noticed, and the Smithcrafter's eyes slid to hers as he pinged the stretched hide of the tambourine with his finger, and raised his eyebrows at the sweet-sounding tinkle of the tiny cymbals under the rim. "So how much were you looking to receive for it?"

"Four marks!" said Piemur with the attitude that he was being eminently reasonable.

"Four marks?" Pergamol feigned astonishment, and the interchange of bargaining began in earnest.

Menolly was delighted, and more than a little impressed by Piemur's shrewdness when the final figure of three and a half marks was hand-clasped. Piemur had pointed out that for a journeyman-made tambourine, four marks was not unreasonable: Pergamol did not have to say who made it, and he saved a thirty-second on turnover. Pergamol replied that he had the carriage of the tambourine. Piemur discounted that since Pergamol might very well sell the item here at the gather, since he could price it under the Harpercraft stall. Pergamol replied that he had to make more than a few splinters profit for his journey, his effort and the rent of the stall from the Lord Holder. Piemur suggested that he consider the fine polish on the wood, listen again to the sweet jingle of the best quality metal, thinly hammered, just the sort of an instrument for a lady to use . . . and a hide tanned evenly, no rough patches or stains. Menolly realized that, for all the extreme seriousness with which the two dickered, it was a game played according to certain rules, which Piemur must have learned at his foster mother's knee. The bargaining for the pipe went more smartly since Pergamol had noticed a pair of small holders waiting discreetly beyond the stall. But the bargaining was done and handsealed, Piemur shaking his head at Pergamol's stinginess and sighing mightily as he pocketed the marks. Looking so dejected that Menolly was concerned, the boy motioned for her to follow him to the spot where the others waited. Halfway there, Piemur let out a sigh of relief and his face broke into the broadest of his happy grins, his step took on a jauntier bounce and his shoulders straightened.

"Told you I could get a fair deal out of Pergamol!"

"You did?" Menolly was confused.

"Sure did. Three and a half for the tambourine? And three for the pipe? That's top mark!" The boys crowded round him, and Piemur recounted his success with many winks and chuckles. For his efforts, he got a quarter of a mark from each of the boys, telling Menolly that that was an improvement, for them, on the full half-mark the Harpercraft charged for selling.

"C'mon, Menolly, let's gad about," Piemur said, grabbing her by the arm and tugging her back into the stream of slowly moving people. "I can smell the pies from here," he said when he had eluded the others. "All we have to do is follow our noses . . ."

"Pies?" Master Robinton had mentioned bubbling pies.

"I don't mind treating you, since today is your first gather . . . here . . ." he added hastily, looking to see if he'd offended her, "but I'm not buying for those bottomless pits."

"We just finished dinner—"

"Bargaining's hungry work." He licked his lips in anticipation. "And I feel like something sweet, bubbling hot with berry juice. Just you wait. We'll duck through here."

He maneuvered her through the crowd, going across the moving traffic in an oblique line until they reached a wide break in the square. There they could see down to the river and the meadow where the traders' beasts were grazing, hobbled. People were moving up all the roads, arriving from the outlying plain and mountain holds. Their dress tunics and shirts made bright accents to the fresh green of the spring fields. The sun shone brilliantly over all. It was a glorious day, thought Menolly, a marvelous day for a gather. Piemur grabbed her hand, pulling her faster.

"They can't have sold all the pies," she said, laughing.

"No, but they'll get cold, and I like 'em hot, bubbling!"

And so the confections were, carried from an oven in the baker's hold on a thick, long-handled tray: the berry juices spilling darkly over the sides of the delicately browned crusts that glistened with crystalized sweet.

"Ho, you're out early, are you, Piemur? Let me see your marks first."

Piemur, with a show of great reluctance, dragged out a thirty-second bit and showed it to the skeptic.

"That'll buy you six pies."

"Six? Is that all?" Piemur's face reflected utter despair. "This is all me and my dorm mates could raise." His voice went up in a piteous note.

"Don't give me that old wheeze, Piemur," said the baker with a derisive snort. "You know you eat 'em all yourself. You wouldn't treat your mates to as much as a sniff."

"Master Palim . . ."

"Master me nothing, Piemur. You know my rank same as I know yours. It's six pies for the thirty-second or stop wasting my time." The journeyman, for that was the badge on his tunic, was slipping six pies off the tray as he spoke. "Who's your long friend here? That dorm mate you're always talking about?"

"She's Menolly . . ."

"Menolly?" The baker looked up in surprise. "The girl who wrote the song about the fire lizards?" A seventh pie was set beside the others.

Menolly fumbled in her pocket for her two-mark piece.

"Have a pie for welcome, Menolly, and any time you have a spare egg that needs a warm home. . . ." He let the sentence peter out and gave her a broad wink, and a broader smile so she'd know he was joking.

"Menolly!" Piemur grabbed her wrist, staring at the two-marker, his eyes round with surprise. "Where'd you get that?"

"Master Robinton gave it to me this morning. He said I'm to buy a belt and some bubbly pies. So please, Journeyman, I'd like to pay for them."

"No way!" Piemur was flatly indignant, knocking her extended hand away. "I said it was my treat 'cause this is your first gather. And I *know* that's the first mark piece you've ever had. Don't you go wasting it on me." He had half turned from the baker and was giving Menolly a one-eyed wink.

"Piemur, I don't know what I'd've done without you these past few days," she said, trying to move him out of her way so she could give Palim the marker. "I insist."

"Not a chance, Menolly. I keep my word."

"Then put your money where your mouth is, Piemur," said Palim, "you're blocking my counter," and he indicated the hulking figure of Camo bearing down on them.

"Camo! Where've you been, Camo?" cried Piemur. "We looked all over for you before we started for the pies. Here're yours, Camo."

"Pies?" And Camo came forward, huge hands outstretched, his thick lips moist. He wore a fresh tunic, his face was shining clean, and his straggling crop of hair had been brushed flat. He had evidently homed in on the sweet aroma of the pies as easily as Piemur.

"Yes, bubbly pies, just like I promised you, Camo," Piemur passed him two pies.

"Well, now, you wasn't having me on, was you, about feeding your mates. Although how come Menolly and Camo . . ."

"Here's your money," said Piemur with some haughtiness, thrusting the thirty-second piece in Palim's hand. "I trust your pies will live up to standard."

Menolly gaped, because there were now nine small bubbly pies on the counter front.

"Three for you, Camo." Piemur handed him a third. "Now don't burn your mouth. Three for you, Menolly," and the pastry was warm enough to sting Menolly's scarred palm, "and three for me. Thank you, Palim. It's good of you to be generous. I'll make sure everyone knows your pies . . ." and despite the heat of the crust, Piemur bit deeply into the pastry, the dark purple juices dribbling down his chin, ". . . are just as good as ever," and he said the last on a sigh of contentment. Then more briskly, "C'mon, you two." He waved to the baker who stared after them before he uttered a bark of laughter. "See you later, Palim!"

"We got nine pies for the price of six!" she said when they'd got far enough away from the stall.

"Sure, and I'll get nine again when I go back, because he'll think I'm sharing with you and Camo again. That's the best deal I've pulled on him yet."

"You mean . . ."

"Pretty smart of you to flash that two-marker about. He wouldn't have been able to change it this early in the afternoon. I'll have to try that angle again, next gather. The large marker, I mean."

"Piemur!" Menolly was appalled at his duplicity.

"Hmmmm?" His expression over the rim of the pie was unperturbed. "Good, aren't they?"

"Yes, but you're outrageous. The way you bargain . . ."

"What's wrong with it? Everyone has fun. 'Specially this early in the season. Later on they get bored, and even being small and looking sorrowful doesn't help me. Ah, Camo," and Piemur looked disgusted. "Can't you even eat clean?"

"Pies good!" Camo had stuffed all three pies into his mouth. His tunic was now stained with berry juices, his face was flecked with pastry and berry skins, and his fist had smeared a purple streak across one cheek.

"Menolly, will you look at him! He'll disgrace the Hall. You can't take your eyes off him a moment. C'mere!"

Piemur dragged Camo to the back of the line of stalls until he found a water skin dangling from a thong on a stall frame. He made Camo cup his hands and wash his face. Menolly found a scrap of cloth, not too dirty, and they managed to remove the worst of the pie stains from Camo's face and front.

"Oh, blast the shell and sear the skin!" said Piemur in a round oath as he took up his third pie. "It's cold. Camo, you're more trouble than you're worth sometimes."

"Camo trouble?" The man's face fell into deep sorrowful lines. "Camo cold?"

"No, the pie's cold. Oh, never mind. I like you, Camo, you're my friend." Piemur patted the man's arm reassuringly, and the numbwit brightened.

"Cold or not," Menolly said after she took a bite from her third, and cooled, pastry, "they're every bit as good as you said, Piemur."

"Say," and Piemur eyed her through narrowed lids, "maybe you'd better bargain the next lot out of Palim."

"I couldn't eat another . . ."

"Oh, not now. Later."

"It'll be my treat then."

"Sure thing!" He agreed with such amiability that Menolly decided that she'd taken the bait, hook and all. "First," he went on, "let's find the Tanner's stall." He took her by the hand and Camo by the sleeve and hauled them down the row. "So you're really Master Robinton's apprentice? Wow! Wait'll I tell the others! I told 'em you would be."

"I don't understand you."

Piemur shot her a startled look. "He did say that you were his apprentice when he gave you that two-marker, didn't he?"

"He'd told me I was before today, but I didn't think that was unusual. Aren't all the apprentices in the Hall his apprentices? He's the Masterharper . . ."

"You sure don't understand." Piemur's glance was one of undiluted pity for her denseness. "Every master has a few special apprentices . . . I'm Master Shonagar's. That's why I'm always running his errands. I don't know how they did it in your Sea Hold, but here, you get taken in as a general apprentice. If you turn out to be specially good at something, like me at voice, and Brolly at making instruments, the Master of that craft takes you on as a special apprentice, and you report to him for extra training and duties. And if he's pleased with you, he'll give you the odd mark to spend at a gather. So . . . if Master Robinton gave you a two-marker, he's pleased with you, and you're his special apprentice. He doesn't tap many." Piemur shook his head slowly from side to side, with a soft emphatic whistle. "There's been lots of heavy betting in the dorm as to who he'd pick since Sebell took his walk as journeyman . . . not that Sebell doesn't still look to the Masterharper even if he is a rank up . . . but Ranly was so sure he'd be tapped."

"Is that why Ranly doesn't like me?"

Piemur dismissed that with a gesture. "Ranly never had a chance, and the only one who didn't know that was Ranly! He thinks he's so good. Everyone else knew that Master Robinton was hoping to find you . . . the one who'd written those songs! Look, there's the Tanner's stall. And just spy that beautiful blue belt. It's even got a fire lizard for a buckle tongue!" He'd pulled her up and lowered his voice for the last words. "And blue! You let me bargain, hear?"

Before she could agree, Piemur approached the stall, acting casually, glancing over the tabards, soft shoes and boots displayed, apparently oblivious to the belt he'd just indicated to Menolly.

"They've got some blue boot hide, Menolly," he said, to her.

Knowing the shrewdness Piemur had already displayed, Menolly followed his cue, and, glancing at the tanner for permission, touched the thick wherry leather. She could see the belt over his shoulder, and the tongue had been fashioned like a slim fire lizard.

"Now, don't tell me you have money in your trous, short stuff," the tanner journeyman said to Piemur and then peered uncertainly at Menolly's cropped hair, trousers and apprentice badge.

"Me? No, but she's buying. Her slippers are a disgrace."

The tanner did look down, and Menolly wanted to hide her scuffed footwear.

"This is Menolly," Piemur went on, blithely unaware of the embarrassment he was causing her. "She's got nine fire lizards, and she's Master Robinton's new apprentice."

Wondering what on earth was possessing Piemur, she glanced anywhere but at the curious journeyman. She caught a glimpse of bright filmy materials and richly decorated tunics. She steadied her gaze and saw Pona, her arm through a tall lad's. He was wearing the yellow of Fort Hold and the shoulder knot of the Lord Holder's family. Behind Pona came Briala, Amania and Audiva, each of the girls escorted by a well-dressed youth, fosterlings of Lord Groghe's to judge by the different hold colors and rank knots.

"Here, Menolly, what do you think of this hide?" asked Piemur.

"And be sure she has the marks for it," said Pona, pausing. Her voice was too smooth to be insulting, and yet her manner gave her words an offensive ring. "For I'm certain she's only wasting your time and will finger your wares dirty. Whereas I want to commission you to make me some soft shoes for the summer . . ." She held up a well-filled waist pouch.

"She's got two marks," Piemur said, turning to challenge Pona, his eyes flashing with anger.

"If she does, she stole it," replied Pona, abandoning her indolent manner. "She'd nothing on her when she was still permitted to live in the cot."

"Stolen?" Menolly felt herself tensing with fury at the totally unexpected accusation.

"Stolen, nothing!" Piemur replied hotly. "Master Robinton gave it to her this morning!"

"I claim insult from you, Pona," cried Menolly, her hand on her belt knife.

"Benis, she's threatening me!" Pona cried, clinging to her escort's arm.

"Now, see here, apprentice girl. You can't insult a lady of the Holders. You just hand over that mark piece," said Benis, gesturing peremptorily to Menolly.

"Menolly, don't take insult," Audiva pushed her way past the others and grabbed her arm, restraining her. "It's what she wants."

"Pona's given me too many insults, Audiva."

"Menolly, you mustn't—"

"Get the mark, Benis," Pona said in a hiss. "Make her pay for threatening *me!*"

"Out of the way, Benis, whoever you are," said Menolly. "Pona has to answer for the insults she gives, lady holder or not." Menolly moved sideways, countering Pona's attempt to evade her.

"Benis, she can be dangerous! I told you so!" Pona's voice went up in a frightened, breathless squeak.

"You mustn't, Menolly," Audiva said, catching Menolly's sleeve. "She *wants* you to. . . . Piemur, help me!"

"Don't you dare, Audiva!" Pona's voice was now edged with angry malice. "Or I'll settle you good as well."

"Come, girl, the money. Hand it over and we'll say no more about attempted insult . . ." said Benis in a patronizing tone.

"Pona's insulted Menolly!" cried Piemur indignantly. "Just because you're a—"

"Close your mouth!" Benis wasted no courtesies on Piemur. He took a stride to close the distance between himself and Menolly, his jaw set in a disagreeable grin as he disdainfully measured the three slight and defiant adversaries.

Pona gave a little squeal as Benis left her standing on her own. Then, another as Menolly, stepping away from Benis, made a lunge at her, trying to catch her long plaited hair.

"Hey, now just a minute, you," said the tanner in a loud voice, sensing an imminent fight. He ducked under the counter of his stall, emerging into the walkway. "This is a gather, not a . . ."

Benis was quick on his feet, too, and he grabbed Menolly by the shoulder, spinning her towards him and securing her left arm, which he immediately twisted up behind her. With a cry of triumph, Pona darted forward, her hands busy with Menolly's belt pouch. Piemur sprang to Menolly's assistance, kicking Benis in the shins and grabbing Pona by the hair. The kick made Benis loosen his hold on Menolly's arm. With a strength developed by Turns of hauling and handling heavy nets, she wrenched free of his grasp, dancing out of his way.

"I settle Pona!" She shouted to Piemur, beckoning him away.

"Benis, save me!" Pona screamed, rushing to the young Holder, but Piemur was still hanging onto her plait.

Benis let fly a kick at Piemur, tripping him up and added another one to the ribs as the boy measured his length in the dust.

"Leave him alone!" Forgetting her quarrel with Pona, Menolly launched herself at Benis. Putting shoulder and body behind her fist, she drove it right into Benis's face. He staggered back, roaring in outrage and pain. One of the other fosterlings came charging forward, fist cocked to slam Menolly, but Audiva hung onto his arm.

"Viderian! Menolly's a seaholder! Help us!"

Startled, her escort bounded in to help Audiva, just as Menolly ducked under Benis's swing and tried to protect Piemur, who was struggling to get to his feet, blood streaming from his nose.

The next moment, the air was full of shrieking, clawing, fighting fire lizards. Piemur was screaming that Benis better not hit the Harper's apprentice, or there'd be real trouble; Camo was howling that his pretty ones were afraid, and he waded in, thick arms flailing, hitting indiscriminately at friend and foe. Menolly got a clout across the ear as she tried to restrain the misguided Camo.

"Shells! It's the Hall's dummy!" "Scatter!" "Get her!" "Knock him down!" "Got her, Menolly!"

The fire lizards were not hampered by Camo's inability to distinguish friend and foe. They went for Pona, Briala, Amania, Benis and the other lads. Menolly, trying to catch her breath, realized that things were completely out of hand and desperately tried to call off the fire lizards. The girls were scattering, screaming, vainly trying to cover their heads, hair and eyes. Attacked from above, so did the fosterlings.

Be still! Everyone! The bellow was stentorian enough to penetrate shriek, howl and battle cries, and stern enough to command instant obedience. "You there, hang on to Camo! Douse him with that skin of water! You, tanner, help them with Camo. Sit on him, knock his feet out from under him if necessary. Menolly, control your fire lizards! This is a gather, not a brawl!"

The Harper strode into the midst of the melee, yanking a fosterling to his feet, spinning one of the girls to the arms of the folk who had converged on the scene, giving a bloody-nosed Piemur a hand up from the dust. The Masterharper's actions were somewhat hampered by the distressed squeals of the little bronze fire lizard clinging tightly to his left arm, but there was little doubt of the Master's fury. A silence broken by the gulping sobs of Pona and Briala held attackers, attacked and witnesses alike.

"Now," said the Harper, his voice controlled although his eyes were flashing with anger, "just what has been going on here?"

"It was her!" Pona staggered a step towards Master Robinton, jabbing her finger at Menolly and struggling to control her sobs. Long scratches marred her cheeks, her head scarf was torn and her hair pulled from its plaits. "She's always causing trouble—"

"Sir, we were minding our own business," said Piemur indignantly, "which was buying a belt that you said Menolly ought to have, when Pona here—"

"That little sneak tripped me as we were passing, and then her hideous beasts attacked all of us. They've done it before. I have witnesses!" She stopped mid-gulp, arrested by the look on the Harper's face.

"Lady Pona," he said in an all too gentle voice, "you are overwrought. Briala, take the child back to Dunca. The excitement of a gather appears to be too much for such a fragile spirit. Amania, I think you ought to help Briala." Though his voice expressed concern for their well-being, it was obvious that the Harper was disciplining the three girls who bore evidence of the unfriendly attentions of the fire lizards.

Now he turned to the Hold fosterlings. Benis, his left eye already bruising, his lip cut, his hair tousled and forehead bearing fire lizard marks, was straightening his tunic and brushing dust from his sleeves and trousers. The other youths who had been escorting the now banished girls maintained the rigid stance they had adopted as soon as they recognized the Masterharper.

"Lord Benis?"

"Masterharper?" Benis continued to adjust his garments, awarding the briefest of glances to the Harper.

"I'm glad you know my rank," said Robinton, smiling slightly.

Menolly had been soothing Beauty and Rocky who had refused to leave when she sent the others away. At his tone, she looked at the Harper, amazed that he could express so profound a reprimand with a brief phrase and a smile.

One of the other fosterlings jabbed Benis in the ribs, and the young man looked angrily about.

"I expect you have business elsewhere . . . now!" said the Masterharper.

"Business? This is a gather day . . . sir."

"For others, indeed, it is, but not, I think, for you," and the Masterharper indicated with his hand that Benis had better retire. "Or you, and you, and you," he added, indicating the other fosterlings who displayed claw marks. "Will you occupy yourselves quietly in your quarters or will I have to mention this to Lord Groghe?" He accepted the frantic shakings of their heads.

Then he turned his back on them and pleasantly indicated to those who were avidly observing his summary justice that they should now continue their interrupted pursuits. He walked to where Camo was still being restrained by three large journeymen, blubbering noisily about his pretties being hurt and struggling to free himself.

"The pretties are not hurt, Camo. Not hurt. See? Menolly has the pretties." The Harper's voice soothed the wretched man as he gestured for Menolly to come forward into Camo's line of sight.

"Pretties not hurt?"

"No, Camo. Brudegan, who else is about?" the Harper asked his journeyman. Several other harpers obediently moved against the tide of the dispersing crowd. "Camo had better go back to the hall. Here," and the Harper reached into his pouch and passed Brudegan a mark piece. "Buy him a lot of those bubbly pies on your way back. That'll help settle him."

The crowd had melted away. The Masterharper, stroking his gradually quieting fire lizard, turned back to the small group still clustered together. He gestured them to the unoccupied space between the nearest stalls.

"Now, let me hear the sequence of events, please," he said, but his voice no longer held that chilling note of displeasure.

"It wasn't Menolly's fault!" said Piemur, batting at Audiva's hands as she tried to staunch the flow from his nose with the berry-stained cloth used earlier on Camo. "We were looking at belts . . ." He turned to the tanner for confirmation.

"I don't know about belts, Master Robinton, but they weren't causing any trouble when the blonde girl, Lady Pona, started pulling rank on your apprentice. Made a nasty accusation about the girl having money she oughtn't to have."

A look of dismay crossed the Harper's face. "You didn't lose the mark in the fuss, did you, Menolly?" He scuffed around the trampled area with his boot toe. "I don't have many two-mark pieces, you know."

The tanner stifled a bark of laughter, and the Harper sighed with almost comic relief as Menolly solemnly displayed the cause of the trouble.

"That's a mercy," Master Robinton said with a smile of approval for Menolly. "Go on," he added to the tanner.

"Then this lass," and the tanner gestured towards Audiva, "took Menolly's part. So did the young seaholder. I think all would have come to nothing if Camo hadn't got upset, and the next thing I know the air's full of fire lizards. Are they all hers?" He jerked his thumb at Menolly.

"Yes," said the Harper, "a fact that ought to be borne in mind since they do seem able to recognize Menolly's . . . ammm . . ."

"Sir, I didn't call them . . ." Menolly said, finding her voice.

"I'm sure you didn't need to." He closed his hand reassuringly on her shoulder.

"Master Robinton, Pona bears a grudge against Menolly," said Audiva in a rush as if she had to make the admission before she could change her mind. "And she's got no real cause at all."

"Thank you, Audiva, I've been aware of the prejudice." The Harper made a slight bow, acknowledging the tall girl's loyalty. "The Lady Pona will not trouble you further, Menolly, nor you, Audiva," he continued, that hint of implacability tinging an otherwise pleasant tone. "Good of you, Lord Viderian, to support another seaholder, though it is a loyalty I would prefer to render unnecessary."

"My father, Master Robinton, is very much of your mind, which is why I am fostered in a landbound Hold," said Viderian with a respectful bow. He stiffened, his eyes widening at some disturbing sight. He swallowed hard, anxiety plainly written on his face.

"Ah," said the Harper, having followed the direction of Viderian's gaze. "I wondered how long it would take Lord Groghe to respond to promptings. . . ." He grinned, highly amused at some inner reflection. "Viderian, do make off with Audiva. Now! And enjoy yourselves!"

Audiva needed no urging and grabbed the young seaholder's arm, hastening down the aisle until they were lost in the crowd.

"It's Lord Groghe!" said Piemur in a croak, pulling at Menolly's sleeve.

The Harper caught the boy by the shoulder. "You'll stay by me, young Piemur, so we may have an end of this affair now!" Then he turned to the tanner. "Which belt tempted Menolly?"

"The one with the fire lizard on the buckle," said Piemur in an undertone to the Harper and then edged himself carefully so that the Harper was between him and the oncoming Lord Holder.

"Robinton, my queen's doing it again. . . . Ah, Menolly, just the person!" said Lord Groghe, his florid face lighting with a smile. "Merga's been . . . humph! She's stopped!" The Holder regarded his queen accusingly. "She's been fussing! Right up until I reached the square . . ."

"That's rather easily explained," said Robinton in an offhanded manner.

"Is it? Both of 'em are at it now."

Menolly had been aware of it first, because Beauty was chirping and squeaking at Merga through Lord Groghe's conversation. She felt color rising in her cheeks. The discourse finished as quickly as it had begun.

The two little queens flipped their wings closed on their backs and became totally disinterested in each other.

"What was that all about?" Lord Groghe demanded.

"I suspect they were catching up on the news," said Robinton, with a chuckle, for that was what it had sounded like: a spate of urgent gossip. "Which reminds me, Lord Groghe; I heard that the wineman has a keg of good, aged Benden wine."

"He does?" Lord Groghe's interest was diverted. "How did he get his hands on it?"

"I think we ought to check."

"Humph! Yes! Now!"

"Wouldn't do to waste good Benden wine on people unable to appreciate it, would it?" Robinton took Lord Groghe's arm.

"Not at all." But the Holder could not be completely diverted and turned to frown at Menolly. She steeled herself before she realized that his frown was not menacing. "Want a chance to talk to this girl. Didn't seem the time or place to do so t'other day with the Hatching and all."

"Of course, Lord Groghe, when Menolly's finished her bargaining . . ."

"Bargaining? Humph. Well, can't interrupt a bargain at a gather . . . humph!" Lord Groghe pushed out his lower lip as he looked from Menolly to the hovering tanner. "Don't be all day about it, girl. Th'afternoon's a good time to talk. Don't have many chances to sit and talk."

"Finish your dicker for that belt, Menolly," the Harper told her, one arm gently propelling the Lord Holder away from the apprentices, "and then join us at the wineman's stall. And you," the Masterharper's forefinger pointed down at Piemur, "wash your face, keep your mouth closed, and stay out of trouble. At least until I've had some Benden wine to fortify me." Lord Groghe humphed at the delay. "If it *is* Benden wine. . . . This way, my Lord Holder." The two men walked off together, in step, each steadying the fire lizards they carried.

A soft whistle at her elbow broke the trance holding Menolly as she stared after the two most influential men in the Hold. Piemur was dramatically dragging a hand across his brow to signalize a close escape.

"What do you bet, Menolly, that the subject of your cracking Benis in the face never comes up? And where'd you learn to punch like that?"

"When I saw that big bully kicking you, I was so flaming mad, I . . . I . . ."

"May I add my congratulations to Piemur's?" asked a quiet voice. The two whirled to see Sebell, leaning against the side of the tanner's stall. The eyes of his young queen were still whirling with the red of anger.

"Oh, no," said Menolly with a groan, "not you, too! What *am* I going to do with them?" She was utterly discouraged and dejected. It had been bad enough to have the fire lizards diving and swooping at plain noise; outrageous of them to have flown at Master Domick because he'd only spoken angrily to her. And now this very public fracas with the son of the Fort Lord Holder.

"It wasn't *your* fault, Menolly," said Piemur stoutly.

"It never is, but it *is!*"

"How long have you been here, Sebell?" Piemur asked, ignoring Menolly's wail.

"On the heels of Lord Groghe," said the journeyman, grinning. "But I caught a glimpse of young Benis making tracks out of the Hold proper, so it wasn't hard to figure out where he got the scratches," he went on, glancing at the perched fire lizards and absently stroking Kimi. "I have only one burning question: Who had the audacity to give Benis a colored eye?"

"A rare sight that was," said the tanner who'd been keeping back, but now stepped up. "The girl landed as sweet a punch in that young snot's eye as ever I've seen, and I've been to many a gather that boasted a good brawl. Now, young harper girl, which belt had you in mind before the fracas started? I thought you was after boot leather." He eyed Piemur sharply.

"Menolly wants the blue one with the fire lizard buckle."

"It'd be much too expensive," Menolly said hastily.

The tanner ducked back under his counter and picked the coveted belt from its hook.

"This the one?"

Menolly looked at it wistfully. Sebell took it from the tanner's hands, examined it, gave it a tug to see if there were flaws or if the hide was too thin to wear well.

"Good workmanship in that belt, Journeyman," the tanner said. "Proper for the girl to have it, with her owning the fire lizards."

"How much were you asking for it?" asked Piemur, settling down to the business of bargaining.

The tanner looked down at Piemur, stroked the belt, which Sebell had handed back to him, then glanced at Menolly.

"It's yours, girl. And I'll not take a mark from you. Worth it to me to see you plant one on that young rowdy's face. Here, wear it in good health and long life."

Piemur gaped, mouth wide, eyes popping.

"Oh, I couldn't," and Menolly extended the two-mark piece. The tanner promptly closed her fist over the marker and laid the belt on her wrist.

"Yes, you could and you will, apprentice harper! And that's the end of the matter. *I've* struck the bargain." He pumped her hand in the traditional courtesy.

"Ah, Tanner Ligand," Sebell stepped up, leaning on the counter and beckoning the tanner to bend close to him. "While I didn't see much of the affair . . ." Sebell began to rub his forefinger on one side of his nose, "it's not exactly the sort of incident . . ."

"I take your meaning, Harper Sebell," the tanner replied, nodding his head in acceptance of the adroit suggestion. His grin was rueful. "Not that the truth doesn't make fine telling. Still, those fire lizards of yours are young, aren't they, girl, excitable-like, not used to a gather, I expect. . . . Oh, I'll say what's proper. Don't you worry, harpers." He patted Menolly's hand, still outstretched with the marker. "Now cheer up, you've a face like a wet Turn. You've done more good than harm this gather day. And when you've the need for slippers to match the belt, just you send me the work. I won't do you in the mark," and he flashed a look at the skeptical Piemur.

"Not that I don't like a good tight bargain now and then . . ."

Piemur made a gargling sound in his throat and would have disputed the statement.

"Let's clean you up, Piemur, as Master Robinton suggested," said Sebell, warning the boy by the tilt of his head to be silent.

"I've a water-carrier at the back of the stall you're welcome to use," said Ligand. "And here's a cleaner cloth than the one Menolly has!" He held out a white square to her and dismissed her profuse thanks with a smile and a wave to be off.

No sooner had Sebell and Menolly pulled Piemur to the back of the tanner's stall than people began to step up to his counter.

"Hah!" said Piemur, looking over his shoulder. "He's sly, that Ligand, *giving* you the belt. He'll get three times as much business because you—"

"Close your mouth," suggested Sebell, as he rubbed firmly at the bloody streaks on Piemur's face. "Hold him, Menolly."

"Hey . . . I . . ." but Piemur's complaints were effectively muffled by the damp cloth Sebell used in earnest.

"The less mentioned about this matter, Piemur, the better. And what I said to Ligand holds for you as well. Here and in the Hall. There'll be enough rumor and wrangle without you adding your bits."

"Do you think . . . mumble . . . mumble . . . I'd do anything . . . leave me alone . . . to hurt Menolly?"

Sebell suspended the cleaning operation and regarded the boy's flashing eyes and the indignant set of his jaw. "No, I guess you wouldn't. If only not to lose your chance at feeding the fire lizards . . ."

"Now, that's not fair . . ."

"Sebell, what am I going to do about them?" Menolly asked, finally getting out the fears she'd been suppressing.

"They were only protecting . . ." Piemur began, but Sebell silenced him with a hand over his mouth and a stern look.

"Today they apparently had cause, as Piemur said. The other evening they reacted to what was going on at Benden Weyr with F'nor and Canth, through Brekke's fire lizard. Again, cause." Sebell glanced back towards the tanner's stall and noticed that some of the throng were surreptitiously regarding the three harpers. He motioned to Menolly and Piemur to walk out of sight, down behind the stalls, away from the curious. "All of this," and Sebell's hand took in the towering face of the Hold cliff behind them, the Harper Hall across the paved square now lined with stalls, "is as new to you as to them. Enough to cause alarm and apprehension. They're young and so are you, for all you've managed to accomplish. It's again a question of discipline," he said, but his smile was reassuring.

"I had no discipline this afternoon," she said, repenting of her attack on Pona. She might well have jeopardized everything, crying insult from Pona.

"What d'you mean? You had a fantastic right punch!" cried Piemur, demonstrating with a grunt. "And you'd every right to cry insult on Pona, after all she's done to you . . ." Piemur hastily covered his mouth, his eyes widening as he realized he was being indiscreet.

"You cried insult on Pona?" asked Sebell, frowning in surprise. "I thought that Silvina and I told you to leave the matter."

"She called me a thief. She tried to get Benis to take my two-marker from me."

"The two-marker that Master Robinton himself had given Menolly to buy that belt," said Piemur, staunchly confirming the affair.

"If Pona has added insult to the injury she's already tried to do you," said Sebell slowly, "then, of course, you had to take action, Menolly." He smiled slightly, his eyes still considering her face. "In fact, it's good to know that you will take action on your own behalf. But, the fire lizards' part . . ."

"I didn't call them, Sebell. But, when Benis tripped Piemur and then kicked him, I was scared. He just lay there . . ."

"Sure, smartest thing to do in a kicking fight," Piemur replied, unperturbed.

"I cannot, however, condone apprentices fighting with each other or with holders . . . especially holders of any rank. . . ."

"Benis is the biggest bully in the Hold, Sebell, and you know we've all had trouble with him."

"Enough, youngster," said Sebell more sharply than Menolly had yet heard him speak. As quiet and self-effacing as the journeyman usually was, when he spoke in that authoritative tone of voice, it would take a stalwart person to disobey him. "That was not, however, what I meant by discipline, Menolly. I meant the ability to stick with a project, like that song you wrote yesterday. . . . Was it really only yesterday?" he added. He smiled tenderly down at Kimi who was now asleep in a ball, snuggled between his body and elbow.

"You wrote a *new* song?" Piemur brightened. "You didn't tell me. When'll we get to hear it?"

"When will you get to hear it?" Menolly heard her voice cracking on the last few words.

"What's the matter, Menolly?" Sebell took her arm and gave her a little shake but she could only stare at them.

"It's just that . . . it's so different . . ." She stammered unable to express the upheaval in her mind, the reversal of all that she had been expected to do. "D'you know . . . d'you know what used to happen to me when I wrote a song?" She tried to stop the words that were threatening to burst from her, but she couldn't, not with Piemur's face contorted with distress for her. And Sebell quietly encouraging her to speak with the sympathy so plain on his face. "I used to get *beaten* by my father for tuning, for twiddles as he called them. When I cut my hand . . ." she held it up, looking at the red scar and then turning it to them, ". . . gutting packtails, they let it heal all wrong so I wouldn't be able to play. They wouldn't even allow me to sing in the Hall, for fear Harper Elgion would figure out that it was me who'd taught the children after Petiron died. They were *ashamed* of me! They were afraid I'd disgrace them. That's why I ran away. I'd rather have died of Threadscore than live in Half-Circle another night. . . ."

Tears of bitter and keenly felt injustice streamed down Menolly's cheeks. She was aware of Piemur urgently begging her not to cry, that it was all right, she was safe now, and he loved every one of her songs, even the ones he hadn't heard. And he'd tell her father a thing or two if he ever met him. She was conscious that Sebell had put his right arm about her shoulders and was stroking her with awkward consolation. But it was Beauty's anxious chirping in her ear that reminded her that she'd better get her emotions under control. Master Robinton and Lord Groghe wouldn't be pleased by a second alarm incited by her lack of self-discipline. Particularly if it dragged them away from good Benden wine.

She dashed the tears from her eyes, and gulping down one last sob, looked defiantly into the startled faces of Sebell and Piemur.

"And I wanted you to teach me how to gut fish!" Sebell let out a long sigh. "I wondered why you were so hesitant. I'll find someone else, now I understand why you hate it."

"Oh, I *want* to teach you, Sebell. I want to do everything I can, if it's gutting fish or teaching you to sail. I may be only a girl, but I'm going to be the best harper in the entire Hall . . ."

"Easy, Menolly," said Sebell, laughing at her excess. "I believe you."

"I do, too!" said Piemur in a low, intense tone of reassurance. "I never knew you'd had *that* kind of hold life. Didn't anyone *ever* listen to your songs?"

"Petiron did, but after he died . . ."

"I can see now why it's been so hard for you, Menolly, to appreciate how important your songs are. After what you've been through," and Sebell gently squeezed her left hand, "it would be hard to believe in yourself. Promise me, Menolly, to believe from now on? Your songs are very important to the Harper, to the Hall and to me. Master Domick's music *is* brilliant, but yours appeals to everyone, holder and crafter, landsman and seaman. Your songs deal with subjects, like the fire lizard and Brekke's call to F'nor and Canth, that will help change the sort of set attitudes that nearly killed you in your home hold.

"There's something wrong in not appreciating one's own special abilities, my girl. Find your own limitations, yes, but don't limit *yourself* with false modesty."

"That's what I've always liked about Menolly: she's got her head on right," said Piemur with all the sententiousness of an ancient uncle.

Menolly looked at her friend and then began to laugh, as much at Piemur as at herself. Her outburst had at long last lifted a weight of intolerable depression. She straightened her shoulders and smiled at her friends, flinging out her arms to signal her release.

They all heard the happy warbling of the fire lizards. Beauty crooned with pleasure, rubbing her head against Menolly's cheek, and Kimi gave a drowsy chirp that made the trio of harpers laugh.

"You are feeling better now, aren't you, Menolly?" said Piemur. "So we'd better follow orders, because it doesn't do to keep a Lord Holder waiting, much less Master Robinton. You've got your belt and I'm washed up, so we'd better get to the wineman's stall."

Menolly hesitated just a moment.

"Well?" asked Sebell, raising his eyebrows to encourage her to answer.

"What if he finds out I'm the one who hit Benis?"

"Not from Benis he won't," replied Piemur with a snort. "Besides, he's got fifteen sons. And only one fire lizard. He wants to talk to *you* about her. Not even the Masterharper knows as much about fire lizards as you do. Come *on!*"

Chapter 10

To Menolly's intense relief, all Lord Groghe did want to talk about was the fire lizards—his in particular and in general. The four of them, Robinton, Sebell, Lord Groghe and herself, sat at a table apart from the others, on one side of the square, each of them with a fire lizard. Menolly was torn between amusement and awe that she, the newest of apprentices, should be in such exalted company. Lord Groghe, for all his clipped speech and an amazing range of descriptive grimaces, was very easy to talk to, once she got over her initial nervousness about the fracas with Benis. She heard, in detail, about the hatching of Merga, smiled when Lord Groghe guffawed reminiscently over his early anxieties about her.

"Could've used someone with your knowledge, girl."

"You forget, sir, that my friends broke shell at about the same time Merga did. I wouldn't have been much help to you then."

"You can be now, though. How do I go about teaching Merga to fetch and carry for me? Heard about your pipes."

"She's just one. It took all nine of mine to bring me the pipes. They're heavy." Menolly considered the problem, seeing the disappointment on Lord Groghe's features. "For just Merga alone, it would have to be something light, like a message, and you'd have to *want* it very badly. It was . . . well, my feet still hurt and it was such a long walk to the cot. . . ."

His eyes, which were a disconcertingly light brown, fixed on hers. "Got to want it badly, huh? Humph. Don't know as I want anything *badly!*" He gave a snort of laughter at her expression. "You want things *badly* when you're young, girl. When you're my age, you've learned how to *plan.*" He winked at her. "Take the point, though, since Merga's a bundle of emotion, aren't you, pet?" He stroked her head with a remarkably tender touch for a big, heavy-fingered man. "Emotion, that's what they respond best to. Want's sort of an emotion, isn't it? If you want something bad enough . . . Humph." He laughed again, this time with an oblique look at the Harper. "Emotion, then, Harper, not knowledge, is what these little beasties communicate. Emotion, like Brekke's fear t'other night. Hatching's emotional, too. And today . . ." he turned his light eyes back to Menolly.

"Today . . . that was all my fault, sir," Menolly said, grabbing at a remark of Piemur's for excuse. "My friend, Piemur, the little fellow," and Menolly measured Piemur's height from the ground with her free hand, "stumbled in the crowd. I was afraid he'd be trampled . . ."

"Was that what that was all about, Robinton?" asked Lord Groghe. "You never did explain," but Lord Groghe seemed more interested in the lack of wine in his cup. Robinton politely topped the cup from the wineskin on the table.

"It never occurred to me, Lord Groghe," said Menolly with genuine contrition, "that I'd be alarming you or the Masterharper or Sebell."

"The young of every kind tend to be easily alarmed," remarked the Harper, but Menolly could see the corners of his mouth twitching with amusement. "The problem will disappear with maturity."

"And increases now with so many fire lizards about her," added Lord Groghe with a grunt. "How much more d'you think they'll grow, girl, if yours are the same age as Merga?" He was frowning at Beauty and glancing back to Merga.

"Mirrim's three fire lizards at Benden Weyr were from the first clutch, weren't they? They're not more than a fingertip longer," said Menolly, eagerly seizing on the new topic. "They'd be older by several sevendays, I think." She glanced at the Masterharper who nodded in confirmation. "When I first saw F'nor's queen, Grall, I thought it was my Beauty." Beauty squeaked indignantly, her eyes whirling a little faster. "Only for a moment," Menolly told her in apology and stroked Beauty's head, "and only because I didn't know the Weyrs had also discovered the fire lizards."

"Any notion how old they must be to mate?" asked Lord Groghe, scowling in hopes of a favorable answer.

"Sir, I don't know. T'gellan, Monarth's rider, is going to keep a watch on the cave where my fire lizards hatched, to see if their queen will come back to clutch there again."

"Cave? Thought fire lizards laid their eggs in sand on the beaches?" Master Robinton indicated that she was to speak freely to the Lord Holder, so Menolly told him how she'd seen the fire lizard queen mating near the Dragon Stones, how she'd happened to be back that way, looking for spiderclaws ("Good eating, those," Lord Groghe agreed and gestured for her to get on with the tale) . . . and helped the little fire lizard queen lift the eggs from the sea-threatened strand into the cave.

"You wrote that song, didn't you?" Lord Groghe's frown was surprised and approving. "The one about the fire lizard keeping the sea back with her wings! Liked that one! Write more like it! Easy to sing. Why didn't you tell me a girl wrote it, Robinton?" His scowl was now accusatory.

"I didn't know it was Menolly at the time we circulated the song."

"Humph. Forgot about that. Go on, girl. Did it happen just as you wrote the song?"

"Yes, sir."

"How come you were there in the cave when they hatched?"

"I was hunting spiderclaws and went further down coast than I should have. Threadfall was due. I was caught out, and the only shelter I could think of was the cave where I'd put the fire lizard eggs. I arrived . . . with my sack of spiderclaws . . . just as the eggs began to break. That's how I Impressed so many. I couldn't very well let them fly out into Thread. And they were so hungry, just out of the shell . . ."

Lord Groghe grunted, sniffed and mumbled to the effect that he'd had enough trouble keeping one fed, his compliments for handling nine! As if mention of food had penetrated their sleep, Kimi and Zair roused, creeling.

"I mean no discourtesy, Lord Groghe," said Master Robinton, rising as hastily as Sebell.

"Nonsense. Don't go. They eat anything, anywhere." Lord Groghe swung his heavy torso about. "You there, what's your name . . ." and he waved impatiently at the wineman's apprentice, who came running. "Bring a tray of those meatrolls from the stalls. A big tray. Heaped. Enough to feed two hungry fire lizards and a couple of harpers. Never known a harper who wasn't hungry. Are you hungry, harper girl?"

"No, sir; thank you, sir."

"Making a liar out of me, harper girl? Bring back some bubbly pies, too," the Lord Holder roared after the departing apprentice. "Hope he heard me. So you're the daughter to Yanus of Half-Circle Sea Hold."

Menolly nodded acknowledgement of the relationship.

"Never been to Half-Circle. They brag about that cavern of theirs. *Does* it hold the fishing fleet?"

"Yes, sir, it does. The biggest can sail in without unstepping the masts, except, of course, when the tides run exceptionally high. There's a rock shelf for repairs and careening, a section for building, as well as a very dry inside cave for storing wood."

"Hold above the docking cavern?" Lord Groghe seemed dubious about the wisdom of that.

"Oh, no, sir. Half-Circle Sea Hold really is a half circle." She cocked her thumb and curved her forefinger. "This," and she angled her right hand to show the direction of the curve, after squinting to see where the sun was, "my thumb is the docking cavern, and this," and she pointed to the length of her forefinger, "is the Hold . . . the longer part of the half circle, and then this much," and she touched the webbing, "is sandy beach. They can draw dinghies up on it or gut fish, sew nets and mend sail there in fair weather."

"They?" asked Lord Groghe, his thick eyebrows rising in surprise.

"Yes, sir, *they.* I'm a harper now."

"Well said, Menolly," replied Lord Groghe, slapping his thigh with a crack that made Merga squeal in alarm. "Girl or not, Robinton, you've a good one here. I approve. I approve."

"Thank you, Lord Groghe, I was confident you would," said the Masterharper with a slight smile, which he shared with Sebell before he nodded reassuringly at Menolly.

Beauty chirped a question, which Lord Groghe's Merga answered in a sort of "that's that" tone.

"Cross-crafting works, Robinton. Think I'll have to spot a few more of my sons about. Seaholds, too."

The notion of Benis in Half-Circle Sea Hold appealed to Menolly, though she didn't know if that was whom Lord Groghe had in mind.

The slap of running feet and hoarse breathing interrupted the conversation as the apprentice lad, juggling two trays, all but slid the contents into the laps of those he served.

As the new fire lizards were fed, Menolly saw that more and more people were filing into the central square, taking seats at tables and benches. At one end was a wooden platform. Now a group of harpers took their places and began to tune up. Immediately sets were formed for a call-dance. A tall journeyman harper gave his tambourine a warning shake and then called out the dance figures in a loud voice that carried above the music while his tambourine emphasized the step rhythm.

Those watching on the sidelines clapped in time to the music, shouting good-natured encouragements to the dancers. To Menolly's surprise, Lord Groghe added a hearty smacking beat of his hands, stamping his feet and cheerfully grinning about at everyone.

Once the music started, the square filled up, and still more benches were angled into any free space. Menolly saw colors of all the major crafts on journeymen and apprentices from the halls of the Fort Hold complex. Groups of men stood about, drinking wine and watching the dancing, their heavy boots and clean, though earth-stained, trousers marking them as small holders in from neighboring farms for the restday and a bit of trading at the gather. Their womenfolk had congregated along one side of the square, chattering, tending smaller children, watching the dancing. When the sets changed, some of the holders dragged their giggling but willing women out to make up new groups as the musicians began another foot-tapping, hand-clapping tune.

The third was a couple's dance, a wild gyration of swinging arms and skipping legs, an exercise that rendered every participant breathless and thirsty to judge by the calls on the wineman's lads when the dance ended.

A change of harpers occurred now, the dance-players giving up the platform to Brudegan and three of the older apprentices who ranged themselves slightly behind Brudegan. At his signal they sang the song that Elgion had sung the night of his arrival at Half-Circle Sea Hold: it was one Menolly had never had a chance to learn. She leaned forward, eager to catch every word and chord. On her shoulder, Beauty sat up, one forepaw lightly clasping Menolly's ear for balance. The little queen gave a trill, glanced inquiringly at Menolly.

"Let her sing," said Master Robinton. Then he leaned forward, "But, if you can keep the others where they are on the roofs, I think that might be wise."

Menolly sent a firm command to her friends just as Merga rose to her haunches on Lord Groghe's shoulder and added her voice to Beauty's.

As the fire lizards' descant rose above the harpers' voices, Menolly was conscious of being the focus of startled attention. Lord Groghe was beaming with pride, a smug smile on his face, the fingers of one hand drumming the beat on the table while he waved the other as if he were directing the extemporaneous chorus.

Wild applause followed the song, and cries of " 'The Fire Lizard Song'!" "Sing the Queen's song!" "Does she know it?" "Fire lizard!"

From the platform, Brudegan beckoned imperiously to Menolly.

"Go on, girl, what's holding you back?" Lord Groghe flicked his fingers at her to obey the summons. "Want to hear you sing it. You wrote it. Ought to sing it. Shake yourself up, girl. Never heard of a harper not wanting to sing."

Menolly appealed to Master Robinton, but the Harper had a wicked twinkle in his eyes, despite the bland expression on his face.

"You heard Lord Groghe, Menolly. And it's time you did a turn as a harper!" She heard the emphasis on the last word. He rose, holding out his hand to her as if he knew very well how nervous she was. She'd no choice now, for to refuse would be to shame him, slight the Hall, and annoy Lord Groghe.

"I'll accompany you, Menolly, if I may. You do remember the new wording?" Robinton asked as he handed her up to the platform.

She mumbled a hasty affirmative and then wondered if she did. She hadn't actually sung the new words, or the tune, for that matter, since she'd composed it so very long ago in the little hall in Half-Circle Hold. But there was Brudegan, grinning a welcome, and gesturing to two gitar players to hand over their instruments to her and the Masterharper.

Menolly turned and saw all the faces, all the people massed on each side of the square. A hush fell, and into that attentive silence, the Harper struck the first chords of her fire lizard song. Master Shonagar's oft-repeated advice flashed through her mind: 'Stand straight, take your breath into your guts, shoulders back, open your mouth . . . and sing!'

> *"The little queen all golden*
> *Flew hissing at the sea.*
> *To stop each wave*
> *Her clutch to save*
> *She ventured bravely."*

The applause that greeted the final verse of the song was so deafening that Beauty rose on wing, squealing with surprised alarm. Then the crowd laughed and gradually the noise subsided.

"Sing something from your Sea Hold," said the Masterharper in her ear as he played a few idle chords. "Something these landsmen might not have heard. You start: we'll follow."

The crowd was noisy, and Menolly wondered how she'd be heard, but as soon as she struck the first notes, the gather quieted. She used the chorus for introduction, giving the Masterharper the chording, and smiling, even as she sang, to find herself so well accompanied.

> *"Oh wide sea, oh sweet sea,*
> *Forever be my lover.*
> *Fare me on your gentle wave*
> *Your wide bed over."*

Over the applause when she finished, she heard the Masterharper saying right in her ear, "They've never heard that one before. Good choice." He bowed, gestured for her to take a bow and then motioned to the harpers waiting just beyond the platform to start the second dance group.

Smiling and waving to various people, he led Menolly from the platform and back to the table where Lord Groghe was still enthusiastically clapping. Sebell grinned approvingly and rose to pass back to the Masterharper the very irritated little Zair.

Menolly would have preferred to sit down and recover from the surprise of her first public appearance as a harper and the warmth of the reception, but Talmor came up.

"You've done your duty by crafthall now, Menolly, let's dance!" He spied Beauty on her shoulder. "But could she sit this one out? No telling how she'd misconstrue my manhandling you in a dance!"

The harpers had already struck a fast prance tune.

"Will she stay with me?" asked Sebell, offering his arm and a padded sleeve. "Zair didn't mind too much . . ."

Menolly coaxed Beauty, who chattered with annoyance but allowed herself to be transferred to Sebell's shoulder. Talmor, one arm about Menolly's waist, swung her expertly and quickly into the whirling dancers.

After that, it seemed to Menolly that she'd no more than time to take a quick sip of wine to moisten her parched throat and reassure Beauty, before she was claimed by another partner. Viderian took her for the next set dance, with Talmor partnering Audiva in the same group. Then Brudegan caught her hand for a dance and, to her complete surprise, Domick after him. She acceded to Piemur's boast that he could dance as well as any journeyman and master and wasn't he her best friend, despite a lack of hands in height and Turns in age.

Quartets of singers spelled the dance players until Menolly was certain that every single harper must have performed. Both of the songs that Petiron had sent to the Harper were so frequently requested that Menolly writhed a bit with embarrassment until Sebell caught her eye, cocking an eyebrow and grinning at her discomfort.

As full dark settled over Fort Hold, the crowd began to thin, for those with a distance to travel had to start their journeys home. Stalls were taken down and folded away, the grazing herdbeasts and runners were captured and saddled to bear their owners down the roads from the Hold. The wineman, since he kept a hold in the Fort cliff, continued to serve those unwilling to end a gather.

Pecking Menolly urgently on the cheek, Beauty reminded her that the fire lizards had politely waited for their supper long enough. Abashed at her thoughtlessness, Menolly rushed back to the Harper Hall. On the kitchen steps, Camo sat disconsolately, his thick arms cradling an enormous bowl of scraps, his eyes on the archway. The instant he caught sight of her and the fire lizards wheeling and diving as escort, he rose, calling to her.

"Pretties hungry? Pretties very hungry! Camo waiting. Camo hungry, too."

From nowhere, Piemur appeared.

"See, Camo, I *told* you she'd be back. I told you she'd want us to feed her fire lizards!"

Piemur stopped her breathless apologies as he handed out gobs of meat to his usual trio.

"Told you gathers were fun, didn't I, Menolly? Told you it was about time you had some, too. And you sang just great! You should always sing 'The Fire Lizard Song'! They loved it! And how come *we* don't know that sea song? It's got a great rhythm."

"That's an old song—"

"I never heard it."

Menolly laughed because Piemur sounded as testy as an old uncle instead of a half-grown boy.

"Hope you know some more new ones like that because I'm so bored with all the stuff I've heard since I was a babe . . . Hey, you had the last piece, Lazy. It's Mimic's turn . . . there! Behave yourself."

The hungry fire lizards made short work of Camo's bowl. Then Ranly leaned out of the dining room window, urging them to come and eat before the food was cleared away. There weren't many in the dining hall: Piemur had been right that they got scanty rations on a gather day, but the cheese, bread and sweetings were all Menolly could eat.

When the Apprentice Master marshalled the younger ones to the dormitory, Menolly quietly ascended the steps to her own room. The lilting strains of still another dance tune drifted on the night air. She'd done her first turn as a harper, and done well. She felt like a harper for the first time, as if she really did belong here in the Hall. Lulled by the music and distant laughter, she fell asleep, the warm bodies of the fire lizards nestling against her.

The next morning, looking from her window to the place where the gather had been held, she saw few traces of litter, only the dew-glistening trampled earth of the dancing square. Holders trudged towards the fields, herdsmen were guiding their beasts to the meadows, and apprentices dashed up and down the holdway on their errands. Down the ramp from Fort Hold paced a troop of leggy runners, fresh after a day's rest, fretting against the slow pace to which their riders held them until they were past the ambling herdbeasts. They disappeared in a cloud of dust down the long road to the east.

Menolly heard the noise from the apprentices' dormitory, and a soft, all but inaudible, creeling closer by. She threw on her clothes and dashed down the steps.

"Knew you wouldn't miss, Menolly," said Silvina, meeting her on the steps from the kitchen. She carried a tray, which she thrust ahead. "Do take this up to the Harper, like a pet, would you? Camo's just about finished wielding that chopper of his for your fair."

Menolly's polite tap at the Masterharper's door brought an instant response. He had a fur clutched around him and an insistently creeling fire lizard clawing at his bare arm.

"How'd you know?" he asked, delighted and relieved to see her. "Thank goodness you did. I really can't appear in the kitchen wrapped in a sleeping fur. There, there! I'm stuffing your face, you bottomless pit. How long does this insatiable appetite continue, Menolly?"

She held the tray for him so he could feed Zair as they crossed the room. She slid the tray onto the middle of the sandtable and, anticipating the Harper's own requirements, offered Zair his next few pieces of meat while Master Robinton gratefully gulped down steaming klah. He grabbed a piece of bread, dipped it into the sweeting, had another sip of klah and then, his mouth full, waved at Menolly to leave.

"You've got your own to feed, too. Don't forget to work on your song. I'll require a finished copy later this morning."

She nodded and left him, wondering if she ought to check and see if Sebell was managing with Kimi. He was, seated at one of the journeymen's tables, with more than enough willing assistants.

Her fire lizards waited patiently at the kitchen steps with Piemur and Camo. Once her friends had been fed, she was enjoying a second cup of klah when Domick came striding across the court towards her.

"Menolly," and he was frowning with irritation, "I know Robinton wants you to finish that song for him, but will it take *all* morning? I wanted you to go through that quartet music with Sebell, Talmor and myself. Morshal has the girls for theory on firstday so Talmor's free. I'll never get that quartet ready for performance unless we have a few more good rehearsals."

"I'll start the copy right now, only . . ."

"Only what?"

"I don't have any copying tools."

"Is that all? Finish your klah quickly. I'll show you Arnor's den. Just as well I'm taking you," Domick said, guiding her towards the door in the opposite corner of the court. "Robinton wants the song done on those sheets of pulped wood, and Arnor won't hand *them* out to apprentices."

Master Arnor, the Hall's archivist, occupied the large room behind the Main Hall. It was brilliantly lit with glow baskets in each corner, in the center of the room, and smaller ones depending above the tilted worktables where apprentices and journeymen bent to tasks of copying fading Record Hides and newer songs. Master Arnor was a fusser: he wanted to know why Menolly was to have sheets; apprentices had to learn how to copy properly on old hide before they could be entrusted with the precious sheets; what was all the hurry about? And why hadn't Master Robinton told him himself if it was all this important? And a girl? Yes, yes, he'd heard of Menolly. He'd seen her in the dining hall, same as he saw all the other nuisancy apprentices and holder girls and, oh, well, all right, here was tool and ink, but she wasn't to waste it now, or he'd have to make more and that was a lengthy process and apprentices never paid close attention to the simmering and if the solution boiled, it would be ruined and fade too soon and oh, he didn't know what the world was coming to!

A journeyman had been unobtrusively assembling the various items, and he handed them to Menolly, giving her an amused wink for his master's querulousness. His smile also conveyed to Menolly the tip that the next time she should come directly to him rather than approach his cranky master.

Domick got her away from the old Archivist after the barest of courtesies. As they walked back to the Hall entrance, he again directed her not to be all morning at the copying or he'd never get the new quartet sufficiently rehearsed before the Festival. As he opened the door to the Main Hall, she heard the Masterharper's voice and sped up the stairs.

As she worked in her room, her concentration was penetrated now and then by voices raised in discussion in the Hall below. Absently she identified the various masters: Domick, Morshal, Jerint, the Masterharper and, to her surprise, Silvina, and others whose voices she couldn't recognize as readily. As the conversations apparently had to do with posting journeymen to various positions about the country, she paid scant heed.

She was, in fact, just finishing the third and looser interpretation of the song when a brisk tapping at the door startled her so much she almost smeared the sheet. At her answer, Domick strode in.

"Haven't you finished yet?"

She nodded to the sheets, spread out to dry. Scowling with exasperation, he strode across the room and picked up the nearest sheet. Before she could warn him about damp ink, she noticed that he took the sheet carefully by the edges.

"Hmmm. Yes. You copy neatly enough to please even old Arnor. Yes, now . . ." he was scanning the other sheets. "Traditional forms all duly observed. . . . Not a bad tune, at all." He gave her an approving nod. "Bit bare of chord, but the subject doesn't need musical embellishment. Come, come, finish that sheet, too." He pointed to the one before her. "Oh, you have! Fair enough." He blew gently across the sheet to dry the last line of still glistening ink. "Yes, that'll do. I'll just be off with these. Take your gitar across to my quarters, Menolly, and study the music on the rack. You're to play second gitar. Pay special attention to the dynamic qualities of the second variation."

With that he left her. Her right hand ached from the cramped position of copying, and she massaged it, then shook her fingers vigorously from the wrist to relieve the strain.

"Now," she heard the Masterharper's voice from the room below, "the point is that all but one of the formalities has been observed. Admittedly, there's not been much time spent in the Hall, but an apprenticeship served elsewhere under a competent journeyman has always been admissible. Does anyone wish to register any reservations about the competence of that journeyman?" There was a short pause. "So that's settled. Ah, yes, thank you, Domick. Now, Master Arnor . . ." and Menolly lost the sound of his voice as he evidently moved away from the window.

She was uncomfortably aware that she was not only an inadvertent eavesdropper on Craft matters not her business, but disobedient to Master Domick's orders. Not that she didn't wish to follow them. She picked up her gitar. Playing with Talmor, Sebell and Domick was a pure delight. Had Master Domick meant to intimate that she'd be part of that quartet in a performance? Well, if yesterday was any sample of being a harper, yes, she probably would be performing in that quartet, new as she was to the Harper Hall. That was part of being a harper, after all.

When Menolly entered Domick's quarters, Talmor and Sebell, Kimi disposed on his shoulder and not looking too pleased to be shifted from the crook of his arm, were already discussing the music. They greeted her cheerfully and asked if she'd enjoyed her first go in a gather at Fort Hold. They both laughed at her enthusiastic replies.

"Everyone's the better for a good gather," said Talmor.

"Except Morshal," said Sebell, and, glancing sideways at Talmor as if they shared some secret, rubbed the side of his nose.

"Let us play, Journeyman Sebell." Menolly thought that Talmor sounded reproving.

"By all means, Journeyman Talmor," said Sebell, not the least bit perturbed. "If you will join us, Apprentice Menolly." The brown man gestured elaborately for Menolly to take the stool beside him.

As Menolly checked the tuning of her gitar, Talmor turned the sheets of music on the rack. "Where does he want us to start?"

"Master Domick told *me* to study the dynamics of the second variation," said Menolly with helpful deference.

"That's right, that's where," said Talmor, snapping his fingers before he flipped the correct sheets to the front. "At the beat then . . . sweet shells, he's changing the time in every third measure . . . what does he expect of us?"

"Are the dynamics difficult?" asked Menolly, feeling apprehensive.

"Not difficult, just Domick all over," said Talmor with the sigh of the long-suffering. But he tapped the appropriate beat on the wood of his gitar and gave a more emphatic fifth beat for them to start.

They'd had a chance to go through the second variation once before Domick entered the room. Nodding courteously to them, he took his place.

"Let's start at the beginning of the second variation, now that you've had a chance to play through it."

They worked steadily, going straight through the music once. The second time they paused frequently to perfect the more difficult passages and balance the parts. The dinner bell punctuated the brisk notes of the finale. Talmor and Sebell put down their instruments with small sighs of relief, but Menolly refingered the final three chords softly before she laid her instrument down.

"Does your hand hurt?" asked Domick with unexpected solicitude.

"No, I was just wondering if the string was true."

"If you heard a sour sound, it was my stomach," said Talmor.

"Too much gathering?" asked Sebell with little sympathy.

"No, not enough breakfast, thank you!" replied Talmor with the brusqueness of someone being teased. He rose and left the room, followed closely by the silently laughing Sebell.

"Master Shonagar has you this afternoon, Menolly?" asked Domick, motioning for Menolly to come with him.

"Yes, sir."

"Well, then you'd have to continue that voice instruction anyway," he said in a cryptic fashion. Menolly decided he must be wishing to have her practice with him more steadily, but Master Robinton had been specific: her mornings were scheduled to Master Domick; afternoons she was to go to Master Shonagar.

When they entered the dining hall, the room was already well filled. Domick turned to the right towards the masters' table. Menolly caught one glimpse of Master Morshal, already seated, his face set in the sourest lines she had yet seen on the bad-tempered old man, so she looked quickly away.

"Pona's gone!" Piemur pounced on her from the left, his face wreathed with smug satisfaction. "So I can sit with you, near the girls, now. Audiva said I could 'cause it was Pona who got snotty. Audiva says will you *please* sit with her."

"Pona's gone?" Menolly, both surprised and nervous, permitted Piemur to pull her towards the hearthside table. There were two empty places, one on either side of Audiva, who smiled hesitantly as she saw Menolly approaching. She beckoned to the seat on her right, away from the other girls.

"See, Pona is gone! She got taken away a-dragonback," Piemur added, his pleasure in her departure somewhat alloyed by the prestigious manner of her going.

"Because of yesterday?" The thin knot of worry in her middle grew larger and colder. Pona in the cot, contained by the discipline of the Harper Hall, was bad enough; but, in her grandfather's Hold, pouring out acid vengeance, she was much more dangerous for Harper apprentice Menolly.

"Naw, not just yesterday," Piemur said firmly. "So don't you go feeling guilty about it. But yesterday was the final crack, the way I heard it, bearing false witness against you. And Dunca's been raked over by Silvina! That pleased her no end; she's just been itching to take Dunca down."

Timiny was straddling three seats across from Audiva, and gesturing urgently to Menolly and Piemur to take them.

"You sit with Timiny, Piemur. I'm going to sit next to Audiva. Looks like she's being put on by Briala with that empty seat and all."

As she stepped to the place, she caught Briala's startled, antagonistic glance. The dark girl nudged her neighbor, Amania, who also turned to glare at Menolly. But Menolly smiled at Audiva and, as she stood by the tall craftgirl, she felt Audiva's hand fumble for hers and the grateful pressure of her fingers. Stealing a sideways glance, she noticed that Audiva's eyes looked red and her cheeks showed the puffiness of recent and prolonged weeping.

The signal to be seated was given, and the meal began. If Menolly felt too self-conscious and Audiva too upset to talk, Piemur suffered no inhibitions and babbled on about how he'd made his marks count.

"I got nine more bubbly pies, Menolly," he told her gaily, " 'cause the baker thought they were for you, me and Camo. I did share with Timiny, didn't I, Tim? And then I won a wager on the runners. Anyone

with half an eye could tell the one with the sore hoof would run faster
. . . so he wouldn't have to run so long."

"So, how many marks did you come back with?"

"Ha!" Piemur's eyes flashed with his triumph. "More'n I went to the
gather with, and I'm not saying how much that is."

"You're not keeping it in the dorm, are you?" asked Timiny, worried.

"Haw! I gave it to Silvina to keep safe for me. I'm no fool. *And* I told
the entire dorm where my marks are, so they know it's no good putting
on me to find out where I've hid 'em. I may be small, but my glow's not
dim!"

Briala, who was pretending to ignore them all, made a disagreeable
sound. Piemur was about to take umbrage when Menolly kicked his
shin to warn him to be silent.

"You know what, Menolly," and now Piemur leaned across the table,
exuding mystery as he glanced from her to Audiva and Timiny,
"they're posting journeymen."

"Are they?" asked Menolly, mystified.

"You ought to know. Couldn't you hear anything in your room? I
saw the windows of the Main Hall open, and you're right over 'em."

"I was busy," Menolly said sternly to Piemur. "And I was brought
up not to listen to other people's private conversations."

Piemur rolled his eyes in exasperation for such niceties. "You'll never
survive in a Harper Hall then, Menolly! You've *got* to be one jump
ahead of the masters . . . and the Lord Holders . . . A harper's supposed to learn as much as he can . . ."

"Learn, yes; overhear, no," replied Menolly.

"And you're an apprentice," added Audiva.

"An apprentice *learns* to be a harper by overhearing his masters,
doesn't he?" demanded Piemur. "Besides, I gotta think ahead. I gotta
be good at something besides singing. My voice won't last forever. Do
you realize that only one out of hundreds," and he waved his arms in
such an expansive gesture that Timiny had to duck, "of boy sopranos
have any voice when they hit the change? So, if I'm not lucky, but if I'm
good at digging things out, maybe I'll get posted like Sebell and have a
fire lizard to take important messages from hold to hall . . ." Then
Piemur froze, and cautiously turned to look at Menolly, his eyes wide
with consternation.

She laughed; she couldn't help it. Timiny, who had obviously heard
Piemur's long-range plan before, gulped so fiercely that his neck carti-
lage bobbed up and down his throat like a net float in a fast current.

"I really do like the fire lizards, Menolly, I really do," said Piemur, trying to undo the indiscretion and reinstate himself in Menolly's good graces.

She couldn't resist a pretense of disdain, and ignored him, but his expression was so genuinely panic-stricken that she relented sooner than she intended.

"Piemur, you've been my best and first friend in the Hall. And I really do think my fire lizards like you. Mimic, Rocky and Lazy let you feed them. I may not be able to help, but if I *do* ever have any say in the matter, you'll get an egg from one of Beauty's clutches."

Piemur's exaggerated sigh of relief attracted attention from the other girls, who were still pretending that that end of the table didn't exist.

Platters of stewed meats and vegetables were now being served, and Menolly took advantage of the general noise to ask Audiva how things were with her.

"All right, once the furor died down. I rank the rest of them, even if rank is *not* supposed to be a consideration while we're at the Harper Hall."

"You're also the best musician of the lot," said Menolly, trying to cheer Audiva. She sounded very depressed, and she must have been crying a lot to have such puffy cheeks.

"Do you really think I can play?" asked Audiva, surprised and pleased.

"From what I heard that morning, yes. The others are hopeless. If there's no reason you *have* to stay at Dunca's when you have free time, maybe you'd like to come to my room. We could practice together if that would help."

"Me? Practice with you? Oh, Menolly, could I please? I really do want to learn, but all the others want to do is talk about the fosterlings at the Hold, and their clothes, and who their fathers are likely to choose as husbands for them, and *I* want to learn how to play well."

Menolly extended her hand, palm up, and Audiva gratefully seized it, her eyes sparkling, all traces of her unhappiness erased.

"Just wait till I tell you what happened in the cot," she said in a confidential tone that reached only Menolly's ears. She saw Piemur cocking his head to try and hear, and waved him away. "It was a treat! A rare treat! What Silvina said to Dunca!" Audiva giggled.

"But won't there be trouble about Pona being sent back? She is the granddaughter of the Lord Holder of Boll."

Audiva's face clouded briefly. "The Harper has the right to say who stays in his own Hall," replied Audiva quickly. "He has equal rank with a Lord Holder, who can dismiss any fosterling he chooses. Besides, you're a holder's daughter."

"Holder's, not Lord Holder's. Only I'm an apprentice now." Menolly touched her shoulder badge, which meant more to her than being her father's daughter.

"You're the Masterharper's apprentice," said Piemur who indeed had sharp ears if he'd heard their whispers. "And that makes you special." He glanced towards Briala, who had also been trying to overhear what Menolly and Audiva were saying. "And you'd better remember that, Briala," he said, making a fierce grimace at the dark girl.

"You may think you're special, Menolly," said Briala in a haughty voice, "but you're only an apprentice, after all's said and sifted. And Pona's her grandfather's favorite. When she tells him all that's been going on here, you may not be *that* any more!" And she snapped her fingers in a derisive gesture.

"Close your mouth, Briala! You talk nothing but nonsense," said Audiva, but Menolly caught the note of uncertainty in her voice.

"Nonsense? Just wait'll you hear what Benis plans for that Viderian of yours!"

They were all distracted by a sudden groan from Piemur.

"Shells, Pona *has* gone! That means that I'm stuck with singing her part! What a ruddy bore!" His dismay was comic, but it turned the talk to a discussion of the upcoming Spring Festival.

Piemur told Menolly that if she thought a gather was fun, she should just wait for the Festival. Everyone in the Hold cliff doubled up so that the entire western half of Pern could be under shelter there for the two days of the Festival. Dragonmen came from all over, and harpers and craftmasters and holders, large and small. That's when any new craftmasters were made, and new apprentices tapped, and it was great fun, even if he would have to sing Pona's role, and there'd be dancing all night long instead of just until sundown.

The gong sounded, and the chores were assigned: most of the sections were to clean up the gather area and rake the fields where the beasts had been tethered. Piemur made a huge grimace since his section drew the field duty. Briala smiled maliciously at his chagrin, and he would have answered in kind, but Menolly toed his shins sharply again. He rolled his eyes at her but, when she cocked her head meaningfully and tapped her shoulder, he subsided, realizing that he would have to stay in her good record to get his fire lizard.

She reported, as ordered, to Master Oldive who checked her feet and pronounced them sound enough. He suggested that she see Silvina about boots. Her hand showed improvement, but she was to be careful not to overstretch the scar tissue. Slowly but surely was the trick, and she wasn't to neglect the healing salve.

As she crossed the courtyard for her lesson with Master Shonagar, the fire lizards appeared in the air. Beauty landed on her shoulder, broadcasting images of a lovely swim in the lake and how warm the sun had been on the flat rock. Merga had evidently been with them, for Beauty projected a second golden queen on the rocks. They were all in good spirits.

Master Shonagar had not moved. One thick fist upheld the heavy head on the supporting arm, his other arm was cocked, hand on thigh. At first Menolly thought he was asleep.

"So, you return to me? After *singing* at the gather?"

"Wasn't I supposed to sing?" Menolly halted so abruptly in her astonishment at the reprimand in his voice that Beauty cheeped in alarm.

"You are never to sing without my express permission." The massive fist connected with the tabletop.

"But the Masterharper himself . . ."

"Is Master Robinton your voice instructor? Or am I?" The bellowed question rocked her back on her heels.

"You are, sir. I only thought . . ."

"You thought? I do the thinking while you are my student . . . and you will remain my student for some time, young woman, until your voice is properly trained for your duties as a harper! Do I make myself clear?"

"Yes, sir. I'm very sorry, sir. I didn't know I was disobeying . . ."

"Well," and his tone abruptly modified to one of such benevolence that Menolly again stared in disbelief, "I hadn't actually mentioned that I didn't consider you ready to sing in public yet. So I accept your apology."

Menolly gulped, grateful for the reprieve.

"You didn't, all things considered, perform too badly yesterday," he went on.

"You heard me?"

"Of course I heard you!" The fist landed again on the table, though with less force than the previous thump. "I hear every singing voice in this Hall. Your phrasing was atrocious. I think we'd better go over that song now so that you can correct your interpretation." He heaved a sigh of profound resignation. "You will undoubtedly be obliged to sing it again in public; that's obvious, since you wrote it, and it is undeniably popular. So you might just as well learn to sing it *well!* Now, we shall start with breathing exercises. And we can't," another crash on the sandtable, "do that when you're halfway across the hall and trembling all over. I won't eat you, girl," he added in the gentlest of the voices he had yet used in her presence. A slight smile parted his lips. "But I will," and his tone took on a sterner note, "teach you to make the most of your voice."

Although the lesson began with a totally unexpected scolding, Menolly left Master Shonagar's presence with a feeling of considerable accomplishment. They had gone over "The Fire Lizard Song," phrase by phrase, occasionally accompanied by Beauty's trilling. By the end of the session, Menolly stood in further awe of Master Shonagar's musical acumen. He had drawn from her melody every possible nuance and shading of tone, heightening its total impact.

"Tomorrow," Master Shonagar said as he dismissed her, "bring me a copy of that latest thing you wrote. The one about Brekke. At least you have wit enough to write music *you* can sing, that lies in the best part of your voice. Tell me, do you do that on purpose? No, no, that was an invidious question. Unworthy of me. Inapplicable to you. Away with you now, I'm excessively wearied!"

His fist came up to support his head, and he was snoring before Menolly could express her gratitude for his stimulating lesson.

Beauty flew to her perch on Menolly's shoulder, chittering happily, and Menolly, beginning to feel as weary as Master Shonagar claimed to be, absently checked to see where her other friends were. As usual, they were sunning on the rooftops, where they'd undoubtedly remain until feeding time.

Menolly entered the Hall, wondering if she should ask Silvina about boots, but she could hear a lot of bustle and noise from the kitchen and decided to bide her time. She made her way to her room, saw the door ajar, and was surprised to find Audiva waiting for her.

"I took you at your word, Menolly, but, honestly, if I had to stay one more moment in that poisonous atmosphere . . ."

"I meant it."

"You look tired. Master Shonagar's lessons are exhausting. We have only one in the week, and you have to go every day? Was he in one of his banging moods?" Audiva giggled, and her eyes sparkled with merriment.

Menolly laughed, too. "I sang yesterday at the gather *without* his express permission."

"Oh! Great stars." Audiva was torn between giggles and concern. "But why would he complain? You sang so beautifully. Viderian said it was the best he'd heard that sea song done. You've made another good friend in Viderian, if that's any consolation. That fist in Benis's face. He's wished so often that he could bang that arrogant booby."

"Audiva, could Lord Sangel of Boll make Master Robinton . . ."

"You didn't pay heed to that spiteful wherry, Briala. Oh, Menolly . . ."

"But can an apprentice . . ."

"An apprentice, an *ordinary* apprentice, yes," Audiva said, with a reluctant sigh for the truth, "because apprentices have no rank. Journeymen do. But you are Master Robinton's *own* special apprentice, just as Piemur said, and it'd take more than a Lord Holder to shift Master Robinton when he's made up his mind. Besides, you weren't at fault. Pona was. Bearing false witness. Now, you listen to me, Menolly, don't you dare let that bunch of sly slippers worry you! They're just jealous. That was Pona's problem, too. Besides," and Audiva's face brightened as she thought of the telling argument, "Lord Groghe needs you here to help him train Merga. There's your new song. Oh, Menolly, Talmor was playing it, and it's the most beautiful thing I've ever heard. 'Live for my living/or else I must die.' " Audiva had a throaty contralto voice that throbbed poignantly on the deep note. "I wanted to weep, and while I know I'm just a silly girl—"

"You're not just silly. You stood up for me against Pona . . ."

Audiva bit her lip guiltily, her expression contrite. "I *didn't* tell you about Master Domick's first message . . ." She paused, full of self-reproach. "I knew about it. I heard him tell Dunca. We all did. And I knew they were trying to make trouble for you because you had the fire lizards . . ."

"But you told Master Domick that I hadn't been told."

"Fair's fair."

"Well, then, if fair's fair, you did stand up with me against Pona *and* all those fosterlings when it really mattered. Let's forget everything else . . . and just be friends. I've never had a girl friend before," Menolly added shyly.

"You haven't?" Audiva was shocked. "Weren't you fostered out?"

"No, being the youngest and Half-Circle being so isolated and with Thread falling, and that's what the Harper usually does, and Petiron never . . ."

"Just as well old Petiron kept you by him, the way things turned out, isn't it?" Audiva grinned. "But *we're* friends now, aren't we?"

And they sealed the bargain with a handshake.

"Are they really practicing my song?" asked Menolly, a little apprehensive.

"Yes, and hating every minute of it because you wrote it." Audiva was delighted. "I'd be obliged if you'd teach me some simpler chords than the ones you've written. I cannot get my hands . . ."

"They are simple."

"For you, maybe, but not for me!" Audiva groaned over her inadequacy.

"Here," and Menolly thrust her gitar at Audiva. "You can start with a simple E chord . . . go on, strum it. . . . Now, modulate to an A Minor . . ."

Menolly soon realized that she didn't have as much patience as she ought to with Audiva, especially since Audiva was her best friend now, and she certainly did try to follow Menolly's instructions; but both girls were relieved when Beauty's creeling interrupted the practice. Audiva declared that she'd have to fly to change before supper. She wouldn't have the time after, or she'd be late to rehearsal. She gave Menolly a quick and grateful embrace, and dashed down the steps ahead of her.

Camo and Piemur were waiting for Menolly at the kitchen level. It seemed incredible to Menolly as she fed her hungry friends that she'd only been at the Harper Hall a sevenday. So much had happened. And yet the fire lizards had settled in as if they'd never lived anywhere else. She had established a routine in her sessions with Domick and the journeymen in the mornings, with Shonagar in the afternoon. Above all, she had the right, the exquisitely sweet right—no, an *injunction* from the Masterharper—to write the songs that had once been totally forbidden her.

Seven days ago, standing in this very courtyard, she'd been scared to tears. What had T'gellan said? Yes, he'd given her the sevenday to get adjusted. And he'd been right in that, though she'd doubted him at the time. He'd also said that she didn't have anything to fear from harpers. True enough, but she had experienced envy and to some extent overcome it: she'd made staunch friends and good impressions on those in Hall and Hold who mattered to her future. She'd made not one, but several places for herself in the Craft Hall: with her songs, her fire lizards and, unexpectedly, her knowledge of seacraft.

Only one small worry nagged at her: what if the vengeful Pona could prejudice her grandfather, Lord Sangel, against a lowly apprentice in the Craft Hall? Not all Lord Holders were tolerant men like Lord Groghe. Not all of them had fire lizards. Menolly had had too much stripped from her before in her home Hold to calm that anxiety.

Chapter 11

O Tongue, give sound to joy and sing
Of hope and promise on dragonwing!

Domick caught her before she left the dining hall the next morning.

"That sea song you sang at the gather? Would it take you long to note it down? I never heard it before." Menolly wasn't sure from his frown if he blamed her for that oversight or not. "Master Robinton wants sea songs inland and land songs on the seaside . . ." Domick looked annoyed, until he saw Menolly's expression. "Oh, I agree with him in principle, but he wants things done *now*. With the journeymen to be posted today, he wants as many copies to go with them as possible. Save trips later . . ."

"I could make several copies as easily as one," she said.

Domick blinked as if he'd forgotten. "Of course, you could. And a mighty neat hand you've got. Even old Arnor had to admit that!" For some obscure reason this amused Domick. He continued in a much better humor. "All right then, to save a lot of useless talk and wasted time, would you please copy that sea song? And do a couple of 'The Fire Lizard Song.' I'm not certain how many Arnor has completed, and you got a taste of his attitude yesterday . . ." Menolly grinned. "You remember who to go to if you need more materials? Dermently's his name."

With that he left Menolly, but he whistled absently as he strode towards the now closed door of the main hall.

Sea songs inland and land songs on the seaside, thought Menolly as she climbed the steps to her room. She wondered just how Yanus, her father, would approve of land songs at Half-Circle Sea Hold. Well and good, and wouldn't it be the best of all jokes if the land songs introduced at Half-Circle by Harper Elgion were ones she herself had written or copied out? Disgrace the Hold, indeed!

Now she wondered if she should write her mother, Mavi, or her sister, and just casually mention that she was apprentice to the Masterharper of Pern. That all her twiddles and tunings had considerably more merit than anyone at Half-Circle had the wit to appreciate. Except, of course, Harper Elgion. And Alemi, her brother.

No, she wouldn't write her mother or her father, and certainly not her sister. But she might write Alemi. He'd been the only one who cared. And he'd keep the knowledge to himself.

But right now she had things to do. She organized her materials, her ink and tools, and carefully set about copying down the sea song. She worked quickly, though she had to sand out several small errors. Nevertheless, she had six fair copies by the time the dinner bell rang.

Domick was in the hallway, in earnest conversation with Jerint who appeared annoyed about something. Domick caught sight of her, excusing himself from Jerint but with just that hint of reprieve that suggested Menolly's appearance was a welcome excuse.

"Six . . ." he leafed through her sheets, "and every one a fair copy. My thanks, Menolly. Can you do. . . . No, you must work with Shonagar this afternoon . . ."

"I'd need more paper, Master Domick, but I'll have time to do two or three more copies before supper, if you need them . . ."

Domick glanced at the slowly filling dining room. He took her hand. "If you could squeeze in maybe three copies of your fire lizard song, I'd be in your debt. Come with me. Arnor should have retreated from his domain, and we can get as much paper as we want from Dermently. At least, today."

They were out the door with no more delay, heading toward the Archive room.

"I don't mean to make a habit of this with you, Menolly, because it's more important that you create than that you copy. Any apprentice can copy. But, with so many journeymen going off. . . . That's why Jerint is looking peeved. And wait till Arnor hears . . ."

"Journeymen going off?"

"You didn't think they stayed here forever and moldered . . ."

Actually Menolly had experienced a swift pang of regret because Talmor and Sebell were journeymen, and Sebell said he "journeyed."

"Don't worry about our quartet," replied Domick with sudden perception. "It's one thing to send away someone who's really needed here and quite another for a master to refuse to let a qualified journeyman go out of the Hall because *he'll* be put to the bother of training a new assistant. The whole point of the Harper Hall is to extend knowledge." Domick's arms swept wide to include all Pern. "Not to confine it," and his right fist made a tight ball. "That's what's been wrong with Pern, why we haven't really matured; everything's been kept in shallow little minds that forget important things, that resist new knowledge, and experience . . ." He grinned at her, "That is why, I, Domick, Composition Master, *know* that your songs are as important to the Craft Hall, and Pern, as my music. They are a fresh voice, fresh new ways of looking at things and people, with tunes no one can keep from humming."

"Would you ever leave the Hall?" asked Menolly, greatly daring. She was storing up his words to think about later.

"Me?" Domick was startled, and then frowned. "I might, but it would serve little purpose. Might be good for me, at that." Then he shook his head again, rejecting the idea. "Perhaps, when there's a big occasion at one of the larger Holds or another Craft Hall . . . Or a Hatching . . . But there really isn't a Hold or Craft that needs a man of my abilities." Domick spoke without conceit and also with modesty. It was a fact.

"Do masters always stay in the Hall?"

"Shells, no. There are any number assigned to the larger Holds and Crafthalls. You'll see. Ah, Dermently, just a moment . . ." and Domick signaled the journeyman who was about to leave by another door at the far end of the Archive's well-lit hall.

Menolly just had time to get to her room with an armload of supplies and off to the dining hall before everyone sat down. It was true that Master Jerint and Master Arnor wore expressions of sullen discontent. She wondered who was leaving. But she had no time to speculate. There was dinner, and then her lesson.

No sooner was she released by Master Shonagar than she returned to her copying, this time of "The Fire Lizard Song." At first she felt awkward copying her own music, then she began to relish the notion. Her songs, going inland so that people would get some understanding of seaside creatures that had once been thought to be pure invention. That lovely old sea song, one she'd heard at Half-Circle since her first conscious appreciation of music, was a fine one to teach inland people how the seaman regards the broad ocean.

Domick's attitude towards her music had been reassuring, too. It was a relief to her to know that there was no awkwardness between them. He thought her songs were serving a purpose, and that suited and pleased her.

It was, Menolly thought, one thing to work hard day in and day out to bring in food enough to feed oneself, one's family and one's Hold; it was quite another thing, and vastly more satisfying, to provide comfort for other lonely minds and tuneless hearts. Yes, Master Robinton and T'gellan had been right: she did belong in the Harper Hall.

Before she realized how time had flown, it was evening. She carefully put away her instruments, the ink and the unused sheets, delivered the music to Master Domick's room, and went to the kitchen level to feed her friends.

Beauty and the bronzes were crowded round her when, though scarcely sated, they suddenly looked skyward. Beauty crooned softly in her throat. Rocky and Diver answered, as if agreeing with her, then all three again demanded food.

"What was all that about?" asked Piemur.

Menolly shrugged.

"Will you look at that?" Piemur cried, excitedly, pointing skyward as three, then four, dragons appeared in the sky, slowly circling down to the wide fields. "And your fire lizards knew! D'you realize that, Menolly? Your fire lizards knew there were dragons coming."

"Why would dragons be coming?" Menolly asked, and that lump of fear grew a few sizes larger. "It isn't time for Threadfall again, is it?" She doubted that Lord Sangel would send dragonriders to discipline a mere apprentice.

"I told you," and Piemur sounded exasperated with her obtuseness. "The masters were closeted yesterday and today, reassigning journeymen. So," and he shrugged as if that explained the presence of dragonriders, "the dragons transport them to the new holds. Two blues, a green, and . . . hey . . . a bronze!" He was impressed. "I wonder who rates the bronze!"

Now the Fort Hold watch dragon bugled a welcome and was answered by the circling beasts. Beauty and the other fire lizards added their trill of greeting.

"Oh, no," Piemur groaned. "They're landing in the field, and we just got it cleaned up!"

"Dragons are not runner beasts," said Menolly in a tart voice. "And don't stuff Lazy, Rocky and Mimic so fast. They'll choke. You'll see the dragonriders soon enough, I expect, if they're coming here for the journeymen."

Piemur was not the only apprentice with sharp eyes. Soon the courtyard was spotted with groups of curious lads. The dragonriders strode out of the shadows of the arch, and Menolly distinguished the colors of Istan, Igen, Telgar and Benden Weyrs on the dragonriders' tunics. And none of them a watch-dragonrider wearing the colors of Boll. Then she recognized the Benden dragonrider as T'gellan.

"Menolly! I've got 'em for you," he shouted across the courtyard, waving an oddly shaped mass above his head. He spoke to his companions, who continued onward to the steps of the Hall where Domick, Talmor and Sebell waited to greet the dragonmen. T'gellan then strode at an oblique angle towards Menolly. As he neared her, she realized that he carried a pair of boots by their laces: boots tanned blue with cuffs of blue-hued wild wherry down.

"Here you are, Menolly! Felena was in a state, worrying that those light slippers would wear out before you got these. I see the toes are going, aren't they? Keeping you on 'em here, are they? But you're looking good. Say, your fire lizards are growing, aren't they?" He beamed approvingly at Menolly, then at Camo and Piemur, whose eyes were enormous at this proximity to a real bronze dragonrider. "Glad you've got some help."

"This is Piemur and that's Camo, and they've both been marvelous help."

"Will this lad be ready for a fire lizard then?" asked T'gellan with a sly wink at Menolly.

"Why do you think he's helping me?" asked Menolly, unable to resist teasing Piemur.

"Aw, Menolly." Unexpectedly Piemur was blushing, eyes downcast and so thoroughly out of countenance that Menolly relented.

"Truly, T'gellan, Piemur's been a staunch and true friend since the first day I got here. I couldn't manage without him and Camo."

"Camo feed pretties. Camo very good feeding pretties!"

T'gellan gave her a startled look, but he slapped the drudge affectionately on the back. "Good man, Camo. You keep on helping Menolly with her pretties."

"More food for pretties?" Camo perked up.

"No, no more now, Camo. Pretties aren't hungry now," Menolly said hurriedly.

"Have you finished with Camo yet, Menolly?" Abuna appeared at the kitchen door. "Oh!" She was startled to see the company her half-witted drudge was keeping.

"Camo help Abuna now. Pretties fed, Camo. You help Abuna!" Menolly gave Camo the customary turn and push towards the kitchen.

"Now, Menolly, you sit there, on the steps," said T'gellan, pointing, "and try these boots on. Felena gave me explicit instructions that I was to see if they fit. Because if they don't . . ." T'gellan left the threat hanging.

"They ought to: the Weyr tanner took my measure . . ." said Menolly as she discarded the worn slippers and put on the right boot. "I don't see how he could miss, even if my feet were still a bit swollen. Oh, it fits! It fits just fine. And so soft inside. Why," and she put her hand in the left boot, "he's lined it with soft hide. . . ."

"You'll need the double protection, Menolly," said T'gellan, and then his face took on a look of pure mischief, "particularly if you do any more running . . ."

"I'm not running anywhere anymore," she said firmly. And hastily forgot about Lord Sangel and Pona. "Please thank Felena, and give my love to Mirrim, and thank Manora and everyone . . ."

"Hey, hey, I just got here. I'm not going anywhere yet. I'll see you before I go, but I'd better join the others now."

"And a dragonrider . . . a bronze dragonrider brings you blue harper boots . . ." Piemur's eyes were enormous with astonishment as they both watched T'gellan's lanky figure striding towards the Hall entrance.

"I don't suppose they wanted to waste leathers they'd already cut to fit me when they thought I'd be staying on in the Weyr," Menolly said, nonetheless deeply touched by the gift. She wiggled her toes against the smooth soft hide. She wouldn't need to bother Silvina for new footwear now. And harper blue! Why, she was harper-garbed from head to toe now.

The supper bell rang, and the curious knots of boys and journeymen blended into a throng, converging at various speeds on the steps. Along the walls opposite the dining hall as she and Piemur entered, Menolly saw backsacks and instrument cases.

"I told you," Piemur nudged her in the ribs. "Journeymen are being assigned tonight. There'll be gaps at the oval tables tomorrow."

Menolly nodded, thinking that there would be some frantic masters, too, with fewer journeymen to help.

T'gellan was at the round table, but Menolly noticed that the other dragonriders were standing on the journeymen's side of the dining hall. She made her way to her seat beside Audiva, still that space left between Audiva and Briala. Piemur stood opposite Audiva and Menolly.

Special meat and fish rolls accompanied the customary soup, and there were sharp cheeses, bread and, afterwards, wedges of beachberry pies. Piemur grumbled because the pies should be hot, and Menolly countered that he ought to be grateful for the treat so soon after a gather!

Talk was spirited throughout the hall, although the seven girls continued their silent treatment of Audiva and Menolly. There was a current of excitement in the air, much of it from the journeymen's tables.

"They're only told in advance that they're being assigned, you know," Piemur told Menolly and Audiva. "Not where. Eight of them going, if I counted the packs right. The Masterharper really means to spread the word."

"Word?" Timiny was baffled.

"Don't you listen to anything, Timiny?" Piemur was disgusted. "Bet you not one of those journeymen is going back to his own hold or crafthall, like they used to do. Masterharper's set on shuffling everyone around. Cross-crafting with a vengeance. They all got copies of your songs, Menolly?"

Suddenly the moment everyone had been anticipating happened. The gong shimmered, and before the metallic tones had died away, the hall was still. Every eye was on the Masterharper who had risen from the table.

"Now, my friends, without further ado and to permit those holding their breaths to breathe, I will announce the postings." He paused, grinning, as he glanced around the hall. Then he looked across the apprentices' tables to the journeymen.

"Journeyman Farnol, Gar is your assignment, in Ista. Journeyman Sefran, please do what you can to improve understanding and extend enlightenment in Telgar at Balen Hold. Journeyman Campiol, you are also Telgar-bound, to the Minercrafthall under Facenden. See what you can do to improve the quality of metal for our pipes and brasses. Journeyman Dermently, I'd like you to assist Wansor, the Starsmith at Telgar Smithcrafthall." There was a murmur of surprise from Dermently's companions. "You have the finest hand with drafting, and while I am sorry to rob Master Arnor of his most accurate copyist, your efforts are essential if Wansor's studies are to progress and be properly recorded.

"There's a small seahold on Igen River mouth that requires a man of your tolerance and good nature, Journeyman Strud. I also want you to keep an eye open on the beaches for possible fire lizard mounds. You are, however, to report them to your Holder, not to me." The regret in the Masterharper's voice caused a ripple of amusement to run through his audience. "Journeyman Deece is also Igen bound, to the Hold. Harper Bantur needs a young assistant. He's a dab hand at bringing on a good harper to understand the complexity of a master harper's job. And you've the new songs to give him as well. Journeyman Petillo, it's no sinecure, but I need your patience and tact at Bitra to bolster Harper Fransman.

"Journeyman Rammany, Lord Asgenar at Lemos has asked for someone from Master Jerint's hands. You'll work principally with Woodsmith Benelek, and I don't think you'll find that too onerous a task with such wood as Benelek dries for us. However, be sure you're on hand to choose the next consignment of wood for our use, and Master Jerint will bless you.

"Will all the journeymen please come to the Great Hall for a farewell cup of wine? Benden wine, of course. But first, I've one more very pleasant and unusual announcement.

"To be a harper requires many talents, as you all ought to realize by now," and he frowned at the very youngest of the apprentices who giggled nervously. "Not all of these skills need be learned within these walls. Indeed, many of our most valuable lessons are more forcefully learned at some distance from this hallowed Hall," and he frowned at the journeymen, who grinned back at him. "However, when the fundamentals of our craft have been well and truly learned, I insist that we hold no one back from the rank they are entitled to by knowledge and ability, and in this case, rare talent. Sebell, Talmor, since neither of you will resign in the other's favor . . ."

A silence emphasized by Piemur's tiny gasp of astonishment fell over the dining hall as Sebell and Talmor rose from their table and walked up the aisle by the hearth. They stopped. Startled, Menolly looked up at Sebell's shy grin and Talmor's broad smile.

She couldn't grasp the significance of their presence, though she heard Audiva's cry of joy and saw the stunned amazement on the faces of Briala and Timiny. She glanced wildly about her, saw Master Robinton grinning, nodding, gesturing for her to rise. But it wasn't until Piemur kicked her on the shins that she shed her paralysis.

"You're supposed to walk the tables, Menolly," Piemur said in an audible hiss. "Get up and walk. You're a journeyman now. You've made journeyman."

"Menolly's a journeyman! Menolly's a journeyman!" echoed the other apprentices, clapping their hands in rhythm to their chant. "Menolly's made journeyman. Walk, Menolly, walk. Walk, Menolly, walk!"

Sebell and Talmor took her by the elbows and lifted her to her feet.

"Never saw an apprentice so loath to take a walk," muttered Talmor under his breath to Sebell.

"We could carry her," Sebell said, in a whisper, "because, between you and me, I don't think her legs are going to walk her."

"I can walk," said Menolly, shaking off their helping hands. "I've even got harper boots. I can walk anywhere!"

The last vestige of anxiety lifted from Menolly's mind. As a journeyman in blue, she had rank and status enough to fear no one and nothing. No further need to run or hide. She'd a place to fill and a craft that was unique to her. She'd come a long, long way in a sevenday. The pulse of her words suggested a tune. She'd think of that later. Now, holding her head high, while the fire lizards swept in from the windows, trilling their happy reaction, she walked between Talmor and Sebell to the oval tables of her new station in the Harper Craft Hall of Pern.

DRAGONDRUMS

This book is dedicated (and about time) to

FREDERICK H. ROBINSON

for many, many, many reasons,

not the least of which is the fact that

HE *is the Master Harper*

At the Harper Craft Hall

Robinton—Masterharper; bronze fire lizard, Zair

Masters: Jerint—Instrument maker
Domick—Composition
Shonagar—Voice
Arnor—Archivist
Oldive—Healer
Olodkey—Drummaster

Masterharper Journeymen: Sebell; gold fire lizard, Kimi
Talmor
Menolly: nine fire lizards
gold Beauty
bronze Rocky
Diver
brown Lazybones
Mimic
Brownie
blue Uncle
green Auntie One
Auntie Two

Drum Journeymen: Dirzan
Rokayas

Drum apprentices: Piemur
Clell

Apprentices: Ranly
Timiny
Brolly
Bonz
Tilgin

Silvina—headwoman
Abuna—kitchen worker
Camo—half-witted kitchen drudge
Banak—head stockman

At Fort Hold

Lord Holder Groghe; gold fire lizard, Merga
N'ton—Weyrleader of Fort Weyr; fire lizard, Tris

At Nabol Hold

Lord Holder Meron
Candler—harper
Berdine—journeyman healer
Deckter—grand-nephew of Meron
Hittet—blood relation of Meron
Kaljan—minemaster
Besel—kitchen drudge

At Igen Hold

Lord Holder Laudey
Bantur—harper
Deece—journeyman harper

At Southern Hold

Lord Holder Toric
Saneter—harper
Sharra—Toric's sister

At Benden Weyr

F'lar—Weyrleader
Lessa—Weyrwoman
Felessen—son of F'lar and Lessa
T'gellan—bronze dragonrider
F'nor—brown dragonrider; gold fire lizard, Grall
Brekke—queenrider; bronze fire lizard, Berd
Manora—Headwoman
Mirrim—fosterling of Brekke; three fire lizards
Oharan—harper

At Southern Weyr

T'kul—weyrleader
Mardra—weyrwoman
T'ron—dragonrider

Craftmasters

Masterherdsman Briaret
Masterminer Nicat

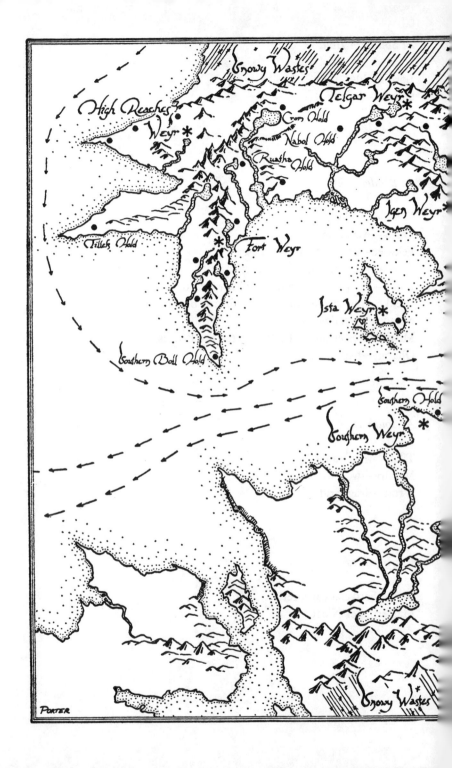

Chapter 1

The rumble-thud-boom of the big drums answering a message from the east roused Piemur. In his five Turns at the Harper Craft Hall, he had never become accustomed to that bone-throbbing noise. Perhaps, he thought, sleepily turning over, if the drums beat every dawn, or in the same sequence, he'd get accustomed enough to sleep through it. But he doubted that. He was naturally a light sleeper, a talent picked up when he'd been a herder's boy and had to keep an ear awake for night alarms among the runner beasts. The facility had often been to his advantage, since the other apprentices in his dormitory couldn't sneak up on him with vengeance in mind. And he was often awakened by discreet, dragon-borne visitors coming to see the Masterharper of Pern, or the arrivals and departures of Master Robinton himself, for he was surely one of the most important men on Pern; almost as influential as F'lar and Lessa, the Weyrleaders of Benden. Occasionally, too, on warm summer nights, when the shutters of the main hall were thrown back, the masters and journeymen assuming all the apprentices slept, he'd hear fascinating and uninhibited talk drifting on the night air. A small fellow like himself had to keep ahead of everyone else, and listening often showed him how.

As he tried to get back to sleep for just a little longer in the gray dawn, the drum sequence echoed in his mind. The message had originated from Ista Hold's harper: he had caught the identifying signature. He couldn't be sure of the rest of the message: something about a ship. Maybe he ought to learn message-drum beats. Not that they came in with such frequency now that more and more people owned little fire lizards to take messages round and about Pern.

He wondered when he'd get his hands on a fire lizard egg. Menolly had promised him one when her queen, Beauty, mated. A nice thought on her part, Piemur reflected, realistically aware that Menolly might not be able to distribute Beauty's eggs as she wished. Master Robinton would want them placed to the Harper Hall's advantage. And Piemur couldn't fault Master Robinton. One day, though, he'd have his fire lizard. A queen, or, at the least, a bronze.

Piemur folded his hands behind his head, musing on such a delightful prospect. From having helped Menolly feed her nine, he knew a fair bit about them now. More than some people who had fire lizards, the same people who'd been claiming for Turns that fire lizards were boys' sundreams. That is, until F'nor, brown Canth's rider, had Impressed a little queen on a beach in the southern continent. Then Menolly, halfway across Pern, had saved a fire lizard queen's eggs from being drowned in the unusually high tides of that Turn. Now everyone wanted a fire lizard, and admitted that they must be tiny cousins to the great dragons of Pern.

Piemur shivered with delighted terror. Thread had fallen over Fort Hold yesterday. They'd been rehearsing Master Domick's new saga about the search for Lessa and how she'd become Weyrwoman at Benden just before the new Pass of the Red Star, but Piemur had been much more aware of the silvery Threads dropping through the skies above the tightly shuttered and sealed Harper Hall. He'd imagined, as he always did during Threadfall, the graceful passages of the great dragons as their fiery breath charred Thread before it could fall to the ground and devour anything living, before it could burrow into the ground and multiply. Even thinking of that phenomenon made Piemur quiver fearfully again.

Before Master Robinton had discovered Menolly's talent at songmaking, she'd actually lived outside her hold, caring for the nine fire lizards she had Impressed from the rescued clutch. If only, thought Piemur with a sigh, he wasn't immured in the Crafthall; if only he had a chance to search seashores and find his own clutch. . . . Of course, as a mere apprentice, he'd have to give the eggs to his Craft Master, but surely, if he found a whole clutch, Master Robinton would let him keep one.

The sudden raucous call of a fire lizard startled him, and he sat up in alarm. The sun was now streaming across the outer side of the Harper Hall rectangle. He had fallen asleep again. If Rocky was screaming, he was late to help feed. With deft movements, he dressed, except for his boots, and thudded down the steps, emerging into the courtyard just as he heard the second, more urgent summons from a hungry Rocky.

When he saw that Camo was only just trudging up the steps outside the kitchen, clutching his bowl of scraps, Piemur drew a sigh of relief. He wasn't all that late! He thrust his feet into his boots, stuffed the laces inside to save time, and clomped across the court just as Menolly came down the steps from the Main Hall. Rocky, Mimic and Lazy whirled above Piemur's head, chittering hungrily at him to move faster.

Piemur glanced up, looking for Beauty. Menolly had told him that when the little queen was close to mating time she'd seem to be more golden than ever. She was now circling to land on Menolly's shoulder, but she seemed the same color as ever.

"Camo feed pretties?" The kitchen drudge smiled brightly as Menolly and Piemur reached him.

"Camo feed pretties!" Menolly and Piemur spoke the customary reassurance in chorus, grinning at each other as they reached for handfuls of meat scraps. Rocky and Mimic took their accustomed perches on Piemur's shoulders, while Lazy clung with far from indolent strength to his left forearm.

Once the fire lizards settled to the business of eating, Piemur glanced at Menolly, wondering if she'd heard the drum message. She looked more awake than she usually did at this hour, and slightly detached from her immediate task. Of course, she might just be thinking up a new song, but writing tunes was not Menolly's only duty in the Harper Hall.

As they fed the fire lizards, the rest of the Hall began to stir: the drudges in the kitchen were roused to breakfast efforts by Silvina and Abuna; in the junior and senior dormitories, occasional shouts punctuated random noises; and shutters on the journeymen's quarters were being opened to let in the fresh morning air.

Once the fire lizards had wheeled up for their morning stretch of wings, Piemur, Menolly and Camo separated: Camo, with a push from Menolly, was sent back to the kitchen; then she and Piemur went up the main steps of the Harper Hall to the dining room.

Piemur's first class that morning was chorus, for they were, as usual at this time of the Turn, rehearsing the spring music for Lord Groghe's feast. Master Domick had collaborated with Menolly this year and produced an uncommonly singable score for his ballad about Lessa and her golden queen dragon, Ramoth.

Piemur was to sing the part of Lessa. For once, he didn't object to having to sing a female role. In fact, that morning he waited eagerly for the chorus to finish the passage before his first entrance. The moment came, he opened his mouth, and to his amazement no sound emerged.

"Wake up, Piemur," said Master Domick, irritably rapping his stick on the music stand. He alerted the chorus. "We'll repeat the measure before the entrance . . . *if* you're now ready, Piemur?"

Usually Piemur could ignore Master Domick's sarcasm, but since he had been ready to sing, he flushed uncertainly. He took a breath and hummed against his closed teeth as the chorus began again. He had tone, and his throat wasn't sore, so he wasn't coming down with a stuffed head.

The chorus gave him his entrance again, and he opened his mouth. The sound that emerged ranged from one octave to another, neither of which were in the score he held.

A complete and awed silence fell. Master Domick frowned at Piemur, who was now swallowing against a fear that froze his feet to one spot and crept up his bones to his heart.

"Piemur?"

"Sir?"

"Piemur, sing a scale in C."

Piemur attempted to, and on the fourth note, though he had hardened his middle to iron for support, his voice again broke. Master Domick put down his stick and regarded Piemur. If there was any expression in the Composition Master's face, it was compassion, tinged with resigned irritation.

"Piemur, I think you had best see Master Shonagar. Tilgin, you've been understudying the role?"

"Me, sir? I haven't so much as glanced at it. Not with Piemur . . ." The startled apprentice's voice trailed off as Piemur, slowly and with feet he could barely force to move, left the chorus hall and walked across the court towards Master Shonagar's room.

He tried to close his ears to the sound of Tilgin's tentative voice. Scorn gave him momentary relief from his cold fear. His had been a much better voice than Tilgin's would ever be. Had been? Maybe he was just coming down with a cold. Piemur coughed experimentally, but knew even as he did so that no phlegm congested his lungs and throat. He trudged on to Master Shonagar, knowing the verdict and hoping against vain hope that somehow the flaw in his voice was transitory, that he'd manage to keep his soprano range long enough to sing Master Domick's music. Scuffing up the steps, he paused briefly in the threshold to accustom his eyes to the gloom within.

Master Shonagar would only just have arisen and breakfasted. Piemur knew his master's habits intimately. But Shonagar was already in his customary position, one elbow on the wide table, propping up his massive head, the other arm cocked against the columnar thigh.

"Well, it's sooner than we might have expected, young Piemur," the Master said in a quiet tone, which nonetheless seemed to fill the room. "But the change was bound to come sometime." A wealth of sympathy tinged the Master's rich, mellow bass voice. The propping hand came away from the head and brushed aside the tones now issuing from the chorus hall. "Tilgin will never come up to your measure."

"Oh, sir, what do I do now my voice is gone? It's all I had!"

Master Shonagar's surprised contempt startled Piemur. "All you had? Perhaps, my dear Piemur, but by no means all you *have!* Not after five Turns as *my* apprentice. You probably know more about vocal production than any journeyman in the Craft."

"But who would want to learn from me?" Piemur gestured to his slight adolescent frame, his voice cracking dramatically. "And how could I teach when I've no voice to demonstrate?"

"Ah, but the distressing condition of your singing voice heralds other alterations that will remedy those minor considerations." Master Shonagar waved aside that argument, and then regarded Piemur through narrowed eyelids. "This occasion has not caught *me* . . ." the thick fingers tapped against the bulging chest ". . . unprepared." Now a gusty sigh escaped Master Shonagar's full lips. "You have been without doubt or contradiction the most troublesome and ingenious, the laziest, the most audacious and mendacious of the hundreds of apprentices and voice students it has been my tiresome task to train to some standard. Despite yourself, you have achieved some measure of success. You ought to have achieved even more." Master Shonagar affected a pout. "I find it altogether too perverse, if completely in character, for you to decide on puberty *before* singing Domick's latest choral work. Undoubtedly one of his best, and written with your abilities in mind. Do not hang your head in my presence, young man!" The Master's bellow startled Piemur out of his self-pitiful reflections. "Young man! Yes, that's the crux. You are becoming a young man. Young men must have young-manly tasks."

"What?" In the single word, Piemur expressed his disbelief and distress.

"That, my young man, is for the Harper to tell you!" Master Shonagar's thick forefinger pointed first at Piemur and then swung towards the front of the building, indicating Master Robinton's window.

Piemur did not dare permit the hope that began to revive in him to blossom. Yet, Master Shonagar wouldn't lie for any reason, certainly not to give him false hope.

Then they both winced as Tilgin erred in his sight reading. Instinctively glancing at his Master, Piemur saw the pained expression on Master Shonagar's face.

"Were I you, young Piemur, I'd stay out of Domick's sight as much as possible."

Despite his depression, Piemur grinned, wryly aware that the brilliant Composition Master might well decide that Piemur had elected to thwart his musical ambition in this untimely voice change.

Master Shonagar sighed heavily. "I do wish you'd have waited a trifle longer, Piemur." His groan was wistful as well as resigned. "Tilgin is going to require much coaching to perform creditably. Now, don't you repeat that, young Piemur!" The thick forefinger pointed unwaveringly at Piemur, who affected innocent shock that such an admonition might be needed. "Away with you!"

Obediently, Piemur turned, but he'd gone no more than a few paces to the door when a second shock stopped him. He whirled towards the Voice Master.

"You mean, just now, sir, don't you?"

" 'Just now, sir?' Of course, I mean now, not this afternoon or tomorrow, but now."

"Now . . . and always?" asked Piemur uncertainly. If he could no longer sing, Master Shonagar would take on another special apprentice to perform those personal and private duties for him that Piemur had been undertaking in the past Turns. Not only was Piemur reluctant to lose the privilege of being Master Shonagar's special lad, he honestly didn't wish to end the very rewarding association with the Master. He liked Shonagar, and those services he had performed for his Master had stemmed from that liking rather than a sense of duty. He had enjoyed above all the droll humor and florid speech of his Master, of being teased for his bold behavior and called to task by a man he had never managed to deceive for an instant with any of his stratagems or ploys.

"Now, yes," and there was a rumble of regret in Shonagar's expressive voice that eased Piemur's sense of loss, "but assuredly not always," and the Master's tone was brisker with only a hint of resigned irritation that he was not going to be forever rid of this small nuisance. "How can we escape each other, immured as we are in the Harper Hall?"

Though Piemur knew perfectly well that Master Shonagar rarely left his hall, he was obscurely reassured. He made a half turn and then came slowly back.

"This afternoon, you'll need some errands done?"

"You may not be available," said Master Shonagar, his face expressionless, his voice almost as neutral.

"But, sir, who will come to you?" and again, Piemur's voice broke. "You know you're always busy after the midday meal . . ."

"If you mean," and Shonagar spoke with real amusement crinkling his eye folds, "do I plan to appoint Tilgin to the vacancy? Sssssh! I shall, of course, have to devote a great deal of time to improving his voice and musicality, but to have him lurking about on tap . . ." The thick fingers wiggled with distaste. "Away with you. The choice of your successor requires considerable thought. Not, mind you, that there are not hundreds of likely lads who would undoubtedly suit my small requirements to perfection . . ."

Piemur caught his breath in hurt and then saw the twitch of Master

Shonagar's expressive brows and realized that this moment was no easier on the older man.

"Undoubtedly . . ." Piemur tried to turn away on that light note but found he could not, wishing that Master Shonagar might just this once . . .

"Go, my son. You will ever know where to find me, should the need arise."

This time the dismissal was final because the Master slanted his head against his fist and closed his eyes, shamming weariness.

Quickly Piemur walked to the entrance, blinking at the bright sunlight after the darker hall. He paused on the bottom step, reluctant to take the final one that severed his association with Master Shonagar. There was a sudden hard lump in his throat that had nothing to do with his voice change. He swallowed, but the sensation of constriction remained. He rubbed at his eyes with knuckles that came away moist and stood, fists clenched at his thighs, trying not to blubber.

Master Robinton had something to tell him about new duties? So his voice change had been discussed by the Masters. To be sure, he wouldn't have been callously thrown out of the Harper Hall and sent in some obscure disgrace back to his herdsman father and the dreary life of a beast farmer simply because he no longer had his soprano voice. No, that wouldn't be his fate, despite the fact that singing was his one undeniable harper skill. As Talmor said of his gitar and harp playing, he could accompany so long as his playing was drowned out by loud singing or other instruments. The drums and pipes he made under Master Jerint's guidance were only passable and never got stamped for sale at Gathers. He copied scores accurately enough when he put his mind to it, but he always found so many more interesting things to do than spending hours cramping his fingers to renew Records someone else could do more neatly and in half the time. Yet, when pushed to it, Piemur didn't actually mind scribing, if he were allowed to add his own embellishments. Which he wasn't. Not with Master Arnor looking over his shoulder and muttering about wasted ink and hide.

Piemur sighed deeply. The only thing he was really adept at was singing, and that was no longer possible. Forever? No, not forever! He spread his fingers in rejection of that prospect and then closed them into tighter fists. He'd be able to sing all right: he'd learned too much from Master Shonagar about voice production and phrasing and interpretation, but he might not *have* a voice as an adult. And he wasn't going to sing unless he did! He had his reputation. Better if he never opened his mouth to sing another note. . . .

Tilgin flubbed another phrase. Piemur grinned, listening to Tilgin repeating the phrase correctly. They'd miss Piemur all right! He could sight-read any score, even one of Domick's, without missing a beat or an awkward interval, or those florid embellishments Domick insisted on writing for the treble parts. Yes, they'd miss Piemur in the chorus!

That knowledge fortified him, and he took the final step onto the flagstones of the court. Clipping his thumbs over his belt, he began to saunter towards the main entrance of the Harper Hall. Not, he reminded himself, that a lowly apprentice who has just lost his privileged position, should saunter when sent to the Masterharper of Pern. Piemur squinted into the sunlight at the fire lizards on the roof opposite. He didn't spot Master Robinton's bronze fire lizard, Zair, among those sunning themselves with Menolly's nine. So the Masterharper wasn't with the day as yet. Come to think of it, Piemur reflected, he'd heard the clear baritone voice of the Harper in the Court late last night and the noise of a dragon landing and departing. These days the Harper spent more time away from the Hall than in it.

"Piemur?"

Startled, he glanced up and saw Menolly standing on the top step of the Main Hall. She'd spoken quietly, and when he peered at her, he knew that she knew what had happened to him.

"It *was* rather audible," she said, again in that gentle tone, which both irritated and appeased Piemur. Menolly, of all within the Harper Hall, would sympathize with him most acutely. She knew what it was to be without the ability to make music. "Is that Tilgin singing?"

"Yes, and it's all my fault," Piemur said.

"All your fault?" Menolly stared at him in surprised amusement.

"Why did I have to pick *now* to break voice?"

"Why indeed? I'm sure you did it only to annoy Domick!" Menolly grinned broadly at him, for they both had experiences with Domick's whimsical temper.

Piemur had reached the top step and experienced another shock on this morning of surprises: he could almost look Menolly squarely in the eye, and she was tall for a girl! She reached out and ruffled his hair, laughing as he indignantly swatted her hand away.

"C'mon, Master Robinton wants to see you."

"Why? What'm I going to be doing now? D'you know?"

"Not for me to tell you, scamp," she said, striding on her long legs across the hall and forcing him to a jog pace to keep beside her.

"Menolly, that's not fair!"

"Ha!" She was pleased by his discomfiture. "You've not long to wait. I will tell you this: Domick may not be pleased that your voice changed, but the Master was."

"Aw, Menolly, one little hint? Please? You know you owe me a favor or two!"

"I do?" Menolly savored her advantage.

"You do. And you know it. You could pay me back right now!" Piemur was irritated. Why did she have to pick now to be difficult?

"Why waste a favor when a little patience on your part will bring the answer?" They had reached the second level and were striding down the corridor towards the Harper's quarters. "You'd better learn patience, too, my friend!"

Piemur halted in disgust.

"Oh, c'mon Piemur," she said, with a broad swing of her arm. "You're not a little 'un anymore to wheedle news out of me. And wasn't it you who warned me that you don't keep a Master waiting?"

"I've had enough surprises today," he said sourly, but he closed the distance between them just as she tapped politely on the door.

The Masterharper of Pern, his silvering hair glinting in the sun streaming in his windows, was seated at the worktable, a tray before him, the steam of hot klah rising unnoticed as he offered pieces of meat to the fire lizard clinging to his left forearm.

"Glutton! Greedy maw! Don't claw me, that's bare skin, not padding! I'm feeding you as fast as I can! Zair! Behave yourself! I'm perishing for a taste of my klah, but I'm feeding you first. Good morning, Piemur. You're adept at feeding fire lizards. Pop sustenance into Zair's mouth so I can get some in mine!" The Harper shot a look of desperate entreaty to Piemur.

He whipped round the long worktable and, grabbing up several chunks of meat, attracted Zair's gaze.

"Ah, that's more the thing!" exclaimed Master Robinton after he'd had a long gulp of his klah.

Absorbed in his task, Piemur wasn't at first aware of the Harper's scrutiny, for the man was applying himself to his own food with his free right hand. Then Piemur saw the keen eyes on him, lids narrowed as if weighty from sleep. He could tell nothing from the Harper's expression, for the long face was quiescent, slightly puffy about the eyes from sleep, the grooves from the corners of the mobile mouth pulled down with age and accumulated fatigue rather than displeasure.

"I shall miss your young voice," said the Harper with a gentle emphasis on "young." "But, while we're waiting for you to settle into an adult placement, I've asked Shonagar to release you to me. I've a suspicion that you won't mind too much"—and a smile twitched the Harper's lips—"doing the odd job for me and Menolly and my good Sebell."

"Menolly *and* Sebell?" Piemur gawked.

"I'm not sure I care for that emphasis," said Menolly in a mock growl, subsiding as the Harper threw her a quieting glance.

"I'd be *your* apprentice?" Piemur asked the Harper, holding his breath for the answer.

"Indeed, you'd have to be my apprentice at that," said Master Robinton, his voice and face turning droll.

"Oh, sir!" Piemur was stunned at such good fortune.

Zair squawked petulantly in the little silence, for Piemur had paused in his feeding.

"Sorry, Zair," and Piemur hastily resumed the task.

"However," and the Harper cleared his throat while Piemur wondered what disadvantage to this enviable status was about to be disclosed (there had to be one, he knew), "you will have to improve your skill in scribing—"

"We must be able to read what you write," said Menolly, sternly.

"—learn to send and receive message drum accurately and rapidly . . ." He looked at Menolly. "I know that Master Fandarel is very keen to have his new message-sender installed in every hall and craft, but it's going to take far too long to be useful to me. Then, too, there are some messages that should remain privy to the Craft!" He paused, staring long at Piemur. "You were bred on a runner beast hold, weren't you?"

"Yes, sir. And I can ride any runner anywhere!"

Menolly's expression indicated disbelief.

"I can, too."

"You'll have ample chance to prove it, I fear," said the Harper, smiling at his new apprentice's stout claim. "What you will also have to prove, young Piemur, is your discretion." Now the Harper was in solemn earnest, and with equal solemnity, Piemur nodded assurance. "Menolly tells me that despite your incorrigibility on many other counts, you're not given to indiscriminate babbling. Rather," and the Harper held up his hand as Piemur opened his mouth to reassure him, "that you keep close about incidental information until you can use it to your benefit."

"Me, sir?"

Master Robinton smiled at his wide-eyed innocent expression. "You, sir, young Piemur. Although it does strike me that you've exactly the sort of guile—" He broke off, then continued more briskly, leaving unsaid words to tantalize Piemur. "We'll see how you get on. I fear you may find your new role not as exciting as you think, but you will be serving your Craft, and me, very well indeed."

If he couldn't sing for a while, thought Piemur, being the Master's apprentice was the next best thing. Wait'll he told Bonz and Timiny; wouldn't they just choke!

"Ever sailed?" asked Menolly with such a piercing look that Piemur wondered if she'd read his thoughts.

"Sailed? In a boat?"

"That's the general method," she said. "With my luck you'll be a seasicker."

"You mean, I might get to the Southern Continent, too?" asked Piemur, having rapidly added up assorted pieces of information and come to a conclusion; all too hastily spoken, he realized belatedly.

The Harper lost all semblance of lassitude and sat bolt upright in his chair, causing his fire lizard to protest vehemently.

Menolly burst out laughing.

"I told you, Master," she said, throwing up her hands.

"And what makes you mention the Southern Continent?" asked the Harper.

Piemur was rather sorry now that he had.

"Well, sir, nothing special," he said, wondering himself. "Just things like Sebell being gone for a couple of sevendays midwinter and coming back with a tanned face. Only I'd known he'd not been in Nerat or Southern Boll or Ista. There's been talk, too, at the Gathers that even if dragonriders from the north aren't supposed to go south, some of the Oldtimers have been seen here in the north. Now, if I was F'lar, I'd sort of wonder what those Oldtimers were doing north. And I'd try to keep them south, where they're supposed to be. And there're all these hold-less men, looking for someplace to live, and no one seems to know how big the Southern Continent is and if. . . ." Piemur trailed off, daunted by the keen scrutiny of the Masterharper.

"And if . . . ?" Master Robinton urged him to continue.

"Well, I've had to copy that map F'nor made of the Southern Hold and Weyr, and it's small. No bigger'n Crom or Nabol, but I've heard from weyrfolk at High Reaches who were *in* the south before F'lar exiled the worst of the Oldtimers, and they said they were sure the Southern Continent must be pretty big." Piemur gestured broadly.

"And . . . ?" The Harper's encouragement was firm.

"Well, sir, if it were me, I'd want to know, 'cause sure as eggs hatch, there's going to be trouble with those Oldtimers south"—he jerked his thumb in that direction—"and trouble with the holdless men in the north," he turned his thumb back. "So when Menolly talks about sailing, I know how Sebell got south without being taken by a dragon. Which Benden Weyr wouldn't permit 'cause they promised that northern dragons wouldn't go south, and I don't think Sebell could swim that far. If he can swim."

Master Robinton began to laugh, a soft chuckle, and he slowly swung his head from side to side.

"I wonder how many more people have put the same pieces together, Menolly?" he asked, frowning. When his journeywoman shrugged, he added to Piemur. "You've kept such notions to yourself, young man?"

Piemur gave a snort, realized he must be more circumspect with the Master of his Craft and said quickly, "Who pays any attention to what apprentices think or say?"

"Have you mentioned these notions to anyone?" The Harper was insistent.

"Of course not, sir." Piemur tried to keep indignation from his tone. "It's Benden's business, or Hold business, or Harper business. Not mine."

"A chance spoken word, even by an apprentice, can sift through a man's thoughts till he forgets the source and remembers the intent. And repeats it inadvisedly."

"I know my loyalty to my Crafthall, Master Robinton," said Piemur.

"I'm sure of your loyalty," the Harper said, nodding his head slowly, his eyes still holding Piemur's. "I want to be certain of your discretion."

"Menolly'll tell you; I'm not a babblemouth." He looked at Menolly for her support.

"Not normally, I'm sure. But you might be tempted to speak when taunted by others."

"Me, sir?" Piemur's indignation was genuine. "Not me, sir! I may be small, but I'm not stupid."

"No, one could not accuse you of that, my young friend, but as you've already pointed out, we are living in an uncertain Turn. I think. . . ."

The Harper broke off, staring out the window, frowning absently. Abruptly he made a decision and regarded Piemur for a long moment. "Menolly told me you were quick-witted. Let's see if you comprehend the reason behind this: you will not be known as *my* apprentice . . ." and Master Robinton smiled understandingly at Piemur's sharp intake of breath. Then he nodded with approval as Piemur promptly schooled his expression to polite acceptance. "You will be told off as apprentice to the Drummaster, Olodkey, who will know that you are under my orders as well. Yes"—and the crispness of Master Robinton's tone told Piemur that he was pleased by this solution, and Piemur had better be —"that will serve. The drummers must, of course, keep irregular hours.

No one would note your absences or think anything of your taking messages."

Master Robinton put his hand on Piemur's shoulder and gave him a little shake, smiling kindly.

"No one will miss your boyish treble more than I, lad, except possibly Domick, but here in the Harper Hall, some of us listen to other tunes and drum a different beat." He gave Piemur another shake, then cuffed him on the shoulder encouragingly. "I don't want you to stop listening, Piemur, not if you can take isolated facts and put them together as well as you just did. But I also want you to notice the way things are said, the tone and inflection, the emphasis."

Piemur mustered a grin. "What a harper hears is for the Harper's ears, sir?"

Master Robinton laughed. "Good lad! Now, take this tray back to Silvina and ask her to fit you out with wherhide. A drummer has to be at his post in all weathers!"

"You don't need wherhide on the drumheight!" exclaimed Piemur. Then he grinned as he cocked his head at his master. "You do need it if you're riding a dragonback, though."

"I told you he was quick," said Menolly, grinning at the Harper's consternation.

"Scamp! Rascal! Impertinent snip!" cried the Harper, dismissing him with a vigorous wave of his hand that set Zair squawking. "Do as you're told and keep your notions to yourself!"

"Then I will be riding dragons!" said Piemur, and when he saw Master Robinton rise half out of his chair, he quickly slipped out of the room.

"What did I tell you, Master," said Menolly, laughing. "He's quick enough to be very useful."

Though the glint of amusement remained in his eyes, the Harper stared thoughtfully at the closed door, his fingers tapping idly on his chair arm.

"Quick yes, but a shade young . . ."

"Young? Piemur? He was never young, that one. Don't let that innocent, wide-eyed stare of his fool you. Besides, he'd got fourteen Turns, almost as old as I was when I left Half-Circle Sea Hold to live in the Dragon Stones' cave with my fire lizards. And what else can be done with all his energy and mischief? He's simply not suited for any other section of this Craft. Master Shonagar was the only person who had half a chance of keeping him out of trouble. Old Arnor couldn't, nor Jerint. It's got to be Olodkey and the drums."

"I could almost see the merit of the Oldtimers' attitudes," said the Harper on the end of a heavy sigh.

"Sir?" Menolly stared at him, startled as much by the abrupt change of subject as the sense of what he said.

"I wish we hadn't changed so in this last long Interval."

"But sir, you've been supporting all the changes F'lar and Lessa have advocated. And Benden's been right to make those changes. They've united Hall and Hold behind the Weyrs. Furthermore," and Menolly took a deep breath, "Sebell told me not so long ago that before this Pass of the Red Star began, harpers were nearly as discredited as dragonriders. You've made this Hall into the most prestigious craft on Pern. Everyone respects Masterharper Robinton. Even Piemur," she added with a laugh trembling in her voice as she struggled to relieve her master's melancholy.

"Ah, now, there's the real accomplishment!"

"Indeed it is," she said, ignoring his facetiousness. "For he's very hard to impress, I assure you. Believe me, too, that he won't be in the least distressed to do for you what he does naturally for himself. He's always heard the gossip at Gathers and told me, knowing I'd tell you. 'What a harper hears is for the Harper's ears.' " She laughed to find Piemur's saucy quip so applicable.

"It was easier during the Interval. . . ." Robinton said, with another long sigh. Zair, who'd been cleaning himself, chirped in a querying way, tilting his head and peering with earnestly whirling eyes at his friend. The Harper smiled as he stroked the little creature. "Boring, too, to be completely candid. Still, it won't be that long an assignment for Piemur, will it? His voice ought to settle within the Turn, and he can resume his place as a soloist. If his adult voice is half as good as his treble, he'll be a better singer than Tagetarl."

Seeing that that prospect cheered her Master, Menolly smiled.

"The drum message was from Ista Hold. Sebell's on his way back with those herbal medicines Master Oldive wanted. He'll be at Fort Sea Hold by late afternoon tomorrow if the wind holds."

"Indeed? I'll be very interested to hear what our good Sebell has for his Harper's ears."

Chapter 2

The tray Piemur was carrying was all that restrained him from jumping into the air and kicking his heels together in his jubilation. Working for Master Robinton, no matter how indirectly, and being apprenticed to Master Olodkey, was no loss of prestige and much much more than he had dared contemplate. Not, Piemur admitted to himself, that he'd given much thought to his future.

Of course, one never saw much of Master Olodkey about the Hall. He kept to the drum height, a lean, slightly stooped figure of a man with a big head and coarse bristling brown hair that seemed to stand out from his skull to give him the appearance, the irreverent said, of one of his own bass drumsticks. Others insisted that he was deaf from years of pounding the great message-drums for the Harper Hall. Except for drumbeats, they hastily amended, which he didn't need to hear: he felt the vibrations in the air.

Piemur considered his new apprenticeship and found it good: there were only four other apprentices, seniors all, and five journeymen serving Master Olodkey. Granted that Piemur had been Master Shonagar's special, but Master Shonagar was responsible for every singer in the Hall, whereas Master Olodkey rarely had more than ten harpers looking to him. Piemur again was in a select group. Even more select if he'd been permitted to announce the full truth.

He skittered down the steps, balancing the tray deftly. Maybe, once he'd proved to the Masterharper that he could keep his mouth sealed. . . . And Master Robinton was wrong to think that any could extract information from Piemur that Piemur didn't care to divulge. Nothing pleased Piemur more than "knowing." He didn't necessarily have to show off to other people how much he "knew." The fact that he, Piemur, an insignificant herdsman's son from Crom, knew, was sufficient.

He wished he hadn't been so brash, mentioning the Southern Continent, but the reactions had proved that his guess was accurate. They had been down to the south: at least Sebell had, and probably Menolly. If they'd gone, then the Harper needn't risk the trip with such eyes and ears to do the hard work.

Piemur hadn't had much to do with the Oldtimers before F'lar had ordered them exiled to the Southern Continent. For this he was fervently grateful as he'd heard enough about their arrogance and greed. But if he, Piemur, had been exiled, he wouldn't have just stayed put. He couldn't understand why the Oldtimers had quietly accepted their humiliating dismissal. Piemur calculated that some two hundred and forty-eight Oldtimers and their women had gone to the Southern Continent, including the two dissatisfied Weyrleaders, T'ron of Fort and T'kul of the High Reaches. Seventeen Oldtimers had returned north, accepting Benden as their leader or so Piemur had heard. Most of the exiled men and dragons had been well on in Turns, so they were no real loss to the dragon strength of Pern. Old age and sickness had claimed almost forty dragons in the first Turn, and almost as many had gone *between* this Turn. Somehow that struck Piemur as being rather careless of dragons, even Oldtimer ones.

He stopped abruptly, aware of a tantalizing aroma wafting from the kitchens. Bubbly berry pies? And just when he needed a real treat! His mouth began to water in anticipation. The pies must be just out of the bake oven or surely he would have discerned that fragrance before.

He heard Silvina's voice rising above the working noises and grimaced. He could've got a few pies out of Abuna with no trouble. But Silvina wasn't often taken in by his starts and schemes. Still. . . .

He let his shoulders sag, dropped his head and began to shuffle down the last few steps into the kitchen level.

"Piemur? What are you doing here at this hour? Why do you have the Harper's tray? You should be rehearsing . . ." Silvina took the tray from his hands and stared at him accusingly.

"You didn't hear?" Piemur asked in a low, dejected voice.

"Hear? Hear what? How could anyone hear anything in this babble? I'll. . . ." She slipped the tray onto the nearest work surface and, putting her finger under his chin, forced his head up.

Piemur was rather pleased to be able to squeeze moisture from the corners of his eyes. He narrowed them quickly for Silvina wasn't easily fooled. Though, he told himself hastily, he *was* very sorry he wouldn't be singing Domick's music. And he was sorrier that Tilgin was!

"Your voice? Your voice is changing?"

Piemur heard the regret and dismay in Silvina's hushed tone. It occurred to him that women's voices never did change, and that she couldn't possibly imagine his feelings of total loss and crushing disappointment. More tears followed the first.

"There, lad. The world's not lost. In a half-Turn or less your range'll settle again."

"Master Domick's music was just right for me . . ." Piemur did not need to fake the ragged tones.

"To be sure, since he wrote it with you in mind, scamp. Well, wouldn't you know? Though I can't for the life of me believe you could contrive to change your voice to spite Domick—"

"Spite Master Domick?" Piemur widened his eyes with indignation. "I wouldn't do such a thing, Silvina."

"Only because you couldn't, rascal. I know how you hate singing female parts." Her voice was acerbic, but her hand under his chin was gentle. She took a clean corner of her apron and blotted the tears on his cheeks. "As luck would have it, I seem to be prepared with an easement for your tragedy." She propelled him before her, motioning towards the trays of cooling pies. Piemur rapidly wondered if he ought to dissemble. "You can have two, one for each hand, and then away with you! Have you seen Master Shonagar yet? Watch those pies! They're just out of the oven."

"Hmmmm," he replied, biting into the first pie despite her admonition. "It's the only way to eat 'em," he mumbled through a mouthful so hot that he had to suck in cool air to ease the burning of his gums. "But . . . I'm to get wherhide clothes."

"You? In wherhide? Why would you need wherhide?" She frowned suspiciously at him now.

"I'm to study drum with Master Olodkey, and Menolly asked me could I ride runners, and Master Robinton said I was to ask you for wherhide."

"All three of them in it? Hmmm. And you'd be apprenticed to Master Olodkey?" Silvina considered the matter and then eyed him shrewdly. He wondered should he tell Menolly that Silvina hadn't been taken in by their stratagem of making him a drummer. "Well, I suppose you'll be kept out of mischief. Though I, for one, doubt it's possible. Come on then. I do have a wherhide jacket that might fit." She cast him a calculating look as they moved towards the storage section of the kitchen level. "Let's hope it'll fit for a while because sure as eggs hatch, I shan't be able to pass it on to anyone else the way you mangle your clothes."

Piemur loved the storerooms, redolent with the smell of well-cured hides and the eye-smarting acridity of newly dyed fabrics. He liked the glowing colors of the cloth bales, the jumble of boots, belts, packs hanging from hooks about the walls, the boxes with their odd treasures. Silvina rapped his knuckles with her keys several times for opening lids to investigate.

The jacket fit, the stiff new leather bucking against his thighs as he pranced about, swinging his arms to make the shoulders settle. It was long in the body, but Silvina was pleased: he'd need the length. Fitting him with new boots showed her how ragged his trousers were, so she found him two new pairs, one in harper blue and the other in a deep gray leather. Two shirts with sleeves too long, but which no doubt would fit him perfectly by midwinter, a hat to keep his ears warm and his eyes shaded, and heavy riding gloves with down-lined fingers.

He left the stores, his arms piled high with new clothes, boots dangling from their laces over his shoulder and bumping him front and back, his ears ringing with Silvina's promise of dire things happening to him if he snagged, tore, or scuffed his new finery before he'd had it on his back a sevenday.

He happily employed the rest of the morning by dressing in his new gear, examining himself from all angles in the one mirrored surface of the apprentice dormitory.

He heard the burst of shouts as the chorus was released and peered cautiously over the sill. Most of the boys and young men swarmed across the Court to the Hall. But Master Domick, music rolled in one fist, strode purposefully towards Master Shonagar's hall. The last to exit was Tilgin, head bowed, shoulders slumped, weary from what must have been an exhausting rehearsal. Piemur grinned; he had warned Tilgin to study the part. One never knew when Master Domick might call on the understudy. There was always the chance of a bad throat or a hacking cough for a soloist. Not that Piemur had ever been sick for performance . . . until this one. Piemur gave a sour note. He really had wanted to sing Lessa in Domick's ballad. He'd sort of counted on coming to the Benden Weyrwoman's notice that way. It was always wise to be known to the two Benden Weyrleaders, and this would have been the perfect opportunity.

Ah well, there were more ways of skinning a herdbeast than shaving him with a table-knife.

He folded his new clothing carefully in his bedpress, giving the fur a smoothing twitch. Then quickly glanced out the window again. Now, while Master Domick was busy with Master Shonagar, would be the time for him to slip into the dining hall. Keep out of sight, and soon enough he'd be out of Domick's mind. Not that Piemur was at fault. This time.

A shame really. Lessa's melody was the loveliest Domick had ever written. It had so suited his range. Once again a lump pushed up in his throat at the sadness of the lost opportunity. And probably a Turn before he could try to sing again. Nor was there a guarantee that he'd have anywhere near as good a singing voice as an adult as he'd had as a boy. None at all. He'd miss being able to astonish people with the pure tone he could produce, the marvelous flexibility, the perfect sense of pitch and timing, not to mention his particularly acute skill at note-reading.

His reflections caused him sufficient pangs of regrets so that, when he drifted past the first group of apprentices in the court, they paused in their play and watched his slow progress with awed silence.

He trudged up the steps, past apprentices and journeymen, eyes down, hands flopping at his sides, the picture of dejection. Scorch it, would he have to pretend to have lost his appetite? He could smell roast wherry, succulent, and dripping with juices. And then, berry pies.

However, if he managed his tablemates adroitly. . . . Hunger warred with greed, and there was nothing feigned about his expression of sad reflection when the dining room began to fill.

Piemur, deep in his plans, was aware of being flanked by silent boys. But the chubby fist visible on the left was Brolly's. The stained, dirty, calloused, nail-bitten hand on the right was Timiny's. His good friends were standing by him in this moment of loss. He let out a long, drag-gling sigh, heard Brolly shift his feet uncomfortably, saw Timiny extend his hand tentatively to draw it back slowly, uncertain how a gesture of sympathy would be received. Well, Timiny might just give him both pies, Piemur thought.

Suddenly everyone moved, and a quick glance at the round table told Piemur that Master Robinton had taken his place. A flash of blue and gray past his lowered eyes was probably Menolly moving to take her place at a journeyman's table.

Ranly and Bonz sat directly opposite Piemur, regarding him with wide and worried eyes. He gave them a sad half-smile. When the platter of roast wherry slices came to him, he heaved another sigh and fumbled for a slice. He stared at it on his plate instead of attacking it immedi-ately. But then, generally, he'd have taken as many slices as he could knife onto his plate without raising uproars from his mates. He did like roast tubers, but restrainedly took only a small one. He ate slowly so that his stomach would think it was getting more. A rumbling belly would ruin his ploy for bubbly pies.

None of his friends spoke, either to him or to each other. At their end of the table, gloomy silence prevailed. Until the bubbly pies were served. Piemur maintained his air of tragic indifference as the first ripple of delighted surprise sighed down from the kitchen end of the table. He could hear the rise of happy voices, the quick interest of his friends as they saw the burden of the sweet tray.

"Piemur, it's bubbly pies," said Timiny, pulling at his sleeve.

"Bubbly pies?" Piemur kept a querulous note in his voice, as if even bubbly pies had no magic to revive him.

"Yes, bubbly pies," said Brolly, determined to rouse him.

"Your very first favorite, Piemur," said Bonz. "Here, have one of mine," he added and, with only an infinitesimal show of reluctance, pushed the coveted pie across to Piemur.

"Oh, bubbly pies," repeated Piemur on the end of a quavering semi-interested sigh and picked up one of the offerings as though he was forcing himself to exhibit interest.

"It's an awfully good bake, Piemur." Ranly bit into his with exaggerated relish. "Just take a bite, Piemur. You'll see. Get a bubbly or two inside, and you'll feel more like yourself. Imagine! Piemur not wanting all the bubblies he can eat!" Ranly glanced at the others, urging them to second him.

Bravely Piemur ate slowly of the first bubbly pie, wishing they were still hot.

"That did taste good," he said with a trifle brighter tone and was promptly encouraged to eat another.

By the time he had consumed eight because three more were donated from the other end of the table, Piemur affected to lose the edge of his gloom. After all, ten bubbly pies when he might only have had two was a good day's scrounge.

The journeyman rose to deliver announcements and assignments. Piemur toyed with the notion of several different reactions to the news of his change in status. Shock, yes! Delight? Well, some because it was an honor, but not too much, otherwise they might doubt the performance that had won so many pies.

"Sherris, report to Master Shonagar . . ."

"Sherris?" Surprise, shock, and consternation, totally unrehearsed or anticipated brought Piemur straight up off the bench and prompted his neighbors to seize him by the shoulders and push him down. "Sherris? That little snip, that wet-eared, wet-bottomed, wet-bedded—"

Timiny clamped his hand firmly over Piemur's mouth, and the next few announcements were lost to that section of the apprentice tables. Indignation revitalized Piemur, but he was no match for the concerted efforts of Timiny and Brolly, determined that their friend should not suffer the extra humiliation of a public reprimand for interrupting the journeyman.

"Did you hear, Piemur?" Bonz was saying, leaning across the table. "Did you not hear?"

"I heard that Sherris is to be Master . . ." Piemur was sputtering with rage. There were a few truths Master Shonagar ought to know about Sherris.

"No, no, about you!"

"Me?" Piemur ceased his struggles, abruptly horrified by the sudden thought that maybe Master Robinton had changed his mind, that some further investigation had led him to believe Piemur was unsuitable, that all the morning's bright prospect would be wrenched from his grasp.

"You! You're to report to . . ." and Bonz paused to give additional weight to his final words, "Master Olodkey!"

"To Master Olodkey?" Relief gave Piemur's reaction genuine force. Then he looked wildly around for the Drummaster.

Bonz's elbow suddenly digging into his ribs alerted him, and there was Dirzan, Master Olodkey's senior journeyman, staring down at them, fists against his belt, a wary and disapproving expression on his weathered face.

"So we get saddled with you, eh, Piemur? I'll tell you this, you watch your step with our Master. Quickest man in the world with a drumstick, and he doesn't always use it on the drums!" He eyed Piemur significantly and then, with a sharp gesture, indicated that Piemur should follow him.

Chapter 3

The rest of that day was not quite as joyful for Piemur. At Dirzan's order, he moved his gear from the senior apprentice dormitory to the Drummers' quarters, four rooms adjacent to the height, separate from the rest of the Hall. The apprentices' room was cramped and would be more so when the spare cot for Piemur was added. The journeymen's quarters were hardly more spacious, nor Master Olodkey's, though he had his small room to himself. The largest room was both for the instruction and living. Beyond, separated by a small hallway, was the drum room, with the great metal message-drums shining in the afternoon sun. There were several stools for the watchdrummer, a small worktable to write down the messages, and a press, which became the bane of Piemur's mornings. It contained the polish and cloths required to keep that eye-blinding shine on the drums. Dirzan took evident relish in telling Piemur that, by custom, the newest apprentice was required to maintain their brilliance.

The drumheights were always manned save for the "dead" time, four hours in the depth of night, when the eastern half of the continent was still sleeping and the western half just retiring. Piemur wanted to know what happened if an emergency occurred in the dead time and was crisply informed that most drummers were so attuned to an incoming message that even in the shielded quarters the vibrations had been known to alert them.

As part of his apprentice training, Piemur had dutifully learned the identifying beats of each of the major holds and crafthalls, and the emergency signals, like "threadfall," "fire," "death," "answer," "question," "help," "affirmative," "negative" and a few useful phrases. When Dirzan first showed him the mass of drum messages that he would be expected to memorize and perform, he began to wish fervently that his voice would settle before winter came. Dirzan ruthlessly loaded him down with a column of frequently used beat measures to learn by the next day, telling him to practice quietly, using sticks on the practice block, and left him.

In the morning, writhing under Dirzan's full attention, Piemur struggled through the lesson. He almost cried out with relief when Menolly appeared. She ignored him.

"I need a messenger. Can I steal Piemur?"

"Certainly," Dirzan said without surprise, since that task was also a function of drum apprentices. "He can practice his lesson on his way, I expect. I expect he'd better."

Piemur groaned to himself at this partial reprieve, but kept a carefully contrite expression on his face for Dirzan's benefit.

"Did you get riding gear yesterday from Silvina?" Menolly asked him, her face unrevealing. "Get it on," she said when he nodded, gesturing him to be quick about changing.

She was laughing with Dirzan when he reappeared, but broke off her conversation, motioning Piemur to follow her. She took the steps from the drumheights at a clip.

"You said you'd ridden runners?" she asked.

"Sure. I'm herder bred, you know." He was a bit miffed.

"That doesn't necessarily mean that you've ridden runners."

"Well, I have."

"You'll have a chance to prove it," she said, awarding him a curious smile.

Piemur stared hard at her profile as they made their way out of the arch entrance and across the broad Gather meadow in front of the Harper Hall. To their left towered the cliff that housed Fort Hold, and the rows of cots that huddled in the bosom of the sturdy precipice. On the fire heights of the Hold, the brown dragon stood, looking more massive silhouetted against the bright sky, one wing extended, which his rider was grooming.

Piemur felt a surge of reverence for dragons and their riders, reinforced by the sight of Beauty, Menolly's queen fire lizard, alighting on her friend's padded shoulder, while the rest of Menolly's fair cavorted in the air above them.

Her head raised, Menolly smiled at her playful friends and told them they were going for a ride. Did they care to come along? Chirruping and excited aerial displays greeted her question, and Piemur watched, as ever envious, while Beauty stroked Menolly's cheek with her wedge-shaped head and crooned into her ear, the jewel-faceted eyes bright blue with pleasure. Grimly, Piemur forebore to ask the questions that seethed in his mind as they walked in silence towards the great caverns carved into the Fort cliff to house the herdbeasts, wherry flocks and runners. Inside the cavern, the head stockman approached with a smile for Menolly. Her fire lizards whirled into the cavern and sought perches on the curious beams that supported the ceiling, beams that had been fashioned by long-lost skill of the ancients. No one even knew from what substance they had been contrived.

"Off again, Menolly?"

"Again," she said with a slight grimace. "Banak, have you gear for a beast for Piemur, too? As easy for me to have the second runner ridden as led."

"A' course," and the man led the way to the enclosure where the backpads and headgear were hung on racks. After a close look at Piemur, he selected pad and gear, handed Menolly hers. They followed him down the aisle of open-ended stalls. "Your usual is third down, Menolly."

"See if Piemur remembers how to go on," she said to Banak.

The man smiled and handed Piemur the gear. With a degree of assurance he didn't feel, Piemur made the clucking sound it was wise to use to announce human presence to a runner beast. They weren't intelligent creatures, responding to a narrow set of noises and nudges, but, within that limited scope, quite useful. They weren't even pretty, being thin-necked, heavy-headed, long-backed, lean bodied, with spindly legs. Their hide was covered in a coarse fur and ranged in color from a dirty white to a dark brown. They were more graceful than herdbeasts but by no stretch of the imagination as beautiful as dragons or fire lizards.

The creature Piemur was to ride was a dirty brown. He threw the mouth rope over its neck, and by pinching its nose holes, forced it to open its mouth to receive the metal mouthpiece. Quickly grabbing its ear, Piemur managed to get the headstall in place. It snorted as if mildly surprised. Not half as surprised as Piemur that he'd remembered that little trick. He heard Banak grunt. He slapped the pad in place and tightened the midstrap, wondering if this thing would give him any trouble once he was astride it.

Untying its halter, he backed it out and found Menolly in the aisle, holding her larger beast. She examined the gear on his.

"Oh, he did it right," said Banak, nodding approval and waving them to go on as he turned to the rear of the cavern on his own affairs.

It had been a long time since Piemur had been astride a runner. Fortunately, this creature was docile, and its pacing stride smooth as Menolly set off briskly down the eastern roadway.

There was a knack of easing yourself on a runner's pad. Piemur found himself almost unconsciously assuming the position; sitting on one buttock, extending his left leg as far as the toe-hold strap would go, while cocking the knee of his right leg firmly against the runner's side. A rider would change sides often in trip. For a girl seahold bred, Menolly rode with the ease of much practice, Piemur noted.

All the way down to the sea hold, Piemur kept his mouth shut. He'd be scorched if he'd ask her why they were going there. He doubted that the sole purpose of this excursion was to see if he could ride runners or keep his mouth shut. And what had she meant by easier to have a second runner ridden than led? This reticent, assured Menolly on Harper business was quite different from the girl who let him feed her fire lizards, and a long stride from his recollections of the shy and self-effacing newcomer to the Harper Hall three Turns back.

Once they reached Fort Sea Hold, Menolly tossed him her beast's mouth rope, told him to take them to the hold's beastmaster, ease the backpads, water them and see if they could have some feed. As Piemur led the creatures away, he noticed that she went to the harbor wall, shading one hand as she peered at the eastern horizon. Why was she waiting for a ship? Or had that something to do with the drum message from Ista Hold the other morning?

The beastmaster greeted him cheerfully enough and helped him attend the runners.

"You'll be likely heading back to the Hall as soon as the ship docks," said the man. "I'll pad up Sebell's beast, so he's ready. Soon's we got these comfortable, you just pop into my hold there, and my woman'll fix you a bite to eat. Boy your age could always do with a bit, I'm sure. One thing about seaholding, you've always the extra to feed, even in Threadfall."

His hospitality included Menolly when she came in; after Piemur too had seen the speck far out on the sea. He knew that he'd have a chance to rest his weary bones as well as exercise his jaw.

Sebell had a runner stabled here, huh? Sebell borne by a westbound ship. Which suggested that Sebell had also sailed from this seahold. Piemur tried to remember how long it had been since he'd seen Sebell about the Hall, and couldn't.

Fort Sea Hold possessed a natural deep harbor so that the incoming ship sailed right up to the stone-lined side. Seamen on shore as well as on the ship neatly tied her thick lines to the bollards on the wall. Sebell was not immediately visible, though as Menolly's fire lizards did a welcoming display above the ship's rigging, the westering sun glinted off two golden bodies. Sebell's queen, Kimi, as well as Menolly's Beauty. Piemur didn't spot Sebell in the bustle of people unloading the ship until suddenly he appeared right in front of them, heavy bags draped across his shoulders and arms. A seaman carefully laid two more filled sacks at his feet. Enough to load down a runner beast, all right.

"Good trip, Sebell?" asked Menolly, picking up one of the sacks and slinging it with a deft twist of her wrist to her back. "Give Piemur at least one yoke of those," she added, and Piemur sprang quickly to relieve Sebell of some of his burden, fingering the bulges to see if he could identify the contents. "And don't maul it, Piemur. The herbs will be crushed soon enough!"

Herbs?

"Piemur? What're you doing here? Shouldn't you be rehearsing?" began Sebell. His smile was pleasant and the whiteness of his teeth stood out against dark tanned skin.

Herbs and a tan? Piemur would bet every mark he had that Sebell had just returned from the Southern Continent.

"Piemur's voice has broken."

"It has?" There was no doubting Sebell's pleasure at the news. "And Master Robinton's agreeable?"

Menolly grinned. "With a slight variation, according to the wisdom of our good Master!"

"Oh?" Sebell glanced first at Piemur and then back to Menolly for explanation.

"He's been told off as apprentice to Master Olodkey."

Sebell began to chuckle then. "Shrewd of Master Robinton, very shrewd! Right, Piemur?"

"I guess so."

At such a sour rejoinder, Sebell threw his head back and laughed, startling his queen who'd been about to land on his shoulder. She flew about his head, scolding, joined by Beauty and the two bronzes. Sebell threw an arm across Piemur's shoulders, telling him to cheer up, and draped his other arm about Menolly. Then he guided them towards the holdstables.

There was a look on Sebell's face that suggested to Piemur that the companionable arm about his shoulders had been an excuse for the one about Menolly's. The observation cheered Piemur for he knew something no other apprentice did. Maybe not even Master Robinton. Or did he?

Variations on that notion contented Piemur on the initial leg of their hallward trip. The last three hours were spent in increasing physical discomfort. For one thing, he had sacks strapped front and back of his pad and another slung over his shoulder. It was difficult to adjust his rear end and find a spot not already beaten to a pulp by the runner beast's action. Rather unfair of Menolly, Piemur thought with some rancor, to include him on an eight-hour ride his first time on a runner in Turns.

He was immensely relieved that he wasn't expected to tend the mounts, too, as they handed mouth ropes to Banak. Then, Piemur wished he'd been able to dismount in the Harper Hall courtyard, for his stiff and seemingly reshaped legs made the short walk from beasthold to

Hall an unexpected torture. Sourly he listened to Menolly and Sebell chatting as they preceded him. They talked of inconsequentialities so that Piemur couldn't even ignore his aches by concentrating on their comments.

"Well, Piemur," said Menolly as they climbed the steps to the Hall, "you haven't forgotten how to pace a beast. Shells, what's the matter with you?"

"It's been five bloody Turns since I've ridden one," he said, trying to straighten his sorely afflicted back.

"Menolly! That's plain cruel," cried Sebell, trying to keep a straight face. "Into the hot baths with you, lad, before you harden in that posture."

Menolly was instantly contrite, with protests of dismay and apology. Sebell guided him to the bathing room, and when Menolly brought a tray of hot food for them all, she served Piemur as he floated in the soothing water. To Piemur's utter embarrassment, Silvina appeared as he was patting his sore parts dry. She proceeded to slather him with numbweed salve and, making him lie down, massaged his back and legs. Just when he thought he'd never move again, Silvina made him get to his feet. Strangely enough, he could walk more normally. At least the numbweed deadened the muscular aches enough for him to make his own way across the court and up the three flights to the drumheights.

He slept through three drum messages the next morning, the fire lizards' feeding and half the chorus rehearsal with instruments. When he woke, Dirzan gave him time for a cup of klah and a meatroll, then quizzed him on the drum measures assigned him the day before.

To Dirzan's amazement, Piemur beat them out timeperfect. He'd had plenty of hours in which to memorize them on that runner ride. As a reward, Dirzan gave him another column of measures to learn.

The numbweed salve had worn off, and Piemur found sitting on the stool during his lesson agonizing. He had rubbed his seat bones raw, a combination of the stiffness of his new trousers and the riding. This affliction provided him with an opportunity to visit Master Oldive after lunch. Although Sebell's sacks were in evidence in Master Oldive's quarters, even to some herbs piled on the worktable, Piemur pried no new snippets of information from the Master Healer. Not even if this had been the first shipment of such medicines. He did learn that galls hurt more when treated than when sat on. Then the numbweed took over. Master Oldive said he was to use a cushion for sitting for a few days, wear older, softened pants, and ask Silvina for a conditioner to soften his wherhide.

No sooner had he returned to the drumheights, than he was sent with a message for Lord Groghe to Fort Hold, and when he came back, set to stand a listening watch.

He saw Menolly and Sebell the next morning when he fed his trio of fire lizards but, apart from a solicitous inquiry about his stiffness, the two harpers were not talkative. The next day Sebell was gone, and Piemur didn't know when or how. He was able, however, to observe, from the drumheights, the comings and goings, in and out of Fort Hold, of riders on runners, of two dragons and an incredible number of fire lizards. It occurred to him that while he had been congratulating himself on knowing most of what went on in the Harper Hall, the drumheights let him observe the larger world which, up till that day, had been unremarked by himself.

Several messages came in that afternoon, two from the north and one from the south. Three went out; one in answer to Tillek's question from the north; an originating message to Igen Tanner Hall; and the third to Master Briaret, the Masterherdsman. To tantalize him, all the messages were too quickly delivered for him to recognize more than a few phrases. Infuriated to be in a position to know more and unable to exercise the advantage to the full, Piemur memorized two columns of drum measures. If his zeal surprised Dirzan, it irritated his fellow apprentices. They presented him with several all too forceful arguments against too much application on his part. Piemur had always relied on being able to outrun any would-be adversaries, but he discovered that there was no place to run to in the drumheights. While nursing his bruises, he stubbornly learned off three more columns, though he kept this private, tempering his recitations to Dirzan. Discretion, he was learning, is required on many different levels.

He was not sorry six days later to be told to take a message to a minehold situated on an awkward ridge in the Fort Hold Range. With a signed, Harper-sealed tube of record hide, he mounted the same stolid runner beast Banak had given him for the previous trip.

Gingerly settling the seat of his now well-softened wherhide pants onto the pad, Piemur was relieved to feel no discomfort from his tail bones as the creature moved off. The journey should take him two to three hours, Banak said, as he'd pointed out to him the correct southwestern track. Three hours was probably correct, Piemur thought as his efforts to increase the pace of his runner failed. By the time the wide track had narrowed to a thinner trace, winding against a stony hillside, with deep gorges on the outside, Piemur was quite willing to let his runner go at that steady, careful pace. As he figured it would have taken the Fort Hold watchdragon only a few moments to make the trip, and the watchdragon's rider was quite willing to oblige the Masterharper of

Pern, he wondered why he'd been sent. Until he delivered his message tube to the taciturn mineholder.

"You're from the Harper Hall?" The man scowled at him dubiously.

"Apprentice to Master Olodkey, the Drummaster!" This could be some sort of test of his prudence.

"Wouldn't have thought they'd send a boy on this errand," he said with a skeptical grunt.

"I've fourteen Turns, sir," Piemur replied, trying to deepen his tone without notable success.

"No offense meant, lad."

"None taken." Piemur was pleased that his voice remained steady.

The Miner paused, his gaze drawn upward. Not, Piemur noticed, in the direction of the sun. When the Miner began to scowl, Piemur also looked up. Though why the Miner should register displeasure at the sight of three dragons in the sky, Piemur couldn't guess. True, Thread had fallen only three days before, but you'd think dragons would be a reassuring sight at any time.

"There's feed and water in the shed," said the Miner, still watching the dragons. He gestured absently over his left shoulder.

Obediently Piemur started to lead the runner around, hoping that there would be something for himself as well when he'd tended the beast. Suddenly, the Miner let out a startled oath and retreated into his holdcot. Piemur had only reached the shed when the Miner came striding after him, thrust a small bulging sack at him.

"This is what you were sent for. Tend your beast while I tend these unexpected arrivals."

Piemur's trained ear did not miss the apprehension in the Miner's tone nor the implicit command that Piemur was to remain out of sight. He made no comment, stuffing the small sack in his belt pouch while the Miner watched. The man left as Piemur vigorously pumped water into the trough for his thirsty beast. As soon as the Miner reached his cot, Piemur changed his position so that he had a clear view of the one reasonably level area of the minehold where dragons could land.

Only the bronze did. The two blues settled on the ridge above the mine opening. Sight of the great beast that backwinged to the ground told Piemur all he needed to know to understand the Miner's grimness. Before their exile south, the Oldtimers from Fort Weyr had made few appearances, but Piemur recognized Fidranth by the long sear scar on his rump and T'ron by the arrogant swagger as he strode up to the minecot. Piemur didn't need to hear the conversation to know that T'ron's manner had not altered in his Turns south. With a very stiff bow, the Miner stepped aside as T'ron, slapping his flying gloves against his thigh, strode disdainfully into the cothold. As the Miner followed, he glanced towards the shed. Piemur ducked behind the runner.

It needed little wit now to realize why the Miner had thrust the sack at him. Piemur investigated the contents: only four of the blue stones that spilled into his hand had been cut and polished. The others, ranging from one the size of his thumbnail to small uneven crystals, were rough. The blue sapphires were much prized by the Harper Hall, and stones as large as the four cut ones were mounted as badges for Masters of the Craft. Four cut stones? Four new masters walking the tables? Would Sebell be one of them, Piemur wondered.

Piemur thought a moment and then slipped the cut stones carefully, two and two, into his boots. He wiggled his feet until the stones settled, sharp lumps against his ankles but they'd not slip out. He hesitated as he was about to stow the sack in his pouch. He doubted T'ron would stoop to searching a lowly apprentice, but the stones made a suspicious bulge. Checking the leather to make sure it bore no miner's mark, he wrapped the thong on the backpad ring beside his drinking flask. Then he took off his jacket, folding the harper badge inside before he slung it over the pump handle. Trail dust had turned his blue pants to a nondescript gray.

A clink of boot nails on the ridge stone warned him and, whistling tunelessly, he picked up the beast's feet in turn, checking for stones in the cleft hooves.

"You there!"

The peremptory tone irritated Piemur. N'ton never spoke like that, even to a kitchen drudge.

"Sor?" Piemur unbent and stared around at the Oldtimer, hoping his anxious expression masked the anger he really felt. Then he glanced apprehensively at the Miner, saw a harsh wariness in the man's eyes and added in his best hillhold mumble, "Sor, he was that sweated, I've had a time cleaning him up."

"You've other work to do," said the Miner in a cold voice, jerking his head towards the cothold.

"A day too late, am I, Miner? Well, there's been yesterday's work and this morning's." The Oldtimer superciliously gestured the Miner to precede him towards the open shaft.

Piemur watched, keeping a dull expression on his face as the two men disappeared from sight. Inwardly he was right pleased with his dissembling and was positive he'd seen an approving glint in the Miner's eyes.

By the time he had finished grooming the runner from nose to dock, T'ron and the Miner had not yet reappeared. What other work would he have to do if he were a genuine miner's apprentice? It would be logical for him to stay far away from the shaft at the moment, for he'd be scared of the dragonrider if not of his master. Ah, but the Miner had indicated the cothold.

Piemur pumped water into a spare pail and lugged it back to the cothold, ogling with what he hoped was appropriate fear the blue dragons ensconced on the ridge, the riders hunkered between them.

The minecot was divided into two large rooms, one for sleeping, the other for relaxing and eating, with a small portion curtained off for the Miner's privacy. The curtain was open, and plainly the disgruntled dragonrider had searched the press, locker and bedding. In the kitchen area, every drawer was open and every door was ajar. A large cooking pot on the hearth was boiling so hard its contents frothed from under its cover. Not wishing what might be his meal in the ashes, Piemur quickly swung the pot away from the full heat of the fire. Then he began to tidy the kitchen area. No lowly apprentice would enter the Master's quarters, however humble, without direct permission. He heard voices again, the Miner's low comments and T'ron's angry reproaches. Then he heard the sounds of hammers against stone and ventured to look cautiously through the open slit window.

Six miners were squatting or kneeling, carefully chipping rough dark stone and dirt from the blue crystals possibly within. As Piemur watched, one of the miners rose, extending the palm of his hand towards the Miner. T'ron intercepted the gesture and held the small object up to the sun. Then he gave an oath, clenching his fist. For a moment, Piemur thought that the Oldtimer was going to throw the stone away.

"Is this all you're finding here now? This mine produced sapphires the size of a man's eye—"

"Four hundred Turns ago it did indeed, Dragonrider," said the Miner in an expressionless voice that could not be construed either as insolent or courteous. "We find fewer stones nowadays. The coarse dust is still good for grinding and polishing other gems," he added as the Oldtimer stared at the man carefully brushing what seemed like glistening sand into a small scoop, which he then emptied in a small lidded tub.

"I'm not interested in dust, Miner, or flawed crystals." He held up his clenched fist. "I want good, sizeable sapphires."

He continued to stand there, glaring at each of the miners in turn as they tapped cautiously away. Piemur, hoping that no larger sapphires would be discovered, made himself busy in the kitchen.

By the time the sun was westering behind the highest of the ridges, only six medium to small sapphires had rewarded T'ron's afternoon vigil. Piemur was not the only one to watch, half-holding his breath, as the Oldtimer stalked to Fidranth and mounted. The old bronze showed no faltering as he neatly lifted in the air, joined by the two blues. Only when the three had winked out *between* did the miners break into angry talk, crowding up to the Miner, who brushed them aside in his urgency to get to the minecot.

"I see why you're a messenger, young Piemur," said the Miner. "You've all your wits about you." Grinning, he extended his hand.

Piemur grinned back and pointed towards his backpad and the sack with its precious contents, looped in plain sight to the ring. He heard the Miner's astonished oath, which turned into a roar of laughter.

"You mean, he spent all afternoon facing what he wanted?" cried the Miner.

"I did put the cut gems in my boots," Piemur said with a grimace for one of the stones had rubbed his ankle raw.

As the Miner retrieved the sack, the others began to cheer, for they'd had no chance to learn that the Miner had managed to save the product of several sevendays' labor. Piemur found himself much admired for his quick thinking as well as his timely arrival.

"Did you read my mind, lad," asked the Miner, "to know that I'd told the old grasper I'd sent the gems off yesterday?"

"It seemed only logical," Piemur replied. He'd taken his boots off just then, examining the scratches the sapphires had made. "It would've been a crying shame to let old T'ron get away with these beauties!"

"And what are we going to do, Master," asked the oldest journeyman, "when those Oldtimers come back again in a few sevendays' and take what we've mined? That placer's not played out yet."

"We're closing up here tomorrow," said the Miner.

"Why? We've just found more—"

The Miner signaled silence abruptly.

"Each craft has its privacies," said Piemur, grinning broadly. If the Miner felt an apprentice required no apology for such curtness, he would not be admonished for impertinence for repeating a well-known rule. "But I shall have to mention this to Master Robinton, if only to explain why I'm so late returning."

"You must tell the Masterharper, lad. He's got to know if no one else. I'll tell Masterminer Nicat." Then he swung about the room with a warning look at each of his own craftmen. "You all understand that this matter goes no further? Well and good. T'ron got only a few flawed stones—you were all very clever with your hammers today, though I deplore cracking good sapphires." The Miner sighed heavily for that necessity. "Master Nicat will know which other miners to warn. Let the Oldtimers seek if it amuses them." When the older journeyman laughed derisively, the Miner went on, raising an admonishing finger at him. "Enough! They are dragonmen, and they did help Benden Weyr and Pern when aid was badly needed!" Then he turned to Piemur. "Did you save any of our stew, lad? I've the appetite of a queen dragon after clutching."

Chapter 4

That day held one more event! At sunset, as Piemur was helping the apprentice bring in the miners' runners from the pasture, he heard the shrill cry of a fire lizard. Glancing up, he saw a slender body, wings back, drop with unnerving speed in his direction. The apprentice dropped to the ground, covering his head with his arms. Piemur braced his legs, but the bronze fire lizard did not come to his shoulder. Instead, Rocky spun round his head, berating him, his jewel-faceted eyes spinning violently red and orange in anger.

It took Piemur a few minutes to talk Rocky into landing on his shoulder and even more time to soothe the little creature until his eyes calmed into tones of greeny blue. All the time the miner apprentice watched, eyes bugged out.

"There now, Rocky. I'm all right, but I have to stay the night here. I'm all right. You can tell Menolly that you've found me, can't you? That I'm all right?"

Rocky gave a half-chirp that sounded so skeptical Piemur had to laugh.

"Is that fire lizard yours?" asked the Miner curiously as he approached Piemur, eyeing Rocky all the time.

"No, sir," said Piemur with such chagrin the Miner smiled. "This is one of Menolly's, Master Robinton's journeywoman. His name is Rocky. I help Menolly feed him mornings, because she's got the nine and they're a right handful, so he knows me pretty well."

"I didn't think the creatures had enough sense to find people!"

"Well, sir, I have to say it's the first time it's happened to me," and Piemur couldn't suppress the smug satisfaction he was feeling that Rocky had been able to find him.

"Now that he's found you, what good will that do?" asked the Miner with a revival of his skepticism.

"Well, sir, he could go back to Menolly and make her understand that he's seen me. But it would be much more useful if you'd let me have a bit of hide for a message. Tied on his leg, he'll take it back, and they'll know exactly. . . ."

The Miner held up his hand admonishingly. "I'd rather nothing in script about the Oldtimers' visit."

"Of course not, sir," replied Piemur, offended that he needed to be cautioned.

A terse message was all he could scribe on the scrap of hide the Miner grudgingly produced for him. The hide was so old, had been scraped so often for messages, that the ink blurred as he wrote. "Safe! Delayed!" Then it occurred to him to add in drum measures, "Errand completed. Emergency. Old Dragon."

"You've a way with the little things, haven't you?" said the Miner with reluctant respect as he watched Piemur tying the message on Rocky's leg, an operation the fire lizard oversaw as carefully as the Miner.

"He knows he can trust me," said Piemur.

"I'd say there were not many," replied the Miner in such a dry tone that Piemur stared at him in surprise. "No offense meant!"

Piemur had to concentrate just then on imagining Menolly as strongly as he could in his mind. Then, lifting his hand high, he gave a practiced flick to send Rocky into flight.

"Go to Menolly, Rocky! Go to Menolly!"

He and the Miner watched until the little fire lizard seemed to disappear in the dimming light to the east. Then the apprentice called them to their meal.

As he ate, Piemur wondered what the Miner had meant by that remark. "Not many that fire lizards could trust?" "Not many people that trusted Piemur?" Why would the Miner say a thing like that? Hadn't he saved the miners' sapphires for them? It wasn't as if he'd told any lies to do so. Further he'd never taken any real advantage of his friends in bargaining at a Gather or failing to keep a promise. All of his friends came to him for help. And, Shells, wasn't the Masterharper entrusting him with this errand? And knowing about Harper Hall secrets? What had the Miner meant?

"Piemur!" Someone shook him by the shoulder.

Abruptly the young harper realized that he'd been addressed several times.

"You're a harper! Can you not give us a song?"

The eagerness of the request from men isolated for long periods of time in a lonely hold gave Piemur a genuine pang of regret.

"Sirs, the reason I'm messenger is that my voice is changing and I'm not allowed to sing just now. But," he added seeing the intense disappointment on every face, "that doesn't mean I can't talk them to you. If you've something I can drum to give the rhythm."

After several attempts, he found a saucepan that did not sound too flat, and while the men stomped their heavy boots in time, he talked the newest songs from the Harper Hall, even giving them Domick's new song about Lessa. The Shell knew when they'd hear it sung, though no one was supposed to hear it until Lord Groghe's feast. If the performance of the spoken song lacked much in Piemur's estimation, Master Shonagar couldn't hear, Domick would never know, and the men were so grateful that he felt completely justified.

He left the minehold with the first rays of the sun and made the trip back to the Harper Hall at a downhill pace that all but forced his voice back up to the treble range. At times his runner slithered unnervingly down tracks that they had laboriously climbed the day before. Piemur closed his eyes, held tightly to the saddle pad, and fervently hoped not to go sailing off the track into the deep gorges. When he returned the stolid runner to Banak, it was barely sweated under the midstrap while Piemur knew that his armpits and back were damp with perspiration.

"Safe back, I see," was Banak's only remark.

"He may be slow, but he's sure-footed," said Piemur with such exaggerated relief that Banak laughed.

As Piemur jogged into the Harper Hall court, he heard Tilgin bravely singing his first solo as Lessa. Piemur grinned to himself, for Tilgin's voice sounded tired even if he was note-wise. None of Menolly's fair was sunning on the ridge, but Zair was sprawled on the ledge of the Harper's window so Piemur took the steps two at a time. While he sort of wished someone would encounter him on his triumphant return, he was also relieved that he'd have no temptation to blurt out his adventures.

Master Robinton's greeting, however, was warm enough to make Piemur puff his chest out in pride.

"You make the most of your opportunities, young Piemur—but kindly explain your cryptic measures before I burst with curiosity! 'Old dragon' does mean oldtimers, I take it?"

"Yes, sir," and Piemur took the seat the Harper indicated and began. "T'ron and Fidranth with two blue dragons came to relieve the Miner of his sapphires!"

"You're positive beyond doubt that it was T'ron and Fidranth?"

"Positive! I did see them once or twice before they were exiled. Besides, the Miner knew them all too well."

The Harper gestured for him to continue, and the day's events made good telling with the best of all audiences in the Masterharper, who listened intently without a single interruption. He then asked Piemur to repeat, this time questioning a detail here, a response there, and extracting from Piemur every nuance of the confrontation of Miner and

Oldtimer. He laughed appreciatively at Piemur's strategy and lauded his caution of putting the four cut gems in his boots. It was only then that Piemur remembered to hand the precious stones to the Harper. The sun sparkled off the facets as the sapphires lay on the table.

"I'll have a word with Master Nicat myself. And I think I'll see him today," said Robinton, holding up one of the gems between thumb and forefinger and squinting at it in the sunlight. "Beautiful workmanship! Not a flaw!"

"That's what the Miner said," and then Piemur daringly added. "I gather it's not easy to find the right blues for masterharpers."

Master Robinton regarded Piemur, a startled expression on his face, which changed to amusement. "You will keep that to yourself as well, young man!"

Piemur nodded solemnly. "Of course, if I'd had a fire lizard of my own, you wouldn't have had to worry about me and the stones, and perhaps something could have been done about T'ron."

The Harper's face altered and the flash in his eyes had nothing to do with amusement. Now Piemur couldn't imagine what had prompted him to say such a thing. He didn't even dare look away from the Harper's severe gaze, although he wanted more than anything else to creep away and hide from his Master's disapproval. He did stiffen, fully expecting a blow for such impertinence.

"When you can keep your wits about you as you did yesterday, Piemur," said Master Robinton after an interminable interval, "you prove Menolly's good opinion of your potential. You have also just proved the main criticism that Hall masters have expressed. I do not disapprove of ambition, nor the ability to think independently, but," and suddenly his voice lost the cold displeasure, "presumption is unforgiveable. Presuming to criticize a dragonrider is the most dangerous offense against discretion. Further," and the Harper's finger was raised in warning, "you are rushing towards a privilege you have by no means earned. Now, off with you to Master Olodkey and learn the proper drummeasure for 'Oldtimer.' "

The kindly note in his tone was almost too much for Piemur, who could more easily have borne blows and a tirade for his transgressions. He made his way to the door as fast as his leaden legs could bear him.

"Piemur!" Robinton's voice checked him as he fumbled for the latch. "You did handle yourself very well at the Minehold. Only do," and the Harper sounded as resigned as Master Shonagar often had, "do please try to guard your quick tongue!"

"Oh, sir, I'll try as hard as I can, really I will!" His voice cracked ignominiously, and he spun around the door so that the Harper wouldn't see the tears of shame and relief in his eyes.

He stood for a moment in the quiet hall, intensely grateful that it was empty at this time of day as he conquered dismay at his untimely insolence. The Harper was so right: he had to learn to think before he spoke; he never should have blurted out that unfortunate criticism of dragonriders. He'd've rated a right sound beating from any other Master. Domick wouldn't have hesitated a moment, nor even languid Master Shonagar, whose hand he'd felt many a time for his brashness. But how had he dared criticize dragonriders, even Oldtimers, to Master Robinton? Certainly that took the prize for impudence, even from him.

Piemur shivered and vowed fervently to mind his thoughts and, even more carefully, his tongue. Particularly now, when he did know something of real significance. For he had been aware, previous to his imprudent comment, that the appearance of the Oldtimers at the mine, not to mention their errand, was unwelcome news to the Harper.

Besides, what *could* have been done about the Oldtimers' illegal return to the North?

Piemur gave his own ear a clout that made his eyes swim and then started down the corridor. Now, how was he to find out the drum code for Oldtimers? Under the circumstances he couldn't just ask Dirzan outright without having to explain why he needed to know. Nor could he ask one of the other apprentices. They were annoyed enough with him and his quick studying. There'd be a way, he was sure.

Then he wondered why Master Robinton had asked him to find out. Was it a code he'd need? Did that mean the Harper expected this wouldn't be the first such visit by the Oldtimers? Or what?

The speculations on this subject occupied Piemur's mind off and on for the next few days until he did have the chance to check the code.

Somewhat to Piemur's disgust, Dirzan treated him as if he had deliberately protracted his errand to avoid polishing the drums. This was his first task, and because Piemur couldn't polish when the drums were in use, it dragged on until the midday meal.

That afternoon Piemur began to participate in another activity of the drumheights, since he had unfortunately learned the drum measures so well. All apprentices were supposed to stop and listen when messages came in and write down what they heard, if they could. Then Dirzan checked their interpretations of the message. It seemed harmless enough, but Piemur soon learned that it was one more road to trouble for him. All drum messages were considered private information. A bit silly to Piemur's way of thinking, since most journeymen and all masters had to be adept in drum messages. A full third of the Harper Hall would understand most of a drum message booming across the valley. Nonetheless, if word of something especially sensitive became common knowledge about the Hall, it was deemed the fault of a gossipy drum apprentice. Piemur was twigged for that role now!

When Dirzan first accused him of loose talk, a day or two after he started writing messages, he stared in utter astonishment at the journeyman. And got a hard clout across the head for it.

"Don't try your ways on me, Piemur. I'm well aware of your tricks."

"But, sir, I'm only in the Hall at mealtimes, and sometimes not even then."

"Don't answer back!"

"But, sir . . ."

Dirzan fetched him another clout, and Piemur nursed his grievance in silence, rapidly trying to figure out which of the other apprentices was making mischief for him. Probably Clell! And how was he going to stop it? He certainly didn't want Master Robinton to hear such a wretched lie.

Two days later a rather urgent message for Master Oldive was drummed through from Nabol. As Piemur was on duty, he was dispatched with it to the Healer. Mindful of a possible repeat accusation, Piemur noted that no one was about in court or hall as he delivered his message. Master Oldive bade him wait for a reply which he wrote on a then carefully folded sheet. Piemur raced across the empty court, up the stairs to the drumheights and arrived out of breath, shoving the note into Dirzan's hand.

"There! Still in its original folds. I met no one coming or going."

Dirzan stared at Piemur, his scowl deepening. "You're being insolent again." He raised his hand.

Piemur stepped back deliberately, catching sight of the other apprentices watching the scene with great interest. The especially eager glint in Clell's eyes confirmed Piemur's suspicion.

"No, I'm trying to prove to you that I'm no babblemouth, even if I did understand that message. Lord Meron of Nabol is ill and requires Master Oldive urgently. But who'd care if *he* died after what he's done to Pern?"

Piemur knew he'd merited Dirzan's blow then and didn't duck.

"You'll learn to keep a civil tongue in your head, Piemur, or it's back to the runner hold for you."

"I've a right to defend my honor! And I can!" Piemur caught himself just in time before he blurted out that Master Robinton could attest to his discretion. As rife with rumor as the Harper Hall generally was, there hadn't been a whisper about the Oldtimers' raid on the mine.

"How?" Dirzan's single derisive word told Piemur forcibly how very difficult that would be without being rightfully accused of indiscretion. "I'll figure a way. You'll see!" Piemur glared impotently at the delighted grins of the other apprentices.

That night, when everyone else slept through the dead hours, Piemur lay awake, restless with agitation. The more he examined his problem, the harder it was to solve it without being indiscreet on some count or another. When he'd still been free to chatter with his friends, he could have asked the help of Brolly, Bonz, Timiny or Ranly. Among them, they'd surely have been able to discover a solution. If he approached Menolly or Sebell about such a piffling problem, they might decide he wasn't the right lad for their needs. They might even consider his complaint a lack of discretion in itself.

How right Master Robinton had been when he said that Piemur might possibly be plagued into disclosing matters best left unmentioned! Only how could the Harper have known that Piemur was stuck in the one discipline, as a drum apprentice, where he was most likely to be accused of indiscretions?

One possibility presented itself to his questioning mind: the apprentices, even Clell as the oldest, were still plodding through the medium hard drum measures. Therefore some parts of every long message reaching the Harper Hall were incomprehensible to them. Now, if Piemur learned drum language beat perfect, he'd understand the messages in full. Not that he'd let Dirzan know that when he wrote the message down for him. But he'd keep a private record of everything he translated. Then, the next time there was a rumor of a half-understood message, Piemur would prove to Dirzan that he had known *all* the message, not just the parts the other apprentices had understood.

To further achieve his end, Piemur kept to the drumheights even at mealtimes. Preferably within the sight of Dirzan, the Master, or one of the other duty journeymen. If he wasn't near others, he couldn't be accused of gossiping to them. Even when he was sent on message-runs, he made the return trip so fast no one could possibly accuse him of dawdling and gossiping on the way. The only other time he was in the court was to help Menolly feed the fire lizards. Messages came through, some of them urgent, some tempting enough, Piemur would have thought, for one of the apprentices to repeat, but no whisper of rumor repaid his immolation. In despair he gave up his plan and tore up the messages he had written. But he still held himself away from others.

He wasn't certain how much more of this he could endure when Menolly appeared in the drumheights just after breakfast one morning.

"I need a messenger today," she said to Dirzan.

"Clell would—"

"No. I want Piemur."

"Now, Menolly, I wouldn't mind letting him go for a minor errand but—"

"Piemur is Master Robinton's choice," she said with a shrug, "and he's cleared this with Master Olodkey. Piemur, get your gear together."

Piemur blandly ignored the black looks Clell directed his way as he crossed the living room.

"Menolly, I think you ought to mention to Master Robinton that we haven't found Piemur too reliable—"

"Piemur? Unreliable?"

Piemur had been about to whip round and defy Dirzan, but the amused condescension in Menolly's tone was a far better defense than any he could muster under his circumstances. In one mild question, Menolly had given Dirzan, not to mention Clell and the others, a lot to think about.

"Oh, he's been bleating to you, has he?"

Piemur could hear the sneer in the journeyman's voice. He took a deep breath and continued to gather his things.

"In point of fact," and now Menolly sounded puzzled, "he's not been talkative at all, apart from commenting on the weather and the condition of my fire lizards. Should he have reason to bleat, Dirzan?"

Piemur half-ran back into the room, to forestall any explanation by the journeyman. This opportunity was playing beautifully into his hands.

"I'm ready to go, Menolly."

"Yes, and we have to move fast." It was obvious to Piemur that Menolly had wanted to hear Dirzan's reply. "I'll be back to you on this, Dirzan. C'mon, Piemur!"

She led the way down the steps at a clatter, and only when they had passed the first landing did she turn to him.

"What have you been up to, Piemur?"

"I haven't been up to anything," he replied with such vehemence that Menolly grinned at him. "That's the trouble."

"Your reputation's caught up with you?"

"More than that. It's being used against me." As much as Piemur wanted to expand, the less he said, he decided, even to Menolly, the stronger his position.

"The other apprentices against you? Yes, I saw their expressions. What did you do to set them so?"

"Learned drum measures too fast is all I can think of."

"You sure?"

"I'm bloody sure, Menolly. D'you think I'd do anything to get in the Masterharper's bad record?"

"No," she said thoughtfully as they skipped down the last flight. "No, you wouldn't. Look, we'll sort it out when we come back. There's a Gather today at Igen Hold. Sebell and I are to be there as harpers, but Master Robinton wants you to play scruffy boy apprentice."

"Can I ask why?" Piemur delivered the question on the end of a long suffering sigh.

Menolly laughed and reached out to ruffle his hair.

"You can, but I've no answer. We weren't told either. He just wants you to wander about the Gather and listen."

"Has he got Oldtimers on his mind?" Piemur asked as casually as he could.

"I'd say he probably does," Menolly answered after a thoughtful moment. "He's been worried. I may be his journeywoman, but I don't always know what's on his mind. Neither does Sebell!"

They had reached the archway now and turned towards the Gather meadow.

"I'm to ride a dragon?" asked Piemur. He lurched to a stop, his eyes bunging out at the scene before him. Bronze Lioth was shaking his wings out in the sun, his great jeweled eyes gleaming blue-green as he turned his head to watch the antics of the fire lizards. Dwarfed by his bulk, the tall figures of N'ton, Fort Weyrleader, and Sebell stood by his shoulder.

"C'mon, Piemur. We mustn't keep them waiting. The Gather at Igen is already well started."

Piemur struggled into his wherhide jacket, making that an excuse for falling behind Menolly. Actually he was both terrified and overjoyed at the prospect of riding a dragon! All those cloddies up there in the drumheights! He hoped that they were watching, that they'd see him riding off on a dragon! That'd teach them to smear his reputation. He pushed from his mind the corollary that the privilege of flying a dragonback would make his lot with his fellow apprentices that much harder. What mattered was the now! Piemur was going to ride a dragon.

N'ton had always been Piemur's ideal of a dragon rider: tall, with a really broad set of shoulders, dark brown hair slightly curled from being confined under a riding helmet, an easy, confident air reflected by a direct gaze and a ready smile. The contrast between this present Fort Weyrleader and his disgruntled predecessor, T'ron, was more vividly apparent as N'ton smilingly greeted the harper's apprentice.

"Sorry your voice changed, Piemur. I'd been looking forward to Lord

Groghe's Gather and that new Saga I've heard so much about from Menolly. Have you ridden dragonback before, Piemur? No? Well, up with you, Menolly. Show Piemur the knack."

As Piemur attentively watched Menolly grab the riding strap and half-walk up Lioth's shoulder, swing her leg agilely over the last neck ridge, he still couldn't believe his good fortune. He could just imagine T'ron permitting a journeyman, much less an apprentice lad, to ride his bronze.

"See how it was done? Good. Up with you then, Piemur!" Sebell gave him an initial boost, and Menolly leaned over with a helping hand and a guide rope. It seemed a long way up a dragon's shoulder.

Piemur grabbed the rope and just as he planted his booted foot on Lioth's shoulder, he wondered if he'd hurt the dragon's smooth hide.

N'ton laughed. "No, you won't hurt Lioth with your boots! But he thanks you for worrying."

Piemur was so startled that he almost lost his grip.

"Reach up, Piemur," Menolly ordered.

"I didn't know he'd hear me," he said in a gasp as he settled astride Lioth's neck.

"Dragons hear what they choose to," she said, grinning. "Sit back against me. Sebell's got to fit in front of you!"

The words were barely out of her mouth before Sebell had swung up with the ease of considerable practice and settled himself before Piemur. N'ton followed, passing back the riding straps. Piemur thought that a needless caution. His legs were wedged so tightly between Menolly's and Sebell's, he couldn't have moved if he had to. Then Sebell peered over his shoulder at him.

"You'll have heard a lot about *between,* I expect, but I'll warn you now: it's scary even when you know what to expect."

"Right, Piemur," Menolly added, circling his waist with her arms. "I've got you tight, and you hang on to Sebell's belt."

"You won't feel once we're *between,*" Sebell continued. "There's nothing *between* except cold. You won't be able to feel Lioth beneath your legs nor our legs against yours, nor your hands about my belt. But the sensation lasts only a few heartbeats. They'll sound very loud to you. Just count 'em. We'll be doing the same thing, I assure you!" Sebell's grin absolved Piemur from any expression of fear or doubt.

Piemur nodded, not trusting himself to speak. He didn't care what happened *between.* At least, he would have experienced it, which very few apprentice harpers could say.

Suddenly there was a great heave, and he cracked his chin against Sebell's shoulderblade. Inadvertently looking down, he saw the ground moving away from him as Lioth sprang skyward. He could feel the great muscles along Lioth's neck as the fragile-seeming wings took their first all-important downsweep. Then the Gather meadow and the Harper Hall seemed to rush away, and they were on a level with the Hold fire-heights.

Sebell gave Piemur's hands, clutching his belt, a warning squeeze. The next heartbeat and there was nothing but a cold so intense that it was pain. Except that Piemur couldn't feel pain with his body, only sense that his lack of tactile contact with reality included everything except the wild beating of his heart against his ribcage. Ruthlessly he clamped down on the instinct to scream. Then they were back in the world again, Lioth gliding effortlessly down to the right, a tremendous expanse of golden ground beneath his wings. Piemur shuddered again and kept his eyes fixed on Sebell's shoulders. Hard as Piemur wished he wouldn't, Lioth continued to glide downward, dipping sideways at unnerving angles. Suddenly Piemur could hear fire lizards chittering, and despite his resolve not to look around, found himself watching them zip about the dragon.

"It is scarey to look down," Menolly's voice said in his ear. "It's worse when they . . . ahhhhh. . . ."

Piemur felt his stomach drop and, to his horror, his seat seemed to leave the dragon's neck. He gasped and clutched more tightly at Sebell, feeling the man's diaphragm muscles move as he chuckled.

"That's what I mean!" said Menolly. "N'ton says it's only air currents, pushing the dragons up or letting them down."

"Oh, is that all?" Piemur managed to get the words out in a rush, but his voice betrayed him. "All" came out in a two-octave crack.

Menolly didn't laugh, and he felt more kindly toward her than at any other time in their association.

"It always scares me," she said in a comforting shout by his left ear.

He was just getting accustomed to this additional hazard of flying dragonback when Lioth seemed to be diving straight for the Igen River bed. He was pressed back against Menolly and didn't know whether to clutch more fiercely at Sebell's belt or relax into the pressure.

"Don't forget to breathe!" Menolly was shouting and, at that, he barely heard her words as the wind ripped sound away.

Then Lioth leveled and began to circle at a gentler rate of descent towards the now-visible rectangle of a Gather. To the left was the river, a broad, muddy stream between red sandstone banks. Small sailing craft skimmed the surface on a current that must be swifter than the turgid surface suggested. To the right was the broad, clean-swept rock shelf that led up to Igen Hold, a safe distance above the highest flood marks left by the river on the sandstone banks. Behind Igen Hold rose curious, wind-fashioned cliffs, some of which made additional holds for Igen's people, for there were no rows of cotholds adjoining the main Hold here. Igen Hold also had no fire-heights, not needing any since there was nothing but sand and stone around the Hold proper, to which Thread could do no harm. The lands that supplied Igen Hold were around the next bend of the river, where the waters had been led inland by canals to supply water-grain fields.

Piemur wasn't sure that he would like living in such a barren-looking Hold, even if no Thread could ever attack it. And it was hot!

Red dust puffed up as Lioth landed, and suddenly Piemur was unbearably warm. He began to unbelt his wherhide jacket before he released the riding strap and noticed that Menolly was as quick to strip helmet, gloves and jacket.

"I always forget how hot it is at Igen," she said, fluffing out her hair.

"The dragons love it," said N'ton, pointing beyond the Hold to where the rough shapes that Piemur had assumed were rock now became recognizable as dragons, stretched out to bake in the sun.

It was as he was sliding down Lioth's shoulder that Piemur noticed the curious construction of the Gather rectangle. There didn't seem to be any walkway. The only open space was the customary central square for dancing. Though who'd have the energy to dance in this heat he didn't know.

Then Piemur ducked while Lioth showered them all with sand as he vaulted into the air and winged to join the other sunbathing dragons. The fire lizards—N'ton's Tris, Sebell's Kimi and Menolly's nine—swirled up and away and were met, midair, by other fire lizards, the augmented fair swirling higher and higher in the joy of meeting.

"That'll occupy them for a while," said Menolly, then she turned to Piemur. "Give me your flying gear and I'll leave it at the Hold till you need it again."

"We must pay our respects to Lord Laudey and the others," said Sebell, bringing out a handful of marks from his pocket. He presented Piemur with an eighth piece and two thirty-seconds. "I'm not being stingy, Piemur, but you'd be questioned if you had too many marks about you. And I don't think Igen Hold runs to bubbly pies."

"Too hot to eat 'em anyway." Piemur mopped his sweaty forehead with one hand as he gratefully slid the marks into his pouch.

"But they do make a confection of fruits that you might like," said Sebell. "Anyway, move around and listen. Don't get caught being nosy and come up to the Hold for the evening meal. Ask for Harper Bantur if you have any trouble. Or Deece. He remembers you."

They had reached the edge of the Gather tents, and now Piemur realized that walking space existed but was considerably covered with tenting to deflect the worst of the sun's baking heat. It was simple now for Piemur to move away from the journeymen harpers and the Weyrleader in the steady flow of people sauntering past the Gather stalls. He saw Menolly turn about, trying to see where he had got to, then Sebell spoke to her, and she shrugged and moved on with him.

Almost immediately Piemur noticed one great difference between this and the Gathers he had attended in the west: people took their time. In order to separate himself from his craftmates, Piemur had deliberately lagged behind, but when he would have stepped out again at his customary pace, he hesitated. No one was moving briskly at all. Gestures and voices were languid, smiles slow, and even laughter had a lazy fall. A great many people carried long tubes from which they sipped. Stalls dispensing drinks, chilled water, as well as sliced fruits, were frequently placed and well-patronized. About every ten stalls or so, there were areas where people lounged, either on the sand or on benches placed about the edges. The tenting was raised in corners to catch breezes sweeping up from the river, cooling the lounge areas and the walkway.

Piemur did one complete walkabout of the Gather rectangle. He could appreciate that, despite breezeways and the expenditure of the minimum of physical effort, people did not do much talking as they strolled from stall to stall. The talking, either conversation or bartering, was done while both parties sat comfortably. So he used one thirty-second piece on a long tube of fruit juice and some succulent slices of a rind-melon, found himself an inconspicuous spot in one lounge area, and settled to listen as he sipped his drink and ate.

At first he didn't quite catch the softer drawl of these south-easterners. The low-pitched conversation between two men on his left turned out to be the innocuous boasting of one about the breeding lines of the splay-footed runners he was hoping to barter profitably while the other man kept extolling the virtues of the currently favored strain. Disgusted at such a waste of his time, Piemur focused his ears on the group of five men on his right. They were blaming the weather on Thread, the bad crops on the weather and everything else except their lack of industry, which Piemur thought would be the real problem. A group of women were also murmuring against the weather, their mates, their children and the nuisancy children of other holds, but all in a fairly comfortable, tolerantly amused fashion. Three men, with their heads so close together no sound passed their shoulders, finally parted, but not before Piemur saw a small sack pass from one to another and decided that they must only have been bargaining hard. The runnermen

left and a new pair took their places, composed their loose robes about
them, leaned back and promptly went to sleep. Piemur found himself
growing more heavy-eyed and sipped the last of his juice to keep him
awake, wondering if he would find another lounge area as dull.

A combination of excited voices and a chill breeze woke him. He
stared about him, wondering if he had missed a drum message, and then
oriented himself. Night had fallen and, with the set of sun, the cooler
winds of evening blew cheerfully through the raised flaps. There was no
one else in the tent with him, but he could smell the aroma of roasting
meats and scrambled to his feet. He'd be late at the Hold for his supper,
and he was hungry.

Cool evening had enlivened everyone, for the walkway was now full
of quickly stepping, chattering people, and Piemur had to duck and dart
his way out of the Gather tents. The dragon lumps on the Hold cliff
turned their brilliant lanterns of eyes on the doings below them, rivaling
the blazing glow baskets set on high standards about the Gather
grounds.

No one challenged Piemur at the Hold courtyard gates, and he found
the main Hall by simply following the general drift of the well-dressed
people.

Lord Laudey, according to Harper Hall gossip, was not a very outgo-
ing man, but at a Gather, every Holder did make an effort. The princi-
pal men and craftmasters of his Hold were invited with their immediate
families to dine in the Hold Hall, as well as such dragonriders and
visiting Lord Holders, Craftmasters and Masters who might be attending the Gather.

By custom, the harpers ate at the first table below the main one.
Piemur had never seen the resident Harper, Bantur, and hoped that
Menolly and Sebell were already at the table. They were, and chatting
in high spirits with Deece, who'd been seconded to Bantur the night
Menolly had walked the tables to become a journeywoman, and with
Strud, who'd been posted to a sea hold on Igen River that same night.
Gray of hair but with bright and unusually blue eyes, Bantur welcomed
Piemur with such friendliness for a mere apprentice that Piemur was
made more uncomfortable by kindness than he would have been by
taciturnity. Bantur insisted on getting him fresh meats and tubers from
one of the drudges and heaped his plate so high with choice cuts that
Piemur's eyes goggled.

The other harpers talked while he ate, and when he had finally swallowed the last morsel, Bantur suggested they all leave to make room for
more of Lord Laudey's guests. Then Bantur asked if Piemur would take

a harper's turn on drum or gitar and, when Piemur saw Sebell's discreet nod, he agreed with a show of enthusiasm to take a gitar part.

"Why Piemur, I thought sure you'd take a drum part," said Menolly, her expression so bland that he nearly rose to her bait.

Piemur restrained an urge to kick her in the shins and smiled sweetly at her instead. "You heard today what the drummers think of me," he replied so demurely that Menolly chortled until her eyes filled.

As the harpers filed out of the Hall for the Gather, Sebell fell in step with Piemur.

"Heard anything of interest?"

"Who talks during the day's heat?" asked Piemur with heartfelt disgust. He suspected that Sebell had known about desert daytime indolence.

"You'll notice the change in them now, and you'll only need to do the dance turns. If I gauge the Gather right," said Sebell, glancing ahead at Menolly's slender figure in harper blue, "they'll keep her singing until she's hoarse. They always do."

Piemur glanced swiftly at Sebell, wondering if the journeyman was aware of showing his feelings for the harper girl so openly.

The first dance turn was the longest and the most energetic. The crisp night air stimulated the dancers' gyrations until they were energetic beyond Piemur's credence. Quite a transformation from the languid manners of the afternoon. Then, as Bantur, Deece, Strud and Menolly remained on the platform to sing, Sebell nodded to Piemur to work his way from the square's attentive audience towards the smaller groups of men, drinking tubes in hand, conversing in quiet tones.

The subdued level, Piemur decided, was out of courtesy to the singers and their audience, but it made it hard for him. He was about to give up when the word "Oldtimers" caught his ear. He sidled closer to the group and, in the light of the glow baskets, recognized two as seaholders, a miner, a smith and an Igen holder.

"I don't say it was them, but since they've gone south, we've had no more unexpected demands," said the smith. "G'narish may also be an Oldtimer, but he follows Benden's ways. So it had to have been Oldtimers."

"Young Toric often sends his two-master north for trade," said one of the seaholders, in a voice so confidential that Piemur had to strain to catch the words. "He always has, and my Holder sees no harm in it. Toric's no dragonman, and those that stayed south with him don't fall under Benden's order. So we trade. He may bargain close, but he pays well."

"In marks?" asked the Igen holder, surprised.

"No. Barter! Gemstones, hides, fruit, such like. And once"—here Piemur held his breath for fear of missing the confidential whisper—"nine fire lizard eggs!"

"No?" Envy as well as surprised interest were expressed in that startled reply. The seaholder quickly gestured the man to keep his tone down. "Of course," and there was no disguising the bitter jealousy, "they've all the sand beaches in the world to search in the south! Any chance . . ."

The fascinating conversation broke off as another seaholder joined them, an older man, and possibly superior to the gossiping seaman, for talk turned to other things, and Piemur moved on.

Then Menolly began to sing alone, the other harpers accompanying her. All conversations died as she sang, with what appeared to Piemur to be incredible aptness, the "Fire Lizard Song."

Her voice was richer now, Piemur noticed with a critical ear, the tone better sustained. He couldn't fault her musical phrasing. Nor should he be able to after three Turns of severe instruction by Master Shonagar. Her voice was so admirably suited to the songs she sang, he thought, and more expressive than many singers who had even better natural voices. As often as Piemur had heard the "Fire Lizard Song," he found himself listening as intently as ever. When the song ended, he applauded as vigorously as everyone else, only then aware that he had been equally captivated. Putting words to music was not Menolly's only talent; she put her music in the hearts and minds of her listeners, too.

While her enrapt audience started shouting for their favorite tunes, she beckoned Sebell to the platform, and they sang a duet of an eastern sea hold song, their voices so well blended that Piemur's respect and admiration for his fellow harpers reached unprecedented heights. Now, if only his voice turned tenor, he might have the chance to sing with. . . .

He played three more dance turns, but Sebell had been correct: the Igen gatherers wanted Menolly whenever she would favor them with song. Piemur also noticed that for every solo she sang, there was at least one group song and a duet including the Igen harpers. Clever of her to forestall ill-feeling. Too bad such discretion did not translate into his particular problem with the drum apprentices!

Whether it was because he'd had a sleep in the afternoon or because the desert air was particularly bracing, Piemur was never sure, but it was only when he noticed the thinning of the crowd around the dance area, and the increased number of people rolled up in their blankets in the Gather tents, that he began to feel fatigue. He looked around then for Sebell and Menolly. When he saw nothing of them, he finally sought a weary, yawning Strud, who advised him, with a grin, to find a corner and get some sleep, if he could.

It had been easy enough to sleep that afternoon, but now, with no heat to lull him, the things he had heard—music as well as malice—danced about in his mind. One positive fact emerged: the Oldtimers' descent on the miner in Fort Hold was not an isolated incident. He also knew that while G'narish, Igen's Oldtime Weyrleader, was respected, Igen Holders would have given much to be beholden to Benden instead.

A sharp peck on his ear woke him, and he had a momentary fright before he focused his eyes on Rocky's cocked head and heard the reassuring soft chirrup. Someone was snoring lustily beside him, and Piemur's back was warm. He cautiously eased away from this unknown sleeper.

Rocky chirped again and, hopping off his shoulder, walked a few paces away with exaggerated steps before looking back at Piemur. He wanted Piemur to come with him, and while his eyes were not red with hunger, they were whirling fast enough to indicate some urgency.

"I don't need a drum to get your message," Piemur said under his breath as he moved further away from his snoring bed companion. He really must have been tired to sleep through that sort of racket.

Rocky landed on his right shoulder, poking at his cheek to force his head left. Piemur obediently ducked under the tent flap and, in the glows that were shedding a subdued waning light on the sands before Igen Hold, he saw the dark bulk of a dragon and several figures.

Rocky called in a sweet light voice and then took off towards the group. Piemur followed, yawning and shivering in the chill pre-dawn breeze, wishing he had some klah. Especially if the presence of a dragon meant he had to go *between;* he was cold enough already.

The dragon was not Lioth, as he'd half expected, but a brown nearly as big as the Fort Weyr dragon. It had to be Canth. And it was, for as he neared the group, he saw the scars on F'nor's face from the dreadful, near-fatal scoring he'd taken on his famous jump to the Red Star.

"C'mon, Piemur," called Sebell. "F'nor's here to take us to Benden Weyr. Ramoth's latest clutch is Hatching."

Piemur started to whoop with joy, then bit his tongue, choking off his jubilation. Bad enough he'd been to a Gather, but when Clell and that lot heard he'd been to a Benden Hatching, his life wouldn't be worth a wax mark! He saw in the same instant that the others were expecting him to react with appropriate anticipation and, loudly damning his changing voice, he affected as genuine a smile as he could manage. The groan that escaped him as he climbed to Canth's back was for the inexorable forces he couldn't resist rather than the physical effort. He endured in silence Sebell's teasing about the miseries of an apprentice's life, and then Menolly's for his silence, which she attributed to either hunger or sleepiness.

"Never mind, Piemur," she said with an encouraging smile, "there's bound to be some klah left in the pot for you at Benden Weyr." She peered down at his face. "You are awake, aren't you?"

"Sort of," he said, yawning again, then added for her benefit, "I just can't take it that me, Piemur, gets to go to a Benden Weyr Hatching!"

Should he ask Menolly not to tell the Drum Master and Dirzan? Could he ask her to say he'd been left at Igen Hold until they could collect him? No, he couldn't, because she'd want to know why. And he couldn't tell her because that would mark him a blubber-baby, bleater, babblemouth. There had to be some way he could settle Clell and Dirzan by himself!

Despite his misgivings, Piemur succumbed to the fear-charged thrill of Canth's initial vault into the air, the sensation of being pressed down, the breathlessness as the huge wings beat powerfully, and he felt the effort of Canth's neck muscles under his buttocks. It wasn't quite as scarey flying in this predawn darkness because he didn't know how far he was above the ground, particularly since his face was turned away from Igen Hold's fading lights; but he caught his breath in a spurt of pure terror as F'nor gave Canth the audible request to take them *between* to Benden Weyr. He was again alone in the intense, sense-deprived, utter cold, and then, before the cold could sink to his bones, they had emerged into the brightening day, momentarily suspended above the massive Bowl of Benden Weyr.

He'd been to Fort Weyr once, by cart, with a group of harpers, when Ludeth, the Weyrqueen, had her first queen egg hatching. He'd thought that Fort was huge, but Benden seemed much bigger. Perhaps because he was seeing it from dragonback, perhaps because of the light, touching the far edges of the Bowl, gilding the lake. Perhaps it was because this was Benden, and Benden figured so hugely and importantly in his eyes, and the eyes of everyone else on Pern.

Without Benden and her courageous leaders, Pern might have been half-destroyed by Thread.

Another dragon appeared in the air just above them, and instinctively Piemur ducked, hearing Menolly laugh at his reflex. A third and then a fourth dragon arrived even as Canth began to glide down to the bowl floor. By the time Piemur could slide from the brown's shoulder to the ground, he marveled that the dragons hadn't collided midair, appearing as they had with such startling frequency.

Beauty, Kimi, Rocky and Diver popped in above Menolly's head, caroling with excitement, and suddenly they were joined by five other fire lizards Piemur had never seen before. When Menolly muttered worriedly about feeding fire lizards before they disrupted the Weyr, F'nor laughingly told them to find Mirrim. She was likely to be supervising breakfast in the kitchen caverns. Sebell's nudge in his ribs reminded Piemur to thank the brown rider and his dragon. Then the three harpers made their way across the Bowl to the brightly lit cavern.

The enticing aromas of fresh klah and toasted cereals quickened their steps, Menolly leading the way towards the smallest hearth, away from the bustle and hurry of weyrfolk at the larger fires.

"Mirrim?" she called, and the girl at the hearth turned, her face lighting as she recognized the new arrivals.

"Menolly! You came! Sebell! How are you? What have you been up to recently to get so tanned? Who's this?" Her smile disappeared as she noticed Piemur bringing up the rear, as if such a scruffy apprentice shouldn't be in such good company.

"Mirrim, this is Piemur. You've heard me speak of him often enough," said Menolly, putting her hand on Piemur to draw him forward and closer to her, the intimacy a guarantee of him to Mirrim. "He was my first friend at the Harper Hall, as you were mine here. We've all been at the Igen Gather. Baked yesterday, frozen this morning, and very hungry!" Menolly let her tone drift upward plaintively.

"Well, of course, you're hungry," said Mirrim, breaking off her stern appraisal of Piemur to turn to the hearth. She filled cups and bowls and set them out on one of the small tables with such alacrity that Piemur changed his first, unflattering impression of her. "I can't stop long with you. You know how things are at the Weyr when there's a Hatching; so much to do. The important details you really have to see to yourself to be sure they're done right." She flopped gracelessly into a chair with an exaggerated sigh of relief to underscore the weight of responsibility on her shoulders. Then she ran both hands through the fringe of brown hair on her forehead, ending the gesture with pats at the neat plaits that hung down her back.

Piemur eyed her with a certain skeptical cynicism but, when he realized that Menolly and Sebell took no notice of her mannerisms and had sought out her company from everyone in the busy cavern, he came to the reluctant conclusion that there must be more to her than was obvious.

Beauty landed on Menolly's shoulder just then, chirruping with some petulance, her eyes whirling reddishly. Diver swooped to Menolly's other shoulder just as Kimi landed on Sebell's. Rocky, to Piemur's intense delight, came to roost on his.

"I thought that was Rocky," Mirrim said, pointing accusingly at Piemur as if he oughtn't to have a fire lizard anyhow.

"It is," said Menolly with a laugh, "but Piemur helps me feed him every day so Rocky's just reminding us he's hungry, too."

"Why didn't you say they hadn't been fed?" Mirrim bounced to her feet, scowling with disapproval. "Really, Menolly, I'd've thought you'd take care of your friends first. . . ."

Sebell and Menolly exchanged guilty smiles as Mirrim stalked off to a table where women were cutting up wherries for the Hatching Feast. She returned with a generous bowlful of scraps, three fire lizards hovering anxiously above her. She shooed them away, reminding them with gruff affection that they'd already been fed. To Piemur's relief, because he was developing an antipathy to her manner, Mirrim was called away to one of the main hearths. Rocky poked his cheek imperiously, and Piemur concentrated on feeding him.

"Is she a good friend of yours?" Piemur asked when the first edge of fire lizard hunger had been eased.

Sebell laughed, and Menolly made a rueful grimace.

"She's very good-hearted. Don't let her ways put you off."

Piemur grunted. "They have."

Sebell laughed again, offering Kimi a large chunk of meat so he could get a swallow of his klah while she struggled to chew. "Mirrim does take a bit of getting used to but, as Menolly says, she'll give you the shirt from her back . . ."

"Complaining all the time, I'll wager," Piemur said.

Menolly's expression was solemn. "She was fosterling to Brekke, and Manora's always said that it was Mirrim's devoted nursing that helped Brekke live after her queen was killed."

"Really?" That did impress Piemur, and he looked for Mirrim among the knot of women by the hearth as if this disclosure had caused her to change visibly.

"Don't, please don't judge her too quickly, Piemur," said Menolly, touching his arm to emphasize her request.

"Well, of course, if *you* say so . . ."

Sebell winked at Piemur. "She says so, Piemur, and we must obey!"

"Oh, you," and Menolly dismissed Sebell's teasing with a scowl of irritation. "I just don't want Piemur jumping to the wrong conclusion on the basis of a few moments' meeting—"

"When everyone knows," and Sebell rolled his eyes ceilingward, "that it takes time, endurance, tolerance and luck to appreciate Mirrim!" Sebell ducked as Menolly threatened him with her spoon.

They had finished feeding the fire lizards and sent them out to sun themselves when Mirrim popped up before them again, exhaling a mighty sigh.

"I don't know how we're going to get everything finished in time. Why those eggs have to be so awkward in their timing. Half the western guests will be dead of sleep and need breakfast. . . . See?" She waved towards the entrance where dragons were depositing more passengers. "There's so much to be done. And I particularly want to get to this Hatching. Felessan's a candidate today, you know."

"So F'nor told us. I could manage the breakfast hearth, Mirrim," said Menolly.

"Just set us a task," said Sebell, throwing his arm across Piemur's shoulders, "and we'll do our best to assist."

"Oh, would you?" Suddenly the affected manners dropped, and Mirrim's scowl gave way to a incredulous smile of relief, illuminating her face and making her a very pretty girl. "If you would just set up those tables," and she pointed to stacks of trestles and tops, "that'd be the greatest help!"

She was again summoned across the cavern and dashed off with a smile of such unaffected gratitude that Piemur stared after her in astonishment. Why did the girl act oddly? She was much nicer when she was just herself!

"So, Felessan stands on the Hatching Ground," said Sebell. "I missed that this morning."

"Sorry, thought I'd told you," said Menolly, rising to clear the table of their dishes. "I wonder if he'll Impress."

"Why shouldn't he?" asked Piemur, startled by her doubt.

"He may be the son of the Weyrleaders, but that doesn't necessarily mean he'll Impress. Dragon choice can't be forced."

"Oh, Felessan'll Impress," said a dragonrider, approaching the small hearth, two others just behind him. "Are you tending the pot, Menolly?"

"And a good day to you, T'gellan," Menolly said with a pert smile for the bronze rider as she poured klah for him.

"How's yourself, Sebell?" T'gellan went on, seating himself on the bench and gesturing to the other riders to join him.

"Hard put upon," said Sebell in a long-suffering tone that sounded suspiciously like an imitation of Mirrim. "We just got organized to set up the tables. C'mon, Piemur, before Mirrim lays about us with her ladle."

Because Menolly had so stoutly championed Mirrim, Piemur kept an eye out for the girl as he and Sebell arranged the additional tables. He spotted Mirrim dashing from one hearth to another, called to assist in trussing wherries for roasting, herdbeasts for the spit. He watched her organize one group of youngsters to peel roots and tubers and another to laying the tables with utensils and platters. He decided that Mirrim had not been puffing up her responsibilities.

Menolly, too, was kept busy, feeding dragonriders and their sleepy-eyed passengers, dragged from their beds for the imminent Hatching.

Sebell and Piemur had just set up the last table when a faint hum reached their ears. Fire lizards reappeared in the cavern, the high notes of their chirruping a counter-cadence to the low bass throb of the humming dragons.

Mirrim, divested of her apron and brushing water stains from her skirt, came dashing towards them.

"C'mon, Oharan promised to save us all seats by him," she cried and led the way across the Bowl at a run.

The Weyr Harper had kept them places in the tiers above the Hatching Ground, though, he informed them, his life had been threatened by Holders and Craftmasters. Piemur could see why as he settled down, for this was a splendid position, in the second tier, close to the entrance so that the view of the entire Ground was clear. There was no queen egg for Ramoth to guard, so the Benden queen dragon was standing to one side of the ground, Lessa and F'lar on the ledge above her. Occasionally the enormous golden dragon looked up at her weyrmate, as if seeking assurance or, Piemur thought, consolation, since the eggs she had clutched were shortly to be taken from her care. The notion amused Piemur, for he'd never have ascribed maternal emotions to Benden's preeminent queen dragon. Certainly Ramoth with her yellow flashing eyes and restless foot-shifting, wing-rustling, was a far picture from the gentle concern herdbeast females or runners showed their offspring.

A blur of white, seen from the corner of his eye, drew Piemur's attention to the Hatching Ground entrance. The candidates were approaching the eggs, their white tunics fluttering in the light morning breeze. Piemur suppressed his amusement as the boys, stepping further on the hot sands, began to pick up their feet smartly. When they had reached the clutch, they ranged themselves in a loose semi-circle about the gently rocking eggs. Ramoth made a noise like a disapproving growl, which the boys all ignored, but Piemur noticed that the ones nearest her edged surreptitiously away.

A startled murmur ran through the audience as one of the eggs rocked more violently. The sudden snapping of the shell seemed to resound through the high-ceilinged cavern, and the dragons on the upper ledges hummed more loudly than ever with encouragement. The actual Hatching had begun. Piemur didn't know where to look because the audience was as fascinating as the Hatching: dragonriders' faces with soft glows as they relived the magic moment when they had Impressed the hatchling dragon who became their life's companion, minds indissolubly linked. On other faces was hope, breathless and incredulous, as guests and parents of the candidates waited for the moment when their lads would be chosen, or rejected, by the hatchlings. Fire lizards, respectfully quiet, perched on many shoulders in the Ground. And Piemur, who could never aspire to Impress a dragon, was reminded of that unfilled promise, that he would have a fire lizard one day. He wondered if Menolly remembered her promise to him. Or if he'd ever have the opportunity to remind her of it.

"There's Felessan," said Menolly, nudging him sharply with her elbow. She pointed to a leggy figure with such a luxuriant growth of dark curling hair that his head seemed oversized.

"He doesn't even look nervous," said Piemur, as he noted the signs of apprehension in other candidates who shifted uneasily or twitched unnecessarily at their tunics.

A concerted gasp directed their attention from Felessan, and they saw that several more eggs were rocking violently as the hatchlings struggled to be free. Abruptly an egg split open, and a moist little brown dragon was spilled to his feet on the hot sands. Dragging his fragile-looking damp wings on the ground, he began to lunge this way and that, calling piteously, while the adult dragons crooned encouragement, reinforced by Ramoth's half-hum, half-howl.

The boys nearest the dragonet tried to anticipate his direction, hoping to Impress him, but he lurched out of their immediate circle, staggering across the sands, his call plaintive, desperate until the next group of boys turned. One, prompted by some instinct, took a step forward. The little brown's cries turned joyous, he tried to extend his wet wings to bridge the distance between them, but the boy rushed to the dragon's side, caressing head and shoulders, patting the damp wings while the little hatchling crooned with triumph, his jeweled eyes glowing the blue and purple of love and devotion. The day's first Impression had been made!

Piemur heard Menolly's deep and satisfied sigh and knew that she was reliving the moment she had Impressed her fire lizards in the Dragon Stones cave three Turns ago. He was again assailed by a deep stab of envy. When would he rate a fire lizard?

Excited cries brought his attention back to the Hatching Ground as more eggs cracked, exposing their occupants.

"Watch Felessan, Piemur! There's a bronze near him . . ." cried Mirrim, grabbing Piemur's arm in her excitement.

"And two browns and a blue," added Menolly, scarcely less excited as she canted her body in a mental effort to direct the little bronze towards Felessan. "He deserves a bronze! He deserves one!"

"Only if the dragon wants him," said Mirrim sententiously. "Just because he's the Weyrleaders' son—"

"Shut up, Mirrim," said Piemur, exasperated, clenching his fists, urging the Impression to occur.

Felessan was aware of the bronze's proximity, but so were a handful of other candidates. The little creature, rocking unstably on his wobbly legs, seemed not to see any of them for a moment. Then the wedge-shaped head fell forward and got buried in the sand as his hind legs overbalanced him. It was too much. Felessan gently righted the little beast and then stood transfixed, the expression on his exultant face plainly visible to his friends as Impression was made.

Ramoth's bugle astonished everyone into a long moment of silence; but it was no wonder, Piemur thought, that F'lar and Lessa were embracing each other at the sight of their one child Impressing a bronze!

The excitement was over too soon, Piemur thought, just moments later. He wished that all the eggs hadn't hatched at once, so this dizzy happiness could be extended. Not that there wasn't some disappointment and sadness, too, because far more candidates were presented to the eggs than could Impress. Only one little green had not Impressed, and she was mewling unhappily, butting one boy out of her way, lurching to another and peering up into his face, obviously searching for just the right lad. She had worked her way towards the tiers, despite the efforts of the remaining candidates to attract her attention and keep her well out into the Ground.

"Whatever is the matter with those boys?" demanded Mirrim, frowning with anxiety over the little green's pathetic wandering. She stood up, gesturing peremptorily to the candidates to close around the little green.

Just then the creature began to croon urgently and made directly for the steps that led up to the tiers.

"What is possessing her?" Mirrim asked no one in particular. She looked behind her accusingly, as if somehow a candidate might be hiding among the guests.

"She wants someone not on the Ground," rang a voice from the crowd.

"She's going to hurt herself," said Mirrim in an agitated mutter and pushed past the three people seated between her and the stairs. "She'll bruise her wings on the walls."

The little green did hurt herself, slipping off the first step and banging her muzzle so sharply on the stone that she let out a cry of pain, echoed by a fierce bugle from Ramoth who began to move across the sands.

"Now, listen here, you silly thing, the boys you want are out there on the Ground. Turn yourself around and go back to them," Mirrim was saying as she made her way down the steps to the little green. Her fire lizards, calling out in wildly ecstatic buglings, halted her. She stared for a long moment at the antics of her friends, and then, her expression incredulous, she looked down at the green hatchling determinedly attacking the obstacle of steps. "I can't!" Mirrim cried, so panic-stricken that she slipped on the steps herself and slid down three before her flailing hands found support. "I can't!" Mirrim glanced about her for confirmation. "I'm not supposed to Impress. I'm not a candidate. She can't want *me!*" Awe washed over the consternation on her face and in her voice.

"If it's you she wants, Mirrim, get down there before she hurts herself!" said F'lar, who had by now reached the scene, Lessa beside him.

"But I'm not—"

"It would seem that you are, Mirrim," said Lessa, her face reflecting amusement and resignation. "The dragon's never wrong! Come! Be quick about it, girl. She's scraping her chin raw to get to you!"

With one final startled look at her Weyrleaders, Mirrim half-slid the remaining steps, cushioning the little green's chin from yet another harsh contact with the stone of the step.

"Oh, you silly darling! Whatever made you choose me?" Mirrim said in a loving voice as she gathered the green into her arms and began to soothe the hatchling's distressed cries. "She says her name is Path!" The glory on Mirrim's face caused Piemur to look away in embarrassment and envy.

For one brief moment, Piemur had entertained the bizarre notion that maybe the little green dragon had been looking for him. A deep sigh fluttered through his lips, and a hand was laid gently on his shoulder. Schooling his expression, he turned to see Menolly watching him, a deep pity and understanding in her eyes.

"I promised you Turns ago that you'd have a fire lizard, Piemur. I haven't forgotten. I will keep that promise!"

As one they turned their heads back to watch Mirrim fussing over her Path, her fire lizards hopping about on the sands, chattering away as if welcoming the little green in their own fashion.

"Come on, you two," said Sebell, as Mirrim began to encourage Path to walk out of the Hatching Ground. "We'd better see Master Robinton. This is going to cause problems." The last he said in a low voice.

"Why?" asked Piemur, making sure they weren't overheard. But everyone was filing out of the tiers now, eager to congratulate or condole. "She's weyrbred."

"Greens are fighting dragons," began Sebell.

"In that case, Mirrim's well paired, isn't she?" asked Piemur with droll amusement.

"Piemur!"

At Menolly's shocked remonstrance, Piemur turned to Sebell and saw an answering gleam, though the journeyman turned quickly and started down the steps.

"Sebell's right, though," Menolly said thoughtfully as they started across the hot sands, quickening their pace as the heat penetrated the soles of their flying boots.

"Why?" asked Piemur again. "Just because she's a girl?"

"There won't be as much shock as there might be," Sebell went on. "Jaxom's Impression of Ruth set a precedent."

"It's not quite the same thing, Sebell," Menolly replied. "Jaxom is a Lord Holder and has to remain so. And then the weyrmen did think the little white dragon mightn't live. And now he has, it's obvious he's never going to be a full-sized dragon. Not that he's needed in the Weyrs, but Mirrim is!"

"Exactly! And not in the capacity of green rider."

"I think she'd make a good fighting rider," said Piemur, keeping the comment carefully under his breath.

When they located Master Robinton, he was already earnestly discussing the matter with Oharan.

"Completely unexpected! Mirrim swears that she hadn't been in the Hatching Ground at all when the candidates were familiarizing themselves with the Eggs," Master Robinton told his craftsmen. Then he smiled. "Fortunately, with Felessan Impressing a bronze, Lessa and F'lar are in great spirits." Now he shrugged, his grin broadening. "It was simply a case of the dragon finding her own partnership where she wanted it!"

"As Ruth did with Jaxom!"

"Precisely."

"And that is the Harper message?" asked Sebell, glancing about the Bowl where knots of people surrounded weyrlings and dragonets.

"There doesn't seem to be any other explanation. So let us drink and be merry. It's a good day for Pern! And I'm terribly dry," said the Masterharper as the Weyr Harper solemnly proffered a cup of wine. "Oh thanks, Oharan. Must be the heat of the Hatching Ground or the excitement. I'm parched. Ahhhh." The Harper's sigh was of relief and

pleasure. "A good Benden vintage . . . ah, an old one, the wine has a
mellowness, a smoothness . . ." He glanced about him as his audience
waited expectantly. Oharan's hand casually covered the seal of the
wineskin. The Harper took another judicious sip. "Yes, indeed. I have it
now. The pressing of ten Turns back, and furthermore . . ." he held up
a finger, ". . . it's from the northwestern slopes of upper Benden."
Oharan slowly uncovered the seal, and the others saw that the
Harper had been absolutely correct.

"I don't know how you do it, Master Robinton," said Oharan, having
hoped to confound his master.

"He's had a lot of practice," said Menolly at her driest, and they all
laughed as Master Robinton started to protest.

They had time for a quiet glass before the admiring guests had exhausted all the possible things one could say to a newly impressed pair.
Then the Weyrlingmaster took his charges off to the lake where the
newly hatched would be fed, bathed and oiled, and the guests began to
drift towards the tables, seating themselves for the feasting that would
follow.

Master Robinton led his craftsmen in a rousing ballad of praise to
dragons and their riders before he joined the Weyrleaders and their
visiting Lord Holders. Oharan, Sebell, Menolly and Piemur did the
courtesy round to the tables where the parents of new dragonriders
were seated, singing requests. Menolly's fire lizards sang several songs
with her before she excused them, explaining that they were far more
interested in the new dragons than singing for mere people. Then she
got involved with a group from the crafthall at Bitra, and the other
three harpers left her explaining how to teach fire lizards to sing as they
continued the rounds.

The tradition was that a harper's song deserved a cup of wine. Chatting as they drank, Sebell and Oharan took turns directing conversation
where they wished it: Mirrim's unexpected Impression.

There was, to be sure, considerable surprise that Mirrim had done so,
but most of those queried found it to be no large affair. After all, they
said, Mirrim was weyrbred, a fosterling of Brekke's, had Impressed
three of the first fire lizards to be found at Southern, so her unexpected
rise to dragonrider was at least consistent. Now Jaxom, who had to
remain Lord of Ruatha, was a different case entirely. Piemur noticed
that everyone was a good deal interested in the health of the little white
dragon and, while they wished him the best, were just as pleased that
he'd never make a full-sized beast. Evidently that made it easier for
people to accept the fact that Ruth was being raised in a Hold instead of
a Weyr.

Holdlessness was a topic to which conversations returned time and again that evening. Many lads, growing up in land crafts, would not find holdings of their own when they were old enough. There simply weren't any old places left. Could not more of the mountainous regions of the far north be made habitable? Or the remote slopes of High Reaches or Crom? Piemur noted that Nabol, which actually had tenable land uncultivated, was never cited. What about the marshlands of lower Benden? Surely with such a competent Weyr, more holds could be protected. Occasionally Piemur, standing or sitting at the edges of groups, would overhear fascinating snatches and try to make sense out of them. Mostly he discarded them as gossip, but one stuck in his tired mind. Lord Oterel had been the speaker. He didn't know the other man, though his lighter clothes suggested he came from the southern part of Pern. "Meron gets more than his share; we go without. Girls impress fighting dragons, and our lad stands on the Ground. Ridiculous!"

Piemur found it getting progressively harder to rise from one table and move to another. Not that he was drinking any wine; he had sense enough not to do that. He just seemed to be more tired than he ought to be; if he could just put his head down for a few moments.

He was scarcely conscious of the cold of *between,* only annoyed because he was being forced to walk when he wanted to sit down. He did recall some sort of argument going on over his head. He could have sworn it was Silvina giving someone the very rough edge of her tongue. He was mercifully grateful that finally he was permitted to stretch out on a bed, feel furs pulled over his shoulders, and he could give in to the sleep he craved.

The bell woke him, and his surroundings confused him. He looked about, trying to figure out where he was, since he certainly wasn't in the drum apprentices' quarters. Further he was on a rush bag on a floor— the floor in Sebell's room, for the clothes Sebell had been wearing for the past two days were draped on a nearby chair, his flying boots sagging against each other by the bed. Piemur's empty clothes had been neatly piled on his boots at the foot of the rush bag.

The bell continued to ring, and Piemur, keenly aware of the emptiness of his belly, hastily dressed, paused long enough to splash his face and hands with water in case anyone, like Dirzan, wanted to fault him on cleanliness and proceeded down the corridor to the steps and the dining hall. He was just turning into the hall when Clell and the other three came in the main door. Clell flashed a look at the others and then strode up to Piemur, grabbing him by the arm roughly.

"Where've you been for two days?"

"Why? Did you have to polish the drums?"

"You're going to get it from Dirzan!" A pleased smirk crossed Clell's face.

"Why should he get it from Dirzan, Clell?" asked Menolly, quietly coming up behind the drum apprentices. "He's been on Harper business."

"He's always getting off on Harper business," replied Clell with unexpected anger, "and always with you!"

Piemur raised his fist at such insolence and leaned back to make the swing count in Clell's sneering face. But Menolly was quicker; she swung the apprentice about and shoved him forcefully towards the main door.

"Insolence to a journeyman means water rations for you, Clell!" she said and, without bothering to see that he'd continue out of the hall, she turned to the other three who gawked at her. "And, for you, too, if I should learn of any mischief against Piemur because of this. Have I made myself perfectly clear? Or do I need to mention the incident to Master Olodkey?"

The cowed apprentices murmured the necessary assurances and, at her dismissal, lost themselves in the throng of other apprentices.

"How much trouble have you been having in the drumheights, Piemur?"

"Nothing I can't handle," said Piemur, wondering when he could get back at Clell for that insult to Menolly.

"Water rations for you, too, Piemur, if I see so much as a scratch on Clell's face."

"But he . . ."

Bonz, Timiny and Brolly came flying into the hall at that point and hailed Piemur with such evident relief that, after giving Piemur a long, forbidding glance, Menolly went off towards the journeymen's tables. The boys demanded to know where he'd been and he was to tell them everything.

He didn't. He told them what he felt they should know as far as the Igen Hold Gather was concerned, an innocuous enough tale. And he could, and did, describe in great detail the Impression of Path to Mirrim. The bare bones of that unexpected event was already the talk of the Hall, and Piemur had heard the public version so often that he knew he wasn't committing any indiscretion. He was careful to play down, even to his good friends, the circumstances that had brought him to Benden Weyr at such an auspicious occasion.

"No dragonrider was going to take me, an apprentice harper, all the way back to the Hall when there was a Hatching, so I had to stay."

"C'mon, Piemur," said Bonz, thoroughly disgusted with his indifference, "you can't ever get me to believe that you didn't enjoy every moment of it."

"Then I won't. 'Cause I did. But I was just bloody lucky to be at the Igen Gather right then. Otherwise I'd've been back polishing the big drums yesterday!"

"Say, Piemur, you getting on all right with Clell and those others?" asked Ranly.

"Sure. Why?" Piemur kept his voice as casual as he could.

"Oh, nothing, except they're not mixers, and lately, they've been sort of asking about you in a funny sort of way." Ranly was worried, and from the solemn expressions on the other faces, he had confided their concern.

"You just haven't been the same since your voice changed, Piemur," said Timiny, blushing with embarrassment.

Piemur snorted, then grinned because Timiny looked so uncomfortable. "Of course, I'm not, Tim. How could I be? My voice is changing, and the rest of me, too."

"I didn't mean that . . ." and Timiny faltered in a muddle of confusion, looking at Bonz and Brolly for help to express what puzzled them all.

Just then the journeyman rose to give out the day's assignments, and the apprentices were forced to be quiet. Piemur held his breath, hoping that Menolly had not made Clell's discipline a public one and felt relieved when it was obvious that she hadn't. He was going to have enough trouble with Clell as it was. Not that he worried about the apprentice going hungry. He'd seen the other three secreting bread, fruit and a thick wherry slice to smuggle out to him.

As the sections dispersed for their work parties, Piemur went to the drumheights, wondering exactly what awaited him. He was not surprised to find that the drums had been left for him to polish, or that Dirzan grumbled about his absence because how could he learn enough to be a proper drummer. And it was only to be expected that there was no word of praise from Dirzan when he came out measure perfect on all the sequences Dirzan asked him. What Piemur wasn't prepared for was the state of his belongings when Dirzan dismissed him. He got the first whiff when he opened the door to the apprentices' room. Despite the fact that both windows were propped wide open, the small room smelled like the necessary. He opened the press for clean clothes and realized where the worst of the offending stench lay. He turned, half-hoping this was all, but as he ran his hand over his sleeping furs they were disgustingly damp.

"Who's been . . ." Dirzan came striding into the room, finger and thumb pinching his nose against the odor.

Piemur said nothing, he merely let the soiled clothing unroll and held the furs up so that the light fell on the long, damp stain. Dirzan's eyes narrowed, and his grimace deepened. Piemur wondered what annoyed Dirzan more: that Piemur's unexpectedly long absence had made the joke more noisome than necessary, or that here was proof positive that Piemur was being harassed by his roommates.

"You may be excused from other duties to attend to this," said Dirzan. "Be sure to bring back a sweet candle to clear the odor. How they could sleep with that. . . ."

Dirzan waited until Piemur had cleared the noxious things from the room, and then he slammed the door with such force that the journeyman on watch came to see what was the matter.

With everyone scattered for work sections, Piemur managed to get to the washing room without being stopped. He was so furious he wouldn't have trusted himself to answer properly if anyone had asked him the most civil of questions. He slapped the furs, hair side out into the warm tub, sprinkling half the jar of sweetsand on the slowly sinking bedding. He shook the half-hardened stuff out of his clothing into the drain, and then, with washing paddle, shoved and prodded the garments to loosen the encrustations. If there were stains on his new clothes, he'd face a month's water rations but he'd pay them all back, so he would.

"What are you doing in here at this time of day, Piemur?" asked Silvina, attracted by the splashing and pounding.

"Me?" The force of his tone brought Silvina right into the room. "My roommates play dirty jokes!"

Silvina gave him a long searching look as her nose told her what kind of dirty jokes. "Any reason for them to?"

In a split second Piemur decided. Silvina was one of the few people in the Hall he could trust. She instinctively knew when he was shamming, so she'd know now that he was being put on. And he had an unbearable need and urge to release some of the troubles he had suppressed. This last trick of the apprentices, damaging his good new clothes, hurt more than he had realized in the numbness following the discovery. He'd been so proud of the fine garments, and to have them crudely soiled before he'd worn some of them enough to acquire honest dirt hit him harder than the slanders at his supposed indiscretions.

"I get to Gathers and Impressions," Piemur drew a whistling breath through his teeth, "and I've made the mistake of learning drum measures too fast and too well."

Silvina continued to stare at him, her eyes slightly narrowed and her head tilted to one side. Abruptly she moved beside him and took the washpaddle from his hand, slipping it deftly under the soaking furs. "They probably expected you back right after the Igen Gather!" She chuckled as she plunged the fur back under the water, grinning broadly at him. "So they had to sleep in the stink they caused for two nights!" Her laughter was infectious, and Piemur found his spirits lifting as he grinned back at her. "That Clell. He's the one who planned it. Watch him, Piemur. He's got a mean streak." Then she sighed. "Still, you won't be there long, and it won't do you any harm to learn the drum measures. Could be very useful one day." She gave him another long appraising look. "I'll say this for you, Piemur, you know when to keep your tongue in your head! Here, put that through the wringer now and let's see if we've got the worst out!"

Silvina helped him finish the washing, asking him all about the Hatching and Mirrim's unexpected Impression of a green dragon. And how did he find the climate in Igen? It was as much a relief for him to talk to Silvina without restraint as to have her expert help in cleaning his clothes.

Then, because she said nothing would be dry before evening, she got him another sleeping fur, and a spare shirt and pants, commenting they were well-enough worn not to cause envy.

"You'll mention, of course, that I tore strips out of you for ruining good cloth and staining fur," she said with a parting wink.

He was halfway out of the Hall when he remembered the need for a sweet candle and went back for it, bearing her loud grumbles to the rest of the kitchen with fortitude.

Afterwards, Piemur thought that if Dirzan had ignored the mischief the way Piemur intended to, the whole incident might have been forgotten. But Dirzan reprimanded the others in front of the journeymen and put them on water rations for three days. The sweet candle cleared the quarters of the stench, but nothing would ever sweeten the apprentices towards Piemur after that. It was almost as if, Piemur thought, Dirzan was determined to ruin any chance Piemur had of making friends with Clell or the others.

Though he did his best to stay out of their vicinities, he was constantly having benches shoved into his shins in the study room, his feet trod on everywhere, his ribs painfully stuck by drumsticks or elbows. His furs were sewn together three nights running, and his clothes were so frequently dipped in the roof gutters that he finally asked Brolly to make him a locking mechanism for his press that he alone could open.

Apprentices were not supposed to have any private containers, but Dirzan made no mention of the addition to Piemur's box.

In a way, Piemur found a certain satisfaction in being able to ignore the nuisances, rising above all the pettiness perpetrated on him with massive and complete disdain. He spent as much time as he could studying the drum records, tapping his fingers on his fur even as he was falling asleep to memorize the times and rhythms of the most complicated measures. He knew the others knew exactly what he was doing, and there was nothing they could do to thwart him.

Unfortunately, the coolness he developed to fend off their little tricks began insidiously to come between him and his old friends. Bonz and Brolly complained loudly that he was different, while Timiny watched him with mournful eyes, as if he somehow considered himself responsible for Piemur's alterations.

Piemur tried to laugh it off, saying he was drum happy.

"They're putting on you up in the drumheights, Piemur," said Bonz glowering loyally. "I just know they are. And if Clell—"

"Clell isn't!" Piemur said in a tone so fierce that Bonz rocked back on his heels.

"That's exactly what I mean, Piemur!" said Brolly, who wasn't easily intimidated by a boy he'd known for five Turns and still topped by a full head. "You're different and don't give me that old wheeze about your voice changing and you with it. Your voice is settling. You haven't cracked in days!"

Piemur blinked, mildly surprised at the phenomenon of which he'd been unaware.

"It's too bad. Anyhow, Tilgin's got the part down . . . finally, and it wouldn't sound the same with you as baritone," Brolly went on.

"Baritone?" Piemur's voice broke in surprise and, when he saw the disappointment on his friends' faces, he started to laugh. "Well, maybe, and then, maybe not."

"Now you sound like Piemur," said Bonz, shouting with emphasis.

Isolated as he'd been in the drumheights, Piemur had easily managed to forget the fast approaching feast at Lord Groghe's and the performance of Domick's new music. Two sevendays had passed since the Benden Hatching, and he'd been too engrossed with his own problems to give much attention to extraneous matters. His friends now underlined the nearness of the Feast, and he was sure that he couldn't escape attending it and wondered how he could. He'd prefer to be out of Fort Hold altogether on the night of the performance because, sure as eggs cracked, he'd have to go to it.

Then it occurred to him that he hadn't been on any trips with Sebell and Menolly lately. He forced himself to laugh and joke with his friends in a fair imitation of his old self, but once back in the drumheights, while he stood his afternoon watch, he began to wonder if he'd done something wrong at Benden Weyr or Igen Hold. Or if, by any freak chance, Dirzan's tittle-tattle had affected Menolly's opinion of him. Come to think of it, he hadn't seen Sebell at all of late.

The next morning, when he was feeding the fire lizards with her, he asked her where the journeyman was.

"Between you and me," she said in a low voice, having seen Camo occupied with the greedy Auntie One, "he's up in the Ranges. He should be back tonight. Don't worry, Piemur," she said, smiling. "We haven't forgotten you." Then she gave him a very searching look. "You haven't been worried, have you?"

"Me? No, why should I worry?" He gave a derisive snort. "I put my time to good use. I know more drum measures than any of those dimwits, for all they've been mucking about up there for Turns!"

Menolly laughed. "Now you sound more like yourself. You're all right with Master Olodkey then?"

"Me? Sure!" Which, Piemur felt, was not stretching the truth. He was fine with Master Olodkey because he rarely came in contact with the man.

"And that rough lad, Clell, he's not come back at you for the other day, has he?"

"Menolly," said Piemur, taking a stern tone with her, "I'm Piemur. No one gets back at me. What gave you such a notion?" He sounded as scornful as he could.

"Hmmmm, just that you haven't been as—well . . ." and she smiled half-apologetically. "Oh, never mind. I expect you can take care of yourself any time, any where."

They continued feeding the fire lizards, and Piemur wished heartily that he could tell Menolly the real state of affairs in the drumheights. But what good would it do? She could only speak to Dirzan, who would never accept Piemur for any reason. Asking Dirzan to discipline the other apprentices for what was only stupid petty narking wouldn't help. Piemur could see clearly now that his well-founded reputation for mischief and game playing were coming back at him when he least expected, or even less, deserved it. He'd no one but himself to fault, so he'd just have to chew it raw and swallow! After all, once his voice settled, he'd be out of the drumheights. He could put up with it because he'd have the odd Gather out with Sebell and Menolly.

Chapter 5

That afternoon a drum message came in from the north. Piemur was in the main room diligently copying drum measures that Dirzan had set him to learn by evening, although he already knew them off rhythm perfect. He translated the message as it throbbed in. "Urgent. Reply required please. Nabol." To himself Piemur smiled as the rest of the message pounded on, because he had the sudden suspicion that the Nabol drummer had begun with those measures to soften the arrogance of the main message. "Lord Meron of Nabol demands the immediate appearance of Master Oldive. Reply instantly." Had the drummer added "grave illness," the signal "urgent" would have been appropriate.

Piemur continued his copying smoothly, aware of the eyes of the other apprentices on him. Let them think that he understood little beyond the first three measures, which was about all they'd know.

Rokayas, the journeyman on duty, came into the room a moment later.

"Who's running messages today?" he asked, the thin, folded sheaf of the transcribed message in his hand.

The others all pointed to Piemur, who immediately put his pen down and rose to his feet. The journeyman frowned.

"You were on yesterday."

"I'm on today again, Rokayas," said Piemur cheerfully and reached for the sheaf.

"Seems to me you're always on," Rokayas said, holding the message away from Piemur as he glared suspiciously at the others.

"Dirzan said I was messenger until he said otherwise," said Piemur, shrugging as if it were a matter of indifference to him.

"All right, then," and the journeyman surrendered the message, still eyeing the other four boys, "but it seems queer to me you're always running!"

"I'm newest," said Piemur and left the room. He was rather pleased that Rokayas had noticed. Actually he didn't mind because he got a brief respite from the sour presence of the other apprentices.

He dashed down the three flights of steps in his usual fashion, one hand lightly on the stone rail, plummeting down as fast as he could go.

He burst out into the courtyard, automatically glancing about. The raking team was at work. He waved cheerfully to the section leader and then took the main steps to the Hall three at a time. His legs must be getting longer, he thought, or he was improving his stride because he used to be able to leap only two.

Slightly puffed, he tapped politely at Master Oldive's door and handed over the message, wheeling instantly so that no one could say he'd seen the message.

"Hold a moment, young Piemur," said Master Oldive, unfolding the sheaf and frowning as he read its contents. "Urgent, is it? Well, it could be, at that. Though why they wouldn't in courtesy send their watch dragon. . . . Ah well. Nabol hasn't one, has it? Reply that I'll come, and please ask Master Olodkey to pass the word to T'ledon that I must prevail on his good nature for passage to Nabol! I shall go straight to the meadow to wait for him."

Piemur repeated the message, using Master Oldive's exact phrasing and intonation. Released by the healer, he sped back across the court with another wave to the section leader. He was halfway up the second flight when he felt his right foot slide on the stone. He tried to catch himself, but his forward motion and the stretch of his legs were such that he hadn't a hope of saving himself from a fall. He tried to grab the stone railing with his right hand but it, too, was slick. He was thrown hard against the stone risers, wrenching thighs and hips, cracking his ribs painfully as he slid. He could have sworn that he heard a muffled laugh. His last conscious thought as his chin hit the stone and he bit his tongue hard was that someone had greased the rail and steps.

His shoulder was roughly shaken, and he heard Dirzan's irritated command to wake up.

"What are you doing here? Why didn't you return immediately with Master Oldive's request? He's been waiting in the meadow. You can't even be trusted to run messages!"

Piemur tried to form an excuse, but only a groan issued from his lips as he groggily tried to right himself. He was dimly conscious of aches and pains all over his left side and sore stiffness across his cheek and under his chin.

"Fell on the steps, did you? Knocked yourself out, huh?" Dirzan was unsympathetic, but he was less rough-handed as he helped Piemur turn and sit on the bottom step.

"Greased," Piemur mumbled, waving with one hand at the steps while with the other he cushioned his aching head to reduce the pounding in his skull. But every place he touched his head seemed to ache, too, and the agony was making him ill to his stomach.

"Greased! Greased?" Dirzan exclaimed in acid disbelief. "A likely notion. You're always pelting up and down these steps. It's a wonder you haven't hurt yourself before now. Can't you get up?"

Piemur started to shake his head, but the slightest motion made him feel sick to his stomach. If he had to spew in front of Dirzan, he'd be doubly humiliated. And if he tried to move, he knew he would be ill.

"You said it was greased?" Dirzan's voice came from above his head. The agitated tone hurt Piemur's skull.

"Step there and handrail . . ." Piemur gestured with one hand.

"There's not a sign of grease! On your feet!" Dirzan sounded angrier than ever.

"Did you find him, Dirzan?" Rokayas called. The voice of the duty journeyman made Piemur's head throb like a message drum. "What happened to him?"

"He fell down the steps and knocked himself *between.*" Dirzan was thoroughly disgusted. "Get up, Piemur!"

"No, Piemur, stay where you are," said Rokayas, and his voice was unexpectedly concerned.

Piemur wished he wouldn't shout, but he was very willing to stay where he was. The nausea in his belly seemed to be echoed by his head, and he didn't dare so much as open his eyes. Things whirled even with them shut.

"He said it was greased! Feel it yourself, Rokayas, clean as a drum!"

"Too clean! And if Piemur fell on his way back, he was *between* a long time. Too long for a mere slip. We'd better get him to Silvina."

"To Silvina? Why bother her for a little tumble? He's only skinned his chin."

Rokayas' hands were gently pressing against his skull and neck, then his arms and legs. He couldn't suppress a yelp when a particular painful bruise was touched.

"This wasn't a little tumble, Dirzan. I know you don't like the boy . . . but any fool could see he's hurt. Can you stand, Piemur?"

Piemur groaned, which was all he dared to do or his dinner would come up.

"He's faking to get out of duty," Dirzan said.

"He's not faking, Dirzan. And another thing, he's done too much of the running. Clell and the others haven't moved their butts out of the drumheights the last two sevendays I've been on duty."

"Piemur's the newest. You know the rule—"

"Oh, leave off, Dirzan. And take him from the other side. I want to carry him as flat as possible."

With Dirzan's grudging assistance, they carried him down the stairs,

Piemur fighting against his nausea. He was only dazedly aware that Rokayas shouted for someone to fetch Silvina and be quick.

They were maneuvering him up the steps to the Main Hall, towards the infirmary, when Silvina intercepted them, asking quick questions, to which she got simultaneous answers from Dirzan and Rokayas.

"He fell down the stairs," said Rokayas.

"Nothing but a tumble," said Dirzan, overriding the other man. "Kept Master Oldive standing in the meadow. . . ."

Silvina's hands felt cool on his face, moved gently over his skull.

"He knocked himself *between,* Silvina, probably for a good twenty minutes or more," Rokayas was saying, his urgent tone cutting through Dirzan's petulant complaint.

"He claimed there was grease!"

"There was grease," said Silvina. "Look at his right shoe, Dirzan. Piemur, do you feel nauseated?"

Piemur made an affirmative sound, hoping that he could suppress the urge to spew until he was in the infirmary, even as a small spark of irreverence suggested that here was a superb opportunity to get back at Dirzan with no possible repercussions.

"He's jarred his skull, all right. Smart of you to carry him prone, Rokayas. Here, now, set him down on this bed. No, you fool, don't sit him. . . ."

The tipping of his body upward triggered the nausea, and Piemur spewed violently onto the floor. Miserable at such a lack of control, Piemur was also powerless to prevent the heaving that shook him. Then he felt Silvina's hand supporting his head, was aware that a basin was appropriately in position. Silvina spoke in a soothing tone, half-supporting his trembling body as he continued to vomit. He was thoroughly exhausted and trembling when the spasms ended and he was eased back against a pile of pillows and could rest his aching head.

"I take it that Master Oldive has already gone off to Nabol?"

"How did you know where he went?" demanded Dirzan, irritably astonished.

"You are a proper idiot, Dirzan. I haven't lived in the Harper Hall all my life without being able to understand drum messages quite well! Not to worry," she said, and now her fingertips were delicately measuring Piemur's skull inch by inch. "I can't feel a crack or split. He may have done no more than rattle his brains. Rest, quiet and time will cure that thumping. Yes, Master Robinton?"

Silvina's hands paused as she tucked the sleeping fur about Piemur's chin.

"Piemur's been hurt?" The Harper's voice was anxious.

As Piemur turned to one elbow, to acknowledge the Harper's entrance, Silvina's hands forced him back against the piled pillows. "Not seriously, I'm relieved to say, but let's all leave the room. I'd like a word with these journeymen in your presence, Master Robin—"

The door closed, and Piemur fought between the overwhelming desire to sleep and curiosity about what she had to say to Dirzan and Rokayas in front of the Masterharper. Sleep conquered.

Once she'd closed the door, Silvina gave vent to the anger she'd held in since she'd first glimpsed the gray pallor of Piemur's face and heard Dirzan's nasal complaints.

"How could you let matters get so out of hand, Dirzan?" she demanded, whirling on the astonished journeyman. "What sort of prank is that for apprentices to try on anyone? Piemur's not been himself, but I put that down to losing his voice and adjusting to the disappointment over the music. But this . . . this is . . . criminal!" Silvina brandished Piemur's begreased boot at Dirzan, backing the astonished journeyman against the wall, oblivious to Master Robinton's repeated query about Piemur's condition, to Menolly's precipitous arrival, her face flushed and furrowed with anxiety, and to Rokayas' delighted and amused observation.

"Enough, Silvina!" The Masterharper's voice was loud enough to quell her momentarily, but she turned to him with an injunction to keep his voice down. Please!

"I will," said the Harper in a moderate tone, keeping Silvina turned towards him, and away from the subject of her ire, "if you will tell me what happened to Piemur."

Silvina let out an exasperated breath, glared once more at Dirzan and then answered Master Robinton.

"His skull isn't cracked, though how it wasn't I'll never know," and she exhibited the glistening sole of Piemur's boot, "with stair treads coated with grease. He's bruised, scraped and shaken, and he's definitely suffering from shock and concussion. . . ."

"When will he recover?" There was an urgency behind the Harper's voice that Silvina heard. Now she gave him a long keen look.

"A few days' rest will see him right, I'm sure. But I mean rest!" She crossed her hands in a whipping motion to emphasize her verdict, then pointed to the closed infirmary door. "Right there! Nowhere near those murdering louts in the drumheights!"

"Murdering?" Dirzan gasped an objection to her term.

"He could have been killed. You know how Piemur climbs steps," she said, scowling fiercely at the journeyman.

"But . . . but there wasn't a trace of grease on those steps or the railing. I tested them all myself!"

"Too clean," said Rokayas, and earned a reprimanding glare from Dirzan. "Too clean!" Rokayas repeated and then said to Silvina. "Piemur's decidedly odd man. He learns too quickly."

"And spouts off what he hears!" Dirzan spoke sharply, determined that Piemur should share the responsibility for this untoward incident.

"Not Piemur," Silvina and Menolly said in one breath.

Dirzan sputtered a moment. "But there've been several very private messages that were all over the Hall, and everyone knows how much Piemur talks, what a conniver he is!"

"Conniver, yes," said Silvina just as Menolly drew breath to defend her friend. "Blabberer, no. He's not been saying more than please and thank you lately either. I'd noticed. And I've noticed some other things happening to him that ought not to have! No mere pranks for the new lad in the craft, either!"

Dirzan moved uneasily under her intense stare and looked appealingly towards the Masterharper.

"How much of drum message has Piemur learned in his time with you?" asked the Harper, no expression in voice or face other than polite inquiry.

"Well, now, he does seem to have picked up every measure I've set him. In fact," and Dirzan admitted this reluctantly, "he has quite a knack for it. Though, of course, he's not done more than beat the woods or listen with the journeyman on duty." He glanced at Rokayas for support.

"I'd say Piemur knows more than he admits," said Rokayas in a droll tone, grinning when Dirzan began to mouth a denial.

"It'd be like Piemur," said Menolly with a grin and then, touching Silvina's arm, "does he need someone with him right now?"

"Rest and quiet is what he needs, and I'll look in on him every little while."

"Rocky could stay," Menolly said. The little bronze fire lizard put in an immediate appearance, chittering worriedly to find himself in such an unexpected place.

"I won't deny that would be sensible," said Silvina, glancing at the closed door. "Yes, that would be very wise, I think."

Everyone watched as Menolly, stroking Rocky gently, told him that he should stay with Piemur and let her know when he spoke. Then she opened the door just enough to admit the little fire lizard, watched as Rocky settled himself quietly by Piemur's feet, his glistening eyes on the boy's pale face.

"Rokayas, would you help Menolly collect Piemur's things from the drumheights?" asked the Harper. His voice was mild, his manner unexceptional but, unmistakably his attitude informed Dirzan that he had misjudged Piemur's standing in the eyes of the most important people of the Hall.

Dirzan offered to do the small task himself, and was denied; offered to help Menolly, who awarded him a cool look. He desisted then, but the set look to his mouth and the controlled anger in his eyes suggested that he was going to deal sternly with the apprentices who had put him in such an invidious position. When he was unexpectedly placed on duty for the entire Feastday, he knew why the roster had been changed. He also knew better than to blame Piemur.

Once Menolly and the journeymen had left them, Robinton turned again to Silvina, showing all the anxiety and concern he had kept hidden.

"Now, don't you worry, Robinton!" Silvina said, patting him on the arm. "He's had a frightful knock on his skull, but I could feel no crack. Those scrapes on chin and cheek'll mend. He'll be stiff and sore from the bruising, that's certain. If you'd only asked me," and Silvina's manner indicated that she'd have her say any road, "I'd have said there were much better uses for Piemur than message drumming. He's been a changed lad since he went to the heights. Not a peep of complaint out of him, but it's as if he wouldn't speak for fear of saying something that was the least bit out of line. And then Dirzan has the nerve to say that Piemur babbled drum messages!"

They were at the Harper's quarters now, and Silvina waited until they were within before she had her final words. "And don't I know what he'd never whispered!"

"And what would that be?" Robinton eyed her with wry amusement.

"That he brought the masters' stones down from the mine, and something else happened that day to keep him overnight, which I haven't discovered as yet," she added with a sigh of regret as she seated herself.

Robinton laughed then, rubbing his fingers gently on her cheek before he came round the table and poured wine, looking at her as he suspended the wine skin above a second glass. She nodded agreement. She needed the wine after the excitement and worry over Piemur, and with the little bronze watching the boy, she didn't need to hurry back.

"The whole accident is my fault," said the Harper after a long sip of wine. He seated himself heavily. "Piemur *is* clever, and he *can* keep his tongue still. Too still for his own good health, I see now. He hasn't hinted of any trouble in the drumheights to either Menolly or Sebell. . . ."

"They'd be the last he'd tell, except for yourself, of course." Silvina gave a snort. "I only knew about it after the Impression at Benden. The others . . ." and Silvina wrinkled her nose in remembered distaste, ". . . treated his new clothes. I came upon him washing them, or I'd never have known either." She chuckled with such malice the Harper had no trouble following her thought.

"They did it while he was at Igen Hold, not knowing about the Impression?" He joined in her laughter, and Silvina knew that she'd restored his perspective on the unfortunate affair. "And to think that I placed him in the drumheights to safeguard him! You're sure he's sustained no lasting hurt?"

"As sure as I can be without Master Oldive to confirm it." Silvina spoke tartly, for Master Oldive's attendance on that worthless Lord of Nabol when he was urgently needed in the Hall aggravated her intensely.

"Yes, Meron!" The Masterharper sighed again, one corner of his expressive mouth twitching with irritation and an inner perplexity.

"The man's dying. Not all of Master Oldive's skill can save him. And why bother with Meron? He's better dead after all the harm he's done. When I think that Brekke's queen might still be alive today . . ."

"It's his dying that will cause even more trouble, Silvina."

"How?"

"We can no more have Nabol Hold in contention than we can Ruatha Hold—"

"But Nabol has half a dozen heirs of full blood—"

"Meron won't name his successor!"

"Oh." Silvina's exclamation of startled comprehension was followed quickly by a second of utter disgust. "What more could you expect of that man? But surely steps can be taken. I doubt that Master Oldive would scruple against. . . ."

Master Robinton held up his hand. "Nabol has been cursed with Holders either too ambitious, too selfish, or too incompetent to render it in any way prosperous . . ."

"To be sure, it's not the best of Holds, stuck in the mountains, cold, damp, harsh."

"Quite right. So there's little sense in forcing combat on the full-Blooded heirs when one might just end up with another unsympathetic and uncooperative Lord."

Silvina narrowed her eyes in thought. "I make it nine or ten full-Blooded close male heirs. Those daughters of Meron's are too young to be married, and none of them will ever be pretty, taking after their sire as they all seem to have had the misfortune to do. Which of those nine—"

"Ten . . ."

"Which would get the most support from the small holders and crafthalls? And how, pray tell, does Piemur fit into . . . ah, but, of course." A smile smoothed Silvina's frown, and she raised her glass to toast the Harper's ingenuity. "He did well then at Igen Hold?"

"Indeed he did, though Igen's a loyal group under any circumstances."

Silvina caught his slight emphasis on the word "loyal," and scrutinized his thoughtful face. "Why 'loyal'? And to whom? Surely there's no more disloyalty to Benden?"

Robinton gave a quick negative shake of his head. "Several disquieting rumors have come to my notice. The most worrying, the fact that Nabol abounds with fire lizards . . ."

"Nabol has no shoreline and scarcely any friends in Holds that do acquire what fire lizards are found."

Robinton agreed. "They have also been ordering, and paying for, large quantities of fine cloth, wines, the delicacies of Nerat, Tillek and Keroon, not to mention every sort of mongery from the Smithcrafthall that can be bought or bartered, quantities and qualities enough to garb, feed and supply amply every holder, cot and hold in Nabol . . . and don't!"

"The Oldtimers!" Silvina emphasized that guess with a snap of her fingers. "T'kul and Meron were always two cuts from the same rib."

"What I cannot figure out is what besides fire lizards the association gains Meron . . ."

"You can't?" Silvina was frankly skeptical. "Spite! Malice! Scoring off Benden!"

Robinton reflected on that opinion, turning his wine glass idly by the stem. "I'd like to know. . . ."

"Yes, *you* would!" Silvina grinned at him, tolerance for his foibles as well as affection in her glance. "You and Piemur are paired in that respect. He has the same insatiable urge to know, and he's a dab hand at finding out, too. Is that why you want his head mended? You're sending him up to Candler at Nabol Hold?"

"No . . ." and the Harper drawled the word, pulling at his lower lip. "No, not directly to Nabol Hold. Meron might recognize him: the man's never been a fool, just perverted in principle."

"Just?" Silvina was disgusted.

"I'd like to know what's going on there."

"Today is not likely to be the last time Meron summons Master Oldive. . . ." she said, raising her eyebrows suggestively.

Robinton brushed aside the notion. "I hear that a Gather's been scheduled at Nabol on the same sevenday as Lord Groghe's. . . ."

"Isn't that just like Meron."

"Consequently, no one would expect Hall harpers to be in attendance," and Robinton ended his sentence on an upswing of tone, eyeing Silvina hopefully.

"The boy'll be fit enough for a Gather, and undoubtedly it's kinder to send him away from the Hall on that particular day. Tilgin's come along amazingly."

"Could he do aught else?" asked Robinton with real humor in his voice, "with both Shonagar and Domick spending every waking moment with him?"

Chapter 6

Piemur drifted in and out of sleep for the rest of that day and most of the next, immeasurably reassured and comforted by the presence of Rocky or Lazy and Mimic who spelled the bronze fire lizard. If Menolly's fire lizards were with him, he reasoned, during the moments he drifted into consciousness, then Master Robinton couldn't be annoyed that he'd been stupid enough to fall and hurt himself just when the Harper needed him. For that was how Piemur construed the Harper's urgent query about his injury. He fretted, too, about what Clell and the others might do with his possessions until he saw his press against the wall beside his bed.

The first time Silvina appeared with a tray of food, he didn't feel like eating.

"You're not likely to be sick again," she told him in a low but firm voice, settling on his bed to spoon the rich broth into him. "That was due to the crack you gave your head. You need the nourishment of this broth, so open your mouth. Too bad we can't numbweed the inside of your head, but we can't. Never thought to see the day *you* weren't ready to eat. Now, there's the lad. You'll feel right as ever in a day or two more. Don't mind if you seem to want to sleep. That's only natural. And here's Rocky to keep you company again."

"Who's been feeding him?"

"Don't sit up!" Silvina's hand pressed him back into the half-reclining position. "You'll spill the broth. I suspect Sebell gave Menolly a hand. Not to worry. You'll be back at that chore soon enough!"

Piemur caught at her skirt as she made a move. "There was grease on those steps, wasn't there, Silvina?" Piemur had to ask the question, because he couldn't really trust what he thought he'd heard.

"Indeed and there was!" Silvina frowned, pursing her lips in an angry line. Then she patted his hand. "Those little sneaks saw you fall, scampered down and washed the grease off the steps and handrail . . . but," she added in a sharper tone, "they forgot there'd be grease on your boot as well!" Another pat on his arm. "You might say, they slipped up there!"

For a moment, Piemur couldn't believe that Silvina was joshing him, and then he had to giggle.

THE HARPER HALL OF PERN

"There! That's more like you, Piemur. Now, rest! That'll set you right quicker than you realize. And likely to be the last good rest you'll get for a while."

She wouldn't say more, encouraging him to go back to sleep, and slipping out of the room without giving him any hint to the plans for his future. If his things were here, he didn't think he'd be going back to the drumheights. Where else could he be placed at the Hall? He tried to examine this problem, but his mind wouldn't work. Probably Silvina had laced that broth with something. Wouldn't surprise him if she had.

Complacent fire lizard chirpings roused him. Beauty was conferring with Lazy and Mimic, who were perched on the end of the bed. No one else was in the room, and then Beauty disappeared. Shortly, while he was fretting that no one seemed to be bothering about him, Menolly quietly pushed the door open, carrying a tray in her free hand. He could hear the normal sounds of shouting and calling, and he could smell baked fish.

"If that's more sloppy stuff . . ." he began petulantly.

" 'Tisn't. Baked fish, some tubers, and a special bubbly pie that Abuna insisted would improve your appetite."

"Improve it? I'm starving."

Menolly grinned at his vehemence and positioned the tray on his lap, then seated herself at the end of the bed. He was immensely relieved that Menolly had no intention of feeding him like a babe. It had been embarrassing enough with Silvina.

"Master Oldive checked you over last night when he returned. Said you undoubtedly have the hardest head in the Hall. And you're not going back to the drumheights." Her expression was as grim as Silvina's had been. "No," she added when she saw him glance at his press, "no more pranks. I checked. And I checked with Silvina to be sure all your things are accounted for." She grinned, then, her eyes twinkling. "Clell and the other dimglows are on water rations, and they won't get to the Gather!"

Piemur groaned.

"And why not? They deserve restriction. Pranks are one thing, but deliberately conspiring to injure—and you could have been killed by their mischief—is an entirely different matter. Only . . ." and Menolly shook her head in perplexity, ". . . I can't think what you did to rile them so."

"I didn't do anything," Piemur said so emphatically that he slopped the water glass on his tray.

Rocky chirped anxiously, and Beauty took up the note in her trill.

"I believe you, Piemur." She squeezed his toes where they poked up the sleeping furs. "I do! And, would you also believe, that that's why you had trouble? They kept expecting you to *do* some typical Piemur tricks, and you were so busy behaving for the first time since you apprenticed here, no one could credit it. Least of all Dirzan, who knew all too much about you and your ways!" She gave his toes another affectionate tweak. "And you, bursting your guts with discretion to the point where you didn't tell me or Sebell what you bloody ought to have. We didn't mean for you to stop talking altogether, you know."

"I thought you were testing me."

"Not that hard, Piemur. When I found out what Dirzan . . . no, eat all your tubers," and she snatched from his grasp the plate with the still bubbling pie.

"You know I only like 'em hot!"

"Eat all your dinner first. You'll need your strength, and wits. You're to go with Sebell to Nabol Hold for Meron's Gather. That'll get you away from here during Tilgin's singing, though he has improved tremendously—and no one at Nabol will be expecting any extra harpers. Not that they've all that much to sing about in Nabol Hold anyhow."

"Lord Meron's still alive?"

"Yes." Menolly sighed with distaste, then cocked her head slightly. "You know, your bruises might just come in very handy. They're just purpling beautifully now, so they won't have faded. . . ."

"You mean," and Piemur affected a tremulous whine in his voice, "I'm the poor apprentice lad whose master beats up on him?"

Menolly chuckled. "You're on the mend."

Late that evening, a dust-grayed, raggedly dressed man peered round the door and shuffled slowly into the room, never taking his eyes from Piemur's face. At first, Piemur thought that the man might be a cotholder, looking for Master Oldive's quarters on the Hall's second level; but the fellow, though initially hesitant and almost fearful in his attitude, altered perceptibly in manner and stance as he came closer to the bed.

"Sebell?" There was something about the man that made Piemur suspicious. "Sebell, is that you?"

The dusty figure straightened and strode across the floor, laughing.

"Now I'm sure I can gain a discreet arrival at the Nabol Hold Gather! I fooled Silvina, too. She says you still have some rags that will be appropriate to the status of a rather stupid herder's boy!"

"Herder's boy?"

"Why not? Kum in handy, like, tha' knowin' the way from tha' bluid, like." As Sebell affected the speech mannerisms of the up-range herders, he became completely the nondescript person who had first entered the infirmary.

Despite his chagrin at being told to resume a role he'd hoped never to play again, Piemur was enchanted by the journeyman's dissembling. If Sebell would do it, so would he.

"Master Robinton's not angry with me, is he?"

"Not a mite." Sebell shook his head violently for emphasis. Kimi swooped in, scolding because Sebell had made her wait outside. Then his expression became serious, and he waggled a finger at Piemur. "However, you will have to watch your step with Master Oldive. We've sworn blue to him that this isn't going to be an energetic adventure for you. Even heads as hard as yours must be treated with caution after such a fall. So, instead of hiking you in from Ruatha Hold as I'd planned," and Sebell gave a mock scowl at Piemur's burst of laughter, "N'ton will drop you off at dawn in the valley before Nabol Hold. Then we'll proceed at a proper pace with beasts suitable for sale at the Nabol Gather."

"Why?" asked Piemur bluntly. Discretion had got him nothing but misery, confusion and unwarranted accusations. This time he would know what he was about.

"Two things," Sebell said without so much as a pause for consideration. "If it's true that there are more fire lizards in Nabol Hold than—"

"Is that what they meant?"

"Is that what who meant?"

"Lord Oterel. At the Hatching. I overheard him talking to someone . . . didn't know the man . . . and he said, 'Meron gets more than he ought and we have to do without.' Didn't make sense then, but it would if Lord Oterel was talking about fire lizards. Was he?"

"He very likely was, and I wish you'd mentioned that snip of talk before."

"I didn't know you'd want to know, and it made no sense to me then." Piemur ended on a plaintive note, seeing Sebell's frown of irritation.

The journeyman smiled a quick reassurance. "No, you couldn't've known. Now you do. We know that Lord Meron had his first fire lizards from Kylara nearly four Turns ago, so they could have clutched at least once, possibly twice. And he'd've made certain he had control of the distribution of those new eggs. Nonetheless, he has distributed more in Nabol than we can account for. What is equally important is the amount of other supplies that are being brought into the Hold and . . . disappearing!"

"Meron's trading with the Oldtimers?"

"Lord Meron, lad and don't forget the title even in your thoughts . . . and yes, that's the possibility."

"And he's getting whole clutches of fire lizard eggs for trading for 'em? As well as the eggs of his original pairs?" Piemur was assailed by a variety of emotions: anger that Lord Meron of Nabol Hold was getting more than a fair share of the fire lizard eggs when other, more worthy persons, Piemur included himself, ought to have a chance to Impress the precious creatures; a righteous indignation that Lord Meron (and he slurred the title into an insult in his thoughts) was deliberately flouting Benden Weyr by trafficking in any way with the Oldtimers; and an intense excitement at the possibility that he, Piemur, might help discredit further this infamous Lord Holder.

"Those are two of the main things to listen for. The third, which is the most important in some ways, is which of Lord Meron's male heirs would be most acceptable to craft and cot."

"He is dying then?" He'd been sure that the message to Master Oldive was spurious.

"Oh, yes, a wasting disease." Sebell's grin was malicious, and there was an unpleasant gleam in his eyes as he met Piemur's astonished gaze. "You might say, a very proper disease to fit Lord Meron's . . . peculiar ways!"

Piemur would have liked to have particulars, but Sebell rose.

"I must be away now, Piemur. You're to rest, without getting into any mischief."

"Rest? I've been resting—"

"Bored? Well, I'll ask Rokayas to give you drum measures to learn. That ought to ease your boredom without taxing your strength." Sebell laughed at Piemur's snort of dismay.

"As long as it's Rokayas."

"It will be. *He's* of the mind that you learned a great deal more than Dirzan believes."

Piemur grinned at the subtle question in Sebell's words, but before he could retort, the door was closing behind the journeyman and Kimi, who fluttered above him. Piemur hugged his knees to his chest, rocking slowly on his tail bones as he thought over all that Sebell had confided to him. And tried to figure out what it was Sebell hadn't told him.

One thing Sebell hadn't mentioned was how cold and how dark it would be when N'ton collected him before dawn. Menolly with Beauty and Rocky had roused him from a fitful sleep, for he'd been afraid he'd oversleep and consequently spent a restless night. He could sense Menolly's amusement as the two of them, guided by the encouraging chir-rups of the fire lizards, stumbled across the dark courtyard towards the Gather meadow. Then Lioth turned his brilliant jewel-faceted eyes in their direction, and they moved more confidently forward.

Menolly giggled as she boosted Piemur up to catch the fighting straps, and then he felt N'ton's downstretched hand and was aided into position. He heard her softly wish him luck, then she blended into the shadows, her actual position discernible only by four points of light that were fire lizard eyes.

"D'you want the fighting strap about you, Piemur? Night flying un-nerves a lot of people."

Piemur wanted to say yes, but instead took a good hold on the leathers that encircled Lioth's neck. He replied that since this was only a short trip, he wouldn't need them. Then clutched convulsively as Lioth sprang upwards. They were above the rim of Fort Hold's fireheights before Piemur caught his breath. N'ton gave the bronze dragon the audible command to Nabol, and Piemur knew he screamed into the nothingness of *between*. He choked off the noise as he felt the change from intense cold and blackness to frosty chill and the faint lightening in what must be the eastern sky.

Two whirling points of light danced above N'ton's left shoulder, and a fire lizard's complacent chirp informed Piemur that N'ton's bronze, Tris, had turned to look at him. Then Lioth swerved and Piemur's fingers became numb as he increased the pressure on the straps, uncon-sciously leaning backwards against the angle of descent into darkness. Tris chirruped encouragingly, as if he were completely aware of Piemur's internal confusion. Piemur prayed fervently that Tris wouldn't inform N'ton of how scared he was. Abruptly the bronze dragon backwinged and settled with the lightest of bumps in black shadow.

"Lioth says there are people not far down the road, Piemur," said N'ton in a low voice. "Give me your flying gear."

"Isn't it Sebell?" asked Piemur, shedding helmet and jacket and thrusting them blindly toward N'ton.

"Lioth says no, but Sebell is not far behind. He hears Kimi."

"Kimi?" Piemur's surprise made him speak louder than he intended, and he winced at N'ton's warning.

"You forget," whispered N'ton, "Sebell can bring Kimi because fire lizards are so common here in Nabol. Or so we're led to understand." Displeasure colored the Fort Weyrleader's amendment. Then Piemur felt the strong gloved hand curl about his wrist, and he obediently threw his right leg back over Lioth's neckridge, sliding down the massive shoulder, aware as he slipped beyond N'ton's guiding hand, that the dragon had cocked his leg to allow an easier slope of descent. He let his knees take the shock of his landing and patted Lioth's shoulder, wondering as he did so if that were bold of him.

"Good luck, Piemur!" N'ton's muted voice just reached his ears. He stepped back, turning his head against the shower of dust and sand as the huge bronze launched himself skyward.

Once his eyes were accustomed to the variations of black and dark gray, Piemur located the winding road and whistled softly as he realized how accurately the dragon had landed in the one flat area big enough to accommodate him. Piemur's respect for draconic abilities rose to new heights.

He heard now the occasional sound of voices and saw the erratic wavering of light from the glowbaskets of the leading file. A creaking of wheeled carts and the familiar *sluff-sluff* of plate-footed burden beasts reached his ears. He looked about him for a place to hide. He had a choice of boulders and ledges, and found a shielded spot that faced the track but gave him a clear view of the dimly seen exit. He curled up small, hugging knees to chest, secure in the belief that he couldn't be seen.

A chirrup disabused him of that notion and, startled, he glanced up and saw three pairs of fire lizard eyes gleaming at him.

"Go away, you silly creatures. I'm not even here!" To prove this, he closed his eyes and concentrated on the awful nothingness of *between*. The fire lizards responded with an agitated chorus.

"What's the matter with them?" a gruff male voice called over the creaking of cartwheels and the shuffling sound of the burden beasts.

"Who knows? Who cares? We'm most to Nabol now!"

Piemur redoubled his efforts to think of nothing, and heard the faint flutter of fire lizards taking flight. To think of nothing took more effort than to concentrate on something. A great many carts, too, Piemur thought, for a Nabol Gather when there was another, better one at Fort Hold. He opened his eyes now and saw the flicker of winging fire lizards in the gathering daylight, and the point-lights of their eyes in gloom. And these were carters? Small holders? The anger that injustice roused warmed Piemur long after the caravan and the comfort of their glowbaskets passed from his angle of vision.

The cold dawn wind rose, and Piemur wished that Sebell would put in his promised appearance. He ought to have asked N'ton if Lioth had seen Sebell as he glided to his landing. Then Piemur chided himself that this was scarcely the first time he'd waited on his lonesome in the dark of dawn. He'd done his watches with his father's herds. Of course, there'd usually been someone sleeping in the cot within voice range during those long, slow hours. What if something had happened to Sebell? Or he was delayed? Should Piemur go on to Nabol by himself? And how was he to return to the Harper Hall? He'd forgotten to ask N'ton that, presuming it was the Fort Weyrleader who'd collect him. Or was he to be collected? Did Sebell plan to sell those suitable beasts of his during the Gather? Or would they have to herd them back whence they'd come? There was a great deal that Sebell hadn't told him in spite of the journeyman's candid explanation about their surreptitious appearance at Nabol Hold.

Piemur relieved his anxieties by remembering that he wasn't going to have to attend the Fort Hold festivities, or listen to Tilgin sing music that Domick had written for *him.* He sighed, depressed that he wasn't going to be singing the role of Lessa, that he wasn't still comfortably in his bed in the senior apprentices' dormitory, waking to anticipate the applause of Lord Groghe's guests, the accolades of his friends and Domick. And quite likely Lessa's approval, since the Weyrwoman was Lord Groghe's special guest today.

Here he was, cold, miserable, and uncomfortably aware that he hadn't had so much as a cold cup of klah before he was bundled onto a dragon's back and dumped here to await a man who might not arrive for hours if he was walking a herd of beasts in from Ruatha Hold all by himself!

And when they found out what they'd come to discover and returned to the Harper Hall, what would Piemur do tomorrow?

He grinned, hugging his knees in smug satisfaction, remembering Rokayas' surprise the day before when he had perfectly dead-sticked the complicated message Rokayas had thought up to test his knowledge of the drum language. Piemur was almost sorry he wouldn't be—

He groped on the ground beside him and found a rock, gave it an experimental whack against the boulder that sheltered him. The resultant sound echoed about the small valley. Piemur found another rock and, rising, went to the now visible track. He beat the rocks together in the monotone code for "harper," adding the beat for "where," grinning as the sharp staccato sounds reverberated. He repeated the two measures, then waited. He beat his measures again to give Sebell time to find his own rocks. Then in the pause he heard distantly a muffled reply: "journeyman comes."

Immeasurably relieved, Piemur was wondering whether to proceed down the track and intercept Sebell when he heard a "stay" as the message was repeated. He was a bit daunted by the "stay" and restlessly scuffed at the loose gravel on the track. Surely Sebell wasn't far away. What did it matter if Piemur did go to meet him? But the message had been clear—"stay"—and Piemur decided that Sebell must have a reason, other than obedience to Master Oldive's instruction about Piemur's dented head.

Sullenly, Piemur resumed his position behind the boulder. And none too soon. He heard then the sharp clatter of hooves against stone, the jangle of metal against metal, and a rumble of encouraging shouts. A fair of fire lizards arrowed out of the graying southern skies, heading straight up the track. Piemur thought of cold *between*'s nothingness, as the fire lizards, intent on keeping ahead of the swiftly pacing riders, swept on. The ground beneath Piemur's rump trembled with the runners' passage.

There was so much dust raised that Piemur couldn't be sure how many rode by, but he estimated a dozen or more. A dozen riders with a full fair of fire lizards escorting them?

Again anger consumed Piemur. He knew that he wouldn't have resented this latest concentration of fire lizards, obviously companioning holders prosperous enough to own fast pacers, if the earlier caravan hadn't been just as well favored with the creatures. It wasn't fair. He agreed wholeheartedly with Lord Oterel! There were many, too many fire lizards abroad in Nabol.

He was so incensed over such inequity, since the caravaners obviously hadn't appreciated the capabilities of the little creatures, that at first he didn't hear the *shluff-shluff* of the approaching herd.

Kimi's quizzical cheep nearly frightened him out of his wits. She cheeped again, apologetically, and her eyes whirled a little faster as she peered at him from the top of the boulder.

"Well?" asked Sebell, appearing around one side. "You took me too literally."

"They all have fire lizards," cried Piemur, too indignant to make polite greeting.

"Yes, I had noticed."

"I don't mean that lot," and Piemur jerked his thumb in the direction of the riders. "There was a caravan that had two or three full fairs—"

"Did they see you?" asked Sebell, suddenly wary.

"The fire lizards did, but no human paid any attention to their alert!" Then Piemur caught sight of the beasts that Sebell had herded and whistled.

"So? They meet with your approval?"

The leader had ambled past, eyes half-closed against the dust, and the rest, nose to the tail in front, with eyes fully closed, followed. Piemur counted five: all were well-fleshed, with good, thick, furry hides, moving steadily without a stumble, which meant their feet were sound.

"You'll sell them all right," said Piemur.

"Happen Ah will!" said Sebell in proper accent and, passing his arm about Piemur's shoulders, urged him ahead of the herd. "Here," and Sebell passed Piemur a padded flask. "It should still be hot. I only broke camp when Kimi told me Lioth had flashed by."

Piemur mumbled his gratitude for the klah, which was hot enough to warm his belly. Then Sebell handed Piemur a dried meat roll of the sort that was standard journey rations, and Piemur began to view the imminent day in a much improved frame of mind.

As soon as he'd finished eating, he voluntarily dropped back to the apprentice's uncomfortable position at the end of the single file. He'd be properly coated with dust by the time they arrived at Nabol Hold.

The first thing Piemur did when they got to the Gather meadow was head towards the nearest watering trough, fighting against his thirsty charges for a space at the edge. He also remembered exactly where to pinch their noses to make them turn from him.

"Ar, lad, let th'beasts drink deep farst!" Sebell unceremoniously hauled him away, his voice angry, though his eyes twinkled as he warned Piemur to play the proper part.

"Ar, sor, tongue that dry can't move."

Two young boys were approaching the trough with pails, but they waited, as custom dictated, until the beasts had drunk their fill and the cold mountain water flowed clear again. Piemur and Sebell then herded their charges towards the area of the meadow set aside for animal sales. The Hold Steward, a pinch-faced man with a runny nose, all but pounced on them, demanding the Gather fee. Sebell immediately protested the amount, and the two set to haggling. Sebell brought the fee down a full mark before he surrendered his token, but he didn't protest when the Steward waved them contemptuously towards the smallest enclosure at the end of the rank. Piemur was about to object when Sebell's hand closed warningly on his shoulder. Looking at the journeyman in surprise, Piemur saw the imperceptible jerk of his head over his shoulder. Piemur waited a few discreet seconds and then casually glanced about him. Three men had started to follow them towards their allotted space. A thrill of fear made Piemur catch his breath until he recognized the unmistakable herder gait and knew these were prospective buyers.

"Tol'ya Ah'd suitable beasts, di' Ah no?" drawled Sebell under his breath.

"Ar, an yull drink th' profit again, like as not," replied Piemur in a sullen tone, but his shoulders shook with the effort to control his amusement. He hadn't a single doubt in his mind that Sebell would also play the happy drunken herdsman to perfection. And manage to say without offense what would be impossible for a sober man anyplace.

They got the beasts enclosed, and Piemur was sent with a worn mark of the Herdsman's Crafthall to haggle for fodder. He managed to save an eighth on the dealing, which he pocketed as any apprentice would. Sebell was already deep in bargain with one of the men while the others were examining the beasts with pinch and prod. Piemur wondered where under the sun Sebell had managed to acquire such proper moun-tain-bred creatures, with rock-worn hooves and shaggy coats. He could no more account for the good flesh on them after this long winter than the prospective buyers, so he hunkered down and listened to Sebell's explanation.

Trust a harper to weave words well, and Piemur's respect for the journeyman increased proportionately to the elaborations of the tale he told. Sebell would have his audience believe that he merely used an old trick handed down from grandsire to grandson: a combination of herbs and grasses sweetened with just the right amount of berries and well-moistened dried fruits. He also said that he and his did without some-times to improve their beasts, and Piemur promptly sucked in his cheeks to look suitably haggard. He saw the eyes of the men linger on his bruises, showing yellow on his chin and cheek, while Sebell rambled on about his holders scrambling up and down the southern face of his hold hill to find the sweet new grasses that produced such spectacular results.

The earnest knot of listeners attracted more who stood respectfully back but close enough to hear. What Piemur couldn't figure out was that, while the beasts had very old marks of Ruathan breeding, the secondary marks were also well-worn. Then he was annoyed with him-self: Sebell must have pulled this sort of stunt before. Undoubtedly somewhere in Ruatha was a cotholder who kept a few special beasts for the Harper Hall's convenience. He began to relax and enjoy Sebell's tale-spinning thoroughly.

The sun was well over the mountains by the time Sebell had struck hands on the bargains—for there were three. One man bought three of the beasts, and the others one apiece, at what Piemur knew was a bloody good price. He wondered if that had covered their original pur-chase and their keep. Appropriately sober-faced during the bargaining, Sebell permitted pleasure to glow on his dirt-smeared face as he care-fully stowed the mark pieces in his belt pouch while the beasts were prodded away by their new owners.

"Didn't think I'd make that much, but the trick always works!" said Sebell in a low mutter to Piemur.

"Trick?"

"Sure," said Sebell softly as he patted dust from his clothing. "Arrive dusty, early, with well-fleshed beasts, and they're on to you fast, hoping you're tired enough to be stupid."

"Where did you get 'em?"

Sebell flashed Piemur a grin. "Craft secret. Get along with you now," and he gave Piemur a wink and a rough shove. "See t'Gather!" he added in a louder tone. "Ah find thee when Ah wish to go."

This wasn't much of a Gather, Piemur decided when he'd done one round of the small nestle of stalls. They didn't even have bubbly pies at the baker's, and the Crafthalls had obviously sent very junior men to represent them. Still, a Gather was a day to be enjoyed, and not many were held at Nabol even when restdays were Thread-clear, so the Nabolese were making as much of the occasion as they could.

The wineman was doing a brisk trade by the time Piemur returned that way. He squatted at the corner of the stand, munching slowly away at another meatroll, listening to comments and noticing with deep chagrin and a growing wrath how many fire lizards flitted about, resting for a moment on the stall tops, wheeling up in fairs to dance in the air a bit before settling on their friends' shoulders or on a new position where they could overlook. At first Piemur tried to convince himself that he was only seeing the same group again and again. He did notice that most were greens with a sprinkling of brown and blues—the lesser fire lizards. When he saw bronzes, they were always on the shoulder or arm of the more prosperously dressed. Yet no matter how Piemur argued the matter in his mind, it was clear that Nabol Hold boasted more fire lizards than he had seen even at Benden Weyr during the Impression.

Suddenly a phrase stood out from the murmurous conversation about the winestand.

"There'll be a few more happy holders today, I hear!"

Piemur turned to scratch his shoulder fiercely and located the man who had spoken from his knowing smirk, a smith from his clothing. His companion, a miner by his shoulder badge, was nodding in comprehension.

"Nabol don't take proper care of 'em, he don't. Three never shelled. My master was fair upset about that. Means to have three more today or his name's not Kaljan."

"Is that so?" The smith bobbed his head up and down to show regret. "We'd one that didn't hatch, too, but no joy did we get above! Eggs we was promised and eggs we was given. Up to us to care for 'em proper enough to make 'em hatch. That one," and his head jerked towards the

Hold cliff to indicate Lord Meron, "enjoys putting a snake among the wherries!" He snorted derisively. "Happen it's his only pleasure now." Both men guffawed with malicious delight. "Happen we'll not need to worry about him much longer, I hear tell." The smith winked broadly at the miner. "Couldn't be soon enough for me. Well, see you at the dancing?" "Going so soon?" "Had my glass. Must get back."

The disappointment in the miner's face made Piemur think that the smith's departure was precipitous. Going to tell his master about the eggs that were up at the Hold, was he? Piemur decided to tag along.

Eggs handed out in quantities, eggs that had been badly handled and wouldn't hatch. Unless . . . and Piemur reflected over something that Menolly had said about fire lizard eggs. Green fire lizards laid eggs as well, having been fertilized by a mating flight with a blue or brown, sometimes even a bronze. But green fire lizards were stupid: they'd lay a clutch, ten at the most, Menolly said, and leave them with such a shallow covering of beach sand that they were easy prey to wild wherries or sand snakes. Very few green-laid clutches survived to Hatch. Which, as Menolly had succinctly stated, was just as well or Pern would be up to the eyeballs in little green fire lizards.

Piemur wondered if anyone in Nabol realized that a deception was being practiced on them, and green fire lizard eggs were what were dispersed so lavishly. Then he realized that he'd lost sight of the smith and, cursing his inattentiveness, began to retrace his steps, turning with assumed idleness to peer between the stalls. He spotted the smith, urgently speaking to a man with a smithmaster's badge and, as the man reacted to his journeyman's excited words, his master's chain sparkled. Piemur managed to duck away as both men suddenly turned towards him. When they had passed him on their way to the Hold, Piemur followed, restlessly scanning faces in the hopes that he might see Sebell and tell him what he'd overheard. Sebell might wish to investigate.

As the two smiths turned from the Gather area towards the Hold, Piemur had to pause or be noticeable. The smiths strode purposefully up the ramp towards the main Hold gates. They were challenged by the guard and, after some moments of arguing, the guard summoned another from the gatehouse and sent him to the Hold with the smithmaster's message.

While the messenger was gone, two men emerged from the Hold, well wrapped in their cloaks, though the air had lost its chill. Something about the way they walked, carefully; the way they carried their heads, proudly; the way they nodded and smiled at the guards, smugly; and most of all the way they pointedly avoided contact, struck Piemur as significant. He continued to watch them as they turned towards the Gather meadow. As they approached him he caught sight of their figures in profile and realized that each man carried something hidden in his cloak, held tight against his side. It couldn't have been a large object. But, thought Piemur, putting expression, manner and profile together, an egg pot wouldn't be large. He wanted to follow the men to see if his suspicion was correct, but he also didn't want to leave the Hold until the message from the smithmaster had been answered.

A new party, holders by the look of them, now made themselves known to the guards and were admitted, to the angry chagrin of the smithmaster. Then three carts, heavily laden to judge by the straining of the burden beasts struggling up the ramp, forced the smithmaster to one side. The guard waved the carts toward the kitchen courtyard. The last cart jammed a wheel against the ramp parapet, the driver thudding his stick against the burden beast's rump.

"Wheel be jammed," yelled Piemur, not liking to see any animal beaten for what was not its fault.

He jumped forward to help guide the carter. The man now backed his stolid beast, swinging its head left. Piemur, setting his shoulder to the tailgate, gave a push in the proper direction. He also tried to peek under the covering to see what on earth was being delivered to the Hold on a Gather day when most business was done in the Gather meadow. Before he could get a good look, the cart had picked up speed as it reached more level ground.

He was past the guards, arguing with the smith and paying no more attention to the procession of carts. Ducking quickly to the side of the cart away from the carter, Piemur gained access to the Hold proper.

As the carts rumbled on into the kitchen court, Piemur rapidly wondered how he could turn this opportunity to advantage and remain in the Hold after the carters had unloaded and left. Certainly if he was actually in the Hold, he might find out more than he could possibly learn wandering about the Gather. If nothing else he could discover what the carter had delivered.

Then he spied a line of coveralls bleaching in the spring sun. He darted over and removed one, ignoring the slight dampness as he slipped it over his head. Kitchen drudges were never noted for cleanliness, and once the beast dirt and stains on his tunic were covered, the dust on his boots and trousers would be unremarkable.

"Hey, you!" Piemur tried to ignore the call, but it was repeated and could only be directed to him. He turned towards the speaker, affecting a stupid expression. "I mean you, with the empty arms!"

Obediently he trudged back to the carter, who slung a heavy sack across his back. At that point, the kitchen steward bustled out to supervise, and Piemur, bent double under the sack, passed him without a glance. The steward alternated between chivvying his drudges out to help unload, and the carter for his ill-timed arrival. The carter replied with equal heat that he had heavy carts and slow beasts and had had to give way and eat dust from those hurrying to this bloody Gather. Meron ought to be pleased he'd got here within the day allotted, much less at an earlier hour.

The steward hushed him and began shouting orders, ordering Piemur on to the back stores rooms. Piemur got inside the kitchen, not knowing where the stores rooms were, so, making a business of wiping his face and easing his shoulders, he waited until someone brushed past him and turned down the proper corridor.

"Don't know where Ah'm t' put more as is plenty here a'ready," muttered the drudge as Piemur followed him.

"A-top them others?" suggested Piemur helpfully.

In the dim light of waning glows, the Nabolese peered at Piemur. "Never saw you afore."

"Nor you haven't," Piemur agreed amiably. "Sent from t'Hold to help in kitchen for t'Gather."

"Oh!" And the sly gleam in the man's eyes suggested to Piemur that he had just let himself in for the worst and dirtiest of the chores about a Hold on a Gather day when the Lord was feasting guests.

Haste appeared the vital factor in unloading the carts, so Piemur didn't see many of the seals on the sacks, barrels and boxes he humped out of sight. But he saw enough to realize that the delivery came from a variety of sources: tanner, weaver, smithcraft for the heaviest boxes, wine from many of the yards, but none, he was pleased to note, from Benden. When the last bundle was stowed in the now-bulging stores rooms, Piemur's sigh of relief was echoed by Besel, the sly drudge, who had managed to stay close to him during the unloading. Piemur had no sooner lowered himself to a sack to rest than the man snatched him to his feet.

"C'mon, we've no time to rest t'day."

Nor did Piemur, who was set first to scrape out ashes from the secondary hearths and then to gutting beasts and wild fowl, thankful that he'd watched Camo often enough at that task to know the tricks. He scoured extra plates, encrusted with the dirt and grime of Turns, until his fingers shriveled. When he'd done that, and peeled a dragonload of tubers, he was allowed a breather so long as he kept one of the five spits turning.

Chaos broke loose when the Hold Steward arrived to inform the kitchen that Lord Meron chose to eat in his own quarters and these were to be prepared while he walked the Gather.

The kitchen steward obsequiously took the change of order, having only that hour completed the feast arrangements in the Great Hall. The moment the heavy door had swung shut on the Hold Steward's back, however, he burst into obscenities that won him Piemur's astounded approval.

If Piemur had thought he'd worked hard already, he was soon disabused of that notion by the rate at which he was sent flying about the kitchen to collect cleaning and polishing tools and preparations. Then he was sent on ahead with Besel and a woman to start cleaning the Lord's rooms. Already weary from an early rising and more hard labor than he'd known since he'd left his native cothold, Piemur tried to cheer himself by imagining Master Oldive's reaction to his "quiet day" at Nabol Gather.

"Who'd a thought *he'd* walk t'Gather?" the woman was saying as they trudged up the steep steps from the main hall to Meron's apartment.

"Had to. Didncha hear what they be saying at Gather? Meron dead a'ready and none know his heir. Some as want to turn Gather Day into Duel Day."

That remark set both Nabolese into cackles of laughter, and Piemur wondered if he could be ignorant enough of Hold problems to ask why they were so amused.

"Ah saw 'em comin' in, Ah did," said Besel, again with that sly, knowing expression on his face. "Ev'ry one of 'em was with 'im some time t'day, they was. Outsides with him now, shouldn't wonder."

"He'll have his li'l game wi'em, he will, each thinking he's been named," said the woman and dug her elbow into Besel's ribs which sent them both off into malicious laughter again.

"Hope it's not just us as has to do all the cleaning here," Besel said, putting his hand on the door handle. "Hasn't been done in . . . faugh!" He turned his head away, coughing against the stench that wafted out to them from the opened door.

As the smell reached Piemur's nostrils, sweet, cloying, sickening, he felt his stomach turn in protest and tried not to inhale. He hung back, hoping the fresher air of the corridor would cleanse the room of its stink.

"Here, you get in and open shutters. You're used to stinking messes, guttingman." Besel grabbed Piemur roughly by the arm and propelled him violently into the room.

How Piemur managed not to vomit from the odor of the room before he reached the shutters and flung them open, he didn't know. He half-threw his body up the deep sill, gasping in fresh, cool air.

"Other windows, too, boy," ordered Besel from the doorway.

Piemur filled his lungs and opened the other windows, staying by the last until the chill air dissipated the odors of decay and illness. And Lord Meron's heirs had had to attend him in this funking atmosphere? Piemur spared them a moment of sympathy.

Then Besel shouted for him to go into the other rooms and open them up to air properly. "Else no one'd eat his food, like as not, and we'm to clean up their messes."

The foul odor hung heaviest in the last of the four large rooms that comprised the Lord Holder's private apartments in Nabol. It was then that Piemur blessed the happenstance that had sent him in here ahead of the others. Reposing on the hearth were nine pots of exactly the size in which fire lizard eggs were placed to keep warm and harden. Mastering his urge to gag, Piemur ducked across the room to investigate. One pot was set slightly apart from the others and, lifting the lid, Piemur scraped enough sand away to see the mottled shell before he covered it carefully over. He took a quick look at the contents of the first pot in the other group. Yes, the egg was smaller and of a different hue. He'd wager every mark he owned that the separate pot contained a fire lizard queen egg.

Quickly he switched pots. Shielding his actions with his body in case Besel ventured this far to check on him, he dumped the sand with deft speed into the cinder shovel, removed the egg and shoved it up under his coverall and into his shirt above his belt. Poking among the cinders, he selected one that had a slightly rounded end and neatly inserted it into the egg pot, replaced sand and lid and stood the rifled pot back in line, straightening up just as the woman crossed the threshold.

"That's the lad, tend the fire first. And you'll need to bring up more blackrock from the yard. *He* likes his warmth, he does." She cackled again as she roughly pushed carven chairs out of her way to sweep under the worktable. "To be sure, he'll feel the cold soon enough, he will!"

Besel joined in her laughter.

The fire was hot as Piemur shook the grate free of ashes, and his face burned by the time he had cleared the debris. The heat also warmed the egg, lying against his ribs.

"Hurry it up, you guttingman," said Besel when Piemur began to lug the heavy ash bucket out. "No slouching, or I'll take me hand to you."

He raised a big fist and Piemur ducked away, feeling the egg pinch his skin and worried he might crack it prematurely.

As he strained with the heavy bucket down the long steps, he wondered how ever was he going to keep the egg safe. Certainly not on his person. And he'd have to keep it warm, too. As well as in someplace to which, in his guise as a lowly guttingman, he'd have easy access.

The solution came to him just as he was about to dump the ashes. He checked the swing of the bucket and glanced about the ashpit. Then very carefully, he emptied the ashes in a pile just to the left of the ashpit opening. Anyone emptying ashbuckets tended to fling the contents to the back wall where the cinders spread downward from the top of the accumulated pile. The molding on either side of the opening kept ashes from tumbling back into the courtyard until the pit was full. Its capacity was by no means reached at this moment. With his booted toe, Piemur made a small depression in the warm ashes, quickly inserted the egg, covering it first with warm ashes, then with a coating of cold cinders to insulate it. Glancing at the sun as he filled his bucket with fresh blackstone from the dump next to the ashpit, Piemur saw that the sun was lowering. Which was a mercy he thought, lugging the blackstone back into the Hold, because he wondered if he'd manage to last through the most arduous day of his life.

They'd have the Feast soon; more than likely as soon as Lord Meron returned to his freshened quarters. What caused that noxious stink? Certainly not Master Oldive's medicines, for the healer believed in fresh air and freshening herbs, which at their worst were pungent but could not cause the odor in Lord Meron's rooms. No matter. Once the Lord and his guests were served, the drudges would get what remained on the serving platters and that would mean everyone could relax for a while. He could, perhaps, sneak away then, before Sebell got anxious. And did he have a lot to tell Sebell!

Half the workers in the Hold were now running up and down the steps, pursued by the strident voice of the Hold Steward who had arrived to direct the freshening. Piemur was promptly given another ashbucket to empty and fill with blackrock. On his way back through the kitchen this time, he sneaked a breadroll, which heartened him considerably.

By some miracle, they were just about finished when a messenger arrived from the guard to say that Lord Meron and his guests were returning. The Steward shoved and pushed everyone out, even to the point of collecting abandoned cleaning tools. As the last of the drudges scurried back into the kitchen, the laughter of the returning Gatherers was heard at the Hold doors.

Piemur had to assist the cook turn the roast for carving, and nearly had his fingers sliced thinner when the cook caught him taking bits that dropped to the table. Then he had to mash endless kettles of tubers. As fast as a dish was served up and garnished, it was despatched above. At one point, Piemur thought he might be sent, but it was decided he was much too dirty to carry food. Instead he was sent to the bowels of the Hold for more glowbaskets as Lord Meron complained that he couldn't see to eat. Piemur had to make three trips to satisfy the need. By that time, the platters were coming back to the kitchen. The drudges and lesser stewards stripped food off as it passed them by. The kitchen began to quiet as mouths were stuffed too full to permit speech. Piemur managed to secure a meat-rimmed bone and, grabbing a handful of the sliced breads, he retired to the darkest corner of the huge room to eat.

He applied himself ravenously to his food, having decided to leave as quickly as possible now. The sun had set during the furor of serving the feast, so he had the cover of darkness to retrieve his egg. And he'd have the excuse for the guards, if they stopped him, that he was finished with his duties. Lord Groghe always gave his drudges time to attend the Gather dancing. Piemur was looking forward to encountering Sebell again. He might not have heard much to the point of which heir the Hold staff preferred, but he had proof that Lord Meron was getting far more fire lizard eggs than a small Hold like Nabol ought to receive; that his stores rooms were full of more supplies than he and his could ever use in a full pass much less a Turn.

Hungry though he was, Piemur couldn't finish all the meat on the bone. He was too tired to eat, he thought, and before he did collapse from exhaustion, he'd better retrieve the egg and slip out to meet Sebell. How he longed for his bed at the Harper Hall.

The regular kitchen drudges were too busy grumbling about the poor selection left for them to eat and how much those blinking guests were eating and drinking to notice Piemur's deft exit.

He took possession of the precious egg, warm to the touch, and wrapping it carefully in a wad of rags, thrust the bundle once again under his tunic. He jauntily approached the main gates, whistling deliberately off key.

"And where do you think you're going?"

"T'Gather," Piemur replied as if this was all too obvious.

He was as surprised by the man's guffaw as he was by being swung around and roughly propelled back the way he had come.

"Don't try that one on me again, guttingman!" called the guard as the force of his push sent Piemur stumbling across the cobbles, trying not to fall and damage the egg. He stopped in the darkest shadow of the wall and stood fuming over this unexpected check to his escape. It was ridiculous! He couldn't think of any other Hold in all Pern where the drudges were denied the privilege of going to the Hold's own Gather.

"G'wan back to the ashes, guttingman!"

It was then that Piemur realized his coverall, none too clean in the light, was still visible in the shadows, so he slunk past the opening into the kitchen court. Out of sight, he stripped off the betraying coverall and flung it into a corner. So he wasn't allowed to leave, was he?

Well, the guests would have to be passed. He would simply bide his time and slip out of Nabol Hold the same way he'd gotten in.

Taking heart in that notion, he looked about him for a suitable place to wait. He should remain in the courtyards, where he would hear the commotion of leave-taking. He'd better not return to the kitchens, or he'd be put to work again. His roving eye caught the blackness that was the ash and blackstone pits, and that solved his problem. Keeping to the shadows, he made his way to this least likely of all hiding spots and settled on the spongy surface at the right hand side of the opening to the ashpit. Not the most comfortable place to wait, he thought, removing a large cinder shell from under his tail bone before he achieved some measure of comfort. The night wind had picked up a bit, and he felt the chill when he poked his nose over the coping. Ah well, he shouldn't have long to wait. He doubted anyone would tolerate Lord Meron's smell longer than absolutely necessary.

He was awakened from a fitful doze by the sound of shouting and much running about in the main courtyard, and then a nearer, more frightening clamor in the kitchen itself. Above the shouts and slammings, he heard a pathetic wail.

"Ah dunno 'im. Ah tell yuz. First time today Ah saw 'im. Said he was here to help t'Gather, and we needed help."

Trust Besel to clear himself of any blame, thought Piemur.

"Sir, gate guard says a boy answering his description tried to pass out to the Gather awhile back. He couldn't say if the drudge carried anything about him. Wasn't looking for stolen items."

"Then he didn't leave?" The voice was a snarl of fury.

Lord Meron? wondered Piemur. And then realized that the unexpected had happened. The substitute in the egg pot had been discovered. There'd be no way he could creep out of this Hold in the shadow of departing guests. With the way men were dashing about lighting up every crook and corner of the courtyards, he'd be lucky to remain undiscovered. Some eager soul would certainly think to prod a spear through the ashpit just on the off-chance . . . especially if Besel remembered that he'd emptied ash buckets and might have hidden the egg there.

Frantic now, Piemur glanced up at the walls about him. Carved from the cliff itself, they were, and he could never climb straight up unseen. He caught sight of a rectangular darkness just above his head to the left of the ashpit. A window? To what? This side of the kitchen was devoted to stores rooms, but what window. . . . The stores rooms were backed from the corridor side. No searcher would believe him able to open locked doors without a key. Which the kitchen steward kept on a chain about his waist at all times. He couldn't ask for a safer hiding place. And if he closed the window behind him. . . .

He had to wait until the kitchen courtyard had been thoroughly searched . . . except for the garbage and ashpits. The shout went up that the thief must be hiding in the Hold. The searchers swarmed back inside, and he leaped to the top of the ashpit wall. His fingers just reached the ledge of the window. Taking a deep breath, Piemur gave a wriggling jump and succeeded in planting both hands over the sill. It took every sinew in his body to secure that awkward and painful grip. He felt as if he'd scraped the skin from all his fingers as he clung and worked his body up until his elbows had purchase on the sill. With another mighty wriggle and kick, he managed to propel himself up and over, falling on his head on the topmost sack. Groaning at the pain of that contact, he twisted about, and reaching up, drew the shutter tightly but quietly across, barring the window. Then he felt the egg to be sure his fall had done it no harm.

He tried to imagine this room from the perspective of the door side, but all the stores rooms had seemed the same. He crouched in terror as he heard shouting in the corridor. Someone rattled the bolts of the door.

"Locked tight, and the steward has the keys. He can't be here."

They might just take a look, thought Piemur, when they didn't find him anywhere else. He crawled cautiously over the stacked bundles until he found one with enough slack at the top to admit him. He opened the thong, and just as he was crawling in, wondered how under the sun he was going to tie it up again, the stitching at the side began to give in his hands. Smiling happily at such a solution, he rapidly undid the stitching down the side. Crawling out, he retied the knot about the mouth of the sack, then slid through the undone seam, which, once inside, he could do up, slowly but enough to pass a cursory inspection. It was hard to do, feeding the thick thread through the original holes from the inside, and his hands and fingers were cramped when he finally accomplished the feat.

He was in a sack of cloth bales and, despite the cramped confines, he was able to wiggle down between bolts so that he was standing on the bottom of the sack and both he and the egg were cushioned on all sides by the material.

Between fatigue and the scant supply of air in the sack, he found his eyes drooping, and surrendering to the combination of exhaustion and safety, he fell fast asleep.

He was roused briefly when the door was unlocked and thrown open. But the inspection was cursory, since the Hold Steward kept insisting that the doors had been locked since the morning and he wouldn't let them poke any spears lest they harm the contents of the bales.

"He could have hid in the glow room. He was sent there several times."

The door was duly shut and locked.

Piemur was conscious of more activity, but his sleep was so deep that he wasn't certain later whether he dreamed the noise or not. He wasn't even conscious of being moved or of the cold of *between.* What woke him was a strange difficulty with breathing, a sense of heat and the terror of suffocating in his own sweat.

Gasping, he tore at the thread he had reworked, hard to undo with moist trembling hands that had no strength, and with sight impeded by perspiration pouring down his forehead.

Even when he had forced a small hole in the sack, he still couldn't seem to breathe. Weeping in terror, even to the point of forgetting the egg that had brought him to this extremity, he squirmed out of the sack to discover himself in a small space among other sacks. The heat was unbearable, but caution returned and he listened for any sounds. Instead of noise, his senses reported sun-heated material and hides, sun-warmed metal, and the sour sweat of hot wine.

He tried to shove the nearest sack away from him and couldn't shift it. Feeling the contents, he realized that it was metal. Twisting around, he tested the sack above him and gave an experimental heave. It moved, and a whoosh of slightly cooler air rewarded his efforts. Dragging breath into his lungs, he waited until his heart stopped its frantic pounding. And then, belatedly remembering the egg, he felt the rags about the precious burden. It seemed to be whole, but he didn't have sufficient space to get it out and look. He gave another shove at the upper bale with no success. Angling so that his shoulders were against the unyielding metal, he levered his feet and pushed as hard as he could. It moved farther, and he saw a crack of sky so brilliantly blue that he gasped at the color.

It was then that he realized he wasn't in Nabol Hold any longer. That the heat was not due to the unventilated stores room beyond Lord Meron's kitchen, but the sun pouring down from southern skies.

Once he was able to breathe easily, Piemur became aware of other discomforts: parched mouth and throat, a stomach gnawing with emptiness, and a head that banged with a distressingly keen ache.

He repositioned himself and shoved the sack a little further to one side. Then he had to rest, panting with the exertion as sweat trickled down inside his clothes. He had made enough space to take a look at the egg, and he fumbled under his tunic for it with trembling hands. It was warm to his touch, almost hot, and he worried that an egg could be overheated. What had Menolly said about the temperature required by hatching eggs? Surely beach sands under the sun were hotter than his body. He could see no fracture marks on the shell and fancied he felt a faint throbbing. Probably his own blood. He squinted at the blue sky, which meant freedom, and decided not to put the egg back in his tunic. If he held it in front of him, then it didn't matter how he twisted and squeezed his body past the sacks and bales, the egg would take no harm and there was no way it could fall far.

When he was breathing more easily, he gathered his body, egg-holding hand above his head, and began to squirm upwards. Just as he thought he was free, the sack behind him settled agonizingly on his left foot, and he had to put the egg down to free himself.

Bruised—torn in muscle, skin and nerve—Piemur slowly dragged himself out of the carelessly piled goods. He lay stretched flat, mindful that he might be visible. The unshielded sun baked his dehydrated and exhausted body as he listened beyond the pounding of his heart and the thudding of blood through his veins. But he heard only the distant sound of voices raised in laughing conversation. He could smell salt in the air and the odd aroma of something sweet, and perhaps, overripe.

His tired mind could not recall much of what he'd heard of the Southern Weyr. Vague flashes of people saying you could pick fresh fruit right off the trees reassured him. A breeze fanned his face, bringing with it the smell of baking meats. Hunger asserted itself. He licked his dried, cracking lips and winced as the salt of his sweat settled painfully in the cuts.

Cautiously he raised his head and realized that he was at the top of a considerable mound that was braced against the stone walls of a structure of some height. To one side there was open space, to the other the crushed green of leaves and fronds, half-trapped by the bales. He inched himself cautiously towards the foliage, the egg considered at each movement. But even with caution his heart all but stopped when his motion caused one of the bundles to settle abruptly with what seemed to him a lot of unnecessary noise.

He listened intently for a long moment before continuing his crawl towards the foliage. Now, if he could climb up that tree. . . . One look at the horny bark decided him against that. His hands were sore, scratched and bleeding from past efforts. He was about to crawl down the mound instead when something orangey caught his eye. A round fruit slowly swayed just above his head. He licked his dry lips and swallowed painfully against the parched tissue of mouth and throat. It looked ripe. He reached out, scarcely believing his luck, and the fruit rind dented softly at his touch.

Piemur did not remember picking the fruit: he did remember the incredibly delicious, wet, tangy taste of the orange-yellow meat as he tore juicy segments out of the rind and crammed them into his moisture-starved mouth. The juice stung his cracked lips, but it seemed to revive the rest of him.

It was while he was licking his fingers clean of the last of the fruit that he noticed the change in the laughing and talking. The noise was coming nearer, and he could hear individual phrases.

"If we don't get some of that stuff under cover, it'll be ruined," said a tenor voice.

"I can smell the wine, in fact, and that better be taken out of the sun or it will be undrinkable," said a second male voice with some urgency.

"And if Meron's ignored my order for fabric *this* time. . . ." The woman's sharp alto left the threat unspoken.

"I made it a condition of that last shipment of fire lizard eggs, Mardra, so don't worry."

"Oh, I won't worry, but Meron will."

"Here, this one bears a weaver's seal."

"At the very bottom, too. Who piled this so carelessly?"

Piemur, scurrying down the other side as fast as he could, felt the shiver as someone began tugging at the sacks in the front. Then he was sliding and grabbed the egg more tightly, exclaiming as he hit the ground with a thud.

Immediately three fire lizards, a bronze and two browns, appeared in the air about him.

"I'm not here," he told them in a soundless whisper, gesturing urgently for them to go away. "You haven't seen me. I'm not here!" He took to his heels, his knees wobbling uncertainly, but as he lurched down a faintly outlined path leading away from the voices and the goods, he thought so fiercely of the black nothingness of *between* that the fire lizards gave a shriek and disappeared.

"Who's not here? What are you talking about?" The strident tones of the woman's voice followed Piemur as he careered away.

When he could run no more for the stitch in his side and the lack of breath, he dared no more than pause until he'd gotten his wind. He did stop longer when he came to a stream, rinsed his mouth out with the tepid water and then splashed it about his heated face and head.

A noise, to his apprehensive mind like the querying note of a fire lizard, set him off again, after nearly falling into the stream. He plunged on, tripped twice, curling his body each time as he fell to protect the egg; but the third time he fell, he had reached the end of his resources. He crawled out of the line of the faint path to a place well under the broad leaves of a flowering bush and probably slept even before his labored breathing quietened.

Chapter 7

Sebell had not really worried about Piemur throughout the Gather day as he wandered—or staggered—about in his assumed role of wine-happy herdsman. And when word flashed through the crowds that Lord Meron was to walk the Gather, Sebell had no time to look for his apprentice. He had to concentrate on listening to the mutterings about Lord Meron and his curious generosity with fire lizard eggs that only hatched greens.

If Lord Meron's appearance gave the lie to rumors that the man was dead or dying, it was apparent to Sebell's sharp eyes that the Lord Holder needed the support of the two men who walked beside him, arms linked in his. Some of his heirs, Sebell heard whispered in glum and disgusted tones.

When the roasted beasts were being sliced for distribution to the Gather crowd, Sebell did begin to search for Piemur. Surely the boy wouldn't miss free meat at Lord Meron's expense. Not that the beasts were juicy, probably the oldest creatures in the Hold herds, Sebell thought, endlessly chewing on his portion. He had placed himself at an end table about the Gather square where Piemur ought to be able to see him.

By the time the dancing started, Sebell began to worry. N'ton would be returning for them at full dark, and he didn't want to impose on the bronze dragonrider by requiring him to wait about or return at a later time.

It was then that Sebell wondered if Piemur had somehow gotten into trouble and maybe left the Gather area. But, if Piemur had gotten into trouble, surely he would have set up a howl for Sebell to rescue him. Perhaps he had only crawled away for a nap. He'd had an early rising and he might not be completely recovered from his fall. Sebell sent Kimi about the Gather to see if she could locate the boy, but she returned, cheeping anxiously at her failure. He sent her then to the allotment, in case Piemur had gone there to wait. When that errand too was fruitless, Sebell appropriated a handy, fast-looking runner beast from the picket lines and made his way to their original meeting place, on the offchance that Piemur had returned there, to wait for him and N'ton.

Though Sebell searched the valley carefully, he found no trace of his young friend. He was forced to admit that something had indeed happened to Piemur. He couldn't imagine what, nor why Piemur, or whoever the lad might have crossed, had not sent for him as Piemur's master.

He sped back to the Hold, retied his borrowed mount, and reached the Gather just as news of the theft of the queen egg rippled through the crowds. Feelings were mixed as that news spread; anger from those who had received lesser eggs, and amusement that someone had outsmarted Lord Meron. By the time Sebell got to the Hold gates, no one was being allowed in or out. Glowbaskets shone on empty courtyards, and every window of the Hold was brilliant with light. Sebell watched with the rest of the curious gatherers while even the ash and refuse pits were searched. Wagers were being laid that somehow Kaljan the Miner had managed to steal the egg.

Sebell was there when the minemaster was escorted by guard into the Hold after the man's baggage was thoroughly searched. An order was circulated, and additional guards posted, to prevent anyone's leaving the Gather. Sebell positioned himself along the ramp parapet leading to the Hold, where Piemur could easily spot him in the light from the Hold's glows. Surely if the boy had only fallen asleep, the noise would rouse him.

It was only when word filtered through the crowd that some unknown drudge had made off with the precious egg that Sebell came to the startling conclusion that that drudge could have been Piemur. How the boy had managed to enter the guarded Hold, Sebell couldn't figure out, but trust Piemur to find a way. Certainly it was like the boy to steal a fire lizard egg, given the opportunity. A queen egg at that! Piemur never did anything by halves. Sebell chuckled to himself and then sent Kimi flying with the other agitated fire lizards to see if she could discover where Piemur was hiding.

She returned and conveyed to Sebell that she couldn't get close to Piemur. It was too dark and too full. When Sebell questioned her for more details, she grew distressed and repeated the image of darkness and her inability to reach the boy.

The frenzy of the search mounted. Guards were now dispatched on fast runners up every road leading from the Hold to find any travelers journeying from the Gather. Sebell sent Kimi to the valley to warn N'ton away in case the bronze rider was awaiting them. When Tris accompanied her back, Sebell knew that his warning had been timely. Tris chittered at him and then settled beside Kimi, giving Sebell the opportunity to send the fire lizard to bring N'ton should he be needed.

Both moons had risen by now, adding their soft light to the glows, but despite the fact that the guards endlessly searched and researched the Hold and yards, their efforts proved vain. Delighted with Piemur's elusiveness, Sebell settled himself to wait out the night in the shadowy corner of the first cot below the ramp. He had a good view of the guards and, by carefully looking over the ramp wall, could see most of the courtyard.

He was roused from a half-doze by the shouts and angry muttering as the guards prodded those who had lingered about the gates back down towards the Gather area.

"Go on now," the guards kept saying. "Go to your cots or your allotments. You'll be allowed to leave in the morning. No need to linger here. Go on with you, now!"

The moons had set, and gone, too, were all the glowbaskets that had illuminated the courtyards. Even the Hold was in darkness, though some light seeped through the shutters of the Lord Holder's apartments on the first level. Curling himself into a tight ball in the shadows, Sebell hid his face and hands and ordered Kimi to tell Tris to be quiet and for both to keep their eyes closed.

When the guards disappeared, he wondered what was happening. The Hold was virtually unguarded as well as unlit. Was this some sort of trap to catch Piemur? Or should Sebell take advantage of this opportunity and sneak into the Hold? Kimi rattled her wings in alarm, and through narrow slits her eyes gleamed yellow with worry. Tris, too, stirred nervously.

Then Sebell picked up from Kimi's mind the image of dragons; furthermore, dragons that neither fire lizard knew! Just as that image faded in his mind, Sebell heard the sound of dragon wings. Gliding from the northern shadows of the Hold cliff, he saw the black bulks of four dragons, wing on wing. Two settled neatly into the kitchen courtyard while the other pair landed in the main yard. Sebell heard hushed commands and then an unusual, muted hubbub. Grunts and muffled oaths punctuated the activity. Sebell was considering moving out of his protective shadows for a better view when he heard a heavy groan, the unmistakable scrabble of talons on stone, and the equally identifiable swhoosh of mighty wings making a powerful downstroke.

In the one band of light in the kitchen courtyard he saw the belly of a heavily laden bronze dragon struggling to rise, his sides bulging. No sooner had the first one cleared, then the second dragon launched himself skyward. The two in the main courtyard moved to the kitchen yard. More activity ensued, conducted with hoarse whispers and low voiced commands.

All during this, Kimi and Tris shivered, clinging to Sebell in a fashion they had never exhibited in the vicinity of other dragons. It took no great effort for Sebell to conclude that he had witnessed Lord Meron delivering goods to the Oldtimers from the Southern Weyr. That queen fire lizard egg had probably been prepayment for whatever the dragons had lugged away.

Sebell heard the sound of low voices coming from the direction of the Gather, and he hastily nipped back to his dark corner, warning the two fire lizards to close their eyes as he hid his face and hands again.

After moments of boot scuffing and muttered phrases, there was silence. Cautiously raising his head, he saw that the guards were back in position and that the glowbaskets again glowed on ramp and Hold walls, illuminating the roads leading up to the Hold. He was trapped in his shadowy corner. Nor did he dare to send Kimi or Tris from him, for their flight would surely be noticed when there wasn't another fire lizard to be seen. With a sigh, he settled himself as comfortably as he could, Kimi draped warmingly about his shoulders, and Tris curled at his side.

He couldn't have slept very long before he was rudely awakened by the boom of the message drums. "Urgent to the Healer! Lord Meron very ill. Masterharper required. Urgent! Urgent! Urgent!"

Had they then caught Piemur and, recognizing him, summoned Master Robinton to account for the misbehavior of one of his apprentices? Lord Meron would like nothing better than to be able to humiliate Master Robinton, for any censure of the Masterharper would also touch the Benden Weyrleaders, whom Lord Meron hated. Oh, well, if that were the case, at least the boy had been found. Sebell felt certain that Master Robinton could handle Lord Meron's accusations. And yet, why was Master Oldive so urgently required? No Hold drummed that measure unless the emergency was critical.

The Hold's fire lizards had been awakened by the boom of the big message drums and now wheeled about in the glowlight. Sebell unwrapped Kimi's tail from his neck, and holding her slender body in his hands, compelled her to look at him while he gave her directions to Menolly. He thought hard about clean clothes and imaged himself dressed in harper blue. Kimi chirruped understandingly and, after stroking his chin with her head, launched herself up. Tris chirped questioningly, tugging at Sebell's sleeve. N'ton would be a good ally, but strictly speaking the Fort Weyrleader had no genuine business here since Nabol was beholden to T'bor of the High Reaches Weyr. So Sebell looked deeply into Tris's lightly whirling eyes, thought hard that N'ton need not come to the valley, and sent the little brown back to his friend at Fort Weyr.

The message drum boomed a repeat, emphasizing again the urgency. Sebell strained his ears for the relay drums at the next point, but a handful of guards quick-stepped down the road towards the Gather and their passing masked the distant sounds.

Dawn was just breaking when Sebell, scanning the lightening skies, saw a dragon emerge. As the creature circled gracefully down, Sebell was relieved to note the silhouettes of four riders. He was perplexed because the dragon's spiraling descent would not put the party in the Hold's courtyard, where logically they would be expected to land. Abruptly, Kimi appeared in the air above him, chittering excitedly and darting off towards the Gather meadow. Her mind pictured Menolly. When Sebell did not move quickly enough to please her, she hovered at his shoulder and tugged at his dirty tunic, darting off again towards the meadow.

"I understand, of course. I'm tired, that's why I'm slow, Kimi," he said. Sticking to the shadows, he skirted the cot and started down the deserted road until he was far enough away from the guards. Then he picked up his feet and ran down the deserted road towards the new arrivals. He reached them just as the blue dragon left.

"Ah, Sebell," said the Masterharper, for all the world as if he were welcoming his journeyman into his rooms at the Harper Hall instead of surreptitiously meeting on a dark meadow in early dawn. "Menolly, hand him his clothes. He can tell us what has been happening while he changes. Is Lord Meron so desperately ill?"

"Probably. Of temper if nothing else," replied Sebell, stripping off his tunic and getting a shower of dust and grit in his hair and face. "He walked the Gather last evening . . ."

"He what!" exclaimed Master Oldive, cocking his head up at Sebell in surprise.

"He had to. And then someone stole a fire lizard queen egg from the hearth of his bedroom . . ."

"No?" Laughter as well as amazement colored the Harper's exclamation.

"Piemur?" asked Menolly at the same moment. "Is that why he isn't with you?"

"Is that why I've been summoned? To witness the punishment of a thieving apprentice?" Master Robinton was no longer amused.

"I don't know, Master. Kimi located Piemur in the Hold, but she couldn't explain where, said she couldn't get to him because it was too dark. I know the guards spent hours searching the Hold. Presumably they know it better than Piemur could. But—" Sebell paused. "I'm bloody certain they would have made some sort of commotion if they had found him and recovered that egg."

"Nothing would give Lord Meron more satisfaction than to force me to punish an apprentice thieving in his Hold."

"The message clearly states that Lord Meron is ill," said Master Oldive. "If he was foolhardy enough to walk his Gather and then agitate himself over the loss of a queen egg, he could indeed be very ill in his condition."

"It's accepted fact among the Nabolese," said Sebell, gratefully throwing aside his herdsman's cracked boots, which had rubbed his heels raw, "that the man's dying." He glanced up at Oldive and saw the Healer's head move affirmatively.

"Did you find out whom the Nabolese prefer as heir?" asked Master Robinton.

"A grand-nephew, Deckter. A carter who runs a steady business between Nabol and Crom. He's got four sons that he keeps firmly in line. He's not a friendly man, but he's got the grudging respect of those who know him." Sebell had finished dressing and now gestured the group towards the Hold. "I have also discerned that there are more fire lizards in and about Nabol than there ought to be. Most of them . . ." and he paused to give his words more weight, ". . . are green."

"Green?" Menolly swung on him in surprise.

"Yes, green."

"You mean," Menolly went on, "he's been distributing eggs from green fire lizard clutches? Why, the bloody beast!"

"On top of that insult, a lot of the eggs don't hatch at all, so you can imagine how little his generosity endears Lord Meron to the recipients," Sebell added grimly. "Of more importance," and Sebell held up his hand to forestall her angry words, "just after moonset, four dragons landed right in the courtyards and lifted off again so heavily laden you could hear their wings creaking!" Sebell grinned at the expressions of shock from his companions. "Further, Kimi didn't know those dragons and their presence frightened her."

"Now that is the most interesting piece of news you've given me," remarked the Masterharper.

He said no more because they had reached the foot of the ramp to the Hold and the group of men waiting there impatiently rushed down to meet them. Sebell recognized the Hold's harper, Candler, and the healer, Berdine. Of the other three, he recognized the two men who had supported Lord Meron on his Gather walk. The fatter man barged straight up to the Harper.

"Master Robinton, I am Hittet, of the Blood, and you simply must assist us. The situation must be clarified with all possible dispatch. As I'm sure Master Oldive will tell you, there is no time to be lost. . . ." The others exclaimed in support of his words. "I fear that after the alarms and excitements of this night, the poor man cannot long survive. But come, we must hurry." Then he took the Harper by the arm and urged him towards the Hold.

"Alarms and excitements? Ah, yes, you had a Gather yesterday. . . ." Master Robinton was saying.

"I can't thank you enough for responding, Master Oldive," said Berdine falling in step with the Healer as the others followed Hittet and Master Robinton across the Court. "I know you said that there was nothing more you could do for Lord Meron, but the truth of the matter is that he has sadly taxed what strength was left him. I warned him, oh I did most explicitly, that he ought not walk the Gather, but he was adamant. Had to reassure his holders. I think that would have been safe enough, but then he insisted on having guests in his apartments . . . so much excitement. And then, to discover the queen egg had been stolen!" Berdine fluttered his hands in distress. "Oh my, oh my. I was beside myself trying to calm him. He wouldn't take that draught you left me for such an emergency. He became utterly uncontrollable when they couldn't find that wretched drudge who'd stolen the egg—"

"Journeyman Berdine," said Hittet in chilling tones, whipping about to stare warningly at the healer.

That interruption was timely made, for none of the Nabolese saw the looks of relief that the harpers exchanged.

"A drudge stealing an egg?" asked the Harper, as if he didn't believe his ears.

"Yes, if you must know," began Hittet, still glaring at the indiscreet healer. "Lord Meron was recently given a clutch of fire lizard eggs, one of which was thought to be a queen egg. He naturally took the best care of such prizes, kept them on his own hearth. He has had a lot of experience with fire lizards, you see. He was to distribute the eggs to deserving people as the high point of the Gather Feast. When his rooms were being freshened, one of the kitchen drudges had the audacity to steal the queen egg. How, we can't yet understand. But it's gone, and that wicked lad is somewhere in the Hold." Hittet's tone augured ill for Piemur when he was found.

None of the Nabolese noticed Beauty, Zair and Kimi peeling off from airy escort and darting out an open window as the group traversed the Main Hall. Sebell gave Menolly's hand a reassuring squeeze. She didn't look at him, but her lips curved slightly in a smile of relief.

"You can appreciate how upset Lord Meron was when the theft was discovered, and I fear this, and our pressing him to name an heir, resulted in his collapse," Hittet was saying to Master Robinton.

"Collapse?" Master Oldive looked sternly at Berdine, who immediately got his tongue twisted, trying to vindicate himself to his craft's Master. Master Oldive now brushed past Hittet and Master Robinton and, with the still apologetic Berdine on his heels, ran up the steps with no regard to his physical handicap or dignity.

Master Robinton also quickened his pace until the fat Hittet was forced to run to keep up. Sebell and Menolly deliberately slowed, to give their fire lizards a chance to range through the Hold and locate Piemur.

"If you could know how good it is to see a friendly face," said Candler, quite willing to match their laggard advance to the Lord's apartments. "If anyone can make that dreadful man see reason, it's Master Robinton. Lord Meron won't name an heir. That's why he collapsed, to avoid it. He was furious about the egg theft, to be sure, but while they were searching, he was more like himself—totally disagreeable and planning all kinds of fiendish punishments when they caught the drudge. Frankly, Sebell, he wants the Hold in contention. You know how he hates Benden. And now," and Candler laughed sourly, "none of the relatives who've been badgering him to name one of them wants to be the heir. I don't know why. They changed their tune abruptly this morning. Just as well." Candler snorted with disgust. "Any one of the lot would create disorder in next to no time."

"Changed their minds early this morning, did they?" said Sebell, grinning at Menolly.

"Yes, and I can't figure out why. Every single one of them has done all he could to secure the nomination. Now. . . ."

"I'd heard that Deckter was an honest man."

"Deckter?" Candler swung towards Sebell in surprise. "Oh, the carter." He gave a mirthless laugh. "I suppose he could be considered an heir, couldn't he? Grand-nephew, isn't he? Forgot about him. Which is probably Deckter's doing. Said he could make more money carting than he could holding. He's probably right. How'd you know about him?"

"Looked up the Nabol bloodline."

Beauty flitted back, skimming so close to Candler that he ducked. Rocky, Zair and Kimi followed her, all chittering in some distress. All had the same message: Piemur was not in the Hold. Sebell and Menolly exchanged glances.

"Would he have hidden somewhere outside?" Menolly asked.

Sebell gave a quick shake of his head. "Kimi couldn't find him."

"Rocky and Beauty have been much closer to Piemur than Kimi."

"Can't hurt to try!"

"Piemur?" asked Candler, mystified by this cryptic exchange.

"I've reason to believe that the theft was accomplished by Piemur," said Sebell. He and Menolly gave their fire lizards new instructions and watched them dart out the Hold door.

"Piemur? But I remember Piemur. The boy with the fine soprano. I didn't see him anywhere—" Candler broke off and pointed at Sebell. "You *were* there when Lord Meron walked the Gather. The very drunken herdsman. I thought there was something familiar about him. It was you! Well. And Piemur here, too? On harper business? I thought it odd for one of Meron's drudges to have so much initiative. Well, I'll tell you one thing, Piemur is not in this Hold."

"How could he have gotten out?" asked Sebell. "I was just beyond the ramp all night. Even if I didn't see him, Kimi would have."

They had reached the Lord's apartments now, and Candler opened the door, gesturing them to precede him.

"What's that smell?" asked Menolly softly, grimacing in distaste.

"Smell? Oh, you get used to it. Disgusting, I know, but it has something to do with Lord Meron's illness. We try to mask it," and Candler gestured to the sweet candles alight in containers about the room. "I often think that it's only justice," he added in a careful whisper, "for the suffering he's given others, but it's a terrible way to die."

"I thought Master Oldive had given him. . . ." Sebell began.

"Oh, he has. The strongest there is, according to Berdine. But the medicine only dulls the pain."

The doors to the next two rooms were open, and the harpers could see the clusters of men standing about, in silence, all avoiding each other's gaze. Suddenly, in the third room, there was a brief flurry as the Harper appeared at the door to the Lord's private room.

"Sebell!" Master Robinton's calm request carried clearly, and everyone turned to watch the journeyman hurry to his master's side. "Please send a drum message to Lords Oterel, Nessel and Bargen, and to Weyrleader T'bor. Would they please attend us here at Nabol immediately. Double urgency on the beat, please."

"Yes, sir," said Sebell with such unexpected vigor that Master Robinton gave him a mild second look. But Sebell turned on his heel and walked swiftly out of the apartments, motioning as he passed them for Candler and Menolly to come with him. "I don't know why I didn't think of it earlier, Menolly. *If* Piemur got out of the Hold and is hiding somewhere in the hills, he'll surface to a drum message aimed at him. Lead us to your drumheights, Candler."

The big message drums needed only to be uncovered. Sebell stood for a moment, beaters poised over the taut hide as he composed his message. The opening roll boomed across the valley, the urgent measure following as the last echoes died. Then Sebell, eyes half-closed in concentration, beat out the recipients' names, the Harper's request, and the urgent measures once again to insure immediate reply and attention. Menolly positioned herself at the window then, ears straining to catch the pass-along roll from the next drumheights.

"There it is from the east," she told the two men. "What's wrong with the northern listeners? Still asleep? Ah, there they are."

"Candler, any chance of some food?" Sebell asked the Hold Harper. "We'd best wait here for replies."

"Yes, let's eat here where the air is clear," said Menolly, with a shudder as she thought of the thick, distasteful odor in Lord Meron's rooms.

"Of course, of course. I apologize for not offering sooner." Candler was away down the stairs.

Sebell picked up the sticks again and beat a quick measure. "Apprentice. Report. Urgent." He waited a few breaths and then repeated the measure.

"If he's anywhere between here and Ruatha or Crom, he'll hear that," Sebell said, carefully replacing the drumsticks on their hooks before he joined Menolly at the window.

Her face was sad and her brows constricted in a tiny frown as she gazed across the huddle of cots below the Hold ramp and over the disorganized Gather square, still tenanted by those unwillingly held over by the emergency. Few sounds wafted to their ears at this height, and the scene was unrealistically calm.

"Don't fret over Piemur, Menolly," Sebell said, trying to sound more lighthearted than he felt. "He has a knack of landing on his feet." He smiled down at her, allowing himself the luxury of putting his arm lightly about her shoulders.

"Except when the steps are greased!" Menolly's voice had an angry edge, and he gripped her shoulder reassuringly.

"Look at it this way: just see how that misadventure has worked to his advantage. He's got out of the drumheights and acquired himself a queen fire lizard egg. For all we know, he may meet us at the Hold gates with it, smiling in that ingenuous fashion of his, when you and I know he's as devious as Meron!"

"I wish I could believe you, Sebell," Menolly said sighing heavily, but she leaned trustingly against him for his comfort. "If he was anywhere in the vicinity, Beauty and Rocky ought to have found him."

"He's somewhere," replied Sebell firmly, and daring more than ever, he gave her a quick hug, turning abruptly from her as he caught her startled look. "The wretch!" he added, more of a growl than a comment. At that moment, they both heard the message drum roll across the mountains, and Sebell hastily strode back to the drums.

Candler arrived just as Sebell beat "receive" for the last of the messages. The Nabol Harper was panting with the exertion of his climb, for he carried not only a well-laden tray, but a full wine skin slung over his shoulder. The three harpers had time to make a leisurely meal before the first of the visitors arrived. The harpers then escorted the Lord Holders and T'bor to the Master Harper.

Sebell almost gagged and lost his breakfast when he brought Lords Holder Nessel and Bargen into Lord Meron's inner room. Menolly was already there with Lord Oterel and Weyrleader T'bor. He saw her mouth working to control the revulsion she was obviously feeling. Only Candler seemed impervious to the odor.

Although Sebell had seen Lord Meron the day before, he was appalled by the change in the man propped up in the bed: the eyes were sunken, pain had lined his face deeply, his skin was a pale yellow, and his fingers, plucking nervously at the fur rug that covered him, were claws with hanging bags of flesh between the knuckles. It was as if, Sebell thought, all life was centered in those hands, feebly holding onto life through the hair of the fur.

"So, I'm granted my own private gather, is that it? Well, I've no welcome for any of you. Go away. I'm dying. That's what you all wished me to do these past Turns. Leave me to it."

"You've not named your successor," said Lord Oterel bluntly.

"I'll die before I do."

"I think we must persuade you to change your mind on that count," said the Masterharper in a quiet, amiable tone.

"How?" Lord Meron's snarl was smug in his self-assurance.

"There is friendly persuasion. . . ."

"If you think I'll name a successor just to make things easy for you and those dregs at Benden, think again!" The force of that remark left the man gasping against his props, one hand feebly beckoning to Master Oldive, whose attention was on the Harper.

". . . Or unfriendly persuasion," continued Master Robinton as if Lord Meron hadn't spoken.

"Ha! You can do nothing to a dying man, Master Robinton! You, Healer, my medicine!"

Master Robinton lifted his arm, effectively barring Berdine from approaching the sick man.

"That's precisely it, my Lord Meron," said the Harper in an implacable voice, "we can do . . . nothing . . . to a dying man."

Sebell heard Menolly's catch of breath as she understood what Master Robinton had in mind to force this issue with Lord Meron. Berdine started to protest, but was silenced by a growl from Lord Oterel. The healer turned appealingly to Master Oldive, whose eyes had never left the face of the Harper. Although Sebell had known how desperately Master Robinton wished for a peaceful succession in this Hold, he had not appreciated the steel in his pacific Master's will. Nabol Hold must not come into contention, not with every Holder's younger sons eager and willing to fight to the death to secure even as ill-managed a Hold as this. Such fighting could go on and on, until no more challengers presented themselves. What little prosperity Nabol enjoyed would have been wasted in the meantime with no one holding the lands properly.

"What do you mean?" Meron's voice rose to a shriek. "Master Oldive, attend me. Now!"

Master Oldive turned to the Lords Holder and bowed. "I understand, my Lords, that there are many seeking my aid at the Hold gates. I will, of course, return when my presence is required here. Berdine, accompany me!"

When Lord Meron screamed for the two healers to halt, to attend him, Master Oldive took Berdine by the arm and firmly led him out, deaf to Meron's orders. As the door closed behind him, Meron ceased his entreaties and turned to the impassive faces that watched him.

"You wouldn't? Can't you understand? I'm in pain. Agony! Something inside is burning through my vitals. It won't stop until it's eaten me to a shell. I must have medicine. I must have it!"

"We must have the name of your successor." Lord Oterel's voice was pitiless.

Master Robinton began to name the male relatives, his voice expressionless as he intoned the list. When he had completed it, he recited it again.

"You've forgotten one, Master," Sebell said in a respectful tone. "Deckter."

"Deckter?" The Harper turned slightly towards Sebell, his brows raised in surprise at being corrected.

"Yes, sir. A grand-nephew."

"Oh." The Harper sounded surprised, at the same time dismissing the man with a flick of his fingers. He repeated the list to Lord Meron, now mouthing obscenities as he writhed on his bed. Deckter was added as an afterthought. Then the Harper paused, looking inquiringly at Lord Meron, who responded with another flow of invective, demanding

Oldive's presence at the top of his voice. Again, the effort rendered him momentarily exhausted. He lay back, panting through his opened mouth, blinking to clear the sweat from his eyes.

"You must name your successor," said T'bor, High Reaches Weyrleader, and Meron's eyes rested on the man whose private grievance with him ran deepest. For it was Lord Meron's association with T'bor's Weyrwoman, Kylara, that had caused the death of both Kylara's queen dragon, Prideth, and Brekke's Wirenth.

Sebell watched Meron's eyes widen with growing horror as he finally realized that he would have no surcease from the pain of his body until he did name a successor, confronted as he was by men who had excellent reason for hating him.

Sebell also noted that T'bor forgot to mention Deckter. So did Lord Oterel when he took his turn. Lord Bargen recited the name first, with a glance at Oterel for his omission.

Sebell knew he would always remember this bizarre and macabre scene with horror as well as with a certain awful respect. He had long known that Master Robinton would use unexpected methods to maintain order throughout Pern and to uphold the leadership of Benden Weyr, but he had never expected such ruthlessness in the otherwise gentle and compassionate Robinton. He schooled his mind away from the stink and closeness of the room, from Meron's pain, by trying to appreciate the tactics that were being used as Lord Meron was deftly maneuvered into choosing the one man the others preferred among his heirs by their seeming to forget Deckter half the time. For a long while afterward, the flickering of glows would remind Sebell and Menolly of those eerie hours while Lord Meron tried to resist the will of his inflexible peers.

It was inevitable that Meron would capitulate: Sebell thought he could almost feel the pulsing of pain through the man's body as he screamed out Deckter's name, thinking he had chosen to displease the men who had so tormented him.

The instant he spoke Deckter's name, Master Oldive, who had gone no further than the next room, came to give the man relief.

"Perhaps it was a terrible cruelty to inflict on anyone," Master Oldive told the Lords when they left Meron in a drugged stupor, "but the ordeal has also hastened his end. Which can only be a mercy. I don't think he can last another day."

The other heirs, Hittet the most vocal, now barged in from the entry room, demanding to know why they had been excluded from their kinsman's presence, berating the Lord Holders and Master Robinton for this unconscionable delay and finally remembering to ask if Lord

Meron had indeed named an heir. When they were told of Deckter, their reactions were compounds of relief, consternation, disappointment and then incredulity. Sebell extricated Menolly from the knot of chattering relatives and guided her to the steps down to the Main Hall and out of the Hold where they could breathe the fresh, untainted air.

A considerable and silent crowd lined the ramp, held back by the guards. At the sight of the two harpers, they began to shout for news. Was Lord Meron dead? What was happening to bring Lord Holders and the Weyrleader to Nabol?

As Sebell raised his hands for silence, he and Menolly scanned the faces, looking for Piemur in that crowd. When he had their attention, Sebell told them that Lord Meron had named his successor. A curious rippling groan came from the crowd as if they expected the worst and were steeling themselves. So Sebell grinned as he called out Deckter's name. The multiple gasp of astonishment turned into a spate of relieved cheers. Sebell then told the head guard to send for the honored man, and half the crowd followed the messengers of this mixed fortune.

"I don't see Piemur," said Menolly in a low anxious voice, her eyes continually scanning. "Surely with us here, he'd come forward."

"Yes, he would. And since he hasn't . . ." Sebell looked about the courtyard. "I wonder . . ." As he twisted slowly in a circle, he realized that there would have been no way for Piemur to climb out of the Hold yards. Not even a fire lizard could claw its way up the cliff above the Hold's windows. Especially not in the dark and encumbered by a fragile fire lizard egg. His eyes were drawn by the ash and refuse pits, but he distinctly remembered their being vigorously spear-searched. His glance traveled upward and paused on the small window. "Menolly!" He grabbed her by the hand and started pulling her towards the kitchen yard. "Kimi said it was dark. I wonder what's . . ." In his excitement, Sebell reversed back to the guard, hauling the complaining Menolly with him. "See that little window above the ashpit?" he asked the guard excitedly. "What does it open on? The kitchen?"

"That one? Naught but a stores room." And then the guard clamped his teeth shut, looking apprehensively back to the Hold as if he had been indiscreet and feared reprisal.

His reaction told Sebell exactly what he needed to know.

"The supplies for the Southern Weyr were stored in that room, weren't they?"

The guard stared straight ahead of him, lips pressed firmly together, but the flush in his face was a giveaway. Laughing with relief, Sebell half-ran towards the kitchen yard, Menolly eagerly following him.

"You think Piemur hid himself among the stuff for the Oldtimers?" Menolly asked.

"It's the only answer that suits the circumstances, Menolly," said Sebell. He halted right in front of the ashpit and pointed to the wall that separated the two pits. "That wouldn't be too high a jump for an agile lad, would it?"

"No, I wouldn't think so. And just like Piemur! But, Sebell, that would mean he's in the Southern Weyr!"

"Yes it would, wouldn't it," said Sebell, unutterably relieved that the mystery of Piemur's disappearance could be explained. "C'mon. We'll send a message to Toric to be on the lookout for that rascal. I think Kimi knows Southern better than Beauty and Rocky."

"Let's send them all. Mine know Piemur best. Oh, just wait till I get my hands on that young man!"

Sebell laughed at Menolly's fierce expression. "I told you he'd land on his feet."

Chapter 8

The change in temperature roused Piemur, his mouth dry and sour, his body stiff. He couldn't think for a moment where he was or why he ached and his guts rumbled.

He sat bolt upright as he remembered and felt inside his tunic for the beragged egg. He tore the covering in his frenzy to check the precious shell and was trembling with relief when he touched its warm shape. The quick tropical dusk was nearly on him, the vivid glimmer of the sun coating the foliage about him with gold. He heard the lap of water and, peering towards the sound, realized that he was close to a beach. The call of a nest-homing wherry startled him as he crept stiffly from under his bush. He knew he'd have little time and light to settle the egg in warm sand for the night. He staggered to the beach, praying it would be a sandy one, crying out in relief when he saw that it was, dropping to his knees to burrow into the warm sand and bury the egg safely.

Wearily he built a pile of rocks to mark the spot and then pulled himself back to the jungle, using the last light to locate a tree with orange fruit. The first few he batted down from the branches with a long stick were too hard to be edible, another fell with a liquid splot. He scooped up the overripe fruit and swallowed it down, grimacing at the slightly rancid taste. Then he managed, after several more attempts, to get two edible fruits. Barely satisfied, he propped himself against the tree's trunk and slept fitfully through the night.

Piemur stayed in that area all the next day, resting, washing his scratched and bruised self in the warm seawater, rinsing out his stained and torn clothes. He had to seek the concealing shelter of the forest several times as first fire lizards and then dragons flew overhead. He was too close to the Weyr, he realized, and he would have to move on. But first, something to eat: more orange fruit and redfruit, which seemed to grow in profusion. He also picked up several dried hulls, one for carrying water and another for carrying his fire lizard egg buried in warm beach sand.

When he saw fire lizards and dragons returning to the Weyr, he waited for a spell before he retrieved his egg, packing it well in the hot sands, and headed westward, away from the Weyr.

Afterwards, he never could figure out why he felt the Weyr and the

Southern Hold were dangerous to him. He just felt he ought to avoid any contact with them, certainly until his egg had hatched and he had Impressed his own fire lizard. It wasn't logical, really, but he'd endured a harrowing experience, had already been in the role of the hunted, and so he continued to run.

The first moon rose early and full, lighting his way along the shore, up the rocky banks and steep sand dunes. He traveled on, occasionally eating fruit as he plodded and pausing three times for a small nap. But each time anxiety snapped him wakeful and set him on his way again.

The second moon rose, doubling the quantity of light but striking curious shadows against its companion that often made Piemur detour around rocks made gigantic by the mismatched illumination. He knew that strange things could happen to travelers under the double moons, but he persevered until both moons had set and the darkness forced him to seek refuge under the trees, where he'd be safely hid if he slept and dawn came before he knew.

He woke when a snake crawled over his legs, scraping against his bare skin where the trousers had been torn. He clutched feverishly at the egg, for snakes liked fire lizard eggs. The sand about his precious possession was cool and that brought him to his feet. He emerged onto a small cove, baking in a midmorning sun. He scooped out a hole and buried his egg, marking the spot with the upturned fruit shell ringed by beach stones. Then he returned to the jungle to seek his breakfast and water.

The diet of fresh raw fruit was affecting his digestion, and he spent some uncomfortable moments before he realized he would have to have something else to eat. He remembered what Menolly had said about fishing from her cave in the Dragon Stones, but he hadn't so much as a line. Then he noticed the thick vines clinging to tree trunks and viewed the thorns on the orange fruit trees with new sight. Using his belt knife and a little ingenuity, he shortly had himself a respectable fishing line. He baited his hook with a sliver of orange fruit, having nothing better.

The western arm of the cove had been swept into a long rocky hook and Piemur climbed and scrambled to the furthest point. Casting his hook and line into the foaming waves that lapped the base of the rock, he sat down to wait.

It was a long time before he had any luck in landing a fish, though he had pulls on several occasions that lost him his bait. When he finally hauled in a medium-sized yellowtail he had every right to be jubilant and think longingly of roast fish. But as he rose from his cramped position and turned, he realized he'd been very stupid. His rock was now isolated from the cove's arm by active surf. With a shock, he realized his second mistake: he had buried the egg in sands that would shortly be underwater. His yellowtail was considerably mangled by the time he had paddled, jumped and splashed ashore. His immersion in salt water had disclosed another shortsightedness on his part: his face, particularly his nose and the tips of his ears, had been badly sunburned, as well as the parts of his body showing through rents in his tunic.

He rescued his egg first, burying it in the shell with the hottest sands he could scoop about it. Then he hurried on to the next cove and a spot well above an obvious high-tide mark.

It took him time, too, to find rocks that would spark and light his fire of dried grasses and twigs. Eventually, he got enough of a blaze and he stretched the gutted yellowtail over the fire to broil, barely able to contain his impatient hunger until the meat darkened. Never had fish tasted so sweet and delectable! He could have eaten ten or twelve the same size and not had too much. He gazed longingly out at the sea, and to his disgust saw fish leaping out of the waters as if to tantalize him. Then he remembered that Menolly had said the best times to fish were sunrise and sunset or after a hard rain. No wonder he'd had such a wait, fishing at midday.

His face and hands burned now from too much sun, so he hiked deep into the woods that lined the beach, looking for fresh water, for ripe fruit, and seeing in the luxurious undergrowth, familiar, but oddly out-sized, leaves of tuber plants. Experimentally he yanked on a handful of stems and up came a huge tuber root, which he dropped when he saw the small gray grubs that swarmed over it. But they disappeared quickly back into the rich loam, leaving clean the enormous white tuber. Suspiciously Piemur picked it up and examined it from all sides. It looked all right, even if it was much bigger than any tuber he'd ever seen. He was certainly hungry enough to eat all of it.

Taking it back to his dying fire, he fed the flame to a good height, washed the tuber in some of his precious fresh water, and sliced it thinly. He toasted the first slice on the end of his knife and broke off a tiny piece for judicious tasting. Maybe it was his hunger, but he decided he'd never tasted such a delicious tuber, crisp on the outside and just soft enough on the inside. He made quick work of cooking the remaining slices and felt immeasurably better.

Retracing his steps, he found tubers in quantity, but took only what he could carry.

When the tide had begun to recede from his boulder that evening, he splashed out to it again and was rewarded with several yellowtails of respectable size. He broiled two for his dinner, toasted another huge tuber and then undug his egg, arranging it in its carrying shell with plenty of warm sand.

He walked that night again until both moons had set. When he found a place to sleep on dried tree fronds, he arranged himself so that the rising sun would shine in his face and wake him. That way, he would be up in time to catch fish.

He followed this routine for two more days and nights, until the last night he realized that for some time he had seen no fire lizards nor dragons, nor any other living creature, except windborne wild wherries soaring high above the ground. He told himself that the next day, as soon as he found fresh water and a good cove with a wide sandy beach well above high-water markings with convenient fishing points, he would settle. The egg was perceptibly hardening and surely must be close to hatching time.

That evening he began to wonder why he had continued moving away from hold and Weyr. Of course, it was kind of fun, discovering each new cove and the vast stretches of sandy beach and rocky strand. To be accountable to no one except himself was also a new experience. Now that he had enough to eat and some variety of food, he was enjoying his adventure very much indeed. Why, he'd wager anything that he'd set foot on places no other person had ever trod. It was exhilarating to be first at something, instead of following others and doing just what every other apprentice had done before him Turn after Turn after Turn.

He fished in the morning, catching a packtail and being mindful of Menolly's experience with the tough, oily flesh as he gutted it. He smeared oil on face and body to ease the rough skin the sun had burned, reasoning that if Menolly had used fish oil for her fire lizards' flaking hides, it would do for his as well.

Retrieving and inspecting his precious egg, he was now certain it must be close to hatching, the shell was so rock hard. He packed it in the fruit shell with warm sand and proceeded westward, striking off through the shadier forest for a while.

At midmorning he stumbled out of the shade onto a wide expanse of gleaming white sand that forced him to squint against its glare. Shading his eyes, he saw a lagoon, partially sealed off from the sea by a jagged barrier of massive rocks, which must once have been the original coastline. Carefully climbing along that rocky arm, he could see all kinds of fish and crawlers in the clear water, trapped there after the higher tides had retreated. Just what he needed, his own private fishing pond. He retraced his steps and continued along the beach. Parallel to the point where the lagoon broke into the sea, he discovered a small stream emerging from the jungle, feeding into the lagoon. He followed it far enough up its course to clean water untainted by the sea.

He was jubilant and amazed that anywhere in this world of sun, sea and sand could exist that was exactly right to suit his requirements. And it was all his! Here he could stay until his egg hatched. And he'd better make the right preparations for that event now. It wouldn't do to miss Impressing simply because he had no food for the hatchling.

He had seen neither fire lizards nor dragons in the sky for the past two days, so afterwards he thought that might be why he had given no thought to Thread. In hindsight he realized that he had known perfectly well that Thread fell on the southern half of Pern just as it did in the North. His preoccupation with the fire lizard egg and his efforts to supply himself with food had simply divorced him from the concerns and memories of life in craft and hall.

He was fishing that dawn, lying prone on the grass pad he had made to protect his bare chest from the harsh rock surfaces when he experienced a sudden sense of alarm so intense that he glanced over his right shoulder and saw in horror the gray rain hissing into the sea not a dragon's length beyond.

He remembered later that he glanced for the reassuring sight of flaming dragons just before he realized that he was completely unprotected from Thread whether dragons were in the sky or not. That same instinct sent him plunging into the lagoon. Then he was in the midst of violent activity as half the fish in the ocean seemed to crowd against him, eager to consume the Thread that was diving to feed them. Piemur propelled himself up out of the water, flailing his arms to keep water about his body in the notion that water might protect him from Thread, as he gulped air into his lungs.

His shoulders were stung while he fell back under the water. He pushed himself down, down again. But before long, he had to repeat the cycle of emerging, gulping air into his laboring lungs, then retreating to a depth that was free of viable Thread. He'd done this six or seven times before he realized that he couldn't sustain such activity for the length of Threadfall. He was dizzy with lack of oxygen, pinpointed by Threadscore that burned and stung in the salty water. Menolly had at least had a cave in which to shelter and. . . .

If he could find it, if it were sufficiently above the surface of the lagoon at this time of the tide, there was an overhanging rock. . . . He desperately tried to place its location on the lagoon arm the next time he surfaced, but he could barely see with eyes red and stinging. He was never sure in the midst of panic and anoxia how he found that meager shelter. But he did. He scraped his cheek, right hand and shoulder in the process, but when the redness cleared from his eyes, his nose and mouth were above water and his head and shoulders protected by a narrow roof of rock. Literally, just beyond the tip of his nose, Thread sheeted into the water. He felt fish bump and dive against him, sometimes sharply nibbling at his legs or arms until he flailed the attacked limb and the fish darted after their customary food.

Part of his mind knew when the menace of Thread had passed, but he remained where he was until the cloud of falling Thread moved beyond the horizon and the sun once more shone in unoccluded splendor on a peaceful scene. The terrified core of his soul, however, was slower to acknowledge that danger was over, and he remained in the shelter of the ledge until the tide had receded, leaving him stranded like a white fish on his portion of the reef.

Anxiety for his egg finally drove him from his sanctuary to check it in its beachy nest. The first scoop of sand he threw violently from him for it contained hundreds of the gray, squirming grubs. They reminded him so forcefully of Thread that he scrubbed his hands against his sides. Could Thread have penetrated the egg? He dug frantically until he reached it. He caressed the warm shell in relief. Surely it would hatch any time now!

Abruptly he hoped it wouldn't happen just now. He had no fish handy, and with their bellies full, he doubted if he'd catch any before sundown. If then. And how would he know precisely when the egg was going to hatch? Dragons always knew when a clutch was ready and warned their riders. Menolly said her fire lizards began to hum and their eyes whirled purple-red. He had no such forecasters to aid him.

Seized by a sense of urgency, he foraged in the jungle for vines to make another line and thorns from the fruit trees for hooks. But just to be safe, he gathered some fruit and some tough-shelled nuts. Hatchlings needed meat, he knew, but he supposed anything edible would be better than an empty hand.

It was while he was fitting the thorn hook into the end of the vine that the impact of the day started to hit him. His fingers trembled so that he had to pause. He, Piemur of . . . well, he wasn't a herdsman's boy anymore, and he wasn't a harper's apprentice either . . . Piemur . . . Piemur of Pern. He, Piemur of Pern, he went on more confidently, had survived Threadfall holdless. He straightened his shoulders and smiled broadly as he glanced proudly across his lagoon. Piemur of Pern had survived Threadfall! He had overcome considerable obstacles to secure a queen fire lizard egg. It would hatch, and he would, at long last, have a fire lizard all his own! He glanced fondly at the mound in the sand that was *his* little queen.

Was he certain, though, that it was a queen? Doubt assailed him briefly. If it wasn't, it might be a bronze and that was every bit as good. But it had to be a queen egg, separated as it had been from the others warming by Lord Meron's fire.

Piemur chuckled at his own stupidity. He ought to have realized that Lord Meron would present the eggs as the climax to his feasting. Of course, the recipients would check, out of joy. Or maybe, out of distrust for Lord Meron's generosity. He really ought to have gotten out of the Hold before the feast had ended. How, he couldn't imagine, but he just might have done it if he'd tried. Certainly he wouldn't now be isolated on the Southern Continent. He put a final twist in the vine to hold the thorn hook firmly.

He gazed northward across the heat hazy sea in the general direction of Fort Hold and the Harper Hall. He'd been gone eight days now. Had they tried to find him at Nabol Hold? He was a bit surprised that Sebell hadn't sent Kimi or Menolly's Rocky to look. But then, how was anyone to know where he was? North or south? And fire lizards had to have directions, just like dragons. Sebell might not have learned that Lord Meron was dealing with the Southerners, or that there had been a collection that night.

A splash in the lagoon attracted his attention. The fish were back with the tide. He rose and made his way across the exposed rocks, affectionately patting the ledge that had sheltered him.

It took him longer than usual to catch a fish that evening. And he only landed a small yellowtail, too small to satisfy his hunger, much less provide for a voracious hatchling. Soon the rising tide would isolate him on this section of the lagoon so if he didn't hook shortly, he'd have to retreat to where the fishing was always poorer.

Controlling his impatience as best he could, for Piemur was certain that the fish heard sound, else why were they avoiding his hook, he also held his breath as he jerked his line in an imitation of live bait. That's when the curious noise came to his ears. He raised his head, looking about, trying to locate the source of that odd sound, so faintly heard above the lap of wave against rock. He scanned the skies, thinking there might be wild wherries or fire lizards above him. Or worse, dragonriders to whom he would be extremely visible, stretched along the reef rock.

It was the movement on the beach that caught his eye, more than placing the sound there. Just then the line in his hand jerked. In a panic of comprehension, he nearly let go but a reflex prompted him to haul the line in rapidly, rising to his feet as he did so, his eyes on the beach.

Something moved on the sand. Near his egg! A sandsnake? He picked up the first yellowtail, poked a finger in the gills of the hooked one, and made for the beach. Nothing was going to. . . .

Surprise and consternation halted him for one panic-filled instant as he saw the cause of the motion; a tiny glistening golden creature flapping awkwardly across the sands, piteously screaming. Wild wherries materialized in the sky, drawn by some uncanny magnet to this birth moment.

"All you have to do is feed a hatchling!" Menolly's calm advice rang in his ears as he stumbled across the sand and nearly fell on the tiny queen. He fumbled at his belt for his knife to cut up the fish. "Use pieces about the size of your thumb or else the hatchling will choke."

Even as he tried to cut through tough fish scale, the little fire lizard darted forward, screaming with hunger.

"No. No. You'll choke to death," cried Piemur, pulling the fish tail from the fire lizard's grasp and hacking chunks from the softer flesh along the spine.

Shrieking with rage at being denied food, the little queen began to tear at the fish flesh. Her talons were too birth soft to perform their function, so Piemur had time to slice suitable portions for her. "I'm slicing as fast as I can."

A race ensued then, between the hunger of the little queen and Piemur's knife. He managed to keep just a slice ahead of her voracity. When his knife opened the softer fish gut, she pounced, mumbling in her haste to consume it. Piemur wasn't certain if fish entrails, full of Thread no doubt, were a suitable diet for a newly hatched fire lizard, but it gave him time to cut more flesh.

He started on the second yellowtail, gutting it first to occupy her while he hacked rapidly at the flesh. He knew one was supposed to hold the fire lizard while one fed it, to form the Impression, but he didn't see how he could contrive that until he had food enough to coax her into his hand.

Finished with the offal, she turned back to him, her rainbow eyes glaring at him as they whirled redly with hunger. She gave a scream, opened her still wet wings and dove on the small mound of fish pieces. He caught her first, holding her body firmly just under the wings and then proceeded to feed her piece by piece until she stopped struggling in his grasp. The edge of her hunger assuaged, she paused long enough to chew, and her voice took on a new, softer note. He loosened his hold and began to stroke her, marveling at the wiry strength in the slender body, at the softness of her hide, at the liveness of her, his very own fire lizard.

A shadow crossed them, and the queen raised her head and rasped out a warning.

He looked up and saw that the wherries had boldly circled down and were just above him, talons poised to grab. He waved his knife, the blade sparkling and glinting in the sun, frightening the wherries into wider, higher circles.

Wild wherries were dangerous, and he and the hatchling were unprotected on the open beach. He gathered her carefully into the crook of his arm, grabbed the line from which the fishhead still depended and started to run toward the jungle.

She shrieked in protest as he broke into a full run just as the wherry leader made its first pass. He sliced upward with his knife, but the wherry was clever and, adding its piercing scream to the fire lizard's, veered away from him. Holding the struggling queen against his chest, Piemur hunched his shoulders and concentrated on reaching the forest as fast as he could. He'd always prided himself on his speed: right now that ability had to save two lives.

He saw the shadow of another wherry dive at them and swerved to the left, grinning with satisfaction at its shrill call of anger when it was balked of its prey.

The queen's talons might not be dry but they scrabbled painfully against his bare chest as she struggled to grab the fishhead that dangled enticingly from the line in his hand. Piemur ducked right as he avoided a third wherry's dive, and the queen missed her lunge for the fishhead.

The fourth attack occurred so quickly that Piemur couldn't duck in time and felt a sharp pain as the wherry's talons scraped across his shoulders. Twisting upwards, he slashed out with his knife, tripping as he did so and instinctively rolling to the right to protect his precious burden. He saw the wherries trying to veer fast enough to come at him on the ground, shrilling out that their prey had fallen and was at their mercy.

The little queen was now aware of their peril and slipping from his grasp, jumped to his shoulder, spreading her wings and screaming defiance at the attackers. She was so valiant, the little darling, so small in comparison to the wherries that her courage gave Piemur the impetus he needed. He scrambled to his feet, felt her cling to his hair, her tail tightly wound about his neck, continuing her stream of defiant cries as if by her fury she could repel their attackers.

Piemur ran then, pumping his legs as fast as he could, his lungs straining for breath to sustain the speed. He ran, expecting momentarily to feel the wherry talons rending his flesh. But abruptly their cries turned from triumph to fear. Piemur launched himself into the thick bushes, grabbing at his queen to keep her secure. Safe under the wide leaves and among the thick stalks, he turned to see what had frightened their pursuers. The wherries were flying away as fast as they could flap their wings, and he had to crane his neck eastward until he saw a flight of fire lizards arrowing in pursuit of the wherries. Just as he drew back under the concealing bush, he saw five dragons gliding above the sea.

His queen gave another cry, softer now, in protest that the fishhead still dangled beyond her reach. Afraid that somehow the dragons might hear her, he gave her the head, which she contentedly tore and consumed while Piemur watched the dragons circling the spot where she had lain enshelled. Without waiting to see if the dragons landed, Piemur pushed his way deeper into the jungle, trying to remember if Menolly had ever said anything about fire lizards tracing newly hatched ones.

But fire lizards only knew what they'd seen, and he'd been under-cover by the time the winged rescuers had reached the lagoon area. The wherries' shrieks would have masked any sound she'd made, and as Piemur plunged past thorn trees and undergrowth, her cries became softer. Weariness overcame the last vestiges of her shelling hunger.

Piemur was more aware of her contentedness than his rasping breath as he continued to put as much distance between him and the lagoon, and possible discovery, while light remained to guide him in the murky jungle.

In the same hour Kimi returned with a message from Toric, answering the Harper's query about young newcomers in the southern settlement, the drum beat the news of Lord Meron's death.

"Eight days it's taken him to die," said the Harper on the end of a long sigh, "when Master Oldive thought one."

"Determined to disoblige us, I imagine," said Sebell, dismissing the man as he concentrated again on Toric's message. "No one has applied to him for shelter. There's been no outburst from the Weyr, which he's certain would have been made if a stowaway had been discovered. But that doesn't mean," said Sebell hurriedly, raising his hand to forestall Menolly's protest, "that Piemur didn't get there. Toric says that the Weyr has been barred to his holders for the last sevenday, but his fire lizards imaged a pile of strange shapes by the Weyrhold, so he suspects that a shipment has arrived from the north. They don't let the mere holders in the Weyr grounds to celebrate. So if Piemur smuggled himself out of Nabol Hold in one of the Oldtimers' sacks, he also got out of it and made himself scarce."

"Which is sensible of Piemur," said the Harper, idly twirling his wine glass with one hand. His face was expressionless, but his eyes moved restlessly with his thoughts. "Piemur would undoubtedly deem it discreet not to come to the Oldtimers' notice."

"At least not until that egg of his had hatched," added Menolly. She had so hoped that Piemur would have gone to Toric. She was certain he would know that Toric was friendly with the harpers. She turned to Sebell. "Candler will let us know the instant the other eggs from the clutch have hatched, won't he?"

"Yes, he said he would," the journeyman replied, but then he made a face, scratching his head. "But we don't know if that queen egg came from the same clutch as the others."

"But we do know the others weren't green's eggs; they were too big. And that's the only time scale we have to work with. I'm positive that Piemur won't attempt to seek anyone out until that egg has hatched and he's Impressed. I know I wouldn't if I were in Piemur's boots. Oh, I wish I knew if he were all right." She beat her thighs with her fists at her helplessness.

"Menolly," said the Harper soothingly, "you're not responsible for—"

"But I feel responsible for Piemur," she said, and then shot her Master an apologetic look for interrupting him so rudely. "If I hadn't encouraged his interest in the fire lizards, if I hadn't filled his ears with the pleasures they bring, he might not have been tempted to steal that egg and get himself into such a predicament." She looked up because both men started to laugh, and she exclaimed with exasperation at their callousness.

"Menolly, Piemur has been getting in and out of trouble since long before you arrived here," said Sebell. "You and your fire lizards calmed him down considerably. But I think you're right about Piemur not showing himself until Impression's been made. And Toric is on the alert for him. He'll show up."

"Meanwhile," said the Harper, rising from his chair and reaching for his flying gear, "I'd best go and assist the new Lord Deckter to secure his Hold."

Chapter 9

Afterwards, Piemur wasn't certain why he had run from the dragonriders. He seemed to have been running from or to something ever since his voice had changed. In his panic, he supposed he aligned the Oldtime dragonriders with Lord Meron, and he did not want to encounter anyone connected with Lord Meron just then. Whatever, that night he plunged through the jungle until lack of breath, the painful stitch in his side and the darkness forced him to halt. Sinking to the ground, he rearranged his fire lizard comfortably and then fell asleep.

Just as the sun was rising the next morning, she awoke him, snappy with hunger. He eased the worst of her pangs and his own with fresh redfruit, cool from the night air and succulently sweet. Then he turned north, to make his way back to the beaches and fish for Farli, for that was the name he gave his little queen. Pushing his way through the underbrush, he tripped over a half-eaten runner beast carcass. Farli chattered with delight and ate flesh from bone, humming at him in pleasure.

"You'll choke like that," he said, and proceeded to hack smaller pieces, keeping about one knife slice ahead of her voracious appetite.

When Farli had curled herself about Piemur's neck, thoroughly sated, her belly bulging, he sliced more meat from the dead runner. He figured the creature must have been killed during Threadfall so the meat wouldn't as yet be tainted. Not only would it be a welcome change for him from fish, but red meat was better for Farli as well.

Comforted by her sleeping weight about his neck, Piemur found thick grasses and wove a rough envelope in which to carry the meat. He estimated he had enough for several meals for himself and Farli, but if he could cook it, the meat wouldn't spoil as quickly in the heat.

Continuing on a northwestern course back to the beach, he collected dry grass and sticks with which to build a fire. He was still heading generally north when he saw the unmistakable glint of water through the thinning trees to his left. He stopped, stared, unable to think how he could have mistaken his direction. A lake? However, if water was this close now. . . .

He pushed his way through the thinning screen of trees and bush and came out on a small rise. Below him were wide tidelands, which swept from the forest in an undulating grassy plain, broken by thick clumps of a gray-green bush. The plain continued on the other side of a broad river, which gradually widened until, in a distant point now hazy with heat, it must open its mouth into the sea. A breeze, scented with an oddly familiar, pungent odor, dried the sweat on his face. Squinting against the sunlight, Piemur could see herdbeasts grazing on the lush grass on both sides of the river. And yet there'd been Thread here the day before, and no dragonriders flaming to prevent the deadly stuff burrowing into the ground and eating the land barren.

As if to reassure himself, he poked at the soil with one of the sticks he'd collected, lifting up a clod of grass. Grubs fell from the roots, and Piemur was suitably awed by the abilities of those little gray wrigglies, which could, all by themselves, keep such an enormous plain free from the ravages of Thread. And those bloody Oldtimers hadn't so much as stirred from the Weyr during yesterday's Fall. They weren't proper dragonriders at all. F'lar and Lessa had been right to exile them here to the South, where the insignificant grubs did their work for them. Why, he could have been killed during that Threadfall, and not a dragonrider around to protect him. Not, Piemur honestly admitted, that he hadn't been well able to protect himself.

He gazed across the river, now noticing the swifter moving current that rippled towards the sea. He'd have fresh water for drinking here as well as a retreat from Thread. The jungle behind him would provide fruit and tubers; the meadow's inhabitants red meat for Farli. There was no need to trek to the sea again. He could stay here until Farli had lost the worst of her hatchling appetite. Then he'd better start back to the Southern Hold. If he was careful, he could avoid being noticed by the Oldtimers until he'd made contact with the holder . . . what was his name? He was certain he'd heard Sebell mention the man by name. Toric! Yes, that was it. Toric.

He set about making a rough circle of stones to protect his fire from the breeze, whistling softly. A fresh breeze brought him another whiff of that odor, sun-warmed and so puzzlingly familiar. Whatever it was must be down on the plain for the wind came from that direction. Leaving his meat to roast at his fire, Piemur made his way down the slope, looking about at the tiny blooms in among the grasses with Thread-pricked blades. He almost passed the first clump of bushes before he realized that their leaves were definitely familiar. Familiar, he thought as he reached out to touch one, but so much larger. He bruised the leaf as the final test and sure enough, had to jerk his hand back as his fingers smarted and then lost all feeling. Numbweed! The whole plain was dotted with numbweed bushes, growing bigger and fuller than any he'd ever seen in the north. Why, if you harvested even one side of this plain, you'd keep every Weyr on Pern in numbweed for the entire Pass. Master Oldive ought to know about this place.

A petulant squeak in his ear warned him that Farli had roused, probably smelling the roasted meat. He carefully broke off some large numbweed leaves, and wrapping their cut stems in a thick blade of grass, returned to the fire. When he had given Farli a few half-done pieces of meat, she was quite content to curl up for the rest of her nap. Then Piemur bruised a numbweed leaf between two flat, clean stones. He rubbed the wet side of the stones against his cuts, shivering at the slight sting of the raw numbweed before its anesthetic properties took effect. He was careful not to rub the stone too deep, for raw numbweed must be used sparingly or you could get horrible blisters and end up with scars.

As he settled by the fire to wait for his meat to cook, he knew he'd be sorry to leave here.

He said that to himself the next morning when he rose, and that evening when he curled up in the shelter he'd made for Farli and himself. He really ought to try to get word back to the Harper Hall.

Each day, however, found him too busy catering to the needs of a rapidly growing fire lizard to make provisions for a journey of possibly several days. He spent a whole day trying to catch a fish for the oils needed to soothe Farli's flaking skin.

Then Thread fell again. This time he was adequately prepared, and forewarned. Farli went hysterical with alarm, her eyes wheeling furiously with the red of anger as she rose on her wings and, shrieking defiance to the northeast, suddenly flicked out. When Piemur called her, she popped back in, scolded him furiously, and then disappeared. She had gone *between* before, inadvertently scared by some odd noise or other, so that it wasn't until she remained away for much longer than before that Piemur began to wonder what had frightened her. He looked northeast, noticing as his eyes swept across the plains, that the animals were all moving towards the river with considerable haste. The quick blossom of flame against the sky caught his eyes, and he saw, not only Thread's gray rain, but the distant motes of dragons.

He had made preparations against the next Fall of Thread, determined never to spend another eternity under a rock ledge. He had found a sunken tree trunk where the river flowed out of the forest. Diving into the water, he kicked down to the depth at which drowning Thread could no longer sting. There he hooked his arm around the tree trunk and poked back to the surface a thick reed, through which he then was able to breathe. It was not the most comfortable of hideaways, and fish constantly mistook his arms and legs for outsized Thread so he had to keep moving. Time, too, seemed motionless, and it felt like hours had passed before the impact circles of Thread on the water surface ceased. He was glad when with a mighty kick of his legs, he burst back into the air, nearly overturning a small runner. In fact the shallows seemed to be blanketed with animals. As if his eruption from the depths had been a signal, or perhaps his presence had frightened them, the creatures began to struggle towards the shore, shake themselves, and then rapidly take off down the plain. Some were bawling with pain, and he saw a number with bloody face scores where Thread had stung them. He also noticed some of the injured making to the numbweed bushes and rubbing against the leaves.

Piemur waded to the bank, calling for Farli as he sank to the solid ground. His arms and legs felt leaden from his efforts to discourage fish from eating him.

Farli burst into view just above him, chittering with relief and anxiety. She landed on his shoulder, wrapping her tail about his neck and stroking his cheek with her head, one paw wrapped around his ear, the other anchored to his nose. They comforted each other for a long moment. Then Piemur felt Farli's body go taut. She peered around his face and began to chatter angrily. Twisting about, at first Piemur saw nothing to alarm him. Farli loosed her hold on his nose, and he realized that she was pointing skyward. He saw the wherries then, circling high, and knew that something had not survived the Fall. If wherries were after it, it was something that would also feed him and his fire lizard.

Farli seemed as eager as he to beat the wherries to their victim, and she chattered encouragement as he found a stout stick and made his way up the riverbank.

Most of the creatures that had taken refuge in the river had disappeared, but he kept a wary eye for snakes and large crawlers that might also have found sanctuary in the river.

He saw the bulge of the fallen runner beast, half-hidden under a large numbweed bush. To his surprise, it heaved upwards, its bloodied flank crawling with grubs. The poor thing couldn't still be alive? He raised his stick to put an end to the creature's pain when he realized that the movement came from under the animal, spasmodic and desperate. Farli hopped from his shoulder and chittered, touching a tiny protruding hoof that Piemur hadn't noticed.

It had been a female runner beast! With an exclamation, Piemur grabbed the hind legs and pulled the corpse from the youngster the female had given her life to protect from Thread. Bleating, it staggered to its feet, shedding a carpet of grubs, and hobbled the few steps to Piemur, its head and shoulders scored here and there by Thread.

Almost absently, Piemur stroked the furry head and scratched behind the ear cup, feeling its rough tongue licking his skin. Then he saw the long shallow scrape on the little beast's right leg.

"So that's why you didn't make it to the river, huh, you poor stupid thing?" said Piemur, gathering it closer to him. "And your dam sheltered you with her body. Brave thing to do." It bleated again, looking anxiously up at him.

Farli chirped and stroked her body against the uninjured leg before she moved on to start making a meal off the dead runner. With a sense of propriety, Piemur took the youngster off to the river to bathe its wound, treat it with numbweed and wrap it with a broad river plant to keep off insects. He tethered it with his fishing line and then went back to slice off enough meat for several meals. The wherries were closing in.

Farli was sated enough not to resist leaving the carcass. Nor did she object when Piemur carried little Stupid back to their forest shelter.

As Piemur settled down to sleep that night, he had Stupid curled tightly against him along his back and Farli draped across his shoulders. He had fully intended to use the interval between this Fall and the next to make his way to the Southern Hold, but he really couldn't leave Stupid, crippled as well as motherless. The leg would heal with care and rest. Once Stupid was walking easily, after the next Threadfall, he would definitely make tracks to Southern.

Despite the lateness of the hour, the Masterharper could see light coming from his study window as he wearily made his way from the meadow where Lioth and N'ton had just left him. He was very tired, but well satisfied with the results of his efforts over the last four days. Zair, balancing on his shoulder, cheeped an affirmative. Robinton smiled to himself and rubbed the little bronze's neck.

"And Sebell and Menolly are going to be satisfied, too. Unless, of course, there has been word from that scamp that they haven't been able to send me."

He saw the half of the great Hall door swing into darkness and wagered with himself who waited for him there in the dark.

"Master?"

He was right; it was Menolly.

"You were away so long, Master," she cried in a soft voice as she closed the door behind him and spun the wheel to lock the bolts tightly in floor and ceiling.

"Ah, but I've accomplished much. Any news from Piemur?"

"No," and her shoulders drooped noticeably. "We would've sent you word instantly."

He put his arm around her slender shoulders comfortingly. "Is Sebell awake as well?"

"Yes, indeed!" She gave a chuckle. "N'ton sent Tris to warn us. Or you'd've been locked out of your own Hall."

"Not for long, my dear girl, not for long!"

They were climbing the steps now, and he noticed that she slowed her pace to match his. He was tired, true, but, worse, he no longer commanded the resilience that made no bother of late hours.

"Lord Groghe was back two days ago, Master. Why did you have to stay so long at Nabol?" He felt her shoulders give a convulsive shudder under his arm. "I wouldn't have stayed at that place a moment longer than I had to."

"Not the most of congenial of Holds, to be sure. I can't think what can have happened to all the wine Lord Fax appropriated in his conquests. He had some good pressings, too. Meron can't have drunk it all in a bare thirteen or fourteen Turns."

"You'd no Benden wine, then?" Menolly teased him.

"None, you unfeeling wretch."

"Then I'm more amazed than ever that you stayed so long."

"I had to!" he replied, amazed at the irritation in his voice. But they had reached his rooms now, and he opened the door, grateful for the sight of the familiar disorder of his workroom and the welcoming smile on Sebell's face. The journeyman was on his feet, helping his master out of his flying gear and guiding him to a chair, while Menolly poured a goblet of a decent Benden wine.

"Now, sir, have you a tale to tell?" asked Sebell, lightly taunting with his Master's usual greeting. "Could we not have come to Nabol and helped speed matters?"

"I would have thought you'd seen enough of Nabol Hold to last a Turn or two," said Master Robinton, sipping at his wine.

"He's got news, Sebell," said Menolly, narrowing her eyes to glare at her master. "I can tell that look on his face. Smug, that's what he is. Did you learn what happened to Piemur at Nabol?"

"No, I'm afraid I didn't find out about Piemur, but among other, equally important, things, I have arranged matters so that we don't have to worry about Nabol Hold supplying the Oldtimers with northern goods or receiving a further embarrassing riches of fire lizard eggs in that otherwise impoverished Hold."

"Then, none of the disappointed heirs caused trouble during the confirmation?" asked Sebell.

Master Robinton waggled his fingers, a sly smile on his face. "Not to speak of, though Hittet is a master of the snide remark. They could scarcely contend the nomination, since it had been made before such notable witnesses. Besides, I never bothered to disabuse them of the notion that Benden and the other Lord Holders would call the heir to account for the sins of his predecessor." Master Robinton beamed at the reactions of his journeyman to his strategy. "It afforded me considerable pleasure to help the new Lord Deckter send the worthless lot back to improve their beggared holds."

"And Lord Deckter?" asked Sebell.

"A good choice, however unwilling. I pointed out to him, adroitly, that if he merely regarded his Hold as a flagging business and applied the same ingenuity and industry with which he had built a flourishing carting trade, he would find that the Hold would respond and repair. I also pointed out that in his four sons he has able assistants and ministers, a fortune few Lords can enjoy. However, he did have one matter he was particularly anxious to resolve." The Harper paused. He looked at the expectant faces. "A matter that just happens to march kindly with a problem we face." He turned to Menolly. "You'd best ready that boat of yours. . . ." he had started referring to her skiff in that manner after he and Menolly had been storm-lost on his one voyage to the southern hold the previous Turn. Now Menolly's face brightened, and Sebell sat up straight, eyes wide with anticipation. "We won't locate Piemur by whistling for him from the north. You two go south. Make certain that Toric lets the Oldtimers know, if you can't carry the message discreetly to them yourselves, that Meron is dead and that his successor supports Benden Weyr. I believe that Master Oldive wants you to bring back some of those herbs and powders. He used up a large portion of his supplies on Meron.

"But don't you dare return until you've found Piemur."

Chapter 10

Stupid bleated, his rump, as he struggled to his feet, pushing sharply into Piemur's belly. Curled on Piemur's shoulder, Farli gave a sleepy complaint, which rapidly changed to a squeak of alarm. Piemur rolled over, away from both his friends for fear of injuring either and got stiffly to his feet. There wasn't anything alarming in the clearing about his small shelter but, as his eyes swung about, he caught the unexpected distant blur of bright red on the river. Startled, he brushed aside an obscuring bough and saw, just where the river began to narrow between the plains, three single-masted ships, carrying brilliant red sails. Even as he watched in surprise, the ships altered course, their red sails flapping as they were first turned into the wind and then were carried by momentum up onto the muddy beach.

Fascinated at the sight of ships on his river, Piemur moved further from his shelter, stroking to reassure Farli, who chittered questions at him. He was marginally conscious of Stupid brushing against his bare leg as he reached the outermost screen of trees. Not that anyone from the ships could possibly see him at this distance. He watched, as one will review a dream, while people jumped out of the ships: men, women and children. Sails were furled fully, not just thrown across the boom. A line was formed to convey bundles and packages from the ships across the muddy beach to the higher, dry banks. Holdless men from the north? wondered Piemur. But surely he'd heard that they were passed through Toric first, so that their inclusion in the Southern Hold was unobtrusive and the Oldtimers had no cause to complain. Whoever these people were, they looked as if they intended to stay awhile.

As Piemur continued to watch the disembarkation, he became aware of a growing sense of indignation that anyone would dare invade his privacy, would have the audacity to make a camp and set up cooking fires with great kettles balanced on spits across the flames, just as if they belonged here. This was his river, and Stupid's grazing grounds. His! Not theirs to litter with tent, kettle and fire!

What if the Oldtimers just happened to fly this way? There'd be trouble. Didn't those folk know any better? Setting up in the sight of everything?

Farli distracted him by protesting her hunger. Stupid had fallen to his customary sampling of every type of greenery in his immediate area. Absently, Piemur reached in the pouch at his belt for a handful of nutmeats he'd kept there to pacify Farli. Daintily she took the offerings, but informed him with a querulous cheep that this had better not be all she was given to eat that morning.

Piemur chewed on a nut himself, trying to figure out who these people were and what they were about. One group was now separating itself from those bustling about tents or filling the huge kettles with water drawn from the river. This group moved purposefully towards the far end of the field and then the individuals spread out. Long chopping blades flashed in the sun, and suddenly Piemur knew who they were and what they were doing.

Southerners had come to harvest the numbweed bushes, now full of sap and strong with the juice that eased pain. He wrinkled his nose in disgust: it'd take them days to harvest that field; and each kettleful would require three days of stewing to reduce the tough plant to pulp. Another day would be required to strain the pulp, and the juice had to be simmered down to the right consistency to make the numbweed salve. Piemur knew that Master Oldive took the purest of the resultant salve and did something else with it to make it a powder for internal use.

He sighed deeply, because the intruders would be here for days and days. The camp may have been set up a good hour's walk from him and undoubtedly he could keep from being noticed. He wouldn't escape however, even at this distance, from the stench of boiling numbweed, for that smell was pervasive, and the prevailing breeze right now was from the sea. It was infuriating to be forced out of *his* place just when he'd gotten everything arranged to his convenience so that he could feed himself, Farli and Stupid, had shelter from the tropical storms at night and safety from Threadfall whenever it came.

Then it occurred to him that perhaps these weren't Southerners, but a work party from the north. He knew that Master Oldive preferred southern grown herbs; that was why Sebell had made that trip not long ago to bring back sacks and sacks of medicinal things. Surely he'd brought enough or maybe this was a new arrangement with the Oldtimers, who surely couldn't object to the Healer.

But northern ships had many-colored sails; Menolly had told him that seaholders prided themselves on the intricacy of their sail patterns. Plain red sail did suggest Southerners, whom everyone knew broke northern tradition whenever possible. Also those work groups were moving with the familiarity of much practice.

Piemur grinned to himself. One thing sure, he wasn't going to announce his presence right now. Sure as eggs hatched, he'd get himself included in harvesting numbweed. He'd just take what he needed and work around them, through the forest, until he got to the seashore, well east of them. And well away from the stink of boiling numbweed.

So he made a neat bundle of his woven mat and tied it with a vine thong, ignoring the chittering of Farli, who disapproved of his activity and of the fact that he was ignoring her gradually more insistent requests for food. He stared at the walls of his little shelter and decided that there was just the chance that someone might hunt in the forest and discover his rude hold. He dismantled the sheets of woven grass and hid them in the thick leaves of nearby bushes. He couldn't remove the clearing he'd made, but he scuffed up the tamped-down earth and scattered dead fronds here and there so that a casual glance would make it appear a natural clearing. He silenced Farli's now-urgent complaints by heading for the river. His fish trap, tied to his sunken Threadtree, held more than enough to feed her amply. He gutted what remained after she was sated, and wrapping them in broad leaves, added that to his bundle. He hesitated a few moments before tossing the fish trap back into the water. Surely no one would notice it unless someone tripped over the silly thing, which seemed highly unlikely, and the fish it captured wouldn't suffer. He'd leave it, and then he'd have ample eating when he returned here.

He made his way through the forest, skirting the wide plain, pausing to drink when he crossed a small contributory stream and to let Stupid rest awhile. The little fellow's short legs tired quickly, and while the creature was no great weight, he did seem to get heavier on those occasions when Piemur took pity and carried him awhile. Farli flitted ahead of them and behind, venturing up through the trees into the sky occasionally, twittering a scold that Piemur didn't understand but assumed was directed at the invaders.

"At least, you're not afraid of them," said Piemur, when she returned to her perch on his shoulder, begging caresses. She leaned against his finger as he stroked her neck, murmuring sweetly for him to continue, and she twined her tail lightly about his neck. "If only they weren't making numbweed, I'd be willing to introduce us all."

Or would he? Piemur wondered.

It would have been so simple to go down and find out if they were Southerners. Imagine their surprise when he wandered in, as easy as you please. They'd be startled, they would! And amazed when he told them his adventures here in the south. Yes, but then they'd want to know how he'd got here, and he wasn't at all certain he ought to tell the exact truth. Surely it wasn't unusual for a bold holdless man to try to sneak south, particularly if he had merited his Holder's displeasure! Piemur didn't have to mention that he'd acquired Farli in the north and certainly not that he'd removed her from Meron's hearth in Nabol Hold. Southerners would naturally assume that he'd found the little queen fire lizard here in some beach clutch. Stupid's acquisition posed no problem at all. He could tell the truth there. Piemur could always pretend that he didn't know where the Southern Hold was, and had been endlessly searching. Yes, that was it, he could say he'd stolen a small boat and had had an absolutely ghastly trip south, which was only the truth. Yes, but where had he sailed from? Ista? That was too small a hold to steal a boat from. Igen? Maybe even Keroon? The Southerners were not likely to check with anyone . . .

"Hello! What are you doing sneaking around here?"

A tall girl stepped into his path, blocking his way. On one shoulder was a bronze fire lizard, on the other a brown, both eyeing Farli intently. She let out an apologetic *squak,* as startled as Piemur. As she also dug her talons into his shoulder and tightened her tail about his neck, all that came out of his mouth was a choked cry of astonishment. A quick chirp from the little bronze caused Farli to relax her tail. Piemur turned his head towards her, annoyed that she hadn't warned him.

"It's not her fault," said the girl with a wide smile, easing her weight to one leg as she enjoyed Piemur's discomfiture. She had a pack strapped to her shoulders; a belt with a variety of pouches, some empty; dark hair wrapped with a band tightly about her head so strands wouldn't tangle in branches; and thick-soled sandals on her feet as well as shin guards tied about her lower legs. "Meer," and she indicated the bronze, "and Talla know how to be silent when they wish. And when they realized that she was already Impressed, we all wanted to see who had got a gold. I'm Sharra from the Southern Hold." She held out her hand, palm up. "How'd you get down here? We didn't see any wreckage as we came along the coast."

"I've been here three Threadfalls already," said Piemur, crossing her palm quickly in case she was the sort of person who sensed when someone lied. "Landed up near the big lagoon." Which was also partially true.

"Near the big lagoon?" Sharra's face expressed concern. "Then you weren't alone? The others were killed? That lagoon is treacherous in high tide. You don't see the outside shelf of rocks until you're right on them."

"I guess being little, I sort of slid over okay." Piemur felt it was safe to seem sorrowful.

"That's all past history for you, lad," said Sharra, her deep, musical voice compassionate. "If you survived the southern seas, and three Threadfalls holdless, I'd say you belong in the south."

"I belong here?" Suddenly the prospect heartened Piemur. Sharra was as perceptive as the Harper. The thought of being permitted to stay on in this beautiful land, walking where no one else, maybe not even Sharra, had ever trod before, made Piemur's heart tip over.

"Yes, I'd say you belonged," said Sharra, wide mouth curled in a smile. "So, what name shall I call you by?"

If she hadn't given him the option to state a name, any name, not necessarily his own, Piemur might have prevaricated. Instead, he answered her with a grin. "I'm Piemur of Pern."

Sharra threw back her head and laughed at his audacity, but she also laid her arm about his shoulders and gave him a companionable squeeze.

"I like you, Piemur of Pern. What have you named your little queen? Farli? That's a pretty name, and is that little runner beast a friend of yours, too?"

"Stupid? Yes, but he's just joined us. His mother was threadscored last Fall, but he keeps up with us—"

"Keeps up with you? You mean, you saw the ships land?"

"Sure. Saw 'em going to harvest numbweed, too."

Sharra laughed again at the intense disgust in his tone, and Piemur found himself grinning at the infectiousness of her humor. "And that decided you to make tracks away from wherever you were? Can't blame you, Piemur of Pern." Her eyes glinted with humor and she added in a conspiratorial tone. "I make it my special job to gather other leaves and herbs that grow in this area. Generally takes me the entire time they're rendering the numbweed."

"I wouldn't mind helping you with that, you know," suggested Piemur, slyly giving her a look. He was only just aware of how much he had missed the interchange with someone of like mind.

"I'd be glad of the right sort of help. And you'll have to keep up with me. I've got a lot to do while they muck about with the numbweed. There's a northern Healer who's sent me a special request."

"I thought you Southerners kept away from the north?" Piemur decided it was time to be ignorantly discreet.

"Well, there are some things that need to be traded back and forth."

"But I thought Benden Weyr doesn't permit—"

"Dragonriders, yes," and there was a curious tone in her voice when she said "dragonriders" that caught Piemur's quick ear. It was a mocking derision that surprised him, accustomed as he was to the respect with which all dragonriders—except the Southern Oldtimers—were treated. But Sharra meant the Southern Oldtimers when she said "dragonriders." "No, we trade with Northerners." Again that odd derision, as if Northerners weren't up to southern standards. "All manner of southern plants grow bigger and better than the same things in your old north. Numbweed, for one, feather herb and tuft grass for fever, red wort for infection, pink root for bellyache, oh all manner of things."

She had begun to walk now, gesturing Piemur to follow her deeper into the forest, her stride swinging as if she knew exactly where she was going in the tangled depths, had traveled this way many times before.

At some stages of the next few days, Piemur had occasion to regret not harvesting numbweed, a comparatively simple task compared to Sharra's search, which included digging, scrambling under thorny bushes that scratched his back raw, and climbing trees for parasitic growths. He felt he had found a taskmaster in her equal to old Besel at Nabol Hold. However, a taskmaster far more interesting, for Sharra talked about the properties and virtues of the roots for which they dug, the leaves for which they climbed only the healthiest of trees, well-sheltered from the worst ravages of Threadfall, or equally elusive herbs that lived obscurely where other bushes had thorns to scratch. Sharra had a wherhide jacket with her, but he had nothing to shield him from lacerations. She was quite ready and prepared to daub him with numbweed whenever necessary, but she did have to point out that his size made him the logical person to pursue the shyest herbs in their protective environment. Nothing would permit Piemur to lose honor in Sharra's eyes.

The first evening, she built a tiny, hot fire, knowing which of the southern woods burned best, and cooked him the finest eating he'd had since he'd left the Harper Hall; his contribution was fish and hers a combination of tubers and herbs. The three fire lizards devoured their portions of the stew with as much gusto as he did.

To Piemur's pleased surprise, Sharra did not question him again about his journey south nor his imaginary companions. When she commented on his knowledgeable handling of little Stupid, he did admit to having been a herdsman's boy in mountain holds. Otherwise Sharra seemed determined to introduce him to the south and gave him endless lectures on its beauties and advantages. She told him of explorations up the river—his river—which had ended in an unnavigable and dangerous marshland of tremendous breadth. The explorers had reluctantly decided that rather than get lost one by one up blind waterways they had better abandon the search until they could make an aerial survey of the

area; a survey unlikely to be accomplished until one of the Oldtimers
boredly agreed to the outing.

Piemur hadn't been in Sharra's company for more than several hours
before he learned how poor her opinion was of dragonriders. While he
had to agree to her estimate of the Oldtimers, he found it very difficult
not to call N'ton to her as comparison. He felt he was being disloyal to
the Fort Weyrleader when he forced himself to keep silent. But a
favorable mention of N'ton might bring a query as to how he, a lowly
herdsman's boy, came to know so much about a Weyrleader.

Sharra had a light blanket, which she was quite willing to share with
Piemur at night. She also acquainted him with the thick bush leaves,
which made a more fragrant and comfortable bedding than the spring-
ier fronds he'd been using. The leaves also had no tendency to drive
annoying splinters into soft flesh.

Sharra knew a great deal, Piemur realized, for she also had him
feeding Stupid on a particular plant that would make up for the lack of
nourishment from his dead mother. Piemur would never have known
that that was why Stupid had browsed so continuously; a dietary instinct rather than an insatiable appetite.

The second day, after a light meal of fruit and tubers, which Sharra
had baked in the ashes of the fire, the two continued on a steady course
south. The thick forest gave occasionally onto grassy meadows, dotted
with herdbeasts and runners who would gallop wildly away when the
first scent of the humans reached them. By the middle of the next day,
they had reached higher ground, more frequently broken by meadows,
until suddenly, they came to a low bluff, as if the land had suddenly
fallen away from the level on which they stood. Below, stretching to the
far hazy horizon, was a marshland, fingered with black strips of water,
which wove and disappeared about the clumps of drier land on which
grew giant bushes of stiff, tuft-topped grasses.

"We were well met, Piemur," said Sharra. "With you to help, we can
get twice as much, manage a larger raft with two to steer it, and return
down the river to the ships in very good time. But not," she grinned
down at him, "until they've had time to barrel the numbweed. Here's
what we do now."

She showed him, by a map she scratched in the dirt at their feet with
her belt knife, and by pointing in the appropriate directions. The third
large channel to their right was actually the river that led to the sea.
That much the earlier exploration had determined. There was plenty of
the valuable tuft grasses between the bluff and that safe, third channel.
They would be able to half-swim, half-wade across the intervening
channels, using the fire lizards to scare away the water snakes, which

could wring the blood out of a person's arm or leg. Piemur didn't believe that water snakes could grow that big, but he had to credit her warning when she showed him the fine band of puncture marks on her left arm where a water snake had wound its coils and left the myriad points of its toe-teeth. Not a denizen of these parts, Sharra assured him blithely, and brushed aside his pity by saying that the marks would fade gradually. Then she suggested that, being taller, she'd better carry Stupid across the waters on her shoulders.

As they reached each grassy island, they cut the tufts from the grass for the therapeutic seeds that grew along each stem. The larger branches were laid aside and tied in bundles to be bound together for the raft. Sharra said that the branches absorbed water gradually, but the raft would float long enough to get them safely to the river's mouth. The heart of the grass plant, just above the root ball, was its most important part. This was dried and pounded into a powder that was the best medicine known for reducing fever, especially firehead fever, about which Piemur had never heard. Sharra told him that it seemed to occur only in the south, and generally only during the first month of the spring season, now well past. Something, they thought, rolled up on the spring tides so that beaches were avoided during that month by everyone.

Piemur might have avoided both numbweed stench and water snake puncture, but he certainly worked as hard beside Sharra, as he had that one day in Nabol Hold, a day that seemed to belong to another boy entirely, not this one that was alternately soaked and dried to parchment as they harvested the precious fruits of the swamp grass.

The fourth day they made the raft, binding layer after layer of the grass stalks and then forcing them into a vaguely boatlike shape by tying the ends into stubby prows, leaving a central hollow for their precious cargo and Stupid.

Sharra had taught her fire lizards to hunt when they were in the wild, but she had also managed to train them to bring their catch to her. They returned that fourth evening with the strangest-looking creature Piemur had ever seen. Sharra identified it as a whersport. It was far too small to be like the watchwhers that Piemur knew as nocturnal hold guardians in the north, but it was bigger than fire lizards, which it also somewhat resembled. Fortunately it was almost dead when the delighted Meer and Talla deposited it on the ground by Sharra's feet. She dispatched it with a deft prick of her knife and, grinning at Piemur for his horrified expression, proceeded to disembowel it, throwing the offal far out into the black waters, which ruffled briefly as the snakes took the offering.

"May look a sight, but roasted in its skin, a whersport is very good eating. So, we'll stuff it with a bit of white tuber and some grass shoots, and we'll have a meal fit for a Lord Holder."

When she saw Piemur's dubious expression as she completed her arrangements, she laughed.

"There're a lot of strange beasties in this part of the south. As if all the animals you have up north got mixed up somehow. A whersport isn't a fire lizard, and it isn't a wher. For one thing it's a daytime beast, and whers are nocturnal; sun blinds them. Then there's far more varieties of snake here than in the north. Or so I'm told. Sometimes I'd like to go north, just to see all the differences, but then again," and Sharra shrugged, her eyes wandering over the lush, deserted and strangely beautiful marshlands, "this is where I hold. I haven't seen half enough of it yet to begin to appreciate all its complexity." She pointed due south with her bloody knife blade. "There're mountains down there that never lose their snow. Not that I've seen snow, on them or on the ground, though my brother has told me about it. I wouldn't like to be as cold as he says it gets in the north when there is snow on the ground."

"Oh, it's not bad," replied Piemur reassuringly and a trifle pleased to be able to talk on a subject he did know, "rather invigorating, in fact, cold is. Snows are fun, too. Then you don't have to—" He caught himself. He'd been about to say "you didn't have to report to all work sections at the Harper Hall." "—do as much work."

Sharra didn't seem to notice his brief hesitation or that he had substituted another phrase. She gave him a grin.

"We don't always work this hard in Southern, either, Piemur; but now it's time to harvest numbweed and get the tuft seeds and bush hearts. If we didn't have them. . . ." and she shrugged to indicate a very unpleasant alternative. Then she made a trench in the red ashes of their fire, lined it with thick water plant leaves, which began to hiss and exude a steamy fragrance, deftly inserted the stuffed whersport, folded over the leaves, then carefully knifed the hot ashes in place, and sat back. "There. Dinner won't be long, and there's enough for all."

Chapter 11

Once out of the grip of the Great Current, Sebell wrestled with the gaudy striped mainsail, untying it from the runners on the boom and folding it away neatly in its bag. Then he and Menolly bent the bright red southern sail to the boom and mast. Practice had made it a smooth operation, though the first time Menolly and he had changed the sail halfway to the Southern Continent, it had taken them hours, with him cursing at his ineptness and she patiently explaining the trick.

No sooner had they hauled the red sail up the mast than the wind, which had so favored their journey, dropped to a mere whisper.

With a sigh, Menolly surveyed the bright blue and cloudless sky and then laughed as she sank to the deck by the all but motionless tiller handle.

"Wouldn't you just know?"

"All right, weather eye, breeze at sunset?"

"Possibly, usually does come up again, then," she replied, squinting up to see what made Sebell so irritable.

"Sorry, Menolly," he said, running his hands through wind-disheveled hair. He dropped to the deck beside her.

"You're not worried about Piemur, are you? Something you've kept from me?"

"No, girl, I've kept nothing from you." Her anxious query seemed at this moment more of an accusation to him than a plea for reassurance, and he had answered with more asperity than was customary for him. She was quiet, though he could sense her confusion at his manner; he was unable to explain it to himself. "I didn't mean to snap, Menolly," he said, realizing that she wouldn't speak until he had. "I just don't know what's gotten into me. I honestly believe we'll find Piemur in the south."

"Maybe we ought to have taken someone else to help with the sail-ing—"

"No, no, it's not that!" Again his tone was churlish. He bit his lips together, took a deep breath and carefully added. "You know I like sailing. Better, I like sailing with you alone!" That came out sounding more like himself, and he gave her a smile.

Menolly started to respond to his oblique apology, but then stared at his face, her eyes widening. Suddenly, she glanced skyward, where the fire lizards were aerially following the skiff in swoops and glides. She watched them for a long moment, frowning slightly as she saw one dive into the waves. Sebell, puzzled by her abrupt curiosity, identified the fisher as his own Kimi and smiled indulgently as she brought the neatly captured yellowtail back to the prow of the ship. Oddly, the others stayed aloft while Kimi tore savagely into the flesh of her still-struggling prey.

Sebell wondered why the other three fire lizards didn't come to share the feast, but the thought didn't absorb him long. The ferocity with which Kimi ate fascinated him; he felt as if he were somehow involved in tearing the strips, as if he could savor the warm salty flesh in his mouth, as if—

"I'm sending Beauty to Toric at Southern Hold. She can't stay here now, Sebell."

Sebell heard Menolly's voice but made no sense of the words, his entire attention was concentrated on the unusual actions of his fire lizard queen. He wanted to go to her, but he couldn't move. He found that he was alternately clenching his hands and then rubbing his sweating palms against his legs. He was unbearably hot and tore at his shirt to open the throat.

"Oh!" he heard Menolly exclaim. "Oh, what else can I do? I can't send Rocky and Diver away. That's not fair to Kimi. We're too far from land to raise more fire lizards, and there's not a breath of wind to attract them here!"

Sebell pulled off his shirt and tossed it aside. The coolness of the day seemed to have no effect on the heat that consumed him. Then he noticed the two bronze fire lizards, crouching on the roof of the small cabin. They made no attempt to join Kimi in her feast. She was growling, too, her eyes glowing orangely at the two impertinent bronzes, and she seemed to be glowing in the sunlight.

Glowing? Unwilling to share food? What had Menolly mumbled about sending Beauty away? And to Toric? Why would she send Toric another message? What *was* the matter with Kimi?

He wanted to reprimand her but could frame no message in his mind. And why were those bronzes waiting? Why didn't they go away and leave Kimi? Why . . . ?

The "why" suddenly penetrated Sebell's fire-lizard-linked confusion. Kimi eating alone, savagely; Menolly sending Beauty, another queen, away; Kimi, glowing golden and taunting the bronzes, her good friends, with her staring, whirling orange-red eyes! Kimi was about to fly. And it was Menolly's bronzes who would fly her. A surge of elation swept Sebell, who could scarcely believe his good fortune. And yet. . . .

"Menolly?" He turned to her, hands outstretched, palms up, pleading with her and apologizing for what he knew was about to happen since there were only the two of them on this becalmed boat in the middle of the windstill sea. He hadn't wanted Menolly coerced, as she now must be; he'd wanted to be in full command of himself, not overridden by the mating instinct of Kimi.

"It's all right, Sebell. It's all right."

Smiling, Menolly put her hands in his and let herself be drawn into his arms where he had so yearned to have her.

As if their contact had been a signal, Kimi uttered a shriek and flung herself skyward from the prow, the two bronze fire lizards a length behind her. Sebell wasn't standing on the deck with Menolly in his arms; he was with Kimi, exulting in her strength, in her flight, determined to outsmart those who pursued her. Just let them try to catch her!

Never had her wings responded so fully to her demands. Never had she flown so high, soaring, veering, gliding. The sun flowed across her body, its rays burning into her eyes as she flew on and ever upwards. The heat was unendurable. She glided obliquely to the right, caught movement below her and, sweeping her wings back, dropped down, screaming with delight as she fell between the two startled bronzes.

One of them tried to entangle her with his lashing tail and fell, his flight rhythm disrupted. She beat upwards again, calling defiance and deliberately cutting across the path of the second bronze. But, in her desire to flaunt her flight superiority, she brushed just too close to him, and he veered, jamming his wing tip against hers. Her forward speed was momentarily checked. Before she could get away from him, he had caught her, neck twining hers in that instant. Locked together, they fell towards the shimmering sea so far below.

On the tiny bright oblong that was but a mote on the glistening water, Sebell and Menolly, too, were together, lips, bodies, hearts and minds as they, linked by and in the love of their fire lizards, experienced and repeated the joy that enveloped Kimi and Diver.

The flapping of the untended sail roused Sebell first, the rising sea breeze cooling his cheek. He moved aside, shaking his head, trying to orient himself. Menolly stirred against him, awakened by the same sea sounds. Startled, she opened her eyes and saw him, propped on his elbow above her. Surprise, and then memory, changed the color of her sea green eyes. Holding his breath, Sebell watched, fearful of her reaction. Her smile was tender as she lifted her hand and brushed his hair back from his eyes.

"What chance did you have, dear Sebell, with Rocky and Diver so determined?"

"It wasn't just Kimi's need," he said in a hurried voice, "you know that, don't you?"

"Of course, I know, dear Sebell." Her fingers lingered on his cheek, his lips. "But you always stand back and defer to our Master." She did not hide from Sebell then how much she loved Master Robinton, nor would that ever come between them since they each loved the man in their separate ways. ". . . but I have so wished—"

The ominous creak of the boom swinging across the cockpit warned her just in time to pull him back against her, out of its way.

"I wish," said Sebell in a growl, "that the bloody wind didn't choose to rise right now."

"We need the wind, Sebell," she replied, laughing with a spontaneous gaiety that drew a laugh from him because they had finally spoken of what had kept them apart too long.

He put up his hand to grab the boom before it could swing back. She half rose and reached the lines to secure the boom, then pulled herself onto the seat to unlash the tiller. As Sebell rose to join her, he caught sight of a curled ball of bronze and gold on the forward deck, but Kimi and Diver were too soundly asleep to be roused by considerations of sea and wind. He envied them.

"Where did Rocky go?" he asked Menolly, who frowned slightly in thought.

"He either joined Beauty . . . or found himself a wild green. I suspect the latter."

"Wouldn't you know?" asked Sebell, surprised.

Menolly shook her head from side to side, with a half-smile, and Sebell realized that she'd been unaware of anything except their rapport with their two fire lizards. He relaxed, thoroughly content with their new understanding.

"If this breeze continues to follow, we'll make Southern by tomorrow high sun," she said and deftly played out the line, making the most of the wind that filled the red sail. Then she indicated that Sebell should bridge the distance between them in the cockpit.

Neither left each other for very long all through that brilliant, lovely night.

Menolly's sea-sense was acute, for the sun had just reached its zenith when they eased the little skiff into the pleasant cove that served the Southern Hold as harbor. Sebell counted the ships bobbing at anchor and wondered where the largest three vessels were. They'd seen none fishing as the Great Eastern Current had raced them towards their destination. Not that Sebell expected anyone in the Southern Hold to be moving about in the heavy heat of high sun.

Suddenly Beauty appeared, chittering a wild welcome. Rocky arrived more sedately, settling on the tied boom. Menolly scooped him from his perch and caressed him, murmuring loving reassurances until Sebell heard her laugh.

"What's so amusing?"

"He must have found a green. He looks far too smug, but he's trying to make *me* feel guilty!"

"Not your fault Diver lived up to his name!"

"Hello down there!" The loud hail attracted their attention up to the small precipice that bulged out above the harbor. The tall, tanned figure of the Southern Holder, Toric, waved an imperious arm at them. "No use sweltering! Come where it's cool!"

With Beauty and Rocky as escort, they waded ashore, leaving Kimi and Diver still asleep. Sebell firmly captured Menolly's hand as they raced across the hot sand to the steps that would lead to the top of the white stone cliff, which rose above the sea to make a safehold for its inhabitants.

Toric was gone from the halfway lookout when they reached it, but they were both accustomed to the southerner's habits, and indeed, it was only sensible to get out of the burdening heat.

Toric had been able to keep the lush vegetation of the south only so far from the entrance to the cool white caves by strewing the area deeply with seashells. The crunch and break of shell also served to warn the hold of visitors. Toric awaited them just inside the hold's entrance, gripping each by the arm with fingers that threatened to leave bruise marks.

"You were mighty short on words with that message Beauty bore me," he said as he escorted them to his private quarters.

The Southern Hold differed from northern ones in many respects, and, at this time of day, was uninhabited. The large low cavern was used for mealtimes, bad storms or Threadfall. The Southerners preferred to live apart, in shelters set in the shade of the thick forest of the bluff. When the wind was from the wrong quarter, this cavern could be breathlessly hot. Today, however, as Toric handed them each long tubes of cooled fruit juices, the temperature was a distinct drop from the heat without.

"To expand on Beauty's terse message," said Sebell, without the usual harper preambles, for Toric was a blunt-spoken man and appreciated the same in return. "Meron is dead and his successor, Lord Deckter, wishes it clearly understood that he is in no way to be bound by previous commitments."

"Fair enough. I'd expected it. Mardra and T'kul won't *like* it, and they may try Deckter's resolve—"

"He'll remain firm—"

"So he has no problem." Then Toric laughed to himself, shaking his head from side to side in his amusement. "No, Mardra won't like it, but it'll do the old one good to be thwarted. She was going to give Meron every dead fire lizard egg she could find for sending her a half-empty sack."

"Half-empty?" Sebell caught Menolly's eye.

"Yes, the sack arrived with the top loosened and she's certain some of the shipment, some materials she's been plaguing the Masterweaver for, dropped out *between*. Why?" Toric caught the significant glances between the harpers. "Oh, that missing lad you queried me about several sevendays back? You think *he* came south in it?"

"It's a possibility."

"Never occurred to me to connect the two before now." Toric stroked his cheek thoughtfully. "A small lad? Yes, he'd doubtless have fit in that sack. Anything else about him I should know perhaps?"

Sebell thought how like Toric to want answers before he gave his own.

"A queen fire lizard egg was involved. . . ."

"Oh ho," and Toric's eyes crinkled with satisfaction. "Then it's not a possibility anymore, but a probability that your lad got here." He stressed the word "got," strangely, but went on before Sebell could question his emphasis. "Four, no three Threadfalls ago, weyrmen went after a wherry circle. Most of the time that means fire lizard hatchings so they do stir themselves to investigate." Toric gave a sour laugh. "Not that that energy will profit them now if this Deckter fellow won't follow Meron's ways. The strange thing was that when they reached the area, the wherries flitted away through the forest, and they found only a queen's shell on the beach. They spent a good deal of time going up and down that strand, but there wasn't any trace of a full clutch."

"Piemur does have his friend after all," cried Menolly, grabbing Sebell and dancing about with him in her relief.

"Piemur? That's your missing boy? Hey, stop that, you'll set every fire lizard in the place a-wing."

Kimi and Diver swooped into the cavern at that point, and with Beauty and Rocky bugling their delight, some of the southern fire lizards were also reacting. Sebell and Menolly called their four to order, and Toric sent his away.

"Yes, it's Piemur who's been missing, our apprentice," said Menolly, so jubilant that for a moment Sebell thought she'd swing Toric into their joyful antics.

"He and I were at Meron's Gather," said Sebell. "Somehow he got into the Hold itself and purloined the queen fire lizard egg. Meron was livid. . . ."

"I can well imagine," said Toric with a snort.

"Only none of his men could find Piemur or the egg. Kimi said she couldn't reach him," Sebell went on.

"That was when he'd hidden in the sack," Menolly said. "Oh, that wretched, that clever rascal."

"More clever than he knew, or could guess," Sebell continued, for Toric's expression told him that he didn't think so highly of Piemur's escapade. The harper explained to Toric all that had occurred after Piemur's daring theft: the fear of the main contenders for the Holding that Benden Weyr would discover Meron's dealings with the Southern Oldtimers. The heirs apparent now wanted no part of the succession, nor did they want the Hold in contention, so they pressured Meron to name a successor, who would then try to placate the Benden Weyrleaders. But Meron had collapsed, and both the Master Healer and the Masterharper were summoned, for the Harper could act as mediator. He convoked other Lord Holders and the High Reaches Weyrleader to force Lord Meron to name his successor. About the methods, Sebell remained discreet. Nor did Toric inquire, since Sebell's recitation was limited to facts rather than story-telling embellishments.

"So we think," Sebell finished, "that since Kimi specifically said it was too dark, as in a sack, and she couldn't 'find' Piemur, or room enough to get to him, he did secrete himself in a sack, which the Oldtimers collected that night—I saw the dragons—and brought here. That would also explain why none of our fire lizards could find a trace of him anywhere in Nabol."

Toric had listened with keen attention to Sebell's summary, but now he cocked his head to one side and made a rueful noise with his tongue against his teeth.

"It's true a boy could have fit in that sack, and it's true that a queen fire lizard egg was found. But . . ." and he held up his hand warningly, ". . . Thread fell that day . . ."

"Piemur knew you could live holdless through Threadfall!" said Menolly with the firmness of one trying to convince self.

"Wherries were circling that shell. They could have got the little queen at hatching—"

"Not if Piemur was alive! And I *know* he was," said Menolly more stoutly now and utterly convinced. "Is that place far from here? Could your queen take our fire lizards? If Piemur's anywhere about, *they'll* find him."

Toric was dubious, but he called up his queen. To the surprise of both harpers, the queen didn't, as Kimi or Beauty would have done, land on Toric's shoulder, but hovered awaiting his pleasure. Toric issued the sort of order one would give a stupid drudge. She chirped at Kimi and Beauty, disdaining the two bronzes, and flitted out of the cavern, the other four fire lizards right behind her.

"Lord Meron's death won't bother *them,*" and Toric jerked his head in the direction of the Southern Weyr, "for a while. They just brought in all they'll need for some time. I would prefer that we somehow keep them supplied. *I . . .*" and he jerked his thumb at his chest in emphasis, ". . . do not wish to jeopardize my arrangements with Lessa and F'lar. *They*" and again he meant the Oldtimers, "don't care how they get what they think they need. Meron was just convenient." He took the harpers' solemn assurance of assistance as his due, but then grinned, not pleasantly. "Has any one of Meron's people figured out just how many green fire lizards eggs got foisted off on 'em?" Toric plainly thought little of people who would be taken in by such a deception.

"You forget that the small holders don't know much about fire lizards," said Sebell. "In fact, the enormous fire lizard population at Nabol is one of the reasons why Piemur and I were there: to make certain Meron was the source of so many green fire lizards."

Toric half-rose, his usually controlled expression showing anger. "No one suspected *me* of cheating traders?"

"No," Sebell said, though that had been one of his problems. "Don't forget that I collected the clutches you've sent north in barter, but it was necessary for the Harper to find the real culprit. Green clutches could have been brought in by sailors who have been so conveniently losing themselves in southern waters."

"Oh, all right then." Toric subsided, his honor unchallenged.

"The Oldtimers have not questioned those lost sailors?"

"No," said Toric, shrugging negligently. "So long as the sails are red. They never have bothered to count the number of ships we really own."

Toric then noticed that they had drained their juices so he replenished the cool drinks.

"Have you some ships out now?" asked Sebell, because he had thought it odd to see so few at anchor when the sun was high.

Toric smiled again, his good humor completely restored by Sebell's observation. "You are well come, Harper, since the ships have sailed on your account. Or, I should say, Master Oldive's. It's harvest time for the numbweed, and for certain other herbs, grasses and such like that Sharra says the good man requires. If you stay until they return, then you can sail home full laden."

"Good news, Toric, but we'd best sail home laden with Piemur as well."

The southerner clicked his tongue pessimistically. "As I said, there've been three, maybe four Threadfalls since that queen egg shell was found."

"You don't know our Piemur," said Menolly, so insistent that Toric raised his eyebrows in surprise at her fervor.

"Maybe, but I know how other Northerners act in Threadfall!" Toric was plainly contemptuous.

"You're having trouble with their adaptation here?" asked Sebell, worrying that the Harper's masterful solution of sending holdless men south to Toric in unobtrusive numbers was in jeopardy.

"No trouble," said Toric, dismissing that consideration with a wave of his hand. "They learn to cope holdless, or stay holdbound without the additional privileges of being ranked as holders here. Some have adapted rather well," he admitted grudgingly. Then he noticed Menolly's anxious glances towards the entrance. "Oh, I told her to give the forests a good raking, too. The fire lizards'll take a while if my queen has followed her orders. Now that drink is not enough to soothe a sea thirst; there's sure to be ripe fruit cooling in the tanks." He rose and went to the kitchen area of the cavern where he scooped a huge green-rinded fruit from a tank set in the wall. "Generally we save heavier eating for the evening, when the heat has eased." He sectioned the fruit and carried a platter of the pink-fleshed slices to the table. "Best fruit in the world for quenching thirst. It's mainly water."

Sebell and Menolly were licking their fingers for the last of the succulent juices when a twittering fair of fire lizards swooped in. Beauty and Kimi made immediately for their friends' shoulders, Rocky and Diver settled near Menolly on the table, but Toric's queen hovered, chirping out a message, her eyes whirling with the orange-red of distress.

"I told you he might not survive," said Toric. "My queen really looked for any trace of a human, too."

Menolly hid her face on the pretext of reassuring her fire lizards, who were imaging to her endless distances of forest and deserted stretches of beach and sandy wastes.

"You sent them west," said Sebell, grasping at any theory that would give them hope, "to the place where the egg shells were discovered. If I know Piemur, he wouldn't have stayed anywhere that he had left clues. Could he have worked his way east? And be further down this side of the Southern Weyr?"

Toric gave a snort of laughter. "He could be any bloody where in the whole great southlands, but I doubt it. You Northerners don't like to be holdless in Threadfall."

"I managed quite well, thank you," said Menolly, her face bleak despite the sharpness of her reminder.

"There are undeniably exceptions," said Toric smoothly, inclining his head to indicate he meant her no insult.

"Piemur avoided discovery by fire lizards at Nabol, he told me, by thinking of *between,*" said Sebell. "He could have tried that trick again today. He'd have no way of knowing they were our friends. But there's one call he won't ignore or hide from."

"And what would that be?" asked the skeptical holder.

Sebell caught Menolly's suddenly hopeful expression. "Drums! Piemur will answer a call on drums!"

"Drums?" Toric threw back his head in an honest guffaw of surprise.

"Yes, drums," said Sebell, beginning to find Toric's attitude offensive. "Where's your drumheights?"

"Why would we need drumheights in Southern?"

It took the astounded harpers a little while to understand that drumheights, traditional in every hold in the north, had never been installed in the Southern's single hold. Granted, there were now small holdings established as far to the east as the Island River, but messages came back and forth either by fire lizard or by ship.

To Sebell's impatient query for any sort of drums in the hold, Toric said that they had a few to aid rhythm in dances. These were found in the quarters of Saneter, the hold's harper, who roused from his midday rest to show them to Sebell and Menolly. They were, as Sebell sadly found, no better than dance drums, with no resonance to speak of.

"Still and all, message drums would be handy to have nowadays, Toric," Saneter said. "Easier than sailing down the coast to discuss something. Just drum 'em up here. Safer, too. Those Oldtimers never learned drum measures. Come to think of it, I'm not sure how much I remember myself." Saneter regarded the journeymen harpers with an abashed surprise. "Haven't had to use drum talk since I came here with F'nor."

"It wouldn't be hard to refresh your memory, Saneter, but we must have proper drums. And that would take time with all the Master

Smith has on his plate right now," said Sebell, shaking his head with the disappointment he felt. He'd been so sure. . . .

"Must drums be made of metal?" asked Toric. "These have wooden frames." He tapped the stretched hide across the larger drum, and it rattled in response.

"The metal message drums are large, to resound—" Sebell began.

"But not necessarily metal; just something big enough, hollow enough over which to stretch your hide, and resonate?" asked Toric, ignoring the interruption. "What about a tree trunk . . . say . . ." and he began to hold out his arms, widening the circle while Sebell started in disbelief at the area he encompassed. ". . . about this big? That ought to make a bloody loud drum. Tree I'm thinking of came down in the last big storm."

"I know things grow bigger here in the south, Toric," said Sebell, skeptical in his own turn, "but a tree trunk as big as you suggest? Well, now, they don't *grow* that big."

Toric threw back his head, laughing at Sebell's incredulity. He clapped Saneter on the shoulder. "We'll show this disbelieving northerner, won't we, Harper?"

Saneter grinned apologetically at his crafters, spreading his hands out to indicate that Toric was indeed telling the truth.

"Further, it's not all that far from the hold. We could make it there and back before dinner," said Toric, well pleased with himself, and strode out of the harper's quarters ahead of the other three to rouse assistants.

While Sebell didn't doubt that the fallen tree was "not far" from the Southern Hold, it was also not an easy trek through steamy hot forests where the trail had to be hacked out afresh. But, when they finally reached the tree, it was every bit as large in girth as Toric had promised. Sebell felt much like Menolly, awed, as they reached out to caress the smooth wood of the fallen giant. The insects that had burrowed out the monster's core had also made meals of its bark until only a thin shell remained, the last skin of the once-living tree. Even that shell had begun to rot away in the steam and rain of its environment.

"Will this make you enough drums, harperman?" asked Toric, delighted to confound them.

"Enough for every holding you've got, with more left over," said Sebell, running his eyes down the fallen trunk. Surely it must be several dragon lengths: queen dragons! It must be the biggest, oldest tree ever grown on Pern. How many Threadfalls had it survived?

"Well, how many shall we cut you today?" asked Toric, gesturing for the double-handed saw that had been carried by his holders.

"I'll settle for one just now," said Sebell, "from here . . ." and he marked the distance with an arm and his body, pointing to the limit with his right forefinger by his ribs, ". . . to here. That would make a good, deep, long-carrying sound when hide is stretched."

Saneter, who had come with them, stooped to pick up a thick, knobby-ended branch and pounded the tree trunk experimentally. Everyone was surprised at the hollow boom that resulted. The fire lizards, who'd been perched on the surface, lifted with shrieks of protest.

Grinning, Sebell held out his hand to Saneter for the stick. He beat out the phrase "apprentice, report!" He grinned more broadly as the majestic tones echoed through the forest and started a veritable shower of tree-dwelling insects and snakes, shaken from their perches by the unexpected loud reverberations.

"Why move it?" asked Toric. "You could hear this at the back of the mountains."

"Ah, but site this on that landing over your harbor, and a message would carry to that Island River of yours," said Sebell.

"Then we'll cut your drum, Harper," said Toric, gesturing for another man to take the opposite handle of the big saw. He held the blade for the initial cut. "Then we shall . . . take the rest . . . out in sections . . . as big as we . . . can carry them," he said, thrusting mightily at his end of the saw.

With a man of Toric's brawn and the willing help of the other holders, the first drum section was quickly detached from the trunk. A long pole was cut, vines quickly laced to secure the section to the carrier, and the party was soon making its way back to the Southern Hold.

By the time they had arrived, Sebell and Menolly were dripping with sweat, tortured by scratches and insect bites, which did not seem to bother the tougher, tanned hides of the Southerners. Sebell wondered if he could find the energy to cover the drum that day. Toric had firmly assured him that there were hides large enough—since herdbeasts also grew larger here in the south—to fit this mammoth drum. But the journeyman was determined to work as long and hard as the Southern Holder if he had to. And he had to, to find Piemur.

They had positioned the drum in front of the cavern "for the sun to dry up the insects," so Toric announced, when the big holder frowned at his guests.

"Man, you will die an early death if you work this hard all the time." Toric waved towards the westering sun. "The day is nearly over. This drummaking can wait till morning. Now we all need a wash," and his gesture went seaward. "That is, if you harpers swim . . ."

Menolly gave a sigh, partly composed of relief that Sebell was not going to insist on finishing the drum tonight and partly of disgust since Toric would never remember that she had not only lived holdless but had been a seaholder's daughter and could outswim him. Sebell hesitated briefly before he surrendered to Toric's suggestion.

The seawater, not as warm as Sebell had anticipated, was indeed refreshing as well as relaxing. The four fire lizards zipped in and out of the gentle evening waves, chittering with delight to frolic with their friends, though if Menolly disappeared for long beneath the waves, her three fire lizards dove after her, pulling her surfacewards by her hair.

Suddenly Toric's queen, who had held herself aloof from the antics of the visitors, hovered about Toric's head, twittering urgently. Toric glanced around. Following his gaze, Menolly and Sebell saw three red-sailed sloops, their sides lined with people, rounding the arm of land that protected the southern harbor.

"The harvesters have returned," said Toric to the harpers. "I'll just see if all is well. Stay on and enjoy yourselves."

With strong strokes of his powerful arms, he made a diagonal line to the shore that would intercept the landing of the lead ship.

"Sometimes that man is too much," she said, shaking her head at this latest exhibition of the southerner's strength.

"Which is as well for me," said Sebell, laughing, and pulled her under just to let the fire lizards rescue her.

They played that game a bit, reveling in the freedom of the water and its coolness until Menolly suddenly wondered if she had enough energy left to swim back to shore. But they got there safely, fire lizards escorting, and paused to lean against the seawall to catch their breaths before continuing back up to the hold.

Toric was now directing the unloading, his tall figure moving here and there. Abruptly, they saw a tall, dark-haired girl, only a head shorter than the big Holder, approach him and hold him in a long conversation.

"That must be Sharra," Menolly said, noticing several fire lizards converge over the girl's head. One of them landed on her shoulder, and Menolly gave a snort. "Toric certainly has his queen well-trained, hasn't he?"

Suddenly a sound paralyzed them: the sharp thudding of a practiced hand against what could only be the newly acquired drum round. A practiced hand that beat a measure, "Harper here, anyone else?" and the staccato that was a question.

"It has to be Piemur!" Menolly's cry was half-gasp, half-scream, but the words weren't quite out of her mouth before both harpers were on their feet and running towards the ramp up from the harbor.

"What's the matter?" they heard Toric yelling after them.

"That was Piemur!" Sebell managed to gasp out as he charged a bare stride ahead of Menolly. But when they skidded to a halt on the shell-strewn area before the cavern, there was no one about.

Sebell cupped his hands about his mouth. "PIEMUR! REPORT!"

"Beauty! Rocky! Where is he?" gasped Menolly, half-angry with Piemur for that heart-stopping shock.

"SEBELL?"

The harper's name echoed and re-echoed coming from the cavern. Sebell and Menolly were halfway there when a tanned, bare-legged, shock-haired figure ran straight into them.

Menolly, Sebell and Piemur were entangled in mutual cries and thumpings of rediscovery when a tiny fire lizard queen began attacking Sebell, and a small runner beast tried to butt Menolly's knees from under her. Beauty, Rocky and Diver immediately drove off the little queen, but it wasn't until Piemur, dashing tears of relief and joy from his eyes, called Farli to order and reassured Stupid, that any sort of coherent conversation was possible. By that time, Sharra, Toric, and half the Southern Hold were aware that the lost had been found.

A celebration for the successful return of the harvesters would have been held in any case, but the evening was certainly crowned by Piemur's appearance, especially after he was reassured that his absence would be forgiven by the Masterharper in view of the extraordinary outcome of the initial folly of stealing the queen egg from Meron's hearth.

Sebell and Menolly listened intently when Piemur accounted for his continued absence once Farli had been Impressed.

"He was wiser not to come back right then, anyhow," said Sharra before Toric could speak. "If you remember, Mardra was in a taking over that unclosed sack and ready to flay the hide off the back of the culprit. Though what she wants with more to wear here, I don't know!"

"The wilderness has its own thrall," said Toric, eyeing Piemur so closely that the boy wondered what he'd done wrong now. "Tell me, young apprentice harper, how did you survive Threadfall the day your queen hatched?"

"In the water, under a ledge in the lagoon," said Piemur as if that ought to have been obvious. "Farli didn't hatch until after Threadfall."

Toric nodded approval. "And the other Threadfalls?"

"Under water. Only by that time I'd sort of found a camp by the river, above the numbweed meadows. . . ." He glanced at Sharra, whose eyes twinkled at the truth he now chose to speak, "where I found a submerged log to hold onto and a long reed to breath through."

"Why didn't you come back after the second Fall?"

"I found Stupid, and I couldn't travel far or fast until he was grown up."

Sharra bubbled with laughter then, for the ingenuous expression of Piemur's face was just short of impudence.

"You were certainly making tracks eastward to the sea when our paths crossed," she said.

"You expected me to stay anywhere near people making numbweed?" asked Piemur with such disgust that everyone laughed.

"I'll bet there were times in the marsh when you wished you were back just harvesting numbweed," said Sharra, grinning at Piemur, who rolled his eyes upward.

"You went alone to the marshes?" Toric was not pleased.

"I know the marshes, Toric," said Sharra firmly, as if this were a continuation of previous arguments. "I had my fire lizards and, in fact, I had Piemur, Farli and little Stupid. And I'll add one thing"—now she turned to the harpers—"your young friend is a born Southerner!"

"He's apprentice to Master Robinton," said Sebell, with a warning to Piemur that brought a sudden silence to the main table.

"He's wasted as just a harper," said Sharra after a moment. "Why, I—"

"And I'm not really a harper right now, either, am I, Sebell?" asked Piemur, suddenly collecting his wits. "I was only good as a singer, and I have no voice. Is there *really* a place for me at the Harper Hall? I mean," and he rattled on, his eyes going from Sebell to Menolly, "I know you and Menolly thought you could get me to help you two, but a fine help I turned out to be, getting sacked up and sent south without even knowing it. It's not as if I was good at anything except getting into trouble—"

"Useful trouble, as it turned out," said Sebell, "but I just had an idea . . . to keep you out of trouble for a while." The journeyman turned to the Southerner. "You rather like the idea of message drums, Toric? And, Saneter, you say you've forgotten most of the measures you learned. Well now, Piemur hasn't."

"I could be drum messenger here?" Piemur was suddenly open-mouthed with shock.

Sebell held his hand up to get a word in, and the radiance in Piemur's face faded. "I can't be certain until I've asked Master Robinton, but frankly, Toric, I think Piemur could serve his Hall very well right now as drum . . . no, drum apprentice-master . . . if Saneter wouldn't mind being taught by one of lower rank." Sebell then turned to the startled hold harper to explain. "Rokayas, who is Master Olodkey's senior journeyman, said that Piemur was one of the quickest, cleverest apprentices he's ever had to beat measures into. If you wouldn't mind him refreshing your memory. . . ."

Saneter laughed and beamed encouragingly at Piemur, whose face once again shone. "If he can put up with a fumble-fingered old harper . . ."

"Toric, as Southern Holder?" Sebell paused delicately, for he had caught the narrowing of the big man's eyes and wondered if he had presumed too much.

"Troublemaker in the Hall?" Toric frowned, giving each one a long, expressionless look, pausing to stare hard at Piemur. The boy held his breath so long his face began to turn bright red under his tan.

"Actually, not a troublemaker, Toric," said Menolly. "He just has a lot of energy."

"We could certainly use drums for messages to the coastal holds," said Toric in a slow drawl, his face closed on his thoughts. "Can Piemur make the drums?" he asked Sebell.

"I'd prefer to stay and supervise," Sebell murmured.

"Well, in the ordinary way I wouldn't accept another Northerner, but as Piemur has already proved he can survive on southern lands, I will make an exception in his case."

At the shouts of joy, he held up his hand once more, commanding instant silence. "Contingent, of course, on the approval of the Masterharper."

"He'll be so glad to hear that Piemur's alive and well," cried Menolly, fumbling in her pouch for the message tube.

"Aw, Menolly, it's not as if I hadn't listened to everything you told me about fire lizards and your life in the Dragon Stones cave and all—"

"You'll find this lad has ears in every pore of him," said Sebell, giving Piemur's right one an affectionate twist.

"And tell Master Robinton I've got a queen and a tame runner beast," Piemur told Menolly who was busily writing. "I wouldn't have to leave Stupid behind if I have to go back to the Harper Hall, would I, Sebell?"

Sebell said something soothing and watched as Menolly made the message tube fast to Beauty's leg, told her to go back to Master Robinton and return as soon as possible.

"D'you think he'll let me stay?" Piemur asked Menolly then, his eyes round with hope and anxiety.

"You did put your time in the drumheights to good advantage," Menolly said, hoping that this solution to the problem of Piemur's immediate future did indeed meet with Master Robinton's favor. The

boy so clearly had thrived in his few sevendays' here. She could swear
he was taller and had broadened through chest and neck. And there
was no question but what his unexpected trip to Southern had altered
him in many subtle ways. She caught Sebell's glance and knew that he
had observed those changes, too. That the journeyman must see that
this broad and unexplored southern land could absorb the energies and
intelligence of their young friend far better than the more traditional
Harper Hall. "Bet you didn't think it would result in an opportunity
like this?"

Solemnly Piemur shook his head from side to side. Then the laughter
that always lurked in his eyes shown through. "Bet you didn't, either."

Most of the Southerners then prevailed on the two visiting harpers
for the latest northern songs, always a happy importation. So the time
passed quickly for most while Beauty delivered her message.

The moment the little golden queen swooped into the cavern, every
sound died, for by now the prospect of Piemur as drum messenger had
filtered to every Southerner present and the suspense was universal.

But Beauty was so attuned to the message she carried that her carolling answered Piemur's question before the confirming words were read
aloud.

"Well done, Piemur. Safely stay. Drum-journeyman!"

Congratulations were loud and cheerful, with Piemur's back being
thumped and hand shaken until he was nearly dizzy with such sudden
acclaim after so much solitude. When Sebell saw him take an opportunity to leave the cavern and the continuing festivity, he started to follow, but Menolly shook her head, already halfway to the door.

So it was only Menolly who heard Piemur say to the tired little
golden queen that clung to his neck: "I wish I had a drum big enough to
tell the whole world how happy I am!"

Anne McCaffrey

Anne McCaffrey has this to say about herself.

"Born on April first, I did nothing else of particular significance until I wrote my first novel during Latin class. I think things would have worked out better if I'd written it in Latin, but I didn't. Then, I wrote *Flame, Chief of Herd and Track,* an impossible western. I gave up writing in favor of the theater and, among other things, was involved in the first musical tent circuses in summer stock, directed operas and operettas and studied voice for nine years. I also got married and had three children, two boys and a girl. All of us write, and so do my older brother and three of my nieces.

"Now I live and work in Ireland with my two younger children who are still in school. I can sew for anyone except myself, embroider, knit an Arran sweater in ten days, cook well (I've edited a cookbook), play some bridge and particularly enjoy taking care of my heavyweight, dapple-gray gelding, Mr. Ed. He answers as readily to "Horseface" because he knows he's beautiful, and he bullies all of us, including the cat, Mr. Magoofey.

"My hair is silver, my eyes are green and I freckle: the rest is subject to change without notice."